WHEN THE
SKYLINE
CHANGES

James B. Fitzgerald

Dedication

Without so many, this would not have been possible. You allowed me to do this, so I dedicate this book to:

My Mother – In so many ways, if it were not for you, I would not be me.

My Father – You were not always there, but you were always there. I wish you were here for this.

My Wife – For sacrificing the time I needed to complete this project, and for standing behind me, no matter what.

My Sister – My coach, cheerleader, proofreader, enforcer, and sounding board.

My Friends – My Expediters of Dreams. Without my "EODs" this book would not exist. I'll never be able to fully repay you, but I can try!

The Bravest (Fire Departments), The Finest (Police Departments), The Doctors and Nurses and Hospital Staff, and The Unfortunate – Except for those who planned and executed the attacks, this is for the thousands who lost their lives on September 11th, 2001, their friends, their families, and for those who suffered the effects for the weeks, months, and years beyond that day.

Table of Contents

Chapter 1 – Close Enough

The ridiculous sound of a jumbo jet landing on a runway, which his computer had just made, signified that Willem Kelly had received a new email. It registered in his subconsciousness but didn't stop the daydream of him being wherever else he was in his head, and not in his office on the 48th floor. He was looking out of the window of his corner office, mostly at the facades of other buildings, but if he adjusted his seat and craned his neck, he could see the busy doings of some of the people; so far away that they appeared like ants that swarmed on the sidewalks and crosswalks below, all bordered by a sea of yellow taxis. He envied all of them. Free. Not stuck to his desk, like he was. One day, somewhere off in the distance, he would be free, too. Free to roam, away from his desk, his cell phone, his mortgage, his BMW, his responsibilities, and his soon-to-be ex-wife, Kathleen. Nothing to tie him down. He would be out of work, out of his marriage, and out of the city. He couldn't wait until his current life became his past life. The second line of his phone buzzed, rattling him from his thoughts. He watched the little red light blinking, blinking, blinking, and left it untouched. He was still on the other line, phone resting between his ear and his shoulder, though there was no one on the other end. It was a trick he had started using months ago, especially late in the day, to ensure he was able to leave the office on his own terms, and not after some last-minute late afternoon meeting was called to discuss financial figures.

It was 4:37 p.m. on a Monday. Twenty-three minutes to freedom from his desk for another day. Twenty-three minutes until he could take that leisurely, almost one-hour drive to his now empty house, he and his wife had once shared. Twenty-three minutes and almost one-hour until that first cold beer. Beer was a new thing in the house. When he was still happily married and sharing a roof and a bed with Kathleen, keeping any alcohol in the house, other than wine for dinner, was highly frowned upon. He would sometimes stop at a bar on the way home, but the first time she smelled it on him, his pillow and a blanket soon found their way to a couch in the den for a few nights. He wasn't an alcoholic by any means, but he couldn't wait to be able to drink what he wanted and when, without the scrutiny.

Snapping back to reality once again, he remembered the screech noise of the airplane and the unread email in his inbox. Focusing on the grey box on his computer screen, he clicked on the "open" button and began reading. As he finished reading, he collapsed back in his office chair, and his mind began to run with more thoughts than it could handle. The email frightened him enough that after time passed, he realized he needed to close his mouth, which had slackened open sometime during his reading of the email. He immediately felt sick. He always knew this day would come; in fact, he had been planning on it for quite some time. But he wasn't ready. There was still so much to do. And now there would be so many loose ends. Loose ends he had meticulously planned over time that would be tied up. He stood up and walked across the floor to the door of his office, almost tripping on the chairs that were there for his guests. *No more guests,* he thought to himself. He felt as if in a daze, his head swimming with plans and sacrifices and adjustments. The near future just became now. He had to act, and he had to act right. He opened his office door to the normal din of the noise of afternoon commerce and business that filled every square inch of the office.

"Jeannie," he called.

"Yes, Mr. Kelly?" Jeannie, his administrative assistant, was just over fifty years old, looked forty, and sounded twenty. He never really cared for her voice, but she did great work and kept his schedule straight. She had been working for him for just over three years. Before Jeannie, it was Lydia, who retired at sixty-five after forty years with Pickwick. She was a machine for him for six years, up until the final year, when the writing of her retirement was on the wall, and she let some things slide, such as record-keeping and filing. Jeannie spent months catching up, but soon every paper clip was in its place and every pencil had a sharpened point.

"Will you book me a meeting with Mr. Dickey tomorrow at 9:00?"

"Let's see. Mr. Dickey has an off-site appointment until 8:30 but should be in shortly after. So, 9:00 looks good," she said. "I saw the email. Should I be worried? Is everything okay?"

"Set it for 8:45. I'll be waiting for him in his outer room. And everything is fine. You'll know that tomorrow when you, me, and Mr. Dickey hash this thing out in the morning. Everything is going to be fine."

"Then the meeting request is sent! We'll give em' hell in the morning!" she shrieked with a smile.

Ugh, that voice, he thought. He wouldn't miss it at all if he never heard it again. He crossed the floor and flopped down in his office chair, and read the email again.

From: dickey.francis@pickwickfin.com

To:kelly.willem@pickwickfin.com; raines.jeanette@pickwick.com

CC:

higgins.james@pickwick.com;

lossprevention@pickwickfin.com

Subject: Discrepancy Report

William,

Upon review of last quarter's financial reports, we are showing some possible issues for some of the customers for which you have provided business loans. Specifically, we cannot prove they exist. I don't have to tell you that this looks very bad. A full investigation will begin immediately, and consider this a notice for required attendance for a meeting tomorrow at 11:00 a.m. with Loss Prevention & Security (LPS), your assistant Jeanette Raines, and myself. Bring a CD copy of your files for the following clients:

Harp & Co. – Account 298759874

The Holy Cow – Account 298759880

Humbarton, Humbarton, & Lye – Account 298759962

Be prepared to discuss the discrepancies. Bring any relevant material.

F. Roger Dickey

Chief Financial Officer

Pickwick Financial Services.

Shit, he thought. *I guess this is it. I guess they found out.*

Will was stuck between being angry at the carelessness of the spelling of his name and trying to remind himself to remain calm. It was at that time he first noticed the beads of sweat that had formed on his brow. *Stay calm, stay calm,* he thought. *They don't want to see you until tomorrow. They didn't bust down the door with security and police with handcuffs and batons, all ready to beat the hell out of me over some missing money.* He had fired the perfect retaliation shot. Setting the meeting earlier than what Dickey had set would accomplish multiple things. First, it would put Dickey's mind at ease about him being a no-show. *Let him think I am eager to fix the problem, to correct whatever errors I had made.* It would also set Dickey scrambling in the morning to make sure he had everything ready for the investigation. *He'll be running around when he gets back from his early appointment to get things in order. I can see it now with his glasses fogged up and his bald head beading sweat.* Lastly, it would probably anger Dickey, having his own investigation meeting rescheduled without his knowing. *We're gonna do this on my terms, old boy.*

As he suppressed a smile regarding the disarray in F. Roger Dickey's morning the following day, he knew he needed to get his big plan in motion, although a bit earlier than he thought he would need to. He should have hidden more of the money, but that probably would have set off alarms even before the ones now going off in his brain. So much to do, and so many steps to take, and so very little time. He didn't think the day would come so soon, so he was not completely prepared. But he was close. *Close enough*, he hoped. He had money, he had a plan, and he had taken smart steps to be ready. He had a most critical step already in place and waiting. He opened his cell phone and dialed. Two rings later, a voice responded.

"Yo."

"Archie, are we clear?"

"Hold on." Will heard a click in the background of the phone call. The voice on the other end then returned. *"Yeah, go ahead."*

"It's Will. Will Kelly. It's time, Arch...and I mean, it is *really* time. See you tonight."

<h1 style="text-align:center">Chapter 2 – Dissolving</h1>

Three months prior...

The alarm went off at 5:30 a.m. as it did every other day of the week. Willem Kelly woke up the same time every day, whether it was a weekday, weekend, or holiday. He kicked his legs over the side of the bed and rubbed the sleep out of his eyes, and finally smacked the top of the clock and made the buzzer cease its annoying sound. He glanced over his shoulder to her side of the bed and wasn't surprised. Kathleen had slept in the den again, and his goal, again, would be to get out of the house before she woke up. He didn't need the hassle. He got up from bed and used the bathroom. He splashed cold water on his face to help himself wake up and dried his hands on the towel that hung from the wall. It had been a few days since its most recent washing, just one more thing they were letting slide as they went through the motions of a dissolving relationship. They had promised at the beginning, six years ago, that chores would be shared and no one certain chore was to always be handled by one certain member of their team. Except for the towels, wash cloths, and bathroom rugs. They were her "thing," and until recently, she had always made sure they were fresh and clean. Now he dried his face with a used towel.

He donned a set of grey running shorts and a tank top, and when he was done pulling on a fresh pair of white tube socks, he crept down the main stairwell, through the sitting room and peeked around the corner into the den, where Kathleen was turned on her side, facing the back of the couch, shutting out as much of the world as possible as she slept. On the table next to the end of the couch closest to her head was a wine bottle and a glass, both drained of most of their contents. *Hmmph,* he thought. *I can't keep beer in the refrigerator, and she's allowed to pass out on wine. Whatever. I hope she sleeps until 10:00.* The wine was usually saved for dinner and special occasions. But they currently were not eating dinner together too often, and maybe she thought that *was* a special occasion. He continued into the kitchen to the laundry room and out to the mud porch, where he grabbed his running shoes and a headband. It was now 5:45 a.m. as he headed out the back door to stretch on the back patio.

When he felt limber, he took off at a leisurely jog, continuing a morning tradition that he had not missed since his junior year in high school. He had joined the wrestling team and had a winning record, but some of his wins were default wins because there were no other wrestlers in the opposing schools that were in his weight class. For him to actually be able to compete against real opponents on a consistent basis, he needed to shed at least twelve pounds. His wrestling coach got him into a running program, with the dual benefit of losing weight and strengthening his legs. The daily workout paid off, and his high school team won the County Championship in his junior year, and just missed the State Championship as a senior. He had been running every morning since then, no matter the day or the weather.

The near five-mile run route was the same each day, up the hill for a mile or so, and then at the turn of a side street, he sometimes reversed the direction just to change things up, but the distance was static, and usually took him about forty minutes. Coming back down the hill, he hit a patch of pebbles that could have just as well been marbles, and his feet kicked out from under him, and he went down hard. He had fallen on the same route before, so it was not really a big deal. Some scrapes on the leg, and no doubt the bruises would follow. He pulled himself up off the ground, dusted himself off of all road debris, and began to jog the last quarter of a mile. His left knee wouldn't cooperate, though, sore from the fall, and he hobbled the rest of the way.

It was early June and fairly warm, so he was covered in sweat from the run when he got to the house. He checked the front door, but it was still locked from the previous night, and the newspaper was on the porch, undisturbed. These were two signs that Kathleen had not woken from her wine-induced slumber. He went around the back of the house and stopped, looking at their beautiful pool. As was with his morning ritual, he went to the pool house and found his bathing trunks hanging up from yesterday's plunge. It took him less than a minute to pull off his shoes, socks, and tank top, exchange his shorts and underwear for the swim trunks, and dive headfirst into the pool for a quick cooling down. Directly next to the pool was a whirlpool spa, and after a few minutes, he pulled himself over the pool wall and into the smaller spa and turned on the water jets. He closed his eyes and thought about the day ahead. Meetings and clients and people asking for money to be able to start a business, and unfortunately, starting the awful process of suing those who were not successful, not able to repay the loans. He hated that part of the business. He had extended a handshake across his desk to some eager families or young upstarts with dreams of their own restaurant, or retail shop, or tax attorney office, or whatever dream they had, and now he was going to begin their nightmare. He *hated* that part. A bird squawked in the tree next to the house and caused him to open his eyes. He glanced at the tree as the bird flew away and then fixed his eyes on the house. He saw Kathleen peering out of the window in the kitchen. She looked at him and then turned and disappeared into the house. Unfortunately, it was 6:45 a.m. now, and time for him to go into the house as well and prepare for another day of sitting at his desk, awarding money to those he felt could eventually pay it back.

He hopped out of the spa, went to the pool house, hung up his swim trunks, changed back into his underwear, and then walked into the house where, in past times, there used to be coffee waiting. Now they had a coffee maker that used little plastic disposable cups to brew a single cup at the touch of a button. Kathleen had already made her cup. He sighed and noted that it was just one more thing that they used to share but could now do separately. He shook his head and headed up the steps in the kitchen to the second floor. As per usual, Kathleen had taken the liberty of using the shower in the bathroom in their bedroom, leaving him the smaller version in the guest bathroom down the hall. One more thing he had gotten used to and just let go. It wasn't even worth the confrontation anymore. Besides, if he really wanted to use the better shower, he could wake up earlier.

He got out of the shower and popped the door open to let out the extra steam that wasn't sucked up by the fan. He cocked his head to listen to what stage Kathleen was on in her showering process, and heard the hair dryer. He hung up his towel, tossed his underwear in the laundry chute, and strode naked into their bedroom and into his walk-in closet. He chose underwear, blue socks, a blue suit, a white shirt, and a red tie from the ridiculously ordered hanger and shelving system Kathleen had painstakingly designed during one of her upgrades to the resale value of the house. The closet was her favorite of the improvements. Still naked and wet from the shower, he came out of the closet and ran almost straight into Kathleen, who, startled, dropped her towel to the floor. They both stood there, face to face, naked, and contemplated the moment. A few years ago, there would have been no pause, no thought, just the immediate joining of their bodies in an early morning love-making session, which would have made them both blame traffic for being late for work.

She just picked up her towel, moved to the side, and said, "Sorry. I need to borrow a pair of your gym socks. Mine are all dirty."

As he pulled on his suit pants and tucked in his shirt, a million comments he could have said about her doing laundry instead of letting it pile up entered his head, but he let them all fly away unspoken, and instead, just said, "Sure. Early gym day?"

"Yes. I don't have any clients until ten-thirty, so I'm going early. But I won't be home until after eight o'clock, so unless you're making dinner, you may want to grab something while you're out."

"I can make something for dinner, and we can eat when you get home."

Kathleen exhaled and walked back to her side of the room. "Okay," she said. "Just make sure we have a good bottle of wine to go with it."

"Absolutely," Will said. "There is something I want to discuss with you tonight, and dinner and wine will help."

"What are we discussing, and why are you limping?" she asked.

"Not now," he said. "I need to leave to go to work. See you tonight." He no longer made the effort for a quick kiss on the cheek. He felt those efforts were shunned a while ago.

Chapter 3 – Running Late

Will, through with his call to Archie, snapped his mobile phone shut and exited his office, locking the door behind him. He said goodnight to Jeannie and a few others as he wove his way out of the company's business space and to the elevators. The multiple-elevator ride down to the garage was not long enough to even begin to organize his thoughts. He got to his dark blue BMW and exited the garage, his car pouring out into the city traffic with thousands of others as countless workdays ended and their owners wove their ways into the busy metropolis. He finally got his thoughts focused and what he needed to do to put the remainder of his plan into motion. Tomorrow was going to be a big day. Tomorrow was going to be the first page in the new book that his life was going to become. It was going to be his restart. It would be his reset button. His life, he imagined, unplugged, and then plugged back in. A suddenly dark screen lay in front of him, then just as fast, it would be flashing with white light and an infinite number of possibilities. It would also be the first day he would probably be officially recognized as a criminal, as a law-breaking individual, as a wanted person, as an outlaw. He liked the way 'outlaw' sounded, but was nervous about his future, nonetheless.

He had a lot to do. He really wanted to avoid Kathleen tonight, which was probably not an issue, unless she called him, as she had moved out three months earlier. But she had been calling him almost nightly. Their calls were quick. How are you? How was your day? Everything okay? Okay, talk to you later. *It was kind of weird,* he thought. They were broken up, lived in separate locations, and probably talked more now than they did in the last year of their marriage. His mind drifted back to that night when he had made chicken parmesan over angel hair pasta for dinner. That night, he didn't know it, but he had put his grand plan into action. That night, when he poured the wine, they ate in near silence until he was halfway done with his meal, and then began his monologue as to why he wanted them at this dinner, at this time. Who were they kidding? The romance was gone. The attraction had fizzled. No spark, and no fire. No children for whom to stay together. And he remembered her face, lacking surprise, sorrow, or any other telling emotion. There was no blame from either side. They had simply grown apart. As he spoke, she simply agreed as she ate her chicken, and as the meal ended, they had mutually decided that she would be the one to vacate the premises and find a new place to live. And she did just that when she found an apartment just a mile away from the dentist's office where she was a partner with three others in the same field. *Good for her,* he thought. A great place to live near her work. A place she could afford and live happily alone. Or otherwise. The "otherwise" made him shake his head. He wished her no ill will, and they had no interest in each other sexually anymore, but he just couldn't picture her with anyone else. *Yuck,* he thought.

As he made his way through traffic, he finally got to the Brooklyn-Battery Tunnel and entered the quiet of a busy city underground. He cleared his head and focused on what he had to do. Time was short. He had to book a flight to Florida, and then another to Grand Cayman Island. He had thought about that for weeks. In all the movies he had seen, and in all the books he had read, when someone wanted to hide money, they mostly either moved it to the Cayman Islands or Switzerland. Switzerland seemed more like the big-time crooks' destination, so he chose the Caymans as part of his misdirection escape plan. Two fake flights and, assuming someone was chasing him, they would be chasing ghosts, at least at the beginning, and it would be enough for him to get a head start.

The flights weren't the only distraction, he was thinking. He would call a cab from his house, from the dispatch desk, and actually make the trip to Newark Liberty International as if he were flying. That way, there would be a record of him doing so. But he would leave by another cab, one he had just hailed from the hundreds that hung around the arrival terminals. Just a random guy getting in a random cab going to a random place. Then he would be harder to trace because they wouldn't be searching for a cab ride. They would be investigating two flights that had at least one similar passenger ending up in Grand Cayman. The misdirection he was planning was all he could think of as he rode down Route 276 toward the Verrazano Narrows Bridge and Staten Island.

He had thought about packing clothes for his fake destination. He thought that actually checking his baggage at the ticketing desk, so it would look more like he was heading for the islands, would be a good idea. However, the image of a bag perpetually circling the luggage carousel in Florida, catching the eyes of security guards as it made laps around the room with no one claiming it, made him decide against it. So, he squashed that idea then and there. Just the two plane tickets would do, although he was worried that the passenger manifest for the flight to the Caymans might be missing a name, just as the plane was missing a body. He had the flight to Fort Lauderdale covered. He would fumble for his ticket and have his bags in disarray. Once the frantic traveler found his boarding pass, he would then excuse himself and gather his strewn about belongings, and once all together, simply walk around the corner and disappear into a throng of other travelers. He'd dump one of his bags, free of any identification, in a bathroom or a locker on his way back to the airport loop and just keep the important stuff. A few changes of clothes and the money–.

The brakes squealed and the tires left a layer of rubber on the road as he pulled to the shoulder and yelled *"Dammit!"* He had just remembered the keys. He remembered that he had *forgotten* the keys. The keys were everything. The keys were *everything.* The keys were to the money he had stolen. What would he do now? He had to go meet Archie. He had to get the keys. He doubted there was time to do both, but he had to try. He flipped open his phone and dialed.

"Yo."

"Are we clear?"

"Hold on," came the voice from the other side, and then a clicking noise. *"Yeah."*

"Archie! Will Kelly. I'm running late, and I have to go back to the office. Can I come by later than I said?"

"I close at seven, dude," Archie said.

"Come on, man," Will yelled, hoping his Motorola phone wouldn't give out. "I'm in a time crunch here. Can't we do this later tonight?"

"You paid me a lot of money for a service I suspect is needed now. If it's not that important to you, then I'll see you

whenever. Otherwise, tonight, I close at seven. I have stuff to do after work, plus the Giants are playing tonight. You know how I roll."

The line went dead. Will couldn't believe he forgot the keys. He looked at the clock on his car. It said five forty-two. There was no way he could make it back to the building, get to his office, and then get to Archie in time before seven o'clock. He sat in his car on the shoulder and thought about which direction was more important, and lightly banged his head on the wheel. The horn honking was activated by his forehead and returned by a passing motorist. He felt lost, screwed, stupid, and helpless all at the same time. The keys to the lock that hid the money were the most important thing. But it was useless without Archie's part of the puzzle. Five minutes after Archie terminated their phone call, he eased back into traffic and kept going until he saw the Narrows Road exit. He took the exit and navigated the ramps until he was headed south on Hylan Boulevard, where he drove for nearly thirty minutes until he found a strip mall with a dollar store, a nail salon, a coffee shop, and a television repair service. He parked in front of the coffee shop and walked to the entrance of the television repair store. He went right to the counter in the back, where the clerk didn't say a word, but opened the access panel of the counter and motioned him through. As the clerk, whose name tag read "Charly," swung the hinged countertop upward, Will stepped through to the other side of the counter and turned to the clerk.

"I'm here fo-" He was cut off by Charly the clerk, who pointed down an aisle of television tubes and spare parts. Will finally got to a door that swung open as he approached.

"Hey, Will," Archie said.

"Hi, Arch. Good to see you again."

"Yep. And since you're here, now, I guess this is the last time?"

"Nothing against you, but I hope so," Will said.

Chapter 4 – Say Cheese

Archibald Eklund, or Archie, as anyone who was on a first name basis with him addressed him, was the owner of "Boob Tube Service and Sales," a television sales and repair store just off Hylan Boulevard in the New Dorp Area shopping district on Staten Island. He had owned the shop for years, getting a startup loan from his father that he never paid back before the old man found a permanent resting place in Althea Gardens. Archie was a whiz at taking things apart and putting them back together, which made him a great fit for running the shop. Archie was thirty-one years old, unmarried, and kept his business open from seven o'clock in the morning until seven o'clock in the evening. He worked there every day, and he rarely left the building. A room in the back held a bed, a bathroom with a shower, a refrigerator, and all of Archie's possessions. He lived in the back of the store. If he wanted to watch television, he had his pick of the floor models that he offered to his customers, and right now, it was a 44-inch beauty that he had claimed as soon as it came off the truck from the manufacturer. Archie's business, on the books, earned a small profit, enough to keep the lights on and the doors open each month. But it wasn't the television sales and repairs, however, that made Archie the bulk of his earnings.

Archie lit a cigarette, pointed to a chair, and told Will to have a seat. He pulled out a clipboard from the bottom drawer of a desk and flipped a few pages. The cigarette hung at the very edge of his mouth as it burned.

"So, the only thing I can't get right now is the passport," he said, exhaling smoke. "I'm out of books."

Will shifted in his chair. "I don't think that's too much of an issue. I don't plan on leaving the country. Not right away, at least."

"Okay," Archie exhaled. If you want to give me a forwarding address, I can mail it to you."

"Forget it. I don't even know where I'm going yet."

Archie moved to the other side of the room and, from a rafter in the unfinished ceiling in the room, drew down a shade with a blue background and placed another chair upon a set of "x" marks which were etched into the floor, and were barely noticeable.

"Okay, D.B. Cooper, you know the drill," Archie mused, cigarette still dangling. "Let's get started. Sit here. Take off the suit jacket and shed the tie. You don't wanna look too important."

Will moved across the room to the chair that Archie had placed in front of the blue screen. He did as he was told and sat motionless as Archie pulled out a camera and attached it to a tripod that he pulled out from a closet. Will watched him twist knobs and make adjustments, sticking his eye against the eyepiece and looking at Will through the device at least a half dozen times. Finally, Archie told him not to say "cheese," or anything else, but to stay still. Will steeled himself as Archie took his photograph, and he stayed motionless, waiting for the next instruction.

Archie went over to a computer on his desk and punched a few keys. "Where are we from again?" he asked, smoke billowing around his head, although he already knew, and he motioned Will over to the desk. "Philly, right?"

"That's it," Will said, as he sat down in yet another chair in the small room. "76 Sylvester Street. 19149 is the zip."

Archie removed the cigarette from his mouth, holding it between two fingers and pointing it at Will. "That seems awful particular."

"I have it memorized already. Stallone played 'Rocky,' which came out in 1976, and was filmed in Philly, so I did 76 Sylvester Street in Philly, just in case I get asked sometime by someone. Besides, Kathleen's parents live in Philly, and over time, I think I have become familiar enough with the major landmarks that I can fake it if needed."

Archie shook his head and exhaled smoke. "You're still a weird dude... even for a jock."

Will shook his head. "I'm not that much of a jock anymore. You know, I just go on daily runs. That's about it."

"All right," Archie said. "You know I usually don't have you wait for this shit. This is going to take a few minutes. Hang tight. I'll be back in a few. I gotta close the store." He crushed out the cigarette into an ashtray holding several other butts.

Will relaxed in his chair. He thought it was odd that Archie still thought of him as a jock. Sure, he was, in high school where they met, being part of the wrestling team, running track, and trying his hand at baseball, but never really excelling at it. He watched the computer whizzing and whirring away, creating his new identity, and thought back to high school and how Archie was back then. To put it mildly, Archie was a high school nerd. He was great at Math, terrible in Gym, a superstar in Electronics, and alone at his lunch table. He was a target for a lot of the student body, but Will developed a soft spot for him after a summer of math tutoring kept Will from failing a grade in their junior year. He had let his studies slip in favor of his sports schedule, and his math teacher, a big fan of Will's accomplishments on the track and wrestling mat, allowed Will to take his final exam after the tutoring session with Archie. After that, in their senior year, Will kept the bullies and jocks off Archie's back whenever he was around. Will's protection of Archie paid off as well, and Archie had a top-of-the-line model computer and could work wonders as his fingers touched the keys. After a while, Archie had created fake IDs for most of the senior class. There was a friendly cashier at one of the local liquor stores who didn't seem to think it was odd that all these younger men and women, all twenty-one years old, of course, had memberships to the same video store. After graduation, Archie and Will went to different colleges and lost touch. Fortunately for Will, he had stumbled across Archie at their graduating class's ten-year reunion. As they mingled around a decorated firehall for the occasion, Will and Archie bumped into one another, and Will was amused to find that Archie was still in the fake ID business, albeit under the front of a legitimate business. It was this knowledge that solidified Will's plan to escape his current life. He could get his hands on the money. He could get out of town. Those were easy enough. But to reinvent himself, to give himself a new identity and a new background? It was Archie to the rescue.

The whirring and clunking noises of the printer jolted Will out of his memory and back into reality. He turned to the computer and focused his attention on the small print, which was barely readable from where he was sitting. He looked at what was coming out of the printer. It was a Pennsylvania driver's license. Or at least it was supposed to be, and looked like one. As the carriage moved back and forth across the target page, Will watched it create a new version of him, one line at a time. He peered over the edge of the printer, and he was able to get a glimpse of the new him. William Robert Lomax. 76 Sylvester Street, Philadelphia, Pennsylvania, 19419. He was thinking he'd probably go by Bill, or Billy. It would take some getting used to on a constant basis.

As the printer continued its magic that would change Will's future, possibly forever, Archie strolled back into the back room and threw a set of keys on the desk. He walked over to a wall with a set of light switches and turned most of them to the down position, and Will could sense the darkening of the front of the store.

"It's just us now," Archie said with a grin. "And now I have to ask you something. You are married, you have a decent-looking wife, a house on a golf course, and a great, well-paying job." Archie lit another cigarette and squinted his eyes, looking at Will. "So, why?"

Will leaned back in the chair, trying to avoid the smoke, and crossed his legs. "Because I can't stand any of it," he said. "Kathleen and I split up. She's not even living at the house anymore. She's got her own place near where she works. Before we officially split, we barely talked, let alone anything else. No spark there anymore. The house, I can't afford the house by myself on my salary alone, so that's a dead end that will just cost me money until I can unload it. Not a great market, right now, by the way. And it's across from a golf course, not on it. I sneak on to play a few holes in the evening if I can, but I don't have any rights as a member to be there. And the job? The job is boring, and it is without a heart. I can't stand to look into these people's eyes and tell them their dream is stupid and they will never make a dime with their ridiculous ideas of owning their own business, staking a claim for themselves in an oversaturated market in a city that is bursting its own seams with other people who have the same dream. I made a terrible choice when I took the position at Pickwick. The money spoke too loudly, and I answered the call too eagerly. I need to get out. I want to do something that is rewarding. I don't feel like I can look at myself in the mirror at the end of each day and say, 'Dammit, Will, you did a good job today. You made a real difference.' It is a terrible position, and I hate it. Thoroughly. And my boss is a jackass."

"Uh, don't sugar-coat it," Archie quipped. They shared a small chuckle, and Archie continued. "I get it, I guess. If you're that unhappy, I can see making a change. But this is a *big* change. Maybe just quit your current job and find something else to do? Maybe move, legally?"

"Arch," Will broke in. "It's not completely about that anymore. You know what's going on. I have done some things that I am not really proud of, things I have to get away from, or there will be serious repercussions. For instance, this work we're doing here—" he stopped himself. "What are we waiting for anyway? This is taking forever."

"You paid quality dollars, mon frere," Archie said, extinguishing the cigarette. "You are going to get quality work. Keep going with the story."

"Okay," Will said, still glancing at the printer. "What are we doing here? I paid you, as you say, quality dollars. Twenty-five thousand of them, now, to be exact. Do I look like a guy who has twenty-five thousand dollars lying around? Show me what that guy looks like. I want to meet him. You know I have been slowly, over about the last three months, stealing funds from my company to fund this little endeavor. Not only to pay for your fine work here, but for the rest of the cover story, and my future, as a new person, an unknown, in a new place, wherever that may be."

Archie had grabbed his chair in the middle of the story and now sat in it. "Umm, you're probably going to go to prison," Archie said.

Will smiled. "They are going to have to find me first. I figure I am going to have a decent head start by the time whoever may be chasing me will figure out I am not where I am pointing them to think that I will be."

"So, you're going to leave a trail of money on the sidewalk going one direction and you'll go the other?"

"Well, not exactly," Will said. "But I've got a plan, and the less you know about it, the better off you and I will be. By the way, if they ever figure this out about me, and come to you asking what you did to help, just tell them I held you at gunpoint."

"Dude, you're off your rocker. How much money are we talking about here? How much did you steal?"

"Well," Will said as he stood from his chair. "It's in the mid-six figures. Where's the bathroom?"

"Get the hell outta here!" Archie said, shocked. He sat in his chair and looked at Will, waiting for the punchline, but Will just nodded and said it was true. "I should have charged you more."

"I think it was enough. You don't have any expenses here, remember? Now, the bathroom?"

The printer had finished, and Archie was using a laminator to make the IDs look official. He pointed to the very back room where his apartment was.

"Use my personal one... in the back."

Will went into the back room, turned the light on, and marveled at Archie's setup. The bed, desk, couch, refrigerator, shower, and one of the biggest televisions Will had ever seen. As he was washing his hands, he looked in the mirror and questioned himself, not for the last time, *'What are you doing? How can you ever expect to get away with this?'* And he still had to go back for the keys. The keys were in his office. They were the keys, both figuratively and literally, to his future. He grabbed a paper towel and dried his hands, tossing the towel into the trash as he left.

"That's a pretty sweet setup you have back there," Will said. "Do you sleep here often?"

"I live here," Archie said, lighting his third smoke since Will had arrived. "The only time I ever really leave here is if we need something for the store or if I need something for myself, such as food and whatnot. I use the twenty-four-hour laundry next door that I don't have to pay for because I threw the owner a couple of floor model TVs. I have food options all up and down the street, I have my pick of televisions to watch, and my cable service is written off as a store expense. I have everything I need here. I'm just waiting to meet the right lady who will screw it all up for me."

As he was explaining his living arrangements, Archie had been carefully using various tools and machinery to make the laminate used on the driver's license look used and aged. He snipped off one corner of the license's laminate and used a buffer wheel to make the edges smooth, yet worn. He used a different attachment on the wheel to fog the lamination covering so that it did not look brand new. When he was done, he wrapped a rubber band around the cards and handed them to Will.

"Here you go," Archie said, cigarette bobbing up and down as he spoke the words. "You got your driver's license, which is the most important one, then you got some support IDs there to give you some backup."

"Seriously, Arch," Will interrupted, stuffing his tie in his pocket. "With the video store card?"

"I'm partial to them. They have worked for a long time. Although I think I'm going to have to move on to something else. Technology is catching up with me. Mail order DVDs and shit..." Archie was closing the programs on his computer and cleaning up from the process of putting some wear on the IDs. "Listen...wherever you go, you're going to want to establish yourself. Get a residence, I'm guessing you'll rent at first, but open a bank account with a little money, nothing too extravagant, rent a storage facility, even if you don't put anything in it for a while. Get a library card. Get some bills with your new name and address on them, cable television, and get a job, something other than being a loan officer. Try to blend in. Hide in broad daylight...that kinda thing."

He put the cigarette on the ashtray, stood up, and closed the closet where he stored the camera.

"So, I hope the weather is nice down there," he said.

"Down there?" Will questioned with an eyebrow up. "Where do you think I'm going?"

"I don't know. I guess you were heading down south to a non-extradition country, some island somewhere, maybe like Fiji or something. Oh, that's right. No passport!" Archie reached out a hand as Will rose to his feet from his chair. Will accepted it and gave it a shake. "Anyway, wherever you're going, don't ever come back. Blend in. Disappear. Be William Lomax, and be him well, because Willem Kelly is dead."

Will shook his head. "Not just yet. Kelly has a little work left to do, or this little escape plan becomes much harder. I'm only half done."

Archie let go of Will's hand and shook his head. "Ballsiest thing I think I've ever seen, man. Take care of yourself, and get out of here."

Will smiled, then turned towards the exit and headed out of the self-locking front door with part of his ticket to a new life in his pocket. Now he had to get the rest.

Chapter 5 – See You Tomorrow

It was a quarter to eight when Will left Archie's store. He stopped at an automated teller machine and took out his daily maximum from his bank. Unfortunately, he would be leaving some of his balance behind as there wasn't enough time to take out the entire amount from the machines, and he didn't dare go inside the bank and work with a teller to close his account. *That might be a red flag,* he thought. He made his way back to Interstate 278 and then headed back across the Verrazano Narrows Bridge. He was heading back to the office. He had to try to get those keys tonight, even though he had never gone to the office this late, and it would probably be eight- thirty when he got there.

"Lomax," he said out loud. "Lomax. William Lomax. Billy Lomax. Bill Lomax. Will Lomax. Willy Lomax. Willy...with a 'y'? Or with an 'ie?' No. Billy. Billy with a 'y.' Billy Lomax. Billy Bob Lomax? No, Billy Lomax. Billy Lomax. Billy Lomax," he repeated. *This would take some getting used to, and a lot of practice,* he thought. *What the hell are you doing,* he thought to himself again as the scenery zoomed by. *This all seemed like a good idea a few months ago. It's stupid, selfish, risky, and you have to give it a two-percent chance of working. Probably the best-case scenario is that they put you in a low-security prison with a room to yourself. Worst case, well...* He laughed out loud, and then actually laughed about himself laughing at the concept of the worst-case scenario. He tried to clear his head of that as the BMW streaked back through the Brooklyn-Battery Tunnel and back into the city. He loved the city at night when he was younger, and this was a nice flashback in, presumably, his last night to see it.

He pulled the car into the parking garage and parked next to the elevator to the lobby. He rushed inside and punched the "L" button, the doors closed, and he was whooshed up to the main floor. From there, he needed to take an express elevator which would take him to the second third of the building, where he took yet another elevator up some seventeen more floors. The elevator doors slid open, and he walked out into the hallway towards his office. When he got there, he began to worry as all of the lights were off. *Nobody works late around here, you idiot,* he thought to himself. *Don't blame them. You don't ever want to be here a minute longer than you need to.* He pulled on the right handle of the double glass doors that opened into Pickwick Finance. Nothing happened. The door was locked. He knew it was probably a futile effort, but he pulled on the left side door as well. Still nothing. These were the only doors into the office, and they were locked. And his office was locked inside as well. And his desk was locked inside, and his keys to a storage facility locker were locked inside as well.

Dammit! he almost said out loud, but kept it in his thoughts as he turned around and backed up against the glass. *What are you going to do now?* He looked around the hallway and saw a fire extinguisher mounted on the wall. *You could throw that through the glass,* he thought, but that thought quickly dissipated with visions of alarms blaring and security guards meeting him at the shattered glass doors on his way out, handcuffs at the ready. No, that wouldn't do. *You're going to have to come back tomorrow. Early tomorrow, before anyone gets here. The office opens at eight o'clock, but what time do the doors get unlocked? Who even has the keys? Whoever it is, you'll be waiting here for them in the morning.*

With that, Will made the three-elevator gauntlet run back down to the parking garage, got into his car, exited back out into the city, and took the drive through the tunnel and over the bridge, paying his three-dollar and fifty cents and seven-dollar tolls, respectively, for the fourth time that day, and headed for home. His daily drive from the city was usually peaceful, but that was mostly because he kept the windows up and listened to books on tape. One thing he and Kathleen had always agreed on was their taste in literature. They liked the same authors, and had full libraries of some of their favorites, and were still building those of others at the time of their separation. As he drove on and mindlessly listened to the audio version of a book that he had previously read a handful of times, he wondered what would become of those collections, of everything in the house, and even the house, when he was gone. They would look for him, to be sure, but if they never found him, he wondered if the powers that be would give Kathleen a chance to take anything more for which she felt a value. *What does it matter?* he thought. *You'll be gone, you don't care about it, and she will be able to afford to replace anything she wants, including you.*

When Will pulled up to the house that he now identified as *his* empty house, now that Kathleen had moved out, he activated the garage door opener and whipped the BMW into the space on the left-hand side of the two-car shelter. This was a habit. When Kathleen was there, Will had always granted her the right side, because it was closest to the indoor entrance to the house. Will had the left side, which was fine for him, as he usually used the breezeway entrance, which opened into the laundry room. As he did so this night, he looked at all his clothes in the hamper at the bottom of the laundry chute, and realized he was going to be up for a while washing the clothing he was going to need to pack for his great escape in the morning. Most of it was standard clothing, such as golf shirts, khakis, jeans, and socks. There were a few pairs of suit pants, but he wasn't planning on taking any of those with him. He had one suit left to wear before he ran, and it was hanging up in his closet with a half-dozen others he hoped he would never see again.

He immediately started the washing machine and grabbed all of the clothes he felt were important, stuffed them into the front-loader with a cup full of detergent, and shut the door. The machine started immediately as he slipped off his shoes, emptied the contents of his pockets, and laid them atop the dryer, then he shed his suit, and tossed it to the floor. *Screw it,* he thought. *Don't need that one anymore, either.*

He reached into a closet in the laundry room and pulled out a duffel bag. This would do well for the regular clothes he would take with him. He threw the bag on top of the dryer to pack his clothes in after they were clean and dried. He turned and left the laundry room and came out into the sitting room on his way up to his bedroom. He noticed the red light blinking on the phone and checked the readout. Three messages, but he decided to leave them alone and tend to the matters at hand. He had to pack his bogus bags, as he called them. These would be the bags that pulled off the ruse at the airport, and the bags that he would leave behind, stuffed in some lockers. He figured two bags would be enough. His suit bag and a small overnight bag should suffice. They should not need to be checked, and he would have clearance to carry them onto the plane as carry-on luggage. He'd store his duffel bag in a locker when he got to the airport, and then pick it back up when the bag shenanigans at the ticket desk were over and he was on his way to a new life. He threw two suit jackets in his suit bag and stuffed the other overnight suitcase with random items, such as t-shirts, sweatpants, beach towels, and dress socks. Not too heavy to be unmanageable, but not too light to be suspicious if someone else happened to pick them up before he was done with them. He had to make sure he had one other bag with him when he left tomorrow. He needed it for the money. He wasn't really happy about the thought of traveling with a bag full of cash, but what other option did he have? He needed the money for his travel and escape, and couldn't take the risk of it leaving his possession. He reached into the top of his closet and pulled out another gym bag. It was a blue New York Giants duffel bag that he had gotten as a gift two Christmases ago from Kathleen's parents. It would work fine. It even had a zipper on the inside, giving the bag two sections. *Maybe you can hide some of the money in that inside pouch*, he thought. *Idiot,* he laughed to himself. *It's still in the same bag!*

Will sighed and shook his head. He would have to deal with his insecurities about carrying the money. He needed it, and he couldn't trust anyone to hold it for him or send it to him when he decided he had found home. He decided the bag would be fine, and he would watch it like a hawk, and maybe he would use the same idea again when he got his new life situated. Maybe he would store it in public storage again. He certainly wasn't going to keep it in the freezer or under his mattress. Too many movies had taught him that. He would figure it out later. *Of course, this is all assuming you still can get to the money. Why didn't you keep an extra key? Why didn't the owner of the stupid storage place make you give him a key in case you lost one?* But no, both keys were on the same ring inside the little box, locked in his desk.

Enough, he told himself. *You're going to drive yourself nuts. Calm down. Have a beer.* He walked back through the house to the kitchen and opened the refrigerator door. He grabbed a bottle of beer from the top shelf, twisted off the lid, and tried to toss it into the trash, but it sailed wide and clanked against the wall and fell to the floor. He watched it as it settled, turned away, and thought, *like you care. Someone else's problem after tomorrow.* He took a long pull from the beer and smacked his lips, refreshed by its coolness. It was September, but the weather had yet to start to make the turn toward the chilly Fall, and the cold beer felt good going down. He walked back to the sitting room, turned on the television, and found the Giants playing the Broncos, a game the Giants were losing. He shook his head and laid the remote control on the table next to the couch, and put his beer on a coaster right next to it. The red blinking light from the phone caught his eye once again, and he remembered the messages. He grabbed the remote control again and hit the mute button, and the television instantly went silent. He pushed the button on the phone to play the messages.

The first message was from Jeannie, his assistant at Pickwick.

"Mr. Kelly, it's Jeannie. I won't be able to make it into the office for the meeting tomorrow with Mr. Dickey. My grandson has a dentist appointment in the morning, and I have to take him because his mother is unable to miss work. Sorry for the short notice. Good luck tomorrow, and let me know if you need anything from me. I'll be home until around 10 o'clock, and then I will probably be in the office around lunchtime after I take him back to school."

Well, that gets her out of the immediate line of fire, at least, he thought. *She probably won't be collateral damage in the one-sided war that will happen tomorrow. Good for her.* He took another sip from his beer and punched the button on the phone to delete her message.

The second message started, and it was from his doctor's office.

"This is a courtesy message for Willem Kelly. We are calling to remind you of your appointment with Dr. Dougherty tomorrow at 3:30 p.m., regarding your knee. Please remember to bring your insurance card, and we will see you then!" said the cheery voice on the other end of the call.

Will took another sip of his beer. *Ol' Doc Dougherty is going to have some free time tomorrow afternoon,* he laughed to himself. *You're not going to make that one. Your knee. Three months ago, you take a tumble on your run, and then get the brilliant idea that you might want to get it looked at. It's fine. Sayonara, Doc. It's been fun."* Then he thought about the day he fell, and remembered that was the day he and Kathleen decided over dinner to separate.

He reached over and hit the button on the phone, and as if on cue, Kathleen's voice poured from the speaker.

"Hey, you," she said. *"Just thought I would call and see how you're doing. I also had a reminder that your doctor appointment for your knee is tomorrow at 3:30. Don't forget. And make sure you have your insurance card. Anyway, hope you had a good day. Call me if it's not too late. Bye, now."*

He sat back on the couch with his head against the pillow and rubbed his eyes. It was getting late. It was after 10 o'clock now, and he still had things to do. He needed to check to see if the washing machine had stopped so he could dry his clothes. He needed to get his clothes all together and by the door so he could just grab them on his way out in the morning so they would be for the charade at the airport. *The airport! Idiot,* he thought.

He ran to the laundry room, where the washer was still going, grabbed his wallet from the top of the clothes dryer, and then headed back to the couch and grabbed the phone. He pulled a piece of paper from the wallet, which had two phone numbers, and slid his Visa card out from one of the card slots in the wallet. He dialed the first number. American Airlines' recorded menu gave him a maze of several options to navigate by pushing buttons on his phone. Eventually, he got to a ticketing agent, who was more than happy to book him a flight for 9:17 a.m. to Ft. Lauderdale and take the sixteen-digit number on his credit card in exchange. The agent told him his boarding pass would be available for pickup at the main American Airlines desk.

Will hung up the phone and then picked it back up again to schedule the second flight, when he had an idea. *Why point them to a specific place like Grand Cayman, when you can leave them an empty canvas of places to look? They will see you've booked the plane to Florida because you're on the run, but then they won't have anything else to go on.* He put the receiver back into its cradle on the phone. *They won't know if you went to the islands, they won't know if you went to Mexico, and they won't know if you went to Argentina or Siberia. Oh, Willie Boy, this might be your best idea so far!*

He heard the washing machine stop and immediately ran in to turn the clothes over to the dryer to do its part. He stuffed the clothes in and dropped in a dryer sheet, shut the door, set it to high, and started the machine. He grabbed the duffel bag from the top of the dryer and ran up the stairs. He opened his top drawer and grabbed every pair of his underwear he could find. He selected two folded white t-shirts and two pairs of cotton shorts. His golf shirts and two pairs of jeans were down in the laundry still. He added two pairs of white tube socks to the bag and then zipped it up, grabbed his suit bag, the overnight bag, and the duffel bag, and headed down the stairs. He laid them all by the door and went back to his beer and the football game.

Ohhh, is it too late to call Kathleen? he asked himself out loud. "It's almost eleven o'clock," he said aloud. He took the last swig of beer from the bottle and hopped up from the couch. He headed into the kitchen to the refrigerator and grabbed another beer from the top shelf. He popped the cap and made the effort to hit the trash can again, with this one hitting its mark. "Two points!" he exclaimed, heading back to the couch. He sat down and looked at the phone. Why did he feel obligated to call her? He was never going to see her again. She would have her life, and he would be a fugitive.

But he wanted to hear her voice one last time. He picked up the phone and hit the first number on the phone's speed dial options. The phone began to ring as expected, but kept ringing without an answer. He hung up the phone after the fourth ring as he did not want to wake her if she was sleeping. *Don't poke the bear,* he thought. *Now, that wasn't really fair, you jerk. Be nice. She's been even-tempered lately, so you can be nice.* He was still scolding himself when the phone rang, making him jump. He saw the number on the caller ID, but didn't need it.

"Hello," he said.

"Hello yourself," Kathleen answered. *"Why are you calling me this late. I'm sure it could have waited until tomorrow."*

"Well," he paused. "You called me, and I didn't want to leave you hanging. I didn't wake you up, did I?"

"No, not yet. I was sitting here reading, trying to finish this book."

"What book?" he asked.

She exhaled and paused. *"It's a new Grisham book. It's called <u>A Painted House."</u>*

"Another legal thriller?"

"Not even close," she said. *"It's about a family in Arkansas that farms cotton. It's rather good, actually. You can have it when I'm done if you want to read it. I can drop it off tomorrow."*

"Sounds good. You want to make it a dinner? I can cook something." He hated lying to her, but normalcy was part of his great plan. He immediately thought of her knocking on the door and realizing she was being stood up, and quickly wished he could retract the offer.

"No," she said, and he instantly felt relief. *"Maybe another night. The girls and I are going out for drinks tomorrow. But I will still bring you the book."*

"Another night, then," he said. Then, thinking about tomorrow, he said, "You can leave it on the porch if I'm not there." A pause, and then he said, "I'll let you go. It's getting late. Take care."

"Good night, Will. See you tomorrow."

He hung up the phone and began questioning himself again. But he had to do it. Tomorrow would be a big day. He finished off his beer, went to the kitchen, and dumped the empty bottles into the trash can. He also picked up the bottle cap he had previously let stay on the floor and tossed it into the garbage as well. He walked back into the sitting room and looked at his bags piled onto the floor. His future is there now, just in a few bags. He grabbed the duffel bag and went to the laundry room to pack the rest of his clothes he was taking with him, and once again laid the bag by the door with the rest of the others. He turned out the lights, went upstairs, sat on the edge of the bed to set his alarm for 5:00 a.m., and crawled into his bed and went to sleep.

Chapter 6 – The 94th Floor

When Will woke up on Tuesday to the blaring sound of his alarm clock, he immediately felt the difference in the day. Today was the day, and it would be a brand-new start. He hopped out of bed and jumped into the shower. For the first day since his wrestling days in High School, he wasn't going for his morning run. He was going on *the* run, and he just had to do a few things first to make it all happen. He was going to get to the office early, and as soon as it was open, he would run in, do what he needed, and run out, hopefully before anyone saw him, especially Frank Dickey. But he remembered Dickey had an appointment in the morning, so Will thought he could avoid him, and Jeannie was not coming in until noon. He should be able to get in and out without too much trouble.

When he was dressed in what he thought and hoped would be the last suit he would ever wear, he grabbed the bags by the door and headed through the laundry room to the breezeway entrance to the garage, locking the doors behind him. He tossed the bags into the trunk of the BMW, backed out of the garage, and said goodbye to his house. He would miss the pool the most and cursed himself for not getting one last use out of it last night. He clicked the button on the remote control to close the garage door, pulled out of the driveway, and made what he hoped was his final drive to work at Pickwick.

The traffic was lighter this early in the morning, and he made the drive quicker than he thought he would. *Thirty-eight minutes*, he thought to himself. *Not too bad.* He pulled into the parking garage and headed for the elevator, repeating his process from the night before. When he got to the floor where Pickwick was located, he turned the corner and was shocked to find the office dark and the doors still locked. He sat on the bench in the hallway and looked at his watch. It was a quarter after six. He decided he would give it some time for the doors to be unlocked, but when no one unlocked them at six-forty, he got back on the elevator and headed back down to the garage. He would wait it out there, gauge it by the number of cars that came into the garage, and then head back upstairs. He stopped in the lobby and once again extracted some cash.

He entered his BWM, closed the door, and turned on the radio, selecting an easy listening station. It was too early for Limp Bizkit and Kid Rock. He pulled his wallet from his back pocket and looked at the worn edges and the scratched leather. *You should get a new one,* he thought. He opened the billfold and took out his new identification cards, and put them in his breast pocket. Leaving anything that said he was Willem Kelly in his wallet, he opened the glove compartment and tossed in the wallet. Thinking twice, he pulled the wallet back out, removed all of the identifications, credit cards, receipts, and business cards he had within and put them all into the glove box, placed his new identifications into the wallet, and placed it back into his breast pocket. He looked at his watch again. Ten of seven. Probably still too early to get in. He closed his eyes and let his head fall against the headrest, and within a few minutes, he fell asleep. He was awakened, however, by a loud rapping on his window. A security guard was knocking. Will lifted his head and pushed the button, which lowered the window on the passenger side of the car.

"Hey, you can't sleep here," the guard bellowed.

"I'm sorry," Will said sleepily and nodded. "I work in this building, and I was waiting for my office to open."

"Well, get a move on," the guard said. "You can't sleep here."

Will nodded at the guard again and turned the key off, silencing the radio. He looked at his watch and saw it was seven-fifty. *I can't believe I fell asleep for almost an hour!* He needed to hurry to get from the car to the elevator, as the garage was filling up, hopefully with none of his co-workers. He had to get back up to Pickwick, and quietly, and with any luck, no one would see him.

He grabbed his briefcase and entered the building, and took the elevator ride up to the 48th floor, where Pickwick called their corporate home. As he came off the elevator, he bumped into Jerry Nichols, one of his buddies from his company softball and bowling teams, and another loan officer at Pickwick.

"Hey Will!"

"Morning, Jerr," Will replied.

Jerry followed along as Will navigated the various doors and hallways to get to his office. Jerry said, "You look a little frazzled today. Hair on the back of your head is mussed up. Party too much last night?"

"No parties. Just in a hurry."

"What's up? Big meeting?"

Will stopped in his tracks and looked at Jerry. "As a matter of fact, I do have a big meeting. How did you know?"

"Just a guess, man. You look like you're on a mission."

"You know how it is... business never sleeps," Will said as he unlocked the door to his office.

"You ain't kiddin'," Jerry said as he continued down the hallway. "I got seven on my calendar already today, and that's before my day even starts! Everyone wants money!"

Will closed his door behind him, leaning against it and wondering how he was going to pull this off. He was leaving his estranged wife and his current life behind in hopes of a new start. His wife would get over it. She would be mad when he didn't answer the door, and then concerned thereafter, when he didn't show up anywhere, ever. But she had moved on, and she would be okay. And good for her. They were a great match when they were younger, but situations caused them to outgrow each other, and now she had secured a career where she would live comfortably without him dragging her down.

Will left the security of his locked door and went to his desk, which he unlocked with yet another key. He opened the drawer and drew out a small tin of what used to be breath mints. Underneath some cotton batting was a ring with two small bronze keys. The keys to a lock on the door of a small unit in a storage facility. The keys to his future. The keys to his freedom. Now, he just had to get out of there.

He closed the desk drawer, locked it out of habit, shook his head, and looked at his key ring. *You'll be able to get rid of a lot of these soon, Willie Boy,* he said to himself. He grabbed his briefcase from the top of the desk and walked to his door, peering out the thin floor-length window on the left side. No Jeannie in sight, and he didn't expect her there. He really didn't want to see anyone else. He opened the door and started walking down the hallway. He reached the copy machine and made a left toward the door, and found himself staring right into the face of one Francis Roger Dickey, the last person he wanted to see. Behind Dickey was a large man in a black suit that Will had never seen before, but was immediately intimidated by him.

"Hello, Willem, we have not met in person, but I am Roger Dickey," Dickey said, raising an eyebrow. "This is James Higgins. He's with Loss Prevention and Security, and LPS makes sure all the money that is supposed to go to the bottom line gets there. Where are you headed so fast?"

At least he got your name right today, Will thought. *Dammit, why him, and why right now, and how does he know it's you? He's never seen you before.*

"Good morning, Mr. Dickey. Mr. Higgins. Nice to meet you. I was headed to the men's room, then the coffee room. Big day today. Gotta get ready for our meeting. I can't wait to explain it to you. It's a little embarrassing. I made an error in the numbers in the reports, but I can show you."

Dickey put his eyebrow back where it belonged on his face. "That will be good news, Kelly. I would hate to think we had a loss issue, and you were involved. Get your coffee and your information and head up to the big office on 94. Let's get this over with."

"I'm halfway there already. See you up there," Will stammered. *Wow,* he thought. *They were pulling out the big guns. The big office on the 94th floor? And this guy Higgins? No, sorry guys, there's only one direction that elevator is going when this guy gets on it, and that's down.*

The Dickey and Higgins party turned and walked to the double glass doors that led out into the hallway while Will cringed, watching them, until the elevator doors closed them inside. He waited about two minutes to make sure they would be done when he got there, and almost ran to the elevator. Once he was in the elevator, he opened his cell phone and called the TOP taxi company, and requested a taxi to meet him at the southeast corner of Murray and West at eight forty-five. He thought again about saying the destination was Newark Airport, across the river, but what would that accomplish? He was second-guessing himself now. But he decided not to provide the destination and let fate decide what would happen based on that decision. He'd ask the driver to make a quick stop at the public storage facility on North Moore. Time was precious now. The three-elevator ride seemed to take forever, and he was leaving for the garage below, while everyone else was taking elevators up to their workplaces. He finally made it down to the garage and to the BMW. He looked at the car one last time as he pulled his bags from the trunk. He tossed the car keys into the trunk, along with his cell phone, and shut the lid. Now it was time to bolt. He only had a handful of minutes left to meet the taxi.

Will exited the garage on foot, lugging his bags and briefcase, looking around to see if he recognized anyone. He had to hurry to get to the taxi, though, and began his walk at a quick pace. When he reached Barclay, he turned left, and then a right turn onto West. He picked up his pace and ran almost full speed to Murray. As he neared the corner, he saw the taxi waiting for him. Then, he heard a terrible shriek from above. He dropped his bags, covered his ears, stopped, and looked for the source of the noise up in the sky, and then he saw and heard the most terrible thing he had ever seen. And it was the worst sound he had ever heard, as he looked on with total disbelief as the terrorist-hijacked American Airlines Flight 11 disappeared in an explosive fireball into the north side of the World Trade Center's North Tower.

Chapter 7 – Under Attack

Detective Brian Greco ran from his house to his car in the driveway of his house and sped off, leaving tire marks in the road. He had heard on his radio about the tragedy of an airplane crash at the World Trade Center, and everyone was being called in to the crash site to assist. As he sped through the neighborhood, he grabbed his radio microphone from the dashboard of the car and pushed the button on the side.

"Stevo, I'm on my way. I should be there in less than ten. What do we know?"

The voice on the other end of the radio appeared after a crackle of static. *"Greco, it's a damned mess down here, man. I've never seen anything like this. A minute or two ago, a plane flew into the North Tower of WTC. It left Logan in Boston at seven fifty-nine, headed for Los Angeles."*

"Was it rerouted for some reason?" Greco asked. "Why would it be coming so far south if it's going to LA?"

"Don't know yet," Steve Angelucci reported over the radio. *"It took off fine, and at eight-thirteen, Air Traffic Control lost contact. A few minutes later, they took a hard left and went south. Jesus, just get here ASAP."*

"10-4." Greco got as close to the World Trade Center compound as he could before he was stopped by roadblocks built of police cars. He got out of his car and flashed his badge to the police at the barricades, and they waved him through. Debris from the crash was raining down from the top of the North Tower, where the plane had crashed. He put on his sunglasses and looked up toward the top of the building. His view was partially blocked by the South Tower of the World Trade Center, but what he was able to see was horrifying enough. The North Tower was on fire, with heavy smoke billowing from the crash. It looked to be limited to the top third of the building, but he couldn't tell for sure. People were streaming away from the building in mobs, and he felt like he was swimming upstream against them. "Stevo, where are you?"

Angelucci keyed his radio while trying to advance on the building. *"I'm near the doors, closest to West. All of NYPD and FDNY are here, I think. We're trying to get in while everyone else is trying to evac. Hurry."*

"I'm here," Greco yelled. He was stopped at the barricades that were being constructed all around the area. "Detective Brian Greco!" he yelled as he flashed his badge once again. Once inside the barricades, he located Angelucci.

"Can we get up there?" Greco yelled at his partner. The debris was still falling around them, some of it still on fire as it landed behind them. It added to the deafening roar which engulfed the scene, comprised of members of the police and firefighter units giving orders, the constant blaring sirens, and the chilling screams of civilians.

"There's a ton of cops heading up there already. FDNY is also heavy inside, climbing the stairwells. It's a human traffic jam between them going up and civs coming down!" Angelucci yelled above the clamor.

Greco looked around and saw dozens of FDNY and NYPD members headed toward the building entrances as hundreds of employees were evacuating in the other direction.

"Get clear of here and get on the horn and find out what else there is to know," Greco said. He looked back up toward the top of the North Tower again. The smoke was getting worse. Find out who is coming to help, what's the plan, are we getting National Guard, anything? I'm going to work on getting some of these people out of this area until we figure out what's going on."

Angelucci nodded and began to head across the street when he stopped and pulled out his cellular phone. He grabbed Greco's shoulder before his partner could get away. Greco turned and saw Angelucci holding up a finger as if to say, "one minute." Then he pulled down the phone from his ear and closed it.

"This was no accident. The plane was hijacked!" Angelucci screamed. "FDNY has ordered a mandatory evac of the North Tower. We gotta get these people outta here!" They moved back toward the building but got stuck in a mob of barricades and evacuees.

Greco yanked on Angelucci's arm and yelled, "Let's try another entrance!" and he was suddenly aware that the noise around them was getting louder, to the point that Angelucci almost didn't hear him from inches away. Then Greco pulled away; his eyes widened in horror as he looked to the sky, and saw another airplane flying low, and then directly into the south side of the South Tower.

"My God," Greco said. "We're under attack."

Chapter 8 – Desperate And On The Run

Will opened the back door of the taxi, tossed his bags to the other side, and took the seat behind the driver. "Let's get out of here now. Something bad is happening!" Will shouted.

"Ya think?" the driver retorted sarcastically. "Where are we going?"

"I need to make a quick stop first at a public storage place, first!" Will shouted above the constant wail of sirens from passing police cars and ambulances.

"No side routes, Buddy. Especially right now with this shit going on. Where's the storage place?"

Will almost considered getting out of the cab and finding another way to go, but things were getting hectic. "I'll throw you a hundred if you make the stop, and another hundred if you wait for me while I'm there."

The driver looked at Will in the rearview mirror. Will opened his billfold and pulled out two one-hundred-dollar bills to show the driver.

"Half now," said the driver. Will agreed and slid one of the bills through the slot in the plexiglass window. The driver took the cash and shoved it in his pocket. "This public storage place, where is it?"

Will was looking at his bags to make sure he still had them all. A lot had happened in the last seventeen minutes, and he wasn't sure he was altogether together. After he had heard the terrible noise and seen the aftermath of what had happened, he turned around and continued to the corner, where he was to meet his taxi, and his escape from whatever was going on right now, and hopefully everything that was going on before. He had stopped on the sidewalk next to the taxi, and found the driver outside of his door, staring on with dozens, maybe hundreds of others on the sidewalk who had started the morning in their normal fashion. That morning was now disrupted by confusion, chaos, and utter awe. Sheets of paper were falling around the area like eight-and-a-half-by-eleven-inch snowflakes, flitting around, turning over themselves, and looking for a place to settle.

Will heard the murmurs of others close to him, even through the shrieks around the mob. Some of those around him were supposed to be in that building. Will stopped short of exclaiming that he had just left, as that may have raised an eyebrow or two from others, who were asking anyone willing to share information.

A woman put a hand on his shoulder, and Will turned to see her. "Is it a bomb?" she asked in a thick Brooklyn accent.

"An airplane," he said.

Another man offered, "Crashed into the building about ten minutes ago. I saw the whole thing. I was supposed to be there already."

Will turned back around and looked at the wreckage that was burning at the top of the building, and he thought about himself and the fact that he was supposed to be there, too. And he thought of his co-workers. Jerry, whom he had spoken to just this morning. Will wondered if he was going to be okay. And Jeannie, who would have been there, but now had other things to do. He thought about those with whom he had built relationships over the years, and wondered what they must be thinking right now. And then he thought about the meeting he was supposed to be in, up on the 94th floor, and the others, Mr. Dickey and Mr. Higgins, who, up until a few minutes ago, were probably wondering where he was.

Will was looking at the top of the building, burning with fire, ash flying, office papers falling like snowflakes all around. Suddenly, he saw another explosion near the top of the building, this one just as horrific as the first. A gigantic fireball flew from several floors of the building and then upward, and Will could not stop staring. In the back of his head, though, something was nudging him along, to get on with his plan, even through this terrible scene, and he bolted for his taxi.

Will shook himself out of his memory of the past few minutes and looked beside him in the back seat of the taxi. After he counted three bags and a briefcase, he said, "Uh...it's on North Moore." With that, the driver slammed the car into drive and headed for their destination. From the opposite direction, police cars, fire trucks, and ambulances were streaming toward the crash site by what seemed like the dozens. The driver turned on the radio, and they listened to the news talk about the horror of the tragedy. He approached the entrance to the storage facility, but the gate was locked. Will stepped out and punched a code into a keypad, and the gate began to slowly open. He jumped back into the back seat of the cab, and when the gate rolled open enough, the driver rolled through. He kept going until Will told him to stop.

"Remember, you have to wait for me, please," he said.

"Gimme the other hundred now or I roll," the driver said. Will looked around. They were blocks from the crash site, but there was still chaos everywhere. He put the other hundred through the slot.

"And I'll give you another one when I get back," he said. "Just wait." He grabbed the duffel bag, left the taxi's door open, and walked over to a small garage door, not even wide enough to fit a car through. He bent down, grabbed the lock, and used one of his precious keys that were the source of so much trouble. The keys that, oh, if he had just remembered them yesterday, he would be on the road with his plan in full action. The lock snapped open, and he pulled the rolling door up. He walked into the small room and into the back corner and opened a paper box that he had gotten from an office supply store. He removed a small lock box and began rolling the combination wheels until he hit his birthday, 10-30-69. The box opened, and he made his biggest withdrawal of the day, just over four hundred and twenty-five thousand dollars in cash.

The horn of the taxi honked, and Will snapped up the cash and shoved it into his bag. He ran out of the small garage, left the door open, and the lock on the ground. He tossed the keys toward a storm drain in front of the taxi, but couldn't tell if they fell into the underground drainage system as desired. He didn't care. He tossed the bag in the cab and followed it in, shutting the door behind him. The driver looked at him, and Will pulled out his billfold and grabbed two more one-hundred-dollar bills, and slid them through the slot. The driver grabbed them, looked at them, and at Will through the rearview again.

"What are you doing?"

Will looked back at him through the mirror. "What do you mean?"

The driver sniffed and looked at him. "You got your bags, you're throwing money at me like crazy so that I don't leave you stranded, and you seem desperate. You look like you're going on the run."

"Mister," Will said, looking out the window. "I just saw an airplane crash into the building where I work. There are crazy people running all around, there is shit falling from the sky, every emergency vehicle from four states is heading to the same place I was supposed to be today. You're God-damned right I'm desperate and on the run. Away from here. Right now. Now you can profit from it, or you can let me out, but I'm getting out of here before there's another explosion up there and it starts raining more debris, or worse."

The driver threw the car into drive and began to navigate out of the parking lot of the storage facility. "Sir," he said. "That wasn't an explosion. I heard on the radio that it was another airplane. We're under attack by somebody. Where do you want to go now?"

"Newark Airport," Will said.

"Newark? In Jersey?"

"Yeah," Will said in disbelief, and he looked at his watch. It was eleven minutes after nine o'clock in the morning on September 11, 2001.

Chapter 9 – Newark

They headed for the Holland Tunnel, listening to the breaking news that came through the radio every few minutes or so as new developments happened. The driver turned off his dispatch radio, and neither of the men, Will nor the taxi driver, spoke. They just listened as they traveled, and for a period, while going through the tunnel, they lost radio reception. It was the driver who first broke the silence.

"Do you have any family in the area?"

Will leaned back and put his head on the headrest and exhaled. "I have a wife. But we are separated. So, technically, yes. I'm sure she's fine, though. She works on Staten Island. Meier's Corners area. How about you?"

The driver looked at Will in the mirror again. "Two kids, one in high school, the other in college, both are far enough away from all that shit earlier, so I know they are fine. I'm sure we'll talk later. Where are you headed from Newark? Although I'm not sure you could get *me* on a plane today."

Will wanted to keep up the ruse. "I'm headed down to Florida, on business."

"Business!" the driver exclaimed. "According to you, one of those airplanes just hit your building. You sure you still have a job?"

Will didn't really know how to answer the question, so he let it pass for a moment without one. The driver was taking Will exactly where he wanted to go, and that was away from the city, and that's all he cared about right now. He'd get to Newark, pull off his boarding scam, dump some baggage, and then hire a new hack to get him where he needed to go.

"Until they tell me I don't, I will do what they say," Will fibbed.

They drove the rest of the way through the tunnel in silence, and the lack of radio signal kept them from learning a lot of things as they rode. The Federal Aviation Administration had initially grounded all flights that would go through New York airspace, but after the crash of Flight 77 at the Pentagon at 9:37 a.m., of which the driver and his passenger would also learn later, the FAA would start the process of grounding all flights nationwide to the nearest able airport, and no new flights were taking off, meaning Will wasn't flying anywhere, not that it was ever in the plan anyway. He'd be traveling on the ground. Will was thinking about his ground travel when the driver interrupted his thoughts.

"Hey, did you hear that? No flights. They have all been grounded."

Will nodded and then said, "I heard."

The taxi driver looked back at him in the mirror and asked where he wanted to go instead of the airport.

"I still need to get to the airport. They won't ground the flights forever. They will probably be running later today. I still have to get where I am going."

"It's your money, pal," said the driver. "And I'll take you wherever you want to go, but it seems silly to me right now. If I were you, I'd be on the phone with my wife, separated or not, and letting her know that I was okay."

"I don't have a mobile phone," Will said, looking out the window of the cab and thinking about the mobile phone he tossed into the trunk of his BMW, both of which were in the garage under the North Tower. The cab was through the tunnel and in New Jersey now, and on Interstate 78 heading south to get to the airport. Will could now see the two buildings of the World Trade Center burning as he looked across the Hudson. It was an eerie sight. Two of the largest buildings ever created, and were burning near the top of each. "I'll call her when I get to the airport."

"Well, I get that. Not everyone's lucky enough to have one," the driver said, as they crawled along in traffic. "I don't have one. I call the dispatch on this radio. I was going to ask if I could use yours for a few minutes to call my kids."

Will was still looking at the buildings, bathed in black smoke. He couldn't *not* watch it. "Looks like we both need a pay phone," Will said, and at that moment, the South Tower, suffering so much structural damage from the impact and the burning fires within, began to collapse. Will watched in horror as it disappeared from view and became a terrible cloud of dust and rubble. "It's falling...Oh my God, those poor people," he said, eyes still fixed on the scene. And he found himself wiping tears from his face. The driver had not noticed that the traffic in front of him was moving again as they inched along, because he was turned toward the scene and watching as well, and a gap began to grow in front of the taxi. But no one noticed. No one blew their horns in their cars. They were all watching.

They were still tuned to the radio, learning all they could learn about this terrible day, and who was responsible for it. Three airplanes, supposedly all hijacked by terrorists, attacked high-profile targets. *What is left,* Will wondered. *How many more planes are in the sky? How bad is this going to get? What is yet to come?* They navigated a curve in the turnpike, and the scene was now at their backs, but Will continued to crane his neck to see it. One of the Towers was gone. The news on the radio claimed it was the South Tower, but Will wasn't sure. He couldn't wrap his mind around what he was seeing and think about it in a logical way. There was so much smoke, so much dust, and that was just what he could see. He couldn't imagine what was happening at the street level, where everything... *everybody,* had succumbed to gravity and now lay on or close to the face of the Earth. *What the hell is happening...*and then, he began to feel guilty. If he hadn't stolen money, if he hadn't been a criminal, and if he hadn't hatched what he thought was a master plan of escape, he would probably be in the middle of all of the horror that was unfolding. He finally looked away from the site and wiped another tear from his face.

"That's some scary shit, man...all those poor people," the driver said. "My name's Ed, by the way. I don't know why I didn't tell you before. Guess I was a little sidetracked."

"I'm W—Billy," Will caught himself.

"You don't look like a Billy. Billy's usually don't wear the corporate type clothes, huh?"

Will thought about it, but not really. He was preoccupied with what he had seen today, and it was burned into his memory. "Yeah, I guess," was all he could muster. He was still listening to the news radio that Ed had turned on earlier. And the news was getting worse. The Sears Tower in Chicago was evacuated as a precaution, and part of the wall at the Pentagon had collapsed. They still moved along slowly in traffic, and the more they traveled toward the airport, the more they learned how devastating the attacks would be. Bridges and tunnels into New York City had been closed, all roads around the crash site were closed, and covered with debris and ash. Will wasn't even looking at the terrible scene anymore. It was too terrible to think about what else could happen there. And then the newswoman spoke even worse words, and she reported that the South Tower of the World Trade Center was collapsing as well. Will turned around in the car to see, but all he saw in the distance was more smoke, dust, and ash.

A frantic voice broke into the morose report on the radio. Another plane had crashed, but not in a city, or into a building, but in a field in Pennsylvania, not too far from Camp David, across the state line in Maryland. The voice said they didn't have any details, but would be sure to share them when they became available.

"Camp David...are they going after the President now?" Ed questioned. It was rhetorical, the question, but for some reason, Will felt the need to answer it.

"I guess so," he said, sullen. "I guess nothing is off limits." It was in that moment that another voice came across the radio and stated that a car bomb had exploded outside the State Department in Washington. *What the hell,* he thought. *This is like a bad dream.* But it wasn't a dream, and he knew it. They continued the journey to the airport in silence for what seemed like forever as the news continued to pour from the speakers of the taxi, and it continued to get worse. When they reached the airport, a destination Will had wanted to get to as soon as possible to begin the next stage of his escape, he did not want to get out of the taxi. However, taxi driver Ed shifted the car to park and turned towards Will.

"Uhh, that's $53.50, sir."

Will looked up from his lap, where he had been looking since he lost sight of the horror across the Hudson River, just listening to the news, and wondering what was going to happen next. He stared blankly at the driver for a few seconds, until he finally blinked and shook himself out of the stupor that he was in.

"Oh, right," Will said, and slipped another one-hundred-dollar bill through the slot. "Thanks for getting me here, through all this. How are you going to get back to the city?"

"I don't think I am, man," he said, turning the dispatch radio back on and hearing only static. "I was thinking about this on the way. With the bridges and tunnels closed, I am going to try to go over to Caven Point, park this bitch, sit on the pier and watch this from across the harbor. I'll find a pay phone along the way and call my kids, let 'em know I'm okay."

"Well, thanks again," Will said. "Take care of yourself, and--good luck, with—everything, I guess." Ed nodded as Will grabbed his bags and closed the door. Ed drove off into the traffic of the departure area of the Newark airport and blended in amongst the other throng of taxi cabs. Will watched him go and then turned around to face his next challenge, the airport. But he noticed that it was more hectic than usual. More crowded. And then he remembered that there were no flights leaving. Anyone who was showing up to go elsewhere was stuck, and Will guessed it was happening all over the country. He sighed and he started his walk, and then he stopped, and sat on a bench. *What's the plan now? Do you even need to go in to the airport? With no flights, the hoax at the boarding counter won't work. Other than the cab, there's no proof you were even here.* He pondered his next move, but his mind was clouded, confused by what he had seen today. He was having trouble thinking straight, but he knew he had to be smart about his next move. He was originally supposed to dump the bags so that he could travel lighter and – *the bags,* he thought. *What if you check a bag? They must still be processing flights. Planes won't stay grounded forever.* Then he remembered his ticket. His flight was for a nine-seventeen takeoff. He was so caught up in the events of the day that he didn't even notice that he missed his flight. He walked inside the airport and looked around, and he saw a bank of lockers a short walk away on his right. He opened the locker, shoved his duffel bag with the money and some clothes into the locker along with his briefcase. *Why are you still carrying the briefcase? You don't need it. You should have left it in the car in the garage.* And then the memories of the morning all flashed through his head again, and all at once. He shut the locker door and pressed his head against it. He was still carrying the suit bag, draped over his shoulder, and looking like any other businessman on any other day, trying to get to his flight. He began walking across the concourse until he saw the American Airlines desk and made a beeline for it. A short, round woman with curly hair and glasses greeted him in a sober tone.

"Can I help you, sir?" she said, peering up at him from across the desk.

"Yes," Will said with a faint smile, and noticed the name on her lapel tag said "Marcy". "Marcy...Hi. I was supposed to be on a flight this morning to Ft. Lauderdale at 9:17, and I need to reschedule it for the next flight if possible."

Marcy straightened her glasses, but cocked her head to the side like a dog hearing another bark somewhere off in the distance. "Sir, I am not sure if you have heard...I can't imagine you haven't, but there are no flights leaving right now. The Federal Aviation Administration has grounded all flights for now."

"Right, because of the—yeah...Okay, but I just need to get a ticket for the next flight to Ft. Lauderdale, whenever it may be."

"Well, Sir, we have cancelled all of our flights for now, and even *we* don't know when we will resume. We have our standard schedule, which could resume as soon as tomorrow, but we don't know for sure yet."

"Uh, can you book me for my same flight tomorrow?"

"Sir," Marcy sighed, "We are not taking any reservations right now. When the FAA lifts the mandate, you can make an appointment. What I can do is refund your ticket because of the inconvenience, if you would like that, and then you can reschedule your flight when we resume service, and it is convenient for you. Can I have your ticket?"

Will didn't answer her. He didn't even hear her offer. His eyes were fixed on a television behind the desk above Marcy's head. He watched in horror as the scene unrolled, and the North Tower of the World Trade Center—The North Tower, *his tower*, began to crumble and fall into the city below. For the first time, he was seeing the news footage of the dreadful scene, and the debris, and the smoke, and the people running, covered in rubble, and dust, and blood, choking on the cloud that was enveloping the area at an alarming rate. Will's mouth was agape, and he, in instinct, put his hand over it because everyone he saw on the television news cast running from the area was doing the same thing. They were trying to escape, just like him. He never answered Marcy. He couldn't. He just backed slowly away from the desk, still watching, still covering his mouth, still agonizing over what he was seeing.

Chapter 10 – Diego

Thirty minutes later, Will sat on a bench in the concourse, still digesting what he had seen. He was not a very religious person. He went to church as a youth, mostly forced on him by his parents, but when he grew, he grew out of the weekly ritual. Though even as an adult, he and Kathleen would go on Easter and Christmas Eve, but going to church was not a normal Sunday activity. Still, he found the words *"my God"* running through his head on a minute-by-minute basis after what he had seen lately. He kept trying to shake himself out of this paralysis he found himself in, sitting on this bench, but his legs wouldn't move. His brain told him to go, but his body wasn't listening. He was glued to what he was watching on the televisions mounted on poles above his head. There were reports of more hijackings, but they were believed to be false, along with more acts of terrorism on the East Coast.

A businessman who had obviously been stranded by the FAA mandate sat down on the bench next to Will and pulled a mobile phone from his breast pocket. He opened the face of the phone and extended a small antenna, and when he was finished dialing, he held the phone to his ear. After a few seconds, the man frowned, pulled his phone from his ear, looked at it, and finally closed the device and put it back in his pocket. Will had seen the same activity and reaction from others and guessed that there was an interruption in service. He looked around and found a set of pay phones against a wall in the concourse. His legs, finally working, allowed him to stand and walk over to the phones. He was going to call Kathleen. He would tell her he was okay so that she wouldn't worry. He would tell her not to come to the house to drop off the book they had discussed the previous night. And then he would disappear, and he would never speak to her again.

The bank of phones was a mess. There were lines of people behind each phone, and it was not a nice environment. People were pushing and shoving to be the next to make a call to a loved one or a business contact. There was an altercation between two women, and Will thought an all-out fight may happen, but calmer heads prevailed, and the women separated. Will stood in line for over half an hour, but his line was not moving, stalled by a man making an extremely long phone call. Perturbed, Will got out of line and went back to his bench, only to find his seat filled by an obese man with a stain on his shirt. Will thought it might be mustard or egg yolk. Will then realized he had not eaten anything all morning, and it was now nearly noon. The country was in turmoil; how could he be expected to remember something as silly as food? But he had to eat, and he spied a sandwich shop not too far away from his location in the concourse. He bought a toasted ham and cheese on rye and a soda and sat down at one of the small tables. He knew he had to get on the run to keep his plan moving forward, but he had to consider his next move. He ultimately decided he would not call Kathleen. He knew it was wrong, not letting her know, but it would be another clue left under another stone to be unturned by anyone who might be searching for him. *If there's anyone left to search,* he thought to himself. He took a bite of his sandwich. On any other day, it may have had a decent taste, but not today. He couldn't taste any part of the sandwich. He washed it down with a drink from his soda, which also may have been just soda water, the way it was lacking flavor. He exhaled, let out a small burp, and sat back in his chair. *What's the right play, now?* he asked himself. *Take the money and run,* his instinct screamed. And he decided his instinct was correct. He needed to get moving. No calls to anyone, no contact with anyone unless it was absolutely necessary. And if it was necessary, it would only be with strangers. *Will Kelly is dead now,* Will thought. *Now, you're Billy Lomax. Time to get to being Billy Lomax.*

He made his way back to the lockers and used the orange key he was given when he rented it. When the door opened, he saw the briefcase, the suit bag, and the duffel bag, which contained his clothes and the money. He pulled out all three and looked at them on the floor. He thought about transferring the cash to the briefcase. It had a set of combination locks on each side to keep the contents secure. But he didn't like the idea of carrying a duffel bag and a briefcase. He thought he would look silly, and he didn't want to draw any unwarranted attention to himself. He put the briefcase and duffel bag back into the locker and paid the small change fee again to get the same key back from the one-time-use contraption. He picked up his suit bag and went into the men's room. He picked a clean stall and closed the door, locking it behind him. He hung the suit bag from the top of the door and unzipped the front. Inside were the suits he had packed for the ticket desk fiasco that he no longer had plans to execute, and a pair of jeans, a black t-shirt, and a light black jacket. His escape clothing. He exchanged the suit he was wearing for the casual wear, yanked off his black socks, and replaced them with a pair of white tube socks, and switched the loafers he had been wearing all day for the tennis shoes he had stowed away in the suit bag. He tucked in the t-shirt and donned the jacket, zipping it up halfway. He closed the zipper on the suit bag and exited the bathroom stall to the main sink area. He hung the bag on a hook on the wall where another similar bag was hanging, waiting for its owner to finish his business and claim it. Will washed his hands and splashed some cold water on his face. He grabbed a paper towel from the dispenser and dried his face and hands. He looked into the mirror and saw his reflection. Black jeans, black t-shirt, black jacket. All he needed was a black cowboy hat, and he could have been a bandit in the Old West. *You are a bandit,* he thought, looking at himself. *You're a thief, a liar, a coward...You're a criminal. What have you gotten yourself into? There's no going back, but seriously, what in the hell were you thinking?* Another man came into the restroom and began washing his hands, and he was followed by a young Hispanic man in an airport custodial uniform, who began cleaning up paper towels that were thrown towards the trash can, but missed their mark. Will looked at his own paper towel in his hands, which were still wet, and grabbed another from the dispenser. When he was finished drying his hands, he walked over to the trash can. There was another crumpled-up ball of the rough material sitting on the sink where the other man had been washing his hands. Will grabbed it with his own paper towel clump and placed it in the trash can.

"Gracias Señor," the attendant, whose name tag Will read as he passed said "Diego," stated in his native tongue.

Will flashed back to his high school foreign language class and paused. "De nada, amigo," he said, and started for the exit.

"*Señor*, is that your bag?" Diego was pointing to the two suit bags hanging from the wall.

Will turned and looked at the two bags, one of them his, and then looked at Diego. "Not mine," he said. "Must belong to someone else here." With that, Will turned and exited the restroom, leaving one more piece of his past behind.

Diego turned back towards the stalls and bent down. He counted one set of feet under the doors of the stalls. He looked back at the two bags on the wall, shrugged, and left the restroom.

Chapter 11 – Cleo

Will was out on the sidewalk of the terminal, dressed in black from head to toe, his duffel bag slung over his shoulder. He had ditched the briefcase, leaving it in the locker he had rented, and he was still holding the round orange key in his pocket. It would never see its counterpart again. He went to the first taxi he saw and opened the back door.

"Will you take me to Jersey City?" he asked.

The taxi driver turned around, took a cigar from his mouth, and said abruptly, "I'm off duty."

Will looked at the top of the cab. "Your light is on," he said.

The driver faced the front of the car again, reached across the steering wheel, and flipped a small switch on the dashboard. The light on the top of the car went out.

"Now it's off," the cabbie barked. "And I'm off duty."

Will slammed the door and muttered under his breath, equating the driver to male genitalia. He looked up when he heard a car horn honking, and saw the driver of the next taxi waving him over. The cab was yellow, just like most of them, but had one red fender. He ran over to the car, toting his bag over his shoulder. When he got to the car, he opened the door and asked the same question he had asked the previous driver, and this time got the answer he was looking for.

The driver got out of the car and approached Will on the passenger side. "Yes, get in, mon, I take you to Jersey City," he said in what Will thought was a thick accent. "Yah want me to put yah bag in de trunk?"

The driver reached for Will's duffel bag, but Will yanked it away and put it on the other side of his body in a protective manner.

"No," Will almost yelled, and then caught himself. "No... I can get it. I'll just keep it with me in the back seat."

"Fine, mon," the cabbie said, holding his hands up. "No worries, mon... get in. I take yah where yah want to go."

Once they both got settled in the car, Will said, "I'm sorry. I didn't mean to yell. It's been a crazy day so far."

"Yah ain't got to tell me, mon. People are edgy today, and with good reason. I was not born here in dis country, but it is my home. I 'ope they murder de bastards dat did dis."

The driver pulled away from the curb, and they edged their way through the traffic of the airport and out onto the main road.

"Whacha down for in Jersey City, mon? It's pretty close to de action down dere," the driver asked.

Will was looking out the window. The traffic from the airport had eased, and they were moving at a normal speed. "I have to go to the bus station there. Journal Square," Will said.

"Yah runnin' de gauntlet today, mon. Yah get off de plane, and get in mah cab for a ride to de bus."

Will had to stop himself from correcting the driver and saying he didn't come from an airplane. That would have just brought more questions. Why was he catching a cab from the airport if he wasn't getting off an airplane?

"Something like that," he said. Will took notice of the cab driver's hack license attached to the Plexiglas which separated the front and back seats. The driver's name, according to the little paper, was Cleo Baptiste. "Mr. Baptiste," Will said.

"Yah can call me 'CB, '" the driver interrupted. "Just CB. Everyone call me dat."

"Okay, CB, how long do you think it will take to get to the bus station?"

"Prob'ly ten tah twelve minute from 'ere, dependin' on de traffic."

"Got it," Will said. "Thanks." Will leaned back in the seat and closed his eyes for a few minutes, and they drove in silence. He opened his eyes when the tone of the road changed, and as they crossed over the Newark Bay Bridge, he shifted in the seat to try to get a view of the tragic site across the Hudson River. He stared and stared until they were nearly over the bridge. He could make out some of the buildings in other parts of the city, but where the Twin Towers of the World Trade Center should have been, there was nothing. Smoke billowed up from the ground as the fires still burned, but the buildings had been destroyed completely.

"It's so peculiar," Will almost said in a whisper.

"What's dat, mon?" Cleo was looking in the rearview mirror at him, chewing on a toothpick.

"How different the world feels when the skyline changes," Will said.

"Yah, mon... I tink tings gon' be different for a long time after dis."

Will exhaled and sat back in the seat. They rode in silence for a while with the news radio playing at a low level in the background. Every now and then, the radio in the taxi would squawk with the high pitch of a woman's gravelly voice, and after a few seconds of silence, someone would respond to her, and Will felt that almost all of it was unintelligible. The car began to slow, and Cleo pointed it toward the exit ramp of the turnpike. They came to a stop at the bottom of the hill, and after a few more minutes of turns, they arrived at the bus station. Cleo turned and gave Will the total. Will slipped a fifty-dollar bill through the window and told Cleo to keep the change.

"Ayyyy, tanks, mon," Cleo said, smiling and revealing a gold tooth. "You be careful on dat crazy bus, okay?"

"I'll do my best, CB," Will responded. "You take care of yourself and be safe." Will shut the door of the taxi and headed through the doors of the bus terminal. He found an empty ticket window and approached.

"Help ya," the man behind the counter asked, hardly looking up. He was wearing black pants with a white long-sleeved shirt and a red jacket on top. Will thought he looked like a lawn jockey, except he was taller.

"I need to get to Indianapolis," Will said.

The man punched some keys on his computer for what seemed like an eternity to Will, but finally hit the right combination to find what he wanted.

"The Indy bus doesn't run from here," he said, and began to chew on a fingernail, still staring at the screen. When he didn't say anything else, Will broke the silence.

"Your web page says it runs from here. If not from here, where does it run from?"

"Ehhh," he said, clacking a few more keys. "Gotta go over to Newark. Use the main terminal on 1 Raymond Plaza West in Newark. We moved a lot of departures over there because of the... the uh... the plane... crashes."

Exasperated, Will thanked him and turned around to leave, almost hitting another man with his bag.

"Hey, watch it, jackass!" the man said.

"Sorry about that," Will managed to say over his shoulder. The man told Will what he could do with his apology, but Will let it go. *I can't wait to get out of here... away from all of this,* he thought.

He walked back outside and looked for a cab at the stand, but there were none to be had. He looked down the street and saw a yellow cab. Mostly yellow. It had one red fender. Will started running with his bag weighing him down, but he reached the cab fairly quickly. He opened the back door and poked his head in.

"Hi, CB."

Cleo turned around with his mouth full of a bite of a sandwich. "What's de matta, mon," he said through the food. "Yah forget some ting?"

"No, I need another ride. My bus doesn't run from here."

"I'm takin' mah lunch and eatin' mah sandwich, mon. Can't yah find another cabbie?"

"There are none at the stand, and I don't want to wait for one." He pulled out his wallet and picked out a one-hundred-dollar bill. "I'll give you this if you let me screw up your lunch."

Cleo sighed, turned his head back to the front, and shook it gently. "All right, mon. Get in. Where are we going now?"

"The main bus terminal back in Newark. On Raymond Plaza."

Cleo shook his head again. "Yah goin' in circles, mon." He laughed as he started the meter and pulled away from the curb. "'ey mon... yah got some kinda ting about you. Whachu running from?"

Will picked up his head and looked at Cleo in the rearview mirror. "Nothing," he said. "Aside from the airplanes crashing into buildings. I'm running from nothing."

"If yah say so... just sayin' it seems like yah got out of somewhere in a hurry, protective of yah bags, lookin' ovah ya shoulda, and yah are payin' me cash well over the wage, so I tink yah looking for escape, for convenience, quiet, or both. Truth, mon... I don't care... just trying to make conversation for de long ride."

Will smiled and chuckled at Cleo's insight. "Well, there's no real story to tell," he said. "The building I work in was hit by an airplane today, so I have no work future right now, and I'm done with the city life. You can probably guess that some of this was already in the works, and I'm just choosing today to act on it. But I don't know what tomorrow holds. I don't think anyone of us do. I'm getting as far away from the cities as fast as possible, and I can't fly. So, here I am, and that's it."

Cleo glanced at Will in the rearview mirror for a second, and then turned his attention back to the road. "It's okay mon... we all got our secrets. You tink my dream was to come to da United States and drive dis silly yellow car?"

"With a red fender," Will said, laughing.

"Ya mon... another secret," Cleo laughed. "Nah... I come here from Trinidad with my wife and two sons to try to open my own restaurant offering da best food from Trinidad & Tobago. We found de perfect location in de city. Low rent, ample space, but we are short on de money. We would not make it long enough to get established. We go to several banks and loan businesses, but no one will approve it, so, we all drive taxis except my wife, who works at the cab company.

When we make de money, we will try again. So, life is what you imagine? Nah. Yah perfect picture goes to hell at some point, and yah pick up de pieces and make yah own paint by number with what's left. Anyway, mon... I'm not pryin'... just chattin'."

Will mused on the little things in Cleo's story. He thought about Cleo's situation and wondered if he had tried for a loan from Pickwick. The thought of his former workplace then triggered memories of his coworkers, and Will wondered if they had survived. He glanced to his left in the back of the taxi as they travelled the turnpike, and looked across the Hudson. The giant dust and smoke cloud was not dissipating, and Will thought about all those that were at the crash site, either workers in the building, or the police and firefighters who had sacrificed everything to save others. And then he looked away, determined that he would never look again.

Chapter 12 – Let Freedom Ring

When the cab pulled up to the curb at the bus station, Will paid the cab fee along with the promised bonus, grabbed his bags, and wished Cleo well once again. All the pieces of his escape puzzle were now in place, he felt. He was a new person, and it was time to get on with his new life. He bought a ticket at the ticket window from a much more friendly and helpful attendant than the one he faced in Jersey City. His departure time was not until 10:35 that evening, so he had about seven hours to wait. He left the terminal and walked a few blocks to find some real food. He noticed that some places were closed and assumed owners and managers excused everyone for the day to tend to their families. He finally found a Mexican restaurant that was open and serving, and not far from the bus terminal.

He walked through the door and was greeted by a hostess. Will asked if he could sit at the bar, and she guided him to the bar area where he took a seat on a tall stool. There was a man and a woman seated together on the other side of the U-shaped structure, engaged in conversation about what was on the television above Will's head. A bartender appeared from the entrance to the kitchen area, wiping his hands on a towel which he folded and laid on the narrow indentation on the bar furthest from Will.

"Hey there, how you doin'?" he asked. The bartender looked to be in his early to mid-forties, and was clean-shaven and completely bald. The lights shining down from above the bar appeared as bright orbs on his shiny head.

"Given the circumstances of the day, I'm okay," Will said.

"Yeah, this is terrible. Do you know anyone who might have been in there?"

Will was going to say, "I used to work in one of those buildings. I was in it this morning, and then left minutes before the first plane hit," but he caught himself. He decided on the cab ride to the bus terminal that he shouldn't tell anyone he worked there, and that he was in the building earlier in the day. It invited too many questions that he wasn't ready to answer. Instead, he just said, "Some friends worked there. I don't know what their status is right now. I hope they are okay."

"Well, I hope they're okay. I saw you come in. Reminded me of Johnny Cash, wearing all black."

Will looked down at himself and his dark clothing and harrumphed. "I didn't really plan it that way, but I guess it's a good day to be wearing black."

"Or red, white, and blue, maybe."

Will nodded and said, "No doubt."

"What can I get you?" said the bartender.

Will looked at the selection of beer offered on the menu. He was going to order a Mexican import, but then decided he needed to be American on that day. "I'll take a draft beer, please. The one on the end."

"You got it," the bartender said, and left to pour the beer from a blue and white handled tap. When he returned, he placed a coaster on the bar and the beer on top of it in front of Will. "Anything to eat today?"

"I'll take a look at the menu and see if something grabs my attention."

"Sounds good," the bartender said. "My name is Morris, just shout if you need anything."

Will nodded to Morris and took a long pull off the beer. It was cold, and the glass had come from a freezer to help keep it that way. He looked through the menu and decided on an enchilada. Will was watching the news on the television across the bar from his seat, and he relived each terrible moment of the day again. *And what is yet to come*, he thought. *At least all of the planes have been grounded, so there won't be any more of that.*

"How's the food? Want another beer?" Morris asked.

"I'm not really tasting anything today, so I can't speak on the food," Will replied. "But the beer is cold, and I'd love another. And a shot of whiskey while you're at it." Will picked up his glass and finished off his first beer as Morris brought him another, along with a shot glass full of brown liquid. They repeated the transaction once again, twenty minutes later, and Will was beginning to feel the effects of the alcohol. He pulled out his itinerary from his bus ticket. The bus would leave at 10:35 at night, and travel to Harrisburg, where, according to the paper he held, it would stop at 1:20 in the morning for 20 minutes to allow for bathroom breaks, food purchases, and general leg stretching. He knew it was going to be a long trip, and he should end up in Indianapolis sometime in the afternoon on the next day. He folded the paper and put it back in his pocket, picked up his fork, and finished off his enchilada. He downed the last swallow of his beer and asked Morris for his check. When Morris returned with the small slip of paper recounting Will's lunch, he also had two shots of whiskey.

Morris said, "This one's on me."

"Thanks," Will said and took the shot glass. "Cheers, to finding the bastards responsible for today and shoving a nuke up their ass!"

"Cheers to all of that!" Morris said, and the two men downed the alcohol.

Will picked up the bill and looked at the total. He reached for his wallet and opened the billfold to pull out some cash. But his wallet was empty other than a five-dollar bill and a few singles, not nearly enough to cover the check. He looked down at his feet to find his bag, from which to pull some cash from his hidden bonanza. No bag. He immediately froze and was horrified. Where was his bag? He dropped his hands to his knees and felt a lump in his pocket, and then remembered he had stuffed it into a locker in the bus terminal. He now had two orange keys in his pocket, and did not remember which key was for the locker he used at the airport and the one at the bus station. *Now, about Morris*, he thought.

"Uhh, Morris? Can you come over here?"

Morris walked the length of the bar until he got to his place in front of Will's seat. "Whacha need?"

"I have a bit of an embarrassing situation. I didn't bring enough cash to pay the bill. I can get it, but I would need to leave and come back," Will said.

Morris was wiping spots off of glasses. "Have a credit card?"

Will seethed. "I do," he lied, "but not with me."

"We have an ATM out in the vestibule if you have a bank card," Morris said, putting his towel on the bar.

Will lowered his head. "It's in the same place as my credit cards. I will leave and get the cash, and come right back. I just don't want you to think I'm pulling a 'dine and ditch'."

Morris exhaled, picked up his towel, and started cleaning the glass again. "I'll tell you what. You look a little frazzled, like you've had some kind of day. I guess we all have. Don't worry about it. It's on us today."

"No, I can't let you do that," Will said. "That's not right."

"I insist," Morris said. "No more thoughts about it." He took the bill from the bar in front of Will and ripped it into small shreds and tossed them into the trash.

Will dropped his head again. "Well," he said. "Thank you. That's very kind. I do have eleven dollars in cash as a tip."

"Tips on you, buddy. Whatever you want to do," Morris said, walking back into the kitchen.

Will watched him go and found his eyes a little watery, emotional that a stranger would buy his lunch. And maybe it was just the day that was catching up with him. He got up from his seat and left the restaurant, with his eleven dollars still in his wallet. He walked the return route back to the bus terminal, and when he got there, he went directly to where his rented locker was located. He tried one of the orange keys in his pocket, and the first one fit, but didn't turn. Will felt like his heart stopped for a second, and then he tried the other key. It worked! He pulled his duffel bag out and found a quiet corner in the far end of the bus station. He reached into the duffel bag and grabbed one of the stacks of bills he had stuffed in there earlier. He peeled off ten crisp one-hundred-dollar bills and refilled his wallet. He thought back to early that morning when he made the last withdrawal from the ATM, and was surprised he had run through all of the cash he had. It did make sense, though, and he remembered taxi rides, incentive cash, and the bus ticket he bought. He closed up his duffel bag again and decided he would carry it with him for now. He then retraced his steps back to the Mexican restaurant in search of Morris. He bypassed the hostess and made his way back to the bar, where he was surprised to see a tall, dark-haired woman behind the bar. He stopped, looked around for Morris, and then back at the woman.

"Are you gonna stare at me all night or are you gonna sit down?" she said in a thick Bronx-ish accent.

"I'm sorry... I was looking for Morris."

"Morrie's on his break right now. He went home to be with his kids for a while. He'll be back in a few hours for the night shift."

She turned away and started wiping the counter where the man and woman had been earlier. Will looked around again. "Excuse me, would you have to have a piece of paper, a pen, and an envelope, would you?"

"Well, you're a needy somebody, eh? Yeah, maybe. Get a beer and I'll go look for it while you drink."

Will paused for a minute. It wasn't like he was short on time. He still had four-plus hours to go before his bus left. He sat down and asked for the same domestic beer he had earlier, this time without the whisky. Doreen, as her name tag said, poured his beer and walked back toward the kitchen. He took a sip of his beer from an even colder mug than before. The television across from him seemed like it was showing the events of the day on a loop. He had seen it enough.

Doreen returned with an envelope and a check pad and placed them in front of Will. She pulled a pen from her pocket and placed it on the bar. "Don't lose my pen, and don't steal it, neither."

"Doreen, I promise I won't steal your pen. Thanks for getting these for me."

"It's Dorrie. And you're welcome."

Will opened the envelope and tucked in a one-hundred-dollar bill. On one of the guest checks he ripped from the pad, he wrote a note and placed it in the envelope, which he sealed with moisture from his beer glass. He turned it over and wrote "For Morris" on the front.

"Dorrie, can you make sure Morris gets this? I wasn't able to tip him earlier, and I want to rectify that."

"I'll leave it under the drawer in the register and tell Morrie about it when he gets back," she said.

"Do you and 'Morrie' work together a lot?" Will asked her.

"Five dinner shifts a week. Why do you ask?"

"I just got it. 'Dorrie and Morrie.' It's cute. Anyway, thanks for your help. What do I owe you for the beer?"

"Two ninety-two. It's still Happy Hour."

He pulled the eleven dollars out of his wallet and placed them on the bar. "Keep it," he said.

"Thanks," she said, and tossed the change into a bucket. She pulled on a chord by the register, and a bell rang, saluting his tip. He smiled at her and turned to leave. "Have a good night," he said. She waved at him as she turned to head to the kitchen.

Will made his way back to the bus terminal. He was tired and considered taking a nap before his trip, but he was worried about missing his bus. He decided the best place for him to wait would be in a busy section of the terminal, so hopefully he would not be mugged, or worse. He found a chair up against the wall facing the ticket booth. He tucked his duffel bag under the chair and stuck his foot through the straps, so if anyone tried to steal it, he'd be sure to wake up.

He began to watch people as they came and went, the looks on their faces, and their mannerisms, and he came to one conclusion. No matter what race the passers-by were, Black, White, Asian, Latino, everyone, overall, just seemed to be a little *scared*. People were jumpy at sharp noises, nervous, and just scared. And tired. Everyone just looked exhausted. He kept his eye open for anyone who he felt didn't look scared or exhausted, but he soon grew tired of not finding anyone like that. As he kept watch, though, his eyes became heavy, and he fell asleep.

* * *

At 8:00 p.m. that night, Morris arrived back at work and was ready to finish off the dinner shift and any late-night traffic they might see. He thanked Doreen for covering for him. His children were shaken up by the day, but they were fine. Doreen opened the cash drawer, pulled out an envelope, and gave it to Morris. He took it, opened it, and found the cash and the note that Will had left. Doreen watched him; as the guardian of the envelope for the past couple of hours, she was interested in what was inside. He read the note, smiled, and shook his head. He took the one-hundred-dollar bill from the envelope and placed it in the tip bucket by the register. He would split it with Doreen. He showed her the note, and she read it out loud. "Thanks for lunch. Let Freedom Ring!" She smiled and nodded, and walked away, her own eyes wet with moisture. He read it again. And then he folded the note and tucked it into his pocket. He pulled the chord by the register, and the bell rang loudly once again. "Let Freedom Ring, indeed," he said.

Chapter 13 – Dawn Of A New Day

Will awoke to a shaking hand on his shoulder. He was startled, and it took a minute for him to remember where he was. He looked around, eyes wide, and saw it was the agent who sold him his bus ticket who was shaking his shoulder.

"Sir, sir...," she was saying. "Your bus is getting ready to depart. I just wanted to make sure you were on it before it did."

"Thanks," he said, rubbing his eyes and getting his bearings. "I set the alarm on my watch, but I guess I didn't hear it. Thank you. Where do I go?"

"Right through the doors over there on the right. Make sure you get onto the bus with 4461 on it. That one is yours. The other bus is going to Philadelphia."

"Thanks again," he said. Will stood up and forgot he had wrapped his foot in the straps of his bag and nearly fell. He grabbed the bag and headed through the doors as he was instructed. The engines of the buses outside were growling heavily, and the air smelled of exhaust fumes. He found his bus and approached the door, anxious to find a seat where he could stretch out and not have to share his seat with another traveler. He didn't want to get involved with anyone else's troubles or their sad stories. He had enough on his mind. As he went to step onto the bus, a gruff voice came from behind him.

"You wanna store your bag under the bus?" Will turned around and saw a large black man wearing a jacket and hat with the bus company's name on it.

"No, I'll hold on to it on the bus." Will turned back around and started to climb the steps on the bus.

"It wasn't really a question, sir. You need to put your bag underneath."

Will looked at his bag slung over his shoulder. "You don't allow bags on the bus?"

"We allow some smaller bags on the bus," he said. "But not that big. It's gotta fit in the overhead, and that's not gonna fit."

Will pulled the bag off his shoulder and set it on the ground. He looked for a name tag on his counterpart, but didn't see one. "Sir," he said. "This is everything I own in the world right now. I'd rather not let it out of my sight."

"Here, take this," and he gave Will a tag that he ripped off from a small red and white card. "You keep this. This is how you claim your bag when we get to wherever you're going. Jus' whenever you get there, get off and come out here, and someone like me will get your bag for you."

Will exhaled and shook his head. He took the ticket and shoved it down the pocket of his jeans. He felt sick. He didn't trust not having the bag with him. It actually *was* everything he owned, other than what he was wearing. He again questioned himself about what he was doing, but it was far too late to go back. He watched the attendant take his bag and tie the other half of the tag to one of the straps. Once the attendant put the bag in the compartment underneath the bus, Will climbed the steps and found an open set of seats in the fifth row. He turned towards the back of the bus and saw that there was a small restroom. He went back and squeezed through the small door. He wanted to clean up a little, but the small room didn't really allow for that. He settled for washing his hands and splashing some water on his face. He looked up and saw himself in the mirror. He felt like it was getting harder and harder to be able to look at himself, the deeper into his escape plan he got. And after everything else that had happened during the day, he felt even worse. He exited the restroom and found that the seats he had previously chosen were now occupied by a man in a Pittsburgh Steelers hat, so he took an open row of seats two rows back. There was a television on the bus about every 6 rows of seats, and one in the front, but all were switched off. *Just as well,* he thought. *You don't really need any more news today.* He looked at his watch, and the digital numbers showed it was 10:33 at night. Just then, another man in the same type of jacket and hat as the attendant outside had stepped aboard the bus and settled down in the driver's seat. He grabbed the microphone on his left.

"Good evening, Ladies and Gentlemen. We will be pulling out in a few minutes, but before we do, there is a bathroom in the back of the bus for your comfort. We ask that you only throw toilet paper in the commode, and that trash and feminine hygiene products be thrown into the trash can. Please do not open the windows on the bus. If the temperature is not comfortable to you, let me know, and I will try to adjust it to a comfortable level. We will be traveling straight through to Harrisburg, Pennsylvania, and it should take a little under three hours. We will stop there for about 20-25 minutes. There is food available there as well as bathroom facilities. There are a few other stops along the way until we reach Pittsburgh around 5:50 in the morning. I will give you notice of our approaching stops and what is available as we go. When we get to Pittsburgh, anyone going further west will need to change buses. You should have this information in your itinerary. If you have questions or need something, my name is Joe."

With that, Joe put down the microphone, closed the door to the bus, and began backing out of the long parking space it had been occupying. When he cleared the pillars that provided light and presumably held the roof up, the bus squeaked and hissed and slowly began to roll forward. *Well, this is happening,* Will thought. *You're actually leaving.*

The bus headed south on Rt. 21 for a few miles before turning onto the expressway. Will was looking at some of the restaurants that were still open and wished he had gotten some type of snack to munch on during the trip. Three hours seemed like a long time on the road with no food, but at this point, he was stuck. And his bag, with most of his money and all of his clothes, sat a few feet beneath him in the belly of the bus. He tried not to think about that, but he couldn't. If he could get a smaller bag in Pittsburgh when they stopped to change buses, he would transfer some of the clothes and all of the money to the smaller bag so it would be close to him. The bus was soon on the Newark Expressway, which was lined with trees that blocked Will's view of everything except for the shoulder most of the time. He thought he should go back to sleep to make the time pass, but he decided he wouldn't force it. He wouldn't fight it either unless they were close to a stop. He looked around the bus and counted twenty-two other passengers. The bus was built for about fifty passengers, go there was plenty of room. Most who were traveling together did just that, sharing the two connected seats, and everyone who seemed to be alone was.

Will was thankful for his aloneness at the time, but he also couldn't help but think back to the good days with Kathleen, when they were still in love. They used to go on road trips, to Upstate New York, to the mountains in Pennsylvania, south to Philadelphia to see her parents, and to Delaware for some quiet weekends in a rented beach house where they would sit in the sand just to watch the waves roll in. He caught himself in the reflection of the bus window, and saw he was smiling at the memories. And then the smile faded, and he felt terrible the more he thought about it. She was supposed to drop off the book they talked about the night before. *She had probably called you during the day as the attacks unfolded,* he thought. But he wasn't at his desk, and he wasn't home, and he didn't have any mobile phone coverage. *She probably got worried, and she probably did go to the house, and she probably knocked on the door, and got no answer. She probably thinks that you're dead.* And then he became very sad, to have had to put her through that. And it wasn't even the lie about the book. Without a doubt, she would have tried to get in touch with him anyway, and the results would have been the same, based on where he worked. She would think him dead.

The bus moved on along the expressway, and he shed his saddened spirit as they did. And then he let himself relax, and his eyes got heavy. They passed the exits for towns like Milburn, Berkeley Heights, Bernardsville, and Lamington, but Will did not see them. He had dozed off again, but he woke up to see the sign for Clinton and stayed awake until Philipsburg. He told himself that, along with some food and a smaller bag, he would buy something for his entertainment as he travelled, such as a pocket compact disc player and radio, some headphones, and maybe a few CDs, depending on what he could find. The bus passed a sign for Lehigh

University, and Will knew they were somewhere near Bethlehem and Allentown, Pennsylvania. He looked at his watch and frowned. There was still a long way to go before they got to Harrisburg for the first break in the trip. They reached Fogelsville, and when they passed, the sky got darker again, lacking the reflection of city lights below. Will began thinking about how he would miss the city lights. The city he could do without most days, but he loved the lights. That was the only good thing about winter as far as he was concerned. The earlier it got darker, the earlier the lights came on, and he would see them as he drove home. It made the trip less mundane, he thought, because he often noticed new things on some of his travels. Will's watch made a beeping sound. He looked down at it. It was midnight. It was now September 12, 2001. What he considered to be the most terrible day had finally come to an end.

He scooted down in his seat as they passed the town of Hamburg, Pennsylvania, and wished he had a hat to put down over his eyes. The man in the seat two rows from him had turned on his reading light above his head. He could not see what the man was reading, but Will wished he would stop. And then he thought about the hat again and realized he should have been wearing one all day. It may have helped keep him under cover from anyone who had spotted him. The good thing was that no one he ran across should have been looking for him, and while he did not wish ill will on anyone, it would be ideal if the entire loss prevention department of Pickwick no longer had reason to chase him. He thought about growing a beard to help disguise his face. Since he did not shave yesterday morning, he already had a decent amount of stubble, and after a few more weeks, it should provide some good coverage. He had never been one to grow his beard, but even back in High School, after a few days, he had a shadow. So, he thought maybe the beard was a good idea, and in the more immediate future, a hat to shadow his face. He closed his eyes again, but he did not sleep. The man in front of him may have been trying to sleep because his light was now out. Will's light would stay out, too.

Chapter 14 – Harrisburg

The bus and its passengers were continuing their congruent journeys through Pennsylvania, still along Interstate 78. It was very dark now, and Will imagined them passing farmland or forest as the only light he could detect was oncoming traffic and the lights on the exit signs that passed overhead. Will noticed that when they passed by Bordnersville, they merged with Interstate 81, which seemed to come from the north. He noticed off in the distance the bright lights of what he could only guess was Muir Army Airfield, as he had seen signs for it as they traveled. They continued on and Will was beginning to feel like they would never reach their destination when he heard Joe, the driver, come over the loudspeaker of the bus.

"Good evening, Ladies and Gentlemen. We will be pulling into our first stop at Harrisburg, Pennsylvania, in about twenty minutes or so. We will stop there for about 20-25 minutes, departing at 1:40 a.m. and arriving at our next destination around 3:30 a.m.. There is food available there as well as bathroom facilities. There will be one other stop along the way before we reach Pittsburgh around 5:50 in the morning. I will give you notice of our approaching stops. When we arrive at the Harrisburg station, please do not stand up until the bus has come to a complete stop. If you have questions or need something, my name is Joe."

Joe hung the microphone up on its clip once more and returned both hands to the wheel of the massive transport. Will was getting itchy about getting off the bus and getting the items he needed. He didn't want to waste time at the stop using the bathroom, so he got up and walked to the back of the bus. He pulled on the door, but it did not open. Will looked above the door for the light, which should have been illuminated if someone were inside. It was not. Will pulled on the door once again to no avail, and from the other side of the door, he heard a voice utter the word "occupied". Will turned around and sat on an empty seat next to the bulkhead of the bathroom. He'd give it a minute, but if he had to use the bathroom at the upcoming stop, he would. He had an odd feeling, not that they had not all been odd recently, and he turned to his left to see a small boy peering at him from one row of seats up and across the aisle that separated the two long rows of seats. The boy could not have been more than five or six years old. He waved at Will, and Will waved back, making the boy smile. Finally, the bathroom opened up, and a portly man in a tan coat squeezed through the door. He saw Will sitting in the empty seat waiting, and then looked back at the bathroom, and then back at Will.

"Might want to give that a minute," he said.

Will decided to take his chances. He only had so much time before the bus stopped, and then so little time to acquire the things he needed. He went through the narrow door and closed it behind him, and immediately regretted his decision. He pulled his shirt up over his nose, hoping to filter out the smell, but it helped little, and he began to gag. He would have to wait. He unlocked the door and exited the small room as fast as possible. The kid waved at him again as Will walked by, but Will did not see him, and therefore did not wave. He was keeping his eyes on the carpeted strip in front of him that ran between the two rows of seats. He didn't want to make eye contact with the man in the tan jacket who was in the bathroom before him. He found his seat just as Joe was picking up the microphone.

"Good morning, ladies and gentlemen. We should be pulling up to the station in about five minutes. I ask that you remain seated from now until then as we will be making a few stops and some turns. We don't want you to fall. Thank you."

Joe hung up the microphone again, and the bus immediately began to slow as it took an off ramp, which dumped them into Harrisburg. They turned on Market Street and found an empty bus parking spot at the terminal. It was Joe's turn to speak again.

"Ladies and Gentlemen, we have arrived at Harrisburg. It is now 1:17 a.m.. We will depart promptly at 1:40 a.m., giving you twenty-three minutes. There are food and bathroom facilities here for your convenience." Will could not be sure, but he thought Joe was looking at the man in the tan jacket. "Please do not be late for your return to this bus, as if you are, we will be forced to leave you behind. If this is anyone's destination, thank you for riding with us, and you can pick up your bags in a few minutes outside the bus. Thank you."

Will was the first to stand as he headed for the door of the bus. The driver opened the door for him, and Will climbed down the steps. He pulled his claim ticket from his pocket and waited patiently for the attendant to arrive so he could get his bag. Finally, after a few minutes, a red-haired, scrawny kid came to do the job. Will wondered if the boy could lift his own weight, let alone some of the bags. He took Will's ticket and looked at it.

"It says you're with us 'til Pittsburgh," he said in a squeaky voice.

"I am, but I need my bag. I have to get something out of it."

The kid shrugged and searched the cavity under the bus. He pulled and pushed and yanked, and finally pulled the duffel bag out. He stared at the two halves of the ticket and then at Will, and then back at the tickets.

"You're going to have to recheck this when you get back on," Squeaky Voice said.

"I understand." Will took the bag from the kid and headed into the terminal. First thing he needed was a smaller bag. He saw a newsstand further down the concourse and headed for it. When he got there, he looked around for what he needed. He grabbed a Pittsburgh Steelers hat from a rack and tried it on. *A good fit,* he thought. He pulled the tag off the back of the hat and kept it on. From a rack, he grabbed a pair of black plastic-framed wraparound sunglasses and put them on the bill of the hat. He went to the snack area and bought several bags of potato chips, cheese puffs, and pretzels. He grabbed a bag of sugar-covered candy worms as well. He went up to the counter and put his duffel bag down on the floor, and his newly acquired bounty on the counter.

Will looked at the girl behind the counter, who could not have been much older than her late teens. Her name tag said

"Destiny." He thought that was interesting. It was her name, and he had no idea what his would come to be. He reached for his wallet and asked, "Do you have any bags?"

Destiny said, "Yeah, I'll get you one for all this," and reached for a plastic bag from the rack with the store's name printed on it.

"No," Will said. "Like a bigger, more permanent bag. Like a gym bag."

"We have some backpacks over in the corner, around from the magazines."

Will held up one finger. "Great," he said. "Can you give me a minute?"

She nodded, and he picked up his duffle bag and walked around the corner of the store. He found what he was looking for, but not really. All of the bags were very small and had images of cartoon characters or superheroes on them. A lot of good his disguise would do now; hat, dark glasses, beard, and a bright yellow backpack with a cartoon train with a face on it, or a pink one with three big-eyed girls flying on it. He spotted a dark colored bag near the back with only a yellow bat insignia on it. It would have to do. He grabbed a few magazines and brought them back up to the counter, where the man with the tan jacket from the bus was buying some pork rinds and cheese curls. *Yeah,* Will thought. *By all means, eat something that will make you go to the bathroom again.* Then he remembered that he still needed to go himself and was running out of time. He grabbed two packs of chewing gum and a travel-size deodorant and added them to his pile of snacks.

"Oh, the hat and the glasses, too," Will said. He finished his transaction with Destiny and immediately headed for the bathroom. He had seven minutes until the bus left. He entered a stall, which he was thankful for its cleanliness, and put the backpack on top of the toilet tank and the duffel bag on the commode seat. He opened the duffel bag and found the stacks of cash he had put in there the day before. He grabbed about half of the stacks, mostly all those made up of larger bills, and put them carefully at the bottom of the backpack. He pulled the glasses, chips, pretzels, gum, magazines, and candy from the newsstand bag and threw them on top of the stacks of bills, and zipped the bag. He rezipped the duffel bag and then unzipped his pants, finally relieving himself of things he had consumed the evening before.

Over the loudspeaker, he could hear the announcer calling for occupants of bus 4461 with a final destination of Pittsburgh. He finished up and washed his hands in one of the many sinks in the row against the wall. He grabbed his two bags, duffel over his shoulder and the backpack by the scruff, and the bag hung like a kitten in the mouth of its mother. He walked out onto the deck where the bus was parked and handed his big bag back to the attendant, who ripped a ticket in half, gave one half to Will, and tied the other end to the duffel bag. Will climbed the steps to the bus to find his old seat taken up by another traveling soul. In fact, most of the bus was full now, and there were only shared seats to be had. *Why is this bus so crowded at quarter to two in the morning?* he thought. *These people should be home in bed.* Then it hit him. There were no airlines right now. People were stranded, away from home, and they wanted to get there as fast as possible. He was thankful that he did not have a job that required him to travel much. And then he thought again, and reminded himself that he had no job at all. He was just a traveler now, but at some point, that would change. He chose a seat next to a small man in a newsboy hat and a blue pinstriped suit and gave a quick smile as he sat and laid his backpack between his legs. The man nodded and opened a newspaper, a clear sign that he was not ready to chat, which was fine with Will.

"Good evening, ladies and gentlemen." It was Joe again, back on the microphone in the bus. "We will be pulling out in a few minutes, but before we do, there is a bathroom in the back of the bus for your comfort. We ask that you only throw toilet paper in the commode, and that trash and feminine hygiene products be thrown into the trash can. Please do not open the windows on the bus. If the temperature is not comfortable to you, let me know, and I will try to adjust it to a comfortable level. We will be traveling straight through to Midway Plaza in Bedford, Pennsylvania, and it should take a little under two hours. We will stop there for about thirty minutes. There is food available there as well as bathroom facilities. Once we get moving again, we will go straight through and should reach Pittsburgh around 5:50 in the morning. I will give you notice of our approaching stops and what is available as we go. When we get to Pittsburgh, anyone going further west will need to change buses. You should have this information in your itinerary. If you have questions or need something, my name is Joe."

This is a recording, thought Will. It was almost the same speech he had heard in Newark. *Newark*, he thought. Newark seemed so far away to him now. Taxi drivers, and bus terminals, people he had met, Morrie and Dorrie at the Mexican restaurant, and he wondered if Morris had gotten his tip. Dorrie had seemed trustworthy, so Will had a feeling he did.

The bus jerked out of the tight-fitting space at the terminal and began its slow roll back through the town of Harrisburg and back onto Route 22 going north, where they would pick up Interstate 81 once again and begin the trip west. Will had the bag to his side, filled with snacks and stacks of cash. *Snacks and Stacks,* he thought. Almost as cute as Morrie and Dorrie. He looked at the back of his feet and remembered the magazines. As long as News Boy was next to him reading his paper, Will may as well take advantage of the light. He had grabbed the books at random when checking out and didn't really take notice of what he was buying. He kept them in the bag as he looked at their titles. He had a magazine for sports, outdoor living, one of those satirical magazines, and the last was what was clearly a magazine designed for women. *Good job,* he thought. He grabbed the outdoor living magazine and checked the table of contents. There was a story on white water rafting, one on hiking, one on living on a boat, one on mountain biking, and one on living in a log cabin in the woods. He started with the hiking story, but after a while, it began to bore him, and he put it in the pocket in the back of the seat in front of him. Then he slinked down in the seat, pulled the hat down over his eyes, and tried to sleep until they reached the next stop.

Chapter 15 – Collapse

When the South Tower of the World Trade Center began to collapse, Detective Brian Greco began a dead sprint, running as far away as he could get as fast as he could. He was three blocks north of the site and another three to the east before he stopped to turn around. The dust cloud was immense and still growing. He hid in a parking garage vestibule with about a dozen others who were fleeing the scene as well. They waited. They waited there for what seemed like an eternity, yet it wasn't. They waited for their small shelter to be compromised by the flying debris, yet it never was. They waited until the cloud passed, yet it never did. It hung in the air, and it would cling to everything. But it was slowing down, and as they kept waiting, finally it was thinning. It diffused the sunlight to make the day appear as if it were foggy. He saw his reflection in the glass of the vestibule, and the man he saw staring back at him was just as tired, just as sweaty, and just as scared, just as confused. But it was calling him a coward. It was shaming him for running when there were so many still there. So many responders, and so many victims. His partner was still there, too, for all he knew.

"Okay," Greco said, when the cloud had thinned. "Everyone, cover your nose and mouth with whatever you have, shirts, jackets, whatever, and get out of here, and keep moving east if possible. Get as far away as you can." He was gasping for air, they all were, and his lungs felt like they were going to explode. His chest was pounding, and he was extremely sweaty. And all he could think about was getting back to the site as soon as possible. He exited the vestibule, and he went in one direction, while everyone else did as they were told and went in the other.

He peeled off his blazer, unbuttoned and shed his shirt, and took off his t-shirt. On a different day, the scene may have seemed strange, but no one gave him a second glance. Everyone was running from the ever-growing cloud. He put his shirt back on and buttoned it near to the top. He spun his t-shirt into a makeshift bandana and tied it around his face, hoping it would keep the contents of the cloud out of his lungs. His next move was to get back to the site as fast as he could. He began to run, as fast as he could, to the source of the cloud. But then, stopped short.

He was standing next to one of those stores at the foot of a skyscraper where everything is priced at one dollar or less. He pulled on the door, but it was locked from the inside. He was about to pull his service pistol and shoot the lock, but a small man of Asian descent with big-framed round glasses came to the door. The look on his face was one of pure terror. "Can you let me in?" Greco yelled. The man shook his head from side to side and pointed in the direction of the crash site. "I know," Greco said, and then he showed the man his badge. The man reached for the door and turned a small knob on the lock, and the door opened. Greco stepped in. "I need your help," he said. "I need some supplies."

"We not open. What you need?" the man asked.

"I'm not sure yet," Greco said, "But I'll know it when I see it." Greco grabbed a cart and started racing through the store, looking at the items until something struck him as useful. When he found the hardware section, he grabbed all of the safety goggles off of the hooks from where they hung, nine pairs in all, and then all of the painting masks. He kept going, grabbing a case of twelve water bottles, and he tossed them in the cart as well. He counted the remaining cases of water: sixteen. Then he began to sprint around the store again with the little store owner chasing him around. He stopped at a free hanging display of bandanas, took the entire display, dropped it in the cart, and then took all of the hand towels. The last thing he grabbed was a box of large trash bags. He wheeled the cart to the front, and the store owner counted the items.

"Forty-seven dollars. I pay the tax for them. You go, go help!" he said.

"You have sixteen cases of water back there as well. I want those as well."

"Sixty-three—No, I buy, just...just take! Go!"

"Okay, but I still need *your* help. Go get those water bottles and bring them outside, and anyone who runs by your store that needs one, give them one!" Greco took the cart outside and grabbed the box of trash bags. Opening the box, he pulled out one trash bag and put all of the bandanas and hand towels inside. Then he grabbed the case of water and set it on the ground. He ripped open the plastic and grabbed two bottles from the pack, opened them, and poured them into the bag with the bandanas and towels, soaking the pieces of fabric. He grabbed one of the sets of safety goggles and put them on his head. Now he needed to get back to the scene. He looked in the street and saw a frightened man fumbling with his keys.

"NYPD!" he said, flashing the badge. "My name is Detective Brian Greco. I need your car!" he yelled.

The frightened driver opened the door, tossed Greco his keys, and began to run from the scene.

"Thank you," Greco said, and he put the car into reverse at high speed and spun it around in the opposite direction. He zig-zagged for two blocks each way, until roadblocks hindered his progress. He grabbed his badge as he left the car, and he held it in front of him as he ran. The t-shirt around his face made it difficult to breathe, but he was determined to get back to the site to do as much good as he could. The bag he was carrying was getting heavy, so he used his pen to poke holes in the bottom of the trash bag, and the water began to drain from the bag. People around him were all running in the opposite direction after directives given by anyone wearing a uniform. He wove his way through them all, yet trying to make eye contact with everyone he could in case Steve was on his way out. He handed out the wet bandanas to anyone who would take them, advising that it would help them breath without ingesting the contents of the cloud. His main problem was that *everyone looked the same*. No matter what they were wearing, no matter what color it had been earlier in the day, it was a light gray now, covered in the dust from the cloud. He was telling everyone he came across to get as far away, and to find clean air if possible. He wasn't sure if anyone could hear him through the t-shirt, but he was telling them, *he had to tell them,* anyway.

He finally saw a familiar face, a uniformed officer whom he knew from his precinct. Officer Timothy Jenkins was covered head to toe with the dust, and coughing heavily as he moved slowly down the sidewalk.

"Jenkins!" Greco yelled, but Jenkins didn't hear him and kept his pace. Greco ran over to him and grabbed him by the shoulders. "T.J.!" he yelled, trying to get Jenkins' attention again. Jenkins, startled, was wide-eyed and looked confused. "T.J., it's me, Greco." Jenkins looked at him again and seemed to recognize him. He pointed to his ear and shook his head, indicating he was unable to hear anything. That's when Greco noticed the blood coming out of his ear and all over the back of his head. He pulled out one of the wet bandanas and held it against the bloody area of Jenkins' head, and pulled Jenkins' arm up to encourage him to hold it there. "Have you seen Angelucci?" Greco yelled through the din that encompassed the area. Jenkins shook his head from side to side and shrugged, still not able to hear.

"Okay," Greco said, giving him one of the painter's masks. "Get outta here and get that taken care of." He patted Jenkins lightly on the back and continued moving toward the crash site, avoiding those coming towards him.

As he got closer and closer to the site, it became more and more difficult to see, and his eyes were beginning to burn. He pulled the goggles down over his eyes, and it did seem to help, and he began to direct those who were either gawking at the mayhem, or confused, or hurt, or in shock, away from the scene. He reunited a wandering boy with his mother, and helped multiple people off the sidewalk and helped get them on their way.

After a few minutes of searching, he thought he saw his partner, Steve Angelucci, and began to run to him. "Steve! Angelucci! Stevo!" he yelled, but whomever it was, he was running away from Greco toward the site. Greco repeated his calls as he chased his partner, but he was not closing the gap. He removed the t-shirt from his face and yelled again, but even he didn't hear his own voice. Something was wrong.

And he saw it as he looked up toward the source of a noise so loud, so terrible, and he saw the North Tower of the World Trade Center collapse. He looked back down to ground level and saw his partner, still running toward the crash site.

"Steve!" he yelled, as another cloud of debris began to form. "Steve!" he called again, in an extended yell, but no one heard him, not even Greco himself.

Chapter 16 – Midway

Will woke up to a nudging on his arm. "Hey, buddy," he heard. "Hey. Buddy." He opened his eyes and found himself staring into the news boy hat, worn by his new traveling companion.

"What's up?" Will asked. "Are we there already?"

"No," News Boy said. "We're about forty minutes out. I gotta pee."

"Oh," Will said, and he straightened himself up in the seat. "I need to stretch my legs, too." Will stood up and let the man through, and the little man hurried back to the bathroom with urgency. *Don't take the window seat next time, Pal,* he thought. Will looked down at the floor and found his bag where he left it, and it appeared to be undisturbed. He turned and looked toward the front of the bus and out the front window, but all he saw was a dark road illuminated by the headlights of the bus. News Boy was back and took his seat in the one next to Will's and said a polite 'thank you' as he sat back down. Will took his seat with a nod.

"Name's Max," he said, and offered a hand. Will cast a wary eye at the hand, and Max caught it. "I washed it," he said, scowling.

"Billy," Will said as he shook Max's hand. "Nice to meet you."

"Some shit yesterday, huh? I was supposed to fly from Texas to Maine, but they grounded us, made us land in Newark. So, I'm taking a bus back home. Going to take me two and a half days. How about you?"

"Pretty much the same," Will lied. The fewer details he gave, the better off he would be. "Taking this bus to Pittsburgh and then a transfer to Indy."

"Ha," Max said. I had you pegged for being from P-A, what with that Pittsburgh hat. What do you do in Indy?"

"I, uh, I sell shoes. Travel around with samples and try to get retailers to sell our brands." The lying was becoming easier. "You got on at Newark. I didn't see you on the bus earlier, only when we became seatmates at Harrisburg."

Max took his hat off. "I wasn't wearing my hat. You weren't wearing yours, either."

Will thought that was an odd thing to say. Has this guy been watching him? *Following him?* The thought made Will uncomfortable, and he said nothing for a moment. Then he answered with another lie.

"Just picked it up at the last stop. I usually pick up a souvenir or two, mostly hats, from places where I travel for work."

"Ah," Max said. "Want to read my paper? I'm done with it."

"No thanks," Will said. "I have a few magazines with me to read."

"Suit yourself," Max said, and he pulled his hat down low, laid his head back, and closed his eyes. Will was thankful that Max had finally gone quiet. He was worried about slipping up and making an error in his fake story, but even if he did, what would it hurt? *Old man probably won't even remember me after tomorrow,* he thought. *None of them will. We're all just passengers on a shitty ride after a really shitty day.* He let his head fall back against the chair and closed his eyes as well. He was behind on sleep. He guessed most of those on the bus would be as well. It was less than twenty-four hours since the worst thing most of them had ever seen had happened. His eyes popped open quickly when he heard Joe's voice over the loudspeaker of the bus.

"Good morning, ladies and gentlemen. We will be pulling into our next stop at Midway Plaza in about five minutes. We will stop there for about thirty minutes, departing at 4:00 a.m. and arriving at our next destination around 5:50 a.m.. There is food available there as well as bathroom facilities. This will be the last stop along the way before we reach Pittsburgh. I will give you notice of our approaching stops. When we arrive at the Midway Plaza station, please do not stand up until the bus has come to a complete stop. If you have questions or need something, my name is Joe."

Will began mouthing the last sentence of Joe's monologue, knowing it fairly well after hearing it so much. He looked out of the front window of the bus, and it was still dark, other than the headlights from the bus shining on the road ahead. He thought about what he was going to need when they stopped. He really wanted a set of headphones, a player, and some compact discs, but he'd settle for a radio with headphones if that's all he could get. He had no idea what the stop at Midway Plaza was going to be like. He'd never even heard of Midway Plaza. The lights in the distance brought his eyes to life, and as they approached the Plaza, he realized this was just a rest stop, a gas station, and maybe a few small restaurants inside.

When the bus stopped out front of the building, Will grabbed his bag, got off the bus, and went inside. He looked around for what he needed, but there was no source of anything he was looking for. He shouldered his backpack and went into the Men's room to refresh himself. He dropped his bag on the edge of the sink and let some cool water from the spigot run through his fingers, and then he splashed water on his face, using a paper towel from the rack beside him to dry himself off. He removed his jacket and pulled up his shirt to apply the deodorant that he purchased at the previous stop. He studied his face in the mirror. His stubble was slightly more than a five o'clock shadow, and the bags under his eyes made him appear five years older. *With the hat and sunglasses in a few days, and different traveling partners, no one will recognize me*, he thought. *Not that anyone would anyway.* He put his jacket back on, feeling a little refreshed, and headed over to the sandwich shop to get some real food, *or as real as they have, anyway*, he thought.

There were mostly people from the bus in the shop, and he was third in line, which was fine for him as it gave him a chance to check the menu. He'd been to the national chain before, but he was not a regular. It wasn't his normal go-to for quick food. He liked to use the local one-location shops in New York when he went out for lunch. The classic deli-style places. He realized he had been eating lunch at these places more and more recently. And he knew why. He used to take leftovers from the previous night's dinners, when he and

Kathleen would eat together, but as that phased out, so did the leftovers, and so became the need to either make it himself in the morning, go out for lunch, or have it delivered.

When he got to the counter, he ordered an Italian Cold Cut and a soda. He recognized that he had not had very much to drink that day, and he was feeling it. He grabbed a bottle of water as well when he checked out and stuffed it, with the sandwich, in his bag, which he slung over his shoulder. He carried his soda in the other hand, but it never saw the bus. He drank it down quickly as he walked through the plaza building back towards the bus parking area. He dumped the empty soda cup into the trash can at the exit and made his way out to the bus, checking the number to make sure he was getting on the right one. When he got on the bus, he found a woman sitting next to Max in Will's previous seat. He went to the back of the bus and found a set of two empty seats. He tossed his bag into the seat next to the window and sat down in the aisle seat. It was ten minutes to four, ten minutes before the bus was scheduled to leave, so he ate the sandwich quickly. When he was done, Will sat back in the seat, which had more legroom than his previous seat, and he was thankful. It was the restroom next to him that caused the extra foot room. He pulled his hat down over his eyes and slumped down lower in the seat, with a strap of the backpack he was carrying weaved around his left arm. Joe would be getting on the bus soon, and his speech would be forthcoming. Will didn't care to hear it again. He had almost two hours until they got to Pittsburgh, and he was determined to sleep through as much of it as he could.

Chapter 17 – Great Kills

If you're going to do this, Will thought, *you have to do it right. No half-assed nonsense. You're a professional at what you do, be a professional doing this. Use your contacts, and be smart. Focus your dislike, and use that power to do what you need to do, and do it right.*

Will was sitting at his desk in the office at Pickwick Finance on the 49th floor of the World Trade Center, twisting a rubber band around one wrist and then switching it over to the other, just thinking about what he needed to do.

You're going to get caught. At some point, they will figure it out, and you've got to be ready. There's no way to do this without getting caught. He looked out the window and down at the traffic below. *You'll never escape by car. Too damned crowded. No, Willie Boy, you have to leave work one day when everything is fine, and then never come back. Disappear. Completely. Lead whomever may follow on a wild goose chase in the opposite direction. And then there's the money, the workload, and the time to prepare. Your assets are your brain and your contacts. You've got to build everything else around that.* He pulled a small black book from the breast pocket of his suit and flipped a few pages. He found what he wanted and pulled his mobile phone from the same pocket. He dialed the numbers and waited as the phone rang in his ear.

"*Boob Tube,*" said the voice on the other end of the line.

"Yeah," Will said. "Can I speak with Archie?"

"*Is there something I can help you with?*"

"You can help me speak with Archie," Will said.

"*He ain't here,*" the voice said in a droning voice.

"Uh, Archie ordered a special part for me, I wanted to check to see if it was in."

"*What's the name? I can check the deliveries log.*"

Will thought for a half-second. "Miller," he said.

A few minutes of silence passed between the two, and finally the voice on the other end of the line said, *"No, we ain't got nothin' for Miller."*

Will shook his head, disgusted. "Are you sure I can't speak with Archie?"

"I said he ain't here right now."

"Okay, I'll try later," Will said, and he snapped his phone shut. *Jackass,* he thought. *I can't do anything without Archie. Archie is step one. The rest can't fall into place without him.* He was still stewing about it when his mobile phone began chirping.

"Yello," Will said, and listened for the response.

"Will, it's Arch."

"Hey man, how's it going? The guy told me you weren't there."

"Yeah, well," Archie said with a laugh. *"He doesn't work here anymore."*

"Holy hell, man, you didn't have to do that."

"That's one of the best perks of being the boss, dude," Archie snickered. *"You get to fire people. Don't worry about him. I'll call him back in a few days and give it back to him if he wants it, at fifty cents less per hour. Now, what can I do for you? Need a deal on a wide screen?"*

"Nothing like that. Can you meet me for a drink tonight?"

"I'm not going on any more dates with you, man, I told you, we tried that and I'm not your type!"

Will laughed at the old joke. "Come on, man, just a drink."

"All right," Archie said. *"You know that dive place over by the marina?"*

"By Great Kills?"

"That's the one... meet you there about 8:30 tonight."

"Sounds good," Will said, and snapped the phone shut.

Step one is in play, so far, he thought. *Now, you have to think of the rest. You need to set up accounts, fake accounts. You have to be crafty. You need a place to keep the money until it is go time. Somewhere in your house? Kathleen will be gone in a few days, and you'll have the whole house. Probably not a great idea. That points to immediate guilt if anyone finds it here. You can't keep it in the bank. Too many questions there. You could get a safe deposit box and keep it there, safe inside the walls of the bank. That's probably not a genius move either, you moron. Banks are out. Offshore account? You don't even know where to start with that one. What are your other options? Bury it in the backyard? Keep it in the car? That's just as bad as the house. You've got to think of something. You've also got some time before you get your hands on any real cash.*

The alarm on his watch beeped, and it was finally the end of another day. *Get out of here, Willie, Boy,* he thought to himself. *Your countdown is on, but you don't know when your last day here, day zero, will be. You'll have some time, but not a lot of it, and you need to act natural about everything you do. No screw ups.*

He left the building and drove his car out of the parking garage to head home. Traffic was heavy, but he had plenty of time before he would meet Archie. He figured he would stop home anyway and change clothes before he went. When he got to his house, Kathleen was still not home. He ran in through the breezeway entrance and up the step to the bedroom, changed into black jeans and a black t-shirt and tennis shoes. He sat around for a while to kill time until he had to leave. He looked at the front door, which was still locked, and the porch light was still on. Then he got up and checked the backyard, looked in the pool, and then went back inside. Still no Kathleen, he determined, as he looked around the house. What did he expect? They had agreed to part company just two days before, so she had no real obligation to be at the house any longer.

He went back through the house and through the breezeway entrance to the garage, hopped in the BMW, and headed south on Richmond toward Amboy, zigzagging until he reached the marina. He found a parking spot next to the water and put the top up on the car. He walked in and found Archie already sitting at the bar, half of a mug of beer already swallowed. Will sat down on the bar stool next to him.

"What's going on, man?" Will said, grabbing a coaster and putting it in front of him on the bar.

"Same day, different shit."

The bartender came over and asked Will what he wanted to drink.

"Draft beer, please," he said.

"You got it. My name's Debbie, if you need anything." She placed a small menu in front of Will. It was the same one that sat untouched in front of Archie. "We got bar munchies and a couple-a fried things I can make up in the back if you're hungry. Fries, cheese sticks, onion rings, stuff like that."

"Thanks," Will said. "I'm good for now."

She brought the draft beer over, grabbed another coaster, set it down in front of Will, and put the beer on top of it.

"Start a tab?" she asked.

"Put it on mine," Archie said. Debbie nodded and walked to the other side of the bar to continue a chat with some others, one with a Captain's cap on his head.

"How've you been, Arch?"

"I'm breathing and on this side of the ground, so I can't complain. You?

Will took a long pull on his beer and sat back in his chair. "I'm good," he said. "Married, employed, healthy, can't ask for much more." *But that's exactly what I am going to ask for, and you're going to help me,* he thought, setting his beer back on the bar. "Here's hoping that the TV repair biz and the need for people to borrow money continues far into the future." They touched glasses and each took a small drink.

"So, what's up?" Archie asked, looking across the bar at two young women who had just sat down at a table against the wall.

"Do you still dabble in fake IDs?" Will asked in a lowered voice.

"What are you talking about?

"You know, back in high school, fake IDs so we could get beer. Still doing any of that?"

Archie looked at him with a blank stare. He reached into his back pocket and pulled out his wallet. Opening it, he withdrew a ten-dollar bill and laid it on the bar. He stood up, finished his beer, laid the mug down on the table, looked at Will again, and turned to leave the bar. Will, confused, watched him go until he went through the door and out into the parking lot. He sat there for a minute, then got up, took a drink from his beer, and left the remainder. He followed the path that Archie had taken out of the bar, and when he got outside, he looked around the parking lot, but saw no one. He looked down at the ground and shook his head. *Well,* he thought, *at least I didn't get into this thing too deep before this happened. That would have been bad.* He saw in the corner of his eye what he thought was a light from one of the nearby boats. When he turned to look at it, the light was so intense, he had to look away. It was bright red in color and pinpoint in nature. He looked again and saw a figure by the boat docks, holding something small, which was the source of the red light, which was now pointing down toward the gravel parking lot. Will walked toward the figure, and after a few steps, realized it was Archie.

"What the hell, man?" Will asked.

"Walk with me," Archie replied. They began walking up the dock toward the north end of the marina. When they got to an area where no one was around, Archie stopped and turned to Will.

"Take your shirt off," he said.

"What?"

"Do it, Will, or we're done here."

Will looked at him with wide eyes, which then rolled around as he reached for the bottom of his t-shirt. He pulled it up over his head, and then completely off, and looked at Archie.

"Turn around, all the way." Will sighed and began to turn. As he completed his rotation, Archie told him to put his shirt back on.

"Arch, what the hell?"

"Sorry, man," Archie said, lighting a cigarette. He offered one to Will as he blew the cigarette's exhaust into the air. "Cops. Can't be too careful."

Will declined the cigarette. "Okay, so now you know I'm not a cop," he said, almost as a question, and they began walking again.

"I still do 'fake IDs' as you say. It is a little bit bigger than that, but yes, I still do it. But you're not a teenager anymore, so I am guessing this is a little more than a fake video store card that lets you buy beer?"

"You could say that. How much do you charge for these types of things now?"

Archie laughed out loud. "Depends on what you want. The more intricate your needs are, the more expensive it is. What are we talking about, a simple ID, or a driver's license, or do you want to leave the country?"

Will laughed as well and put his hand over Archie's shoulder. "Well, old friend, if things happen the way I want them to happen, let's just say I'll be moving you up into a higher tax bracket for a while."

Archie looked at him with one eyebrow raised, and said, "Good morning, ladies and gentlemen. We will be pulling into our final stop in Pittsburgh in about five minutes."

Will awoke with a start and realized he had fallen asleep on the bus ride. As he listened to the remainder of Joe's speech, he mused on the memory that had manifested itself into his dream, until Joe's voice snapped him from the slumber. *Pretty close to how it really happened,* he thought.

Chapter 18 – Questions

Will looked at his watch when the bus finally came to a stop and saw it was nearly 6:00 a.m. He stopped at Max's row of seats and grabbed his outdoor life magazine that he had left behind earlier, and stepped off the bus. As he waited to collect his bag from beneath the bus, he looked up at the sky, which was mostly still dark, but not the pitch-black shade it had been. Daylight would break soon and cast light upon a country still hurting from the previous day. As he took his bag from the attendant, he could only imagine what the responders in New York, Pennsylvania, and Washington, DC would wake up to see after a night of trying to pick up the pieces. Will tried to block the thought from his mind, but couldn't, and he found himself wiping tears away as he walked. He desperately wanted a coffee and wasn't impressed with the options inside the bus station. He had just under ninety minutes before his next bus left the station, and was sure he could find something local that would suit him. He started to exit the bus station, but remembered the amount of cash he was carrying, and wanted to lessen that before he went out on foot. He made the familiar purchase of the orange key from a set of lockers and stuffed the two bags inside before shutting the door and removing the key, which he placed in his pocket.

He walked through the door of the bus terminal and out onto the sidewalk. He looked around and decided to head up Penn Street for breakfast and coffee. He wasn't really hungry after eating the sandwich he bought earlier, but he thought it might be a good idea to get some road food for the trip. He found a small coffee shop not too far away from the terminal and decided to give it a shot. He pulled his hat down low before he went inside the door. A bubbly young woman greeted him before the door had even closed.

"Hi, good morning!" she said. "What can I get for you?"

"Good morning," he returned, avoiding eye contact. "Can I get a medium coffee, black, and the ham, egg, and cheese sandwich? Make it two of the sandwiches, please? To go?"

"Sure," she said. "Just a few minutes."

He turned from the counter and walked toward the tables and chairs, spying a half-read newspaper on one of them that someone had left behind. He flipped through it, seeing that ninety percent of it was about the attacks the previous day. He was relieved to see that the remaining ten percent said nothing about a man from a New York finance office disappearing with nearly half a million dollars. *Well, that's one good thing,* he thought. He read that all major sports had been suspended, from baseball to football to auto racing. *Everything is on hiatus, it seems, and rightly so,* he thought. *We need to figure shit out first before we get back to normal. Hopefully, we get back to normal, though.* Then he thought about it and wondered what *normal* would be from now on.

"Sir?" Bubbly Girl said. "Your order is ready."

He dropped the newspaper back onto the table and turned to the counter.

"Seven twenty-eight," she said. He pulled out a ten-dollar bill and gave it to her.

"Keep it," he said, and took the bag and the coffee and headed to the door. As he got back to the sidewalk, he noted that it was considerably lighter outside, but it was still before sunrise. He headed back toward the bus terminal, checking his watch, and when he looked up, he ran right into another man wearing a business suit, and Will's coffee spilled all over the man's suit jacket.

"What the—" the man yelled.

Will winced as the hot coffee sloshed out of the cup and hit the top of his hand. He dropped the cup to the ground, splashing the man's pants.

"Oh, man," Will said, grabbing napkins from the bag. "I am so sorry for that," he said, wiping the man's lapels with the napkins. "It was a mistake; I wasn't paying attention. Completely my fault, I'm so sorry."

"Hey... hey, hey, stop it," he said, waving his arms as Will continued to wipe his jacket. "HEY!" he yelled again, and Will stopped and looked at him. "Don't worry about it. I know you didn't mean it. It's okay. There are bigger things going on right now than my suit," he said, and managed a small chuckle.

Will couldn't believe how well the man was taking the whole thing. He pulled out his wallet and offered the man a hundred-dollar bill, and said, "Sir, can I at least pay for the cleaners?"

But the man waved him off and told Will to have a nice day, and to stay safe, and continued on his way. Will picked up his spilled cup, still not believing the entire scenario, and continued on as well, stuffing the hundred-dollar bill into the pocket of his jeans. He went back into the shop he had just exited, and replaced his spilled coffee with a new one. Bubbly Girl was happy to see him again so soon. He was approaching the entrance to the bus terminal again when he saw a woman sitting against the wall of the building. She had a grocery cart full of blankets and other things that Will could not recognize. It looked to be a lot of aluminum cans and trash, he thought. She appeared to be sleeping as he approached. He looked at her and withdrew the one-hundred-dollar bill from his pocket. He folded it neatly, placed it in her shirt pocket, and entered the bus station. He never saw her look up at him as he disappeared inside the building.

Will stopped at the restaurant inside the bus terminal. He sat down at a small table and sipped the coffee, sitting sideways in his chair as he looked around and waited. He took one of the sandwiches he bought at the coffee shop and took a bite. The station was filling with more and more people as he waited, and he was watching them, not knowing he himself was being watched. He could see people, so many different types of people, walking around the terminal, all heading in different directions, with different agendas, and different destinations. But they all looked the same. Unsure, sad, worried, courteous, heart, soul, and pride wounded. *Most of them probably had other plans yesterday,* he thought. *Now they are most likely just trying to get home. They are going home, and you're running from it,* he told himself. *You're probably doing the opposite of what everyone else is doing today.*

A tap on his shoulder brought him out of his own thoughts and back into the world around him. He turned and looked, and saw the woman he had seen sitting against the wall outside the bus terminal. She looked dirty and tired, and she did not smell as if the clothes she was wearing were recently laundered.

"Hey," she said. She stood there and looked at him as he looked back at her, and after she said nothing more, he simply said, "Hello."

"Who are you?" she asked, almost as a demand, more than a question.

"Why do you ask?" he said.

"Because you stuck money in my pocket, and I want to know why."

He turned around in his chair so he could see her more directly. He kept his head down, though, lifted just enough so he could see her face. His hat shaded most of his face from her. "Why do you need to know? Consider it a gift," he said, and turned his attention toward his coffee.

She looked at him and then around the room. "Look, I gotta know who you are! It's important."

"Why is this so important to you?" he asked.

"Why do you keep answering my questions with questions?" she asked, stomping her foot on the floor.

"Why are you so angry?" he asked.

"Errgh!" she yelled.

"Hey, take it easy, take it easy, I'm just goofing around. My name is Joseph Johnson," he said, smiling at her.

"Was that so hard?" she asked. "Joseph Johnson," she repeated. "Sounds made up."

"I'd show you my ID," he said. "But it's in my bags, locked up."

"No, I believe you, it just sounds like a fake name. Like a porn name or something."

"Anyway," he said. "Why do you need to know my name so badly?"

She looked down and started fidgeting with her hands. Will looked at her for a minute and then picked up his coffee and took a drink.

"If you don't want to tell me, it's okay," he told her.

"No, it's fine, I–" she stammered. "I just want to pray for you." He looked up at her, but they did not make eye contact, as she was looking at her feet. "You probably think that's silly."

"No," he said. "I'll tell you that I am not an overly religious person. I go to church once, maybe twice, per year. But I do believe, and if you believe, then I am grateful for your prayer. What's your name?"

"Mary," she said, looking up. "Why?"

He looked up at her and smiled and said, "So I know who to pray for."

A voice over a loudspeaker said that the bus for schedule 1339 would begin boarding in a few minutes. Will looked at her and said, "Well, Mary, that's my ride. It was nice to meet you, and thank you again. There's another sandwich in here if you'd like it." He pushed the bag with the remaining sandwich inside towards her. She looked at the bag and took it quickly.

"Thank you," she said. "Joseph Johnson." And then she turned to go outside and resume her place near the wall. She turned back toward Will, giggled, and said, "Mary and Joseph."

Chapter 19 – Fiona's Turn

Will boarded the bus and listened to the obligatory speech about the bathroom, where they were going, and when they would get there. The only difference was that the driver was female, and if anyone needed anything, her name was Fiona. Will didn't think she looked like a "Fiona." Maybe a "Betty" or "Edna," but not Fiona. So, it was Fiona's turn to drive. He had chosen a seat in the fourth row, letting his backpack take the window seat. The bigger duffel bag was resting in the belly of the bus, carrying its valuable bounty. Will was feeling less scared about the contents of the bag being out of his sight, mostly because he carried a lot of it with him in the backpack, but also, he had seen the loading and unloading process from start to finish, and he felt the baggage under the bud was secure.

The bus had left the station in Pittsburgh at 7:15 a.m. and was on its way to Indianapolis, with a stop in Columbus, Ohio. *Getting down to the last legs of this initial getaway,* he thought. *I have to figure out what I am going to do and where I want to go.* He dropped his head back and looked at the roof of the bus above him and exhaled. *This is the only part of this deal you didn't figure out ahead of time, you fool. And it would have helped,* he thought. *You should get to Indy probably around 2:45 p.m. Then you have to find Archie's buddy in a city of one and a quarter million people, and then you've got to move the plan forward.* He looked out the window of the bus and saw the morning getting brighter, the morning sun blasting the back of the bus as they drove away from it, and the shadows stretched out long, but getting ever so slightly shorter with each passing second.

He reached into his bag and grabbed a bag of pretzels, and he also wanted to take another look at the outdoor life magazine he nearly left behind on the other bus. He opened the bag of pretzels and began munching on the snacks, and turned to the story about a family who lived on their boat, only touching dry land when they needed supplies that living on the water couldn't provide. *That's a life you could take.*

Very little contact with anyone, living off the water, of course, you'd have to learn to fish, or stock up on peanut butter crackers. And you'd have to buy a boat, which would cut into your money big time. And then you'd have to actually learn how to pilot a boat. That would take a license, which would take lessons, and more money...nah, get that idea out of your head. It's not the answer. He finished off the pretzels, flipped a few pages of the magazine, and settled on a story about rafting in Colorado. The pictures were action shots of rafters dodging rocks and paddling to avoid the dangerous rapids, all while trying to keep their kayaks afloat and the water spray out of their eyes. He read the story, but it soon bored him, and his eyes grew heavy. He scooted down into the seat and wrapped his hand around the straps on his bag. Then he pulled his hat down over his eyes and once again fell asleep.

It was Fiona's voice over the loudspeaker that woke him up. She was giving her speech on how long it would take for them to get to Columbus, and how long they would stay there, and what was available to the passengers. The stop was nearly an hour, and Will thought it might be the perfect time to catch a retail store open and get a set of headphones. *The little luxuries,* he thought. He straightened up his body and lifted his hat slightly. *Looking back, that was the best sleep you've had since Sunday night. You've been a crazy man on the run since then,* he thought to himself. *The email from Dickey came on Monday, and that was a crazy night, running all around New York, and then Tuesday...ugh, Tuesday. So glad to see the sun come up this morning.* As Fiona finished her speech, he was looking out of the bus window at the sprawl that was Columbus, Ohio. It was a lot of residential area, but as they came off the expressway, he began to feel hope that he could find a shopping mall or a retail outlet. The bus pulled into a fenced yard and finally came to rest as it approached the curb. Will stood from his seat and grabbed his bag. He had fifty-five minutes to get out, find somewhere, and then find something that would suit his needs as far as a music source.

He made his way through the terminal and out of the front door, and immediately saw the Columbus City Center to his left, and he made a beeline for it. It was nearing 11:00 a.m., and he was hoping the mall itself was going to be open, as well as the stores inside. He crossed the street and found the entrance to the mall. He pulled on the door, but it was still locked. He checked his watch and saw that it was ten minutes after eleven o'clock. He assumed the mall then did not open until at least eleven-thirty, maybe not until twelve o'clock, if at all, considering the events of the previous day. He couldn't risk waiting around until eleven thirty, as he might not make it back to the bus in time before it left. He looked around and saw a doughnut shop, where he stopped and got a soft drink and a doughnut, which he consumed almost immediately. He sucked down the soda and used the restroom, and headed back to the bus terminal with about twenty minutes to spare. He looked in the cargo area of the bus and saw his duffel bag, safely tucked away. With that knowledge, he relaxed a little bit and climbed back aboard the bus. He returned to his seat to find two young girls in the seat he previously used, and who he assumed were their parents or guardians in the seats behind them. He continued to the back of the bus and found his seat with the extra leg room next to the bathroom once again. And once again, his bag took the window seat, and he held hands with it as usual, wrapping his arm through the straps, and once again, he slumped down in the seat and pulled his hat down over his eyes. It was nearly noon, and Fiona started her monologue, which at this point, Will could have done for her. He never saw any more of Columbus that day, as he was already sleeping when the bus pulled out of the lot on its way to Indianapolis.

Chapter 20 – Big Star

Indianapolis seemed a lot bigger than Will had imagined it would be. More people, more buildings, more streets, and more cars. When the bus was parked, and he was through with cross-country buses, for the time being, anyway, he really took in his surroundings. A lot more, he thought, than in the previous stops along the way, although most of those were in the dark and in the early hours of the morning. He was scruff-carrying the backpack again, and the duffel bag was slung over his shoulder. He was walking west on South Street, and to his right, he saw the enclosed stadium where the Indianapolis Colts called home. It was a massive behemoth of a building with what looked like a pillowy top. He would have loved to do more sightseeing and take in what Indianapolis had to offer, but he needed to keep moving, keep furthering his plans, so that eventually, one day, he might be able to stop running. He caught a taxi at Missouri street, and after stuffing both bags and himself in the back seat, he asked the driver to take him to a motel.

"What kinda motel ya want? Low end, high end, or somewhere in the middle?"

Will thought about it for a minute. "I'm not sure," he said. "I wasn't planning on being here, so I don't have a reservation. What do you recommend?"

"If it were me, and I was in Indy unexpectedly, I'd stay at the Revere. It's the oldest hotel in downtown Indy. Spectacular."

Will wondered if everyone from Indianapolis called the town 'Indy.' He also felt like, after the trip he had just endured, he could use a little pampering. "The Revere sounds good," he said.

"You'll love it," the driver said. "They got a wing joint just down the road with sexy waitresses." With that, they peeled off from the curbside and started toward the hotel. After a few turns, the driver announced they were at their destination. Will paid the cab fare and began to tug his bags out of the car. He shut the door of the cab, and the driver departed to pick up his next fare.

Will looked at the building and started having his doubts. The location was very clean, which was not bad, but when he got inside, he noticed that the decoration was ornate in nature, including a huge chandelier in the lobby. This was much fancier and probably more expensive than he was looking for, but he was already there, so he went to the front desk to find a room.

"Can I help you, sir?" the woman behind the counter asked. Will checked her nametag. It read "Noel," and it appeared that she was an assistant manager.

"Yes, hello... Noel," he said, making use of the name tag. "I'd like to get a room for the night."

"Do you have a reservation?" she asked.

"I do not. Is that a problem?"

"Not at all," she said with a smile. "What brings you to Indianapolis?"

He thought for a second. Being a show salesman from Indianapolis didn't seem to be the right play this time. "I'm just traveling, trying to get home."

"Oh, we're seeing a lot of that," she said. People have been shuffled around because of yesterday. It's really very sad."

"It is indeed," he said.

"Okay," she said. "I've got you in one of our standard rooms, sorry, that's all we have right now. Here is your total right here. How will you be paying?"

Will looked at the quote for the room, and an unintended whistle escaped his mouth. "Uhh, cash," he said, and pulled his backpack up on the counter.

"I will also need a major credit card for any incidentals," Noel said.

"I don't have one with me," he said. "Any wiggle room on that? Can I leave some cash instead?"

"I'm sorry, sir, it's our policy. Are you traveling without credit cards?"

"Uhh, yeah," he stammered. "I uh, I lost them yesterday."

"Oh, well, we can call the credit card company and get approval over the phone!" she said, trying to help, and reaching for her phone.

"No, no, it's okay. I really shouldn't be spending this much on a room anyway. Can you cancel the reservation, and maybe suggest something a little lower in price in the area?"

She smiled in an odd way, Will thought, and tore up the quote, tossing it in the wastebasket behind her.

"Big Star Motel, across the tracks on 17th. Ask for Leon," she said, and disappeared behind a wall in the back of the desk area.

"Thanks," he said. He didn't dare try asking her to call him a cab. He picked up his bags and headed out the front door of the hotel. He tried to flag a cab that went by, but it kept going. *Guess I'm walking for now,* he thought. *That's okay...it will give me time to think. Archie said his guy is on North Delaware. You could go there now if you could find it.* He laughed at himself for being so lost in a city he was not used to, but it was a necessary evil. *Everywhere you go now has to be a strange place. You cannot ever go anywhere you've ever been, and hopefully, you'll never see anyone you met before yesterday ever again.* The thought of that made him shiver a little. *That should be easy enough, you've got the whole country, but it's going to be weird, especially with Kathleen, her parents, and people from work. Just weird, for you, not for them. They all probably think you're dead.* He continued walking down the street he was on, trying to flag down a cab. Then he realized he was walking back toward the bus station he had left not so long ago. *Probably a good place to pick up a cab,* he thought. At that moment, a cab drove by slowly and then parked along the curb about twenty feet in front of Will. Will opened the back door and asked if the driver was on duty.

"Sure am," the driver said.

"Great," Will said. He piled his bags into the back seat of the car and then followed them in.

"Where to?" the driver asked.

"Big Star Motel on 17th," Will said.

"You got it."

Will looked at his watch. *It's nearing 4:30 p.m., and you have accomplished nothing since you've been in Indianapolis. Walking around, taking taxi cabs all over the place, trying to stay in hotels you don't belong in. I hope this dirt motel I'm heading for now doesn't require a credit card. What the hell are you doing?*

"Hmm?" the driver said.

Will looked at him through the rearview, still lost in his own thoughts. "What's that?" he asked.

"Thought you said something," the driver said.

"Oh, no, sorry. Must have been thinking out loud. Do you know how long it will take to get to the motel?"

"Eh, maybe fifteen minutes. Twenty, max, depending on the traffic. In a hurry?"

"Yeah," Will said. "I need to sleep. It's been a weird couple of days."

"I don't doubt it. What brings you to Indy?"

"Just traveling through. Trying to get home."

"Ahh, where's home?"

"Philadelphia," Will said.

"Oh, you can probably get an over-the-road bus that will get you there in a day or so. They make East Coast runs all the time."

"You don't say," Will said with an inaudible laugh. "I might have to try that."

They drove across the city in silence for most of the remainder of the trip. Will looked out the window for most of the ride, taking in the sights of what "Indy" had to offer. He noticed that gradually, just like other cities, the further away they got from the downtown area, the more downtrodden and run down it became, with an increase in both graffiti and vacated housing. They finally crossed a set of railroad tracks, and Will saw the sign for the Big Star Motel. If the Revere was considered a nice hotel, the Big Star was the exact opposite.

It was a two-level dump with what appeared to be half of the lights out in the sign on the road. Or maybe they were all out, and half of the sign was just not dirty. The entrances to the rooms were external, and the office was a small shack that was perhaps attached to the building, but Will couldn't be sure. There were only two cars in the parking lot.

He hopped out of the cab and grabbed his bags. The driver gave him a card with a phone number on it. "Call me if you need another ride somewhere," he said. "I'm over in this area all the time." Will took the card and put it in his wallet.

"Sure," he said, and turned toward the office. The sun was still high in the sky, but definitely on its way towards its slumber as he opened the door to the office and walked in. There was barely enough room for Will and his two bags in the small shack.

"Help ya." The man behind the counter said it as more of a statement than a question. He was wearing a white tank-top t-shirt and black pants. He was balding, and a cigarette was dangling from his mouth.

"Uh yeah," Will said. "I need a room? I was told to ask for Leon?"

The man reached under the desk and pulled out a black handgun and pointed it at Will.

"Jesus!" Will yelled, and he dropped his bags and threw his arms up.

"Who are you" the man said, also not a question.

"I-I-I'm nobody! I'm just traveling! I was just told to ask for Leon!"

"Leon ain't here," the man said. "Who told you to ask for him?" Finally, a question. The gun was still pointed at Will.

"Uh...this woman, at a hotel... uh, N-N–Noel... at the Revere," Will stammered.

"Heh heh heh," the man said, and lowered the gun. "Noel. She's a doll. Can always count on her to send me the castaways." Will, thankful that the gun no longer seemed to be in play, cocked his head to side and looked at the man, much like a confused dog looks at its owner. "Leon is a code.

My name is Nole. Noel is my sister. I'm guessing you had some trouble checking in at Revere?"

"Uh, yeah," Will said, relaxing a little. "I don't have a credit card for, eh, what did she call it, 'incidentals.'"

"Well," Nole said, putting the gun back under the counter. "We don't have any 'incidentals' here. Just a bed, a shitter, a shower, and if you're lucky, a TV. So, you're traveling without a credit card, right? Must be tough."

"Not too bad," Will replied, casting a wary eye at Nole.

"Guess you're carrying a good bit of cash, then," Nole said with a smile.

"I think this is an 'incidental,'" Will said. "How much is this going to cost me?"

"Forty for the room, a C-note for me."

Will snickered and shook his head. Then he pulled out his wallet and withdrew two one-hundred-dollar bills and placed them on the counter. "For your troubles," he said. Nole took the money from the counter, dropped it into the cash register, withdrew two fifty-dollar bills and three twenty-dollar bills, and stuffed them in his back pocket. He then turned and used a key to unlock a box affixed to the wall behind him. He pulled out a key with a large fob attached to it and gave it to Will.

"Thanks," he said.

"No worries, pal. You're in room two. Right next to mine."

Will grabbed his bags and squeezed out of the door with them as Nole watched. He found his room, second door on the lower level, and stuck the key into the lock and opened the flimsy door. The room was small and contained one double bed. There was a stand with a television near the foot of the bed, with barely enough room to walk between the two. Next to the bed was a smaller table with a lamp and a digital alarm clock, which did not seem to be functional, and there was a desk in the corner. He dropped his bags on the bed and went back outside to the office, where Nole was nowhere to be seen.

"Nole," Will said.

There was a grunt from the back room of the shack and what sounded like squeaky bed springs.

"Yeah," Nole said, coming out of the room.

"Uh, there's no phone in the room. Can you call me a taxi?"

"Sure. Probably be here in ten minutes or so."

"Thanks," Will said, and headed back out of the door to the outside, and back to his room. He picked the key up off the table next to the bed where he had laid it when he came in, put it in his pocket, and then went to take a look at the bathroom. He opened the door and noticed a strong smell of bleach. The sink faucet dripped and left a brown stain on the white porcelain of the sink. The shower was a stand-up only type with no bathtub. *You didn't want to take a bubble bath anyway,* he thought. He closed the door and turned the knob on the television. The screen flashed for a minute, but only snow appeared. He turned the channel changer, but it seemed the only thing in northern Indianapolis on television, at least on *this* television, was the weather program, and the forecast was all snow. He heard a horn blast outside, and went to the door, opened it, turned the lock on the back of the knob, and stepped across the threshold. He stopped and turned, and saw his bags, packed with cash, still sitting on the bed.

"Oh, hell no," Will said out loud. He went back inside, grabbed the bags, and walked out the door, closing it behind him.

Chapter 21 – Leon

Will stuffed his bags into the cab as usual and then climbed into the back seat of the familiar-looking cab. The same driver who dropped him at the Big Star was driving the taxi he was in now.

"Hey," the driver said. "I gave you my card. Why didn't you call me?"

"Uh, no phone in the room," Will said. "I asked the guy in the office–"

"Yeah, I know. 'Leon' and I go way back. Where ya headed?"

"One of those big retail-giant stores, if you have one around here."

"Yeah, we got a Super-Jack's not too far from here. What are ya in the market for? Maybe I can help."

"Hey, uh, you didn't turn the meter on."

"Don't worry about it," the driver said. "You tipped me okay before."

Will looked at him in the rear-view mirror and thought for a moment. "I think I'm okay with the Super-Jack's."

"No worries," the driver said.

Will sighed, and after another moment, said, "What's your name? I can't just keep calling you 'Hey' if you're going to be my dedicated driver while I'm here."

"Leon."

Will laughed. "Okay, do you have a real name, 'Leon', or do I just stick with that?"

"Nope," he said. "Just Leon."

"I thought you were going to tell me it was Nole," Will said, looking out the window.

They pulled up in front of the Super-Jack's, and Will got out, taking his bags.

"Hey," Leon said. "Why don't you leave the bags here? I'll wait here until you're done, then take you wherever you want to go next."

"No, I'm good, man, thanks."

"You don't trust me."

"I don't know you and I'm in a strange town, so, yeah, maybe trust is an issue. It has to be earned."

Leon chuckled. "You can put them in the trunk, and take the keys with you."

"Thanks," Will said, "But I'm good." He closed the car door and started walking toward the entrance of the store. He froze when he saw a sign on the front door.

"Due to heightened security precautions, all outside bags will be checked before entry and exit."

Well, isn't that a punch in the nuts, he thought. *What are my options? Go inside, have them search my bags, and find a shit-ton of cash? No, that sure won't raise any red flags. Toss the bags in the trunk of Leon's cab, trusting that he doesn't have another set of keys or a way to get to them? Ugh. Or go back to the motel and sleep with both eyes open. Dammit, this sucks. Things I never planned for.*

The horn on the cab honked, and Will turned to see Leon with his arms up in a 'what are you going to do' motion. He headed back towards the cab, opened the back door and tossed the bags in, and climbed into the seat. He pointed to an empty parking spot and said, "Park there."

Leon looked at him in the rearview, laughed, and started the car. He made a sharp U-turn and parked in the spot as Will directed. "Now what?" Leon said.

"Let's go shopping."

"Damn, son. You do have trust issues," Leon said.

"You have a chance to earn it," Will replied. "Come with me," he said whimsically, "and open the trunk."

Leon opened his door and exited the vehicle as Will did the same, bags in hand. Leon opened the trunk, and Will tossed the bags inside, closing the trunk afterward. Leon flicked a button on the key ring, and all the doors locked. He handed the keys to Will with an arched eyebrow and a wry smile.

"Thanks," Will said, and they headed into the store.

"What are we shopping for today? Hey, I don't know your name, either. I can't just call you 'Hey' if I'm going to be your dedicated driver."

"Joseph," Will said. "Joseph Johnson."

"Sounds like a porn name."

"I get that a lot," Will laughed. "Call me Joey."

"Alright, 'Joey,' what are we buying?"

"I need the electronics department."

"Back this way," Leon said. They weaved through the aisles of the massive store until they reached the electronics department. Will selected a CD player with a radio and a set of headphones. They located the battery section, and Will chose the big pack of "AA" batteries, and they headed to the music department where he picked a few CDs from the rack.

"Now I need, like, the Home section."

Leon pulled a cellular phone from his pocket. "Hey," he said. "No, I'm busy now, get someone else." He snapped the phone closed and returned it to his pocket. "Far corner," Leon said, bored with the exercise already. When they reached the corner area of the store, Will began looking at the items in the bedding section. "What are you looking for?"

"Sheets, for the bed at the Big Star," Will said. "I'm not crazy about sleeping on what is provided."

"Uh-huh," Leon said, casting a wary eye at Will. "You'll probably need a double, and you'll want to get white. Get some pillowcases, too. And while you're at it, I'd actually get new pillows, maybe some towels. That place is kind of a dump."

"Hmm," Will said thoughtfully. "Good idea. Should have gotten a cart." They walked through the area of the store as Will collected the things that would make him feel comfortable sleeping at the Big Star. He also stopped at the front desk of the store and bought a cellular phone with prepaid minutes. When they checked out, Will had spent over four hundred dollars. They made it through the bag check with no incidents and went out to the cab. Will tossed his bags into the back seat and started to climb in.

"Might as well ride up here, now," Leon said. "The seat is cleaner, anyway." Will closed the back door and opened the front passenger and climbed in.

"This is weird," he said. "I don't think I've ever sat in the front seat of a cab, not even back—" Will stopped himself from letting "in New York" finish off his sentence. "Not even when I shared them with people from work back in Philly."

Leon turned on the meter this time as they began to drive out of the parking lot.

"Ah, don't worry about it. I have people ride up here a lot, especially visitors like you." Leon looked at him and grinned.

Will began to feel uneasy. He wished he had sat in the backseat instead. But then he looked at the dashboard of the car and saw a small picture frame of a young woman and a toddler, with Leon behind them. "Who is this?" Will asked.

"Old lady and the kid. My mom took it to the park earlier this year. Took like ten minutes to get the kid to sit still. Old lady kept yelling at me, 'Elmo, hold her still!' We finally got the picture taken, and it was perfect."

"Nice," Will said. "She doesn't look like an 'old' lady, though."

"Nah, I just call her that when she's not around. When she is around, it's usually "Honey' or 'Cookie' or something like that."

"And she calls you 'Elmo.' I thought your real name was Leon. Says so right on your hack license here," Will said, flicking the dash.

"Pet names, Joey," Leon said as he made the turn onto 17th street. They crossed the railroad tracks once again and pulled into the lot of the Big Star. "I'll tell you a story. Leon *is* my real name. Leon Morton Anderson. 'El' for Leon, 'Mo' for Morton. I own the Big Star, and Noel, at the Revere, is MY sister, not

Nole's. If you had asked Noel to call you a cab, she would have called me, and if you had asked me for a place to stay, I'd have taken you to the Big Star. Noel did call me, by the way, and told me which way you were headed when you left the Revere. That's how I came to pick you up. You probably haven't seen a cab back home stop and wait for you too much, have you? We try to keep the income in a closed circle. Noel directs her 'rejects,' forgive the term, to the Big Star, I take you there, Nole cuts you a break for the room, and I cut Noel in for ten percent."

"Who is Nole, then?"

"Just an old friend I'd trust with my life and take a bullet for."

"You know he pulled a gun on me? He's got a gun behind the counter." Will asked.

"Good. I gave it to him."

"Well, that's fair, I guess. Speaking of fare," Will said, pulling out his wallet. "Thanks for toting me around tonight. I told you earlier, trust had to be earned, right? Well, you've earned mine. I'll probably need some rides tomorrow if you're going to be around."

Leon pointed to the picture on the dash. "I do what I do for them. I'll be around."

Will paid the fare and again left a decent tip. As he shut the front door of the cab, Leon gunned the motor and took off. Will was horrified; everything he had just bought and everything he owned started speeding away down the parking lot of the Big Star.

"Hey!" Will yelled. The car stopped, and the backup lights shone brightly, and the car slowly started to come back to Will's location. Will held his arms out as the car came to a stop next to him. The trunk of the cab popped open. "Leon!" Will yelled.

"Just kidding," Leon said loudly with a chuckle. Will pulled everything out of the backseat and the trunk and then shut the lid on the back of the car. As he went to shut the rear door, the driver's window came down.

"Dude, I just crapped in my pants," Will said, and shut the door.

Leon let out a little laugh again. "Yeah, well, make sure you change them before sleeping in my bed. And I'm keeping those sheets and pillows you just bought." He took the lollipop from the corner of his mouth. "Mañana," he said with a smile, and slowly drove away. Will shook his head and entered his room with all of his recently purchased treasures.

Chapter 22 – Something That Matters

Will sat at the desk and stared off into space, not knowing what to write. *You should reach out to Kathleen,* he thought, *but she'd never understand what you're doing. The walls around you feel like they are closing in, but there's nothing you can do about that until you get out of here. Better get started,* he told himself.

He reached into the bottom drawer of his desk and pulled out a manila file folder and laid it in front of him. The office around him was busy as always, and everyone in it was bustling around and hurrying in different directions. It drove him nuts. He had a ton of work to do, but this was more important right now.

He opened the file and extracted the loan application, and laid the folder to the side. He looked at the application from top to bottom. Everything looked to be in order. He opened Pickwick's archaic home-grown loan application entry program and selected "New Account." The screen in front of him changed, and a new account number was created. He noted the account number, 298759874, on the form and began to enter the information from the application in front of him.

'Harp & Company,' he said to himself. *19440 MacArthur Street, New York, New York, 10019. Officers: Johnathan Bryce Harp, Date of Birth is nine, twenty-one, nineteen sixty-four. SSN, enter that, home address: 409 Smithy Drive, Brooklyn, New York, blah blah blah. No wonder I hate this job...so damned boring. Next officer: Lucinda (Lucy) Marino, twelve, fifteen, nineteen sixty-six...*

His phone buzzed, and it made him jump nearly out of his chair. He pulled up a word processing program to cover his screen from any prying eyes that may enter his office. He grabbed the application and the folder and tossed them in the bottom drawer of his desk, and closed it. He looked around the office, and everything looked right. He wasn't sure why he was so jumpy, but he nearly jumped again when his phone buzzed a second time. He hit the button on the phone.

"Yes," he said, frazzled.

"Mr. Kelly, you have a call on line four."

"Thank you, Jeannie." He pushed the fourth button on the right side of the phone. "Will Kelly," he said over the speaker phone.

For the next 22 minutes, Will had a conversation with a man who wanted to enter into a business with a friend. They wanted to open a small bakery in Brooklyn and were sure they had the perfect location and the experience to make the business work, both in the kitchen and in the bank account. Will was looking through the windows in his office that ran nearly floor to ceiling at the city that surrounded him, and marveled at how quiet it was up so high, and yet so loud on the ground. He wanted out, and he would get out.

"Well, yes, sir," he said into the phone. "I think that sounds like a great opportunity. Do you know how much capital you will need to start up?" He listened as the man on the other end of the phone was spitting out numbers. "I see. Why don't you come in, say, one day next week, and we can get some numbers down on paper and see what it looks like." He paused again, listening. "Sure, let me put you through to my assistant. Alright." He pushed a button on the phone and hung up the receiver. He was Jeannie's problem now. In the future, he saw another failed business to which he would try to give money next week. Another failed business that Pickwick would have to chase down at some point to get their money back. Another failed business with someone's broken dreams at the bottom of the rubble.

He opened the loan application program and continued entering the information for the fake business "Harp & Company." He thought about making three or four large loan requests, but thought that might look a little bold, so he decided to do smaller accounts, and more of them. "Harp & Company" was just the first. He had ideas for others, but he had to make sure the rest of the plan would go well. He had to get the fake IDs from Archie, and he had to find banks he could use for his defrauding purposes. He would need a different bank for each business he "opened," and a different ID for each one as well. His mind drifted away from his work, fake work as it was, and he thought about how to make his escape and what he would do with his life. *You've got to do something that makes a difference, or this is all a waste of time. If you want to go to jail, there are easier ways to do it and less expensive ways to do it. No, Willie Boy, you need to do something where you're not stuck in an office all day, doing paperwork for businesses that have a ninety percent chance of failure.*

Jeannie popped her head in the door, and he jumped once again, jolted back to reality by the opening door.

"Wow, sorry," she said. "Didn't mean to startle you."

"That's okay," he said. "What's up?"

"The Milligans are here, the ones for the bodega."

"Ah, yes..." he said. "The Milligans. Please see them in."

Jeannie stepped aside and waved her arm in the direction of the two chairs opposite Will's desk. Will rose from his chair and put on his best smile.

"Mr. and Mrs. Milligan, so nice to meet you, please have a seat." He motioned toward the chairs across from his desk as well. As the Milligans sat in the chairs, Jeannie closed the door to the office, and Will took his seat behind the desk. He opened the top drawer of his desk, and the Milligan file was right on top of the pile. *Thank you, Jeannie,* he thought. *What would I do without you?* "So," he said, grabbing the file and opening it. "We're looking at opening a bodega on 21st Street. Any concerns that 21st is a one-way street? Do you think you'll get enough traffic?"

Mr. Milligan was the first to speak up. "We expect it to be slow at first, but once word gets out, I don't think we'll have any problems."

"I see," Will said, pretending to study the document. In truth, he had memorized all of the details and was well familiarized with the application. "Mmmm hmmm," he said, still perusing. "Mmmmmm hmmm. Well, this looks like a good application to me with a solid business model. You have all of your suppliers listed here, and your financials look good." He pulled a rubber stamp and red ink pad from the front drawer of his desk. "Mmmmm hmmm." He turned to the signature page of the loan application. "Mmm hmm." He opened the ink pad, rubbed the stamp on it, and marked on the signature page with a big red "APPROVED". He wrote the date underneath. "Congratulations, Mr. and Mrs. Milligan. You have been approved for a $50,000.00 loan. A check should be coming to you in a week or so. Takes a little time to process," he said, nodding slightly. "Any questions?" The Milligans both agreed there were none. "You can see Jeannie right outside, and she'll show you the way out," Will said.

Mr. and Mrs. Milligan rose to their feet, their joy almost readable, and took Will's outstretched hand, shaking it heartily. "Thank you so much," they both said, and exited the office. When the door had closed, Will sat back down and swiveled his chair toward the fishbowl in the corner of the room. "Well, Finch, another satisfied customer. Hope they make it." *There's no way in hell they are going to make it. One more broken dream,* he thought. *One more bright day in the life of corporate loans.* And then he went back to entering the fake "Harp & Company" information into the computer. Will wondered what it would feel like at the bank when he opened the first account for "Harp & Company" as he pretended to be Johnathan Bryce Harp, owner of an Art Studio/Antique shop. He completed entering the information into the computer for a $60,000.00 loan. He aimed the mouse cursor, but hesitated before clicking on the "send" button with his mouse. *Yeah, Willie Boy... definitely going to have to do something that matters, and makes a difference, cause this ain't it,* he thought.

Click.

Chapter 23 – He'll Live

It took a long while for the second cloud of dust to dissipate, and even after the massive cloud had covered everything within sight, and even far beyond that, with dust, Detective Greco still found it hard to breathe. He still had the T-shirt tied around his head, and he had his badge pinned to his button-down shirt, and was navigating the area fairly well, as other authorities were allowing him to go where he needed. He only needed one thing: to find Steve Angelucci, his partner for the last eight years. But everyone was covered with the same dust, and everyone looked the same. He would have to look at everyone he came across. Yet there were *so many of them,* he thought, as he wove his way through the snarled mess of demolished cars, wrecked buildings, and worse... *much, much worse*, he thought.

Greco finally made it to an ambulance and found a firefighter searching for supplies. She took one look at Greco and saw the badge, and she shook her head and handed Greco a handful of paper surgical masks. Greco took them, nodded in appreciation, and patted the firefighter on the back in thanks. He had exhausted his supply of moistened bandanas and painters' masks from the supplies he had gotten earlier. Greco removed the shirt from his face and gave it to someone running from the scene.

"It will help you not breathe in the dust!" he yelled. The man took the shirt and put it over his face, continuing to flee the area. Greco was trying to make eye contact with everyone he saw, but with everyone covered in dust and blood, he doubted he would recognize Angelucci anyway. But he had to keep looking for him, through the dust, through the smoke, through the rubble.

"Greco!" he heard from behind. He turned around to see a familiar face, but not the one he was looking for.

"Moss!" Greco yelled as he saw Detective Jason Moss running toward him. They fell just short of a full embrace, but neither of them would have found it odd on that day. "Are you alright?"

Moss nodded and said, "You?"

Greco nodded as well. "But Angelucci was headed full speed into it when it started to fall. I was two hundred yards behind him."

"Oh man," Moss winced.

"Where's Frost?" Greco asked and gave Moss one of the masks.

Moss took the mask and put it around his face, attached to his ears. "That fool picked the right week to go on vacation."

"Good," Greco yelled. "Help me find Stevo?"

"You got it."

The two detectives continued to weave their way through the mess, helping others when they could, directing people away from the crash site. They kept trying to get closer to what was left of the buildings, but were unable to navigate over some of the larger pieces of rubble. They kept searching and eventually, Greco found a way forward.

"Hey, look," he told Moss. "I'm going to go through here and see what I can find. I doubt I'll get too far, but I gotta look."

"Alright," Moss said. "I'll keep on looking out here."

"Sound's good." Greco ducked under a piece of girder and found the opening he was looking for. There was still rubble everywhere, and it was big rubble. He didn't want to lose hope, but from what he saw, if Angelucci was any further in, it was doubtful he wasn't seriously injured, or worse. He stopped his search to check on an injured firefighter to make sure he was okay. The firefighter had a head injury, but was upright and leaning against a fire truck. Greco gave him one of the paper masks and directed him to the ambulance from which he got it.

Oh, this is a mess, Greco thought, and he continued to look around the area where he had last seen Angelucci, but it was buried girders and large sheets of the building facades. Two firefighters approached him and told him that an order had been given that the area be evacuated by all non-essential personnel. Greco tried to tell them he was looking for his partner, but they forced him to leave anyway. One of the firefighters put his hand on Greco's shoulders and told him that if his partner was indeed here, they would find him.

Greco nodded and turned away from the two and made his way back under the girder that had fallen earlier. He had two targets to search for now: Moss and Angelucci, and hopefully, one had found the other, and both were upright and breathing. He was scanning the area for a sign of either, when a shout from behind drew his attention, and as he turned, he was met by a firefighter who was yelling at him.

"Are you Greco?" he shouted over the noise.

"Yeah, what's up?" he shouted back.

"Follow me!" The firefighter weaved through areas of debris and rubble, leading Greco by the arm. They made a turn in front of a damaged ambulance, and the firefighter seemed lost for a minute and looked around. Greco was looking as well. Then the firefighter backhanded Greco's chest lightly and pointed. Greco thought he saw Moss, walking with another survivor, that survivor's arm draped over Moss's shoulder. Greco sprinted to them as best as he could. *It is Moss,* he thought, and then he got in front of the pair.

"Stevo!" Greco yelled, and he hugged his partner, who groaned loudly.

"He's hurting pretty bad, but he'll live," Moss said. "His shoulder is screwed up inside and out, and he's having trouble getting his breath. Probably broke a rib or two, something like that. There's an ambulance one block east waiting to take him."

"Thanks, Moss!" Greco yelled. "I've got him from here. Come on, Stevo. Let's get you some help. Moss, stay safe!" Greco put Angelucci's good arm over his own shoulder, and they limped away from the scene. EMTs had given Angelucci a mask for his face, as well as some oxygen, but he was still labored in his breathing. Greco helped Angelucci, step by step the one city block where he expected to see an ambulance waiting. It wasn't where he expected it to be, however, so he walked with Angelucci, slowly, for another city block. And then, when Angelucci collapsed and could walk no more, Greco picked him up and used a fireman's carry to take Angelucci the next four blocks to the Emergency Room of the nearest hospital.

Chapter 24 – Runabout Man

The alarm went off exactly when he wanted it to, but in retrospect, it still seemed too early. He slapped at the device on the side of the bed, but the noise persisted. He flung the machine from the bedside table, and it flew across the room and landed on the floor, but the noise persisted. He sat up in bed, looked around, and had no idea where he was. But he realized the noise was coming from his wrist, not his clock. He pinched the two buttons on either side of the mechanism, and finally, the ridiculous noise stopped. He looked around and finally remembered. Will wasn't in his room, in his house on Staten Island; he was in the motel room at the Big Star in Indianapolis. It was Thursday, September 13th, 2001.

The sun was out and shining brightly, as it should have been for the time of day, being almost noon. After he had gotten back to the motel, he spent most of the previous night thinking about the day, the past few days, his plans, and the interesting situation he found himself in with a circle of business partners that almost seemed to have trapped him into using their services. *Noel, Nole, and Leon,* he thought. *What an interesting trio. One won't allow me in her hotel, one runs a dirt motel and pulls a gun on you, and one wants to drive you around constantly and be your friend. Not sure what to think of all this. They're definitely shady, but look who's talking. You skimmed nearly half a million dollars from a finance company. Good thing for you that the goofs at Pickwick have their heads so far up their manholes that it took them three months to catch you. But they did catch you, and here you are, executing the 'foolproof' plan you created. You and the money, that's all you really have, and you need to be smart about it. Stop over-tipping. No more frivolity when it comes to the cash. And you've got to figure out where you're going. The longer you float around, the more money you will need to spend. Get done tomorrow what you need to get done, and then get going.*

He had finally drifted off to sleep, against his better judgement and bored with his own thoughts, and now, it was tomorrow. He swung his legs over the edge of the bed and sat there, trying to get his bearings. After a few minutes, he got up from the bed and went into the bathroom and cleaned himself very quickly in the phone booth of a shower. When he got out, he dried himself off with his newly acquired towels and grabbed a set of blue jeans, a collared shirt, some socks, and a clean set of underwear from the duffel bag. Once he was dressed, after two days in the same clothes, he felt like a brand-new man. He grabbed the trash bag out of the small can in the bathroom and stuffed his clothes from the day before in it, tied it at the top, and stuffed it in the duffel bag. He had a few more sets of clothes, but he would eventually need a laundromat to clean the dirty clothes that accumulated.

The cellular phone he purchased the day before was now set up and ready to use, and lay on the table next to the bed. He picked up the useless alarm clock from the floor on his way back to that side of the bed and placed it on the table. He opened the phone and called Leon's number, and advised that he would need a ride if Leon was available.

"Be there in five," Leon said.

Will didn't bother with making the bed, and he did leave the sheets and pillows behind as a gift for Leon. He assumed Nole would be the one to find them. He grabbed his backpack and duffel bag and looked around the room to make sure he wasn't leaving anything behind. Once he was satisfied, he left the room and headed to the small office to turn in the key to Nole, who was nowhere to be found, even after Will called him by name. Will turned to see Leon waiting outside in the cab, and went out to meet him.

"What do I do with the key?" he said to Leon.

"Lock it in the room."

Will went back to the room, unlocked the door, tossed the key on the bed, flipped the little knob on the back of the door to lock it, and closed it behind him. On his way back to the car, the trunk lid popped open, and Will tossed his bags in and shut the lid. He moved to the passenger side of the taxi and pulled on the front door, but it wouldn't open. He then went to the rear door, which was locked as well. He looked in the car and saw Leon laughing.

"I'm just messing with you. Get in here," he said.

Will climbed into the front seat, looked at Leon, and said, "You're twisted."

"Yeah," Leon said, with a lollipop in his mouth. "But what else have I got, right? Where are we headed today?"

"Well, I need to get to West Washington Street. Do you know a place called 'Spectrum Optical?'"

"No, but I know where West Wash is. What's the address?"

Will pulled a small piece of paper from his wallet. He was glad he kept the wallet based on the amount of time it would have taken him to get a new one. He could have stopped after eating at the Mexican restaurant a few days prior, or yesterday at the Super-Jack's, but was glad he'd kept the old one. It was the last piece of normal he had left, and he was thankful for it. He read the address to Leon, and they started on their way. In the front seat, Will still felt odd about sitting there. Leon seemed relaxed as usual and made the trip with the lollipop stuck in the corner of his mouth.

"I know it's real soon to ask for this," Leon said, and Will tensed, not knowing what it was that Leon was going to ask for. "But two days straight with no professional sports is killing me. I need football, I need baseball, hell, I'd even take NASCAR at this point. You like sports?"

Will looked over at Leon. "I can't say I am a superfan, but I'll watch it if there's nothing else to do. I'm glad I watched some of the football game on Monday night, not knowing what Tuesday held."

"Yeah," Leon said. "That was some messed up shit."

"I was traveling most of Tuesday," Will said. "I just found out yesterday about the plane that crashed in Pennsylvania, taken down by a bunch of the passengers."

"Yeah, they figured out it was going bad and took matters into their own hands. Probably saved the White House." Leon made a left turn, and Will saw that they were on West Washington Street. It was a busy part of the town, and the road ran almost diagonally to the side streets, giving most of the businesses on each side an oddly-shaped parking lot. Leon was reading the addresses as he drove and finally found Spectrum Optical between a nail salon and a dentist. "I'm guessing you want me to wait?" Leon asked.

"As you said," Will responded as he got out of the cab. "What else have you got?" He closed the door and headed toward the storefront, walking the sidewalk until he found the door for Spectrum Optical. He walked in the door, and a bell attached to it gave a soft ring. He found himself buried in racks and racks of sunglasses and eyeglasses with frames and tints of all colors. The signs above the counter were close-ups of beautiful male and female face models wearing eyeglasses and smiling brighter than the sun. He didn't see anyone behind the counter, so he looked around at the sunglasses. He still had his pair that he bought the other day, so he wasn't really in the market for a new pair yet. He was looking at how ridiculously high some of the prices for the sunglasses were when a man came out from the back of the store.

"Can I help you?" the man asked with a strong Asian accent.

"Uh, sure. I am looking for Míng jié Zhang?"

The man looked at Will over his glasses and said, "I am Míng jié Zhang. How can I help?"

Will stuttered a little bit, not knowing exactly how to start the exchange. "Uh, my friend, Archie, Ecklund told me to seek you out."

"Ahh, Mr. Lomax, I am guessing?" he asked Will, who was taken aback at hearing his new name.

"Yes," Will said slowly, wondering how he knew.

"Archie, tell me you were coming. Everything ready." He pulled a small envelope from under the cash register and produced two small plastic cards. "So, the way cards work is, money you put up front and give to Archie now held in account by me, Mr. Zhang. Magnetic strip on the back don't call bank, it calls my server. You never get to use money in account. It stay there, but gives you credit through cards. If you need to use credit card to reserve something, like rental car, or airline seat, or hotel reservation, use these cards to make reservation, but you still have to pay cash for it, or trouble happens. The credit is always there because you never use the money. You have five-thousand-dollar credit limit on each card. They have your name on it, through bogus bank, heh heh, Mr. Zhang bogus bank, good for next four years, and you have been member of each card company for eh, about seven years, and credit always look perfect."

Will was amazed. Archie had told him that this was possible, and that he would make the connection to Míng jié Zhang when he got to Indianapolis, but he didn't believe it would actually work.

"So–" Will said, but was stopped by Mr. Zhang.

"Let me show you," Mr. Zhang said, and grabbed the cards out of Will's hand. "You buy some glasses, let's say, three hundred dollars. And let's say I need a credit card deposit to order them for you. I take the card, I swipe card. Transaction is approved. Now, you, criminal man, have a choice. When glasses come in, you pay instead with the cash, and continue to be a free runabout man, or you let charge go through, and I don't get paid, and I investigate, and I call cops, and you have big problem. So, always pay with the cash!"

"Always pay with the cash, got it. Anything else to know?" Will asked.

"You pay me for glasses now."

Will cocked his head to the side a bit and began to reach for his wallet.

"Haha," Mr. Zhang laughed. "I got you. Mr. Zhang just making joke!"

"Ahh," Will said. "Anything else to know?"

"Not about cards. You need glasses? They make great disguise for you, runabout man."

"No, I think I am good for now."

"Then you go," Mr. Zhang said. "Go get out of Mr. Zhang's shop, runabout man. We never meet."

"Works for me," Will said, and headed out of the store. Leon was waiting in the cab as promised, and Will continued down the sidewalks in front of the stores in the strip mall and climbed into the front seat of the cab.

"No glasses?" he asked.

Will shut the door and said, "No. I need a special tint for driving."

"Uh-huh," Leon said. "Where are we headed now?"

Will looked thoughtfully out the window and didn't answer for a minute. Leon backed out of the parking spot and headed northeast on West Washington. He wove his way through traffic and continued toward the city for a while as Will continued to stare out the window. He had noticed yesterday that he was seeing American flags, and they were *everywhere*. Any business with a video marquee sign outside that was able had an American flag streaming across the display, and any business that wasn't able had a real flag flying or hanging. Nearly every house they passed had one flying from a pole, or hanging in a window, or stuck to their fences or mailboxes. Today was no different. Everywhere he looked, he saw red, white, and blue. *Good,* he thought. *Let those colors fly. You have to wonder what's going on back in New York. It's one thing to see it, but it's another thing to live there. You know it's even more true these days. What would you be doing if you were back in New York, you idiot? Not going to work? You've got that covered. Not being in the city? Check. Staying in an empty house? Well, at least your house is empty. Hey, speaking of the house, the house payment is due in two days. That will start the crap machine rolling for sure, well, you know, if it weren't already tumbling full speed downhill because of the whole embezzling thing. Yes, Willie-Boy, the train is definitely off the trac—*

"Hello, there," Leon said. "Anyone home?"

"Home," Will said, thoughtlessly repeating Leon, and then he began to think of New York, and everything that had happened in the past few days. It was still so familiar to him, with its gigantic skyscrapers, rushed activity, and the nighttime lights, but now so far away. And then he looked around where they were in Indianapolis again, where most of the buildings were only a few stories, and there was nothing taller beyond them. "It's so strange," he said out loud, but didn't realize it.

"What's that?" Leon said.

"Oh, what?" Will said, coming out of his thoughts.

"You said, 'It's so strange.' What's strange?" Leon asked.

"I was just thinking," Will said. "How different the world feels when the skyline changes." And then he remembered he had the exact same feeling in the cab with Cleo just days before, when he saw the aftermath of the attacks in New York.

"A little different than the big city at home, huh?" Leon posed.

"No doubt," Will responded, and thought about Leon's words. *Home.* "That's where I want to go. I want to go home." And he thought for a moment. "Yeah, I think I want to go home."

"Goodbye already, eh?" Leon asked. "Back home to Philly. Okay, so, bus station? Train station?"

"No," Will said, still thinking. After a moment, he said, "I want to drive home."

Leon took an extra look at Will and said, "Man, a rental car, even a cheap one, is going to cost you some big dollars to go that far." They pulled up to a red light and stopped, and Leon waited for Will to respond.

"No," Will said again, "no rental car. I want a used car. Private seller. You know anyone?"

Leon looked over at him once again and kept the stare until Will looked back. Finally, Will returned the glance, and he saw Leon with a big smile on his face, a lollipop still stuck in the corner of his mouth. The light turned green, and Leon mashed the gas, leaving tire marks on the road in his wake.

Chapter 25 – Wrestlers!

Will walked around the car, taking a look at the tires with great scrutiny, and the body of the car with little care. "Pop the hood," he shouted. The hood latch released, and the hatch opened slightly. Will ran his fingers under the opening until he found the small lever that allowed him to raise the lid completely. He found the prop rod and stuck it in the receptacle in the underside of the hood. Will stuck his head underneath and searched the seals, mostly, trying to identify any leaks in the engine, but it looked good, and from what he knew of the car so far, it ran well. The tires looked decent, and the interior was mostly clean. "$4500.00, huh?" he said. It was rhetorical, and he really didn't expect an answer. He shut the hood and came to the driver's side door. "Why so cheap for a '98?"

"Because I'm ready for a new cab, man," Leon said. "Gotta keep my ride fresh for all of my reject customers," he said with a laugh.

"Fair enough," Will said. "At least I don't have to take my bags out of the trunk. I assume cash is good?"

"Sure, but I need two days before you take ownership so I can get a replacement set up with the meter equipment, lights, and the interior shield."

"I was thinking more like I would take it now, as is, and technically, you still own the car. No change of ownership. We'd call it an open-ended lease, so to speak." Will said. "What if I gave you five thousand?"

"Alright, Joey," Leon said, exhaling, "You've been pickin' at my radar ever since you got into my cab. Seriously, who are you?"

"What do you mean?"

Leon took the lollipop from his mouth. "You show up out of nowhere, no credit cards, but no spending limit, and apparently, you have a bottomless supply of cash. You're tipping me big, you tipped Nole big, you spent hundreds at the Super-Jack's last night, and you are ditching half the things you bought without a second thought. Oh, and let's see, you're paying me a sum of cash that nobody carries around on them without going to the bank first, and you are avoiding a paper trail of you taking ownership of the car. It's a little shifty to me, so let's have it!"

Will was taken a little aback at Leon's tone, which seemed to be getting louder and more aggressive. Will took a few steps back and turned away. *You've done it now, dum-dum. You were supposed to be careful, but you let this guy in too soon, too fast, and he knows too much. Dammit, you fool. Nah...no, wait...he doesn't know anything, he just suspects something's off. What does he know? He knows that over the span of about twenty-four hours, I have spent over a thousand dollars, and am willing to spend another six. That's about seven thousand, not a huge sum of money, and definitely explainable.*

He turned back around to face Leon. "Hey man, I'm just a guy trying to get back home. My company wired me some money so that I'd be able to do that. That's all it is."

"Where's home?"

"Philadelphia," Will said.

"Uh-huh," Leon said with a sneer. "You already said that before. And you get stuck in Indy, and fall into my lap. Where were you before Indy?"

Will thought quickly. "Louisville. Kentucky."

"What were you doing in Louisville?" Leon snapped.

"Leon, I don't—"

Leon's words became very pointed. "What were you doing in Louisville?"

"Recruiting."

"Recruiting for what?"

"Wrestlers!" Will said, almost yelling, and then calmed his voice. "Amateur wrestlers. I'm a scout for Temple University in Philadelphia. And I want to go home."

Leon looked at Will for a minute, then put the lollipop back in his mouth. "Not that crap on TV at night. You mean real wrestling, like in college, and the Olympics?" Will nodded nervously. "What do you know about wrestling?" Leon asked.

"I wrestled in high school. State Champion in my weight class."

"Really..." Leon said with a bit of a sneer. "Let's find out." He tossed the lollipop to the ground and assumed the neutral position with knees bent and arms ready.

"You want to wrestle?"

"Let's go," Leon said.

Will looked at him, mouth open. "Leon, come on, this is ridiculous."

Leon laughed. "Come on, grappler, let's see what you've got." With that, he reached for Will's legs and executed a double leg takedown, but Will broke free and rolled through it, landing back up on his feet. Leon continued his assault, closing in on his foe. Will backpedaled slightly and waited. Leon reached out with a few feigned grab attempts, and on his third, Will reached out and grabbed Leon's arm, dipped down, and took Leon over in a fireman's carry takedown. The two men wrestled with each other, fairly, in the dusty parking lot of the Big Star Motel. If there had been any passers-by, it would have been a sight to see. As it was, no one saw them, not even Nole, who was holed up in the back room of the motel office. Leon tried to kick out of the position, but Will blocked the first attempt, and when Leon tried to roll out of it, Will used Leon's momentum to force Leon onto his stomach. Will then used his legs to block Leon's attempts to reverse, and hooked his left arm up under Leon's armpit, and clamped his hand down onto Leon's neck, forcing Leon's face into the dirty lot. "Enough!" Leon yelled. Will slowly released the hold, and when it appeared that Leon would not attack him again, Will released him completely.

"Not too bad, Joey, not bad," Leon said as he got off the ground and the two men dusted themselves off. Leon had a small rip in his blue t-shirt and a cut above his left eye, but Will came away mostly unscathed.

"What the hell is your problem?" Will yelled. "We talked about earning trust yesterday. I guess I haven't earned yours yet. What the—ugh!" Will said, frustrated.

Leon reached into his back pocket, pulled out another lollipop, and opened it as he caught his breath. "In this business I am in, I have seen all kinds of frauds, and I know one when I see one, mostly because I am one. I'm not doing anything illegal here, it's just unethical, I guess, directing money into my own pocket at the cost of others." The lollipop went from hand to mouth. "But I can sleep at night because I know that what I do is the right thing for me and the right thing for my family. That's who I am protecting, and I don't wanna get caught up in any bullshit that would jeopardize any of what I have. I just had to get your backstory to know I could trust you. I feel better now."

"Glad *you* feel better," Wil said, still dusting himself off. "I feel like a criminal under investigation." Will almost laughed at his own analogy, but held it back. It wouldn't have been the best thing to happen at the time. "So, what happens now?"

"You buy my car," Leon said, "and I stop asking questions."

Will brushed the last of the parking lot dust from his pants. "Where were we with the car? Five grand?"

"How about six?" Leon said.

"Fifty-five hundred," Will countered.

"Done," Leon said, and the two men shook hands. "Just keep the 'On Duty' light off."

"What about the graphics on the sides and rear?" Will asked.

Leon laughed and grabbed an edge of the graphics on the side of the car, and pulled the magnetic attachment off the side of the cab. He walked to the rear and the far side of the car and did the same. Will reached into the car, popped the trunk, and headed to the back. He reached into his backpack and withdrew $5,500.00, closed the trunk, and met Leon back at the front of the car. He gave Leon the cash and started to get into the car.

"Wait, the cab has just been filled with that much cash this whole time?" Leon asked.

Will smiled. "No. I have headphones and magazines, too," and shut the door. He shook hands with Leon one more time through the window of the car. "Take care, and thanks for everything."

"Have a safe trip home, William," Leon said. Will, from habit, almost let it pass. It was the *'William'* that got his attention, and then he remembered. He cast Leon a look with a raised eyebrow and a tilted head. "What do you think, William, or Will, or Billy, or Willy," he said, and the lollipop came back out. "We talked about trust before. You think we didn't look in your wallet, *William Robert Lomax of Philadelphia?* I told you, I needed the back story. " Will looked at him, mouth slightly agape, and shook his head slowly in disbelief.

"Take care, Leon," Will said dryly. "My best to the family." He put the car into drive and peeled out of the parking lot of the Big Star Motel and out onto the road, where he headed south until he hit Tenth Street, which he thought looked like a main road. He turned right, heading away from the city, but with no destination. *And where are you going now, idiot? You don't know this town and have no idea where you're going. You need a map. No, what you need is a plan. You need to figure out what you're going to do and where you're going to go.* He continued navigating through traffic until he found a convenience store, and he pulled the used-to-be-taxi into the parking lot and found a spot near the door. He exited the car, being sure to lock the door. As he was approaching the front door, he noticed a scrawny man sitting on the curb with a cup in his hands. The man looked dirty, like he had not changed clothes in days. *Who are you to judge?*, he thought. *You wore the same clothes for two days on a bus and rode around Indianapolis in a cab driven by a corrupt motel owner for whom you ended up buying new sheets. The same guy you rolled around on the ground with today, and got your own clothes all dirty.* He shook the thought from his head and continued into the store. The door chimed as he walked in, and he walked the store until he found a rotatable rack with maps. He spun the rack until he found a state map of Indiana.

He grabbed that, one for Indiana, and another for the United States. That would at least give him an idea where to go. He went to the soda fountain and grabbed a cup, filled it with ice, and then held it against a spout until it was full. He snapped a lid on it, grabbed a straw, and headed to the counter to pay, grabbing a newspaper while he was there.

On his way out of the store, he passed the scrawny man with the cup who now seemed to be sleeping. Will dropped his coin change from his purchases into the cup and headed back to the car. He unfolded the map of Indiana that he bought and studied it for a few minutes. *Okay, Willie Boy, - okay, stop calling yourself Willie Boy. You're going to have to be Billy Boy, now. You're going west, now, Billy Boy. That still doesn't sound right. you'll have to come up with something else. Going west was always the plan, but how far west, and how do you want to get there? There's always Interstate 70. You can ride that for a while until you figure something out. You should have figured all of this out already, ya dumb nut. Your greatest plan has so many holes in it that the rats think it's cheese. Ugh, you can see that all of this is starting to get to you, right? You need to reel it in, stop making friends, stick to being the new you, and do your own thing. So, focus on where you're going. Again, west, on Interstate 70, for now.*

He folded the map back to its original form and tossed it on the passenger seat. Then he started the car and backed out of the parking spot and drove back onto the street, heading toward the interchange to get onto Interstate 70 heading west. The sun was starting its descent into its disappearance for the day, but was still high enough that it was not in his eyes. From Route 465, he passed an airport on his right, and then found the exit to get onto Interstate 70, which was currently aimed in a southwest direction. Will drove for about an hour until he hit Terra Haute, and by that time, his drink was gone, and its contents were ready to evacuate his body in a most expeditious manner. He pulled off of 70 and onto Highway 41 heading north to find a place to answer Nature's call. There was a gas station to his right, but a block further, he noticed a pancake house, and it reminded him that he had not eaten since that morning, and it was nearing four in the afternoon. As he waited for the light to change, he again noticed the abundance of American flags flying. *Where was all of this patriotism before,* he wondered. *I mean, it is nice to see it now, but it is a shame that it took the tragedy that happened on Tuesday to bring this out of everyone. We all should be like this all the time.* Will heard a honking car from behind and came back to reality, staring at a green light. He hit the accelerator and made the turn into the pancake house for some much-needed nourishment.

Chapter 26 – Terrorists

It was the Thursday after the terrorist attacks on September 11th, and Brian Greco was peering out of the window at the New York City traffic down below. Because of the attacks, a lot of traffic had to be rerouted from around the World Trade Center site, but the traffic he was looking at was still far less than usual. He considered the fact that the two largest buildings in the area were no longer standing, but also that some people were probably not yet ready to go back to work. Some were probably being encouraged by their management to remain home for the time being. The morning sun was shining through the buildings of the city, hitting the back side of the cars heading west, and into the eyes of those traveling east. Greco could see that most of the eastern-facing cars had their sun visors engaged to combat the morning ball of fire rising in the sky.

Greco reached down to the windowsill and picked up a flimsy paper cup, and took a drink of bad, lukewarm coffee. He winced at the taste of the foul beverage, but then finished it off, crunched the cup into a ball, and tossed it into the trash can behind him. He turned his attention back toward the window, and for the second day in a row, wished that the skies would deliver a nice day of rain. Not just a shower, but an entire day of rain. The city needed a bath, in his opinion. The cursed dust of destruction was still all over much of the city, and Greco wanted it gone. It was a gruesome reminder of all that had transpired a few days ago. No one would ever forget it, to be sure, but he did not feel the need for the minute-by-minute reminder of the dust.

He thought about what had happened, just in the span of the last two days, starting with the wideband alert on Tuesday morning of the first crash. Greco had been sitting at his dining room table, eating his cereal, and reading the morning paper. He was lamenting the outcome of the previous night's professional football game, where his favorite team, the New York Giants, did not take the win. He had stayed up late the previous night to watch the game on television, and for some reason, thought reading about it in the newspaper might have changed the outcome. But much to his chagrin, the 30-21 score remained the same, and his beloved team took the loss. He was just getting ready to flip the sports page to check the baseball scores when his radio crackled from its cradle across the room where it had been charging. He listened intently as the incident was described, and the horror overcame him. He immediately tossed his blazer around himself over his shoulder holster and shoved his arms through the sleeves. He did all of this on the run towards the front door of his house. He ran out of the door, pulling it shut behind him, and he bolted to his car, and nearly flew to the scene of the crash, where for the next few hours, the worst things he could never have imagined would unfold. The bowl of cereal was still on the table, next to the unread baseball scores.

He was jolted out of his memory when he heard a noise behind him. He turned to see his partner, Steve Angelucci, adjusting himself in his hospital bed. Angelucci had a large bandage on his shoulder, another on his head, and his ribs were wrapped tightly.

"Hey buddy," Greco said in a soft voice. "How you feeling?"

Angelucci groaned with a crackle. "Sore. Very sore. And apparently hoarse."

"What are the docs saying?"

"Well, I got a broken shoulder, a lump on my head that won't stop bleeding, and three broken ribs. One of the ribs barely missed piercing my lung, so I guess I can be thankful. They also said my lungs might have some damage from all the stuff I breathed in... dust and smoke and whatnot."

Greco sat on the edge of the bed and put his hand on his partner's knee. "You could have died in there, man. You gotta be careful."

Angelucci groaned again as he shifted in the bed to find the controls. He lifted the head of the bed up about three inches to look at Greco. "Man, what happened? I was out of it for most of yesterday."

Greco walked across the room and looked at a bunch of flowers that some of their friends at the Police Department had sent over. The card read: "To a True Hero, Get Well Soon!" He turned back around to face Angelucci. "Some assholes, directed by another asshole, hijacked a bunch of airplanes, flew two into the Trade Center here, one into the Pentagon, and another was probably headed for the White House, but the passengers took it over and put it down in PA. They were all killed in the process. They are saying it is the Taliban organization that's responsible, all plotted out by their leader, Osama Bin Laden."

"But why?"

"Because they are terrorists, and they hate America, I guess. Anyway, it's just a big mess, and I'm ready to join the Army to find the son of a bitch and take his head." Greco realized how loud his voice was becoming and tried to make an effort to calm down. "Just pisses me off is all, but you don't worry about that. You need to focus on getting yourself better and all healed up. I need my partner out there, right?"

"I'm with you, brother. Just needed a little vacation."

"Alright," Greco said, putting his jacket on. "I'm gonna get out of here. You need your rest. I'll come see you tomorrow."

"Sounds good, man. Try to have a safe day."

Greco turned and looked at his partner from the hospital room doorway. He manipulated his finger into a gun position and clicked his tongue as if he were firing. He said, "You know it, kid!" and exited the hospital room and went on his way down the hall to the elevator.

Chapter 27 – Western Boots

For the rest of that day and the next, Will drove west on Interstate 70, which he noticed was also called Dwight D. Eisenhower Highway. After his pancake dinner on Thursday, he crossed the border from Indiana into Illinois, passing towns like Effingham and Vandalia. He pulled off the highway in a small town called Pocahontas and marveled at how a town this small, slightly larger than a postage stamp town, seemed to have everything it needed, from bars to gas stations to grocery stores. He liked it. It looked like a place he could call home, far away from everyone he knew, and out of the way of anyone chasing him. But it wasn't far enough away, he decided. Besides, we wanted to see more options before he decided. And he wanted to see the West Coast, at least once anyway. *And not California,* he told himself. *Everybody goes to California. That's where people who are on the run from the East Coast go to get caught. You're not going to get caught. You are going to find a nice quiet town, like this, in which to settle down. You just need to find it.*

He left Pocahontas after filling his gas tank and continued westward on I-70, leaving Illinois and into Missouri through St. Louis. He would have liked to have seen the Gateway Arch, but it was out of the way, and it was also dark, and he wanted to keep moving. He kept driving and made it to a town called Kingdom City. It was a little past one in the morning, and he felt like he needed to rest, so he pulled the car over when he found a travel center, but he felt it was too well lit to make it a destination for sleep. He'd have preferred a motel, but he was still iffy on the fake credit cards and didn't really want to spend the cash when Leon's headrest was comfortable enough. He pulled into the parking lot of an all-night restaurant, facing the car away from the building. He rolled all the windows up, reclined the seat so that he was almost lying flat, and locked the doors. Within minutes, he was sleeping and did not wake up until the alarm on his watch went off at six thirty in the morning.

The sun was just getting ready to come up, and when Will opened the car door, he found himself in the middle of nowhere on a brisk Missouri Friday morning. He grabbed his jacket from the back seat and put it on as quickly as possible, and zipped it up to his neck. He needed to eat, and he needed a restroom. He went inside the all-night restaurant and took care of both. He wanted to change clothes, but wasn't sure if the restroom or the parking lot was a better option. He chose neither for the time being and decided it would be best to get back on the road. He still had a long way to go. He got back onto I-70, still heading west, and drove for over five hours straight, through towns like Dafer and Fairfield, and cities such as Kansas City as he crossed over the Kansas River. Then came Topeka, and as he drove further, Junction City and Salina, until he reached the town of Russell, Kansas, where he stopped for fuel, for both him and the car, and a restroom. He noted that Russell was a little larger than Kingdom City, but it still had that small-town feeling. He then decided that they all would have that feeling when compared to New York. He liked the feeling of this one, though, as it was modern enough to have fast food, but still had businesses like a barber shop with a spinning barber pole, and an old-time theater, the kind where they can only show one movie at a time.

When he left the town, Will decided he had seen enough of I-70 for a while, and coming out of Russell, he drove north on Rt. 281 for seventeen miles until he found Rt. 18. The sign pointing west showed the name of the next town as "Paradise." *Too good to be true?* he asked himself. *Guess you'll see.* He turned the car left at the junction and headed west on Rt.18 for about three miles. He made the turn into the town from the main road and onto what he found out was Second Street. *Billy Boy, this town may not be what you're looking for. It's got a church and what appears to be a water tower, a post office, and there are a couple of schools. Maybe three dozen houses in all. Not for you, though. This one's way too small.* He has started to become more and more aware that he was having these internal conversations with himself, and he was almost always referring to himself in the second person, as in "you this" or "you that." He didn't remember doing that before he became a criminal. He thought that it may be his conscience, giving him directions, *but isn't your conscience supposed to guide you in a good way? Yours is telling you how to best escape with the money and hide where no one can find you!*

He continued his drive through the town, checking out what there was to see. A few small businesses spread here and there, but nothing that seemed of consequence. He rode back out onto Rt. 18 and a little after the town of Natoma, turned North on 28 Road, which, for a while, he thought might have been private property. The road was not paved, and there was only farmland and a few pumpjacks on each side. He stayed on it until he hit S Road, and took a quick right-left pattern, and kept following the road north. It was then that he noticed that the pumpjacks were everywhere, trying to pull petroleum out of the land beneath them. And they were all he could see for as far as he could see. He kept going for another seventeen miles until he found the town of Woodston, which was not too much bigger than Paradise. He turned left on what was the first paved road he had seen in a while and found himself heading west on Rt. 24, driving another nine miles to reach Stockton, Kansas. He drove through the town, liking what he saw, and then he saw what he thought he might need as he traveled. It was a sporting goods store, and he was hoping they would be able to accommodate his possible requirements. He parked the car outside, locked the car doors after he got out, and headed into the store, where he was almost immediately greeted by a man in blue jeans, a white button-down shirt with short sleeves, and a white apron wrapped around his waist. The man looked to be in his mid-to-late fifties in age and wore a pair of octagonal frameless glasses.

"Can I help ya?" the man asked in a friendly tone.

"I hope so. I need a tent."

"For camping or for events?" the man asked.

"Camping," Will said. "Nothing too extravagant. It's just me."

The man took Will over to the camping section and pointed out various types and styles of tents. Will looked them over and decided on a two-man tent in which he would almost be able to stand straight up. That would give him plenty of room to change clothes if he needed, and enough room to comfortably sleep. Will also picked out a sleeping bag and a propane lantern from the camp section.

"Will there be anything else?" the man asked, with a hopeful tone.

Will looked around the store. "There's probably a few odds and ends I'll need, but won't know that I'll need them until I see them."

"That's understandable," the man said. "Grab a cart from the front of the store and take ya time. I'll take all this up to the register for ya in the meanwhile."

Will headed to the front of the store, grabbed the cart as directed, and zig-zagged up and down the aisles, picking up what he thought he might need. Matches, toilet paper, insect repellent, a small griddle for cooking, a small cooler, a fishing rod, and a ready-made tackle box. When he got up to the register, the man he had been dealing with before smiled at the number of items Will had in the cart.

"Anything else, sir?" he said.

"I noticed you sell cowboy boots."

The man pushed his glasses up his nose a little and looked at Will. "Eh, we call them western boots," he said. "But, eh, yes, we do."

"Okay," Will said. "I'd like a pair."

"Eh, what size?"

"I don't know."

"We can measure ya for that," the man said. "What kind of toe?"

"I'm not sure."

"You know what kinda heel ya want?"

"Not really," Will said.

The man looked at Will. "First pair?"

Will looked away at a woman who came in the door of the store. She was wearing western boots. "You could say that," he said.

"Well, let's get ya measured," the man said.

For the next twenty minutes, the two men determined that Will wanted a Justin brand, brindle walnut brown leather, pull-on, square-toe, cowboy-heel, casual boot, sized 11D. Will's head was spinning with the amount of information he was learning about a boot. The men returned to the cash register.

"You can pay cash or charge for all the camping gear, but I need a credit card for the boots," the man said.

"I can't pay cash for the boots?"

"You can when they come in," the man said. "I have to order them, and ya have to reserve them with a credit card, so they still get paid if ya don't show up to get them."

"I see," Will said, suddenly nervous about using the fake credit card. But, he figured, a little town in the middle of nowhere might be the best first test. He quickly scanned the store for security cameras, but didn't see any. He paid cash for the camping gear and then gave the man one of the fake cards to swipe in the machine.

He took the card from Will and ran it along a small slot in the side of the cash register. Nothing happened, and the man gave the machine a sideways glance. He looked at the card, closely this time, and then ran it through the slot again. The machine beeped, and then started making a fast-beeping noise that almost made Will run from the building without his camping gear, jump in the car, and hit the road as fast as he could and never look back.

"Oh dear," the man said, looking at Will. "I'm afraid we have a bit of a problem." Will winced, waiting for the worst. "The credit card machine is out of paper." Will nearly made an audible exhale, but held it back. "Give me a second here," the man said. He fixed the paper, and the rest of the transaction went off with no issues and the man handed Will a receipt to bring back to the store to pick up the boots. "They should be here the day after tomorrow," the man said.

"Sounds good," Will said, gathering up all of his purchases. "Oh, I almost forgot. Is there a laundromat in this town?"

The man nodded and pointed east. "'Bout two blocks that way."

"And now, the obvious," Will said, and for the next ten minutes, the man drew a map of the area campgrounds and gave him some pamphlets on each. Will thanked him and left the store with his treasures. He knew he would have to make two trips to the car from the cart, and now wondered if all of his belongings would fit in the trunk of the ex-taxi. But it did, barely, and after refilling his wallet with a fresh set of cash bills, he was on his way down the road once again. But he would not go far. It was nearing late afternoon, and he wanted to find a place to rest, thinking that with all of his new gear, it would be the perfect opportunity to spend the night at a campsite.

Using the directions that the man at the sporting goods store had provided, he found himself at a small campground called Eagle's Nest. The campground was mostly reserved for those campers fortunate enough to have one of those large recreational vehicles, drivable or otherwise, but there was a small area for tent camping. After paying a fee, he found a shady spot under a tree, next to a reservoir, where he parked the taxi and unloaded the tent. He unpacked the tent and struggled to get it together for twenty minutes. Then it took him about ten minutes to erect the thing after reading the instructions. He tossed the sleeping bag inside as well and zipped up the tent.

The sun was beginning to go down and would set before long. It would be cooler as the evening air approached, and he decided he would have a fire to sit next to for the evening. *There's a fire ring here already. You're going to need some small sticks and twigs to get the fire going. And good luck with this, by the way. You've been camping, what, twice in your life? Dad always made the fires when you did go. All you did was collect firewood and then sit by the lake with a fishing rod in your hand, catching nothing because you couldn't hold still long enough. Dad always caught or made the meals, set up the tent, started and tended the fire, everything, really. You could have done more at twelve years old, instead of letting him do all the work.* He thought about the camping trips with his father, one when he was eight years old to explain to him that his mother was dying of cancer, and another at twelve to give him the talk about birds and bees. Will's father was very frank in his description of how babies are made, but Will didn't really understand what birds and bees had to do with it. He already knew what he knew from his friends, and he would learn later in life that half of that was a load of crap. He had also caught two dogs in the process in the alley near his house when he was eleven years old, and he knew what they were doing. *You still miss him,* he told himself about his father. *You miss them both. If they were still around, you would not have had the guts to do all of this and put them through what they'd be going through now. Even without the attacks a few days ago, they would have still had to deal with their son being a thief and a fugitive. How proud they both must be.* He rolled his eyes at the thought.

As he had this internal conversation with himself, he had gathered a substantial amount of small branches. He returned to his campsite and began breaking them up into smaller pieces to make the beginning pile with which to get his fire going. There was plenty of paper in the car to use as well. A bag from a fast-food restaurant, a few receipts, and the instructions for the tent. *Now, crumple them up and place them at the bottom of the fire ring, just like that. Now, some small twigs in a tic-tac-toe style. Now, a few of the bigger branches on top, and –*

"Hey neighbor!"

Will nearly jumped when he heard the voice. He was so busy talking to himself that he didn't hear the stranger coming up behind him.

"Wha!" Will yelped as he spun around. He found himself looking at a man, probably in his forties, wearing jeans, a t-shirt with an American flag on it, and a NASCAR hat, and he was carrying three decent-sized logs in his arms.

"Whoa, sorry there, partner," the stranger said, backing up a step. "Didn't mean to scare you."

"Oh, no, it's alright," Will said, composing himself. "Can I help you?"

"Well, maybe I can help you. Saw you combing the area for wood for the fire. Thought you might need these."

"Oh," Will said, looking at the wood. "Uh, thanks. I sure could use it, but I don't want to take it if you need it."

"Hey, we got plenty there, partner. Probably end up leaving some here anyway, so as not to tote it home. If you're gonna be here a while, I can bring you some more."

"Uh, no, no... this is fine," Will said, and came to a standing position to accept the gift. "I'm only here for the night."

The stranger nodded and placed the wood next to the fire ring where Will had constructed the basis for his fire.

"Name's Phipps," he said, and the two men shook hands. "Lenny Phipps. Listen, if you need any more wood, let me know. I'm over at the big Roadrunner RV just up the way." Lenny Phipps pointed away from Will's campsite to the area where the RVs were camped. "Got our name on the back of a wooden sign. You just come, let me know if you need something."

"I'll do that," Will said.

"What do they call you, partner?"

"Johnson," Will said, mimicking Lenny's last name-first-name-last name pattern. "Joseph Johnson. Joey, if you like." *And if you say anything about a porn name...*

"Well, alright, Joey," Lenny said. "Pleased to meet you. Come on up and meet the missus and the little one if you wish."

"Well, thank you, sir, but I don't want to be a bother. I think I'm just going to lay low tonight and sit by my fire, thanks to your generosity, and for it as well."

"Suit yourself, friend. I'm gonna get on my way now. You take care."

Will gave him a quick wave. The man smiled and turned to leave. "Hey, Lenny," Will yelled. Lenny turned around and saw Will lightly pulling at his own shirt. "God Bless America," Will said.

"God Bless America, indeed," Lenny said, and turned back toward the path that led to the RV area.

Will watched him go and then went to the trunk of the car to get the matches he had purchased earlier in the day at the sporting goods store. He returned to the fire ring, struck a match, and got the paper at the bottom of the pile going. The twigs lit without much delay, and soon Will was piling on the heavier branches. When they were almost burnt down to fiery red coals, he propped one of the gifted logs against the inside of the fire ring. After a minute or so, the log began to smoke and make a sizzling noise from the sap within. Will wished he had bought a chair to sit in so he could enjoy the fire in full comfort, but he didn't, and for now, he was stuck sitting on the picnic table near the fire ring. He sat for a moment and then realized he had forgotten something. He jumped up and went to the car to pull out the small cooler that he bought. It was just big enough to hold a six-pack of beer and a few handfuls of ice to keep it cold. That's exactly what Will had stopped to purchase earlier in the day. He wished he had thought of it when Lenny was there, as he would have rewarded his considerate camping neighbor with a thank-you beer.

He sat back down on the picnic table bench with the cooler beside him. He opened it, pulled out a can of beer, and pulled the tab on the top of the can to open it. He took a long drink, and the beer tasted good to him. He sat there as the darkness began to intensify and surround him. He thought about the day, and the towns he had seen, and the long drive on the highway, and he laughed at himself for taking that ridiculous dusty side road that led him to Stockton, the town still just a few miles down the road. He wasn't crazy about sticking around the same area for two days, but he couldn't head further west right now. He had to pay for those boots. But he would go back there tomorrow, and use the laundromat to wash his clothes, and use the bath house in the campground to take a shower. That would require another trip to a store tomorrow because he had no soap or shampoo for his hair. He wasn't worried about shaving, and his five o'clock shadow from the day he left New York was filling in nicely.

As he considered the activities of the day and what lay ahead of him in the next two, he slowly burned through another log and drank his way through the beer. He still had one log left for tomorrow if he needed it. One of the sticks he had gathered earlier was long and strong enough to be of use as a fire poker. He picked it up and began to spread out the embers so they would cool faster, and he could put this day, and himself, to bed. The end of the stick caught fire, so he banged it on the edge of the fire ring to put out the flame. The end of the stick glowed orange in the darkness. He held the stick up in the air, and it made a trail of smoke from its tip, and he swirled it around quickly to make circles with its glowing tip. *You know what Dad told you about playing with fire,* he thought, and he dug the stick in the dirt until the end was as black as the sky above him. *So many stars,* he thought. *You could never see this many stars at home. Far too much light there. The sky looks so different.* And then he thought about what he had said to Leon the previous day. *"It's so odd, how different the world feels when the skyline changes."* He thought back to the sunset he had seen earlier, and he knew he was right. *You've hardly been this relaxed or this happy.* He finished off the last beer and crunched up the can until it was almost flat. He dumped the melted ice onto the remains of his fire and put all of the empty cans inside the cooler. The cooler went into the back seat of the car, and his bags went from the trunk to the inside of the tent, where they would be close to him. He locked the car and crawled into the tent, zipping it closed behind him. He unrolled the sleeping bag, crawled inside, and within minutes, was fast asleep.

Chapter 28 – The Resurrection And The Life

After his second night of camping, Will felt very refreshed and now very focused. His clothes were all clean except for what he was wearing, the car's gas tank was full, and he had organized everything in the trunk in a manner so that it all fit nicely, and he still had room to spare. He was beginning to regret not buying something more like a minivan or an SUV just for extra room and convenience, but the cab would have to do for now. The tent was put away, and he had cleaned the campsite to a point where he thought it was cleaner than it was when he arrived. There certainly weren't any random sticks lying around anymore. He had burnt them all. It was about 10:30 on Sunday morning, and he was almost itching to get back on the road, but the sporting goods store didn't open until noon on Sundays.

He decided to take a walk around the campground just to pass the time. He walked along the reservoir's edge, trying to see if there was anything worth fishing for. His efforts the previous day with his fishing rod and tackle box produced poor results, netting him only a soggy branch and a lost lure. He saw nothing and continued on his way, past the restrooms and boat ramp, and around in a large circle until he was near where Lenny's RV was parked. He had spent some time with Lenny, his wife Erin, and their ten-year-old daughter Kim the night before, sharing some adult beverages and a fire after the child had been sent to her bed for the night. They spoke of the recent events of September 11th, and the increased level of patriotism that seemed to have sprouted since. They spoke of families, workplaces, and recreational activities. Lenny and Erin were from Phillipsburg, which they joked about renaming it Phippsburg for their last name. Larry was a tractor salesman, and Erin was a math teacher at the high school. Both were tennis enthusiasts and liked to watch auto racing. Will, of course, just told a slew of lies about where he was from and what he did. He had to keep up the "Joey" routine as well, and afterwards swore to himself that he'd never give the name again, as he thought he was far enough away from home now that it didn't matter.

When he got to the site, however, Lenny and family were gone, the camper included. It was time for them to head back home, and so it was time for Will to get on the road as well. He got back to the car and began his egress from the campground. Throughout the property, he saw the same scene repeated over and over. Everyone was packing up and preparing to leave. Single campers with little trailers and families with RVs slightly smaller than the bus on which he rode out from the East Coast. And then it hit him. It was Sunday. People have to go back to work tomorrow, including schoolteachers and tractor salesmen. He, on the other hand, did not, and for that, he was thankful. He went back out onto the main road from the campgrounds and took Rt. 24, heading east for the first time in almost a week, he thought. He drove at a leisurely pace so as not to arrive at the sporting goods store too early, but he was a bit anxious to close out the transaction and get the hold off of the fake credit card. He was actually a little excited about the boots, too. Once he had them, he would put Stockton in his rearview mirror again, and never come back, which was a shame, he thought, because he liked it there. If only he hadn't told the Phipps' that his name was Joey Johnson. He should have gone with Billy Lomax; it was just as easy, but recent habits made him do otherwise. He should have known better. He should have learned from his encounter with Leon.

Your recent activities, Bonehead, do not lend themselves to "should have knowns." You're learning all of this as you go, and every day is a blank canvas. You get to paint it using your colors. Satisfied with winning that internal argument, he found himself on the outskirts of Stockton once again. He passed the park on the right and the high school on the left, and continued on Rt. 24 into the town until he found the sporting goods store. He had to parallel park nearly a block down the street from the store, and he noticed how crowded the street was with parked cars. He exited the car and saw a well-dressed woman hurrying toward her vehicle two cars behind his.

"Excuse me," he said. The woman stopped and looked at him, eyebrows arched. "Can you tell me what's going on here today?"

"What do you mean?" she asked, holding her hat down from blowing off in the wind. He didn't notice it was this windy at the campground that morning. Perhaps a storm was approaching.

"The street is packed with cars. I almost didn't find a place to park."

She dropped her head a little and looked at him. "You're not from around here, are you?" she asked, almost chuckling.

"No, Ma'am, I'm not. Just passing through."

"It's church parking," she said. "Mostly for the churches. Most everyone here goes to Sunday service." She looked at him in his hat, golf shirt, and blue jeans. "You can join us next week if you want. We, uh, accept all kinds."

Will wasn't sure how to take that, being called an "all kind," and he decided not to make an issue of it. "Well, thank you," he said in a measured tone. "If I ever come back through on a Sunday, I'll remember that." He tipped his Steeler's hat to her and left her to her business. *The Steelers hat,* he thought. *It doesn't work anymore. You tried so hard to fit in on the East Coast wearing the damned thing that you didn't realize you wore it right out of its usefulness. Now you stick out like a sore thumb when you wear it.* He was trying to remember if he wore it in front of Erin and Lenny Phipps, but couldn't. Now, he was hoping he hadn't. He tried to remember if he had worn it in front of Leon in Indianapolis, but couldn't. It didn't matter anyway. Leon knew Will wasn't who he said he was, which was Joey Johnson, then William Lomax. *The lies are starting to pile up. You need to stick with the story of being from Philadelphia, and you are William Robert Lomax. You paid a lot of money to become him, so be him.* And he was him. He was reminded of that when he walked into the sporting goods store.

"Ahh, Mr. Lomax," the same little man in the apron said, pushing his glasses up on his nose. "I was wondering if I'd see ya today."

"Just hoping my boots are ready," Will said, looking around the store again. He found the section near the front of the store dedicated to hats and looked to see if a new one felt right. There were football hats for the teams from Kansas City, Indianapolis, Minnesota, St. Louis, Miami, Dallas, San Francisco, Tennessee, and Baltimore. None for Philadelphia. *Not a problem,* he thought, picking up the hat for Baltimore. *You can be a Baltimore fan from Philadelphia. That makes about as much sense as the Pittsburgh hat.* But he didn't care. He liked the hat.

"They are, sir, they are. Actually came in yesterday afternoon."

"Perfect," Will said, now regretting the extra night he had slept on the ground.

"Do ya have your receipt?"

Will thought back to starting the fire in the campsite on Friday night, and using various scraps of paper he had in his car to start it. He couldn't recall if he had used it or not, but regardless, he had no idea where the slip might be located.

"Eh, what if I don't?"

The man behind the counter adjusted his glasses again and looked at Will. "Well, then ya got a problem," he said.

"What kind of a problem?" Will asked nervously. He could almost feel it all crashing down on him when not having the receipt made an issue with the credit card, which might be investigated, and Mr. Zhang would know he had screwed it up on the first try, and Mr. Zhang would get in trouble, and Archie would get in trouble, and-

"I'm just pulling your chain," the man said. "There might be a delay in getting them fixed if they don't fit or something odd happens to them during normal wear. He ya go," he said, setting a large brown bag on the counter. "Wanna keep 'em on the card? I know you said something about paying cash the other day."

"Nah," Will said, relaxing. "Let me give you the cash. The hat, too." They completed the transaction, and Will left the store with his new boots, not even sure for what he would wear them or why, but he's always loved the thought of having some western boots. He could have easily gotten them back in New York, but he just didn't. Now he had them. *The spoils of being a thief,* he thought. *Of being an unknown. A stranger in the lives of everyone you meet. You have the freedom and the means to go pretty much anywhere you want to go. You are your own tour guide.* He was driving on Rt. 24, but turned to head north on Cedar Street, and was saying his goodbyes to Stockton. *It was a nice town, but you can't imagine coming back to it, can you? It's not far enough west, and you're known by multiple names to people who don't live too far away from it. No, sir. Keep on truckin' as they say.*

As he reached the northern limits of Stockton, he immediately noticed that more pumpjacks were sporadically placed about. Up and down, they went, continuing their exhaustive search for petroleum. Cedar Street became RT 183, a road on which he remained for about fifteen minutes until he reached the small town of Glade. He turned left there, though, still wanting to head west as an overall plan. When he came across a town, he would slow and take a quick drive up and down a few streets to see what each was like. He liked Logan, but it didn't feel like home, and Edmund felt too small. After checking out Edmund, he drove another few miles and turned the car right onto Rt. 283 going North, where he stayed for maybe 20 miles or so, when he found the town of Borden, Kansas. The evening would soon claim the day's sunset, and he was thinking that he should find a place to rest for the night. He would have preferred to drive through it, but his rear end was beginning to feel all of the miles that he had traveled over the past week. Sleeping in the car would do him no better, as he would remain in the seat, pressure points relocated as they were. He thought about treating himself to a motel and a real bed, but camping seemed more frugal.

He filled up the car with gas at a gas station, paying cash, of course. When he got settled I his new home, wherever it turned out to be, he would hopefully open a bank account, and get a bank card that could be used for credit purchases. That was down the road, though. For now, it was cash for everything. He also bought some road snacks and a large cup of ice in the store, and got directions to a campground nearby. *You only need one more thing,* he told himself. *Beer. And I see just what I need!* He pulled the car into a spot in front of Liquor Land on First Street. *All these towns have numbered and lettered streets. If you ever try to come back to one of these towns, you're not going to be able to figure out which one you liked because they all have a First Street, a Main Street, and most have an A Street somewhere within the limits. You need to start keeping a log, dummy.*

He got out of the car, being sure to lock it as always, and walked into the store. He found his way to the refrigerated section and grabbed a six-pack of light beer. As he headed for the cash register, he saw a section of items for games. Ping pong balls, playing cards, dice, and poker chips were all part of the display. He, however, chose two items which seemed fate had determined they be there. He picked up a small pad of paper about the size of two index cards and a package of two pens. *Now you can keep your log!* he thought. He approached the counter and greeted the man at the cash register. He put his items up on the counter and looked around to see if anything screamed, "You need me!" before he left, but all of the products were silent. The cashier proceeded to punch the buttons on the cash register, told Will the total, and the transaction was completed without incident, which was something that Will would fret over each time he made one. *You never know who is on the other side of the counter, and who they work for or with.*

"Have a good night," Will said, opening the door to leave.

"You too," the man said, and began stocking cigarettes as Will left the store. On his way out of Borden, he noticed it was very much like Stockton, with a brick main street and buildings that were probably a hundred years old or more. He remembered that he would have to add notes for this town, as well as what he could remember from the others through which he passed.

He found the campground a few miles out of town and paid for his campsite for one night. He stopped in the camp store and bought a pack of split wood for his fire. When he reached the site, the tent went up with very little issue, and within twenty minutes, he was sitting on a log around his fire with a beer in his hand. He decided that tomorrow would be the day he would try to break in his boots. He thought himself silly for not trying them on in the store just in case they didn't fit. But if they didn't, he'd find something to do with them or someone to take them. He used the light of the moon and the fire to make notes about the towns he had visited. Effingham, Pocahontas, Kingdom City, Paradise, Natoma, Woodston, Stockton, Glade, Logan, Edmund, and finally Borden were all part of his notes. He made basic notes of approximate size in relation to other towns, places he stopped, people he met, and anything more that he could remember. He told himself he would keep the list going until he decided it was time to land somewhere, and then he would just pick the best. He was still determined to see the Pacific Ocean, but before the time for that decision came. He let his fire burn down and crunched the can from the beer he had just finished off. He locked the car, crawled into the tent, and into his sleeping bag. Within minutes, it was as if he were dead.

* * *

While yesterday's high temperature had reached more than eighty degrees, the cooler air had come in overnight, putting a dewed wetness on the morning ground that was stubbornly hanging around. It was now 10:20 in the morning on Sunday, and the early sun was shining brightly upon the ground, its light getting caught beautifully in the small beads of water on the blades of grass. A car arrived and parked along the edge of the grass. The woman behind the wheel of the car was wearing sunglasses to shade her eyes from the bright morning sunlight, but perhaps also to hide the fact that she wasn't ready for this. She pulled down the visor and opened a flap to reveal a mirror. Lights illuminated each side of the mirror, and she checked the reflection of her face. It was already a difficult morning, one that had followed some very difficult days. Everyone with a heart was feeling something these days, but there were some who were feeling so much more. She was one of them. She had so many decisions to make, and she was confident she had made the right ones, no matter how difficult they were. Now she had to deal with the consequences.

She had decided that sooner rather than later would be best. Dragging out the process would not do anyone any good as far as closure. She also chose minimal versus more, but mostly because she could not think of anyone to invite. No one else who would have cared was left, as far as she knew. The easiest decision was that there was no question of where. She was sure of that, and no more certain of that than she was now that she was there as well. She looked at herself in the mirror again and removed the glasses. No matter what she tried, she could not get the bags under her eyes to disappear. They were tired and red from days of little to no sleep. She tried valiantly to eradicate them, to be sure, but to no avail. When it became clear that they would be tagging along with her today, the only other companions she'd have, she decided to hide them behind the glasses. Next to no one would see them anyway. She just felt better behind them.

When she decided that she couldn't delay it any longer, she put the glasses back on and steeled herself for what was coming. She exited the car and trudged slowly along the path until she reached the point where she needed to walk on the wet grass to get to her destination. She did so, most unaware of her increasingly saturated footwear, and made it to the small structure on the hill, which was enclosed on two sides and open on each end. Once she stopped walking, the Pastor, who had arrived before her, began to speak.

"And now," he said, "we commit Willem's soul to everlasting life. Jesus said, 'I am the resurrection and the life. He who believes in me will live, even though he dies; and whoever lives and believes in me will never die.' Kathleen, do you have anything you wish to say?"

Kathleen looked at him, and then at the vault in the mausoleum in front of her. It was empty, as Will's body had not been found. She wiped the corner of her right eye, then the left, both still hidden behind the glasses, and then slowly shook her head.

"Let us pray," the Pastor said, and they recited The Lord's Prayer together. When they had finished, the Pastor touched her shoulder gently as she cried, and they both went their separate ways as they departed the cemetery.

Chapter 29 – Rocky

On Monday morning. Will woke up early, put on a pair of shorts and his sweatshirt, and for the first time in a week, he went for a run. He left the campsite and started off on a path that hugged the lake for most of the journey. He went up and down what little hills there were, and when he gauged by time what was about a half mile, he turned around and went back. After five repetitions of the same route, he called it a day. He felt great, his breathing was good, and his legs were still strong enough to continue.

When he caught his breath, he downed half of a bottle of water, then packed up his campsite and hit the road. He grabbed the map out of the glove box before he started his drive, and picked out a few points along the way, of which to take a tour. He wanted to make fewer stops and fewer guesses about where to stop, because it was costing him time. It was six days into his escape, and he'd only made it just over halfway across the country, and his goal was as far west as he could get. *Stop doing stupid things like wasting a day on frivolous things like boots.* He knew he needed to stop traveling the smaller routes and get back on the Interstates, so he mapped his direction north out of Borden, out of Kansas, and into Nebraska.

He bypassed a few towns because the route he took did not directly pass them, and more time would have been spent navigating toward them, and then back onto the highway when he was done investigating. He found one town which he felt was bigger than Borden, but didn't really have the same small-town feel to it. He came to Elwood after about an hour on the road, but he felt it was too small. He started west again, though, and passed Eustice, and then took a turn before he reached Farnham, and after about another thirty minutes, he ran into a town called Gothenburg. He took a ride through the town and thought it was nice and seemed fairly quiet, and he thought it interesting that the town had a Pony Express Station Museum. He found a convenience store with fuel pumps and did the usual list of tasks he did when he stopped. Gas for the car, food, drink, and a bathroom for himself.

When all of the standard duties were completed, he headed south from the town and found the exit for Interstate 80, and he was on his way west again, with a northern taste. As he rode on the Interstate, he had the chance to see places like Maxwell, North Platte, and Ogallala, which had a name that piqued his interest, so he had to investigate. He topped off the car and bought a bottle of water for himself in exchange for what he had just donated to the men's room in the gas station. He searched around the town to see what he could find. Plenty of businesses, a baseball park, and three cemeteries. *Three cemeteries? Any town with three cemeteries is too big, and not for you.* And so, Ogallala was now in the rearview mirror.

Brule, Big Springs, Julesburg, and Chappell were also passed and reviewed quickly, but Lodgepole, Sunol, and Colton were too far out of the way to check out, so he continued on. Brownson, Potter, and Dix, and several other towns were passed up, but Brindle became a stop along the way. He had travelled almost four hundred miles throughout the day; he was getting tired, and it was nearing dinner time. He also decided that he needed a bed to sleep in for the night instead of his sleeping bag. There was no shortage of places willing to lend him a room for the night, but he wasn't interested in the big chain hotels that were found near the highway. On the near side of the town, he found a room at the Motel Brindle for a very reasonable price. He got his key, but didn't move anything into the room yet. He was hungry and took the car out to explore. There were a few places he wouldn't mind giving a shot, but he saw what could have been an oasis in the desert or the pot at the end of the rainbow. His mouth started watering almost immediately, and he pulled into the parking lot of the pizza shop. He can't remember the last time he had pizza. *Sure, you do. It was the Friday before last. You took Jerry and went to that new spot on the corner of West. The one with the brothers' faces painted all over the window. They made a nice foldable pizza with a crispy crust and just the right amount of sauce.*

Will chuckled as his memory reminded him of something that he had forgotten from not so long ago. It made him feel more and more like the days were stretching into weeks, but he was wasting them. He walked into the pizza restaurant, and the host took him over to a table near an unlit fireplace and asked what he wanted to drink.

"Just a water for now," he said, and the young man disappeared from the table and behind the counter, rematerializing a few seconds later with the water in a large red translucent cup, with the name of a cola brand on the side.

"Rocky will be right with you," he said as he set the water on the table with a straw. Will ignored the straw and took a long drink of the water, unsure of why he was so thirsty. He had several bottles of water throughout the day, but this cup of restaurant water put them to shame. It was clear, icy cold, and didn't taste like plastic. It tasted like water. He looked through the menu but already knew what he wanted. And he wanted enough of it so there would be breakfast and maybe a piece or two of road pizza on his ride the following day.

"Hi there," came from a female voice from behind. When the source of the voice came into his view, I saw a woman of medium height, brown hair, and a trim figure. She had her hair pulled back in a ponytail, brown eyes, and looked to be in her mid-thirties. "I'm Rocky," she said. "How are ya today?" Her voice was a little south and a little west.

"Great and hungry," he said.

"Made up your mind?"

"Yes, Ma'am," he said. "I'd like to get a large bacon cheeseburger pizza with fresh tomatoes and mushrooms."

"Sounds good, anything else?"

"No, Ma'am, that'll do." Rocky nodded and walked back toward the kitchen.

That'll do? 'That'll'? You've never said 'that'll' in your entire life. Maybe this relaxed life is getting to you. Just maybe, and maybe you like it. Don't slip up, Billy Boy. But you won't slip up. See? You remembered to call yourself Billy Boy instead of

Willie Boy. Progress, kid! He thought for a minute about the server who just left his table. *Rocky. What female is named 'Rocky'? She's cute, though.*

He extracted himself from within his own head and looked around the restaurant. There were only a few other people in the restaurant, and they were all consumed with their own lives and not interested in him. The tables had no tablecloths, but they were covered in some odd laminate that resembled old newspaper classifieds. The items for sale were strange things, like self-operated tooth extractors, hand-cranked potato peelers, automatic corn-shuckers, and handmade soap. He wondered if the newspaper was from Brindle from years ago. He could ask Rocky, but he thought it better to keep to himself.

"Don't I know you?" Rocky said from behind him again, and she placed his pizza on an elevated stand in the center of the table.

"I'm sorry?" he asked, a little surprised.

"You look so familiar," she said. "I'm sure I have seen you somewhere before," she said, smiling.

"I think I just have one of those faces."

"No," she said, and her gum began to escape her mouth as she chewed thoughtfully. "Hey, Sandy, come here." Will buried his head, not wanting any part of the game. "Sandy, do you know him? I think he looks familiar!"

Sandy took a look from feet to face as Will raised his head to end the guessing game as soon as possible. "He kinda looks like John Cusack," she said in a very Texas voice, and walked away.

"See," Will said. "Just one of those faces."

"Hmmmm..." Rocky groaned. "I guess so. Enjoy your pizza. Let me know if you need anything."

Will knocked out two slices of pizza in just over three minutes. He was in a hurry to get on his way, still slightly spooked about possibly being recognized, even if it was a false alarm. He asked for a box and the check as soon as he saw Rocky again. She boxed his leftover pizza and dropped the check on the table, advising him that he needed to pay up in the front of the restaurant when he was ready to leave. He did so and was on his way to the car when Rocky came out of the restaurant.

"I figured out who you are," she said, smiling through her drawl, gum stuck in her smiling teeth.

"Oh, yeah?" he said nervously. Scenarios flew through his head. *Did you turn her down for a loan, and she was forced to move out here to survive? Is she a friend of Kathleen's that you met and forgot? An old acquaintance from high school or college?*

"Yeah," she said, and then she laughed seductively, moving closer to him. Maybe a little too close, Will thought. "You're the guy who walked out of my restaurant and forgot his to-go pizza." She pulled the box from behind her back and handed it to Will.

"Oh, uh... thanks," he said.

"No problem," she said, pausing as she turned around toward the entrance of the restaurant, and then she continued with "John Cusack!" and he heard her laughing as the door closed.

He shook his head and got into the car. It wasn't part of his plan throughout the day, but he decided to stop at a liquor store and pick up some beer. After the exchange at the pizza restaurant, maybe something stronger was needed. He remembered seeing a liquor store on the way in, but he wasn't sure in which direction he would find it, as he'd been driving around in all of them. He didn't find the one he was looking for, but found another, D&J Liquor on Second Street, and this one had a drive-through window. He decided to go inside, however, just to see the selection available.

The cooler was up against a long wall on the inside of the store, and the selection was rather broad between light beer, regular beer, heavy beer, domestic beer, and imports. He opened the cooler and grabbed a six-pack of light beer. He then put it back and grabbed a thirty-pack so that he didn't need to shop every time he stopped somewhere. He took the case and headed for the front of the store. He approached the cashier, who was of medium height and a little more than slightly overweight. He looked to be about thirty-five to forty years old, and his hair was balding at the top, and his goatee was greying. He was working on what looked to be some sort of small electric motor. Will placed the beer on the counter, and the man slid it across a scanner built into the top of it.

"Nineteen seventy-two," he said to Will. "Good year." Will snickered and produced a twenty-dollar bill. "Out of twenty. Twenty-eight cents is your change." The change came from a preloaded box that distributed the proper coins and sent them down a chute to a dish. Will took the change from the dish and immediately dropped it into the Need-a-Penny dish. "Hey, sir," the cashier said, and Will stopped.

"Yes, sir?"

"Uhh, is that an old taxi you're driving around in?" Will looked outside at the car and the useless "On Duty" light on the roof. There was no point in denying it or lying about it more than he had to.

"It is," Will said.

"Wherdya get it?"

"I, uh, bought it from a cab driver who didn't want it anymore," Will said.

"Ya don't say. Still ride good?"

"Rides fine," Will asked. "It's fairly comfortable, pretty clean for a used cab, and it gets decent gas mileage."

"Huh. Might have to find me a used cab. Get a good price on it?"

Will started toward the door, ready to end the conversation and get on with his evening. "Yes, it was a pretty fair deal. Like I said, the guy was looking to sell it. Have a good night," Will said as he exited the liquor store and headed to his car. *Everyone here is either extremely friendly or extremely nosey. You had better hope it's friendly.*

"You too," the man replied, and went back to working on the motor.

Once in the car, Will took a deeper look around the city. He knew it was a city now because the sign on the edge of it said, "Welcome to the City of Brindle." As he drove, he saw everything from the police and fire stations to the county fairgrounds, and on the outskirts, a golf course. He continued riding through the neighborhood, and when it had gotten dark, he headed for his motel room for the night for some beer and then some sleep.

Chapter 30 – Back On The Interstate

For the next few days, Will followed the same pattern, but with less concentration on the places he was seeing, and more on the places he wanted to see, but had not. That was the West Coast. He knew he wanted to at least *see* the Pacific Ocean. He had always heard that a lot of the West Coast was rocky beaches, and the surf pounded up against the land where there was no beach. He had been to a dozen different beaches in his life, all of them on the east coast. From New York down to Wildwood, New Jersey, Rehoboth in Delaware, Ocean City in Maryland, Virginia Beach, and another handful of them in between. But never on the West Coast. He wanted, no, *needed,* to see the Pacific Ocean. It took him five days to go seventeen hundred miles, and he headed into Wyoming, passing Cheyenne and towards Buford, then through some of the highest land elevation he had ever seen. He made it to Laramie for his scheduled breaks and refuels, and continued west, past places like Arlington, Walcott, and Wamsutter. Then there was Table Rock and Point of Rocks, and finally Rock Springs, where he turned off the Interstate and took a state road north. He passed the towns of Eden and Farson, and thought about stopping for the night. He'd been on the road for nearly eight hours with the travel and the food and fuel stops, covering over four hundred miles. He continued on, however, and found Pindell, Wyoming, and decided to call it a day there.

He grabbed a bite to eat and a beer at one of the local bars. Everyone in the bar seemed to ignore him except for the bartender, who only asked him what he wanted to eat and drink. He felt strange and felt like there was something different. It was not the feeling that there was something wrong, but more that something was *right.* And then he realized what it was. On the television attached to the bulkhead on the other side of the bar, baseball was on. Baseball! Baseball was back, and the San Diego Padres were beating the Los Angeles Dodgers two-to-one in the seventh inning. He decided to stay for another beer and consider his options for sleeping. There was the hotel across the street, and the other on the edge of town; he had passed on his way in. He waved them off to consider his other cheaper options. He had not yet found a campground in Pindell, but he had not really looked for one, either. The evening was on the cold side, and he couldn't imagine crawling into his tent tonight and zipping up his sleeping bag to keep warm. So, he decided to find a quiet side street in the town and sleep in the car for the night. He set his watch alarm for six o'clock in the morning, slept in the back seat of the car, undisturbed through the night, and under his unfolded sleeping bag.

When his watch alarm went off, he pushed the sleeping bag to the side and pulled his running clothes from the front seat. He awkwardly dressed in the back of the car, everything but the shoes, which he added to his ensemble when he got out of the car. The morning air was cold, in the mid-forties, but Will was plenty warm in this sweatshirt and sweatpants that he had picked up a few days ago at one of his stops. They were standard grey, and the sleeves and pant cuffs were elastic, so they fit snug and kept the body heat in. He ran his standard pace that morning and wasn't really concerned about measuring how far he ran. His body would tell him when he was approaching his normal distance. He ran past the bar he stopped in for dinner the night before, and past what he found out was a campground. He turned into the entrance and ran through the grounds. The campground had a few campers, all in the bus-sized RV types. No one was tent camping. He began to end his run for the day, heading back to his car, through the town's main street, which oddly wasn't called "Main Street" for once. He turned down the road where his car was parked, and his heart fell out of his chest, hit the street below him, and bounced into the rain gutter. The car was gone. He had assumed it had been towed from the spot which he called his bedroom the previous evening. He searched around for a sign that may give him an idea of where the car may have been towed, but there was nothing. He called information from his prepaid phone to get the number for the local Police Department. He was connected automatically, and when he got an answer, he asked if there was a location where a towed vehicle may have been towed.

"Pindell Towing on Pine Street," the male voice on the other end of the line said. *"Right across the street from us."*

He hung up the phone when the conversation was over. He remembered passing the Police Department on his run and headed back in that direction. He found the towing company and breathlessly walked in the front door. The woman behind the counter looked at him in his sweaty running clothes and wrinkled her nose. She had white frizzy hair and wore glasses that attached to a chain that went behind one side of her neck and reappeared on the other.

"Can I help you?" she asked.

"Hi, yes," he said. "I think you all may have my car here?"

"Which one?" she asked. Will told her the make, model, and year of the car. She looked it up on a computer on the desk. "I don't see anything. When was it towed?"

"Within the last hour," Will said.

"Oh," she said. "It's too early."

"Pardon me?" Will asked.

"It's too soon to be on the computer," she said. "Wait here. Give me the keys." Will gave her the keys, and the glasses came down to hang around her neck as she walked into another room attached to the office. He could see her through a window, speaking to a middle-aged man with a beard. He nodded, and she came back to the office. The glasses went back onto her face. "He'll get it for you. That will be three hundred and twenty-five dollars."

"Yikes," Will said. "You've only had it for an hour."

"At six tonight, it goes up another hundred. Want it or not?"

"Yes, I want it. My wallet is in the car. I can pay you when he brings the car up."

"Can't release the car until the fees are paid."

"I can't pay you until I can get into the car. My wallet is in the car."

"Hold on. Wait here." The glasses went back down, and she went back into the other room. The man with the beard was there, and they chatted again. Now the glasses came back up, and she walked back to the office. "Go outside, he'll let you into the car, you can get your wallet, and then come back in."

"Sounds good," Will said, and went outside.

The man with the beard, whose name patch said, "George," hit the button on the key fob, and the car unlocked. Will reached into the back seat and grabbed his pants from the previous day. He pulled his wallet from the back pocket and headed back into the office. He tossed three hundred and forty dollars in fifty and twenty-dollar bills onto the counter and slid them over to Glasses. She took the bills and counted them twice. Then she took a set of papers bound at one side, one white, one yellow, and one pink, and signed the bottom of the first page. She pulled off the pink copy, gave it to Will, and told him to show it to George, and he would give Will the keys. She walked to the other side of the room, opened a desk drawer, fiddled around inside it, and then returned to give Will his fifteen dollars in change.

"Thanks," he said, but she returned no such pleasantry. Instead, she told him not to park on public streets to sleep in his car. He didn't stop to think how she knew he had slept in his car; he just kept going. George was as good as Will was led to believe, and turned over the keys when Will showed him the receipt. Will inspected his bags in the trunk and found everything satisfactory, with nothing missing. He climbed in the car and headed to Weston Pine Street, ready to leave Pindell, hopefully for good. He stayed on U.S. 191, which turned north at Daniel Junction, and stayed on it past Bondurant and into Jackson, Wyoming, where he turned on Route 22 past Wilson, up into the mountains, and into Idaho.

Once in Idaho, the road exited the mountains and dumped into the flat lands of the Teton Valley. He travelled through Victor, Chapin, Driggs, and Clementsville, taking notes as he went. About one hundred fifty miles into his day, near Sugar City, he turned south and made a stop for food and fuel in Rexburg. He drove around the city for a little while and liked what he was seeing, but maybe it was just a little too big. He'd definitely keep it on his short list, though. Out of Rexburg, he aimed west until he reached Interstate 15 and went north through Hamer, Camas, and Dubois, then crossed into Montana, and saw Lima and Dell before he stopped in Dillion to fill up once again. He didn't want to take any chances on running out of gas, so he allowed himself no less than three-eighths of a tank of gas as a general rule. As he looked at his road map, he thought Dillon was laid out strangely, and the streets ran diagonal instead of north and south or east and west. It reminded him of Washington, D.C., the few times he had been there. He continued on, and the 15 became Interstate 90, and he made it all the way to Missoula before stopping again, this time more for himself than for the car, but he still filled the tank. He crossed the border of Montana, re-entering the oddly shaped state of Idaho, and was nearing his daily limit for sitting in the car when he entered the town of Mullan, where he considered stopping. *One more town,* he told himself, and kept going through a few small villages, until he reached Wallace. He decided to stop for the night, opting for a real bed in the Stardust Motel, a two-story motel hidden away on Pine Street. He remembered the morning of that day, and his having to free his car from Pindell Towing on Pine Street. *All of these places have a Pine Street now instead of a Main Street!* He ordered a sub from a local restaurant that offered delivery, along with a bag of chips and a soda. He pulled a couple of cans of beer from his case in the car and put them in the refrigerator in his room. He felt like the refrigerator he had in college was bigger than the one in his room.

He walked out of the door to his room and down the steps to the parking lot below to wait for the delivery. From what he had seen, Wallace showed promise, he thought, as it was small, seemed quiet, and was completely surrounded on all sides by mountains covered with trees. *Your own little sanctuary. It is beautiful here. A little chilly right now, but beautiful.* He turned around in a full circle from where he stood in the parking lot of the Stardust. *It is amazing,* he thought, and then caught himself, but couldn't stop what was seemingly becoming his catch phrase. "How different the world seems when the skyline changes," he said out loud.

"What's that?"

Will turned around to see the delivery guy standing behind him. He looked like he was twelve. "Oh," Will said. "Oh, nothing... just thinking out loud. What do I owe you?"

"Twelve sixty," the twelve-year-old said. Will gave him a twenty-dollar bill and told him to keep it. "Thanks, man," the kid said, ducking into his car. He chirped his tires as he exited the parking lot and sped off to his next delivery. Will took the food up to his room, consumed it, and fell asleep watching a baseball game on the small television in the room.

When he awoke, it was nearly eight o'clock in the morning. The television was still on from last night's baseball, but it was a morning program from New York interviewing some celebrity about a movie which was delayed due to the terrorist attacks a week earlier. He had forgotten to set his alarm, and now he was disappointed that he would miss out on his morning run. He liked Wallace and wanted to see more of it. But he got dressed in his regular clothes, and as he was packing his bags and belonging into the car, he saw the boots he had bought in Stockton. Today was the day. *You're going to wear the boots.* He sat on the bumper of the car and pulled the boots out of the box. They were full of brown tissue paper, which he extracted from each boot and put back in the box. He pulled his right foot up, and then the left, adding the boot to each foot in turn. He pulled his jeans down over the tops of the boots and then stood up, tossing his shoes in the trunk as he did.

Where have these been all your life? He asked himself. *These are wonderful. Let's have a walk.* He shut the trunk and took a short walk around the parking lot of the Stardust Motel. The boots fit great, and felt great, and he decided he would wear them for the day. When the car was packed and he was certain he had all of his belongings, he turned the key in the office at the Stardust. He had paid cash for the room, of course, and the faux credit cards were working fine for those reserve charges everyone seemed to enjoy employing. He left the motel office and got into his car and exited the parking lot. When he got to the next intersection, a boy was flinging newspapers into the front yards of the residents across the street. Will had to look twice, but recognized the "kid" as the delivery driver who brought him his food the previous night. *You should have tipped him more.*

When Will got back on the Interstate, he followed it through Osburn, Kellogg, Smelterville, Pinehurst, and many other smaller towns as he pointed his car northwest. After a little more than an hour on the road, he found himself near the Wolf Lodge Campground, which he checked out because it was a campground. There was a small area set aside for RVs, but the rest was open for either tent or RV parking, which triggered an entry in his pad-of-paper logbook in case he needed a place to stop later. It had water at each site, electric at most, and a creek.

He used the restroom at the campground before getting back on the road. In another 20 or so miles, he crossed the border from Idaho into Washington, where he almost immediately hit Spokane, which he drove right through. His overall thought about it was that *it's too big!* He kept going for another hundred miles or so, and got off the Interstate to US Route 2, through Davenport and Creston, until he stopped in Wilbur for refreshing and refreshment. He stopped at a place called Doxie's Diner and had one of the best meals that he could remember. He needed to stop eating all of the pizza and subs, and hamburgers he had been eating on the road and get back to cooking again. But in order to do that, he needed to find a *home.* He needed to get off the road and find somewhere permanent. He got back in the car and pulled out the road map. He followed it west, and finally figured out where he was going, instead of just "west." He circled it on the map. His ultimate destination on the westward road trip would be Seattle, which oddly contradicted his plans of finding a small town to call home.

After another near 200 miles, Will was beginning to tire. He stopped in North Bend, Washington, for a bite to eat and an early bedtime. He wanted to get to Seattle early... but then what? He still wanted to see the Pacific, but Seattle wasn't right on the coastline. It was on a bay, off Puget Sound. But still, he was close. He pulled off the highway and found the

Edgewick Inn, a small establishment right off the highway and across from a travel center. The highway was a major trucking thoroughfare, so the travel center was packed with eighteen-wheelers and very noisy. Will hoped he would be able to find some sleep. He was determined to take a run tomorrow morning, perhaps along the river that ran along North Bend. He would run, and then organize his thoughts, and he would reach Seattle well before noon.

Chapter 31 – I Am Mr. Harp!

Will was gazing at the river, somewhere deep in his own thoughts. The morning was warmer than usual, and the morning sun was reflecting off the water, like a million stars in the nighttime sky. His run that morning was uneventful, but he remembered his knee injury a little bit more that day than he had on other days. For some reason, it seemed to be a nagging injury. But he soon forgot about it as he watched a kayaker paddle by lazily, enjoying the morning weather. Will's daydreaming trance was interrupted when the door to his office flew open and Jeannie poked her head in. He pulled his gaze away from the window and looked at her with arched eyebrows.

"First Regional Bank on line two," she said, and closed the door as she left.

Why can't she ever use the intercom, he thought. *That's why it's there!*

"Thanks," he said, and focused his attention on the blinking red light on his desk phone. He picked up the receiver and punched the button next to the annoying blinking light. Will Kelly," he said.

"Mr. Kelly, this is Mark Finnegan, Bank Manager at First Regional Bank."

"Oh, hi," Will said, as if he wasn't expecting the call. "Thanks for taking the call."

"Not a worry, Mr. Kelly. How can I help you?"

"Uh, call me Will, please. I need to open a new account for a customer."

"Understood. Business or personal?"

"Business," Will said, and looked at the fishbowl in the corner of the office. Finch the goldfish looked on in disapproval.

"Company name?" Finnegan asked.

"Harp & Company. H-A-R-P. Harp."

"Principal names or names on the account?"

"Johnathan Bryce Harp." Will spelled out Johnathan to make sure the spelling was correct. "Also, Lucinda Anne Marino." For the next few minutes, when prompted by Finnegan, Will gave the rest of the information that was required to open the account.

"Now that the boring stuff is out of the way," Finnegan said, and both men laughed. Will had spoken with Finnegan on a few occasions prior about the chore of setting up new accounts. They had never met in person, and Will didn't think Finnegan remembered him. This was all fine and well with Will, who was shaking in his office chair. He had set up thousands of accounts for Pickwick's clients, but this was the first one he was setting up for *himself.*

"What is the total amount of the deposit?"

"Fifty thousand," Will said. He would fluctuate the amounts of the loans for these fake customers he was creating. Thirty, thirty-five, forty-five, and fifty thousand dollars. Substantial amounts, but not enough to raise suspicion, at least not right away, anyway. A reckoning would come, but hopefully he would be a long way gone by the time it did.

"Fifty thousand dollars," Finnegan repeated. *"What kind of business?"*

"Antique shop."

"Sounds delightful," Finnegan said with another laugh. *"So, the account number is... Are you ready?"*

"Yeah, shoot."

"10004597448259."

"Got it," Will said, writing it down. "I'm guessing they will be taking it out as a lump sum. I think they were using it to buy the location." *Why did you say that? Like he cares when or how they draw out the cash, you dummy. Be cool."*

"Whatever they wish," Finnegan said. *"That about does it. Let me know if you need anything more."*

"Will do. Thanks, Mr. Finnegan." Will hung up the phone and looked over the paperwork. Then he opened the desk drawer and pulled out a small brown envelope. He looked at the envelope for a minute or two, as if opening it and allowing the contents to mix with the atmosphere would be the equivalent of opening Pandora's jar or setting off World War Three. Luckily for the rest of the world, it was just the key to Will's future. He dumped the contents onto the desk and peered at a driver's license, worn, but not too worn, and a passport, complete with stamps from airports in New York, Los Angeles, Zihuantanejo, Paris, Marrakesh, and several other international locations. There was a credit card for a gas station, and also a video rental store member card. They all had the name of Johnathan Bryce Harp on them, and the passport, driver's license, and video store card were all emblazoned with the image of Will's face. The big test would be tomorrow, when he showed up at the bank to withdraw the fifty thousand dollars he just transferred to the new account. He had considered using the ATMs to remove the funds, but he would still need so much time, with the maximum daily withdrawal amount, not to mention the cameras catching his every transaction.

He stopped at a local bar for a beer on the way home and thought about his plan. The theft, the account setup, the bank, the withdrawals, each step was a risk. But a risk he was willing, *and needing*, to take. He had no illusions of what history would think of him, assuming it even cared. He was no hero, doing what he needed to do. He was a criminal, doing what he needed to do. He saw his reflection in the mirror behind the bar and immediately felt remorse. But it was too late now, and the only direction to go was forward.

He finished his beer and headed home without incident. The next day, as he got dressed, he didn't shave for the second day in a row, and had a nice shadow of a beard. He also used some hair gel and slicked his hair back, just as it looked in the pictures of Johnathan Bryce Harp on the passport and identification he had with him, bearing the fake name. *Archie really does good work*, he thought. He put on a suit, but not an expensive name-brand suit. He brought out an older one that he thought Johnathan Bryce Harp would have worn on his way to the bank to collect his loan, one he needed because he didn't have his own start-up cash to fund his business. He left his house and drove past his work until he reached First Regional Bank on West. He parked in an open spot on the street a block away from the entrance and made the journey on foot. He slipped on a pair of reading glasses and was a dead match for his pictures on the IDs and passport. He opened the front door to the bank at precisely seven minutes after nine in the morning. He bypassed the tellers against the wall and went toward the desks in the back. He waited by the swinging door until he was noticed, and then proceeded back to the desk of Olivia Morgan.

"How can I help you this morning?" she asked.

"Ms. Morgan, I am here to make a withdrawal from an account that was opened for me yesterday." Will sat back comfortably in the high-backed chair, crossed one leg over the other, and put his hands together, index fingers pointing upward.

"I see, and do you have your account number?"

"10004597448259," he said, as she typed it into the computer on her desk. Ms. Morgan was Black, looked to be in her mid-forties, was wearing red lipstick, and her hair was up. She wore small glasses that were perched on the end of her nose. She looked at the screen and then at him, with only her eyes changing direction. Her head remained in a static location.

"Are you Mr. Harp?"

"I am Mr. Harp!" he said, with confidence.

"May I see your identification? Two forms, please? Also, how much would you like to withdraw?"

Will pulled the passport from his breast pocket and the driver's license from his wallet, and placed both on the desk in front of him. "Eighty-five hundred dollars," he said. He then leaned back and resumed his comfortable position. He watched, growing a little nervous as she punched the keys again.

She then stood up and looked at him, down her nose, over the lenses of the glasses, and said, "Please wait here. I'll be right back."

He immediately became extremely nervous, and thought about fleeing the building, shedding the disguise, and cooking up a story about a mistaken customer to tell the bosses at Pickwick. He could feel himself starting to sweat, beads beginning to pop slowly from just behind his hairline. He could see Ms. Morgan at a desk in the back, talking to someone, waving her arms around. She finally turned and headed back toward the desk, *and the man was following her!* Will squirmed uncomfortably in the chair as the two approached. Olivia Morgan spoke first.

"This is Mr. Harp," she said, motioning towards Will. "Mr. Harp, this is Mr. Finnegan, one of our bank managers here. Mr. Finnegan has something to say to you."

Mr. Finnegan was looking at the driver's license and the passport, and then back at Will. "Mr. Harp," he said. "I wanted to welcome you to First Regional. I know your loan is through Pickwick, but their confidence in you goes a long way. If you need anything, please let us know." He reached out his hand, and Will stood to shake it, though a bit wobbly.

"Thank you, sir," he said, and sat back down. Mr. Finnegan walked back to his desk and sat down, and Ms. Morgan sat down behind her desk. "Everything okay?" he asked.

"Everything should be fine. Do you want an envelope for your withdrawal?"

"Yes, please," he said, and relaxed. She pulled out a stack of one-hundred-dollar bills from behind the desk, unwrapped it, and ran it through a counting machine to reassure Will it was all there. *Ffffffffffffffffffffffffffffffffffft*, the machine said, and five thousand dollars appeared on the digital readout. She then pulled out another stack, unwrapped it, counted out thirty-five more of the bills, and then ran them through the machine. *Ffffffffffffffffffffffffffffffffffft*, once again the machine said, and thirty-five hundred dollars appeared on the readout. She took each stack and rewrapped it with the appropriate denomination shown on the band. She placed both in a brown envelope and handed Will a paper about the size of an envelope.

"Sign here," she said.

He did, she smiled, he stood, she thanked him, they shook hands, and he walked out of the bank with eight thousand, five hundred dollars that did not belong to him. Over the next eleven weeks, Will repeated the same process, through multiple banks, over fifty times.

Chapter 32 – A Job And A Home

When he reached Seattle, Will parked his car in an open lot across the street from the Public Market Center on Pike and First in Seattle and decided to walk for a while. He had heard about the market through reading and television, and had always found it interesting. Now, he had the opportunity to check it out. He crossed the street and found an entrance. The Pike Place Market was always described as massive when he had heard or read about it, but he didn't think the description was sufficient. He ate food at three of the stands he visited and even got some food to go, which he carried in a handmade bag he had also purchased at one of the craft stands. He read about the history of the market and how it was almost closed in the nineteen-sixties, due to the fact that nearly two-thirds of the vendors were forced into internment camps during World War II. But a resurgence occurred when the area was designated as a historic district and saved, and Will now watched as the market thrived. He even watched the workers of the Pike Place Fish Market throw whole salmon at their fresh seafood stand.

When he had had enough, he left and carried his to-go food in his new bag back to his car. He didn't realize he had spent nearly three hours in the market! He needed to work on the next item on his checklist, and that was finding a place to stay for the night. He didn't want to stay in the main part of the city as it would be too expensive for an acceptable place. He drove up Interstate 5 past Union Lake and got a room at the Columbus Motor Inn on Highway 99. He tossed his takeout food and his remaining beer into the refrigerator in his room on the second floor and opened a newspaper he had bought while he was out. He spread the newspaper onto the bed, and opened a beer. As he read the paper, he saw nothing in the headlines about anyone disappearing from New York after embezzling a large sum of money and traveling across the country, so he searched for things to do. After checking out the Life section, he decided on a list of places to see, then maybe he would catch a movie, and then return to his room for the remainder of the day.

The next morning, after a run around the surrounding area, he showered, dressed, and hopped in the ex-taxi to head back toward Seattle. He would eventually get a new car one day, but it would be after he established himself in his new life with his new name in his new home. For now, Leon's car would suffice. He drove back into the city and parked across the street from the Seattle Aquarium, where he spent four hours staring at beautiful sea life. He thought the aquarium was nice, but decided he liked the one in Baltimore better. After the aquarium, he did indeed go to a movie theater to catch a film, where he ate a small popcorn while watching *Rockstar*, with Mark Wahlberg and Jennifer Aniston. Not a bad flick, he thought, but not totally believable. He was able, however, to suspend his disbelief and enjoy the movie. After watching the film, he drove back up north and took a walk around the docks where the commercial fishing vessels were located, and marveled at the size of the boats. As he was walking past one of the processing facilities, he found the sign that would change his immediate future, although he did not know it at the time.

"Want to make the big catch?" the sign asked. Then, "Want to work on the big boats?" And then finally, "Want to earn a living doing both?" The sign was attached to a power line pole in front of one of the many buildings on the docks. Will moved to get a closer look and saw a phone number, which he punched into his phone to call later. *You're going to be a fisherman? You couldn't catch crap on the pond last week.* As he walked onward, a voice called out to him from behind.

"You going to call?" the voice said. Will jumped and turned to see a man, probably in his mid-to-late fifties, with a worn and faded Seattle Mariners hat on his head and a cigarette in his mouth. He was wearing a sweater with a hole on the neck, a pair of jeans, and dirty boots.

"Um," Will stammered. "Hadn't thought about it."

"What's stopping you?" the man asked.

"I guess I'm not sure I'm 'big boat, big catch' material," Will said.

"Do you have two arms, two legs, a heart, and a brain?" he asked, puffing on the cigarette.

"Last time I checked," Will said.

"If you want a job, follow me," the man said. Will was intrigued, and felt himself a bit fortunate as he had not yet really started searching for employment, but here it was, possibly just falling into his lap. Will followed the man across the lot, out onto the dock, up a small ramp, and onto a large boat. He continued to follow him toward the front of the boat when the man turned the corner and went through a door underneath what Will could only imagine was the control area of the boat. "In here," he said. They continued down a set of steps and into a kitchen area. Will wondered if they were below sea level. "Have a seat." Will sat down at the table in the kitchen. "What's your name?" Before Will could answer, the man asked another question. "Any commercial fishing experiences?"

"My name is Billy, and, uh, no, sir, no experience," Will said, "but I have always enjoyed non-commercial fishing," he said with a slight grin.

"Eh...haven't we all. This is different. My name is Russell. Russell Pierce. I am the Captain of this fishing vessel, The Seafarer. We catch cod, salmon, tuna, crab, hell, anything the market needs. We go out on four-day trips, half day to unload and clean, half day to load supplies and prep, and you get two days off to catch up on sleep in between. See those bunks?" Pierce was pointing to a room off the kitchen with about four or five beds in it, some stacked on top of others. "Think you can sleep in one of those for five days at a time?"

"Yes, sir," Will said.

"Now, when I say 'sleep,' I'm talking about mostly ninety-minute to two-hour naps. Can you cook?"

"I can hold my own in the kitchen," Will said. "What kind of food do you eat out on the water?"

"Casserole. Lasagna. Steak. Sandwiches. Big breakfasts. Hearty food. And this is not a kitchen, it's the galley."

"Galley, got it. Assuming you hire me, what do I call you?" Will asked.

"Cap, Captain, Skipper, Skip, Russ, Russell, Pierce, whatever you want to call me, but it better be respectful. And you're already hired," he grunted. "Just need to fill out some paperwork."

"Uh, okay," Will said, shocked. *Guess you're working on a boat, Billy Jack.* "What will I be doing, aside from cooking, that is?"

"Whatever the Deck Boss tells you to do. Keep your eyes, ears, and mind open, and your mouth closed on the first couple of trips. Just listen and learn. Do what you're told, and ask questions later. No crying, no complaining. Work your ass off." He stood, turned to a drawer in the kitchen, opened it, rifled through some papers, and then returned to the table. "Here, fill these out and bring them back here at six in the morning on Monday. Bring enough clothes for a week, and nothing of value." Pierce got up and started walking out of the galley and back up the steps to the outside of the boat. Will decided he should follow. "See these hanging up here?" Pierce pointed to a rack at the top of the steps with a handful of what appeared to be suspenders attached to rubber pants. "You need two sets of these, and boots with a non-slip sole." Will took note of the name on the gear. Grundéns. "You'll need the overcoat, too. If you can't afford them right now, you can borrow some until you get your own. Get weatherproof gloves, too, like these," he said, pointing again. "Understand?"

"Yes, sir," Will said, following him out. "Uhh, Cap, I'm new to the area and still looking for a place to live. Do you think I might be able to live on the boat until I find something?"

"No. Liability is too high. Like I said, nothing of value comes on this boat."

"Understood," Will said. "I'll find something between now and Sunday."

"See ya then," Pierce said, heading up another set of steps.

See ya then. Will took this to mean he was supposed to leave the boat at this time, which he did. *Well, your last job was sitting at a desk and doing crap work. This is the exact opposite of that. You wanted something different, you got it.*

Will walked back to his car, and when he sat in the seat and closed the door, the gravity of the situation really hit him. *What the hell just happened? You're starting a new job in two days, that's what. Granted, it is one you don't need, and one you could walk away from, but you don't want to. You want this. It's why you left the other world behind.* He had so much to do. He needed to find somewhere to rent, as calling the motel home would get expensive. He also didn't want to leave his bags, belongings, and money in an unsecure place such as his car or the motel if he was gone for five days at a time. He needed something established.

He got back to the motel room and began to search the want ads for rental properties. He found six that were within walking distance to the docks and set up appointments for four. The other two turned him down immediately for various reasons, such as not having an established job or bank account. He wasn't ready for any of that yet. That would take some time.

The next day, he got up early, took a run, as was becoming his habit in the morning once again, packed up his belongings from the motel, and headed back toward the docks for his meetings with renters. The first wanted too much background information that he wasn't prepared to answer. The Philadelphia IDs helped a lot in his background stories, but as each conversation unwound, his prospective landlords were all scared away by his newness to the area and lack of a "real" job, or his reasoning for moving westward, which he blamed on the September 11 attacks. Four interviews for four apartments, and four rejections. *What are you going to do now, Billy Jack?* He wasn't sure where "Billy Jack" came from in his internal conversations, but Will liked it better than "Billy Boy," or "Billy Bob," or anything else he had come up with. *It'll work.*

He was walking back toward his car when he spotted a "For Rent" sign in a window above the garage of a dark blue, well-weathered house. *This is the place for you. It looks like a place that a rambler fisherman would call home.* He walked up the driveway to a set of rickety steps that led to the front door and climbed them carefully. There were so many splintered boards and rusty nails that he put his weight down very gingerly with each step until he reached the door. He opened the screen door, which was nearly off the bottom hinge, and knocked lightly. After a few minutes, he knocked again, louder this time. An elderly man answered the door, and when Will saw him, he immediately thought of the actor, Hal Holbrook. The man opened the door and looked at Will, and then smiled at him.

"Hello, sir," Will said. "I am here about the 'For Rent' sign in the window up there?"

"Oh, oh yes," the man said. "Come in, please. Please come in." He opened the door for Will, but stayed in the door frame so that when Will entered the house, he had to squeeze by the man in an uncomfortable manner. "Come sit down in the kitchen with me. Yes, come sit with me in the kitchen. My wife is not home right now, no, she's not home. Out at the grocery, she is, the grocery." Will couldn't help but laugh at the way the man talked, but he kept it inside. "Can I get you a lemonade or something, something to drink, maybe a lemonade?"

"Oh, no, sir. I'm fine," Will said, hoping he could keep his face straight throughout the interview.

"So, my name is Marv. Marv Kearney. I'm Marv, and you, who are you?"

"Uh, Billy. Billy Lomax."

"Lomax, Billy Lomax. Uh, are ya any relation to Ed Lomax, Ed, over on McGraw? Lomax?"

"Not that I am aware of," Will said.

"Oh, oh, okay. Anyway, the apartment," Marv said. "You want to know about the apartment? What do you want to know about the apartment?"

"Well, how much per month, and anything else I would need to know. I guess," Will said.

"So, it's four hundred dollars per month, four hundred, and it's got power, and cable, yes, cable and power, and water is included too, yes, the water. And maybe you could help us out, maybe help with some maintenance around here, some maintenance."

"Maintenance, such as?" Will asked.

"Oh, the lawn, mowing the lawn, and some yard work, basic yard work. Maybe just upkeep, general upkeep, I say."

"Like your door and porch, maybe? That all sounds fine to me, but the maintenance will have to be during two days of the week. I'll be gone for days at a time, but I can do those things on my days off," Will volunteered.

"Well, we'll need two months' rent, plus a security deposit, a five-hundred-dollar security deposit. You have an entrance, a private entrance, and a spot in the garage there, a spot for your car if you have one, a car. It's unfurnished, unfurnished, nothing up there. Do you have much to move, uh, a lot to move in?"

"No, just some personal items and eventually a bed, maybe a television."

"Oh, oh, not too loud with the television, not too loud."

"Oh," Will said. "Of course not. Like I said, I won't be here most days. When could I move in? I can get you the upfront rent and the security deposit today."

"Well, today, if you can get it all today, today would be fine, yes, fine," Marv said.

"Today sounds good to me," Will said and stood. "I'm going to go get that deposit and rent money for you. Cash is good?"

"Oh, cash, yes, cash is fine, yes, cash is good."

"Well, I'll be on my way, and I'll be back in, say, an hour or so."

"That's good, yes, sounds good," Marv said. With that, Will left the Kearney household and went looking for a marine store. He had some shopping to do and would return with Marv's cash later.

Once the rent and security deposits were made, Marv gave Will a set of keys, with one for the door to the apartment and another for the garage. He spent the rest of the day moving his belongings and recent purchases into the apartment. Sunday found Will organizing what little belongings he had moved into his new apartment and waiting for his new bed and television to be delivered. He had gone to one of the large department stores and bought a queen bed, just for the extra room, and the television was a cable-ready twenty-three-incher with a remote. Nothing too fancy, but a little more than what he really needed. He really had no idea how long he was going to be here, how long he would live in the little apartment above the garage, or how long he would be a "big catch" angler. So far, though, he liked where he was. Maybe Seattle is home, even though its size was much larger than what he really wanted. He had the windows open and the door propped wide to get some fresh air in and some of the stale air out. Will didn't ask Marv about the last tenant. Who they were, when they left, or why they left all remained a mystery. In fact, Will would do just about anything to keep from asking Myna Bird Marvin anything other than what was necessary. He still had not yet met Marv's wife either, but figured that would come in time.

The delivery truck from the department store finally came around two o'clock in the afternoon, and the men struggled getting the bed up the narrow steps and into the apartment, but they were finally able to finish the job. Will tipped each of the two for their arduous work and closed the door behind him. He looked around the apartment and saw his new bed, new television, and the dresser and chair he picked up from the yard sale down the street. The chair was an office chair, an outcast that had seen some use, and he thought he may get a desk one day to go with it. He finally felt free. After almost two weeks on the road, over the road on buses and an old taxi, he was in Seattle, and he finally felt like he was free.

The day before, he had purchased what he thought would be the proper equipment for the boat, including the waterproof gear the Captain had shown him on the boat. He has also purchased some boxes in which he stores a lot of his miscellaneous items. All the things he had picked up along his journey, such as his headphones, the little diary of towns he had compiled, and a deck of cards he bought to amuse himself in downtime. He had hoped the boxes would fit under his bed, but they were a little too tall. *No matter, they will stack in the corner just as easily. What you really need is somewhere to store all the cash you have in that bag over there.* He looked over at the backpack in the corner of the room. The clothes and other items had been removed from the bag and put into other places around the apartment. The only thing that remained in the bag was a lot of organized stacks of cash.

The television hooked up easily to the cable box, and he popped the batteries into the remote control. He turned the television on, and the first channel he found was two men and a woman on a boat, fishing. He laughed as he turned it off, grabbed his keys off the dresser, locked his apartment, and headed down the steps to the ground level. He spent some time getting some dinner at a local eatery. He had smoked salmon, asparagus, and mashed potatoes for dinner, and then spent an hour in the bar having a few beers before he headed home. *Home. You actually have a home now. Saying it feels good. Say it again. Home. Billy Lomax has a job and a home.*

It was raining when Will left the bar, and he cursed himself for not buying an umbrella while he was out, just to keep in the car. It was a nice steady, soaking rain, with the occasional flash of lightning and rumble of thunder. He parked the car in his designated section of the garage, closed the door, and headed back up the steps to his apartment. When he got inside, he hung his jacket on one of the knobs of the dresser. Since he only had a few sets of clothes with him when he was on the road, he had purchased a few new sets the day before for his new career. He bought mostly jeans, sweatshirts, heavy socks, and underwear, and he stuffed them all in his duffel bag along with his outer weather gear. Once he was packed, he prepared for bed, because tomorrow would be there soon, and he had to get up early to make it to the boat by six o'clock.

Chapter 33 – Welcome Aboard

When Will arrived at the docks on Sunday, his watch said it was five-fifty in the morning. He was glad to not only be on time, but a few minutes early as well. *Make a good impression. Don't be late.* He climbed up the plank heading onto the boat, dropped his duffel bag on the deck, and leaned against the railing, waiting for someone to tell him what to do or where to go. The sun was not yet rising behind him, but the sky held the glow of the promise of a clear day. The horizon was beginning to show that it would potentially release the sun to spread its light and warmth upon all who saw it. Off to the west, however, in the darkness, and to where Will could only imagine they would be traveling, was darkness, with no stars, the remnants of the storm from the night before.

Will looked along the side of the boat from where he stood and decided to familiarize himself with the craft. The deck leaned slightly on each side of the wheelhouse toward the sides, and small holes on the bottom of the solid-sided railing allowed for drainage of rain and sea water. The railing went all the way around the boat, and the deck flattened at the bow and stern. The wheelhouse was located toward the stern of the boat with only a narrow passageway on the deck behind it to allow access to what looked to be a storage area, enclosed by a rounded doorway. He proceeded through the passageway to the other side of the ship and up toward the bow, where there was a large crane of some sort. The side railings of the boat increased in height as they moved toward the pulpit, and were much taller than Will as he stood close to them. He finished his tour of the main deck and took his place next to the ramp down to the pier. He was sure they had specific names for them that were nautical in reference, and he was sure he'd learn them in time, but right now, they were what they were. A ramp and a pier. He didn't dare go down the steps he had climbed the other day during his application, interview, hiring, and orientation. He wasn't sure what he would find waiting, and he was the stranger on the boat.

"Hey," a voice said, coming from behind. "What do you think you're doing?"

Will turned around and saw a man of about his own age looking at him, puffing on a cigarette, and giving him a questioning look. "Uh, hi. What am *I* doing? I'm waiting."

"For what?"

"Someone to tell me what to do, I guess," Will said.

"Oh. Well, I guess I can do that," the man said. "Get off the boat!" he yelled.

"But," Will began, and was interrupted by the man.

"Look, I don't know who you are, where you're from, why you're here, and right now, I don't care. But if you think you're supposed to be here, the best thing you can do right now is get off the damn boat."

Will looked at him for a second and then picked up his duffel bag. The man remained right on the edge of the ramp, so Will had to pass him and then stood behind him on the ramp. "Am I allowed to stand up here on this ramp?" Will asked.

"Not a ramp," the man said, blowing out a nose full of smoke. "It's a gangplank."

"Okay," Will said, exhaling. "Am I allowed to stand up here on this gangplank?"

"Depends."

"On what?"

"What are you doing here?"

"I'm here to work. I'm new at this."

"That's what I thought," the man said, taking one last puff of his smoke and flicking the butt onto the dock. He stuck his hand out at Will. "You must be Billy."

Will took the hand and shook it, but was still confused. "I *am* Billy," he said. "And you are?"

The man leaned back on the weathered aluminum rail of the gangplank, and it creaked, showing some age. "Keith," he said. "Everyone calls me 'Chief.' I'm the deck boss. So far, you're oh-for-one on the rules."

"What rules?"

"Rule one is 'Do whatever the deck boss tells you to do.' I know Cap'n told you that."

"Oh, damn, my fault," Will said, shaking his head. "I thought he meant when we were out on the water. I didn't know we were under the rules now."

Keith laughed and lit another cigarette. "Don't worry about it, Rook. I'm mostly just busting your chops, but seriously, if you want to make it on this boat, or any boat in this fleet, and if you want to live longer than one or two runs, remember rule one. Listen to me, and do exactly as I say."

"Got it," Will said.

"Not 'got it,' Rook. It's 'Aye, Captain,' or 'Aye, Chief.'"

"Aye, Chief," Will said.

"Good," Chief said. "Want to know what rule number two is?"

"Aye, Chief."

"Good. I told you to get off the boat because you need to ask permission to come aboard. I'm still out here on the," Chief paused. "On the," and he paused again, arching his eyebrows.

"Oh, gangplank," Will said, smiling like he just got a question right on a test in elementary school.

"Right. The reason I am still out here on the gangplank is because Cap'n ain't here yet. The only one who doesn't have to ask permission to board is the Cap'n."

"Aye, Chief."

"Speaking of," Chief said, and nodded in the direction of the docks.

Captain Russell Pierce was on his way down the docks and made the hard left to climb the gangplank to board the boat.

When he neared the top, Chief turned sideways and leaned back against the rail to let the Captain pass. Will did the same.

"Chief," the Captain said, as he boarded the boat and turned toward the bow.

"Cap'n," Chief said. "Permission to come aboard?"

Pierce looked at him, and then at Will, then back at Chief. "Granted, Chief," he growled, then looked at Will again before walking away. Chief picked up his bag and crossed the rail with a half-leap and landed on the deck. Will looked at him quizzically, as if to ask if he should come aboard or ask the Captain for his own permission. Chief looked back at him and shook his head quickly, and waved him aboard. Honoring rule number one, Will boarded the boat. He followed Chief, and the two men took their belongings down into the belly of the boat to the crew accommodation area, just off the galley.

"You're there," Chief said, pointing to the top bunk of two that were stacked. "Bunk four. That means you get cubby four, and hook four, and everything else that is numbered as well." Chief was pointing to a wall with several doors, each with its own number. Will found number four, opened the door, and put his clothes inside, folded neatly. When he was finished, he pulled his wallet from his pants, which only contained his Driver's license, and put it inside the bag. He took his watch off and left it with his cell phone on the dresser before he left the apartment, so he had nothing else of value. Chief advised him to hang his weather gear at the top of the steps with the others, on hook number four.

He heard a commotion on the deck and peeked around the open door. Two men with duffel bags like his were standing on the gangplank. Will headed down the steps and said to Chief, "I think there's some guys waiting for permission to come aboard."

Chief nodded and ran up the steps, and in a few minutes, was trailed by two others. One looked to be well seasoned and probably in his late fifties, and the other seemed a few years younger than Will. Standing against the bulkhead of the galley, Will let them pass without contact, and each tossed their belongings onto their bunk. Chief finished putting his items away and turned to face them.

"Guys," he said, "Meet the new greenhorn. This is Billy. He's new, inexperienced, and he called the gangplank a 'ramp', so he's going to need help with terminology. Billy, this is Stump & Jelly. They work on the deck as well." Will moved across the room and shook both men's hands. Each one called him 'Rook' as they greeted him. "Guys, stow your gear and meet on deck for supplies." Chief turned and headed up the steps to the main deck.

"Stump and Jelly," Will said. "I'll assume those aren't your real names, and I'll let you decide when the time is right to tell me the story. It's nice to meet you, I'm glad to be here, and I just want to do a decent job and fit in."

"Works for me," one of them said, but Will didn't know which one was which. Nothing about either man in his initial meeting with them screamed "Hey, this guy must be called 'Stump.'" "I'll see ya up on deck, Stump," the same guy said. *Guess he's Jelly, then.* The assumed Jelly started up the steps, and Will decided he'd follow him. Jelly bypassed the weather gear, so Will did the same and continued behind him.

When they reached the deck, Chief was over on the side of the bow deck next to a panel with several levers sticking out of it. He pulled one and looked to the sky as a large boom swept overhead, and then a cable dropped to the deck when he pulled another. He walked over to where Will was standing and said, "C'mon." They walked over to a container on the side of the boat. Chief opened the hinged lid and began pulling on what looked like a net. "Grab and pull," he said. Will began pulling the net out of the box, and when they were finished extracting it from the box, it covered about fifteen feet of deck space. "Find the lashes," he said, and held up a piece of rope which was about five feet in length. "There's six of them." Will found four of the lashes to Chief's pair and was pleased with himself. Chief took them from him and attached them to a hook on the cable that was lying on the deck. He pulled one of the levers on the panel again, and the cable lifted the net up, and Will saw it was circular in shape and about ten feet deep. The net began to swing over the side of the boat and then down to the dock as Chief pulled this lever and that. "Rook, head down to the dock and start loading supplies."

Will looked over the side of the boat and down to the dock where a refrigerated truck was parked. "Aye, Chief," he said, and began the trip down the gangplank to the dock. When he got to the deck, the driver of the truck opened the rear door, and Will was amazed at the amount of food he saw. Jelly and Stump joined him on the dock, and the three began unloading food from the truck and putting it inside the net. The net reeked of fish, and Will wondered if it would transfer to the food that they would be eating later. Once the food was loaded into the net, Chief used the crane to bring it back aboard the boat and set it on the deck. They spent the next two hours putting everything away, either in the refrigerator in the galley or in the freezer boxes located in the belly of the boat.

When they were finished, the Captain came down from the wheelhouse and stood on the deck. Chief, Jelly, Stump, and Will were standing together chatting at the time, but Will was mainly just listening. "Okay, guys," Pierce said, "we got a call for cod, much as we can catch, so I want these wells filled. We're gonna go twelve to fourteen-hour shifts with travel breaks for rest in between. We're leaving in five, get the rookie up to speed on prep and process. Get 'im wet."

Will wasn't sure what getting "wet" meant, but he felt like he was ready to dive into the job headfirst. He watched the Captain climb the steps back up to the wheelhouse and disappear. Chief was the first to speak. "Billy, go with Jelly. He'll show you the bait." Will looked at Jelly, who put his cigarette in his mouth and waved Will back toward the steps down into the boat. He followed Jelly back toward the freezer chests, and Jelly opened one that they had not put food into. There were boxes and boxes of frozen fish and shrimp. Jelly loaded Will's arms up with three boxes of each, took three of each himself, and told Will to head back up to the deck. Jelly led Will to a covered area under the wheelhouse where a table was located next to some other contraption that Will was sure he didn't want to know how it worked.

"Okay, first, put your gear on," Jelly barked, and he started pulling on the pants of his weather gear. Will ran to the rack just inside the door to the belly of the boat and grabbed his pants and coat from the hook labeled number four. He got back to the bait station and began pulling on his rubberized pants. Jelly put on his gloves and said, "This is bait. When someone yells 'bait!', this is where you go, immediately, no matter what else you're doing. See these containers over here? This is what the bait goes in." Will looked toward a bin that was next to the table. There was a pile of containers with lids attached by a zip tie, and each container was perforated with holes. "Take a box of frozen bait, drop it into the chute here, and turn the crank. Keep your hands free of the chute and grinder. The grinder will chop up the bait into a frozen mush that you fill the bait box with. You do this until all the bait boxes are full. Then, when we're dropping pots, it's your responsibility to bring the bait to the pot, hook it to the inside of the pot as fast as possible, and then get out of the way. Stay away from the pots at all times unless you're baiting. Understand?"

"Aye," Will said.

"Good. It will save your life. Try it out." Will grabbed a box of the bait, ripped it open, and dumped the frozen block of shrimp into the grinder. He turned the crank, and the block began to rattle as the teeth of the grinder started to chew the frozen block of future fish food into the messy mix of mackerel that Jelly had made a minute ago. "That's it," Jelly said. "Alternate –" Jelly was interrupted by two short but extremely loud blasts from a horn on the boat. "Ahh, Jelly said, "we are getting underway. Anyway, alternate boxes so it is an equal mix. Keep going, and if you need more boxes, you know where they are. Fill all the containers with the bait mix and then come find me."

The boat began to move away from the dock as Will opened another box of the smelly bait and ran it through the grinder. When he grabbed the next box, the boat was to the left of the 15th Avenue bridge and heading toward the Ballard Locks, which Will was always interested in seeing. He had heard of the Panama Canal locks, where the boats were held in various sections of the canal until the water could be flooded in and brought to the level of the next lock. He wondered if this worked the same way, and wanted to see it, but focused on his job instead. They continued in a northwest direction through Salmon Bay until they reached the locks, and the boat began to slow. Will had just opened another box of bait to grind when Chief came over to the bait table.

"Rook, if you wanna take a break and check this out, come on," He said. "We're going through the locks." Will was reluctant to leave his post at the bait station, but was really interested in seeing the locks. He weighed his options and remembered rule number one. He decided he didn't want to disappoint the Chief, so he took his gloves off, laid them on the table, and joined Chief on the side of the boat. They were just entering the first lock, and Jelly and Stump were tossing ropes to attendees on the side of the locks. The attendees lashed the ropes to the giant cleats on the edge of the locks, and the boat became stationary. Then the water level in the lock began to fall, and the boat with it. Once the water level was equal to that of the next lock, the doors separating the two began to open. The attendees tossed the boat's ropes back over to Jelly and Stump, and the boat began to move forward. Once the boat was in the next section, the doors behind them closed, and the whole process was repeated. Once they were through the second set of locks, the water opened up into what would eventually become Puget Sound.

"Thanks for that," Will said to Chief. "That was pretty interesting." Chief nodded, and Will returned to the bait station and began cranking again to shred the frozen bait. It took him nearly an hour to get the task completed, and then he began to fill the bait containers with the stinky mixture of fish and shrimp. The boat continued its way northward through the Sound, then through the Salish Sea, and then finally entered the Pacific Ocean. Will looked out the side of the boat, watching the land to the left of him as it finally disappeared from his view and went behind them.

Chief came over to check his progress with the bait and said, "USA to the port side, it's an Indian Reservation, and then there's Canada on the starboard." Will nodded and looked in both directions, and the Chief strode away, then turned back to Will. "Left is port. Right is starboard." Will was beginning to understand why they went out for days at a time and didn't just return at the end of each day. It would take them forever to make the trip each day and burn so much fuel. After the morning loading of supplies and the bait grinding and the boat chugging through the water, Will wondered what time it was. The sun was fairly high in the sky, so he was guessing it was around noon, maybe a little after. He grabbed a container from the bin and filled it with the last of the bait mixture, although it was mostly just ice and some fish guts and shrimp parts. When he snapped the lid shut, he pulled off his gloves and set them on the bait table, and went to find Chief or Jelly or Stump to find out what he was supposed to do next.

He didn't get far when he was stopped by Jelly. "Ha, I was just coming for you. How's the bait going?" Jelly asked.

"I think I'm done," Will said, more hoping than thinking. "I did all the boxes we brought up and filled the bait boxes."

"Good. How many containers are left in the bin?"

Will thought back and said, "Maybe five or six?"

"Not bad," Jelly said. "Next time, stretch it out. What you did should be fine, but if Captain wants us to drop extra pots, it's good to have extra bait ready to go."

"Aye, sir," Will said. "Do you know where Chief is? Or can you tell me what I'm supposed to do next?"

"First, don't call me sir. I don't outrank you. Second, that's what I was coming to you for," Jelly said. "Chief said you told the Captain you can cook."

"I said I can hold my own in the kit—uhh, galley."

"Okay, good. We've got about an hour before we start dropping, so let's get some food in us before then."

"Aye, Jelly. What should I make?" *Aye, Jelly' just sounds weird.*

"You're the chef. Dealer's choice." Jelly walked away, back over toward the stack of pots that were on the boat. Will stowed his gloves in the rack by the door and headed downstairs. He looked in the refrigerator and the cabinets, where all the food had been put away. Most everything was still frozen as far as the meat was concerned, and there wasn't time to boil pasta or make a sauce. He found the deli meat they had stored earlier and grabbed the lot of it. In a cabinet over his head, he pulled out a pack of hoagie rolls, took five from the bag, wrapped the rest back up, and put them in the cupboard. He cut each roll along the side and loaded them up with provolone cheese, pastrami, roast beef, capicola, and salami. He cut each in half, so they were about four inches in length. He found a cutting board and chopped some lettuce, tomato, and onions, and placed them on a separate plate. Finally, he put mustard and mayonnaise in separate bowls with a spoon in each. He found a bottle of hot sauce and placed it on the table along with the salt and pepper, then he put a bowl of potato chips in the center, and his lunch-making was completed. He ran up the steps and looked for either Chief or Jelly. Stump never seemed to be around. He found the Chief first.

"Lunch is ready, Chief," he said.

Chief grunted a laugh at him. "We don't eat breakfast, lunch, or dinner on this boat. When you make the food, and it's ready, you find everyone and yell 'Grub' as loud as you can. If they hear you, they'll find it. Give it a shot."

"Just 'Grub'? As loud as I can?"

"Yeah, come on, time's wastin'."

Will cupped his hands around his mouth and let the word fly from deep within his body. Will was pleased to see Jelly and Stump come from around the corner and head down to the mess area. Chief followed, and as Will turned to follow him down, the Captain came over a loudspeaker and said, "Christ, I heard *that* one." Will smiled and headed down the steps. When he got to the mess area off the galley, he saw that Jelly and Stump were already sitting down, fixing their hoagies to their flavor preferences, and munching on chips. Each had grabbed a soda from the refrigerator, and Chief did the same, so Will grabbed one, too, and joined them at the table. They all sat there, eating in what Will considered to be an odd silence, but he didn't want to be the one to break it, nor did he know how. *So many things you need to know, or do you? You can quit the job and be free from it. No, no, you're going to do your job and do it to the best of your ability. You're going to learn what you need to learn. And you're going to make them teach you. You have all of these questions, so ask them. Things like, 'where are we going?,' and, 'what do we do when we get there?,' and 'who makes the next meal?', and 'when does the Captain eat?' That's it...ask them when the Captain eats!*

Before he could stop himself, Will blurted out, "When does the Captain eat? Do I take him a plate?"

The other three men stopped chewing and looked at each other, and then at Will. Will immediately regretted asking the question, and wanted to crawl into his gloves and disappear.

"Um," Chief said, wiping his face with his napkin. "The Captain eats, sleeps, and craps whenever he can, and it's our job to help him."

"Well, not with the crapping," Jelly said, and the three men opposite Will began to laugh. Will looked at them nervously and smiled.

"No," Chief said, brushing off the joke. "Captain will find his own food when he can. It's part of the job. Just make sure when you make food, you make enough so there's leftovers he can get when he can." Will nodded and bit into his sandwich.

"Hey," Jelly said. "You wanna know why they call Stump 'Stump'?"

"Only if Stump wants me to know and only if he wants to tell me," Will said, finishing off his sandwich.

Stump looked at Will for a few seconds, and then he spoke. "Insult me," he said.

"What?" Will looked at him, confused.

"Insult me!" Stump said again.

"I don't think tha–"

"Do it!" Stump yelled and slammed the table hard with his left hand.

"Uh, you're an asshole!" Will said.

"Screw you, Rook," he said softly, and gave Will "the finger" with his right hand, or tried to, anyway. Stump's middle finger was missing two phalanges from the tip. Chief, Stump, and Jelly all had a hearty laugh, and Will checked out the damage. "Never insult Stump!" Stump yelled, laughing.

"Oh," Will said. "I guess that would be a good tip." They all shared a laugh again.

"There is no 'tip,' Rookie!" Jelly bellowed.

"Eh, that's not what I meant!" Will said, shaking his head and slightly embarrassed at his gaffe.

"Keep your hand clear of machinery, including that bait grinder," Stump said. He got up from the table, put his plate in the sink, and turned toward the steps leading to the deck. He slapped Will on his shoulder as he walked by. "Good sandwich, Rook," he said. "Welcome aboard."

Chapter 34 – Johnny On The Spot

Will could only assume it was his task to clean up from the food he had made, and he did so, washing the plates in the sink and those that were used for the accoutrement. He grabbed one of the clean plates, dried the rinse water from it, placed one of the other cut sandwiches on it, added mustard, mayonnaise, lettuce, onion, and tomato, and set it aside. He took a handful of the potato chips from the bowl and placed them on the plate as well. After he wrapped everything in cellophane for future use, he grabbed the plate and took it upstairs, then quietly wrapped himself around the lower floor of the wheelhouse, which was also the entrance to the downward stairway. Once he was on the side of the wheelhouse, he climbed another external set of steps that led to a small alcove where the door to the wheelhouse was located. Will didn't know the proper protocol for interrupting the Captain, so he knocked once and then opened the door.

"Permission to enter, Skip?" Will said.

"Eh?" Pierce said, looking up from a map. "Oh, you. Granted. Come in, what's up?"

"Nothing much," Will said. "I just wanted to tell you how great your crew has been welcoming me aboard, and to bring you some of the lunch I made."

Pierce straightened up in his chair and looked at Will, squinting at him with one eye. Will was thinking he should have done as he was told, and let the Captain get his own lunch, but it didn't seem right to him. "Well, now," Pierce said. "You know, there are strict rules about a Captain eating lunch at the same time as the crew, right?"

Will fidgeted nervously. "I am unaware of those rules, sir. I just figured you might be hungry."

Pierce laughed. "I'm just messing with you, Rook. What do we have here?"

"Cold cut hoagie and chips, with condiments on the side," Will said. "I thought on the first day, the guys could use a big lunch to fuel them up."

"Hmmm. Sounds good. Thanks, Rook," Pierce said. "Now, better get back down there. We'll be setting out soon."

"Aye, Skip." Will headed out of the wheelhouse and down the steps. He saw Jelly with his weather gear on, so Will donned his, grabbed his gloves, and put on his Baltimore Ravens hat. He went out to seek Chief's instructions and found him by the crane controls. He approached and looked out over the ocean, hoping he could see whatever Chief was seeing, but there was nothing but water as far as he could see. "Chief," Will said in a greeting.

"What's up, Rook?"

"Can you give me an idea of what I need to do today?"

"Gopher. You're going to be Johnny-On-The-Spot with everything that we need, and you're going to do bait. Go get me one of those bait containers you filled." Will ran over to the bait station and grabbed the first one he could get his hands on, and then ran back to Chief. In the time Will was gone, Chief had pulled one of the circular pots off the stack and over to a table on the side of the boat. "Take the clip on that container," Chief said, "and attach it to the center of the pot, clipped to the net on the top." Will reached through the netting and tried to attach it, but it was too big to fit through. He looked for another way in, but also could not find one. Frustrated, he looked at Chief with a set of raised eyebrows. "See this?" Chief was pointing to a rope affixed to the side of the pot. "This comes undone, the door swings open, you climb in, hook it, and get the hell out of there. We will open it and close it for you, but your job is to climb in, hook it, and get out. If you're not out quickly, it's going to cause problems, and someone's going to get mad, fired, hurt, or killed."

"Aye, Chief. Johnny-On-The-Spot and quick in and out. Heard loud and clear. When do we start?"

"Well, this one is ready to go, so as soon as Cap'n says, we drop it and get another one ready. When you crawl out of a pot after baiting it, you immediately go grab another bait container so we can do the next pot, and so on until we're done. I'll be working the ramp, so I won't have time to help you, okay."

"Aye." Will calculated the distance from the hydraulic ramp where he would be baiting the pots to the bait table as about twenty-five feet, give or take. He didn't know how often they dropped the pots yet, but he was determined not to be the slow man on the team. He looked around the boat and saw Stump and Jelly next to a stack of pots, waiting for the Captain to give the go-ahead. Will looked out over the edge of the boat again and stared at the vastness of the Pacific Ocean. He remembered feeling the same way every time he had seen the Atlantic Ocean as well, but for some reason, this felt different. He felt more...*free. It's as if you've earned, or been given, a set of wings. Now fly.* At that moment, a horn blew from the top of the wheelhouse.

"It's time," Chief said. "Stand clear." Will moved back, and Leon pulled a lever on the control panel. The ramp began to rise, and the pot slid slowly off of it and then dropped into the water. Stump and Jelly had come out of nowhere, and Stump began throwing coils of ropes attached to the pot into the water, and Jelly tossed a brightly colored float attached to Stump's coiled ropes, and it all went off the side of the boat and into the water.

"Away!' Chief yelled. Will took that to mean that the pot process was completed, and he ran over to get another container of bait. As he did, Stump and Jelly connected the hook on the crane to another pot, and Chief maneuvered it over to and then down onto the ramp. Will grabbed the tie on the pot and opened the flap. He climbed in upside down and hung the container of bait, and climbed back out of the pot. Chief affixed the tie to close the flap. Everyone stood clear, and Chief pulled the lever to drop the pot. Will was already back with the next bait container when the next pot was set down upon the ramp by Chief. For the next three hours, they repeated the process until the deck was clear of pots, and Will's supply of bait containers was almost gone. He walked over to where Chief was standing by the crane.

"What's next?" he asked, and he felt the boat begin to turn.

"Now we straighten this place down, prep, and rest. Jelly will make us dinner, and we'll eat and sleep. We've probably got about 4 hours until we pick 'em up, same order as we dropped 'em. You're doing bait, so you need to repeat what you did this morning. It's going to be a little different this time because when we pick 'em up, you have to take out the old bait box and put in a new one. So those few you have left over from this last string will give you some ready-made boxes to work with, but when they run out, you're going to have to fill them and bring them over to hook into the pot, so you've gotta be quicker."

"Should I grind the bait ahead of time?" Will asked.

"You catch on quick, Rook. Go get six boxes from the freezer and get to grinding. By the time you're done, grub will be ready, and then you can catch some 'Z's.'"

"Aye, Chief," Will said, and headed down the steps into the boat, and returned a few minutes later with his arms loaded. For the next hour, Will ground the bait as he was directed, careful to keep his hands clear of the mechanism for fear he'd end up resembling Stump. When he was finished grinding the bait, he broke the boxes down and took them back down into the trash receptacle located on the second deck. He grabbed a soda from the cooler, ran back up the steps, and cleaned up the area of extra fish guts and shrimp carcasses.

The sun was beginning to set on the western horizon, and the clouds off in the distance seemed to hang just above the surface of water, and they diffused the sunlight into an eerie mix of orange in the sky and purple in the clouds. He sat down on the edge of the side of *The Seafarer* and looked out at the water. He thought about his journey over the past few weeks, and while he was none too proud of his actions to trigger that journey, he was proud of what he had done since it started. He had crossed the country, met new people, and found a new job and a new place to live in a new city. He has seen a few national parks, passed by major landmarks, crossed major rivers, and watched people throw fish in a market just a few days prior. And now here he was on the deck of a boat, fishing for Pacific cod. He was looking around the boat, and some movement caught his eye. It was Chief walking across the deck of the boat towards him.

"What are you doing, Rook?" Chief asked. "Jelly made some noodle-chicken stuff with a sauce. Pretty good for him. Go get some grub and hit the bunks for a while. We've got a lot of work to do tonight."

"I was just catching the sunset. I have seen plenty of them back home, and they're beautiful, but I have never seen one on the open water like this."

Chief pulled out a pack of cigarettes and pulled one from the pack. He offered one to Will, who declined once again. From his pocket, he produced a Zippo light and lit his smoke. Will was instantly reminded of his father, who also used a Zippo lighter. Growing up, Will loved the combination of the fuel within the device and the freshly lit cigarette. There was just something about it. *Maybe it was a comfort thing. You always knew he was going to calm down when he lit one up. Not that he was ever out-of-control angry, at least not that much, but having the smoke would take the edge off of him.* Will thought about this as he watched Chief complete the ritual, and was hoping to catch a nostalgic whiff from Chief's freshly lit vice, but the wind created by the traveling boat was too powerful, and blew the scent in another direction.

Chief exhaled the initial puff, picked a piece of loose tobacco from his bottom lip, and flung it into the ocean. "First time, I understand that," Chief said. "We certainly get our share of them. But don't fall in love with it. We also get some nasty shit blowing around out here. A lot of weather, and a lot of it is bad. You'll get your taste of it, Rook." The cigarette went back in, and Chief took a long pull and eyed Will's hat. "You said you've seen a lot of sunsets back home. Where's home? Baltimore?"

Will took a drink of his soda. "Philadelphia," he said, a touch of nervousness in his voice.

"Not a fan of the Eagles? You chose the Ravens?"

"Philly isn't that far from Baltimore," Will said. "I had two home teams, I just lived in Philly."

"Eh," Chief grunted. "Never been there. I spent some time in New York when I was younger, but then I came out here, oh, probably twenty years ago."

"What did you do in New York?"

"Uh," Chief took his hat off and wiped his forehead with his arm. "That's a different time and a different place, kid."

Will made a 'tsk' noise with his teeth. "Come on," he said. But Chief was shaking his head slowly.

"Maybe when you've been here for a few years and we build some trust, and maybe I'm drunk enough, we'll have that conversation. The odds of all three of those happening are slim, so you might want to push it out of your head."

Will smiled wryly. "No worries, Chief," he said. "I look forward to trying to get through two of those things and then buying you some beer." The two men laughed together for a minute, and then it became silent, other than the sounds of the boat and the ocean. Chief took another puff on his cigarette, and Will took another drink of his soda. For the next few minutes, they stayed in silence as the boat cut through the water, and the two men watched the horizon. The sun began to dip into the ocean after its slow crawl across the sky. First, the basal edge of it, and then the bottom half, as more and more of it began to disappear. Gradually, less than half of the sun was visible, and then even less as the top of the great ball of gas and fire became the target of the unassailable ocean. Then, finally, minute by minute, and then second by second, the very top of the sun dipped down, ever so leisurely, into the ocean, until it was gone. They sat there again for a few minutes, the sky still ignited in a bright orange fire hue, and Will was overcome.

"Get some rest, Rook."

Will looked at him for a second, and then back out to the water under the sky. "You know, it's a little uplifting," he said.

"What's that?" Chief asked. "The ocean?"

Will shook his head slowly and smiled. "How different the world feels when the skyline changes."

Chapter 35 – Initiation

For the next three days, Will ground bait, filled containers, baited pots, cooked, and served food, slept in short increments, stacked pots, and sorted fish by size, keeping those large enough, throwing the small ones back into the ocean, and having fun doing most of it. He was learning to stack pots on this run because the Captain, as they began to pull the string of pots, gave the indicator that they were not going to reset the pots in the same location, but bring them to the deck for storage. They would be heading back to the docks later in the day.

As each pot was hoisted onto the boat's deck, the cod inside were released from the door and dumped into a large box that was at least eight feet wide and long, and about two feet deep. Will asked if it had an industry or nautical term, but Jelly and Stump just called it the sorting table. As the fish flopped around, the trick was grabbing them at the tail and holding them in one place long enough to measure them. The sorting table had built-in markers on the sides, making the task a little bit easier. Once the size of the fish was determined, it was either tossed overboard if too small, or if it was of legal size to keep, it was sent down a conveyor belt into one of the massive wells on the boat. The wells were filled with water from the ocean, and a flow system kept fresh water coming in, and old water going back out into the sea, and this kept the fish alive for the days that the boat was on the water.

If the pots were to be reset back in the same place, the catch would be dumped into the sorting table, and Stump and Jelly would begin sorting while Will would exchange the bait boxes as quickly as possible. Once the bait box was attached, the pot would go back overboard, and Will would help with the sorting of the fish. Now that the pots were coming back to the boat to stay, Will detached the bait box, tossed it into a bin to be emptied and cleaned later, and then helped direct the pots to where Jelly and Stump wanted them stacked on the deck. Once they were stacked, they were lashed together with short lengths of rope, and the process was repeated when the next pot was pulled from the water.

Will was not overly tired, but he could feel the impact of having only the short naps on his body. None of the other crew said anything to him about dragging, but he could feel it, and he was glad when the last pot was pulled from the water. The catch was dumped into the sorting table, and Will pulled the bait box from the pot and tossed it into the bin, which was rather smelly, he noted. He began to help sort the fish as usual and tossed a few of the smaller ones over the side. He grabbed one of the larger ones and was about to toss it onto the conveyor belt chute to the wells below, but Chief stopped him.

"We got this, Rook. Go stand over there," he said. Will saw where Chief was pointing, a narrow strip of the deck between the two wells, and he did as he was told. "You did okay, Rook, for your first time. Now, we got a little initiation tradition here for the new guys. You stand right there, and you'd better not move, or you're gonna fall into the well..."

Will noticed that each of the three men was holding one of the fish they had caught earlier in the day.

"Stump," Chief said. "What's rule number one for the challenge?"

"Catch the fish," he said, with a touch of a snarl that Will found intimidating.

"And Jelly," Chief said. "What's rule number two of the challenge?"

"Don't drop the fish," Jelly yelled. "Ever!"

"Rook," Chief yelled, looking at Will. Can you guess the third rule?"

"Uh, don't fall in the wells?" Will asked, approaching nervousness.

"That's right!" Chief yelled. "You have to catch and hold onto all three fish to pass the test."

"All three at once?" Will asked in disbelief.

No one answered, but they all smiled at him, and before he knew it, Jelly had tossed his fish right at Will. "Shit," he yelled, and had to take a careful step back, but he got one thumb in the fish's mouth and the other in the gills, and he caught the fish, and he was very pleased with himself. He looked at the fish, and then looked up at his shipmates, and another fish was already on its way, this one tossed by Chief. It hit Will in the chest, and he got an arm up, the same arm already holding the other fish. For a second or two, he looked like a fish windmill, but he caught the second fish, and had no idea how he would get the third, but he had a plan of timing, and using his chest, and crossing his arms at the right time. That plan went to hell when Stump threw his fish, high and long. Will jammed his hand into the both of each fish, carrying them like a six-pack of beer. Then he broke like a base stealer heading for second base, both fish still in hand. He took the first three steps gingerly so as not to fall into the wells. He looked over his shoulder, turned, and jumped, taking the fish full in the chest, and wrapping his arms around the flying beast, but it began to squirt out from under his armpit. He shifted his leg and brought his arm forward, locking the fish in a not-so-pretty headlock. He slowly stood up, looking at the three fish pitchers, all three fish in his possession. He smiled a smile that, if he knew how goofy he looked doing it, he would have never done it in the first place, nor would he ever do it again, but he couldn't help himself. He was happy.

"How's that?" he asked, still smiling.

"Rook," Chief said, shaking his head. "I gotta tell you. No one has ever done that before."

"Are you shitting me?" Will said, and his eyebrows went almost to his hairline.

"No, kid," Stump said. "Damnedest thing I have ever seen. Most have caught one, some have caught two..."

"Some couldn't even catch one!" Jelly yelled.

"Yeah," Chief said. "No one has done all three. Let's get a picture!" Jelly ran to the alcove beneath the wheelhouse and grabbed a digital camera.

"Chief, you wanna get in there with him?" Jelly asked.

"Yeah, first to ever catch the three fish, definitely!" Chief yelled. He walked over to the edge of the wells where Will was standing and still holding the three fish, and put his arm around Will's shoulder.

"Okay, ready, on three," Jelly said. "One, two, three!"

And on the three-count, Chief gave Will a shove, and as much as Will tried, he couldn't control his feet, and he went back first into the well on the port side of the ship. All three of the fish went flying, and then all fell into the well, and Will disappeared beneath the surface of the water in the well. As the water settled, Chief, Stump, and Jelly looked into the well, but Will was nowhere to be found. Finally, Stump got down onto one knee to look in the water, peering into the depths. Still, there was no sign of Will, and Chief began to get worried. He thought of calling the Captain to drain the tanks, but at that moment, Stump went down into the well headfirst after taking a mild hand to the posterior, by Will, who had surfaced in the other opening of the well.

As Stump came up from the water and hung on the side of the well, Will did the same on his side of it.

Stump blew a mouthful of water from his lips and breathed heavily for a moment. "How the hell," he said, "did you manage to hold your breath that long?"

Will laughed. "How the hell did you throw a live fish that far?" The two men laughed and high-fived each other, and the Chief and Jelly then helped them each out of the well. Soaking wet, Will and Stump leaned against the railing on the port side of the boat. It had been three days since Will learned it was the *port* side, and not the *left* side, and the other side of the boat was *starboard*, not *right*.

"Chief," Stump said. "Can we get my friend here a beer? Me too?"

"Me three," Jelly yelled from the stack of pots. He had just finished lashing the last pot to the stack, and the work was done for now.

"That sounds like a good idea," Chief said, and disappeared below the deck, only to return a few minutes later with two six-packs of beer in a plastic tub full of ice. He grabbed one of the six-packs and pulled each beer from the plastic ring, then pulled a knife from his back pocket and sliced the plastic circles in half, did the same with the other six-pack, and then tossed the plastic pieces into the garbage drum on the deck. He picked up four cans and tossed one each to Jelly, Stump, and finally, Will. The men pulled the tabs on their beers, each with a satisfying *psshhht* noise, and Chief made a toast to a successful trip and a successful new deck hand. Will smiled, thanked his new shipmates, and took a long drink of his beer. It was cold, and refreshing, and worth the wait since his last one days ago.

"How often do you guys get beer on the boat?" Will asked.

"This is it," Stump yelled, wiping some beer foam from his chin. "There is still some work to do, and we are still out on a boat in the Pacific Ocean. Being drunk ain't gonna do us no good if somethin' happens and we have to either save it or ditch it."

Jelly chimed in. "Yep, it's a little bit of a perk provided by the Captain for a job well done. Do a good job, get a few beers when it's done. Do a shit job, and you scrub the toilets!" Jelly laughed with the rest of them, and then the group settled down into a moment of quiet.

"Thank you, guys," Will said, in the moment of peace. "You've been really nice to me these past few days, and you've shown me a lot. I do appreciate it."

Stump got up from the edge of the sorting table where he was leaning. "Well, don't appreciate it too much yet, Rook. We still gotta unload this haul and get prepped for the next trip. But," he paused, "that's when we get paid!"

"I've been meaning to ask about that," Will said. "Cap never covered that in the interview. How does it work?"

Chief stood up and grabbed another beer. "It all comes down to percentages," He said. "Most goes to the boat, plus some to restock items such as bait, fuel, equipment, food, and all, and this beer. Then what's left we all split, but it ain't equal. Cap takes most of it, we get the rest, and sorry to say that Stump and Jelly get less than I do, and you get less than they do. It's a numbers game. You just have to hope we catch as much as we can and that the market is good."

Will finished off his beer and tossed the can into a bucket on the deck. "Sounds fair to me. I guess it makes sense. Now, when do you guys retire?" They all shared another laugh, and then the wheelhouse let out two short blasts from the horn.

"Time to get back to work," Chief said, and Will followed the other three men down into the second deck.

Chapter 36 – Eddie

While Will was working his new job on the fishing boat, halfway across the country, on Friday, September 28th, 2021, Eduardo Morales woke up and treated it just like every other day. It started out as usual, for him, with the gentle buzzing of his alarm clock at six thirty in the morning. He rolled over and tapped the bigger button on the top of the machine, and stared at the bright red numbers on its display for a moment. He slowly rolled out of the bed and sat on its side for a few minutes until the cobwebs cleared. He looked out the window and saw the top half of the sun piercing the edge of the planet. *Today will be hot,* he thought. He stood slowly and went to the scale in the corner of the room, stood on it for a moment, and then frowned slightly. He was not obese by anyone's measurements, but he longed to lose the "love handles." His lunches were too high in fat, he thought, but he enjoyed the burritos that his wife made far too much. He vowed to work on it. He stepped off the scale and moved to the bathroom for his morning ritualistic shower. When he was finished, he dressed in khakis and a thin white t-shirt, and then added socks and boots to his ensemble. And when he was done getting dressed, he crossed the room, bent over the bed, and kissed his wife on the cheek. She moaned and smiled, but did not fully awaken.

He made it to the kitchen, clicked a button on the coffee maker, and opened the cabinet to find his breakfast, consisting of two bags of instant oatmeal. He heated some water in the microwave and mixed the liquid into the cereal until it was a thick paste. He blew on it and took a bite. Peach and blueberry, his favorite mix. He watched the coffee maker perform its task, without fail, as it had done since someone in the extended Morales family bought it eight years ago. It was a wedding present from when he and his wife, Maria Sofia, were joined, though from whom it came, he could not remember. He turned his attention back to his oatmeal, the amount of which was dwindling rapidly. Someone decided that maple and brown sugar was a good flavor, and for some reason, there were six packets of that flavor in the variety box, and only two each of the blueberry, peach, and strawberry. Eduardo didn't agree, especially since the name on the box advertised a "Fruity Blend."

He grabbed his thermos from the top of the refrigerator, removed the lid, and began to add the coffee from the coffee machine on the counter. He didn't fill his thermos, though. He always left enough for Maria Sofia to have a cup as well. He finished pouring the coffee and affixed the lid to the thermos. He pulled his lunch, nestled in a brown bag, from the refrigerator and set it on the table, then crept into the room of his twin sons, whom they had named Luis and Alex. He looked at his beautiful boys, still sleeping, and touched each lightly on the forehead.

A horn honking from outside pulled Eduardo from his thoughts, as it did every weekday. He lightly walked across the creaky floor of the room, avoiding the places that made noise when stepped upon. He knew them well. He stealthily made it out of the boys' room and back to the kitchen, grabbing his lunch bag and thermos. He left from the kitchen door, closing it lightly behind him. His construction crew was there to pick him up, as they did every weekday, and he was the last stop on the way to work. He lived in Bunker Hill, Kansas, and two guys in the crew lived in Dorrance, about eight miles away. Manny, the driver of the jumbo-sized pick-up truck they used to get to the job site, was from Wilson, about six more miles away. It made sense for Manny to drive and pick up the others as they went, as all of the men were on or just off the highway, and it was a straight line to their work site. They were working for a contractor who was renovating a large gas station near an intersection of Dwight D. Eisenhower Highway.

As they left his house, Eduardo, or Eddie, as the crew called him, began pouring coffee from his thermos into the cups of the guys, something they looked forward to every morning. The coffee was nothing spectacular, as it was bought from a local supermarket, but it was the tradition that the guys liked. For almost four years, the same guys were on the same crew, and wherever there was work, Eddie and his crew were usually the ones awarded the work. They were the best, doing flawless and desirable work wherever they went.

They chatted as Manny drove, and they all enjoyed the coffee, trying to get into the best of moods on what was most assuredly going to be a very hot day. Mateo was the funny one in the group and always had a joke for his team in the morning. He sat in the back of the truck with Eddie. Diego sat in the front passenger seat, and when Mateo told his joke that morning, Diego could not control his laughter and spat coffee all over the dashboard of the truck. Manny told Diego that he owed Manny a car wash at the detailer.

The crew pulled into the job site, and Manny parked in the lot assigned to the workers. They got out of the truck and joined up with the rest of the crew that had arrived a few minutes prior. After getting their work orders from the foreperson, whose name was Catrina, or Trina as she wished, they set out about their business, and as always, took care in what they did and did flawless work. There were no seams in the drywall or molding, no crooked tiles on the floor, and no weak spots in the paint. The wiring for the electricity was run and installed perfectly.

At noon, they dropped their tools and left their equipment and went to sit under the big shade tree on the side of the store. The tree was big enough to cast a plentiful shadow, which the nine-member crew chose to be a place of rest for their lunch. Eddie opened his bag and found a large burrito filled with refried beans and cheese, and he took a large bite to begin his lunch. Manny chomped down on an apple, Diego leaned against the tree, hoping for a quick nap, and Mateo settled for a banana and a tuna fish sandwich. For the next hour, they all relaxed and made fun of Eddie, his burrito, and his love handles. He didn't mind the running joke at all.

At ten minutes to one o'clock, Trina's watch beeped, and the crew knew it was time to go back to work. They used the bathroom and washed their hands, and then the well-oiled machine of Trina's crew was back in action, completing the necessary tasks. They worked until a quarter to five o'clock in the evening, and then began putting tools away and cleaning up. They would be done with the job in a week,

Trina estimated, and that was two weeks ahead of schedule, which would include a pay bonus. Then they would move on to another job where they were needed, which was at the high school in Sylvan Grove. She would have Eddie drive everyone to the site instead of Manny, as it was 45 miles in the other direction from Russell.

The crew had completed the cleanup for the weekend, and it was one of Trina's favorite moments when she got to reward her crew with their paychecks. Most of the guys had their bank accounts in Russell, so each crew would make the short trip north to either deposit or cash their paychecks.

When they got to Russell, Mateo and Eddie were dropped off at one bank, and Manny and Diego drove on to another bank. They would pick up Mateo and Eddie when they were done, and then would take the ride home together. Mateo and Eddie took off their yellow safety vests and left them in the truck. Mateo opened the door, and Eddie entered the bank first, with Mateo following. They waited in the same line for the tellers to call them to the desk. They chatted about the day and the job they were doing.

Mateo was called to the teller first, and he laid his check on the counter. The teller greeted him and asked for his account information. The teller, however, did not make a move. There was something wrong, and Mateo could see it in her face. He looked at her with an inquisitive expression, and she moved her eyes to the left, but not her head. Mateo looked to the left and saw the man with the gun in his hand at the counter. The man with the gun saw Mateo, too, and now pointed it at him. Suddenly, an alarm shrieked, and the noise distracted the robber, and he looked to the ceiling for a second. Eddie rushed him and tried to get the gun, but it became an odd wrestling match, with the two men rolling around on the ground.

Two police officers arrived and ran into the building, just as Eddie threw a punch and landed it on the robber's jaw, stunning him for a second. The gun slid to the ground, and Mateo tried to grab it, but the robber was much closer and too fast. He picked up the gun and aimed it at the police, who ordered him to drop the weapon. A shot rang out from the other side of the room. A citizen had tried to take the situation into his own hands and fired his large revolver, but it was not accurate, and a window behind the counter was shattered. The robber turned and fired at the citizen, but was also inaccurate. Eddie once again grabbed the weapon to disarm the robber. The robber's arm came down, and another shot was fired.

The police began to move closer, and the robber was able to escape Eddie's grasp. He fired at the officers and then ran from the building into a car in the parking lot. The police chased him out and followed on foot, firing their weapons as they ran, but their bullets did not find their mark. Mateo watched the scene unfold and then turned back to see Eddie holding onto the counter. His back was turned to Mateo, and Mateo called out to him. Eddie turned to Mateo with a strange expression on his face. Mateo looked at Eddie, and that's when he noticed the blood on Eddie's shirt. The robber had fired his gun in the struggle with Eddie and had shot him in the chest. Eddie looked at Mateo for another few seconds, only said "Maria," and then dropped to his knees. Mateo rushed to catch him, but it was of no effect. Eddie fell to the floor, face down. Mateo rolled Eddie onto his back, grabbed Eddie's shoulders, shook him, and cried out Eddie's name. But Eduardo Morales, husband to Maria Sofia, and father to Alex and Luis, was dead.

Chapter 37 – Payday

It had been about two weeks since Will had shaved, and his beard was getting pretty scruffy in his own mind, but he doubted that it bothered his shipmates because they all had beards worse than his. Stump's was the worst, and the worst part about it was that he liked to drink milk most of the time. He said it settled his stomach. He'd grab a glass out of the freezer, his own special glass, with "STUMP" etched into a metal plate on the side, and he'd fill it with full-on four percent fat regular milk. It was so thick, and the glass so cold, that the milk would thicken and freeze to the side of the glass. He would then take a serious drink of the viscous milk. When he was done, he'd pull the glass away from his face with a satisfied "ahhhhhhhhh" noise, and there would be more milk on his face than what went down his gullet, Will thought. It gave a new and more graphic picture of the term "milk mustache." Will managed to keep his facial hair out of his food and drink for now, but the growth was itchy. He thought about it every time he sweated, or when his neck rubbed his rain gear jacket, or when he slept. Itch, itch, itch.

Jelly and Stump were cleaning the galley and crew mess, and because Will was the low man on the pole, he was given the bathroom, or "the head" as it was called on the boat. It wasn't too bad, and Will didn't mind much. The guys all knew they had to share the space, and they mostly cleaned as they went. The head had a commode, as most bathrooms do, but it also had a standing urinal, which, as he cleaned it, Will wondered why, with all the improvements he and Kathleen had made on the house, he had never thought of adding a urinal! He scrubbed and scrubbed, and while he considered the nasty business removed from all surfaces, the line of rust down the middle of the urinal from a persistent leak made Will question his judgement. But he let it as he found it, or at least as close to it as possible, and after washing up, went to the galley to see if he could help clean.

"No, Rook," Stump said. "We're good here. You need to go clear your bunk. All your clothes, any personal items, anything you'd want to keep if you didn't come back. You need to take the sheet and blanket out of your rack so all that's left is the mattress. Take it all, and your belongings, your bags and such, and heft them up the steps. Stow your bags and whatnot in the open area under the wheelhouse, and pile the sheets and stuff on the port side of the wheelhouse behind the steps."

"Aye," Will said, and did as he was directed. He had to make two trips, as the steps to the deck were narrow, and the blanket and sheets were a bit cumbersome. He tripped up the steps on his second run and bloodied his lip on the surface of the deck. He decided to keep this one to himself. *You're not telling anyone on this boat about this. Suck it up.*

When all the gear of the crew was out of the belly of the boat, Jelly ran a quick mop through the galley and crew area, and the three men joined the chief on the deck. Will had not even noticed where they were as he was cleaning, but the boat was only about a mile from the dock from which they had left. The crew stood on the deck and watched as the city of Seattle approached and passed. When the unloading docks were in sight, Chief, Jelly, and Stump all left to put on their weather pants and gloves. Will did the same without asking questions. Jelly grabbed a rope from the bow of the boat, and Stump was where the gangplank would be when they docked.

"What can I do?" Will asked.

Stump, cigarette in the corner of his mouth, said, "Grab the rope at the port side of the stern. When I come to you, throw it to me. Don't short it!"

Will grabbed the rope, though it was much heavier than he thought it would be. Stump ran down the gangplank, and Jelly tossed him the rope from the bow. It landed on the dock, and Stump grabbed it before it slithered into the water. He lashed the rope to a large black cleat on the dock, and then Will saw Stump coming towards him. He watched how Jelly tossed the rope, a two-handed throw from his side, like a giant frisbee. Will made sure his feet were clear, half-turned to the side, and heaved the rope as hard as he could. Most of it sailed over Stump's head, who arched his eyebrows at the throw. He backed up, put his cigarette in his mouth, grabbed the rope, and fastened it to another cleat. The boat was now safely docked. A crane from the dock began to move toward the boat, and when it arrived, Jelly hooked it to one of the big metal plates on the deck, and the well of fish was then exposed. Will had not realized how many fish they had caught during the process, but as he looked into the well, he saw it was nearly full.

Chief pulled a lever from a different panel, this one under the wheelhouse, and the tanks began to drain. Stump hooked the large net-basket they had used to bring the food onto the boat to the crane, and he and Jelly stepped into it.

"Come on, Rook!" Stump said from the basket. Will joined them, and the three men rode down into the well, which now only consisted of fish flipping and flopping around. "Try to find the bottom with your feet. If you can't, no big deal. Just start tossing the fish into the basket."

Will put his left foot through the fishy false bottom and was finally able to touch what he thought was the bottom of the well. His right leg was not so fortunate, so he rested his knee on the pile of floppy fish. He began doing as directed, tossing fish after fish into the net until it was full. Chief gave a thumbs up to whoever was operating the crane, and the basket began to rise. When it was clear, another basket began to drop, this one from the crane on the deck of the boat. When it settled, the crew began to fill it with fish, and so it went until the well was nearly empty of fish.

"Here's the fun part," Jelly said. "Catching the loose ones." And he was correct. It was almost comical how the fish were able to evade the crew as they chased them around the floor of the well, as if they were chasing a football rolling end-over-end down a hill. But they finally completed the task, and the fish were cleared from the boat. Chief lowered a hose with a spray nozzle attached to it, and Jelly began to spray out the well, clearing it of fish scales and seaweed. A small bucket came down from the deck as well, and Chief handed a flat shovel to Stump, who put the collection of gunk into the bucket. Chief had also lowered the net-basket into the well, and once the well was clean, the three men hitched a ride back to the deck from the well below. The Captain had already begun to make the trip from the unloading docks to the docks where the boat was when Will first laid eyes on it during his strange interview.

Chief sprayed each of the crew members from the waist down to get any leftover fish particles off of them, and the crew then hung up their gear, so it was ready for the next run. The deck was swept and rinsed, with the scales and such washed overboard. They were careful not to allow any can tabs, cigarette butts, or trash to go over the side of the boat. They repeated the docking process as they had at the unloading dock, securing the boat until the next run in a few days. They grabbed their bags and then disembarked from the boat.

"Follow us, Rook," said Stump, heading towards the door in the large building where Will first met the Captain. They entered the building and dropped their bags against a wall, opposite a row of chairs. They crossed the room and sat in the chairs, staring at a wall with a sliding door window in the center, about halfway up the wall. Will had an arched eyebrow look about him, and Jelly saw it.

"Hold on a few minutes. Cap's coming," Jelly said. At that moment, the door opened, and the Captain and Chief walked in. Chief took a seat while the Captain crossed the room without a look or a word, opened another door, and disappeared. He reappeared on the other side of the windowed wall and sat down at the desk. He was writing something, and running his hand through his greying hair each time he stopped writing. This went on for about ten minutes or so, when he finally opened the slider and called for the Chief, who stood from his chair and crossed the room to the window. The Captain spoke in a low voice, and then Chief reached through the window, appearing to sign something. He stuffed a piece of paper in his pocket, turned, and grabbed his bag.

"See you in a few days," he said, and left through the door. The Captain called Stump next, and the process was repeated, and then Stump left the room. The Captain called for Jelly next, and then Jelly picked up his bag, told Will he'd see him in a few, and left the building.

"Billy. Come on up," the Captain said. Will stood and walked to the window. "I heard you caught all three fish they slung at you."

"Affirmative, Cap," Will said, slightly embarrassed.

"Don't think anyone's ever done that before."

"That's what the guys were saying. I just got lucky," Will said.

"Hmmph," the Captain laughed, if it was a laugh. "I wanna explain this to you this once, so you know. If you want to go through it every time, we can, but this is how payday works." The Captain turned a book that contained a lot of numbers around toward the window, facing Will. Will recognized it from his financial days as a ledger and checkbook. "Alright. So, we caught three thousand, one hundred and sixty-three point zero eight pounds of fish. We get twelve dollars per pound, which makes thirty-seven thousand, nine hundred fifty-six dollars and ninety-six cents. Half goes to the boat, leaving eighteen thousand, nine hundred seventy-eight dollars and forty-eight cents. Fifteen hundred goes to bait, food, and supplies, leaving seventeen thousand, four hundred seventy-eight dollars and forty-eight cents. As the Captain, I get a double share of five thousand, eight hundred twenty-six dollars and sixteen cents. Chief gets a share-and-a-half, for four thousand, three hundred sixty-nine dollars and sixty-two cents. Jelly and Stump get a full share of two thousand, nine hundred thirteen dollars and eight cents. Sorry, Rookie, you get a half-share for now, until you prove yourself. That's one thousand, four hundred fifty-six dollars, and fifty-four cents. You need to figure out and pay your own taxes. I have a friend who is a tax attorney, if you need help. Here, sign on this line to agree that you received the check."

Will signed his name on the line, and Captain Pierce handed him his paycheck. Will thanked him and then asked, "So, I should come back for the next run?"

Pierce raised his head and looked at him. "Kid, I have seen fish take to water slower than you took to this. You keep learning what you can and doing the job you're doing, and you'll have Chief's job someday. Yes, come back on Monday. Now go home and get some rest."

"Aye, sir. Have a nice weekend," Will said, and then he turned to the other wall, grabbed his bag, and headed out of the building and into the fresh air of Seattle. He made the turn at the side of the building to begin the short walk to his rental, and then he stopped. *You're doing it. You're making a difference. You're providing a product that people need. You're helping to feed them, to keep them alive.* He kept thinking and talking to himself about his new role in life. He wasn't doing surgery to save anyone's life, so he wasn't making *that* kind of a difference, but it was better than lending money to people and not seeing anything happen except for most of them going bankrupt. *This is better.*

He made the walk home in just under ten minutes, and as he climbed the steps to the entrance to his apartment, he was reminded of the state of disrepair of the Kearney's house, and his promise to do some maintenance as part of his rental agreement. *You will address that immediately,* he thought, and decided the first thing he would do was fix the porch. But first, tonight, he would rest. When he entered his apartment, everything looked as it should. He looked under the bed and found the box of cash, just where he left it. He tried not to think about it while he was gone, but he admitted to himself that he was worried about the stash.

Chapter 38 – The Porch

Will awoke at 7:30 AM on Saturday, the 29th of September. After his morning run and a quick shower, he got into his car and found the local, gigantic hardware store, right where the yellow phone book said it would be. He bought a tool belt, a circular saw, an extension cord, a set of sawhorses, two gallons of brown paint, one light brown, one dark brown, some paint brushes, a measuring tape, nails, a hammer, some heavy-duty cord, an electric sander, some quick mix concrete, a shovel, a level, a hand saw, and ordered the lumber he needed to completely replace the porch. He didn't ask Mr. or Mrs. Kearney if this would be a good time for them, and hoped that they would not mind his timing. He still had not seen Mrs. Kearney yet, but he had been there only a few days.

He began using his hammer to disassemble the remnants of the old porch. This did not take very long, as it was in such a bad state of disrepair, and most of the wood had rotted. When he had all of the wood cleared, and the lumber was delivered by the hardware store, he had to dig up the big, heavy chunks of concrete that were the base of the previous porch. He had amassed quite a pile of debris in the front yard and was mixing the concrete when Marv Kearney opened the front door.

"Whoa, Mr. Kearney, be careful there. Don't want you falling!" Will said.

"What in the hell do you think you're doing? Who are you? Who are you?" Marv asked, giving Will a wild-eyed look.

"It's me, Mr. Kearney. Billy Lomax? I rent the apartment upstairs?"

"Well, what, what are, what are you doing?" Marv demanded.

"I'm building you a new porch. We talked about this when we first met. I would do some maintenance work around here as part of the rental agreement?" Will was confused about what was happening.

"Oh, oh yes, yes, now I remember. Yes, I remember. Billy, right. But what, uh, what are you doing?"

Will didn't know how to answer this question again with anything but the truth, so he said, "I'm replacing the porch, like we discussed when we first met."

"The po–, oh, oh yes, the porch. Yes," Marv said in his special way. "Well, make sure you, make sure you clean up that mess in the front yard, my front yard. And don't make too much noise and wake up my wife."

"I sure will, sir." Will said, "I sure will. Just make sure you all use the side door for now. I don't want you falling. And I'll be as quiet as possible." When Marv shut the door, Will realized he had repeated himself just like Marv tended to do. He laughed and shook his head, and then went back to mixing his concrete with his shovel. When he had shorn up the corner posts to make sure they were square and level, he decided it would be a good time to take a break for lunch. He knocked on the Kearneys' side door to see if they might need or want anything, but no one answered. He gave up after a second set of knocks and then began to pile some of the old porch debris into his car to take to the local dump. He stopped at a drive-through and got a quick fast-food meal, which he ate while he was driving, and when he got to the North Transfer Station, he paid the fees and emptied the debris from his car. Without a truck of some sort, it would take him at least three more trips, and he had no idea what to do with the clumps of concrete he had unearthed when disassembling the old porch. He would figure that out when the time came. *Bury them. You've already buried a human life and a marriage*, he told himself.

He spent the next two hours at the laundromat cleaning his clothes from the last fishing run on the boat. He didn't bother folding anything as he would have to repack it for the next run. When he got back to the Kearney's house and pulled up into his driveway spot, he checked the concrete. It had begun to harden, but not enough to begin hammering two-by-fours into the posts.

He figured the concrete would need to sit overnight, so he entered his small apartment and decided he would lay low for the night, eating a salad he had created earlier in the day for dinner. He didn't want to waste the night off back on solid land, but he was still tired from his first trip as well as from the events of the day. He thought he should check on the Kearneys in their part of the house below him, but he did not want to intrude. Marv Kearney was a strange old man, Will thought, and maybe the less he engaged with Marv, the better they would all be. So, he decided to let them be, and he would stay in his apartment for the night.

He awoke early the next morning, and after a coffee, went down to the front door to check his work. The concrete was dry and hard, and the posts did not move when Will pulled against them. Satisfied with the work, he began to work on the structure of the porch. He felt bad about hammering so early in the morning, but the unfinished porch and his new career were looming large on his schedule. He had to be back on the boat tomorrow for the next run. He didn't want to rush the porch, but he also wanted at least the structure completed. Painting could come later.

He affixed the platform of the new porch to the concreted posts with lag bolts, washers, and nuts, all galvanized for weather. He measured, measured again, and then cut the pieces of lumber to the lengths needed for the platform, and by noon, he was nearly done with it. He decided to complete the platform before he broke for lunch, and did so by a quarter to one in the afternoon. He opened the cooler he had brought down from his apartment and grabbed the sandwich and apple he had packed to eat, and a cold beer that lay in the ice on the bottom. It made a satisfying noise when it opened, and he drank nearly half of it on his first taste. He finished it off after eating half of his sandwich, and drank another with the other half of the sandwich. The apple went back into the cooler for later, and he returned to his work.

He looked at the instructions again that the hardware store had provided, formulated his plan, and began to work on the railing that would go over the top of the posts he had sunk into the ground with the concrete. He wasn't great with the corners, and glad they were limited in this project. A miter box would have helped him, but he wasn't running back to the hardware store just for that. He did well enough without it, though, as his measurements were meticulous, and he laid the wooden boards in place to measure before he made the cuts.

At nearly eight o'clock that night, he pounded the last nail into the lattice that he had purchased to fill the gap between the deck and the railing of the new porch. He was done! He remembered his conversation with himself two days before, when he talked about making a difference. He looked at the new porch that he had built for the Kearney's home. *Now that's making a difference. You've taken some of the possible danger from an elderly couple and replaced it with a completely new structure. Not bad, Billy Jack.*

He loaded a lot of the debris from the previous porch into his car, just to get it off of the Kearney's lawn. He wouldn't do anything with it until next weekend, but at least it was off the grass. He stepped back and looked at the porch once again, the porch he created, with a little help from the hardware store's blueprint, and smiled. He once again thought of knocking on the Kearney's front door to tell them it was safe to use the front door again, but it was getting late, and he didn't want to get into another weird conversation with Marv anyway. He climbed the steps to his apartment and took a shower to get the grime of the day off himself. Then, he consumed his dinner, took two aspirin, and after setting his alarm for the next morning, his head hit his pillow for the end of a long week, and a very long month. It was the final night of September 2001.

When Will's alarm went off the next morning, he packed his big bag for the next run on the boat. Five sets of everything except socks, which he took every pair he had cleaned, except for the ones he would wear that day. When he had his bag packed, he took all of his valuables and his cellular phone and left them all behind on the dresser. And then he was on his way to another 5 days on the boat, and for a few weeks, that's how it went for Will. He would leave for the boat every Monday, get back every Friday, and work on Kearney's house on his days off.

As they returned to the docks from the previous trip for more cod, he remembered that he still had each paycheck in his wallet from the fishing job, as he had no real reason to cash them at this point. He still had plenty of money in the box under the bed, and the way he was spending it, it would last him for quite some time. He had been feeling a little odd with it underneath his bed in a box where anyone who might find it would certainly have questions, but he didn't risk putting it in a bank. Then he remembered what Archie had told him.

"Get established, get some bills in your name," he said.

So, he did. He did exactly what he did when he was in New York. The previous weekend, he had gotten a self-storage locker at a facility, paid the first month, and got the bill sent to his second-floor apartment above his landlords. He had bought a small lock box and moved fifty thousand dollars from the box under his bed to the lock box and then stored it in the self-storage facility. He also put another fifty thousand in an envelope inside of a zipper-seal food storage bag and put it under the driver's seat of his car in a place where he had pulled up the carpet. He decided the money was better stored in multiple places instead of all of it in one place. It made him feel a little better about it, and he would open other self-storage units around town and repeat the process, he decided.

On his weekends at the Kearney house, he kept up his end of the rental agreement with maintenance. He finished the porch, including painting it, mowed the lawn every Saturday, built a small corral for the garbage cans, replaced the mailbox, repainted all of the window sills, and cleaned out the old couple's garage. After six weeks at the couple's house, he had still not seen Marv Kearney's wife, but he thought he had heard her a few times, yelling at Marv. The arguments from the couple passed through the air ducts of the house, and the few arguments that he heard were fairly loud. He told himself he would make it a point to go down one day when he knew she was home and introduce himself. He didn't want to be known as the weird guy who lived upstairs.

On the boat, he learned nearly everything he needed to learn to be a first mate. Chief showed him the ropes, literally, of how to operate the crane, how to drop the pots into the water, and how to pull them out. Will mostly did the bait, but he also learned everything that would make him an efficient waterman. He got along with Jelly and Stump just fine, as well as the Chief and the Captain, and he was good at what he was doing. But for him, it wasn't enough. He needed more fulfillment, and while catching fish was entertaining and fun, it wasn't what he ultimately wanted, and he thought about turning in his notice after a few weeks, but he didn't want to leave the boat shorthanded. He guessed, however, that the Captain could replace him fairly easily by collaring someone else looking at his hiring poster and dragging them off to the boat for an orientation, which they may not have wanted. He would talk to the Captain as they left for the next run the following week.

Once the boat was finally docked back at its home from the most recent run, the crew grabbed their gear and headed down the gangplank, crossed the street, and into the office for their paychecks. They were excited about this week's pay as they had caught over four thousand pounds of fish, more than eight hundred pounds more than on Will's initial trip. When the checks had been cut and handed out, and Will signed the ledger, he frowned.

"What's wrong, Billy?" the Captain asked.

"Uh, I was figuring on about half of this," Will said. "This is too much."

"We moved you to a full share, kid. You've earned it. You've done a great job up to this point. In a few years, you'll probably have your own boat to crew."

"Well, uh," Will stammered. "Thank you, sir. I,..., I appreciate your confidence in me." And at that moment, Will decided he would stay on as a crewman on *The Seafarer*. He didn't know for how long, but he would stay for now, and maybe forever. He liked the work, and he was good at it. "Have a good weekend, sir. I'll see you on Monday."

"See you Monday, Billy," the Captain said. Billy closed the door to the building behind him, leaving the Captain to do whatever the Captain did each Friday evening. He folded the check and put it into his wallet with the others. He would need to open an account at a bank soon and get them deposited. Not cashing your paycheck is probably not the best way to stay off someone's radar. He began the walk home, crossing West Ewing Street and up the short alley that was 11th Avenue. He crossed Nickerson Street and then walked down the sidewalk to 12th Avenue. He sniffed the air and smelled what he thought was someone barbecuing on a charcoal grill. The smell at first was tantalizing, and he thought what a great idea it would be to grill out on the Kearney's grill, which he would have to clean first, maybe replace it completely. But if he did, he wouldn't mind. He had not had a cookout since the previous summer. Kathleen used to like them, but they fell out of her favor about the same time he did.

His walk, as usual, took him up to Emerson Street, where he took a right down a smaller road, almost another alley, which was where he lived. The smell of the barbecue got stronger, but then became an acrid scent, as if whatever was cooking was well over-cooked, and it burned in his nose. He kept walking, trying to figure out who was doing the cooking or burning, but he didn't see anyone with a grill. When he got to his rental in the Kearney's house, no one was grilling, and he didn't really believe what he saw. He thought it couldn't be real, yet knew that it was real. No one was grilling food in the neighborhood, but the Kearney's house now lay in a blackened pile of burnt building materials. The only thing that wasn't completely burned was the porch he had provided for the Kearney's just a few weeks ago. The rest of the house was just a burnt, smelly black shell that had partially collapsed in on itself.

Will thought about the Kearneys first. And then he thought about the money.

Chapter 39 – Maureen

Maureen Polyniak, one of Pickwick's Senior Account Managers, stared at the printout on the alternately green-and-white barred paper that stretched across her mammoth desk. The report was dated October 26, 2001, and was just run that morning. She was looking at a handful of accounts that were opened by Willem Kelly between June and September. There were ten accounts in total. The first, Harp & Company, was opened by Kelly on June 10, 2001, and the remainder of the accounts were opened at different intervals over the next two months. There was nothing odd about that. The accounts were set up correctly, and the money was deposited into the proper accounts. The thing that all the accounts had in common was that all of them had missed their first payment. *All of them.* Some had missed their second payment as well. Money went out, but never came back in.

The accounts were brought to her attention by Pickwick's Payments and Collections team, or PAC, as the team was called in the Pickwick world. The company used three-letter acronyms for everything. They even used the three-letter acronym TLA when deciding that something needed a three-letter-acronym. *We've created a new team with new responsibilities here at Pickwick. They are the Payments and Collections Team, and the TLA will be PAC.* Primary Account Managers, or PAMs, Judy Schisler, Linda Weissert, Helen Hart, and Kimberly "Kiki" King shared the ten accounts, and had reported them as derelict in their payments at the last ARM, or Account Review Meeting. The accounts opened in June became an issue in August when they did not pay, and the accounts opened in July became an issue in September when they did not pay. After that, everyone took a bit of a pause because of the September 11 events, and all companies that were late on their payments were given a grace period. It was now over a month later, and business at Pickwick was getting back to normal, or as normal as it could after many of the company's employees perished in the collapse of the North

Tower of the World Trade Center. Pickwick was now working out of a triage office located on 9th Street.

The PAM team had done the due diligence of repeatedly trying to contact the customer which owed Pickwick for their loans, but in each case, there was either a wrong number, an infinite ringing of the phone, or a three toned chirp that was followed by a message that the number was not in service, and the caller should check the number and try again. All repeated attempts were unsuccessful.

There was a knock on the door of Maureen's office. She placed a finger on the line of print she was researching so she would not lose her spot, lifted her head, and said, "It's open." Judy Schisler opened the door and walked into the office. "Jutes, don't go breaking my heart today. I don't think I can handle it. What's up?" Maureen asked, almost afraid of the answer.

"Mo, I think I found another one. This was opened in July by Will Kelly. The account is Humbarton, Humbarton, and Lye. They are supposed to be an accounting firm. They are two months in arrears, and the phone is always a busy signal."

"Super," Maureen said sarcastically. "What the hell is this guy doing? Is he setting up false accounts to make his numbers? Jutes, if this is true, that makes eleven accounts that appear to be false."

Judy dropped the folder she was holding in her hand on the massive desk. "I don't think this one appears to be false, Mo. I know it is. The address on this is 150 East 18th Street in Gramercy. It's down the street from Pete's Tavern, and it's a parking garage, and I know this because it is the garage I use when I park my car at home. I did a web search for the parking garage and got their phone number, and I called them, and they had no idea who a Humbarton or a Lye was." Judy sat in the chair on the other side of Maureen's desk and exhaled up in the air, and it made her hair move.

"I don't know what else to do, Jutes," Maureen said. "This looks like fraud, anyway you stack it. Have you tried to contact this Kelly guy yet?"

"No, GAS says that's not our role."

"Ugh," Maureen said, exhaling as well, thinking of the long running joke about using a TLA *within* another TLA. "Guidelines and SOPs are just that. Guidelines. I'm calling him."

"Want me to leave?" Judy asked.

"No," Maureen replied. "Stick around. We might get someone scared enough to sweat." Maureen picked up her phone and dialed the number that was next to Willem Kelly's name on the account paperwork. The opposite end of the phone was picked up almost immediately.

"Hello, this is Jeannie Raines."

"Hi Jeannie, is Willem Kelly available?"

"Who is calling, please?" Jeannie asked.

"This is Maureen in SAM."

"How can I help you, Maureen?" Jeannie asked.

"I'm looking for Willem Kelly. I have some questions regarding some of his accounts."

Jeannie was silent for a moment and then cleared her throat. *"Mr. Kelly disappeared and was presumed to be a victim of the nine-eleven attacks. He was here in the building that morning, and then the attacks happened. He was scheduled to be in a meeting up on the ninety-fourth floor that morning, and,..."* Jeannie's voice trailed off.

"Jeannie, I am very sorry," Maureen said after the silence. "We lost so many that day. I won't take up any more of your time. Thank you." Maureen slouched back in her chair and looked at the ceiling of the room for a minute, and then straightened back up to look at Judy. "Willem Kelly died in the nine-eleven attacks."

Judys eyes increased in size by nearly two-fold. "Oh my God," she said. "So, what do we do?"

Maureen exhaled. "We have to kick it over to CAL. They'll know what to do with it, and someone has to explain to the higher-ups as to why we're not going to be able to retrieve about a half a million dollars that was supposedly lent to customers."

"Does Contracts and Legal do that?" Judy asked.

"CAL does most of the dirty work around here," Maureen said. "Especially when it gets ugly. And this looks ugly. You should probably leave for this, Jutes."

Judy got up and left the room, and as soon as the door closed, Maureen picked up the phone again and dialed the number for David South, who headed up the Contracts and Legal team. On the second ring, the phone picked up, and Maureen heard David answer the phone and identify himself.

"Hi David, this is Maureen Polyniak in SAM. I have something of a weird situation."

"How weird," David said.

"Loan improprieties by a deceased employee."

David exhaled loudly and long enough that Maureen heard it over the phone. *"Can you meet me in the conference room on the fourth floor in ten minutes?"* Nine minutes later, the two were sitting across the conference room table from each other, and Maureen explained the situation of her team uncovering the eleven accounts; they were all past due in payment, they were all non-communicative, and they were all opened by Willem Kelly in the past four months. She described the conversation she had with Jeannie Raines about Willem Kelly, now presumed deceased. He listened intently and took notes as she talked, and only asked questions when she stopped talking.

"So, that's what I know," Maureen said, concluding her presentation.

"Thank you for bringing this to me, Maureen. I appreciate it, and I will take it from here. Please speak of this to no one, and advise your PAMs to do the same. Okay?"

"You got it," Maureen said, and the two departed. Maureen went back and advised her team not to talk about the situation, and David South went upstairs to the 4th floor to Loss Prevention & Security, or LPS. He knocked on the door and was advised to enter. In the outer office, he encountered Kelly Vance, who asked if she could help him.

"Hi, I am David South. I don't think we've met yet. I am from the CAL team, and I need to speak to the head of LPS."

Kelly smiled and said, "Can I ask you to sit for a moment while I see if he is available?"

David smiled back and said, "Absolutely."

Kelly knocked on the door of another office and was advised to enter. The door closed behind her. After a moment, she reappeared and he was shown into the inner office and was invited to have a seat across from James Higgins, the new head of the LPS team.

Chapter 40 – Investigation

Will approached the burnt house and couldn't believe what he was seeing. Everything was burnt, and the second floor of the house was lying on top of the first, and just as burnt. His thoughts immediately went first to the Kearney's, then to the money that was under his bed, and then to the money that was under the seat of his car. He started to run around the back of the house to the garage, where he was told by Marv Kearney he could park when he would be gone for a few days on his fishing trips. He was stopped by a man in a suit with a cigarette who blocked his progression towards the burnt wreckage and asked Will who he was and where he thought he was going.

"I live here!" Will exclaimed. "This is my house!"

"You're Mr. Kearney?" the man asked.

"No," Will said. "I'm Billy Lomax. I was renting the apartment upstairs! Who are you, and where are the Kearneys?"

"Got any ID?" the man asked, puffing on the cigarette.

"Who are you?" Will asked.

"I'm Charles Travis. I'm a fire investigator." Will pulled out his wallet and prayed that Archie knew what he was doing when he created the Pennsylvania driver's license. He handed the card over to Travis. "Philly, huh? What are you doing in Seattle?"

"Working," Will responded.

Travis gave the identification back to Will. "Can I ask you where you were last night?"

Will put the driver's license in his wallet, and his wallet went into the back pocket of his pants. "I was working on a fishing boat for the past four days."

"Witnesses?" Travis asked.

"The other four guys I was on the boat with, I suppose. Where are the Kearneys?"

"What's the name of the boat?" Travis asked, ignoring Will's question.

The Seafarer, Captain Russell Pierce.

Travis tossed the cigarette to the ground and crushed it with his shoe. "Mr. Lomax, I'm sorry to have to be the one to tell you, but we did find the body of an older Caucasian male in the house. Do you know of anyone other than the Kearneys who lived here?"

"Other than me, no," Will said, still looking at the smelly mess.

"We are trying to determine next of kin. If we cannot, do you think you could positively identify him?"

Will looked over the man's shoulder to the burnt heap. "If it's Mr. Kearney, I guess I could," he stuttered. "I guess if I had to," he said, and then became very sullen. "Is there anything left?"

"Not much," Travis said. "The first and second floors are trash, along with the garage. Two cars inside, one was a 1981 Caddy, and the other is a four-door sedan, might have been a cab.. Both are crispy right now."

Will was nearly in tears, and his hands went to his face. He began to pull them away slowly and asked, "How did it start?"

"That's why I'm here. Looks like arson. Smells like gasoline all through the house, and we found that empty gas container on the porch. Did this belong to Mr. Kearney?"

Will had bought the gas can no more than four weeks prior when he began mowing the lawn for the Kearneys. He was glad he paid cash for it and doubted if the receipt had survived the file. He avoided the question anyway.

"What about Mrs. Kearney?" Will asked, though he had never met her.

"No idea. Like I said, we only found one body," Travis said. "How long have you been renting here?"

"This is unbelievable," Will said. "About six weeks."

"Notice anything weird about your landlords?"

Will wondered what he should disclose. "I've never seen Mrs. Kearney, but I have heard them argue sometimes."

"Arguments?" Travis asked. "What kind of arguments?"

"I'm not sure," Will said. "I couldn't hear the content, just the volume."

"Anything else?"

"Marv, –uh, Mr. Kearney had an odd way of talking. He kind of repeated himself a lot."

Travis pulled a card out of his blazer. "Listen," he said. "Here's my card. If you think of anything else, give me a call."

"Sure," Will said, taking the card.

"I also have to ask you not to leave the city. I may have more questions for you."

"Uh, okay," Will said. What should I do now?"

"I'd start with a motel," Travis said, and chuckled as he walked away. "Call me and tell me where you are when you land in case I need to talk to you."

Will watched him go and stood there, looking at the burnt mess. There was yellow police tape all around the site, but he needed to look around. He needed to know *what was left,* if anything. He walked up the driveway and looked around the side of the house and to the garage. Another burnt shell of a building with a blackened hunk of what used to be his car and Marv Kearney's Cadillac. There was no chance the money under the seat survived, but he looked anyway, and his fears were confirmed. Fifty thousand dollars was now part of the pile of muddy black dust under the car. He looked back at the house. The steps to his apartment had collapsed, and everything within it was charred. He lifted up a few pieces of wood to see if he recognized anything, but it was all a big, black, smelly mess. He did find the remnants of his microwave and mini fridge, neither of which served a purpose any longer. He found his bed frame, at least he thought it was his, but there was no trace of the box that had been underneath it, carrying the bulk of his stolen money.

Well, isn't this just about a punch in the nuts, he thought. *You've gone and let all your money and belongings burn up.*

Shut up, he told himself. Self-bashing was not going to do him any good. He was having enough trouble thinking about losing the money as it was. He didn't need his own help. As he turned to leave, he saw his chest of drawers, which was burnt, but not destroyed. In the top drawer, once he wrenched it open, was his watch, which still worked, his cellular phone, which was ruined, his car keys, which were now useless, and the remains of his little booklet he used to take notes on the places he had been. He grabbed them all and filled his pockets with the items, brushing the soot from his hands, and then went to the front yard to grab his bag. As he walked with the duffel bag over his shoulder, he flashed back to September 11ᵗʰ once again, when he carried the same duffel bag, as he walked away from what would become a terrible pile of rubble. And now his future was once again uncertain.

He walked with his bag containing all his possessions slung over his shoulder until he reached 15ᵗʰ Avenue, where he found a payphone and was able to call a cab. He had forgotten what a pain in his posterior it was not to have a car. He would need one, though, and soon. On his walk, he had time to think, and he pulled together a list of things he thought he needed to do. One of them was to go get his fifty thousand dollars out of the self-service storage facility and close that account. Another was to get all of his paychecks cashed. Still another was to get another car, somehow, and the last one was to get the hell out of Seattle as fast as he could. He was under too much exposure with the fire already, and any investigations made by police or the inquisitive Mr. Travis would be even more unwelcome attention. He also thought about *The Seafarer,* the Captain, Chief, Jelly, and Stump. He knew he wasn't going back to work on Monday, and he knew he wasn't going back to work there ever again. He had to call the Captain and give him a heads up, though. He would not have felt right about it if he hadn't. While he was waiting for the taxi, he dropped another quarter into the pay phone and called the Captain's office number. The phone rang, but there was no answer. Finally, a recorded message answered Will's call. It said:

"You've reached the voicemail of Captain Russell Pierce of The Seafarer. If you're answering the ad for the crew member, we're not hiring anyone right now, but leave your name and phone number, and I will call you back if we have an opening."

Will did not want to leave a message announcing his retirement from offshore fishing. He would have rather spoken to the Captain either in person or at least on the phone to let him know, and not just drop the bomb through a voicemail. He decided he would try the number again the following day, and if Will couldn't reach him then, he would seek out the Captain on Monday morning and tell him face to face.

The taxi arrived, and Will asked the driver for his recommendation of a cheap but decent hotel or motel in the area. The driver told him about a place on Queen Anne Avenue, and Will told him that would be fine. As they drove, Will pulled out his wallet and the paychecks he had been accruing for the last six weeks. He estimated that he had a little over twelve thousand dollars in uncashed checks, another fifteen hundred in cash, and then there was the fifty thousand he had put in the self-service storage facility. He would be getting that tomorrow, for sure. Sixty-three thousand, five hundred dollars. That's what Will had, total. And he needed a car, and he needed to get himself gone, soon.

When they arrived at the hotel, Will paid cash for the room and gave one of his fake credit cards for the ever-popular incidentals. His room was on the second floor and gave a decent view of the surrounding area, although he couldn't see too far. Will pulled Charles Travis' business card from his wallet and dialed the number printed on it. Another answering machine, which Will was fine with in the situation. He really would rather avoid any more interactions with the investigator. He then called down to the front desk and asked if they had a laundry service. "No" was the response, but there was a 24-hour laundry on the next block. Will grabbed his bag, exited the hotel, and dumped all of his remaining clothes, except what he was wearing, into the washer, filled it with quarters, and started the machine. He walked back to the hotel, but this time, entered the lounge where he had three beers, two shots of Irish whiskey, and a Croque Monsieur sandwich. After paying the bill, it was back to the laundry to dry his clothes, and then back to the hotel once again, where he entered his room, flopped down on the bed, and was out for the night.

The ringing phone the next morning woke him rudely, and he nearly fell out of bed trying to answer it. He knocked the receiver onto the floor and swiped at it twice before making contact and bringing it up to his ear.

"Hello?" he said sleepily.

"Mr. Lomax?" the voice asked.

"Who?" Will asked, confused. Then he remembered who he was. "Oh, yes," Will said, struggling to recognize the voice.

"This is Charles Travis, the investigator?"

"Uh, yes," Will said, sorry he answered the phone. "How can I help you?"

"Mr. Lomax, we need to talk." The tone of Travis' voice sent a shiver up Will's spine, and he felt his face flush.

"Uh, okay, about what?"

"Not on the phone. There's a coffee shop right next to the laundry that you used yesterday. Can you meet me there?"

He was following you!

"Uh, sure. When?" Wil thought for a second he might have a window to just go get into the wind, but if Travis was following him yesterday, he'd certainly have an eye on him now.

"Now, Mr. Lomax. Right now. I'm at the coffee shop waiting."

"Okay. I'll be there as soon as I can." Will hung up the phone and sat on the edge of the bed for a minute with his head in his hands. *Going to meet him could be a mistake. Just run.* But then he thought, *No, that's probably a bigger mistake. You're going to go meet him and hear him out. He didn't identify you as a suspect. He's just a smug jackass.*

Will got dressed as quickly as he could after making up his mind to go to the coffee shop and brushing his teeth. It would be a while before he drank Irish whiskey again. He loved the taste, but not the hangover. He took the elevator to the main floor and walked across the street at the light, and then down the next block to where the coffee shop was located. He found Charles Travis sitting at the corner table with two paper cups of what Will could only guess was coffee, and a box with at least a half-dozen doughnuts and pastries inside. Will pointed to the chair across the table from Travis, and Travis nodded with a mouthful of cruller.

Once he swallowed, he said, "I didn't know what you wanted, so I got a mix." Will was more interested in the coffee than the doughnuts, and Travis nodded again when Will asked if it was for him. Will pulled the lid off the coffee, added two creamers and a sugar substitute, and began stirring. "Thanks for meeting me, Mr. Lomax."

"You can call me Billy if you want," Will said.

"Fine, Billy. We got in touch with the Captain of your boat, and he verified who you are and where you were."

Will swallowed his coffee and said, "Well, that's good."

"He seemed a bit upset that you were not out there with him now, but we explained the circumstances to him. He said he would talk with you when he returned to port." All Will could muster at that point was a slight shrug and a sigh. "So, we know you could not have started the fire, and we have yet to find a next of kin for Mr. Kearney."

"What about Mrs. Kearney?" Will asked.

"Did you ever meet Mrs. Kearney, Billy?"

"No, like I said yesterday, all I heard from her was arguments."

"We think you heard the television, or something else, Billy. Mrs. Kearney died four years ago from cancer."

"Are you serious?" Will asked, incredulously.

"As cancer," Travis said, and he laughed at his own joke. Will did not. "We think the old man got tired of living alone, doused the house and garage with gas, and struck the match. The knobs on the stove were also all in the "high" position."

None of this was making sense to Will. He knew what he heard, and it was definitely Marv's voice and a woman's voice. *Did you hear him actually arguing with the television? And the knobs on the stove were on? The place should have been blown into matchsticks.* "Wait, why didn't it explode?" Will asked, thankful that the explosion didn't happen, and little bits of his money didn't rain from the sky to invite questions from investigators such as Charles Travis.

"The main gas line was off. From what we can tell from his usage by the gas and electric company, he hadn't used hardly any gas in years. I bet his microwave did most of the work."

"Incredible," Will said, still internally wincing at the loss of over three hundred thousand dollars.

"Yeah," Travis said. "So, can you come identify the body?"

"Uhh, yeah. What's the address? I'll need to take a cab."

"I can drive you," Travis said.

"Oh, that's not necessary," Will said. He didn't want to spend any more time with Travis than he needed. "I don't mind the cab." *Maybe you can get another car from the cabbie.*

"Come on," Travis said. "Cut your taxi bill in half." Will relented finally, and the two took a mostly silent ride that, thankfully for Will, was only about two miles away. "Look at these gas prices dropping. A buck-forty-three now. Last month it was a buck-fifty-eight." Will just nodded, hoping they would not pass anything more that would cause Travis to open his trap about something Will didn't care to hear. He wanted to get this over with, and he wanted to get his money, and he wanted to be gone from this place. Finally, they arrived at the hospital, and Travis took Will through a maze of hallways. They stopped just outside of a door marked "Morgue." Travis looked at Will with a raised eyebrow. "This isn't gonna freak you out, is it?"

"Not sure. I guess we'll find out," Will said, getting ready for something, but he didn't know what.

Travis opened the right side of the double door, and they went into the room. Travis told Will to stand near a window on the left side of the room, and he went to speak to someone on the other side of the room. It smelled weird in the room, Will thought. It smelled clean, yet dirty all at the same time. He wanted to get out of the room as soon as possible and was relieved when Travis came back over.

"Doctor Rosenberg, there, is gonna go into the room and pull out the body. He'll remove the sheet, and all you gotta do is say 'yes' or 'no' for whether or not it's the old man, okay?"

"Sure," Will said, confident he could pull off the seemingly simple task. Doctor Rosenberg entered the room and pulled a cart over to what looked like a big stack of filing cabinets. He raised the cart op to the third level and opened the door in front of it. A body in a black bag was pulled from the door and onto the cart. Will watched Rosenberg drop the cart down to a waist-high level and wheel the cart over to the window. He unzipped the bag from the top and gently peeled back the flaps of the bag to reveal the charred and scarred remains of someone, but Will could not be sure if it were Marv Kearney or not. Will looked over the corpse for a minute until Travis broke in.

"So, whadaya think? Is this our old man?" Travis asked.

"Honestly, I can't tell you. I'm not sure."

Travis exhaled in an annoyed fashion and made a circling motion with his finger in the air. Rosenberg returned to the cart and spun it around one hundred eighty degrees. And that's when will saw it. The left side of the burn victim's face was uncharred, and it bore a striking resemblance to Hal Holbrook. Will now knew without a doubt that it was Marv Kearney. He nodded his head, and Travis gave Rosenberg a thumbs-up. Will turned away from the window. He felt bad for the old man, but at the same time, felt so much rage against him that Will could barely contain it.

"Are we done?" Will asked, slightly anxious.

"Yeah," Travis responded. "Oh, here's this. It's all the information you're gonna need to file insurance claims. It's my report of the incident, putting you clear of any involvement. Use it for your belongings and your car." Travis gave Will a manilla folder, just like thousands he had seen at Pickwick. Will tucked the folder under his arm. "Yep, you're good now, you can go. Go out the double door and follow the blue stripe on the floor."

"Thanks," Will said. He opened the door and located the blue stripe, and played follow the line until he reached the main lobby of the hospital. He wasn't sure what he was going to do next, but almost two months after he left everything behind except for a bag of his belongings, he was still homeless, with no car, and everything he owned was in a bag that he would carry on his shoulder. He got a cab back to the hotel, and when he got there, he sat on the bed for a moment, and his thoughts swirled around him like fallen leaves on a windy Autumn day. Everything was too much right then, and he couldn't take it. He lay face down on the bed and then cried. *What have you done? Was it really all that bad back in New York? Did you really need to do this masquerade? What was so bad that you had to become a criminal to escape it all? And at what cost?* Will didn't have any answers for his own questions, especially now that, when he looked back, everything he had wasn't that bad.

Chapter 41 – Destination

The next morning, Will woke up, not too refreshed, but enlightened. His thoughts throughout the previous day and the night that had just passed had given him clarity. *You can't go back,* he told himself. *What's done is done. Lament it all you want, but you can't undo it. You have to move forward, and you have to move upward, and you have to do it soon.* He made sense to himself, and as the morning found him, he knew his immediate path to what would lie ahead.

He jumped out of the bed and hit the floor in motion. He grabbed a pair of shorts and threw on a t-shirt. A pair of socks, shoes, and an elevator ride later, he was out for a morning run. It had been a while, and he felt a little rusty at first, and his knee still hurt, but then momentum kicked in, and he found his pace. It was nearly back to normal. He liked Seattle and enjoyed the scenery as he ran along Myrtle Edwards Park and Elliott Bay Park. He was nearing the aquarium he had visited not too long before, but decided it was time to make the turn to go back to the hotel. His life was waiting for him. In the lobby of the hotel when he returned, Will asked if he could add an extra day to his stay. The man behind the counter advised that all of his information would carry over to the next day, which Will approved. When he was done at the front desk, Will picked up a copy of two different newspapers and hopped on the elevator. When he got back to his room, he ditched his sweaty clothes, showered, and packed his bags. He didn't have to leave the room until eleven o'clock tomorrow, but he wanted his main duties completed before he took his next step. Besides, if things went well, he would leave early.

After donning a fresh set of clothes, Will sat on the bed, opened up the newspapers, and spread them out before him. He went directly to the classifieds and looked for the auto section. Disappointment hit him immediately as the selection was thin. It wasn't much better in the second newspaper, and some of the same cars were listed in both papers. He scanned each and made a few calls, but only got two that felt right.

They were low-dollar cash deals that the current owner was willing to dump, fast. He took a taxi over to North Beacon Hill and discovered that the first of his possible targets had an owner who may have been a little disingenuous with his description of the car. He said it was a nearly restored classic Volkswagen and that he was the original owner who took good care of it. In truth, it was a 1976 Beetle that had more rust on it than it had paint. A man who Will thought might be the owner was standing outside by the vehicle and rubbing the tetanus trap with a towel, which may have had more holes in it than the car. As the taxi slowed, Will immediately dismissed the stop and asked the driver to take him to the second location, which was in Judkins Park, not too far away. The cabbie obliged, and they rode through Mt. Baker and up 31st Avenue until they found the house. Will asked the driver to wait for him, and the driver gave him a five-minute window and had a cigarette while Will looked at the vehicle. The second car was not a car at all, but was a 1974 Ford Econoline Van that was beige in color. The van started easily, idled well, and the engine sounded great when the pedal was pushed. He was worried about the van sticking out, though, and wondered how easy it would be to recognize or remember if pressured by an authority. So, he passed on both vehicles, and after the cab ride back to the hotel, Will found himself with forty-six dollars less than he had earlier, and nothing to show for it. Not only that, but he was also hungry.

Will went a few blocks away from the hotel to a place he found on his run earlier in the day on Mercer Street. Fortunately for Will, it was Happy Hour when he arrived. He took a seat at the bar, and a young female approached him.

"Hi there, welcome!" she said, a little too cheerfully for Will.

"Thanks," he said.

"My name is Joy. Here's our food menu, drink menu, and specials. Can I get you started with something to drink?"

"Uh," he said, rubbing his eyes to look at the menu. "How about one of the beers you have on tap, there. I'm not familiar with a lot of them. Can you pick one for me?"

"Sure, what do you normally drink? Pilsner, lager, ale?"

He looked at her. "Usually, I just drink beer. Let's go with a lager."

"You got it." He watched her as she went to a cooler, opened the top, and pulled out a frosty and extremely tall glass that was narrow at the bottom and widened at the top before slightly narrowing again at the rim. The glass seemed like it was a foot tall. She poured the beer and brought it over to him and placed it on a coaster on the bar. "Anything to eat or just the beer?"

"I'm definitely getting food," Will said, "but I'm not sure what I want. Any recommendations?"

"You're having a rough go of it today as far as making decisions, no?" She was smiling as she said it, and he had to admit that her smile was refreshing, beautiful. He hadn't seen a smile like that since... "I'd go with the Reuben," she offered. "Corned beef, Swiss cheese, sauerkraut, and our Thousand Island dressing, all on rye bread, and grilled until it's crispy. It's a nice bite."

Will looked at her, smiled his best, handed her the menu, and said, "I trust you."

"Very well then," she said, and there was the smile again. "I'll have that right up for you. Fries or chips?"

"Chips, please," he replied. She nodded and turned, and he watched her walk away to what he assumed was the kitchen. He took a look around the bar and determined that it was definitely a sports-friendly bar, but he wouldn't call it a sports bar. They had a decent space for live music, there was an upstairs bar, and plenty of tables and booths for seating. It wasn't terribly busy, but it was only three-thirty in the afternoon. Aside from an older gentleman at the bar and a man and a woman sitting at one of the tables having some lunch, Will sat alone. He decided he might have to come back later, especially if Joy was still working. *And you can go ahead and get that out of your head already. You don't need any relationship nonsense right now. You're leaving, remember?*

He did remember, and he listened to the voice when Joy returned with the sandwich. He barely looked at her as he thanked her and responded negatively to her question of whether he needed anything more. He ate his sandwich in silence, contemplating his next move, which he really had no idea of what it would be. He knew he had to get his money. *All of it. Everything that's left, and then you have to go. You never opened a bank account, but you have six paychecks to cash, and then you need to get to the storage facility, grab your fifty thousand that you have stashed there, and then you can go.*

"You live around here? I haven't seen you here before."

Will was jolted from his thoughts back to reality by Joy's question. "Huh?!" he said with a start.

"Sorry, I didn't mean to scare you. I was asking if you live around here?"

"Oh, oh, no," Will said. "I'm just kinda passing through."

"Passing through? To where, the Pacific?" Joy gave him a winning smile again, and it was too much for him to keep his comments to himself.

"No, no, I've seen the Pacific, and it's nice," he said. "I used to be a commercial fisherman for a while, but now I need to move on to something else."

"Like moving on, moving on? Or just doing something different?" she asked.

"Uh, a little of both, I guess," he said. "I think I need a change of scenery. Something further East."

"That's too bad," she said with a wink, and disappeared from the bar again.

Will watched her go again and decided he needed to move fast before he lost control of himself and got into a weird situation with Joy. He opened his wallet, dropped thirty dollars on the counter, and was gone by the time she came to pick it up. She took the money from the bar, looked around, shrugged, and went back to the kitchen.

Back in the hotel, Will cleaned up the newspaper he had strewn all over the bed earlier and shoved it into what became an overstuffed mini trash can. He sat back down on the bed for a second and thought to himself, *What are you going to do now?* Nothing jumped out of his brain now that the escape vehicle had fallen through. He let himself fall backward onto the bed, and he landed with enough force that the headboard of the bed knocked against the wall. The sound jolted Will, and he glanced to see what it was. When he saw the headboard still rocking, the mystery was solved. He let his eyes wander from the headboard, down to the pillow, over to the night table, then to the telephone on the table, then to his watch, which lay on the table, and then to the lamp, which– – *your watch,* his interior voice said, *your watch, Billy Jack, your watch.* Will looked at the watch again. *Your watch,* it said again, louder. Will wasn't putting it together, though. He swung his legs over the side of the bed and grabbed his watch from the end table. *Your watch.* He looked at it, put it around his wrist, and secured it. It was still charred a bit from the fire. *The fire.* He knew he would need to have the watch cleaned. *The fire at the Kearney's.* He thought back to the scene where the burnt house remained, and remembered walking through the debris, looking for anything. *But what were you looking for? What was most important to you then? You were looking for your money. You looked for that beautiful box of money that you stupidly stashed under the bed on the second floor of a house owned by a suicidal man who missed his wife.* He looked at the watch again and was about to take it off when it hit him. *You didn't find your money. What did you find? Your watch, your cellphone, and your book. Your book. Your little travel book of places you had seen on your way out here to Seattle. You got suckered into landing and staying out here. That was never the plan, Billy. That Captain grabbed you and got you on the boat so fast that you were spinning around like a top, bouncing between the boat and what you thought was your new home. But it is all a lie. You were never supposed to stay out here. See the Pacific Ocean. That's what you wanted, and you did it. But somewhere along the way, you lost hold of yourself and what you wanted to do. Make a difference. Remember that? You weren't making a difference then, and you're certainly not making a difference now. That book holds all your research about the kinds of places you want to live. That book is the difference maker and the key to your future. Go be a big fish in a small pond. Have some control over your life instead of letting it drag you around. Get the book.*

Will stood up and went to his duffel bag, which was still packed with all of his possessions that he could touch at the moment, and was lying on the table across the room. *It's in the side pocket.* He reached into the side pocket and felt the remains of the book. *There's not much left.* He pulled the book and examined it. There wasn't much left. Most of the pages were gone, some were waterlogged and burned so that he could not read what was written, and some were blackened to the point that they disintegrated when he touched them. He looked through what was left of the book, page by page, and was disappointed at what he saw as each page was turned. This was not providing any answers, and he was getting more and more confused with each page he turned. If there was an answer, he had not found it yet, and he was nearing the last of his entries– –and then, there it was. One page, with the name of the town at the top and his notes underneath. One page survived the fire that cost him his money. He read the name of the town that was listed at the top of the page. *Brindle. The town of Brindle.* He looked through the rest of the book, but Brindle was the only page left that he could read, and the page was nearly untouched by the fire and not damaged by the water. He felt like it had to be a sign.

Brindle. He had his destination.

Chapter 42 – Promise

On Sunday, October 28th, 2001, the sun was shining brightly, but the air temperature was cool and would not rise above fifty-one degrees that day. Most of those walking the streets of New York City were wearing an outer layer of clothing to protect themselves from the early morning chill, but Detective Brian Greco was wearing his normal "uniform," as he called it, comprised of comfortable dress shoes, black socks, and a navy-blue suit with a two-button jacket. He had blue suits and black suits and brown suits and tan suits, and that was what he wore to work every day. He always wore dark shoes, though, and if the weather was going to be cold, he had a shin-length trench coat that he would wear to protect him from the snow and rain, and whatever mixture of the two that New York's atmosphere would throw at him.

He didn't have the trench coat that day, and the brisk air cut through his thin socks and bit at his ankles as he walked along the sidewalk, swimming upstream like a salmon in a river of people headed in the other direction. He finally reached the entrance to the hospital and walked in through the first set of automatic doors. The heat was on inside, and he stood there for a moment to let it hit his chilled extremities. He moved aside as a trainload of hospital employees wearing matching scrub tops and pants hurried through the door on the way to their various units within the hospital. In his mind, they were all heroes and deserved any respect he could offer them. It was nearly seven weeks ago that they had all performed miracles and saved the lives of so many who were injured, bleeding, and barely breathing. He didn't know how many lives were saved that day, but he knew who was responsible for saving them.

Greco entered the second set of doors and walked through the lobby until he reached a wall of elevator doors. He would have punched the "up" button, but it was already lit. The door of the elevator next to him opened, and he slid in amongst other passengers and several young men and women dressed neck to ankle in pink tops and pants, wearing picture IDs on lanyards that hung around their necks. They all stepped off the elevator on the third floor, and Greco rode two more floors upward with a man who smelled of cigars and wore a heavy brown coat. Greco wished the man a good day as he got off the elevator on the fifth floor. He walked down the corridor to room 514 and stopped. He took a breath before entering, and when he finally had himself composed, he knocked on and then went through the slightly opened door.

"Hey," came the voice from the bed. "I didn't order any doughnuts, Michelle, did you?" The word "doughnuts" came out like "doughnits." It was Steve Angelucci; he was speaking to a nurse at his bedside, but the joke was for Greco. "Who ordered doughnuts?" Michelle just smiled at Steve as she wrote notes in his chart.

"Don't listen to him," Greco said. "He's just hallucinating. Give him some more of those wonderful drugs and maybe he'll pass out, then I can leave, and you can tell him I was here for hours before you kicked me out!"

Michelle closed the chart and placed it in a slot at the end of the bed, and smiled again at both of them. "I'll leave you two alone for a while." She looked at Greco. "And you, no work talk. He needs to relax."

"I'll do my best, but you know he drags out the worst in me," Greco said, returning the smile, and he watched her as she closed the door. "Did she change her hair?" Greco asked, after the door was shut.

"Do not hit on my nurses!" Steve yelled, loud enough so that the entire hallway could hear it, even with the door shut.

"You ass." Greco pulled a chair over from the side of the room and sat next to the bed. Steve did not have to share his room with another patient, for which Greco was thankful. He didn't really want to be here for one sick person, to say nothing of two. "So, how are you feeling?"

"About the same," Steve said. "My shoulder is healing, but I breathed in too much of that stuff that day, and it won't come out. It's stuck in my windpipe and bronchial tubes, and it's in my lungs. I have been doing breathing treatments and things like that, but it's not getting much better, if any better at all."

Greco looked down at the tile floor and wished it were quicksand. As he sank, he would at least be away from there, right then, listening to what Steve had just said. Steve had a tube running from under his nose, up each side of his head, and wrapped around his ears, but Greco couldn't figure out to what it was connected. He figured and hoped it was oxygen, there to help Steve breathe and get better. Steve was making a raspy sound when he breathed, and he often tried to clear his throat with small coughs, which looked like they hurt him.

"What else are they saying?" Greco asked. "Any idea when you can get out?"

Steve half-laughed and half-grunted and looked out of the window to his right for a moment. "I'll be lucky to feel warm sunshine again," he said. "They are saying this stuff is cancerous. There are other people sicker than I am right now. But the good thing for them is they aren't stuck having you visit them. I'm just the lucky one, I guess."

Greco laughed at his long-time friend and partner's joke. He stood and grabbed a paper cup from the dispenser on the wall and filled it with some ice water from a pitcher that sat on a rolling table next to Steve. He gulped it down and tried to digest what Steve had just told him. He marveled at Steve's even-toned delivery and his ability to be light-hearted about the entire situation.

"Dude, stop it," Steve said. Greco turned to look at him. "Stop it. Stop feeling all glum and sorry for me. We both knew the risks when we went through the academy and then put our badges on for the first time. I just did my job, and like so many of us, I'm paying a bit of a price for it."

"A bit?"

"Okay, maybe more than a bit." And then Steve laughed, and Greco with him. It was an old joke they had been using for years whenever Steve tried to make a situation seem not as bad as it really was.

They stopped laughing when Steve began to cough. It was a terrible spell, and Greco thought Steve's face was going to turn blue. As he coughed, Steve pointed to a pile of paper towels on his rolling table. Greco grabbed some from the pile and placed them in Steve's hand, and Steve used them to wipe his mouth, which was partially bloodied from the damage done to his windpipe, lungs, and esophagus. He finally stopped coughing and lay back to catch his breath. Greco took the towels from him and tossed them in the garbage can. Then he poured a cup of water from the pitcher and handed it to Steve, who drank it in very small sips.

"Hurts to swallow a little," Steve said, his voice still raspy.

"I can imagine," Greco said, and he sat on the edge of the bed.

"Ohhhh," Steve exhaled, still trying to get his breathing back under control. "Do you remember when we first did the 'a bit' bit?" Steve started to laugh lightly.

"The undercover hostage thing in the bodega, when you were dressed up as the woman—"

"And the guy had me tied up," Steve added.

"And your radio crackled and scared the hell out of him—" Greco said.

"Yeah," Steve laughed, "and he was so clumsy that he knocked the mayonnaise off the shelf, and the jar broke—"

"– And he slipped on the floor and knocked himself out!" Greco joined in for the punch line, and they both laughed heartily until they were able to control themselves.

"Uhh, heh, heh heh...," Steve laughed and exhaled. Then he got quiet and looked out the window at his view of the city. "I love this city," he said. "I'd do anything for it." He looked back at Greco. "Brian, the bodega, with the guy," he said. "I should have died that day. Everything went wrong, and it was a bad deal to begin with. But I knew what I was doing, what I was getting into, and if it happened, and I died in the line of duty, it would have been okay, because I knew the risks, and I accepted them." Steve's voice grew quieter, and he looked Brian in the eye. "Just like I knew the risks on September 11th. This is my job, Brian, but it's also my life. I never knew anything else. I never wanted to do anything else. Do you know how many lives I helped to save, or at least extend that day?"

Greco turned his head and looked outside. He thought back to his act of running away from the falling debris that day, and how he had felt ashamed about it. But he also remembered getting his wits about him and being responsible for assisting in many saved lives himself. "Dunno," he said. "Hundreds?"

"*Hundreds*, Brian. *Hundreds of lives*," Steve said with emphasis. "I'm good with that." He looked out the window and then back at Greco. "Look," he said, "I'm going to get out of here one day. That's my plan. I'm fighting like crazy now, and I'll keep fighting. And I want you to do the same, whether I'm here or not. So, I have to ask you..." Steve paused for a moment.

"What?" Greco asked.

"If I'm not here, you keep doing the job."

Greco pursed his lips and exhaled. "Come on, man!"

"Promise. You're a great friend and partner, but you're also a fantastic detective. So promise."

"Okay," Greco said, smiling. "I promise!"

"Promise what?" Steve was looking at him with a sideways eye.

"I promise I'll keep doing the job if you're not here," Greco said, with half an eye roll.

"Good," Steve said. "Now, where are my doughnuts?" With that, the two friends and partners laughed, and Greco grabbed Steve by the hand. When the laughing stopped, Greco looked at Steve once again.

"That's my Stevo."

Steve smiled. "And that's my Greco."

Chapter 43 – Preparation

Now that Will had some direction and knew where he was going to try to go, in preparation for his trip, needed to figure out how he was going to get there. Since he didn't have, or want to open, a bank account at the time, he decided to go to a check cashing service, several of them actually, and have his payroll checks from his short-lived fishing career cashed. He knew he'd have to bite the bullet on the paychecks and have the service fee deducted from the amount he was given in return. It was, however, only a few dollars per check, so he didn't mind too much. He figured out that he should make three stops, cashing the first and third check at one, the second and fourth check at another, and the fifth and sixth one at the last one. They were all the same company, just in three different locations around Seattle. There were others, but they did not open, or closed early, on Sunday.

All of his methods of finding a car had gone down the river in a swift canoe, but he had one final idea of how to get around to the places he needed to go. He pulled the yellow phone book out from under the table next to the bed and flipped to the "Auto" section. Somewhere after "Auto Insurance" and before "Auto Repair," he found it. "Auto Rental." He looked through the offerings and tried to find one with a special or a coupon that would save him some money. The only thing that popped out at him with that guideline was a one-line advertisement for a place called "AAAbsolute Auto Rental." It said, "We're Cheap!" right after the company name. *Or maybe it is part of the company name*, he thought. Regardless, he picked up the phone and dialed the number shown. The phone rang four times before it was picked up, and then it was only the greeting of *"Hello?"*

"Oh, hi, I was wondering if you have any cars to rent for the day?" Will said. He thought he heard children yelling in the background.

"It's Sunday," the voice said.

"Oh, uh, so it is. Are you closed on Sundays?"

"No, but we ain't got no cars." Then Will's suspicions were confirmed when he definitely heard a screaming baby in the background. The voice on the other end of the line became muffled and sounded like someone was shouting, probably about the screaming baby. *"You wanna try tomorrow? We might get a straggler or two bringin' a car back."*

"Sounds great," Will said, "I'll do just that." With that, he hung up the phone and called Discovery Car Rental, which actually had a panel ad, but also said they had the lowest rate that he had seen. He booked the car to be picked up in thirty minutes and then went downstairs to the lobby to catch a taxi to the Discovery location. He found one waiting outside ready for a fare, and immediately thought back to Leon in Indianapolis. *You could use another guy like Leon right now. Your car problems would be history. Now, just the car is history. And another fifty thousand dollars you could really use right now, too.*

He laughed at his stupid internal joke and opened the door to the taxi. He stepped in and sat down in the seat, and the driver looked at him through the rearview with an inquisitive look on his face.

"Discovery Car Rental on Elliott?"

"You got it," the driver said. He pulled the lever on the meter, and the thing illuminated with red numbers, already charging Will $4.00 just to get going. "You from around here?"

"Yeah, I'm a fisherman up at the docks. Having some car trouble, so I need a rental." Will said.

"You stayin' in the hotel?" he asked.

Will realized he was getting backed into a corner. "Uh, truth is," he said, stammering a bit, "I'm on the outs with the old lady. She needs the car, and I need a place to sleep, so I'm staying in the hotel and getting a rental car to drive around in until we can get our stuff straightened out."

"Been there, pal," he said, as he sped up to run through a yellow light. Will watched as a man on a bicycle took cover from the speeding taxi. "Listen, just do the whole flowers thing, right? Then take her to dinner somewhere nice. It'll all be fine." Will noticed that the driver had a little bit of a New York accent in his delivery, but he decided against asking about it to avoid further intrusive interrogation about his personal life.

"Maybe I'll try that," Will said. "If she ever picks up my calls or answers the door."

"Heh, heh," was all the driver had left to contribute, and Will was thankful when they arrived at the Discovery location. "Thirteen forty," the driver said, and Will gave him a twenty-dollar bill and told him to keep the change. "Thanks, buddy. Good Luck."

"Thanks," Will said, and shut the door to the cab. He walked into the car rental office, which was slightly larger than a backyard shed. "Hi there," he said as he walked through the door.

"Hello, can I help you?" the man behind the desk asked. There was no counter, just two desks in the middle of the floor, each with a chair for the person at the desk, and another at the side of each. A wall of keys hung behind them, and a printer was off to one side of the room. The other side was decorated with a water cooler and a mini fridge.

"Yes," Will said. "I have a reservation?"

"And your name, sir?" he asked as he stood. He had a lanyard around his neck that dropped down almost to where Will assumed his navel would be. There was a laminated placard on the end of the lanyard that had the man's picture on it, and it said his name was Fahad.

"Lomax," Will said. He figured that Fahad must have been working there for a while, because the picture that hung from the lanyard showed Fahad with hair. The live version did not seem to be so fortunate.

"Come sit, please. I will look for your rental information." Fahad looked through a bunch of pamphlet-style folders on his desk until he found the one with "LOMAX" written in thick black marker across the top. "Ah-ha! Found it. Right where it should have been." Will believed Fahad to be from a Middle Eastern country due to his accent, but he wasn't sure where. "Let me see," Fahad said, "I will be needing your identification and your credit card for the reservation you made." Will handed over the fake identification and the fake credit card to Fahad. He was getting used to using them and no longer had any fear when he was asked for them.

He felt it was too soon, after recent events by certain foreign terrorists, to ask Fahad about his accent or where he was from, and he had heard that there were some retaliations and hate crimes directed towards people of Middle Eastern descent, just because they were. Will didn't think that was necessarily fair, but then again, the American patriot inside him could understand why someone who was ignorant of the facts may perceive that everyone of Middle Eastern descent was an enemy. But it just didn't seem right for Will. He never understood bigotry or racism anyway. Fahad brought the rental agreement over to Will at the side of the desk.

"I need you to read through the contract," Fahad said, opening the folder. "You will need to check one of these boxes here, about whether you want the insurance or not. Check this box to indicate that you agree to bring the car back with a full tank of gas, or be charged a fee of three dollars and seventy-nine cents per gallon required to fill the gas tank if you do not. Finally, check this box to indicate that you have read and understood the contract fully, accept the terms and conditions, and to not damage the car intentionally. I will go and get your keys."

Will scanned the document and looked for anything ridiculously harmful in the text, but found nothing that would stop him from renting the car. *Especially with over sixty-five thousand dollars on the line.* Will declined the insurance, checked the box for the fuel clause, checked that he understood the agreement, and then signed his name, William Lomax, on the line by the "x." Fahad looked over the agreement, nodded, and gave Will the key to the rental car.

"Where is it?" Will asked.

"Come with me and I show you." Fahad left the security of his shed-sized office and ventured out into the world of the parking lot full of rental cars. They walked along the rows of cars, and Will noticed the markings on the pavement of the parking lot were letters. He didn't know what letter indicated the last row, but they were on row "E" and heading toward the front of the alphabet. When they got to "A," Fahad said, "This way!" and they turned up the "A" row. The first spot marked on the ground was number 37. It was a shiny blue Ford four-door that Will would have taken with no issue. But they kept walking, through the thirties and into the twenties, and Will was beginning to wonder if the car was in space A-1.

"If you don't want to make the trip, you can tell me which space it is in. I think I can find it," Will said.

"Oh, it is no trouble, sir," Fahad said, smiling. And they continued to walk through the teens and into the single digits until Fahad stopped in front of space A-2. Will looked at the massive sea of cars they passed and then at their location in the upper leftmost corner of Discovery's parking lot. He didn't say anything to Fahad, but it just seemed to him that there may have been an option closer to the office. Fahad insisted that they walk around the car to look for any existing damage. Other than a few door dings and a scratch on the rear bumper, each of which Fahad noted on the folder of the rental agreement, the car looked fine. Will clicked the button on the key fob and the car chirped, announcing it was unlocked. He opened the driver's door and settled in, all while Fahad watched. "Is everything okay, sir?" he asked.

"There appears to be a cigarette burn on the passenger seat floor mat," Will said. Fahad wrote it down in the folder. "Other than that, it looks fine."

"Oh, great, sir. Listen, I hope you have happy travels and safe travels." He handed the rental agreement to Will. "Be sure to turn this in when you get to your destination." Fahad seemed really excited about Will's happiness with the car. He backed away from the car as Will started the engine. It sounded well enough to hit the road, so Will thanked Fahad and began backing the car out of the parking space. "Have a good day, sir!" Fahad said, smiling. Will hit the button that activated the window, and it disappeared into the door as Fahad inched closer. "Is there a problem, sir?" Fahad asked, with a worried look crossing onto his face like the shadow of the sun during an eclipse.

"No," Will said. "I was just wondering if you wanted a ride back to your office. It's a little bit of a hike."

"Oh no, sir. I will enjoy my walk."

"Okay," Will said. "Have a good day." He rolled up the window before he could hear Fahad's response, put the car into gear, and pulled away, through the car lot, and out onto the road. He had written directions to each of the check-cashing businesses, and the first was only a few miles away, then one was near Greenwood, and the last was near Bitter Lake. The storage facility where the bulk of the money was stored was between the last two.

He reached the first check-cashing facility within minutes of getting the rental car. It was located at a counter inside a department store, which is not what Will was expecting. He was picturing a small shop in a strip mall, but ultimately, he didn't care where it was or what he needed to do to get there. He just wanted his money and to get out of Seattle. He tried to calm his nerves before he approached the counter. There was a woman already there making a transaction, dealing with a younger man on the other side of the counter. He didn't really want anyone around the first time he did this, although he could probably learn the process and be more comfortable with it by watching one in live action. He inched a little closer to the counter, pretending to look at a display of batteries, but still could hear nothing. The woman wrapped up her business and left the counter empty. The man started to walk back into the alcove where the counter was, but Will was too quick to let him get away.

"Hi there," Will said with a smile.

"Hello, welcome to Cash Express. How can I help you?"

"Hi." Will looked at the man's name on the tag on his chest. "Abel. How are you today? I need to cash my paychecks. I have two."

"Certainly, sir. May I have the checks and your ID?" Will opened his wallet and pulled out the first and third checks he had received for his work on the boat, along with the phony driver's license. He handed them over to Abel, who took them, studied them, and then cast a frown. "Our normal check cashing fee for this amount is five dollars, but since your ID is from out of state, it will increase to seven dollars and fifty cents."

"That's fine," Will said, just hoping to get through the transaction. Abel ran the first check through a machine that made all kinds of buzzes and clicks as it processed the conversion. When it stopped, Abel asked Will how he wanted his money. Will replied that he would like the largest bills possible, but nothing bigger than one-hundred-dollar bills. They repeated the process for the second check, with the same question and the same response, and a few minutes later, Will was on his way with over three thousand dollars in an envelope in his pocket. At about seventy-thirty that night, Will left the third Cash Express location with his last two checks cashed. That, along with the fifty thousand he had picked up from the self-storage facility and the money he had in his pocket, he had sixty-three thousand, two hundred twelve dollars and seventy-three cents to his name, and all but one hundred dollars of it was now buried in the trunk in the spare tire well. Now, he was ready to leave Seattle. All he had to do was return the rental car, and he could make his plans to get on the road.

What are you gonna do, Billy Jack? You still don't have a car. Not that you could find Brindle again, anyway. Your maps were burned up in the car. And now, because you were stupid, you have limited funds. What's your plan, genius?

Will had no answer for himself, but he just needed to think about it, and he was sure the answer would come. He drove leisurely along the highway and then on the side roads to get the car back to the rental lot. He felt nothing but dismay, though, when he pulled into the lot. It was dark. The parking lot lights were out, and the lights in the shed-office were off. Now, he would have to wait until tomorrow to get Seattle behind him. He had used the phony credit card to make the reservation, but needed to pay in cash so that the rental company would not charge the card. He would have to come back to clean up that little mess. Money wasn't an issue for the car since it was a twenty-four-hour rental, but he was going to need a place to sleep. *Sleep in the car, numb nuts.* He could sleep in the car. He had done it before when he wanted to save money when traveling, so why not? *Save money when traveling. You know how to do that. Go back to the beginning.* That was it. He didn't need to drive to Brindle. He took a bus from Newark to Indianapolis. There had to be buses running out of Seattle!

He threw the car in reverse and drove around until he found a fairly secluded neighborhood, near Marshall Park, where he could park for the night and maybe get some sleep. It was only eight o'clock, though, and he'd never make it through the night sleeping in his car if he tried to sleep this early. He needed beer, and maybe a shot or two. *Or three.* And he realized then that he was only six blocks west and a few blocks north of the bar where he had lunch and met the decision-making Joy with that infectious smile. He was there in less than ten minutes.

He walked into the bar area and took an empty seat that had just been evacuated by a man who had a woman in tow as he left. Maybe they knew each other, he thought. *Maybe they didn't until they sat down in this bar and found a connection.* He told himself it was possible, but then his self responded with *What are you doing here? You're not going to make a connection with this girl. You had this settled.* He then told himself to shut up before the people around him saw him arguing with himself. He thought the whole thing was ridiculous and hoped there were no witnesses.

A man on the other side of the bar with a mustache and a pointy beard appeared and asked what he wanted to drink.

"Draft beer, please, your choice, and a shot of Irish whiskey, please. Is Joy here?"

Pointy Beard looked at him, clicked his cheek, and said, "Just missed her. She got off at eight. Be right back. My name's Bryan, with a 'y' if you need me."

And there it is. No "Joy" in Mudville, Billy Jack! It would have been nice to know if you still have any game, though. His inner voice was talking more and more these days, and it was starting to get on his nerves. He wondered if he might need an exorcist to get rid of it. *But where would you be without it? It has been giving you all of the good ideas lately.*

Bryan, with a 'y,' brought a tall glass of beer over to Will and set it on a coaster on the bar. The shot of whiskey followed. Will took a sip of the beer and looked at the television over his head. Football was on, and the Baltimore Ravens were hosting the Jacksonville Jaguars. There was no score at the end of the first quarter, but a soon as the commercial break was over, Ravens kicker Matt Stover booted a forty-nine-yard field goal to put the Ravens ahead by three. Will checked out the bar again, and it was a lot busier than it had been in the afternoon. Bryan asked him if he wanted anything to eat, but Will politely declined the offer, took his shot, asked for another, and continued to sip on his beer. He was almost sorry he came out to the bar that night, but it was good to be around people who had no idea who he was and wanted nothing from him.

Eventually, he had two more beers and watched the rest of the football game. It was nearing eleven o'clock at night, and the Ravens had pulled off a come-from-behind win, scoring a go-ahead touchdown with about four and a half minutes to go. He paid his tab, said goodnight to Bryan, and quietly left the bar to head back to his Marshall Park sleeping location. Once he parked, he climbed over the front seat and into the back so as not to draw any attention to himself by slamming any doors at this late hour on a Sunday night. He really missed his tent and the ability to stretch out, although it may have been a little cold to sleep outside in the wild. But he was comfortable enough, and in just a few minutes, he was sleeping.

Chapter 44 – Dead Or On The Run

On Monday, October 29th, James Higgins sat at his oversized desk and looked over the paperwork provided to him by CAL team-head David South. South had reviewed the numbers multiple times after showing them to Higgins the first time. No matter how many times South had reviewed the information, the same conclusion was reached every time, and that was that former employee Will Kelly had been a thief. He had created false accounts, and he had to have created false identities, or some other way to get the money from the banks, and he buried the paperwork for as long as he could. And then he died along with thousands of other souls on that terrible day that was still so fresh in everyone's minds, but it seemed so long ago, too. Higgins studied it all, over and over, and his conclusion was the same as David South's, and that was that Willem Kelly was a thief who stole over four hundred thousand dollars, and then apparently died before he could get the rest of it from the banks.

A knock on the door broke his concentration, and his assistant popped her head into the office.

"What is it, Ms. Womack?" Higgins asked.

"There is a detective from the police here to see you," she said with a worried look on her face.

"Ah," he said. "Please see the detective in, and I think we're going to need some coffee, if you don't mind."

"Not at all," she said, and disappeared for a few seconds, only to return with the detective. "Mr. James Higgins, this is Detective Brian Greico from the NYPD. Detective, please feel free to have a seat. How do you take your coffee?"

"It's uh, Greco, actually, not Greico," Greco said, shaking Higgins' hand. "And black is fine," he said. She nodded and disappeared once again, and Greco took a seat in the chair across the massive desk from Higgins. "Mr. Higgins, what can I do for you?"

"James, please," Higgins said. "I think we have a case of company theft, and your office directed me to you."

Greco took out a small notepad from the inside pocket of his jacket. "Why don't you start with the facts about who you think is stealing from the company, and how?" It was then that Higgins sat forward in his chair and talked his way through his notes, advising Greco about Will's activity between June and September, and how Will had opened at least eleven accounts that seemed to be fraudulent in nature. He picked up a box from the side of his desk and told Greco there were copies of all the important documents within. Greco took notes as Higgins spoke, and then Higgins got to the part about how everyone thought that Will had died on September 11, the same day that Higgins and Dickey were going to review three of the accounts that Will had opened. He took the box from Higgins and flipped through some of the contents. "You were having a meeting with him that day?" Greco asked. "Tell me what you can about that."

Higgins sat back in his chair and thought about what had happened. "Well," he began, "as I said, me and F. Roger Dickey had come down to the 49th floor that day because we had a meeting scheduled with Kelly, a meeting that was scheduled for later in the morning, but Kelly himself had bumped it up to earlier in the morning. We met briefly with Kelly in the hallway, and he said he was getting coffee and using the bathroom, and he would be up to the meeting room on the 94th floor in time for the meeting. Mr. Dickey went up to the 94th floor for the meeting. I did not. I stayed on the 49th floor and went to see the SAS because I was down to one pen and needed supplies. I had a quick chat–"

"I'm sorry," Greco broke in. "The SAS? What is that?"

"Oh, I'm sorry," Higgins chuckled. "It's another one of our acronyms. 'Supplies Acquisition Specialist.' When we need to order office supplies, we go see her. So, I had a quick chat with her to order my pens, after which I would have gone to the 94th floor as well. But then it seems while I was doing that, an airplane was flown into the building, and well, you know everything kind of went to hell after that."

"Do you know if anyone saw Mr. Kelly after you met him in the hallway, and he said he was getting coffee and using the restroom?"

Higgins leaned forward in the chair again. "We have asked around, but the only other employee that remembers talking to him was Jerry Nichols earlier that morning, and they just had normal chit chat, according to Jerry."

"And what about Mr. Dickey?"

"Unfortunately, Mr. Dickey is believed to have perished in the attacks as well, as no one has heard from him," Higgins said, a glum expression covering his face. "He was my team leader. I took over his position when we set up in this location. I believe this was once the office of an architectural firm on this floor, a lawyer had the first floor, and the top two floors were an advertising agency. But it was all empty of people when we got here. Just dusty furniture was left over, so we used it."

"I understand completely," Greco said. "We took over a Burger King on Liberty to use as a temporary local station."

Higgins laughed and patted his slightly protruding midsection with both hands a few times. "I knew the place well," and Greco joined him in his chuckle. "Yes, we are still getting our feet under us, but thanks to some watchful eyes here, we think we have found a crime. I'm not sure what you're going to do about it now that he's gone, but company protocol says that we should contact you in this case."

"Right, and you should," Greco said. "And we're definitely going to look into this. We may have some questions for you later, but with your statement and the copies of the paperwork you have provided, I think I have all I need for now."

The two men stood and shook hands again, and when Greco left Higgins' office, he declined the offer from Ms. Womack to escort him to the lobby. He was pretty sure he could find it himself. He studied his notes as he walked along the corridor, and then again when he reached the street and got into his car. Something wasn't adding up. Something wasn't right. A guy works out a way to steal nearly half a million dollars from his company, the company figures it out, and he disappears and is presumed dead on the day they are going to confront him. *Too neat,* Greco thought. *Too clean.*

He drove back to the station, and when he got there, he grabbed the box of evidence from the trunk of his car, entered through the glass double doors, and walked through the hallways until he reached the small office where his desk sat across from the desk of Steve Angelucci, which remained empty. He plopped the box down on his desk, pulled his notes from his pocket, and paged through them again, cursing his handwriting for not being neater. He re-wrote them, this time trying to stay within the lines provided. When he was satisfied with his notes, he walked down the hall to Sergeant Joseph Harding and lightly tapped on the door before entering.

"Brian, what's new?" Harding was looking through a manilla folder with several pieces of paper inside, some were colored pink and others yellow, and still others were white like regular paper. He motioned for Greco to take a seat in one of the chairs across from his desk. "Did you get on that Pickwick thing?"

Greco sat in the chair as requested and pulled his clean set of notes from his jacket. "That I did, Sarge, and this one is pretty weird. So, this guy, uhh, Kelly. He's a loan officer. He sets up at least eleven phony accounts that Pickwick has found so far, then somehow, he frauds the bank into thinking he is the customer and withdraws the cash."

"Did you get footage from the bank security cameras?" Harding asked, pulling one of the pink papers from the file and staring at it.

"I just got the paperwork from Pickwick today. I need to go through the applications he forged and see if there's a way to figure out which banks he had used. Pickwick said they would give us access to their computer system, or what's left of it. They were in the North Tower of WTC."

"Jesus, really?" Harding stopped looking through the file and sat at his desk.

"Yeah," Greco said, "and here's the kicker. No one has heard from this Kelly since that day. He was supposed to have a meeting with his loss prevention team about some of the accounts they found, but that meeting was scheduled for the morning of September 11th. They actually saw him that morning on the 49th floor of the building, and had a meeting with him later on the 94th floor. After they saw him that morning, he was supposed to be up on the 94th floor within a few minutes, but he stalled them, something about coffee and the restroom, and then, of course, the first plane hit the North Tower and no one has seen him since. And another thing, his assistant was supposed to be in that meeting as well, but she never showed up either."

"So, he's dead and she's missing?"

Greco smiled. "For her, no. She's been back to work ever since the 19th of September. As far as him, presumably dead, but that's the mystery, Sarge. And how did he get away with the money?"

"Maybe he didn't get away with any money," Harding offered. "He's dead."

Greco looked at Harding and was silent for a moment. Then he said, "Well, sir, if he didn't get away with it, where is it? He took it from the banks, apparently."

"What's your plan?" Harding asked, getting to the action plan.

Greco stood from his chair. "While we're waiting on the bank videos, I'm going to start with that secretary of his."

Harding looked at him. "Oh, that Janice, whatever?"

"Jeannette, Sarge. Or Jeannie, I think she prefers."

"Yeah, go find out what she knows," Harding said, going back to his folder. "Maybe she was in on it."

Greco left Harding's office, grabbed the evidence box from his desk, and went straight out to his car parked on Ericsson Place. He pulled the car away, and the rear end dropped off the sidewalk as it usually did when he parked there. He had a short ride to get to the new Pickwick building, but he looked at his watch and noticed it was five minutes after twelve, and the morning had quickly turned into the afternoon. He assumed Jeanette Raines would be having her lunch right about now. It seemed like a good time to go see his partner, Steve, in the hospital for a little while. When he got there, Steve was sleeping almost quietly in his hospital bed. He had a slight raspy noise in his breathing when he inhaled. Greco watched him sleep for about ten minutes and then decided to leave, but as he did, his friend awoke.

"Hey," Steve said roughly. "Hey, I'm awake. Don't go."

Greco turned around and smiled at his friend. "Hey, guy! How's everything? How are you feeling?"

Steve looked at his partner and then turned his head back toward the ceiling. "Dude, you just came to see me yesterday. There's no miracle of modern science happening here. I'm exactly the same as I was."

Greco felt bad about pestering his friend. "Sorry, man. I was just hoping you might have turned a corner. Didn't mean to upset you–"

"Dah, it's alright. I know you're just trying to help. I'm just frustrated and beginning to think that there really is no fixing this. All these weeks of breathing exercises and treatments and shit going down my throat, and nothing is better, except for my shoulder."

"Well, that's a plus," Greco said, trying to find a light in Steve's darkness.

Steve exhaled, and it rattled like a penny shaken around in a shoe box. "I suppose. So, what's new, Grecs? How's the job?"

"I pulled a weird one, Stevo. A guy steals about a half-million dollars from his finance company, which is located in WTC, then apparently gets the money from the banks using false IDs, and such, but then on 9/11, he disappears from the face of the Earth. The company thinks he died in the building."

"But you don't," Steve said, matter-of-factly.

"I don't know, man. There's something strange about the whole thing. They caught up to him and were going to meet with him on 9/11, but the craziness happened right before his meeting, and he was never seen again. I think two options–"

Steve broke in. "Dead or on the run?"

"Exactly."

"Where are you starting?" Steve asked, chewing on a fingernail.

"Security camera recordings from the banks when we figure out which ones he used," Greco said, pulling Steve's hand away from his face. "Will you stop? Your fingernails are finally growing. Let them be."

Steve let out a small curse at Greco and returned the fingernail to his mouth. "How do you figure out which banks, and then, how do you get the tapes?"

Greco moved to look out of the window. "I have a lot of paperwork to review to figure out which banks, and then I just have to contact them and work with the manager, I guess."

Steve spat a piece of fingernail across the room, and Greco shook his head. "You got any of the evidence with you?" Steve asked.

"Out in the car, why?"

"Is it official evidence, yet?" Steve continued.

"No," Greco said, flustered. "Why?"

"Bring it in. I'll search the paperwork, organize the data for you."

"No, Stevo, I can check it later," Greco said.

Steve cocked his head to one side and looked at his friend. "I don't really have anything else to do. Let me help."

Greco paused and thought for a minute, and then decided to let his friend be his partner again for this one. "Okay," Greco said, smiling. "I'll be right back." He left Steve in his hospital room and headed for the elevators, taking the first one that opened down to the parking level. He found his car, grabbed the evidence box, and within ten minutes of leaving, he was back on Steve's floor and aiming towards his room.

But there was a crowd around the room, and it scared Greco. He got closer to the door of the room, and then he saw Steve being wheeled out of the room in his bed by two men in pink tops and pants. He didn't get to see Steve's face as they were pointed in the opposite direction. "Steve!" he yelled, but there was no answer. A doctor followed them out of the room and down the hallway, reading a chart as he walked. He walked blindly into the back of one of the men dressed in pink. The two men exchanged apologies, and Greco watched with great interest. Then one of the men in pink turned and walked toward Greco.

"Are you Brian Greco?" he asked in a deep voice.

"Yes, wh-wh-what's going on?" Greco demanded.

"Nothing. Just some tests. He told me to tell you to leave the box in the room, and he'll look at them when he gets back."

"Oh," Greco said, disarmed. "Well, okay. Thank you. Stevo!" he yelled. "Good luck!" Greco watched his friend be turned down another hallway from the corridor he was in, only to disappear. He smiled as he turned into the room and left the box on a spare chair in the room. He took the elevator down to the parking level and started his course toward the relocated offices of Pickwick to speak to Jeanette Raines.

Chapter 45 – Return To Brindle

The start of the next step had already been taken earlier that morning when Will had stopped at a pay phone and made a call to the bus station to purchase a ticket. There was no direct route to Brindle as it did not have its own bus station, but the ticket he bought would get him close. When he pulled the rental car into the lot, he parked it right outside the front of the shed that Fahad had used as an office the previous day. Will was a little shocked to see Fahad come out of the office to meet him. He was wearing a pair of sunglasses to shield his eyes from the morning sun. Will wished that he still had a pair to lessen the glare from Fahad's balding head. Fahad grabbed Will by both shoulders and had a big smile on his face.

He greeted Will warmly and asked him how the car was, which Will said was fine and made no allusions to the fact that he had slept in the back seat the previous night and had a bruise on his back from the seat belt buckle. Will grabbed the rental agreement from his pocket and the two men went into the shed where Will was easily able to convert his payment to cash, and with a quick blessing from Fahad, he was on his way down the road to Wall Street and then over to Alaskan Way, where he walked along the waterfront, taking in the scenery once again before he left Seattle, probably for good, forever. He passed The Edgewater, Pier 66, where the big cruise lines boarded, and where Anthony's was located. He wished that he had more time. He would have loved to have tried Anthony's. He continued on, past the residences on the left and the marinas on the right, and then to the aquarium he had visited nearly two months ago when he first arrived in Seattle. He passed Waterfront Park and kept going, all the way into Occidental Square, where he zig-zagged streets until he found the bus terminal on King Street.

Will entered the terminal, walked to the ticket desk, and picked up the ticket he had reserved that morning. He paid cash, of course, and in twenty minutes, after checking his duffel bag with the attendant, he was on a bus, listening to the driver's monologue, once again, and eventually leaving Seattle. It was a little bittersweet for him because he had enjoyed his time there, but he knew it was time for him to go. There were too many people who knew him, and too much had happened there that could cause an issue. He thought about the guys on the *Seafarer* and was sorry he wasn't going back out on the boat with them that day. The first thing he had done that morning after he woke up and found a pay phone was to call Captain Pierce in his office, and explain to him the events of the previous few days, and that his time on the Seafarer was at an end. The captain already knew that Will would not be back and was not thrilled about breaking in a new rookie. However, he told Will that he had already replaced him in much the same way he had hired him. Will had remembered thinking that Inspector Charles Travis was sketchy, but at least he had gotten Will off the hook from the job, so to speak, and the Captain was able to hire someone to quickly replace him.

The bus had left at eleven-fifty that morning, and was headed first to Ellensburg, Washington, a trip that would take about an hour and forty-five minutes. Will slept through not only the trip, but the fifteen-minute stop there as well. When he awoke, he saw signs for Moses Lake, Washington, which was the second stop along the way. Will took the fifteen-minute break when they arrived at the terminal, where they used the restroom and bought some snacks for the road. The next leg of his journey was another hour and forty minutes away, and this time, he would land in Spokane, and when he got there, he had to change buses. Once settled in the new bus with him in the aisle seat and his bag getting the privilege of the window seat, Will stayed awake for the fifty-minute trip to Coeur d' Alene, Idaho, and then for another fifty minutes for the trip to Kellogg, Idaho, where the bus didn't even park, it just stopped for five minutes to let passengers on or off.

Will couldn't stay awake for the full length of the next trip, however. It was two hours and ten minutes to Missoula, Montana, and he was beginning to tire, so he let himself rest with the strap of his bag of possessions wrapped around his arm. When he had first looked at the time of arrival on the itinerary, he thought it was three hours and ten minutes, but then remembered he was crossing a time zone, which advanced the time by an hour in an instant. He slept for most of that ride but was awake when they arrived at ten past ten local time in the evening. They stayed long enough to buy some snacks and stretch their legs, and then it was on the move once again, this time to Butte, Montana, which was another two hours and ten minutes away. Will was about ready to get into some fresh clothes at this point, but the stop was not long enough to get his duffel bag from underneath the bus. He had bought another backpack, this one plain black, when he was in Seattle, and he had that with him on the bus, but it was full of cash and his stockpile of snacks.

The bus rolled out of Butte at twelve thirty in the morning on October 30th, and Will was beginning to get tired of riding the buses, but it was the only economical way to get to where he was going. Even though civilian air traffic was reinstated a few days after the 9/11 attacks, he wasn't ready to fly yet. Not that Brindle had an airport, but it was still too soon for him to fly. He would only get on an airplane for the sake of necessity if he had any say about it.

At one fifty in the morning, Will watched through the window as the bus pulled into a twenty-four-hour superstore parking lot in Bozeman, Montana. He had fast ideas of a quick shopping trip and maybe a change of clothes. His schedule was in his bag, and he didn't feel like digging it out. If he had, he would have seen that it was another quick stop, just to let two others get on the almost completely full bus. Will had been lucky enough to keep himself single-seated as people moved around the bus and added to the passenger list at the various stops, but he believed his luck may soon run out. Maybe others didn't want to ask him to move. Maybe it was his big, itchy beard that scared them away. Whatever it was,

Will liked it because it was working. The bus began to move again after the two new passengers had found seats next to each other just behind the driver, whose name was Franklin, at the front of the bus. Will knew the driver's name was Franklin because at every stop, he gave the standard directions and told everyone his name.

It took Franklin and the bus two hours and fifteen minutes to get to the next stop in Billings, Montana. Will was going to have to change buses again, but he was thrilled to see that his next bus did not leave for fifty-five minutes! He got his duffel from under the bus and went into the men's bathroom and opened the first stall door, and immediately closed it again. Apparently, the previous user of the stall, at least he hoped it was the last person to use it, may have had some motion sickness and deposited the results all over the toilet. He continued down the row of mostly locked doors and finally found an open stall in which to change his clothes. He rifled through his duffel and found a fresh pair of underwear, jeans, a new t-shirt, and his old black jacket. Once he had donned his new apparel, he grabbed his bags and exited the restroom as soon as he could. Now, even with fresh clothes, after spending time in that restroom, he still didn't feel so fresh. He still had some snacks leftover from his previous purchases, but he didn't want to pass up an opportunity to get more, since he was unfamiliar with the stops. He bought a few bags of chips and pretzels, and then selected a Danish with the rest of his change. He stuffed them all in his backpack and then bought two bottles of water from another machine and boarded the bus with ten minutes to spare. He propped his backpack in the window seat again, wrapped his arm again, and feigned sleeping so that hopefully he could keep the seat next to him open again.

Brandi, the new bus driver, advised that they were on their way to Sheridan, Wyoming, and that they would be traveling near Crow reservation land and Cheyenne reservation land, and that it was beautiful to see as the sun rose. She was right. As they were nearing the crossover point between the borders of Montana and Wyoming, the sun was rising and its light would poke itself out from behind the hills little by little when the land flattened, and then hide behind the hills again for a moment. Will noticed that after a few minutes, the sun was slowly winning the battle of its struggle to surpass the height of the hills, and although for Will it had been for many hours, the new day's light shone on the lands that he surveyed.

The stop in Sheridan was just a pickup spot with no duration, and the next stop was Buffalo, Wyoming, where Will had to change buses once again in a short fifteen-minute window. His new bus took him to Casper, Wyoming, and then to Douglas, and then to Wheaton, where the stop was actually a fast-food restaurant. They stopped to have a thirty-minute lunch break until just past noon. Will took advantage of it by getting his first real food since he was in Seattle the day before yesterday. Once everyone was back on the bus, Brandi spoke her piece, and they were off to Cheyenne, where Will would leave his fellow bus travelers behind. He began to get excited about the start of his new life, again. The bus pulled off the Interstate 25 expressway and then passed under it before it turned into the bus station, which was nothing more than a large gas station and convenience store. Will happily got off the bus, bid Brandi a happy farewell, and slung his bags over his shoulder as he walked into the convenience store.

The store was not a disappointment, and it seemed to have anything that someone may need at any time, quickly. There was food, fuel, and car accessories, and another fast-food place right across the road. The stop was on the outskirts of Cheyenne, but not too far from its hub. Will wasted no time and went up to the counter in the convenience store. There was a man in front of him in the line paying for his fuel, and Will grabbed a candy bar from the rack beside him. Off to the side was a group of older men who looked like they were possibly playing the lottery and drinking coffee. Will thought they just might be loitering. When the man before him finished his business and walked out, Will approached and smiled at the young man behind the counter.

"Can I help ya?" the man asked. Will looked for a name tag, but none was to be found.

"I hope so," Will said, placing the candy bar on the counter. "Do you know how I can get to Brindle?"

"Go an' take a right outta here to the twenty-five innachange, then head nawth and then go east on eighty, you'll run right into it. Fifty-some odd miles." He pointed up to the ceiling when he said "nawth," which made Will question the directions as a whole.

Will chuckled. "Sorry," he said. "I know where it is, but do you know the best way to get there? Are there any buses that run there? I see these train tracks out there; do they go to Brindle?"

He rang up the candy bar and looked at Will. "Eighty-fuh cents. Far as I know, the only way to get to Brindle is to drive if you got a car. If not, I'ma guessin' you can 'thumb it,' but I don't recommen' it. Cops don't like seein' vagabonds on the road 'round here. Dey'll pick you up if yous jus' walkin'."

Will took a minute to decipher and digest what he had heard. He would have to get a ride to Brindle. This was so much easier when he had his own car. "Okay, thanks. Oh, here." Will gave the man a dollar and got his change, which he dropped into a jar advertising a charity. He walked away from the counter and paused at a spinning rack that held maps. *Fifty miles. No way you can run it, even without the bags on your back. You're going to have to take a taxi. That could get pricey, though, and you need to– –*

"Hey," came a voice from behind him, almost whispering. Will turned to find one of the old men who was playing the lottery looking up at him. He had to be at least seventy, wore an old trucker's hat over his white hair, a pin-striped shirt covered by a yellow zipper jacket, and pants that appeared too big. "Hey," he said again. "Meet me outside." He turned and shuffled his way out of the store. Will watched him go and glanced at the remaining old men, who were suddenly interested in the tile on the floor or the panels in the drop ceiling overhead. Maybe "nawth" *was* up there. He walked out of the door and found the man leaning up against the convenience store, drinking his coffee. The man didn't wait for Will to reach him. He just started walking towards a car in the parking lot in front of him and said, "Fifty bucks."

"Excuse me," Will said, putting his hand up to his ear.

"I said, 'fifty bucks.' You want to go to Brindle? A cab will cost you about one hundred and forty bucks. I'll take you there for fifty." The man opened the driver's door of the car and got in, starting the engine. Will looked around and realized he didn't have many better options in front of him. He opened the back door of the car and tossed his bags in, and started to climb into the back seat. "Sit up here," the man said. "I'm giving you a ride, I'm not your goddamned chauffeur." Will sighed, closed the back door, and then took fifty dollars out of his wallet. He opened the passenger door and eased into the car, holding out the money to the man, who just let Will hold it for a few seconds. "Name's Edgar."

"Billy," Will said, and Edgar took the money from Will. He backed out of the parking space and followed the instructions of the clerk in the convenience store, and soon they were on Interstate 80. "Thanks for the ride, Edgar," Will said.

"You don't look like a Billy. And don't thank me until we get there. I might die between now and then."

Will looked over at Edgar and hoped he wasn't right on both statements. And then his brain took over. *Look, if he does die, and you can keep the car out of the ditch, you can stuff him in the passenger seat and still get to Brindle. Then let the authorities figure it out.* Will was surprised at himself for such a thought and cleared his head of it nearly as soon as it arrived. He wasn't sure if Edgar wanted to chat in the hour that it would probably take to get to Brindle, so he kept his mouth shut for the moment and just looked at the scenery of Cheyenne. They traveled for a while, and the land was mostly flat, as he remembered it from his first time through the area on his eventual way to Seattle. A house here, a mobile home there, and a travel center passes behind them on the left.

"Dah," came the noise from Edgar's mouth as he looked straight forward, hands on the wheel at ten-and-two.

"Something wrong?" Will asked, hoping to break the silence to help the trip along.

"Dah," he said again. "That travel stop charges too much for gas. They are on that side of the road, and their gas is four cents more per gallon than the one in Cheyenne. They try to get away with it from visitors, but people who live here, they know." He pointed to his head several times to indicate that 'they know.'

"Well, I guess since you know where to go for the cheaper gas, you're one of the smart ones," Will said, not sure what else to say.

"Damn right," he said, removing his right hand from the wheel with a wild arm wave, and then immediately replacing it upon the wheel in the 'two' position.

Will looked at the old man for a moment, and then his curiosity got the best of him. "So," he began, "do you just wait around the convenience store and look for people who need a ride?"

Edgar either cleared his throat or grunted. Will was not yet sure he knew the difference. "Happens more than you'd think. But truthfully, what Teddy said back there in the store wasn't completely true. Cops won't pick you up for walking. Teddy is my grandson, and he tries to get me extra money now and then. Hope you're not mad."

Will thought for a moment. *You have every right to be mad. You got swindled into paying this old man, Edgar, fifty dollars by his grandson, who worked at the convenience store.* Then he relaxed. *But who are you to judge? You're a criminal. And what other choices did you have? The hundred-and-forty-dollar cab ride? Teddy and Edgar did you a favor.* "I'm not mad at all," Will said. "I don't begrudge anyone for trying to make ends meet."

"Oh," Edgar said. "Well, then, you're a good kid. What's that hat you have on, there? Baltimore? Is that where you're from?"

"Philly," Will said. It was getting easier to be Billy Lomax. "I'm just a Baltimore fan from Philly." He looked out the window, hoping he could find something about which to ask a question to take the focus off himself, but Edgar was too quick.

"What are you doing out here?" Edgar asked.

"Visiting a friend," Will said, not sure of why. He just wasn't prepared to answer questions from Edgar.

"Your friend couldn't come pick you up?"

"Ehh, it's kind of a surprise visit," Will said. "I doubt they know I'm coming."

The noise came from Edgar again, from deep in his throat, and again, Will was not completely sure of the purpose. "Well, that's a nice surprise, I guess. Showing up unannounced."

"I guess we'll see when we get to Brindle," Will said.

"Well, we're nearly there, okay? Any particular place you want to go?" Edgar's right arm came flying wildly once again, and then again, returning to the safe haven of the wheel. Will thought back to his previous trip to Brindle. He could go to the Motel Brindle, where he stayed before, he could revisit the pizza place, and then there was the liquor store. He wasn't sure either of those was the right answer at the time, so he compromised.

"You can leave me at Acorn and Third street," He said. "I can walk from there," Edgar grunted, and Will hoped that was acceptance. When they arrived at the corner that Will had requested, Edgar slowed to a stop, put the car in park, and took his hands from the wheel. He looked at Will and shrugged. "Thanks, Edgar," Will opened the door, stepped from the car, and told Edgar, "Good luck, and don't pull your scam on the wrong person!" He then gave Edgar an extra twenty-dollar bill and shut the door.

When Will opened the back door and grabbed his bags, Edgar said, "You're a good kid, Billy. Let me know if you ever need a ride."

Will smiled and closed the door, watched Edgar drive away, and looked around the town. *You made it. You're home. Now what? Home. Job. Life.*

***

At almost the same time that Will stepped out of Edgar's car in his return to Brindle, the surveillance camera located in a liquor store about two hundred miles from Will, and about two hundred fifty miles away from Russell, Kansas, in a town called Allston, would show a man entering the liquor store. Another camera would show that he would peruse the shelves of bottles until the store was empty of customers, and then withdraw a sawed-off shotgun from beneath his coat. He grabbed a bottle of apricot brandy from the far side of the store and approached the counter. He kept the shotgun low and almost behind him, and put the brandy up on the counter.

The cameras behind the counter and near the exit showed multiple views of when Terry Brewster, the clerk in the store, took the bottle to ring it up, and the shotgun was quickly raised by the man and pointed into Brewster's face. The video showed that Mr. Brewster slowly put the bottle back down on the counter and put his hands in the air. The man would motion at Brewster with the gun, and Brewster opened the cash register and began piling money into a bag. When the register was empty, Brewster set the bag on the counter and put his hands back in the air. The man took the bag from the counter, pointed the shotgun at Brewster again, and fired.

Chapter 46 – Box Of Lies

Greco walked through the mass of desks in Pickwick Finance's triage location, trying to find the one that said 'Donald Hartley.' Hartley was a Loan Officer within the Pickwick company and had thirteen years' experience in his position. Greco didn't really care about Hartley's experience, or even what he did on a daily basis at Pickwick. His interest in Hartley extended only to his assistant, whom everyone called Jeannie, but her real name was Jeanette Raines, previously the assistant to Willem Kelly. He finally found an office with Hartley's name on it near the corner of the building, and began to search the surrounding desks for Jeannie's, but the outer desks had no names on them. He went to the first desk he found that was occupied and asked if the woman could point out Jeanette Raines.

"That's me," she said. "How can I help you?"

Greco pulled out his badge and a business card and handed both to her. "Is there someplace we can talk in private?" he asked.

A confused look crossed Jeannie's face, and she looked toward Hartley's office. "In there," she said. "Mr. Hartley is out for the rest of the day." They walked into Hartley's office, and Greco closed the door. "Do you want to sit down?" she asked and pointed to a chair.

"Sure," he said, taking a seat in the leather swivel chair. "Thanks. Ms. Raines, how long did you know Willem Kelly?"

"Oh, I guess about three years? I became his assistant in June of ninety-eight, so, yes, just over three years."

"I see," Greco said, taking notes in his book. "How well did you know him?"

"Meaning?" Jeannie asked.

"Meaning, how well did you know him? Were you only work acquaintances? Did you go out after work together? Did you share personal information with each other? Have you ever been to his house? Has he been to your house? How well did you know him?"

Jeannie squirmed in her chair a bit and said, "Listen, Mr. Kelly and I were only professional acquaintances. No silliness. I'm old enough to be his mother! I think it's in bad taste for you to accuse a deceased man of these things!" Her voice got more and more shrill as she went on.

"Okay, easy, Ms. Raines," he said, trying to calm her. "I'm just here to find out some information. Do you know if Mr. Kelly was involved in anything sketchy or illegal?"

"Illegal? No, not that I am aware of."

"Do you have a picture of Mr. Kelly?" he asked. "From ID badges or anything like that?"

Jeannie shook her head. "We did, but it was all destroyed when the towers fell.

Dejected, Greco nodded and wrote. "Did anything seem strange or odd about him or his work?"

"Odd? I don't think so – oh, well, there's the mail," she said, as if finally remembering.

"The mail?" Greco asked. "What mail, and what about it?"

"Hold on one second," she said, and stood, and walked from Hartley's office to the main office area. She returned a moment later and handed him a stack of mail. "If anything came in the mail that was business related after, uh, after, well, you know," and her voice trailed off.

"Go ahead," he said.

"Well, if it was business-related, I redirected it internally or gave it to Mr. Hartley. But Mr. Kelly's personal mail, I kept that. I was going to give it to his wife, or mail it to her, you know, after some time."

"I see." Greco started flipping through the mail. He wasn't sure what he was looking for yet, but thought he would know it when he found it. But all there was in the pile was a lot of junk mail, advertisements, a small, padded envelope with no return address, and nineteen other standard business window envelopes from various sources. "Is there anything else?" he asked. "Anything you can think of at all?"

"No, not really," Jeannie said.

"Okay," Greco said as he stood. He was lightly scratching behind his right ear. "You have my card. If you think of anything, please call me."

"Certainly," she said, and they both left Hartley's office and went their own ways.

When Greco got back to his desk at the station, he checked his messages, but had none. He didn't think Steve would have gone through the information yet, but he was hoping. The truth was, Greco didn't really want this case. He wasn't sure it would lead to anything, but if it did, he wasn't sure he wanted to follow it. It just wasn't that interesting to him at that time, and there were bigger things going on, of which he would have rather been a part. Yet, he was a diligent and decorated detective for New York's finest, so he resigned himself to going through the process and looking at every piece of possible evidence to eventually find if there was a puzzle in which to fit the pieces.

The pile of mail provided by Jeannie Raines was his next task. He tossed the junk mail and advertisements for suit makers and jewelers, and began to open envelope after envelope, finding nearly all of them all next to useless. But he made a note of each in his book and wrote who it was from, when it was sent, and what it was about. He did think two of the pieces of mail were interesting. The first was a flight voucher for American Airlines. The note in the voucher explained that they were sorry that he could not take his scheduled flight to Ft Lauderdale on September 11, 2001, and hoped that this voucher for a free flight within the continental United States would satisfy him. The second was a past-due notice for a small locker in a self-storage facility, and he wondered why a self-storage facility in Kelly's name had a bill-to address that was not his home. He called the number on the bill, but an answering machine picked up, so he left a message with only his name and phone number. As he continued writing his notes, he was interrupted by Maryanne Woods, who helped around the station when someone needed to dig through dirt to find something.

"Greco," she said, and it came out 'Graykowe' because of her accent. She was a shapely woman in her early thirties, with dirty-blonde hair and striking blue eyes.

"Yo," he answered, and he straightened up in his chair. He watched her come into the room and once again rued the time he had asked her to go out for a drink. The worst part was that she declined with a simple response that she was busy. Greco took that to mean she wasn't interested, and he left it alone.

"I found the wife of your dead embezzler," she said, with a big smile on her face. "Here." She laid a small sticky-backed square of paper on his desk with a slap, so it would stick to the surface. She half-sat and half-leaned on the edge of his desk and looked at him quizzically. She had been trying to call the Kelly residence with the number provided to Greco by Pickwick, but there was always an answering machine. She did some searching, made a few phone calls, and found that Kathleen Richter Kelly was a dentist and no longer lived at the Kelly house. "Anything else you need on this one?"

"Ah, thanks," he said, looking at the paper. "Bradley Avenue in Meier's Corners? They were split?"

"Looks like it," she said. "Maybe some people aren't meant to be together, and maybe some are," she said with a wink. "Apparently, she's been renting that apartment for a few months now. Need anything else?"

He caught the wink and let it pass. "Where is the dentist's office?"

"On Victory, also in Meier's," she answered. "It's on the back of the sticky note. Greco, do you need anything more on this one? I got stuff to do."

"No," he said. "Thanks, Maryanne, you're a peach."

"I know it," she said in a matter-of-fact tone. "Call me if you need, you know," she paused and looked at him, and then said, "anything." She smiled again and turned to leave, and he could not help but watch her go. He thought that one day, he might try to make that call again. He should, he thought. Maybe she really *was* busy that day, and she had been rather flirty recently, so perhaps she was ready to give him a chance.

He hopped up from his desk, went out to his car, and drove out to Kathleen's dentist office on Victory Boulevard. He found it in a professional building that shared the space with a handful of other businesses. There was a doctor's office, a car insurance agent, the dentist office, and a copy center. Greco entered through the main lobby and followed the numbers on the doors until he found the dental office. He opened the door and walked into a waiting room with a windowed cutout in the far wall, and a young girl dressed in white on the other side of it. He walked to the desk and asked for Kathleen Kelly.

The girl must have been in her teens, twenty years old at the maximum. The name tag she wore said 'Kerry.' "Dr. Kelly is in the middle of a consult right now," she said. "Do you have an appointment?"

Greco smiled. "I'm not here for dental work," he said. "I need to speak to Dr. Kelly as soon as possible." He pulled out his badge and showed it to her.

"Wait here, please," she said. "I'll be right back. Have a seat." She disappeared behind a wall, and Greco took the seat closest to the window. After a few minutes, Kerry came back out and told him Kathleen would be out in a few minutes to get him. He thanked her and picked up one of the magazines that lay on the table next to him. It was an outdoor magazine with a story on white water rafting, one on hiking, one on living on a boat, one on mountain biking, and one on living in a log cabin in the woods. Before he could get into any deep reading, Kathleen appeared at the door.

"Mr. Greco, follow me, please," she said. He stood up and followed her through the doorway and down a hallway to a small room with a table and four chairs. They entered, and she closed the door, and then offered Greco a seat, which he took after she sat down. "What can I do for you, Detective?" she asked.

"Dr. Kelly, let me first say how sorry I am to hear about your husband's passing," he began. "That was a terrible day, and a lot of innocent people were victims of that tragedy."

"We were separated, but thank you, Detective," she said.

"May I ask when the last time was that you spoke to your husband?"

"The night before he died, on the phone."

Greco nodded and took notes as he talked. "Can I ask what you talked about?"

She took a breath, deeper than normal, and then exhaled. "If I remember correctly, it was just to say 'hello' to each other, and then we talked about a book I was reading."

"What book?"

"*A Painted House*, by John Grisham," she said.

"Any significance to that book?" he asked.

"No," she said. "It was just the book I was reading at the time. I was trying to finish it that night, and I was going to bring it to him the next day. Unfortunately, I had to work late that day and never made it to our hou– his house."

"Did he try to contact you on September 11th?" Greco asked.

"Not to my knowledge," she said. "What is this about, Detective?"

Greco scratched lightly behind his ear. "Dr. Kelly, I've been charged with investigating some illegal activity that your late husband was involved in. I can't give you any details right now, but were you aware of anything he may have been planning or doing?"

"Illegal?" she asked, incredulously. "Will? I don't believe that for an instant. MY Will? Will was one of the most straightforward and honest people I know. He was almost boring. I can't believe he would be involved in anything nefarious." She paused and exhaled, looking to the wall, and then the floor. "I don't think he'd have the guts to try to pull off anything illegal."

"Do you have a picture of Mr. Kelly?" he asked.

She cocked her head sideways. "Detective Greco," she said, "not that long ago, my late husband fixed me an Italian dinner, complete with a bottle of wine, and in the middle of it, told me he thought we would be better off separated. If that had happened to you, would you have kept the picture of the person who said that to you?"

"Hmmm..." he said. "Dr. Kelly, did you and your late husband have a public storage locker on Moore Street in the city?"

She looked at him and slightly opened her mouth. "Public stor–, no. Nothing like that. Detective, if you can't give me any details about the issue, I am afraid I'm not going to be much help. Now, I have to go, because I have an extraction waiting for me in the other room."

Greco sighed. "That's okay, Doctor. I understand. Do you mind if I come back at another time and resume our talk if I have more questions?"

"If you think it will help," she said. "But I'm not sure why you're investigating my dead husband. What do you gain?"

"I'm not sure yet. Thanks, Doctor," Greco said. "I can see myself out. Have a nice day, and, uh, enjoy that extraction." Greco left Kathleen's office and headed back to the station. He sat at his desk and looked through his notes, trying to make sense of it all. He didn't have any proof yet, but he had a strange feeling deep down that Willem Kelly may not have perished on September 11th. He knew it was going to take time to figure it out, and then if he did figure it out, what was next? How was he going to track down a person who vanished into a cloud of dust and didn't want to be found?

The buzzer on Greco's phone brought him out of his thoughts and back to the reality of the day. He sat back up in his chair, grabbed the receiver from its cradle, and addressed the caller.

"Greco," he said.

"Mr. Greco, this is Robin calling from Quick-Key Storage, returning your call. How can I help you?"

"Hello, Robin, this is, uh, Detective Greco with the NYPD. Are you the manager or the owner of Quick-Key?"

"I am the manager. Is something wrong?"

"I don't know," Greco said. "That's why I'm calling. Can I get your last name, please?"

"My last name is DeCinces," she said.

"Ms. DeCinces, I have a past-due bill here on my desk addressed to a Willem Kelly. What can you tell me about Mr. Kelly?"

"Hold, please," she said, and there was a thud of the receiver hitting the desk, then the rustling of papers. *"Mr. Kelly opened his contract on June 14th of this year, and he paid the June and July installments, but nothing since."*

Greco thought for a moment. "When are the monthly bills due?"

"The invoice payments are due a rolling month from the day the account is opened. So, the first invoice from June was due on July 14th, the July invoice was due August 14th, the August– –"

"August was due September 14th, got it. Did he close the account?"

"Well, that's the weird thing. He never closed it, but there is a note here that one of our crew found the locker wide open one day. There was nothing inside; in fact, it was spotless, ready to rent again."

"It was open with nothing in it," Greco repeated. "Anything else?"

"The key for the lock was on the ground near a storm drain."

"Ms. DeCinces, do you have surveillance cameras at your facility?"

"Yes, but they are mostly visual deterrents, only," she said. *"The one at the entrance works, but the rest, they have not worked in years."*

It was all Greco could do not to throw his phone across the room. He exhaled into the phone and cringed before he asked his next question. "How far back do the recordings go?" he asked.

"The tape lasts one week," she said. Greco's phone was further nearing its demise after an imminent heave against the nearest wall, but then she continued. *"We keep the tapes*

for years," she said. "We keep them in a storage locker right here on the premises."

"Would I be able to view the tape from the week of September 11th?" he asked, hopeful.

"Of course, Detective. When would you like to view it? I'll need some time, but I'll make sure it is here for you when you arrive."

"Would tomorrow work?" he asked, once again hopeful.

"Sure," she said. "We open at seven in the morning, so anytime after that and before ten at night."

"Great," he said. "I'll be there tomorrow. Thank you, Ms. DeCinces." He hung up the phone and put his arms in the air triumphantly. If he could get an image of Willem Kelly at the Quick-Key, he'd accomplish two things. He'd prove that Kelly was still alive, and he'd know what Kelly looked like, which right now seemed to be a nationally guarded secret.

He sat at his desk thinking while twirling a rubber band around his opposing index fingers. He was still trying to put it all together, but there was still no proof of anything in any direction. The rubber band snapped and fell on his desk, next to the pile of mail. And then he saw the padded envelope given to him by Jeanette Rains with the rest of the mail. He took it from the desk, ripped the perforated top from it, and inside were three pieces of identification for someone named Shannon Fife. There was a New York driver's license with an address listed in Kips Bay, a work identification for Shannon Fife for Replications Printing Company on Lexington, and a video rental membership card for Shannon Fife for a video store Greco had never heard of before.

He looked at the identification cards. The man on the front was fairly young, probably early to mid-thirties. Greco thought he didn't look like a Shannon. Maybe a Mark, or a Bill. He took the cards, headed out to his car again, and looked for the residence in Kips Bay. He found the place and pulled the car into an alley right between the building and a fire station. The bottom floor of the building was occupied by two businesses. There was a sushi restaurant on one side, and a massage parlor on the other. Greco took the middle option and went inside to the lobby of the apartment building above. He scanned the names on the mailboxes for a "Fife," but there were none so named. He wasn't going to waste time knocking on every door, at least not yet. He got back in the car and then drove over to the business on Lexington, which was not called Replications Printing Company, but instead was a children's clothing store.

When Greco was done pounding his hands on the steering wheel, he looked at the video card just in hope that it would offer some sort of clue. It did not. He drove back to the office, completely confused and angry. It wasn't because of the plethora of dead ends, as he had been through many of those before. It was because he knew, deep down somewhere, either in his heart or in his brain, that Willem Kelly was a criminal, a thief, a fraud, and alive. And Greco knew Kelly was getting the best of him.

He got back to the office and tucked the ID cards into an expandable file that he had put the mail into earlier. When he got the box of Pickwick evidence back from Steve, he'd put it all together and either throw it into the Hudson or use it to solve the case. He was hoping for the latter, but for a second imagined himself tossing the box of lies into the river and watching it as it floated for a while, but then, as the box began to saturate with the water from the river, it tilted to one side a little. And then, it tilted more and more, until it turned sideways from the weight of the water within, and then completely submerged, never to be seen by human eyes again. The water that originated in the Adirondack Mountains would engulf it and slowly, methodically, sweep it all out into the Atlantic Ocean.

Greco was enjoying his fantasy of the water-logged box of nonsense floating out to nevermore when the blinking red light on his desk phone caught his attention. He picked up the receiver, thankful that he had not launched it across the room earlier, and hit the flashing button. After a beep, the raspy voice of Steve Angelucci entered Greco's ear.

"Hey Grecs, it's Steve. Listen, I went through all that stuff in the box, and there are eleven loan applications for eleven different banks. This guy was either thorough or careful, or

maybe both. Dangerous combo. Anyway, I had the nurse fax the list over to the office. Take a look. Let me know if you need anything else."

After another beep, Steve was gone, and Greco's phone was left dangling from the edge of his desk. Greco had bolted from his chair to the telecom room where the facsimile machine was located. He looked through the pile of papers discarded by others, and fourth from the bottom was the list that Steve had sent. Greco raced back to his desk and, one by one, called all eleven banks to request the security system videotapes from June through September of 2001. When the last call was made, he hung up the phone, sat at his desk, and mumbled to himself, "I'm gonna catch you, you little bastard."

Chapter 47 – Fortuitous

Rocky was serving a family of four a large extra cheese with mushrooms on half when she spotted what seemed to be a somewhat familiar face near the counter at the front of the restaurant. Once she finished at the family's table, she made her way through the tables, glanced at Will, and walked through a swinging door on the other side of the restaurant that led to the kitchen area. He watched her go, but never saw her reappear, until she came up behind him at the counter.

"Can I help you?" she asked. Will nearly jumped out of his shoes when she spoke, and turned around to see Rocky looking at him, eyebrows arched, and her jaw moving slowly and sideways as she chewed on a piece of gum.

"Uh, yes, I was– –"

"Where do I know you from?" she asked, her eyes closing into a squint.

"Here, I guess," he said. "A couple of weeks ago, I stopped in to have some dinner."

"Hmmm," she said, eyes still squinting.

He rolled his eyes and said, "You and your friend said I looked..."

"Like John Cusack!" she said, and started laughing. "Now I remember. So, Lloyd Dobler, what can I do for you?" she asked, laughing at her own joke.

"Well, I'm thinking of hanging around Brindle for a while, and I'm looking for a job. I was wondering if you were hiring?"

She made a 'tsk' noise with her mouth and said, "Sorry, Vince Larkin. This here well is a bit dry. In fact, if you came to Brindle looking for work, I have to tell you that there's not much out there. I have given up some of my hours to keep a few others on the payroll here. Half the time, I work for free."

"Oh, well, that's nice of you. Do you know of anywhere that might need some help?" He was beginning to think his little charred book of towns and his perception of its direction to go to Brindle may have been misread.

She exhaled into the air through her pursed lips, and the breeze made her hair blow. "You can try D&J Liquors over on 2nd. Perry at Motel Brindle is usually looking for a maid, but you don't really look like the sheet foldin' type. There's, uh, Tumbleweed, that's a restaurant on the other edge of town, they might need a dishwasher or something. Other than that, check the want ads in the paper, or run for public office."

Will thought the last part was a joke, but he wasn't completely sure. "Mayor Billy," he said, and they both chuckled. "Well, thanks anyway," he said. "I'll probably give those other places you named a try." He turned to walk out the door, and she stopped him.

"Hey," she said. He stopped and turned to face her. "I don't think you look much like John Cusack at all," she said.

"No?" he asked.

"Nope." She turned and walked toward the kitchen, but then turned back to him. "You're much cuter," she said, smiling, before disappearing behind a wall.

"Hmph," he said, and turned to leave the pizza restaurant. He walked a few blocks east and passed D&J Liquor, but there was a hand-written sign on the door that said, 'Lunch, back at 3:00 PM!' so he kept walking. He passed a national chain motel and asked the manager for an application, but she said she was out of them, and they weren't hiring anyway. Then he found the Tumbleweed Restaurant and got similar results. He kept walking, though his bags were beginning to weigh heavily on him, and he noticed he was tiring, and walking slower than usual.

A few blocks ahead of him, still going east, was the Motel Brindle, where he had stayed when he passed through town the first time. He stopped in the office and spoke with the desk clerk about a room. When asked for how long, he said for a week, and reserved the room on his fake credit card, but confirmed he could pay cash when his stay was up. He then approached her about possible employment, but before he got the words out of his mouth, she was shaking her head.

There was nothing available, but he could fill out the application if he wanted, in case something opened up. He politely declined, took his room key, went to his room, and finally ditched the heavy bags containing everything he owned. It was nearing three o'clock in the afternoon, and he wanted to go back to the liquor store, not only to ask about a job, but also to get some beer.

He lay back on the bed for a moment to rest his eyes, but he rested them too long and woke up at a quarter past five in the evening. He cursed himself, twice, and made himself look presentable in the clouded bathroom mirror. He headed out of the room, careful to lock the door, and began the half-mile walk to D&J Liquor. When he got to the store, the same clerk who had helped him last time was working again, and he was sipping on a drink from a cup with a straw. On the side of the cup in bold red letters, it said 'Pit Stop.' Will thought that the previous encounter with the clerk could only help his chances of landing some work. He went to the cooler, grabbed a thirty-pack of light beer, and approached the counter.

"Hey there," Will said.

"How do?" asked the clerk. "This be all?"

"For now, yes," Will said, not wanting to seem too eager.

"Nineteen seventy-two," the clerk said.

"Good year," Will said, and the clerk looked at him with an odd face.

"That's what I always say," the clerk said.

"I figured. You said it the last time I was here," Will said.

"Do I know you?" he asked.

"I came through a couple of months ago," Will said.

"Oh yeah. How's that cab running?"

Will grimaced. "It caught on fire and burned. With a lot of my stuff in it."

"That's too bad. Where'd this happen?"

"Seattle," Will said.

"Dang. That's pretty far."

"Yeah, came home from work one day and it was toast," Will said.

"Dang, again."

"Yeah, well, what are you gonna do?" Will said. "Hey, let me ask you a question."

"Shoot."

"You wouldn't happen to know anyone around here looking to hire anyone, would you?" Will asked.

"Well, you can try the Tumbleweed, or one of the hotels. Maybe Rocky's Pizza Oven. What do you do?"

"Anything really. I'm pretty active, I don't mind lifting, and I have a background in accounting."

The clerk looked at him. "Accounting. Like, you can do the books for a business, keep everything straight?"

"Sure," Will said.

"I guess you wouldn't wanna work here, would you? The wife and I never really have time to get everything straight. Got a box full of receipts and bills back there that need attention."

Will was a little giddy at the concept of working with numbers again, but he wasn't sure he wanted to dive right back into the work full-time. On the other hand, what choice did he have right now?

"Sounds good to me. Maybe I can stock shelves or something as well."

"Now that sounds good to me!" the clerk said. He offered his hand to Will. "Name's Jim," he said.

"Billy," Will said, taking the hand. "Billy Lomax." The two men shook hands and went through the particulars of what Will would be doing and how much he would earn. When he was doing the books, Will would earn thirty dollars an hour. When he was working in the liquor store itself, he would earn eight dollars per hour. Will did some quick math and guessed that it would take him probably five hours per week to do the books, which was one hundred fifty dollars, and assuming he got the other thirty-five hours on the floor, that was another two hundred eighty dollars, all before taxes, of course. That was assuming he was forced to pay the taxes. He had a concern about William Lomax suddenly showing up with no history. But he'd worry about that when the time came.

"When can you start?" Jim asked.

"How does tomorrow work for you?" Will asked. "The sooner you get your books squared away, the better off you'll be."

"Tomorrow's fine. Here, take this, fill it out, and bring it back tomorrow with your driver's license. Or hell, just show it to me now, if you want. Just gotta make sure you're you, is all." Will did as requested, and Jim looked at it for a second, and then looked at Will. "You look better with the beard," he said, laughing.

"I think so, too," Will said. He picked up a newspaper from the rack next to the counter. The headline on the front page read:

'ALLSTON LIQUOR STORE ROBBERY
TURNS DEADLY, CLERK KILLED'

"What's all this?" Will asked.

"Yeah, some old boy up in Allston got his head permanently removed by some fool with a shotgun. They said the clerk did everything right, didn't trip the alarm, gave up the cash, and the fool still blew his head off. This area is getting silly with the crazy crimes. There was a bank holdup in Russell, down in Kansas, and a guy who was just there to cash his check got killed."

Will looked through the story and then at Jim. "Are you worried about anyone pulling this on you?"

"Nah, not really. We're a quiet town and don't get too many drifters. People come off the Interstate out there and stop by to piss and eat, but they usually move on with no trouble. Well, except for the Rusty Rail on the northwest edge of town. Plus, I have a little bit of retaliation under the counter here. It's aimed to shoot right through the counter if anyone tries anything."

"What's the Rusty Rail?" Will asked.

"The Rusty Rail is pretty much the only black eye of Brindle," Jim said, shaking his head. "These two boys from up over in Diggs own it. It's not even really in Brindle. Diggs wouldn't let 'em have it there, and Brindle didn't want it either, so they put it right on the outside of Brindle, just across the railroad tracks. It's a hole. There's always fights, and I think they just force you to drink whiskey. I avoid it."

"Ugh, probably a good idea," Will said. "Well, I'm going to take my beer and hit the road. I will see you tomorrow, sir! Oh, what time?"

"How about ten in the morning? You'll do some stocking and then hit the books."

"Sounds good," Will said. "Oh, while I'm here, do you know of anywhere that is renting a place to stay? I'm in the Motel right now, and I think that might end up getting pricey."

"Check the paper, there," Jim said. "Or you can try Brindle Park over on 4th. And then, of course, there's the mobile home park on the east side of town. There's usually one or two for rent over there."

"Thanks, Jim. See you tomorrow!"

Jim took a drink from his soft drink cup. He swallowed and said, "Yup." Will left the liquor store and decided to head back to the Motel to get his beer from the refrigerator to stay cold. He thought about getting a cooler and taking advantage of the free ice, but he decided against the extra expense. He left once again, and it was just past six o'clock in the evening. He wanted to try to get his living situation squared away as soon as he could, so as not to waste money in the Motel Brindle. As he walked toward Brindle Park, he admitted to himself that walking everywhere was getting tiresome and old. He didn't mind walking, but a car would be more efficient for getting around town. He wasn't sure that was in his budget yet, and he was still unsure of his new identity and how buying a car and having it in his name would be affected.

He made the turn at the corner of 3rd Street and walked up to 4th, and found Brindle Park. It was a cute set of one-floor residences surrounding a courtyard and a pool. However, when he stopped in the office and asked about openings, he was told they were all full at the time. He thanked the woman at the counter and continued up the street until he found what he believed was the mobile home park. He entered the park and walked up and down the rows of sporadically placed mobile homes, some of which were actually just recreational vehicles. There were about twenty mobile homes, and most of them looked like they were well-used and currently in use. He did not find anything available, however, and began his long walk back to the motel. He took a different route than he did on his walk to find a place to live, and it was fortuitous that he did. On 6th Street, he was walking by a house, and saw a yard with a recreational vehicle in the backyard. There was a large 'For Sale' sign attached to the front of the shutter covering the front window.

Will stepped up to get a closer look to see if there was a phone number to call, but there was not. He walked down the alley adjacent to the yard to see if there was anything visibly wrong with the camper. He didn't see anything in the body; the inside remained to be seen, and he didn't know about the wheels, axles, and framework. He thought that could probably be overcome with little or no effort, as the trailer only needed to be towed a thousand yards or so. As he was looking over the exterior, he heard a shout.

"Hey!" It came from the other side of the camper, and Will aimed himself back toward the front of the yard. "Hey there," it came again.

"Hello?" Will said, still walking. At the corner of the yard, he met the person who was sending out the call, and he raised his hand to wave. "Hello!" he said.

"How ya doin'?" the man asked.

"Good," Will said. "Just checking out the RV here. Are you serious about selling?"

"Sure am. Name's Gil."

"Billy. Hi." The men shook hands as men do. "Can I take a closer look?"

Gil opened the gate and motioned Will to come inside. "Sure," he said. "I've only had it for a few years, but the kids aren't campers, apparently. I only used it to go hunting. I can bunk with one of my friends instead of keeping this thing around. I need to free up the area in the yard, and I'll use the money to get the swimming pool the kids have been bugging me about. Here, let's go inside."

Gil unlocked the door to the camper and gave Will the grand tour. The camper was about thirty feet long and maybe eight feet wide. There was a sitting area near the rear of the vehicle and a dining area as well. There was a kitchen and a bathroom with a shower. As Gil went through the tour, he explained that the sofa in the sitting area, as well as the dining room table, could both be converted into a bed. Additionally, in front of the camper was yet another bed, this one full-size and up a small set of steps. They exited the vehicle, and Gil gave Will some extra information about the gray water tank, which held the drainage of the sinks, and then there was the black water tank, which held the toilet waste. Will thought it was a little cramped, but it might have actually been bigger than his apartment in Seattle.

"Well," Gil said, as they stepped back onto solid earth, "What do you think?"

"Looks good inside and out. How are the wheels and frame? Is it towable as is?"

"Sure is," Gil said.

"How much do you want for it?" Will asked.

"I'm asking twenty-two thousand," Gil said, causing Will's eyebrows to rise. "I bought it new for thirty-four."

Will thought about the number. *It seems like a big number, especially since it's one-third of what you have left from your ill-begotten cash stash. Plus, you have no idea how this will work on paper, of which you don't want to leave a trail. It was bad enough that you left a small one in Seattle, but trying to own a home in Brindle could definitely lead to trouble. Think of something, or live in the motel if they'll let you. Sure, it is a constant outpour of cash, but you're employed now.* Will stepped away and walked around the camper again, pretending to inspect it as he worked his brain. He knew it would be sufficient for his needs, at least right now. He ignored the voice in his head regarding the motel, but alternative options did seem like a decent idea. He walked back across the yard to find Gil.

"Gil," he said, ready to deal. "I'm sorry, but I don't have that much in my savings right now." Gil looked down at the ground and pursed his lips in disappointment. "But I have an idea that may suit both our needs. What if you rented it to me, indefinitely, and I paid you a cash sum every month? I'm starting a job tomorrow over at D&J Liquor as their accountant and stocker. I know it sounds like a weird mix, but it will work for now until I find something else."

"Workin' over there with Jim at the store, huh? Nice. He's good people. But as far as your offer, uh, no way, man. I'm sorry, but that doesn't get me closer to a pool. The one I want is gonna cost almost twenty thousand. I have half of that in savings, but I have to pay in full."

"So, you need ten thousand more dollars to get your pool installed, correct?"

"That's right," Gil said, hands and arms in the shrug position.

"Done," Will said. "I will give you ten thousand dollars in cash. You'll get rid of the RV, have the space in your yard, and you can start having your pool installed in time for next summer. That leaves the RV. You wanted twenty-two, I'm giving you ten, leaving twelve. I will also pay you three hundred dollars per month in *rent,* and you'll even out at your twenty-two thousand in three and a half years." Will looked at Gil with his eyebrows up and his head slightly cocked to the left. Gil looked at him with a wary eye, his right arm resting on his left arm, and his right hand stroking his goatee as he thought.

"Five hundred per month. When does that get it paid off?" Gil asked.

"Two years, but that's too aggressive," Will countered. "Remember, I work in a liquor store in Brindle. Let's meet in the middle at four hundred per month."

"Give me twelve now," Gil said. "And you got your four hundred per month. What's that work out to?"

Will calculated quickly. "Twelve thousand now leaves ten to be paid, and at four hundred per month, that's twenty-five months." Will looked around the yard and then back to the camper, and in the house's driveway that went into the back yard, he noticed a red pickup truck with a tow hitch. "Does that truck run?"

Gil pulled his head back with an inquisitive look on his face. "Yeah, why?"

"Okay, Gil," Will said with a grin. "Here's my final offer. Twelve thousand now, leaving ten thousand in the balance. Four hundred dollars per month, for twenty-five months, make it twenty-four to round it out and save me four hundred dollars. Finally, you tow it to wherever I decide to take it, probably right up the road here, and you invite me to a pool party next summer. You get rid of the RV but retain ownership until it's paid off, you get your pool, and you get a little bonus cash over the next two years." Will stuck out his hand, head cocked, and eyebrows raised once again. Gil looked at him with stern eyes and pursed lips, but the look eventually softened, and he took Will's hand and shook it. The two men then smiled and congratulated each other on their negotiation skills. They agreed that Will would provide half of the cash payment tomorrow, and the other half when the camper was delivered to its new home.

Will had finished the walk back to his motel room, and he grabbed a beer from the refrigerator, turned on the television, and found the fourth game of the World Series. The Yankees were up two-to-one over the Arizona Diamondbacks, which made Will happy. If the Yanks won the Series, he wasn't going to go whooping and hollering through the town, but he'd enjoy the moment of his hometown team taking the championship.

He sat there, on the bed, for a while, watching until the last pitch was thrown, and the Yankees claimed the victory. The Clemens-Rivera combination worked well that night, and the Yankees tied the Series at two games each. He thought about his day and what he had accomplished. He finished off a trip to Brindle from Seattle. He found a job that would help sustain his life in a place with which he was not too familiar, and he had a temporary, at least temporarily temporary, home to stay in, while he got settled.

Not a bad birthday, Billy Jack. You did well. Then he finished his beer, tossed the can across the room, where it landed directly in the trash can, turned the light off, and called it a night.

Chapter 48 – Trick Or Treat

Will woke up the next morning very refreshed and in a good mood. He was still happy about his accomplishments the previous day, and today was Hallowe'en. He loved Hallowe'en. It started when he was young, trick-or-treating around the neighborhood, and it continued all through his teen years, having parties for the local kids, and then even into adulthood. Will had organized Pickwick's first Hallowe'en party. The rule was, as long as it didn't affect your work, you could participate. He had refreshments brought in, and they even had a costume contest where everyone cast an anonymous ballot. Will even won once, when he dressed as the bearded lady from the circus.

This Hallowe'en was going to be different, he thought. Different town, different people, new experiences. He could only wonder what the day would hold and if Brindle really got into the Hallowe'en spirit. He threw on some shorts and a t-shirt, though he knew it might be a little chilly outside. He tied his shoes and locked his door at the motel, and he hit the road on a run to learn more about the town. He ran by an old gas station that was now just a mechanic's garage, and then by another station that wasn't anything anymore. The grass had grown over the pavement, the windows were boarded up, and there was a tree growing out of the ground where the gas pumps used to be. He ran by Tumbleweed's, a little glad he didn't find a job there, nor at the hotel to which it was connected. He liked the thought of working at the liquor store, and doing the books for Jim would hopefully keep the business afloat and in a better situation. *Making a difference.* There was a tool rental place, and a paint store, there was a church, and a little further down the road, there was an ice cream shop.

He kept going on his run, and he noticed, for the most part, that the business section was in the north part of the town, and the residential area occupied the south side. The high school was on the south side as well, which made sense. He passed by the Brindle fairgrounds, which looked as dormant as it did vacant. The town was small, but there was so much to see and learn about. He had seen the dilapidated and crumbling drive-in theater on the edge of town when Edgar drove him into Brindle. There was the grain company on the north part of town with gigantic silos that stretched into the sky, and there was the prefabricated house company with the humongous building on the southwest side. Will decided he would learn about it all.

He returned to the motel at seven thirty in the morning, took a quick shower, and put on clean clothes, only to head back out ninety minutes later to go to the mobile home park up the street from Gil's house. He had to be at the liquor store an hour after that, so he had to move fast. He half jogged to the mobile home park and half walked. He got to the office and knocked, and was told to enter by a voice within. Twenty minutes later, he walked out of the office with a rental agreement in his hand, which would allow him to park his 1997 Layton camper in spot D-5 for as long as he wished, and as long as he paid the land rental fee of one hundred fifty dollars per month, and the electric bill was his responsibility. He thought it might have been a little bit on the steep side for what equated to a lot, not much bigger than the camper, but it did have water, electric, and sewer hook-ups at the ready. After his initial expenses, assuming that his math was correct and he would get the hours he was expecting, before the electric bill, he would clear enough money to be considered gainfully employed.

On the way to the liquor store, he called Gil quickly and asked him to tow the camper to the D-5 space when he had time, and Will would bring the initial payment to him as soon as possible. Gil agreed and said he would do it that day and leave the key in a magnetic box underneath the pull-out steps under the entrance to the camper. They also agreed that Gil would hook up the water and power to make the trailer livable immediately. With four minutes to spare, Will reached the liquor store and found Jim behind the counter, counting money in the register.

"Hey, there," Will said.

"Morning, Billy." Jim looked at Will's black jeans and golf shirt as he walked by. "Overdress much? There's no one here to impress. It's just me," he said with a grin.

"I wasn't sure what to wear," Will said. "We didn't really cover that."

Jim took a drink from a convenience store cup. "I don't really care. You can come in here in shorts and a t-shirt or a tuxedo, as long as you're on time and don't steal from us."

Will stopped and went back to the counter. "The last thing I want is my hands dirty that way. You were kind to me, and I'll return that kindness. I won't steal from you." Will offered his hand, and Jim took it. "So," Will said. "Where do I start?"

"Well," Jim said, taking another sip from his cup. "We got a delivery this morning, and it's all in the back. It's through the doorway back there. The bathroom is to the right, the office is further in to the right, and the stock room is all the way back through a double door. You can access the cooler from there. All the beer goes in the cooler, and you can stock the shelves from inside the cooler. You see what's back there, and then check the shelf. If we need anything from a ½ case or more, fill the shelf from the back and store the rest. There are different colored paint markers back there. Mark the number of leftover bottles on the box in the upper right corner. Don't combine partial leftover cases. That way, I know what we have for inventory purposes when I do a count. Don't open a new box if there is a previous partial case. So, it's kind of a combo thing. Let's say you find a case of Charley in the back. It's back there because I ordered it, and I ordered it because either we need it now or we're going to need it before the next shipment comes in, back to the case of Charley. You'll see the full case of Charley in the stock that just came in. But you don't use that one yet. You look in the previous partial cases to see if we have any Charley. Let's say we don't. Use the new case if we need more than half of it on the shelf. Suppose we don't write the number of bottles on the case and stack it in the pile of partial cases. If we do have a partial case, use it to fill the shelf. For the previous partial cases, don't leave fewer than three bottles in a case, because it offsets the balance, and they may topple. And always mark the number of leftover bottles in the upper right corner. Any questions?"

Will was catching his breath from Jim's long speech, which he thought was odd because it wasn't even him who was talking. "No, I think I've got it. Anything else?"

Jim looked up at him from the cash he was counting. "Not right now," he said. "Get the stock put away first, and I'll show you the books later."

"On it," Will said and headed towards the door at the back of the store. He pushed through the door in the back of the sales floor and continued to a set of double doors. He pushed them open and walked through, and saw a truly beautiful woman standing near the stack of boxes on the floor with a clipboard in one hand and a pen in the other. "Oh, hi," Will said, a little surprised.

"Hey," she said. "You must be Billy."

"That's me," he said, walking over to her and softly shaking her outstretched hand. "Nice to meet you. And you are?"

"Daria," she said.

"Daria? That's a pretty name."

"Thank you," she said. "My parents gave it to me."

Will snickered a bit at the joke and looked around the stockroom. "So, this is D&J Liquor. Did Jim tell you what I'm going to be doing?"

"Stock and accounting, correct?" she said, counting boxes and writing numbers on a paper on the clipboard.

"Yes, ma'am," Will said. "I guess I'll get started."

"There's aprons over there on the rack outside the office. You don't want to mess up that shirt."

Will looked down at his golf shirt and back up at Daria. "Oh, great," he said. "Thanks!" He walked over to the rack and grabbed one of the aprons from a set of hooks, put it over his head, and pulled the strings around the back and into the front to tie them across his midsection. He pulled a small notebook and pen from his back pocket and began writing down the names of the various boxes of beer, whiskeys, rums, vodkas, syrupy mixers, and whatever else he found. Then he moved to the wall where the previously opened boxes were stored, and he wrote down the number that was written on the upper right corner next to the names he had written down for the new stock. He then took his notepad out to the sales floor, and next to each name he had written down previously, he marked how many bottles would fit on the shelf based on what he saw. He waved to Jim at the register, who was watching intently at what his new employee was doing. Will returned to the back room, knowing exactly what he needed to bring out to stock the shelves fully.

"Do you have a dolly or a hand truck?" he asked Daria when he got back to the stockroom.

"It should be over in the utility cabinet if Jim put it away. Be careful over there." Will walked over to the utility cabinet and opened the door. A pile of brooms, mop handles, dustpans, the hand truck, and if he hadn't kicked it away, there would have been a ladder that fell along with everything else that fell onto Will and knocked him to the ground. "Do you call that being careful?" Daria asked.

Will pushed everything off of him and got to his knees. "No," he said, laughing. "What was I thinking?"

Daria laughed and retreated to the office for a few seconds before returning. "I'm outta here," she said. "Have a good first day. Or a better first day, I should say. Just shove all that stuff back in there." Will made himself a vow to clean up and organize the cabinet, but later. He grabbed the hand truck and began to pile it with the boxes of alcohol that matched his notes. When the cart was full, he wheeled it out onto the sales floor and began stocking the bottles.

"Jim!" Will called out across the store.

"Yo," came the response from the cash register area.

"First in, first out? Or does it matter?"

There was no response for a minute, and Will considered calling out again. But then the hulking figure of Jim appeared and looked at the shelf, and then at Will. "What do you mean?" he asked.

"Well," Will began. "You have two rows of just about everything you offer as far as the hard stuff. If I bring everything to the front and put the new stuff in the back, it rotates, and the older bottles probably sell first."

Jim looked at the shelves again. "Sounds good. Do it if it works."

Will gave Jim the thumbs up and returned to stocking the bottles, and Jim returned to the front of the store. It was nearing noon, and the store would be opening soon. He went to the front windows where the seasonal displays were, and pulled on several strings which turned on the neon lights to which they were attached. Then he propped the door open with a door stop and returned to his soda behind the counter.

"So, I met Daria in the back. She seems nice," Will said.

"Yeah, she'll do," Jim said, smiling.

"Oh, I just put it together," Will said, rolling his eyes. "D&J Liquor Store. Daria and Jim."

Jim slid a carton of cigarettes into the shelf that hung over his head. "Can't put anything past you," he said with a snicker.

"So, are you guys married?"

"Yup," Jim said. "Just over four years now." He was still stocking the cigarettes into the shelf overhead. "You?"

"No, sir," Will said, then his lie immediately bit him in the heart as he remembered Kathleen, and all he could picture was her, standing on the front porch of their old house, *their* old house, John Grisham book in hand, knocking indefinitely. He knew, based on the events of that day, that the image he was harboring would not have happened, but that's what he saw. In reality, he thought that she would think he had died that day. He wasn't sure which was better or worse, but settled on her knowing in finality rather than wondering in perpetuity.

"Something wrong with those bottles?"

"Wha–?" Will asked, awakened from his daydream. "Oh, no," he said, and thought he would try to cover up his contemplation. "I was just checking this bottle. Did you know this stuff is made in Tennessee?"

"Sure did," Jim said. "Comes with the business, I guess. Now I have to ask you, are you going to read every bottle, because if you do, it's going to take you forever to get this store stocked."

"I'm on it," Will said, and got back to stocking the bottles and rotating them so the older bottles were in the front, and the newer ones were in the back. He kept this up until about one o'clock in the afternoon, and customers came in, and customers left, as they will do in a liquor store, and by that time, he was nearly finished with the stock, and Jim came in the back to see him.

"How's it going?" he asked.

"Good, I guess," Will said. "I'm nearly finished. Oh, do you mind if I organize the stack? You have some full cases hidden in the pile of partials. Might be throwing off your counts."

"Sure," Jim said. "If it will help you, go for it. Just make sure you tell Daria when she comes in on Friday."

"She doesn't work here every day like you?"

"Nope," he said, stretching his back. "She's a nurse on other days."

"Really?" Will asked.

"Yep. She works in the emergency department over at Brindle Health. Closest thing we have to a hospital here. The closest big hospital is in Laramie, over in Wyo. Closest one here in Nebraska is in Ogallala."

"Oga–"

"Ogallala," Jim said again. "It's east of here. Anyway, they are both too far to travel for her to work, so she stays in town and works at the Health Center."

"Well, that's interesting," Will said. "I suppose after a while, I am going to have to familiarize myself with the town if I am going to live here."

"Probably a good idea," Jim said. "Listen, I ordered lunch. Hope you like pizza. Bacon cheeseburger. My favorite."

"You're kidding," Will semi-asked.

"No, why?"

Will smiled. "Tell me you got it from Rocky's."

"I did," Jim said. "Why do you ask?"

"Because they make a great bacon cheeseburger pizza."

Jim looked at Will. "And you know this because..."

"First time through town, when I stopped in here, I was coming from Rocky's."

"Now, that's funny," Jim said. "Come on. Let's eat."

They sat near the front counter of the store, each taking a bite of the pizza and enjoying its flavors. Will noticed a bowl of candy on the countertop by the cash register, and he asked if it was always there, or if it was for Hallowe'en. Jim replied that today it was for Hallowe'en. For any other day, it was always there, except for Christmas, and then it was there for Christmas. When a customer would come in, Jim would handle the register, and if needed, Will would help them out to their cars with their fresh purchases. This went on for thirty minutes until Will stood up and claimed that it was time for him to get back to work. Jim retorted that he still had thirty minutes left.

"An hour for lunch?" Will asked?

"Yeah, why not?" Jim said. "Today, anyway. I make the rules here!"

A customer walked in the door, and the sensor at the door made its ding-dong noise. Jim put down his third slice of pizza, although he was only eating the toppings at this point. He asked the customer what he needed, and the reply was two thirty-packs of light beer, a fifth of Stubby's, a carton of King's cigarettes, and a deck of cards.

Will held his hand up to the customer. "I'll grab the beer and the Stub. Be right back." While he was gone, Jim pulled out the cigarettes from a rack over his head and told the customer to pick out which deck of cards he wanted from the rack under the counter. When the transaction was completed, the fifth of Stubby's, the cards, and the cigarettes were in a bag carried by the customer, and Will had the beer, one box held by each hand. He followed the man out to his car and deposited the beer into the trunk, just as directed. He thanked the man for his business and headed back into the store.

"Did you see that guy's boots?" Will asked.

"No," Jim said, replacing the carton of cigarettes in the rack. "Can't say as I've ever seen *him* before. Not in here, anyway, let alone his boots. What's so special about his boots?"

"Designer," Will said. "I couldn't see the brand, but they were nice. Colors were a bit off, though. Looked like a bowlin' shoe." Will realized he was picking up an accent. *No, that's not the right word. You're picking up 'lazy'. You've been here two days, and you're dropping your 'g's.* Will told his inner voice to shut up, but he knew it was right. His diction had changed. *Whatever,* he told himself. *Blend in.* "Okay," he said to Jim. "I'm going to get back at it. I have a few things to finish up here, and then I'll head to the back and clean up my mess--," he paused. "And yours!" Jim shook his head, and Will went to the back room.

Jim mumbled under his breath. "I'm getting to like that boy," he said. "Gotta be something wrong with him."

In the back room, Will took a look at the utility cabinet and decided it needed more help than what he could do that day. So, he stuffed everything back into the closet as neatly as possible, once again placing the vow on himself to organize it as soon as he could. Once he forced the doors closed on the closet, he popped a pen through the holes in the handles to help keep them shut. For the rest of the afternoon and into the evening, Will stocked the beer into the cooler and filled the empty spots in the shelves that had appeared when someone grabbed a six-pack or other product from the front through the cooler doors. He straightened and organized the entire stock room, every now and then asking Jim what he sold, and Will would refill it. When he was done, he noticed it was nearly ten o'clock at night. He'd been there for almost twelve hours and barely noticed it. At Pickwick, he'd have been watching the clock at ten in the morning.

He took his apron off and hung it on the rack with the others. He thought about taking it back to the motel and washing it before returning it, just so it would be clean, but thought differently at the end. He'd wait until he knew exactly what to do with it. He went into the restroom to wash his hands. The dust that accumulated on the boxes was now residing on his fingers, and looking back, he was glad to have the apron. He thought he might get a pair of work gloves to wear as well. He turned off the water and dried his hands on a paper towel, which he tossed in the trash can.

He heard the front doorbell make its noise again for what he assumed was a last-minute customer. *Oh well, one bottle that you'll have to replace tomorrow*, he thought. Will peeked around the corner between the door and saw someone wearing an orange and black pumpkin mask, and pointing a gun right into Jim's face.

"Trick or Treat," said the voice behind the mask.

Chapter 49 – The Ton Of Videotape

Michael Ilario got up from his chair and walked down the hall to the men's room. He stood at the urinal and prepared himself for the activity, and when the activity was completed, he arranged everything as it should be, and he closed off the world's possible view of the star of the previous show. He turned to the sink and washed his hands, dried them with the air dryer hung on the wall, and then rubbed his hands, front and back, on the back of his pants out of habit. He opened the door and walked back out into the hallway, and headed for the coffee room. It was a kitchen with multiple refrigerators, microwaves, and a toaster oven. There was a sink for washing dishes or for use as a water source. For some reason, it was just called the coffee room. He chose his beverage, which was actually a tea, brewed with water from the coffee machine and a tea bag he brought from home. He carefully carried the Styrofoam cup back to his desk and took his seat. He looked at the stack of files in his inbox and shook his head. They just kept coming.

Around the same time, Greco entered the evidence room, laid the videotape box on the table, and popped the tape into the receptacle in the viewer. The machine clinked and clunked for a minute, and then the image appeared on the screen. It was a poor-quality video of the entrance to the Quick-Key storage facility. Greco played with the knobs on the viewer and succeeded in only making the picture worse at first, but then eventually found the magic touch to make the images a bit clearer. He fast-forwarded the video to seven o'clock in the morning, and then sat back to watch it frame by frame. For an hour and forty-two minutes, Greco sat there and watched the same image on the screen. The camera pointed from the top of a fence post to a spot about fifty feet into the lot. There were full-size garage-type lockers on the left, and on the right, he could see a perpendicular set of rows of units.

The camera did not tilt, nor did it pan. It just pointed straight ahead to the same spot. Greco watched and watched, and saw nothing change. Then, when the clock in the upper left corner of the screen read 8:42:40, the screen jumped, as if there was some interference, and the image shook back and forth for a second or two. *Flight 11*, Greco thought after he noted the time, and he kept watching the video. Since the interference and the vibration occurred, nothing had changed on the screen. But then, when the time stamp on the video showed 9:03:02, the same thing happened. The screen flashed, and the picture shook, but then, for about twenty-two seconds, there was no picture. There was just a blank, black screen. Greco made sure the counter was still moving on the viewer, which it was. Finally, though, the picture came back through.

At the 9:07:12 mark, the camera shook again, but not with the same force it had previously. Seconds later, the image of a mini-van type taxicab rolled into the image, and then made a right turn down one of the rows of smaller units. Greco assumed that the shaking of the camera was from the gate to the facility opening for the taxi. Nothing happened on the screen again for a few minutes, and Greco was picturing the image of someone getting out of a taxi, opening the unit door, grabbing what was important, chucking the key, and rolling out in the taxi. No sooner did he get that sequence of images completed in his mind than the taxi appeared from around the corner of one of the perpendicular rows of storage units. He readied his finger over the 'pause' button, waiting for the exact right time to hit it so that he could read the license plate. It happened when the time stamp on the video read 9:12:17. He had a straight-on shot of the license plate, but the picture was too fuzzy. He couldn't read the combination of numbers and letters on the front of the taxi. He was also fuming because there still wasn't an image of Kelly's face in the camera shot. He must have been sitting in the back seat of the cab.

Greco leaned back in his chair and exhaled above his head, trying hard not to kick the stupid viewer into the following week. He looked outside the room, but didn't see anyone.

"Ilario!" he bellowed. Ilario was still at his desk, attempting to take the first sip of his third tea. The previous attempts led to nothing but a quickly burned lip. This time, when Greco yelled, it spilled down the front of his shirt. He got up and walked into the viewing room to find Greco in a chair staring at the screen.

"Yes, Detective?" Ilario asked, wiping the tea from his shirt.

"Look at this. Come over here. Check this out. I need this license plate. I need to be able to read the numbers on the plate. Can you work your magic?"

"Well," Ilario said, looking at the screen. "It looks pretty grainy. Hold on a sec." Ilario backed up from the screen and fished around in his back pocket until he pulled out what looked like a small magnifying glass. He held it up to the screen where the license plate would be on the car. "I don't know. All I can do is try."

"Well, try for Hell's sake, I need this! It's the only thing I have for my case!" Greco said, voice raised.

"I'm on it," Ilario said, and ejected the tape from the viewer. He pulled it from the machine and bolted down the hallway and into a room in which he disappeared quite frequently, often for hours at a time. Inside that room, he would zoom in on and zoom out from and examine and speed up and slow down the tape to a frame-by-frame level to see if he could get a clear image of the front of the car.

Greco looked into the ton of videotape he had brought into the viewing room with him, and grabbed the one that was labeled 'First Regional.' In the past three days, Greco had worked with the various managers of the associated banks, and together they figured out on what date a withdrawal was made by a Johnathan Bryce Harp, or a Lawrence Harold Shields, or a Ryan Charles Robertson. Asking the bank personnel would not be very useful, he thought, since they saw thousands of customers every day, and asking them to remember them a month later would be futile. So, each manager had made the security video of the date of the transaction available at Greco's request, and Greco had sent Ilario all over the city to pick them up. Greco decided he would look at them in chronological order of the date that each transaction occurred. That made First Regional exactly that; first. He popped it into the viewer and started watching.

He didn't really know what he was looking for, as he still had no idea what Kelly looked like. He felt, though, for some reason, he would know him when he saw him. Or at least when he got through half a dozen of the tapes, he might recognize someone.

He went through the first tape of First Regional Bank and scrutinized every person who had walked into and out of the bank that day, and everyone he saw, he felt like he had seen them before. He felt like he was getting nowhere fast. The video was not clear, of course, and he had a hard time seeing what he was trying to see. It had a bit of interference at one point as well, and the recorded image turned into large black and white z-shape images that he could not decipher. He shook his head and exhaled. He had had cases like this before where they dragged slowly, on and on, never seeming to go anywhere. However, then he would find *the one thing. The one thing* was that magical piece of evidence needed, or the account given by an eyewitness, or the review of something that he had reviewed before that didn't make any sense, but because he had more information, it now did. Once he had *the one thing*, he would know that he had his quarry dead to rights. He needed *the one thing* for this case of the missing Kelly. Once he had it, all he would need to do was find the elusive man on the lam.

As he watched, he took meticulous notes, as always. When someone walked in the door of the bank, he noted the time they walked in, and since the video was black and white, he could not use anything other than 'dark suit,' 'white shirt,' or 'light-shaded hat.' When he recognized them on the way out, he noted that time as well and calculated and noted the full amount of time in the bank. He finished the first video after about two-and-a-half hours and four cups of bad coffee, and an even worse doughnut.

Now he had his baseline of people who had entered and exited First Regional Bank on the day of the withdrawal. With high hopes, he inserted the second tape into the viewer, and after the popping and banging had been completed, the image of the bank entrance showed up on the screen. He watched intently, and as people came into the bank, he wrote down their appearance and whatever else he could see. At least this bank's video was in color, so he could write down 'brown suit' or 'red hat' or whatever else he could see about them. As he went through the second videotape, watched the increasing number of fuzzy pictures, and took more and more notes about the people, he was more and more impressed by Kelly's intellect when it came to selecting which banks from which to process the loans. He didn't use big banks. He didn't use Chase, Citi, Morgan, Deutsche, or Bank of America. He used smaller, more regional banks, like First Regional, Trust New York, Third Manhattan, and Secure America. *He really did his homework.* Greco wondered how deep Kelly's crimes actually went. Had he done research on these banks personally, or did he just know them from experiences he had at Pickwick? Greco wrote down another note and noted the time as well. *Slick bastard,* Greco thought. In the next moment, Ilario ran into the door jam, quite out of breath from his run down the hallway.

"You're still in here," he said, panting like a dog in August.

"Still here," Greco said, not taking his eyes from the video.

"I got a plate," Ilario said, sitting in an empty chair across from Greco, still wheezing.

"Shit, Ilario, did you just run the New York Marathon?"

"I ran to your desk first," Ilario said. "I knew this was important to you. When you weren't there, I ran over here."

"Well, what do you have?" As Greco grilled Ilario, on the viewer screen, a man in a dark suit entered the bank and went straight to the counter. He conducted a transaction. Later, it would be known that he was withdrawing nine thousand dollars from an account opened the previous day by Pickwick Financial Services in the name of Leonard H. Tanzey. The man then took his exit from the side entrance of the building, which Greco did not even know existed.

"Hey, is that a bank?" Ilario asked. "Those tapes are pretty cool."

"Yeah, it's a bank. What makes it cool?"

"The different channels and all, that's all." Ilario took another breath. "So," he started, "the plate." He was starting to breathe normally again.

"Forget the plate," Greco said. "What 'channels' do you mean? Wha-... what channels?"

"The different channels within the video. Most banks have them so you can see different areas of the bank at the same time." Greco looked at Ilario like he had four heads and several different channels himself. Ilario said, "Look, give me the... thingy," pointing at the wired remote that connected to the viewer. "Hit this button here, and the view changes. The timestamp stays the same 'cause it's running at the same time. They have the entrance you were looking at–" Ilario paused and hit the button. "And this looks like it's behind the counter where the tellers are. Oh, she's cute." He hit the button again. "Here's right outside the vault, and then this one looks like another entrance. See, the tellers are still on the left, but it's a different angle."

"Let me see that," Greco said, and when Ilario gave him the device, Greco hit the button, and the view changed to inside the vault entrance, and then to the customer service area, then to another view of the teller's desks, and then back to the first entrance again. "Son of a–"

"Greco, I'm kinda in a hurry, so...the plate? On the cab?"

Greco was still looking at the screen and hitting the button on the remote. "Huh. Uh, okay, the plate. What do you have?"

"Look." Ilario shoved a set of stapled papers toward Greco. Greco picked up the papers and looked at the first page for a moment, then the second, and then back again at the first.

"It's only partial," Greco said, and tossed the papers back across the table. "The last two letters are unreadable. There must be dozens of combinations that are possible."

"Two hundred and sixty," Ilario said, and then he smiled. "But I got one better for ya. I ran all two hundred and sixty options."

"Really?" Greco asked.

"Yep."

Greco smiled. "Hit me with it."

"The cab is registered to Union Taxi Company, over in the Meat Packing District. The owner is a guy named Joe

Falkenberg. He couldn't meet with you today, but he'll expect you tomorrow morning between nine and noon."

"Damn, Ilario," Greco said. "I think I owe you a lunch."

"Yes!" Ilario exclaimed. "Lunch on Greco! Pizza time! Oh, well," Ilario paused. "Well, tomorrow?" Ilario asked. Greco looked at him sideways. "Well," Ilario stammered. "I already brought mine for today."

Greco arched his eyebrows, but then smiled. "Tomorrow works for me. We'll make it a working lunch."

"Uh, a worki–" Ilario started, but Greco cut him off.

"Don't make me rescind the offer, Ilario," Greco said, and went back to watching his video. Ilario quietly slipped out of the room and went to his desk. He sat there for a minute with a puzzled look on his face, and then shook his head. He opened the drawer of his desk that was next to his knees and pulled out a small dictionary. He looked up the word 'rescind,' and then put the book away. He felt like lunch with Greco was still on, or at least fifty-fifty. He'd bring a bag lunch tomorrow anyway, just in case.

Greco returned to watching his video, but he backed it up to the point where Ilario had first come into the room. Every few seconds thereafter, he would flip the channel in the video, looking, searching, *examining* to find anything he could. He watched a man in a dark suit enter the bank and go to the counter where the tellers were located. Greco flipped the channel and tried to see him from the teller's camera, but the man was turned away. He quickly tried to flip through the channels to get to the other view of the tellers' station, but he bypassed it once, and tried to flip through the channels again quickly, but he passed it again. Greco made himself calm down and take it one at a time. Once he got around to the view he was looking for, the man was gone from the station. Greco thought about rewinding the tape, but as he moved back to the channel he wanted, he stumbled onto the view of the second entrance, and got a full face look at the man as he exited.

He looked so familiar to Greco. *Who is he? Have I seen him before?* Greco thought for a minute and ejected the tape and replaced it with the one from First Regional back into the viewer. He was disappointed to see that this tape only had four channels. After forty more minutes of viewing the tape again, he thought he had a decent shot *of the same man,* but he couldn't be sure.

"Ilario," he yelled. "Ilario!"

"Yeah, Grecs," Ilario said, standing at the door.

"Can you get me a side-by-side image of these two tapes at the times and channels I have here? A clear one?"

"I'll try. That one is kinda grainy. Be right back."

Ilario took the tapes and Greco's note to his back room again and disappeared. A few minutes later, he appeared back from the doorway, carrying the tapes, Greco's note, and a freshly printed picture on an eight-and-one-half-by-eleven sheet of paper. He got to the viewing room and handed it all to Greco, who picked up the picture and stared at it. When Ilario tried to speak, Greco shushed him by holding up a finger. Greco kept staring at the picture of the two men, *the same man,* side by side. *Where have I seen him before?*

"Wait here!" he shouted at Ilario. Greco bolted out of the room, to the staircase, and up one floor to where his desk was located. He rifled through the papers and the piles of reports, knocking one stack to the floor, until he found what he was looking for. He grabbed it and headed back down to Ilario and the viewing room as fast as he could. "Ilario," he yelled. "Look at this." He gave the printed paper back to Ilario, who took it and looked at it. Greco opened up the small, padded envelope addressed to Willem Kelly and pulled out the driver's license for Shannon Fife, and gave it to Ilario. "Now, look at this."

Ilario looked at the side-by-side image and then at the driver's license. He pulled out his small magnifying glass and checked them again.

"Hmph," Ilario said. "Same guy."

Greco exhaled. "I'll be damned," he said. "That's my guy."

Chapter 50 – Roadwork For Change

Will poked his head around the door and saw the person with the gun, and he saw the gun pointed at Jim. Jim seemed calm enough, though, and Will thought it was probably hard to be calm with a six-shooter staring you right in the face. He tried to think of what he should do, and the only thing he came up with was grabbing a bottle of booze from the stock room and winging it at the assailant. *Probably not the best plan, idiot. You're intelligent. Use your brain. You should just go hide in the bathroom.*

Will pushed that thought out of his head. He wasn't going to let the store get robbed on his first day. He needed the job, and employment around town was thin. He decided he would at least *try* to stop the robbery, especially before it got bloody. He snuck into the back room and looked around. He didn't have much time. He remembered the flashlight in the utility closet, but he didn't dare open it. The noise alone would draw attention, and he didn't need that. He looked in the office for anything that might give him an idea. But nothing was screaming out to him. He went to the back door of the storeroom. It was a grey, metal, heavy door that had a push-release bar bisecting it. He looked at the door and around the metal frame that held it, and saw the sensor, which was mounted to the frame, and the other side of the sensor, which was mounted to the door. He assumed that if the door were opened, an alarm would go off, which would probably spell bad news for Jim. Next to the door was a grey metal box with a keyhole and a red light, which was illuminated. Will thought that the box had to turn off the sensor, though there were no wires connecting the two that he could see. He was hoping anyway.

He snuck back toward the doorway to the front of the store and checked on Jim. Now there was a problem. A late-night customer had come into the store, and now the robber was waving the gun wildly between the two. He ordered the customer closer, and when the young man got closer to the robber, the robber whacked him in the head with the butt of the gun. Will could not hear what was being said by anyone, but he sure heard the sickening sound of the butt of the gun hitting the young stranger in the head. The gun was then pointed back at Jim. Jim was standing there with one hand up, and then with the other hand, he packed a carton of cigarettes into a bag. Then he opened the register and started pulling out the money. Will knew time was short. He picked up the phone on the desk, heard a dial tone, pressed 9-1-1, and then placed the receiver in the desk drawer. In the same drawer, he found a set of keys. If these didn't open the back door, he'd have to think of something else. At least the police would come, he hoped.

He walked to the back door, and the second key on the ring he tried fit into the lock. He slowly turned it, and the red light in the box went off with a quiet click. Will pushed the handle gently, and the door opened. No alarm. He grabbed the handle of the door, shut it quietly behind him, and snuck quietly to the side of the building. In the alleyway next to the liquor store was an older model Chevrolet Monte Carlo, which Will did not remember seeing before. *Get away car? Maybe. Maybe it belongs to the other customer. Best to leave it alone right now.* He kept his body close to the wall and was about ten feet from the corner toward the front of the store when he heard a *boom* sound from inside the building. Will stiffened and imagined the worst. The robber's gun? Had he shot Jim? Or the customer? Or was it Jim's gun, and the robber was shot? He heard some yelling, and then a soft 'ding dong' noise. Someone either entered or left the store and crossed the invisible beam that made the noise when tripped. Off in the distance, Will heard the siren of a police car or a fire engine. He hoped it was the police, or at least an ambulance, for whatever had happened in the store. He heard footsteps coming at a fast rate of speed. He pressed himself up against the wall. When the footsteps reached him, he recognized the pumpkin mask immediately and stuck his foot out. The gun went flying, sailing across the night sky, and crashing down on top of the Monte Carlo, denting the roof.

Will didn't see the gun fly, though. He was too busy watching the assailant get caught up in his own feet after getting tripped up. He nearly fell, but then began to get his feet back under him. That's when Will pounced. He leaped towards the robber and grabbed him by the shoulders from behind, and kicked his leg in front of the robber's left foot for a second time, and this time, the robber hit the dirt. He was able to get back up quickly, though, but then Will was on him immediately. Will ducked a punch from the robber and used the momentum to get behind him. He threw his arms under the robber's and pulled them up and into a Full Nelson, lacing his fingers together behind the robber's head. The assailant whipped his head backwards, trying to headbutt Will, but Will anticipated the move and dogged it perfectly. Will then once again stuck his left leg in front of the robber and thrust forward, and they both tumbled to the dirt. Will held onto the hold and straddled the robber's back. He was trying to use his own leg's to tie up the robber's when he heard a voice shouting.

"Freeze, Sheriff's Department!" came a voice from behind him. Will did as he was told and didn't move a muscle. He saw his shadow on the ground from the beam of the flashlight that was shining on the two men. "You, on the top. Release him, and slowly get to your feet." Will again did as he was told and rose to his feet. "Hands behind your head! Now, walk backward to me slowly. And you, on the ground, stay there." Will did as the voice said once again. His arms were grabbed one by one and wrenched behind his back, then restrained in a pair of handcuffs. Will was then bent over the hood of the Sheriff's Department's car. He watched as Pumpkinhead was also cuffed and bent over the back of the Monte Carlo.

"What are you all doing out here?" came a voice from behind him. Will was relieved to recognize it as Jim's. Jim was okay, apparently. "Let him go, Ogre! Juan, you got the right guy! Ogre's got my employee shackled up over here!" The man who was holding Will down onto the hood of the car looked at Jim, then down at the ground for a second, and then at Will. Then he looked over to the other deputy, holding Pumpkinhead to a similar position, who looked back at him and shrugged.

"Shit, Jimmy. We didn't know. We had no idea what was going on," the first larger and rounder deputy said. "We got a phantom 9-1-1 call, and then Mrs. Detweiler called it in, and said she heard a gunshot from inside the store. We wadn't but a few blocks out, so we come in hot!" He pulled Will up from the car and took the handcuffs off. Will's nose was bleeding, and a puddle of his blood was slowly running down the hood of the patrol car, and also down Will's mustache, lips, and beard. "Sorry about that, sir," the deputy said to Will. "We come up and saw y'all scrappin' and didn't know who was who. Just doing our job."

"No worries," Will said, wiping his nose. "Jim, you all right?"

"Fine," Jim said.

"What was the gunfire inside?"

Jim laughed and nodded over to Pumpkinhead. "Him. He stumbled over the dude he knocked out and fell backward. The gun went off and put holes in my ceiling. I reached down for my gun, but he was up and out the door. I guess that's when he ran into you. You took him down?"

"I guess you could say that," Will said.

"He took him down and had him pinned to the dirt," said the bigger of the two deputies. "Sorry about the cuffs, again," he said to Will and stuck out his hand. "Deputy Ricky Oglethorpe. Everyone calls me Ogre." Will took the hand and gave it a hearty pump. "That's Juan over there. He's a deputy, too," Ogre said. Will tossed a hand up in the air to wave at Juan, who still had his hands full with Pumpkinhead. "Lemme go and help him."

At that time, an ambulance pulled up, and the medics ran inside the store to take care of the unfortunate customer who felt the butt of Pumpkinhead's gun. Will took a few steps over to where Jim was standing. "So glad you're alright. I didn't know what to think when I heard the shot. I about crapped in my pants."

"Billy, you crap your pants at the sound of a gunshot around here, you're gonna need to buy more underwear. Most of it's harmless, though. Wild boys out in the brush pingin' cans, or folks in the hills keeping rodents out of their hopeful but non-producing gardens."

"Most of them are harmless," Will repeated. "You could have died today."

Jim looked at him for a moment, and then at the ground, and slowly nodded.

"Be right back," he said. Will wasn't sure, but he thought he saw Jim wipe his face and *maybe* sniff back a tear. He walked back out to where Will was standing and sat down on the curb in the parking space. "Heck of a first day," Jim said, handing Will a can of beer and cracking one open for himself.

Will exhaled, sat down next to Jim, opened his beer, and said, "I'm quitting."

Jim nearly spit out the mouthful of beer that he had taken in. "Aww, come on, really?"

Will smiled and shook his head. "No," and he took a drink, let it sit, and then swallowed, finishing with an "ahhhh" sound. "Not a chance. I haven't had this much fun since I worked on the boat. Plus, I promised to get your books right." The two men sat on the curb and watched as the culprit, a Mr. Christopher C. Lankston, recently referred to as "Pumpkinhead,' and whose friends called him 'Clank,' was read his Miranda rights and then shoved into the back of the police car.

This was not the Hallowe'en night that Will was looking for. He had images of children in costumes, both purchased and handmade, roaming up and down the streets of this mostly quiet town. Jim looked at Will, pointed at Lankston, and asked, "Think it might be that old boy who has been hitting banks and liquor stores all around the area?

Will looked at him and then back at the ground. "Nah," he said. "It doesn't fit. After the bank robbery in Kansas when that guy was killed, the killer went from a Glock handgun in the bank to a shotty in Kansas. This guy tonight had a revolver, and he was wearing western boots."

"How do you know?"

Will pointed to a spot in the dusty parking lot. "Look at this boot print. See the mark that the heel left? That's a stylized 'D-L'. The boot that made this print was made by Dave Landry in El Paso. This was the guy who was in the store earlier today when I asked you if you saw his boots. Remember, I said it looked like a bowling shoe?"

"He could have changed shoes between the bank job and here, no?" Jim asked.

"Possible, but it's still doubtful this guy and that 'highwayman' guy are the same. We probably don't even know all of his crimes, but your 'highwayman' is getting precise, more gutsy, and he's probably getting better at what he's doing." Will took a drink from his beer and swallowed. "This guy was clumsy, obviously. If you're going to be running, and you know what you're doing, you don't wear a stylized boot to do it."

"How do you know all this?" Jim asked.

Will thought to be careful before he answered. He took a drink of his beer and swished it around before swallowing it down. Then he decided the truth was actually applicable. "I could just be spouting a big pile of bull crap, but, man, I have read every John Grisham book, every Stuart Woods book, every James Patterson book, and every Patricia Highsmith book, and then I read them all again. I watched those crime dramas on TV where they tell the real story of what really happened. I also know a little bit about boots. You just have to put two and two together and come up with four."

"Whatever you say, Billy. I'm just glad you were here tonight."

"You didn't need me. The dude screwed himself up," Will said.

"Not true, my vigilante new-hire," Jim said. "I have a light on the counter that comes on and lets me know the back door is open. When you opened it, the light came on, and ol' Pumpkinhead saw it. He freaked out, I guess he thought it was an alarm or something. He knocked the other customer out, started demanding the money, looked all around, and backed up and fell over that unfortunate soul." Jim was pointing to the customer that Langston had knocked out being rolled away on a stretcher. He was awake and alert, and holding his head. The medics were taking him to the care center for further observation. Will wondered if Daria would be taking care of him.

Ogre and Juan came over to where Jim and Will were sitting. Juan was wearing his uniform as it was designed to be worn, but Ogre had his hat under his arm and was scratching behind his left ear. He finished and put his hat back on his head, and then took out a small notebook and a pen. "What happened?" he asked. Will thought that they should tell the story in a sequential order from both of their points of view. Jim agreed, and they pieced the events of the last half hour together to paint an accurate picture of what had happened. When they were done, Ogre's hat came off again, and the finger went to the back of the ear again. "Sheriff's gonna wanna talk with you," he said.

Will spoke up first. "Which one of us?" he asked.

"Both, I reckon," Ogre said. "Here's my card if you need anything or think of anything else you didn't tell us yet." Will and Jim both took the business card from Ogre and placed it in their respective wallets. "All right, we'll see ya. Oh, Jim, here's a ten-spot. Can you leave me a sixer of Pal's out here somewhere? I'll pick it up later."

"Sure thing," Jim said, and took the ten-dollar bill from Ogre. "It'll be over there behind the tires. Come on, Billy. Let's ring in your first sale." Will followed Jim back into the store, and Jim closed and locked the door behind them. He turned off all of the neon signs in the front window and hit a switch behind the counter. Nearly all of the lights went off, save for one over the counter and one near the back of the store. He hit another switch, and the glowing 'D&J' sign outside, and the lights beneath the soffit, all went off. He then took a six-pack of Pal's Light Beer from the cooler and set it on the counter. "Well, come on," Jim said. "Get behind the counter. You won't be able to wrestle forever, Kurt Angle."

Will laughed at the joke and then got behind the counter. "Okay, Boss, what do I do?"

"Scan the barcode." Will dragged the beer across the cross-hatched red lights that shone from a gun-shaped scanner connected to the cash register. The register beeped. "Now hit the alcohol tax button." Will again did as he was told. "Now tell me the total."

"Five eighteen," Will said, and Jim handed him the ten-dollar bill.

"Punch the sale button," Jim said. Will hit the button, and the register drawer popped open and punched Will in the stomach.

"Oof!"

Jim chuckled. "Shoulda warned you about that, I guess. I'm assuming you know how to make change?"

"Sure, two pennies, a nickel, three quarters, and four ones." Will closed the cash drawer. "Four eighty-two is your change, sir," Will said, and held out the change for Jim.

"Put it in the jar. Ogre always puts the change in the jar, no matter what." Jim picked up the six-pack of beer and another brown bag and said, "Come on, I'll give you a ride home."

"What's in the other bag?" Will said.

"This is the bag of money that the fool tried to take. I'm just gonna take it home for the night so we don't have to deal with it right now."

"Ah. Well, do we need to close out this drawer or anything?" Will asked.

"Nope," Jim said. "You'll figure it out tomorrow." Will followed Jim out the door. Jim closed it tight and turned a key in a lock near the handle of the door, and then another towards the bottom. "The bottom one sets the alarm," he said. They walked around the side of the building, where not long ago, Will had stopped a would-be a robber from escaping. Jim reached behind a tire that leaned against the wall of the building next door and put the beer behind it. "Hopefully, no one comes to get the tire today," Jim said. "It's been there for about three weeks."

"Nice," Will said. They continued around the next corner, and Jim clicked a button on his keys, and the side markers on a black 1990 Dodge Daytona flickered. Jim opened the driver's door, and Will got in the passenger seat. "This is pretty sweet," Will said. "I haven't seen one of these in a while. How old is this?"

"Eleven years," Jim said, starting the engine. "I've had some modifications done, such as the remote door locks and alarm, the sunroof, sound system, paint job, and pinstriping." He flicked a button, and a pair of clamshell headlights lifted from each side of the car, just in front of the hood. He hit another switch, and the windows rolled down, and after another button was pushed, the sunroof retracted. Will looked through the roof and saw the starry sky. Jim put the car into reverse and backed out of the parking spot, and then he dropped it into drive and headed out onto the street, leaving rubber on the dusty road as he did. "Kicked up the engine a bit, too!" Will watched Jim drive and the scenery change as Jim made the correct turns at the right places and then pulled into the mobile home park.

"How did you know I lived here?" Jim inquired.

"No secrets in the town," Jim said. "New guy comes in, there's a shift in the atmosphere, a roadwork for change. You never know what someone new is bringing to the table, and people notice."

"Huh," Will said, taking off his seat belt as they approached his trailer. When Jim stopped and put the car into park, the doors unlocked automatically, and Will opened the door to get out. "Thanks for the ride, Jim. I appreciate it. See you tomorrow."

"Hey, uh, Billy," Jim said, looking at the windshield as Will closed the door. Will turned to look at him through the open window. Jim looked up and caught Will's eye. "Thanks. For today. I mean it."

Will smiled, stood, and patted the car on the roof. He turned again toward his new home and made his way up the sidewalk. He fished around under the metal steps and found the key box. He opened it and found three loose keys. He found the one for the door, unlocked it, and opened it. Jim watched and then pulled away in a dusty cloud after two short toots of his horn. Will would have been worried that the noise might bother or wake the neighbors, but he only had one.

"Heck of a day," he said, looked around, watched as Jim disappeared from the lot, and then went inside his trailer, closing the door behind him.

Chapter 51 – Steered

The following day, Will woke up at seven o'clock in the morning, went out for a run, procured a garbage breakfast from a gas station convenience store on the way home, and then proceeded to have his first meal in his own home for the first time since September 10th. Gil had been good to his word and parked the trailer where it belonged, straight as an arrow, and hooked up the water, sewage, and power before he left Will the keys under the step. Will was looking forward to his first shower in the trailer, but he needed to get his clothes from the motel first. When he was done eating the horrible breakfast, he took another run over to the motel, picked up his things, and quickly checked out, much to the dismay of Perry, the owner, who was expecting a cash payment for more than the three nights Will had stayed. Perry charged him an extra night for the early checkout, which was fine with Will.

Back at his trailer, Will tested the shower and, although small, it passed with flying colors as far as functionality was considered. There was a bathtub at the base of the shower, not that he would consider sitting down in it, and a sink and working toilet in the rest of the small bathroom area. The lights worked, the water was flowing, and the bed was fairly comfortable. He was home.

After he got dressed, Will opened his bags and pulled out the smaller bag that held all of his remaining cash. It looked undisturbed from the last time he saw it, and he was relieved. He felt edgy about leaving it in the motel room unguarded the night before, but he decided that it could not be helped. Jim had driven straight to the trailer park the previous night, and Will did not think it wise to ask him to redirect his route. Will considered going to get his property after Jim had gone, but he left it alone instead. He grabbed a few stacks of cash, counted out ten thousand dollars, and put it into a large, padded envelope he had bought from the convenience store. He used the clip at the top of the envelope to seal it, and then locked his trailer and took the short walk to Gil's house to hand over the envelope and offer Gil an alteration to their deal. When Gil answered his door, he saw the envelope and had a big smile on his face. Gil invited Will into the house, but Will declined and said he had to get to work soon.

"Jimmy givin' you a hard time yet?" Gil asked.

"Not too bad," Will said. "Had a little excitement last night, so it was a bit of an odd first day."

"Oh yeah," Gil said as a fact. "Heard all about that."

"Already?"

"No secrets in this town, Billy," Gil said. "So what's new?"

"I wanted to drop off the down payment and ask you a question about our deal." He handed Gil the envelope. "Feel free to count it; it should be the first ten."

"Later is fine," Gil said. "What's on your mind?"

"Well, I was wondering if you wouldn't mind if I paid off our deal a little faster. I still have some of my savings left and could probably give you another five, and then we can work out the balance with the payments."

"Fine with me," Gil said with a smile, and lightly grabbed Will around the back of the neck. "Whatever you want to do as far as that is good. Just don't screw me over!" They chucked, and Will assured him that everything would be paid as it should. As Will left, he remembered a question that he was going to ask Jim later on, but he figured he would throw it to Gil as well. "Is there any place in town that sells bikes? I don't mind hoofing it to work, but I'd like to get around town quicker if I need to."

"Not interested in a car?" Gil asked, laughing. "I know a guy with a car for sale."

"If the right deal came along, maybe, but I'm a little cash poor right now," Will said, pointing at the envelope he had previously handed to Gil.

"Understood, friend. I'm not sure I can help you with the bike. You might have to travel out to a nearby town if you can't find anyone here to sell you one."

Will rolled his eyes. "Ugh," he said. "Okay, I'll grab a newspaper and look at the classifieds and see what I can find. I gotta get going, Gil. I'll have the extra five thou for you tomorrow, probably."

"Whenever," Gil said. "If you want to stick to our original deal, we can do that too."

"Thanks, man...I'll talk with you later." Will left Gil's house and headed to the liquor store to start his workday. He enjoyed the walk and wondered why he would need a bike to get around when he enjoyed the walk so much. But he still thought it would be better to have some sort of transportation, even if it was two wheels, in case he needed to get somewhere faster than walking, and less sweaty than if he was running.

He made the trip to the liquor store in a few minutes and got there about fifteen minutes early. The store was dark inside, and the door was still locked, so Will sat on the brick ledge outside the window and waited for Jim. He took a minute to look up and down the street, just to see what he could see, which wasn't too much at nearly ten o'clock in the morning. He did see a cat wandering around, though. It was scraggly and skinny and looked like it lived outside. The cat saw him from across the street and sat down. Will and the cat had a staring contest, which the cat won easily. The dusty street of Brindle did not help keep Will's eyes moist.

The cat put its back leg over its head and licked its inner rear thigh, and then stopped to look at Will again.

"Really," Will said to the cat, which appeared to stiffen a bit. "That's *all* you're going to clean? That one spot? You look like a floor mop." With that, Will held out his hand and made a "pss pss pss" noise toward the cat. The cat stood, actually looked both ways, and began to cross the street. At about that time, Jim's Daytona pulled up to the alley between the liquor store and the next building. Jim honked the horn of the little sporty car as he drove by. The cat stopped crossing the street and disappeared around the corner of another building. A few minutes later, Jim appeared from around the corner of the building, and he and Will shared morning greetings. Jim took out his keys, opened the door, and Will followed him inside the building. Jim left the door unlocked and turned on the lights for the room and for the neon signs in the front windows. The sign for Wilson Whiskey flickered twice, lit, and then went dark. Jim pulled the string again, and nothing happened. The silhouetted bull rider that appeared animated as the sign progressed through different stages of lighting remained dark.

"Hmph," Jim said. "Tragic. I like that sign."

Will smiled and said, "I'll get started on restock."

"Sounds good," Jim said and went behind the counter to clean up the close of yesterday's business. It took Will about two hours to get everything stocked and straightened, and he wandered out to the sales floor to see what Jim wanted him to focus on next. He saw the neon sign that had burnt out still hanging in the window, and remembered the stock of other neon signs in the back room. He went back to the back room and looked for another Wilson's Whiskey sign in the pile, but there was not one to be found. He pulled one for O'Farrell's Irish Whiskey from the stack and took it out to the sales floor.

"How's this for a replacement for the Wilson's sign?" he asked.

"Works for me," Jim said. "You know how to hang it?"

"I can try to figure it out," Will said, and Jim laughed. When Will got to the window to take down the Wilson's sign, he understood the joke. Two small chains hung from the top of the windowsill and attached to the sign by a pair of 's' hooks. He unhooked the Wilson's sign and, within a few minutes, the O'Farrell's sign was hanging in its place and shining with a neon glow.

"Looks good," Jim said. "Why don't you run over to Rocky's and pick up lunch?"

"You ordered pizza again?"

"Yeah," Jim said. "And salad. Make sure you get extra dressing."

"I can't be eating pizza every day, Jim. I'm going to blow up! Plus, I don't have a car." Will no sooner said the words than Jim's keys were flying across the room. Instinct on Will's part was the only thing that kept the keys from hitting him in the face. He caught the keys from the air and asked, "The Daytona?"

"Yep," Jim said. "Be careful and hurry back."

Will left the store and went around to the back to find Jim's car in the same place he had parked the day before. He got in the car and fired up the engine, and a few minutes later, pulled into the parking lot at Rocky's. He waited at the counter at the front of the store for a moment, and then saw Rocky coming from the back.

"You again," she said. "What brings you to my restaurant today? Can't get enough of my pie?"

Will let the awkwardness of the joke pass. "Not me," he said. "Jim at D&J's. He's the pizza addict."

"Why are you picking up Jim's lunch?" she asked.

"I'm working over there. He sent me." Will paused, then continued. "But you knew that already, didn't you?"

"Gotcha," she said, smiling with the ever-present gum showing in the corner of her mouth. "Here ya go," she said. "Tell him I just put it on his tab."

Will cocked his head sideways. "How much is his tab?"

"Why do you ask?"

"Curious," he said, then smiled. "But you already knew that, didn't you?"

She opened a book and flipped a few pages. "Hunert and twelve eighty-five," she said.

Will let the use of the word 'hunert' in place of 'one hundred' go past him as well. "Let me take care of that," he said, and put one hundred and fifty dollars on the counter.

"Hold on, I'll get your change," she said with a wink.

"No change," he said. "It's all you."

"How much is Jimmy paying you?" she asked with another smile.

"Enough to stock his shelves, clean up his books, and apparently fetch lunch."

"And chase down stick-up men, apparently," she said.

"Word gets around quickly," Will said.

"No secrets in this town, Billy," she said, and then another smile. "I gotta run. Got customers."

"See you later," Will said.

"Maybe," she said, and walked back into the kitchen.

Will smiled and shook his head and headed out of the restaurant. He drove Jim's Daytona through the town, and, although he was tempted, he left the sunroof and the stereo as they were, and in a few minutes, he was carrying the pizza box and the bag with the salad through the door. When it chimed, Jim looked up from a crossword puzzle, and his face lit up.

"Finally," he said. Will laid the pizza box and the bag of salads on the counter, and Jim pulled some paper plates from under the counter. Will unpacked the salads, and the two men set up across from each other on the counter. After taking a bite from his pizza, Jim picked up the bag and looked inside. "Dude, where is the salad dressing? I ordered extra."

"Aww, I guess they forgot it," Will said. "Want me to run back over and get it?"

At that moment, the front door of the liquor store opened, and Rocky walked in carrying a small takeout bag. She winked at Jim and said, "You forgot your salad dressing, new guy," and tossed the bag to Will.

"I guess I did," Will said, swallowing his bite of pizza and catching the bag, not necessarily in that order.

"Good thing I was here to save you."

"You're a lifesaver," Will said. "I thought Jim was going to kick my ass or fire me. Or both."

Jim swallowed his food. "Fat chance of that, no pun intended." He looked at Rocky. "This dude's like my own Kurt Angle."

Rocky looked at him and said, "Who?"

Will just looked on as the conversation continued and went down a path of which he wanted no part. He felt like he was gathering too much attention.

"Kurt Angle," Jim said. "The wrestler? Olympic gold medalist Kurt Angle? World Champion Kurt Angle?"

Rocky looked at Will, and then back at Jim, and shrugged. Rocky already knew Jim was going to tell the story, and even though she already knew it, let him tell it anyway.

"Anyway," Jim said. "I'm getting robbed last night, gun to my face, and this guy is in the back room. He sneaks out the back door and comes around the side of the building, and then tackles the dude and wrestles him to the ground and holds him until the Ogre and Juan get there. He didn't get away with anything because the guy was a buffoon and really did himself in, but at least he didn't get away."

"So," Rocky said, eyes rolled up and a finger in the air, "you're touting this guy because he tackled and subdued a buffoon? You're not really giving him any credit for anything."

"He helped get a criminal off the streets," Jim said indignantly. "What if he was going to rob you next? Man's a hero if you ask me."

Rocky looked over at Will, who was watching the back-and-forth intently now. "Hmph," she said, looking back at Will. "Maybe. I gotta go... restaurant ain't gonna run itself, ya know." She turned and opened the door to leave, and as she exited, said, "By the way, Chris Triangle, or whatever you called him, over there, paid off your tab." She released the door and let it shut.

Jim looked at Will, and he back at Jim, who only said, "Chris Triangle," and both men began to laugh. "How did she get that out of 'Kurt Angle?'" Jim asked, between laughing and taking breaths.

"Pretty funny, though," Will said. When the laughter subsided, Will asked, "Does everyone in this town know about last night already?"

"Small town, dude," Jim said. At that moment, a gunshot rang out in the distance, and Will noticeably stiffened. Jim didn't budge. "Rifle shot," he said, with a mouthful of salad drenched in Ranch dressing. Will shuddered, regardless, but he didn't know if it was from the gunshot or from watching so much ranch dressing go into one place at the same time. "Small town," he said again. "You know what's good about small towns?"

"What's that?" Will asked.

"Everyone knows everyone, no one has many secrets, if any, and the population pool is limited, so if you're going to hang around here, whether you're male or female, you choose the pick of the pool when it comes to relationships. You take the best available. That's what Daria did with me. She saw me and snapped me up, 'cause she knew it didn't get much better than this." Jim moved his arms from shoulder-length to hip-length as he said 'this' while referring to his ample frame, and Will couldn't help but snicker at Jim's joke.

"Jim, no offense, and I feel like I can say this to you because we've been through so much in such a short amount of time..."

"Speak on it," Jim said.

"You married up," Will said.

"Don't I know it," Jim said with a smile, and the two men laughed again. When the air settled once again and both men had their composure, Jim said, "But really, man, I think Rocky likes you."

Will laughed. "Rocky doesn't know anything about me other than I am new to this town and I work here."

"And that's two good things you have going for you," Jim said. "You're a bit of a mystery, my friend. I'm actually surprised that more fish aren't checking out the fresh bait, if you take my meaning."

Will was straightening the shelves, which had been disturbed by customers since he had last addressed them. He contemplated being equated to fresh bait, but let the thought pass. "That's probably one thing I am not, Jimmy, is a mystery." *Tell that to those who think you're dead or missing.* The internal voice surprised Will a little. Things had been going so well that save for the activity last night, he hadn't heard much of it for a few days. He didn't miss it. Then, however, it was there, *again*, to remind him of who and what he really was. He got out of his own head and returned to straightening the bottles on the shelves again. When the door chimed, as he heard it do dozens of times during his shift, he didn't look up. He was used to it now, although he was thinking he should start getting to know the people of Brindle a little more, and maybe he should interact with them when they came into the store.

"Billy," Jim said, interrupting Will's thoughts.

"Sir," Will said and looked over to the counter. There was an older man, Will thought he had to be in his fifties, wearing a police uniform and standing near the counter. He had a puffy white mustache and no beard, and the mustache curled up on the ends. Will could not see his hair color because of the hat the man was wearing, but he assumed it was white as well. Will walked over to the counter.

"Sheriff, I think this is the man you're here to see," Jim said. The sheriff turned on one heel and propped himself up on his elbow, which was resting on the counter. Will approached and looked at both men. No introduction seemed imminent, so Will started. He stuck out his hand to the sheriff and said, "Hi, Lomax, Billy Lomax."

"Mr. Lomax," the sheriff said, taking the hand and giving it two solid pumps and then holding the hand, looking Will in the eye for what seemed like an uncomfortable amount of time before setting Will free. "Sheriff Wes Tim Utter," he said, the words pouring from under the mustache.

"Sheriff, nice to meet you," Will said. "What can I do for you?"

"Well, Mr. Lomax," Utter began. "Welcome to Brindle. Trust me when I say that I don't want to get started off on the wrong foot with you, but you gotta let me hash this out."

Will suddenly felt uncomfortable. "Okay," he said. "What's on your mind?"

"Well, it seems that right after you roll into town being driven by some old boy from Cheyenne, and on your first day on a new job, the place where you are workin' gets held up."

Will cocked his head a bit, as if trying to understand what the sheriff was implying. "Sheriff, I—"

"Can I see some ID, Mr. Lomax?" the sheriff asked. Will decided to be quiet, and he pulled out his wallet and handed the fake driver's license over to Sheriff Utter. Utter looked at the license, front and back, and then at Will, and then back to the license. "Philadelphia," he said. "What brings you out here?"

"I had enough of big city life," Will said. "Especially after the events in the past few months."

"I can understand that completely," the sheriff said and handed the license back to Will. "But you just uproot from the big city and roll on out to my town?"

"No, there was some thinking along the way."

"Indulge me with a story," Utter said.

"Well," Will said, taking a breath and letting it out audibly, "on nine-eleven, when I saw what was happening, I decided that it could have just as easily been in Philly, or I could have just as easily been in New York, and I had so many plans and things I wanted to do. I wasn't going to let some asshole on a crusade ruin my life. So, I traveled across the country by car, went camping for the first time since my father died, went fishing, again for the first time without my father, saw dozens of cities and towns, fell in love with a few here and there, drove through some Native American reserves, saw a few National Parks, eventually made it out to Seattle, and ultimately saw the Pacific Ocean. When I was done traveling, I tried to remember the cleanest, safest, and most attractive of all the small towns I saw, and Brindle stuck out. So, I traveled here."

"You don't say," Utter said, looking down at the half-eaten pizza on the counter. "Where did you work in Philadelphia?"

"I was self-employed. I was a freelance scout for Temple University's wrestling team."

Utter picked up a piece of the pizza and picked off the black olives. He placed them back in a corner of the box. "Collegiate wrestling. Not like that goofy shit on Monday nights?" he asked, and then took a bite of the slice.

"Don't knock that goofy shit on Monday nights," Jim said, grabbing a slice of pizza and biting into the point.

"No, sir," Will said, laughing at the popularity of Utter's question. "Greco-Roman and Freestyle, like in the Olympics."

"Wes Tim," Jim said, with a mouthful of pizza that he swallowed before he continued, "this guy here is a hero and should be treated as such, at least in my eyes. Yeah, he's been here for only a few days, but he's a good man in my book. I'll vouch for him. He took that guy down and probably saved someone else from another robbery, where someone could have gotten hurt or killed."

"Jimmy, I have no doubt you are correct. I just have to do my job, or I won't get reelected!" Utter started laughing, and Jim joined him. Utter nearly choked on his pizza. When the laughter subsided, Utter reached into his pocket and pulled out his wallet. "Mr. Lomax," the sheriff began, but was interrupted by Will.

"Please, sheriff, Billy is fine."

"All right then, Billy," the sheriff exhaled from under his puffy mustache, pulling a business card from his wallet, "I want you to go see this man. His name is Denny Blewett, and he's the principal at Brindle High School."

"And why am I going to see this man?" Will asked, taking the business card from Utter.

"You'll find out when you talk to him," Utter said.

"What am I walking into here, Sheriff?" Will asked, almost in a frustrated manner.

"Listen, son, I'm just an old man with a star and a gun that the people of this county will let me keep until I can't wear one properly or shoot the other one straight. I try to keep the drunks off the street and the riffraff out of town, and I think I do a pretty good job of it. All I ever wanted to do was help the people of this town, and if I can see a way to do it through another person, I'm going to steer that person in the direction they need to go. So, son, you're being steered, and that's all I got to say about that."

Will nodded and put the card into his own wallet. "I'll go see Mr. Blewett, then, sir."

"Good," the sheriff said. "Tell him I sent you, and tell him about your background. You're not a pedophile, or don't have a criminal record or anything like that, do you?"

Technically, you have not been charged with anything, so that would be a no to both questions, the voice said.

"No, sir," Will said.

"Good. Now, if you boys don't mind, I'll let you get back to your business and I'll get back into mine." Utter tipped his hat and nodded, and both Jim and Will.

When the door closed and the annoying chime was finished with its duty, Will looked at Jim and said, "What the hell just happened?"

Jim stood up straight, placed his hand across his top lip, and let his fingers dangle down to simulate Utter's mustache. "Son," he said, in his best imitation of Utter, "you've just been drafted." Jim took his hand from his mouth and returned to his standard persona. "The high school has a wrestling team, but the coach left the town at the end of the previous season. Looks like Utter wants you to be his replacement. So, it looks like you won't be working here much."

Will looked perplexed. "But I haven't even met this Blewett guy or had an interview, or assuming all that is good, I haven't accepted the job!"

"Billy, if you're going to stay in this town, there's two things you have to know. One, get used to random gunshots, but you knew that already, so you're halfway home. Two, what Utter wants, Utter gets. So, understand this. You're already hired.."

"How much pull does Utter have in this town?" Will asked.

Jim tossed the last part of his piece of pizza into his mouth and began to chew, and then rubbed his hands together to dust them off. When he swallowed the last of it, he looked at Will and said, "All of it."

Chapter 52 – Pimples, Glasses, Buck Teeth

Greco looked at the printout of the two images from the bank videos that Ilario had given him and compared them again. The pictures were grainy, but Ilario thought they were the same guy. In fact, he insisted on it. Greco had no choice but to take Ilario at his word, not that he doubted him, but in Greco's mind, Ilario was young, hadn't really been around the block, so to speak, and he may not know a handcuff from a cuff link. However, Ilario was a techie who graduated from college with a degree in audio-visual technology, and it was Ilario who had set up the new video system anyway. Why should Greco doubt him?

So now, in Greco's mind, he had his guy. He knew what he looked like, and he knew his name. The only thing left to know was if his man was still alive. He had a good feeling that he was alive, and now he just had to prove it. And then he had to catch him.

He picked up his desk phone and dialed a number he had from his notes. It was for the Union Taxi Company. Joe Falkenberg picked up the phone on the other end, and the two men exchanged greetings. Greco was the first to get down to business.

"Mr. Falkenberg, you are the manager of Union Taxi, correct?" When Falkenberg answered in the affirmative, Greco continued. "Just a couple of questions for you, if I could."

"Sure, but can you make it quick? Pretty busy here."

"I'll do my best. If I came to your place of business, could you provide detailed records of your fares?"

"How detailed do you want?" Falkenberg asked.

"Dates, times, locations, distances, things like that," Greco answered.

"Probably all of that, Detective."

"Is now a good time? I can be there in twenty minutes."

"That should work, as long as we're done by noon," Falkenberg responded quickly.

"On my way," Greco said and hung up the phone. On the way to the cab garage, Greco was lucky enough to hit most of the lights as they were lit green, and arrived there in seventeen minutes. He stepped out of the car and entered the garage, and looked for what might be an office. There was a small room built in the back of the garage, and Greco headed for it. He was stopped by a large man in coveralls with smudges and stains all over them. When Greco said he was looking for Falkenberg, he was directed to the back room.

Greco knocked on the door and peered through the window, and the man inside, phone to his ear, waved him in. Greco entered the room, and the man was still talking on the phone, asking questions about deliveries and where his shipment of gaskets might be. Greco learned that the cab company was facing a shortage of available cabs because of the missing gaskets. He could not have cared less about cabs or gaskets; he just wanted the chance to talk to Falkenberg. After a few more minutes of Falkenberg talking on the phone and eyeballing Greco, Greco stood and started looking at the posters attached to the walls around the office. Most of them were of shapely women stretched out onto the hoods of exotic cars or straddling a motorcycle as they turned and looked toward the camera behind them. Greco admitted that the women were as attractive as the cars were beautiful, but it seemed like overkill to him. There was hardly a spot on the walls that was not covered by posters. Finally, the man hung up the phone.

Greco turned toward him. "Mr. Falkenberg?"

"That's me," Falkenberg responded, not looking at Greco, but instead at a catalog of auto parts. *Probably gaskets*, Greco thought.

"Great. I am Detective Brian Greco, NYPD. I just need a few minutes of your time."

"Greco," Falkenberg said, pausing. "I was trying to figure out what kinda name that is. Greek?"

"Italian, actually," Greco said. "But it does mean 'Greek.'"

"Thought so. My mechanic is a Greek, and he's an idiot."

"Mr. Falkenberg, can you bring up your records from September 11th of this year?"

Falkenberg nodded, went over to a wall behind his desk and pulled a blue binder from the shelf, which read 'September '01" on the side, written in some sort of marker. "Here we go. September 11. What are we looking for?"

"A fare with a stop at the Quick-Key Self Storage on North Moore. Would have been pretty early in the morning, and probably right around the time the attacks were going on."

Falkenberg paged through the book of green and white lined paper. "That day was some shit, wasn't it?" Greco only responded with a 'ummhmm' noise as Falkenberg continued to search. After another minute, Falkenberg closed the book. "Nothing for North Moore or Quick-Key."

"Mr. Falkenberg, I have video proof that one of your cabs was at the Quick-Key that morning."

Joe Falkenberg exhaled and pulled the book back open to September 11th. "Got the plate number?" Falkenberg asked. Greco gave him the plate number, and Falkenberg continued his search. "The only thing I have for that cab that morning was a pickup at eight forty-five in the morning at the corner of Murray and West. No name."

"What was the destination of the fare?"

Heavily exhaling, Falkenberg replied, "No idea. I never saw the driver again."

"What?" Greco said in disbelief. "How does that happen?"

"Don't know," Falkenberg said. "These guys are independent contractors. They come and go as they please. Maybe the driver freaked out over what was going on that day. We got notified that the cab was parked over in Jersey. In some park somewhere..." Falkenberg trailed off and began speaking to himself. "Let's see, what's it say, here? Caven Point? Can't really read it too well." Greco stared at him as if Falkenberg were a student who had just told the teacher a story about his homework and a hungry dog.

"So, this guy just up and disappears?" Greco responded as he wrote the word down in his book. "And who was the driver?"

"Uhh, Ed Filardi."

"And you never saw him again?"

Falkenberg closed the book again and headed towards the shelf with it. "Like I said, he doesn't work here anymore."

"Since when?"

"Since that day, probably. Listen, Detective, I have a garage to run, and it's not running really well right now. I have to get back to it, or all hell is going to break loose. Can you get all your questions together and call my girl at the main number? She'll get them to me, and she'll get back to you with any answers you need."

Greco was irritated by Falkenberg and his unwillingness to provide the information Greco sought. But he let it go and left Falkenberg to his cab business. He sat in his car for a few minutes and read his notes. Kelly went to the Quick-Key, but then what else? He needed the cab driver's address and phone number, but that could be later. A horn honked behind him, and he looked in the mirror to see a taxi behind him, trying to leave the garage. Greco waved, put his car into gear, and began the trip back to the station. He was short on temper at the moment, and the traffic was ridiculous. He needed to review the evidence again, as well as the notes. Something wasn't adding up. On top of it all, he remembered he told Ilario he would take him to lunch today.

"Rahgh!" he said out loud. It was just about half-past noon when Greco got back to the station, and he was stopped by Maryanne as he passed by her desk. "What's up?" he asked. Maryanne motioned him closer, and when he leaned down, he could smell her perfume. It was a warm blend of something flowery yet fruity. He liked it. He was now almost in a squat by her desk, waiting for what had to be told to him in such a manner. "What?" he asked, becoming impatient.

"Look, you have a visitor," she said, and motioned toward Greco's desk. Michael Ilario was walking by as nonchalantly as possible, slowing down to pass Greco's desk, and then resuming a normal speed once he had cleared the area. "Just watch," she said. Ilario disappeared around a corner of the room for a few seconds and then reappeared to make the journey past Greco's desk once again. "This has been going on since at eleven-forty-five or so. I don't know if I saw the first pass he made by your desk, but the first time I saw him, his face fell when he saw you weren't there. So, now, this has been going on for over forty-five or so. What's he doing?"

Greco smiled and squatted even lower by Maryanne's desk so there was little chance that Ilario would see him. He wanted to mess with the kid for a minute or two. On Ilario's next pass, he was carrying a manilla file folder that Greco assumed probably had nothing inside. He snickered a little. "Well," he said in a low voice that he hoped only Maryanne could hear, "the kid actually did some good work for me yesterday, and I told him, as a reward, I'd take him to lunch. He played a poker face pretty well, but I can tell he was a little anxious and happy about it. I just wanna mess with him a little. Shh, here he comes again."

"You're mean," Maryanne said with a smile.

"I know it," he said, crouching even lower. After Ilario passed again, Greco stayed for another minute or two, mostly just to hang around Maryanne's desk, but also to watch for Ilario, but he never came back. "Maybe he gave up," Greco said.

"That would be the first thing I think he's ever given up on in my experience," Maryanne said.

"Oh, and what is your experience with Mr. Ilario?" Greco said, teasing.

"Shut up," she said, and whacked him in the head with a folder she was holding. He laughed, got to his feet, and headed to his desk. He dropped off his notes and was going to check his machine for messages, but he decided to let Ilario off the hook first. And he was hungry himself. His cereal breakfast that morning wasn't quite satiating the hunger he was feeling. He really wanted a street dog, but didn't think that was enough of a reward for Ilario's work.

He rounded the corner of the station and went to get Ilario from his desk and get the lunch going, and over with. However, when he got to Ilario's desk, Ilario wasn't there. Greco looked around the busy floor and tried to see if Ilario was walking around anywhere, carrying an empty manilla folder, but there was no sign of him. Greco checked the restrooms with no luck and eventually found him in the breakroom. "Ilario," Greco said, leaning against the wall. "I thought we were doing lunch today?"

Ilario was sitting at a table, alone, eating what appeared to be a tuna salad sandwich. He said with a half-mouthful of food, "I thought you forgot. I went to look for you at noon, but you weren't at your desk."

"I had some running to do. Case work, you know? Wrap that up. Let's go." Ilario stood and grabbed his sandwich as Greco left the room. He watched Greco leave, chewed, and swallowed the rest of the bite of food he had in his mouth. He looked at the rest of the sandwich, then back at the doorway which Greco had just vacated. He tossed the remainder of the sandwich in the trash and exited the room, catching up with Greco on the way out.

"Where are we going?" Ilario asked.

"Dunno. What do you feel like?"

"Man, I could eat a hot dog and be happy with it," Ilario said, hoping that Greco didn't believe him.

Greco looked at him and they sat down into Greco's car. "I love a good dog, too, but I can't just buy you a hot dog. You helped me find my guy!"

"That's my job, Detective."

"Just Greco is fine, or Brian if you prefer."

"Okay," Ilario said, and then smiled. "Brian."

"Yeah?" Greco asked.

"Oh, no, I was just saying your name, like you asked."

"Oh, gotcha. So, whatdaya like? Sushi, pizza, burgers, deli?"

Ilario exhaled. "Any of that is fine. Deli sounds good."

"Boom!" Greco said, and Ilario jumped. "Katz's it is. Hope you like mustard." They made small talk about backgrounds and things they liked to eat, both as children and now as adults. When they got to the deli, Greco found a parking space about a block away, and as they walked, Greco decided he would try to get to know this kid a little better.

"So, how did you end up an AV geek for the NYPD?" Greco asked.

Ilario looked mostly at the sidewalk as he walked next to Greco. He was a little awkward as he moved, often having to take a few extra steps to keep up with Greco. "I've been the geek my whole life. Pimples, glasses, buck teeth, you name it. I was the first kid on my block my age to have a computer. If it had wires, I took it apart; if it had a program, I messed around with it. It's all I was ever good at, really. Now I guess I can be a geek for a good reason."

Greco felt like he hit a soft nerve and decided to back off. "Well, I'm glad you're here now. You may have given me the big break in this case that I needed."

"So, what's the story with the guy on the video?" Ilario asked.

Greco grabbed the door for Katz's and held it open. "I'll tell you in a little bit. Right now, let's order. I'm hungry." They entered the store, and Greco was surprised when Ilario echoed Greco's order of a Reuben. They watched as the sandwiches were built in front of them, and when Greco paid the nearly fifty-dollar bill, they grabbed seats at the first open table they could find. Napkins were placed across the chests of each man, and the corners were tucked into their shirt collars to protect them from the drippings from the sandwich. They each took a bite and savored the wonderful flavors within the two slices of bread, as corned beef, Swiss cheese, and dressing all mixed together in their faces like a well-planned party. Greco took another bite while Ilario still worked on his first

When they both swallowed, Ilario said, "So?"

"Oh yeah," Greco said. "I almost forgot. So, this finance guy works for this company that's located in the WTC. For the past few months, he's been setting up fake companies and embezzling like a half-million dollars. On the day that the company's security guys are going to meet with him about it, it's nine-eleven. So, this guy disappears, and everyone thinks he's dead. But the money is still gone, so I have to look into it and follow the breadcrumbs. I'm pretty sure he's still alive, I just don't have any proof. He's apparently had multiple identifications made up to match the false accounts he has set up at the banks." Greco took another bite of his sandwich as Ilario chewed and listened. Between the chewing of the sandwich, Greco managed to fit in some words. "Dude's smart," he said, wiping some dressing from the corner of his mouth. "I don't know the motive, and I don't completely know how, but I'm gonna get him." More chewing followed, and then a swallow that was a little too big. Greco took a drink from his cup to clear away the food debris. "He set up accounts for different banks, eleven that I know, and at least another that may still be out there. That ID that I found matched up with the video images you made for me. I swear it's the same guy. I just don't know how these guys come up with this stuff." Greco took another bite.

Ilario, who was mostly done with his sandwich, decided he would talk now that Greco's mouth was preoccupied with his food. "If only they'd use their power for good," he said, and then took the last bite of his sandwich.

"Exactly!" Greco added. "What a wonderful world."

After a few minutes of silence between the two that was buried in the din of the restaurant noise around them, Ilario said, "You know, they filmed part of that movie 'When Harry Met Sally' here."

"Really? I never saw it. Not too much of a romantic comedy movie guy."

"It was okay. I wouldn't give up what you want to watch in favor of it. I just watch a lot of movies."

Greco nodded and then sat back in his chair and exhaled, his eyes rolling upward. "But like, seriously though, I wouldn't know how to get a fake ID even if I wanted or needed one. I mean, as a cop, I can probably figure it out and find the right connections, but how does this guy have a dozen different identities?"

"Programs," Ilario said, still chewing.

"What?"

Ilario swallowed his last bite and took a drink while Greco waited. "Computer programs. There's actually software that does it. It does it pretty well, too. They say you can't tell the difference between the real and fake ones."

"Guess not," Greco said, and then asked, "What programs?"

"I mean, it could be one of several. There's FaceSimile, ShadowBoxer, Doppelganger, RenooYoo... there's a couple of them. All black-market stuff, though. You can't go to the computer area of a department store and just pick these off the shelf. From what I hear, there are back-alley deals and clandestine meetings to exchange cash money for the programs."

"How do you know this?" Greco asked. "Let's go," he said, grabbing up the trash and standing from his chair.

Ilario did the same, and they headed for the exit. "Pimples, glasses, buck teeth, and a lot of free time. I read a lot." Ilario said. "Remember, I'm the geek." During the walk to the car, Greco began to think about what Ilario had said, and he was starting to get the feeling that the only experience the kid had growing up was with computers. Real life seemed to have either passed him by or never caught up to him. Greco wasn't sure, and maybe it didn't matter right now. But inside, he felt guilty about calling Ilario an audio-visual geek. They got into the car and sat down, both putting on their seatbelts.

Greco paused for a moment before starting the car. "Look, I didn't mean it like that earlier, calling you the AV geek. It was meant to be a compliment. I'm sorry if it came out wrong." Ilario said nothing and looked out of the front window. Greco thought he saw him nod slightly. He put the key in the ignition and started the car, and they were on their way back to the office. They listened to the radio most of the way back, the voices on the speaker talking sports, mostly about the Giants' upcoming game against Dallas.

When they reached the station, they both removed themselves from the car, still a little stuffed from their lunch. Greco said, shutting the car door, "Ugh...back to it, I guess."

"Thanks, Brian," Ilario said. "For lunch. No one in the department has really reached out to me like that in any way yet. You made me feel like a person today, not just a resource."

"Let's do it again sometime," Greco said with a smile. "You seem like a good kid, and I think you make a great addition to our team here. You're gonna help me catch my guy."

"If you bring me those IDs you have, I'll take a look and see if I can figure out who or what made them."

Greco smiled at him. "You got it."

They went their separate ways once they got into the office. When he got to his desk, Greco remembered that he had to check his messages, but he didn't have any. He organized his notes from when he tossed them onto the desk earlier, and got everything tidy and aligned. He opened his desk drawer and pulled out the false identifications for Shannon Fife.

"What a name. Whatever happened to John Smith?" Greco said aloud. He stood up from his desk and was getting ready to walk to Ilario's desk to hand them over to him for review when his phone rang.

"Greco," he said into the receiver.

"*Detective Greco, it's Kathleen Kelly, returning your call. How can I help you?*"

Chapter 53 – Cat

Will sat on his couch, the "guest bedroom" as he called it, in his mobile domicile, and flashed back to the words that Jim had said regarding the sheriff of the town the previous day as they were having lunch.

"How much pull does Utter have in this town?" Will had asked.

Jim replied: *"All of it."*

He wondered aloud if he even wanted to get mixed up with the Sheriff, who seemed to control the town and get whatever he wanted whenever he wanted it. It seemed like something out of a book he had read or a movie he had watched. *Maybe* Eye of the Tiger, *or something like that. That evil sheriff died in an exploding pick-up truck as Gary Busey escaped it just in time,* he thought. Red Rock West *would work, too. J.T. Walsh played a great bad sheriff.*

Will exhaled and shook his head, got dressed in his black attire, and went to see Denny Blewett at the high school. Will spent about forty-five minutes filling out eleven pages of paperwork, in which some of the information was true, and some was not. Before that, there had been an exchange between the two men which was nothing more than a five-minute question and answer session followed by a handshake between the two men. Will was completely bewildered at what had happened. All he did was stop a robber from getting away, and now he was a wrestling coach. *How did that just happen?*

Will's new job also included nearly year-round work as a base coach for the high school's baseball team and a bench coach for the football team. Will didn't even know what a bench coach was or what he was supposed to do. Blewett told him not to worry about it. The coach would fill him in. Will's salary for the job of the wrestling, baseball, and football coach would replace what he was no longer making stocking the shelves at D&J, plus, he would still work the hours he had set aside for the bookkeeping duties there.

He left the school and found himself walking back towards D&J's Liquor Store to start his shift there, and somewhere off in the distance, he heard the heavy bass of someone's car stereo. He had promised Jim he would finish out the week at the store and hopefully give him some time to find Will's replacement. *Someone is about to luck into an easy job*, he thought. *Hope they like pizza.* He was lost in his walk and his thoughts, and didn't hear the car pull up behind him until the horn was honked, which nearly caused his bowels to empty before he was ready for them to do so. He turned around abruptly and found himself staring into the front windshield of a Honda CR-X Del Sol, bright red in color and not a scratch or mar that he could see. It was gleaming. Behind the wheel of the little toy was the smiling face of Rocky. She pulled alongside him, and the passenger window came down.

"Hey, new guy," she said, smiling. He almost didn't hear her over the radio, which was so loud he could almost not determine who was singing and what was being sung. But then he heard the distinctive '*Uh-oooohhhhh*' from *E.I.* by Nelly. She turned down the stereo in the car, finally, and greeted him again in the same way, as if she knew he had not heard her the first time. "Where ya headed?"

"You nearly scared the hell out of me. D&J," he said, and kept walking as she drove alongside.

"It's not like you can't hear me coming," she said with a wink. "You wanna lift?"

He smiled and looked at the car, which he felt was about the size of a large roller skate. "Unless that's one of those cars where it looks really small until eleven clowns come out of it, I don't think you and I can fit in there at the same time."

She looked over her red-framed sunglasses, which just happened to match the color of the car exactly, and said, "Darlin', you'd be surprised how big this car can get when the cargo is right." He made a chortle sound and rolled his eyes at her as she laughed. "Come on," she said.

He stopped walking, and she stopped pacing him. He looked at her and shook his head. "Alright, but I might need some butter and a shoehorn to get out." He wedged himself into the passenger seat and shut the door. "Are you headed to the restaurant?" he asked.

"Yup," she said, and turned the music off. "Getting a produce delivery today, so there's a lot of chopping and slicing to do. Wanna help?"

"As fun as that sounds," he said. "No, I have to get to work. I promised Jim I'd finish out the week."

"And then do what?" she asked, forgetting the road and eyeballing him.

"Oh, don't tell me an activity happened in this town that you don't know about. You haven't heard anything through the grapevine?"

The smack on his shoulder was followed by, "No, what are you talking about?"

He looked at her, cleared his throat, and adjusted an imaginary bowtie at his neck like Rodney Dangerfield. "You're looking at the new wrestling coach for the Brindle Pronghorns."

"Get the f–," and then she caught herself. "Seriously?" she asked, eyes back on the road.

"Yes, ma'am," he said. "And a base coach for the baseball team and bench coach for the football team."

"Alright, I know what a base coach is, but what the hell is a bench coach?" she asked him.

"You know, I have no idea. I guess I'll find out when the time comes."

She looked over the top of her glasses again. "How did you fall into–oh," she stopped. "Utter. Utter talked to you after you stopped the burglar, found out about your wrestling background, and got you hooked up with Blewett."

"You put that together fast. Any missing pieces?" he asked.

"Nope," she said. "I know how Utter works. You did a good thing by not crossing him on this. Get on his good side, Billy."

More crap about this strong-arm sheriff, he thought. "Is there something I should know about Utter?"

"Nope," she said again. "Just, with him, you can either get along, or get it on. Don't swim upstream with him. He'll make your life miserable. Give you tickets for jaywalking, or having a taillight out, stuff like that. Don't rock the boat."

"I don't intend to, but I don't want to be his pet, either. I appreciate what he did for me, but it's gonna stop. I ain'–." He stopped himself from saying "ain't." This town and the people were invading his dialect and vocabulary. "I won't be told what to do with my life by the town sheriff unless he's arresting me."

"Fat chance of that now," she said. "You're already in his club. Do not fight this, Billy. Look at it as a gift you don't want to return."

Unbelievable, he told himself. *What have you gotten into here? You're either lucky or cursed, or maybe a bit of both.* She stopped the car in front of D&J's and popped the door locks. "Thanks for the lift," he said.

"You got it," she replied. "Come by for lunch soon if you're bored or hungry, or both. I'll make you a nice salad."

Will nodded and thanked her again, and she sped off down the road, lifting a trail of road dust up in her wake. He turned to the front of the liquor store, and all was dark inside. It wasn't ten o'clock yet. He leaned against the wall to wait for Jim to open the store and begin another day, and as he waited, he saw the same cat that he had seen the other day. It was in about the same spot it was in when he saw it before, and it was just sitting there, looking at him. Will held out his hand and made the 'pss pss pss' noise, and the cat looked at him and began to cross the street. It got to the sidewalk where Will was waiting, and then stopped. It then sat its rear end on the sidewalk, licked its paw, and then ran it over its head. It repeated this function several times, but it never took its eyes off Will. "Kitty," he said. "Come here." The cat finally stopped licking itself and took two cautious steps toward Will, who put out his hand to let the cat take a sniff. The cat did so, and after a few seconds, ran its face alongside Will's hand a few times. Will moved his hand to the top of the cat's head and scratched the dirty beast. The cat began to purr and squint its eyes. Will had no idea if the cat was male or female, and he couldn't tell by looking. It wasn't like the cat was one of those large dogs that shouldn't be allowed to leave their houses without wearing some sort of pants to cover their genitalia. The sex of the cat remained a mystery.

Suddenly, the cat darted off between the liquor store and its next-door neighbor. Will wondered what he had done, but then realized it was from the noise of Jim's car approaching. The sunroof was open, the windows were down, and the music was loud, and Will could identify *The Spirit of Radio* by Rush as the song Jim was blasting from his car speakers. Apparently, everyone in the town played their music loudly when they were in their cars on a nice day.

As Jim turned into the alleyway between the two stores, he held his hand up in a way so that his index and pinky fingers were extended, but the rest were not. It was the classic 'rock 'n roll' sign. Jim's tongue was also out, and his head was banging to the music. He drove by and parked his car in the back, and in a few minutes was unlocking the door of the liquor store.

"What's up, short-timer?" Jim said as he opened the door.

"I'm still here for the rest of the week," Will said. "I told you I wasn't leaving completely anyway. Somebody has to keep you in the black and out of jail."

"True, my friend, and I thank you for that!"

They went inside, turned on all the lights, set up for the day, and then just sat around waiting for something to happen. Will couldn't take the boredom anymore after about thirty minutes, and he did a quick check of stock before heading to the back room to grab what was needed to fill in the gaps. The day went without incident, for the most part, and Will headed for home around five o'clock in the evening. He felt something was not exactly right on his way home as he walked along his path to the trailer park. The sun was getting close to setting, and he looked down at his long shadow that stretched out in front of him. But there was another shadow, too. He stopped, and the other shadow stopped as well. He didn't turn around, but restarted his walk. He felt that if he could get home, he could shake his pursuer, even if just for the night. But the shadow continued to match his steps. He stopped again, smiled, and finally turned to face his stalker.

"Cat," he said, "stop following me." The cat just stopped and looked at him. It had piercing yellow eyes, and Will felt as if they were staring right through him. He walked backwards a few steps, watching the cat, and it stayed where it was, but when he turned around to walk forward again, the shadow followed. He ignored it until he got home, and when he unlocked the door to his trailer, the cat was right behind him. He turned, looked, and sighed, and said, "Are you hungry?" The cat offered no answer, but just looked at him. He figured he could spare some milk for the beast, so he said, "Wait here," as though the animal could understand him. Will opened the door, and the cat bolted inside the trailer before Will could stop it. He shook his head and followed the cat inside. When he shut the door, the cat was standing on the top step that led to his sleeping area. Will opened a cabinet and pulled down a Styrofoam bowl from the pack that he bought with the rest of his groceries the previous day. He poured some milk from the container in the refrigerator and set it on the floor in front of the cat. The cat sniffed it, stuck its tongue into the bowl once, and then did not remove its face from the bowl until the milk was gone. When it was, the cat looked at Will, licked around its mouth, and then lay down on the floor.

"You don't smell great, you know that?" Will asked the cat, which again did not answer. Will walked over to the cat and thought he would try to pick it up. He was worried the cat might scratch him; however, he made the attempt anyway, and the cat did not fight him. He took the cat to the bathroom and put him in the shower, and was expecting the cat to run when he turned the water on. It did not. Will did not know a lot about cats, but he was pretty sure he had heard somewhere that most of them did not like water. This one either didn't mind or wanted the bath. The dirt streamed off the cat and down into the drain, and Will attempted some shampoo, which the cat also did not seem to mind. When the ordeal was over, however, the cat did avoid the towel and instead jumped up on the kitchen counter and shook itself to attempt its own method of drying. Will could do nothing but laugh as the cat looked at him with wild eyes and its hair going in all directions. He opened the door to see if the cat wanted to leave, but it just went under the table and began to once again lick itself.

"Suit yourself," he said, and turned on the television. The World Series was on, and the Yankees were winning. He looked at the cat, who eyed him back, and then Will poured it more milk, of which the cat made short work, and then lay down again. As Will sat in his trailer that night, he was a little bit bewildered at the events of the last few days. *You have a new home, a new job, made some acquaintances, if not friends, stopped a buffoon robber from escaping, met the sheriff of the town, apparently have a pet, and have a new career as a coach for the high school. And it is exhilarating! What else can we do?*

At that moment, he jumped up and put his shoes back on, donned his favorite black jacket, put on his Baltimore Ravens hat, and made the ten-minute jog over to Rocky's for a late dinner. He had a salad, and when he was done, he asked Sheree, the young waitress, if he could speak to the manager. Rocky came out a few minutes later and smiled when she saw him. They chatted for a few minutes, and when they were done, Will had Rocky's phone number and promised to call her and ask her to go out on Saturday night.

He wondered to himself if he was moving too fast, too soon in this new town, but everything felt right. He wasn't sure if he was looking for a romantic relationship with Rocky, but he liked that she was spunky and a risk-taker. He just wanted to get to know her more. So, he decided that he would call her to go out tomorrow night. *Guess you're going out on a date with the owner of a pizza shop on Saturday night. You've got her phone number. Now you just need to get a phone, idiot,* he thought to himself. But, he didn't want to wait that long. As he jogged home, he found a payphone on a street corner and made the call to the number that Rocky just gave him. An answering machine picked up, and Will left an assertive message that they would be going out on Saturday night, and it was up to her to pick the place.

Chapter 54 – Leave

Greco sat across from Sergeant Harding's desk on the second floor of the station building and watched as Harding went through Greco's notes and the evidence he had collected. Harding's eyes were squinty, but that was normal for the sergeant. The furrowed eyebrows were what worried Greco. But Greco said nothing and let the note and evidence speak for themselves. Harding squinted more intently, and then his eyes relaxed.

"There are other cases you could be working on," Harding said, and Greco knew his case was on the brink of going cold. "You've got the robbery of that drug store on Church, and the missing husband, what's his name, Scarborough. You have enough on your plate to worry about chasing ghosts."

Greco objected. "I'll have the robbery wrapped up by tomorrow at the latest. The video is clear, and we know where the suspect lives. Grissom and Hagler are watching his house and place of business, and Ripken and Lewis are working the Scarborough case."

"Were," Harding said. "They are off of it."

"Why are they off the Scarborough case?"

Harding exhaled. "Because I'm putting you on it," he said.

"Why?" Greco exclaimed, his frustration level rising.

"Because this Kelly thing is a dead end. Literally. He's dead, he's gone, he's whatever. The company doesn't give a shit, and neither do I. Stop wasting resources on it. It's done."

"It's not done, Sarge!" Greco was almost yelling now. "I'm close on this. This guy is– –"

"Greco," Harding said, but Greco was still talking. Then Harding raised his voice. "Greco!" Greco stopped mid-sentence. "Listen to me," Harding said in a lower tone. "It's done." Both men were quiet and just looked at each other; each was equally frustrated with the other. Harding exhaled, dropped his head, and put his hands against his desk. "You've got today," he said, giving in. "I need concrete evidence that he's alive and on the run by EOD, or it's done. You got that?"

Greco looked at the floor and then out of the window, trying to calm himself. "Got it," he said, grabbed his box of evidence, and headed back to his desk. He thought to himself that he had one sure bullet in the chamber, and that was Kelly's wife, the not-so-cooperative Dr. Kathleen Kelly, with whom he had a scheduled meeting in about an hour. That gave him time to make a phone call.

Maureen Polyniak at Pickwick answered the phone and identified herself, and Greco was relieved that he would not have to wait on hold or get passed around like an old football. Once he had identified himself to Maureen, he got right to the point.

"Ms. Polyniak, did you happen to find any more accounts that you think Mr. Kelly may have opened in an unlawful or questionable manner?"

"Funny you should ask, Detective," she said. *"We found it just this morning. I was going to call you after lunch, once everything settled down."*

Greco listened and took notes in his book. "And was the name on the account for Shannon Fife?"

There was a pause, and then Maureen said, *"It was, Detective. How did you know?"*

"Thank you, Ms. Polyniak. Please call me if you find any more suspicious accounts."

"Will do, Detective."

In his car on the way over to Kathleen Kelly's apartment, Greco was still trying to put the pieces together about how Will Kelly had disappeared into thin air. It didn't make sense. He had to be somewhere, and Greco's hourglass was running out of sand. He had nine hours to put a case together, or he was going to lose it, based on what the sergeant had said.

Greco arrived at the address given to him by Maryanne back at the station for Kathleen Kelly. He knocked on the door of the apartment, and Kathleen answered almost immediately. She greeted him and asked him to come inside, which he did. He stood by the door and waited for her to get settled, moving throw pillows from one couch to another.

"Please, sit down," she said. He took the edge of a gleaming white sofa and pulled out his notebook from under his coat. "Can I get you anything?" she asked him.

"No," he said. "No, I'm fine, thank you."

She glided across the room, and Greco watched as she sat down on the couch across from him, the two of them separated by a wrought iron and glass coffee table. Greco caught himself wondering what she must have done to make Willem Kelly want to leave her so badly that he would fake his own death to get away from her.

"What can I do for you, Detective?" she asked.

"I'm just trying to tie up some loose ends in your husband's case."

"Loose en—you've solved it?" she asked, almost giddy. "What did you find out?"

"Not so fast, Doctor Kelly. We're sitting at a dead end, and my sergeant has me on a pretty short leash. I fear the case is going to go unsolved unless we get some leads. Assuming your husband did not perish in the WTC, he's done a pretty good job of covering his tracks, and, well, he could be anywhere. I came by to see if you had any more information."

She squirmed a little on the couch. "Inform— about what?"

"Your husband's disappearance, Doctor Kelly. Do you know anything more about it?" Greco was getting impatient, and his time was running out.

"Detective, I told you everything I know, and have not learned anything new. It's not like my dead husband called me and told me where he was." She sighed heavily and looked around her apartment. She looked at Greco. "Are your married, Detective?"

"No," Greco responded, a bit taken aback by the question. "I am not."

"Imagine you're me, Detective," Kathleen began. "On the worst day in the history of this country, your spouse dies.

That's bad enough. But now imagine that you find out that your spouse may actually still be alive, but has chosen another life over continuing the one they had with you. How would that make you feel? Trust me, Detective, when I say that you know everything that I know."

Greco leaned forward on the sofa. He almost thought that would have been impossible had he not pulled off the feat himself. His legs were tucked up under himself and crossed, and he had put himself in one of the most uncomfortable positions he recalled ever having sat. Yet, he found himself leaning further forward, defying gravity.

Greco sighed. "Dr. Kelly, let me tell you something. If it comes out that you're withholding information, you're going to be just as guilty as your husband. That's all I'm saying." He awkwardly rose to his feet and nearly lost his balance, and then slapped his notebook against his hand. He nodded to her and said, "Thanks for your time. I'll let myself out." He walked to the door and closed it behind him, but not until after a dramatic pause, when he turned back toward Kathleen, and then back toward the door. He raced back to the office and when he got there, shoved everything on his desk toward the wall, some of which fell on the floor. He ignored it and then overturned the box of evidence he had accumulated for the Kelly case.

As he went through what was the contents of the box, he examined and thought heavily about each piece of evidence he had. The identification cards, the reports from Pickwick, the videos from the bank. He laid it all out, looked at it in different ways, and from different angles. At the end of the day, he came up with a relatively large pile of nothing. No one was left to question. No clues were left outstanding. Ilario's search for the source of the fake identity cards would take longer than Greco had, and Harding put a stop to it. Greco had even had the cards fingerprinted, but he came up empty. He had nothing.

He decided to make one last run at Harding as the day came to a close. He packed the pieces of evidence into the box, neatly and in an organized fashion. He carried the box through the station and to Sergeant Harding's office. He stopped outside the open door and gave a quick two taps on the reinforced glass next to the door frame.

"Come," came from Harding's voice from inside the office. Greco entered, legging the box on his shoulder. He set the box into one of two empty seats across from Harding's desk. "Sit," Harding said. Greco took the other seat and waited for Harding to finish reading the report on which his eyes were fixated. When the paper was finally lowered and put on top of a stack of similar documents, Harding moved his eyes to Greco. "Whadaya got, Greco?"

Greco's eyes moved to the floor as he scratched his left temple. He returned them to Harding's and said, "About the same. The wife was a dead end. Claims she knows nothing more about it. I have to believe her. Nothing in the evidence says otherwise. Also, the financing company confirmed the eleventh account, which matched the name on the last set of IDs we came across."

"Any lead on where the IDs came from?" Harding asked.

Greco had to bite his tongue to keep from lashing out at Harding for taking Ilario off that task. He held his contempt in check, however, and said, "Ilario wasn't able to find out anything yet."

Harding exhaled and leaned up toward his desk. "Leave it open as unsolved," he said. "Don't actively pursue it, though. You have enough to do outside of that case."

"What's up?" Greco asked, wondering what else he would have piled onto his plate.

Harding swiveled around in his chair and retrieved a box of files from a credenza at his back. "They are yours, now," Harding said, standing from his chair, and holding the box out to Greco.

Greco took the box from Harding and placed it on top of the box of evidence from the Kelly case. He flipped through some of the files, and a frown came over his face. "These are Steve's cold cases," he said. "Why are you giving them to me?"

Harding put his hands on his hips, exhaled, and looked down at the floor. "Because Steve's not coming back. Not any time in the foreseeable future, anyway."

A puzzled look came over Greco's face, and Harding's eyes went back to the floor. "What's wrong with Steve?" Greco asked. "I thought he was getting better."

"His wife called earlier today. A blood clot formed in his shoulder, which the doctors were treating with blood thinners. The clot came loose and went into Steve's brain, causing a stroke. I'm not going to lie to you, Greco. He's in pretty bad shape right now." Harding paused and looked at Greco for a second, and then continued. "Now I know this affects you. So, as of now, you're on leave, with pay."

"Leave?" Greco almost yelped. "No, Sarge, I'm good. Let me find this guy!"

Harding interrupted. "You are not thinking clearly. You don't have the evidence. You...you don't have shit! You are not going to find this guy! You are compromised, and so now, now you're on leave! Two weeks!"

Greco exhaled and sat back down. His head shook slightly back and forth. "I can't believe this. I just saw him two days ago, and he was fine!"

"I was just as shocked to hear it, too," Harding said, softening. "He's not alert, but he's not on life support, either, so he's still fighting. He hasn't given up."

Greco looked at the boxes in the chair next to his. He stood up and loaded the boxes into his arms. "Yeah," he said, looking at the boxes, and then at Harding, and then he started for the door. "He's not giving up. There's enough of that going on around here already."

"Hey!" Harding shouted, but Greco kept walking. Harding let him go.

Greco walked down the hall to the floor and found his desk and dumped the stack of boxes on its surface. His brow was furrowed, and his lips were almost pouty with anger. He looked at the two boxes and then down the hall to Harding's desk. He took a deep breath and exhaled, almost audibly, "I'm right on this. I'm gonna go find this son of a bitch, myself."

Chapter 55 – Friends

"Why are you here?" The question had a stern tone to it, and it immediately made Will uncomfortable. A bright light was now pointing right into his face.

"What's that?" Will asked, with a squint, to try to avoid the light.

"Why are you here?" the question came again. "Of all places you could have gone to start over, what brought you here, to Brindle?"

It was a straightforward question, and one that he could answer easily, assuming he wanted to spill his guts about everything that had been going on in the last few months. He was a thief masquerading as a dead man to some, and as a completely different person to others, and he was hiding from them all, and anyone else who might know of or about him. If he did come clean, that would certainly clear the air and remove a weight from his shoulders. However, thinking better of the situation, that response was not his first choice. That would only cause him more trouble. He worked on a version of the truth that he hoped would satisfy his interrogator. He was tired of the big city. He wanted to get away. He didn't want to work on the boat in Seattle anymore. Brindle was just a random choice of places that seemed far away from all of it. That should work, but he was terrified of the follow-up questions before he even knew what they were. This was not how he intended to spend his evening. He tried to look away from the light, but all he saw were a lot of purple dots burned into his field of vision.

"By bus," Will said meekly, and the reaction he got indicated that the interrogation would continue. He had just wanted to have a nice, quiet dinner with Rocky, and get to know her a little, and maybe go see a movie, assuming the town had a theater. He didn't even know if that was the case yet. He would have asked her, but they had dinner, and then the night spun off in this trajectory instead. He wished it had gone the other way. He wished he had some water, as his throat was dry, and all he could taste was garlic from his dinner.

The light burning in his eyes was finally extinguished as the car in the parking lot across the street finally got into gear and went on its way. He turned and looked at Rocky, but still only saw the purple dots.

"No, I mean, how did you get here?" she asked. "Did you choose here, or end up here? It's not like New York or Chicago, where you get offered a great job and you move to it. There are no great jobs here that anyone can't get out of high school."

"I guess we chose each other," he said. "I wanted to get away from the cities, and I had to get off the water. It was just time for something new. My car burned up in a fire the day before I was going to come out here, so I took a bus and rolled on out to beautiful and wild Nebraska."

"So, how did it choose you?" she asked.

"Funny story," he said, and wondered how much of the burnt notebook with only Brindle remaining within it he should tell her. He looked at her, and she looked amused, eyebrows arched. She wanted to hear the story. "When I left Philly and went out to the West Coast, I drove. Being from the big city, the small towns intrigued me. They seemed different, almost special. So, one day, I bought a notebook and started keeping track of all the towns I stopped in. I logged in things like where I slept, if I did, where I ate, if I did, and the general feel of the town. I had decided to get out of Seattle, get out of the fishing business, but I wasn't sure where I wanted to go. I thought about my notebook, but didn't think to look into it until I had no other choice."

"What do you mean by not having a choice?" she asked.

"I told you my car burned, right? Well, the notebook was in the glovebox, and it burned pretty well, but not all the way. In fact, there was only one page remaining that was actually legible."

"Brindle," she said.

"Correctamundo."

"Ugh, don't say that. My ex-husband used to say that all the time. Yuck." She dragged out the 'yuck' into about three different syllables. "He picked it up after about the fourteenth time watching *Pulp Fiction*."

"I'll try to forget the word," he said, smiling, and she playfully pushed him on the shoulder, and he swayed a solid inch away. "My turn," he said. "How does someone like you get the name 'Rocky' hung on her?"

She laughed again. "Took you long enough," she said. "Most people ask in the first five minutes."

"I think you'll find I'm not 'most people,'" he said.

"Hmph. So far, so good, anyway." She looked out into the road as the night wind blew the dust from the road across it, making small dust tornadoes as it did. "What's your name?" she asked.

He cocked his head and looked at her, then decided to play her game. "Billy," he said. "But you know that."

"Your real name," she said.

Will recoiled from the question, but recovered, and said, "William."

She stuck out her hand. "William, nice to meet you. My name is Raquel. My friends, and everyone else, call me 'Rocky.'" He took her hand and gave it two short pumps.

"I guess I could have put that together," he said. "A nickname."

She looked across the street at the parking lot of the Hungry Horse Restaurant, where they had just had their late dinner, and watched as car after car leaving pointed its headlights right at Will's face. "I think a lot of people have nicknames," she said. "Some they are born with, and some they choose, and some that get planted on them for some apparent or otherwise reason. Look at you. You're Billy, which you chose over William. You didn't wanna be called William, so you chose to be called Billy."

Will thought back to all the years that he was called Willem, his real name. He didn't mind it, but he really didn't like Willie or Billy, back then, especially when it was used with his last name. He never liked the almost rhyming end parts of his first and last names used together, as Willie Kelly. He just preferred Will if his last name were to follow. It reminded him of a television show he watched with his father when they were younger, "The Equalizer." The man who played Robert McCall was Edward Woodward. It just didn't feel right coming off the tongue, not to Will anyway.

"I suppose you're right," he said. "I used to work on a boat with two guys, once was named 'Stump', and 'Jelly' was the other one." It was in the middle of this sentence that Will noticed that he had picked up a bit of an accent when he talked. It wasn't Baltimore, not Philly, by no means was it New York, it wasn't Georgia, and it certainly wasn't Texas. It was Brindle, Nebraska. He caught it.

"Hey," Rocky said.

"Wha-?" he said, jolted from his thoughts.

"Where'd you go?" she asked.

"What's that?" he asked her in return.

"I said, 'Where did you go?'" she asked again, a little more sternly.

"Nowhere," Will said. "I'm right here."

"Were you ignoring me? I asked you a question."

"No," Will said apologetically. "I'm sorry. I was thinking back to the boat."

"That's what I was asking you about. Who was 'Stump'?"

"Oh," he said, with a slight smile. "Stump was a deckhand on the last boat I worked on. They had this machine on the boat that chopped frozen bait into little bits and pieces so we could put them in the bait boxes to go into the pots. Stump was grinding bait one day and got a little too close. He lost his middle finger just above the knuckle, so he had a little stump of a middle finger. Crazy bastard made me make him give me the finger before he would even tell me the story."

"Eww," she said, but it came out as 'EE-yoo.' "You saw the accident?"

"No, it happened before I was hired. But, that's how he got his nickname, like you said."

"And the other, 'Jelly', I think it was?" She paused. "Please don't tell me part of him was squished into little bits by a machine and turned into jelly."

"No, nothing like that," Will said, and then he laughed. "You know, it's funny. It took him four trips on that boat before he trusted me enough to tell me."

"Trust issues?" she asked. "From a guy who works closely with others on a small boat?"

"So, there's a story," Will said. "He finally told me this story while we were making a turn to go pick up some pots that we had laid out earlier. It was about a two, two-and-a-half-hour run. The weather was horrible. Just a pounding rain, lightning everywhere, and swells I thought could swallow the boat up at any time. I was actually scared for a little while. It was sketchy. We were lying in our bunks, me up top, and him right under me, and we were talking about life, and past acquaintances, and finally, I asked him where he got the name from. His story took nearly the entire time of that two-and-a-half-hour run. Looking back, I think it really scarred him up as a kid, and he remembered names, and the faces were etched into his mind, and he said he'd never forget how cruel the other kids were to him back then."

"Cruel about what?" Rocky asked.

"Well, turns out, he was chubby as a kid. More than chubby, he told me. Just plain fat, is what he said. The other kids called him all kinds of names, like 'Fatso' and 'Piggy' and all those other names that kids call other kids who are different. Some real mental bullying was going on, ya know? Anyway, all the kid ate for lunch was peanut butter and jelly sandwiches, and he had one every day. No difference any time. Every day for lunch, he had a PB&J. And the kids would crack on him and tell him he needed to eat salad, or carrot sticks, and things like that. One day, some kid made a crack about him eating peanut butter and jelly sandwiches because that was all his mother could afford, making money as a hooker."

"Oh no," Rocky gasped. "How terrible." The breeze blew Will's hair down from his head and into his eyes. She brushed it away and looked at him. "You guys must have really made a connection on that boat for him to trust you with this story," she said, and then she shivered.

Will took off his jacket as he said, "Yeah, I guess we kinda did. I miss those guys a little, and I miss that water and the work on the boat, but I'll never go back to it." He placed the jacket over her bare shoulders and said, "You should have dressed warmer, silly. Come on, let's get back to the car."

"I wasn't shivering at the cold," she said, getting to her feet. "When you were telling about how terrible those kids were to another kid gave me chills. Hatred and bullying, things like that, they just make me ill. It's like spinach. Just turns my stomach. Blechh." She sighed and said, "I'm sorry. I've gone and made your story about me. Please continue."

Will looked up at the night sky and could not wrap his mind around the stars and how bright they were. He quoted:

"I will love the light for it shows me the way,

Yet I will endure the dark because it shows me the stars."

"What's that?"

"Something I read once," Will said. "Augustine Mandino."

"If you say so," she said.

"Where were we?" Will asked, beginning the walk back.

"The hooker," she said.

"Oh, right. So, the kid says that to Jelly, and according to Jelly, he was on the kid in less than a heartbeat, and he started wailing on him, like Ralphie in that movie *A Christmas Story*. Just over and over, lefts and rights, wham, wham, wham. He beat the hell out of the kid, and after that, the other kids saw him differently. Some became his friends, including, eventually, the kid he beat up. One day, one of his new friends asked him about the PB&J sandwiches and the real reason he ate them. He said, 'Hey Elliott, why do you eat peanut butter and jelly every day?' He answered, 'Because I like them, and they are easy to make. It is something I can do myself, so I don't have to worry my parents with it.' And the other kid said, 'Maybe we can call you Peanut Butter and Jelliot!' Jelly said the lunchroom table at which he sat became quiet, and they all looked at Jelly. Jelly said he started to laugh, and for a while, they did call him that, but found it too long, so it was shortened to Jelliot, and then just Jelly."

They kept walking along the dusty road at almost a meandering pace, neither in a hurry to have the night end. They did get back to the car, but instead of sitting in it, they sat on a roadside bench. They looked up at the sky, so bright with stars, and Rocky craned her neck to see a bright one just overhead. Her head landed on Will's shoulder, and she left it there, and he didn't mind.

"So," she said. "How did this little interaction between you and Jelly conclude?"

"Well, it was a bit heavy in the room for most of his story, so I tried to lighten the mood with a joke."

"What did you say?" Rocky asked.

"Well, I said, 'You know, being so young then, that was really thoughtful of you, taking care of making your own lunch. Your mom must have appreciated it, you know, being a hooker and all.'"

"You didn't!" Rocky exclaimed.

"I did, and he was out of his bunk so fast and got me into a headlock, but I turned it around on him and got his arm pinned behind his back, but we were just goofing around. Unfortunately, that was when the captain walked in and saw us rolling around on the floor together. We sat there in silence with him looking at us, and we were looking back at him. He just said, 'I hope you're using a condom,' and he turned around to leave. Then he said, 'When you're done basking in the afterglow and finished with your cigarettes, come to the main deck and let's catch some fish.'"

Rocky laughed and picked her head up from Will's shoulder. "Your captain was a good guy, it seems."

"Yeah, but hard to get to know. One day, I'll tell you how he hired me. That's a tale, too." He took in a breath of the night air and felt cleaner from it. He loved the air in Brindle. It seemed so clean as opposed to that in Seattle or New York.

He looked at Rocky and said, "So, tell me about you. How did you get to be a restaurant owner?"

She sighed and said, "It's a long story, one for another night. I'm getting tired."

"Understood," he said. "Some other time." They sat on the bench for a minute, and Will decided that he was truly happy there. The sun had set, but there was still a purple glow just about the tops of the hills in the distance. A rifle shot in the distance was heard by both of them, yet neither budged. Will looked around and couldn't help what he was feeling. "It's amazing," he said.

"What's amazing," she asked.

"How different the world feels when the skyline changes." She looked at him for a long moment, and he looked back at her. There was an awkward moment between the two, and she moved closer to him, and their lips met for the shortest of moments, and then he pulled back, and then she pulled back.

"What's wrong?" she said, more as a statement than a question. "Did I do something bad?"

"No," he said, exhaling. "It's me, not you." He turned and looked her in the eyes. "One day I'll tell you the full story, but I'm just coming off of another relationship, and I'm not really ready to get back into something until I know it's right. I like you, Rocky, but I don't want to make a mistake we're going to regret later on. I want us to be friends, no matter what."

"Friends," she said, abruptly.

Will became a bit defensive. "Look, Rock—"

She cut him off. "I don't need any more friends, Billy. Christ, I got a whole town full of friends. Anyone who wants a free pizza wants to be my friend! I thought—" The tone of her voice dropped, and she calmed. "I hoped you would be different. I thought you might want something more, but I guess you just want pizza."

"Rocky, I—"

"I have to go," she said. She took off Will's jacket and handed it to him, and then walked expeditiously to her car.

He walked after her, and when he approached her car, he tried to yell through her closed window.

"Rocky, I didn't—" She pulled away in a cloud of dust and left him there in mid-sentence. "—mean it that way," he said, words trailing off. "Do you want to go see a movie?!" he shouted at her rear bumper, but it, along with the rest of the car and Rocky inside of it, continued to disappear into the distance and the dust. *Good job, idiot.* "Shut up," he yelled. Though his comment was directed only to himself, no one was around to hear him anyway. When he could no longer see her car, he turned around, unlocked the Daytona, and climbed inside. His ride back to his trailer, his home, was miserable. He parked the car at the front of the trailer, locked it, and went inside. He hung up his jacket in the little closet by the refrigerator, and then went into the bathroom. When his business was completed, he washed his hands and, as he dried them, he looked in the mirror. His reflection looked back at him, shook its head, and called him an idiot again.

Chapter 56 – Come On Out, Mr. Lomax

Still referring to himself as an idiot the next morning, Will ate a quick bowl of Oat Holes cereal and then put on his running shoes and went for a tour of the city. He had still only been here for a few days and had accomplished a lot. However, he felt like he didn't really know the town yet, not that he could say that he would accomplish that as well with just one run, but if he ran every day, he could get to know more of it over a period of time. He took off from the trailer park, ran past Gil's house on 6th Street, then went a block south to 7th. He stayed there, passing a lot of houses and a funeral home, and kept going until he hit the edge of the main part of town. He followed the road around a curve and found 4th Street and took it all the way back until he ran into the Fairgrounds, where he turned south and then east back onto 4th Street, which led him back to the trailer park. He enjoyed this run and thought he would keep mainly the same path for the next few days, with a little bit of variance just so it wouldn't get stale.

Will crammed himself into his small shower in the trailer and washed off the sweat and debris from the run. When he got out, he wore nothing, as nothing was needed, as he was alone. Or he thought he was, until he remembered the cat, who was sitting on top of the table, looking at him.

"What are you looking at?" Will asked. The cat said nothing, of course, but stretched its back leg over its head and began to lick the inside of the leg again. "Show off," he said, and took the two steps up to his bedroom to get dressed. A few minutes later, he came back down the steps and went to the refrigerator. He opened up a container and pulled out a few pieces of chicken from a leftover chicken Caesar salad. He put them on a paper plate and cut them up into smaller pieces, and then put the plate down onto the floor for the cat. It looked at the food on the plate, and then back up at Will, and then slowly began to eat. Then, the pace of the eating picked up, and within a few minutes, the chicken was gone. Will filled an old butter bowl that he found in the cabinet with water, grabbed his keys, and went outside, with the cat following him out. Will placed the water bowl in a shady spot beneath the trailer. He felt bad about leaving the cat outside, but he figured since the cat was outside for at least days when they first met, it would be okay. Another reason for the cat going outside was that Will had not yet had the chance to pick up a litter box for the beast, and he was a little wary about what the cat might leave behind in his home.

The cat seemed content to stay outside, and Will wondered if it would be there when he got home. Whether it was or not, Will had a feeling that it would be okay. If it stuck around, he'd have to think of a name for the thing. He couldn't just call it "Hey You." He felt like it needed a real name. Finding out the sex was a minor goal, and all of this was assuming the animal stayed with him and that he accepted the animal.

He started his walk to the liquor store for one of his last few days before starting his new position at the high school as a multi-sport coach. He'd never been a coach before. He knew the sport of wrestling, but knowing the rules and having the patience and the ability to teach teenage boys the finer points? Well, that remained to be seen.

He was just past Gil's house when he heard the familiar sound of Rush coming from a car stereo behind him. Before he even turned around, he knew it was Jim. A quick peek over his left shoulder yielded a vision of a black Dodge Daytona, and his suspicions were confirmed. The car pulled up on his left side and slowed, and the passenger window dropped within the door, and the music was suddenly louder, Will noticed.

"Hey Buddy!" Jim yelled out the window.

"What's going on?" Will said, continuing his walk.

"Wanna ride?"

"Nah," Will said. "I'll leave you to your car. I like the exercise."

"Hey, goof, I wasn't asking if you wanted a ride, I was asking if you want *to ride*."

Will stopped. "What are you talking about?"

"Look in the back."

It was at that moment that Will noticed the rear lift gate was propped open on the car. He moved around to the back of the car, and Jim parked the car and met him there. He opened the lift gate, and lying down in the trunk of Jim's car was a bicycle. It was a beautiful midnight blue and appeared only slightly used.

"You bought a bike?" Will asked.

"I bought *you* a bike!" He stopped, began taking the bike from the back of the car, and then spoke again. "Actually, I traded for the bike. Ryan Busch picked up quite a little bit of a tab over at the store, and he traded me this to pay it off."

"And you want to give it to me."

"And I am giving it to you!"

Will's hands went to his hips. He looked at the bike gleaming in the morning sun and thought about how good it would feel to ride again. It had been too long. "Alright," he said, knowing that Jim had gone through some effort to do this for him, and also that he would not take 'no' for an answer.

"Get on and get going," Jim said. "I don't want to see you in the store until at least noon. Give it a shake down, figure out what needs to be fixed!" Jim started laughing on the last part. "But that's your responsibility!" He hopped back into the Daytona and sped away, music still blaring.

Will pulled the bike over to the curb and checked the tightness of the seat, then lifted the bike from the seat and turned the pedals. No rubbing of the tires, and no squeaking from the chain, Will noticed. He shook his head and exhaled, then straddled the bicycle. And kicked up the kickstand. He began to pedal the bike, and before he knew it, he was rolling along at a decent speed, and the wind in his face and hair felt electrifying. He'd never had a beard like this before, and the wind flowing through it felt off, but welcoming. He made a left turn at Maple, and then a right on Seventh, and took the same route he did when he took his previous run, straight up Seventh, past the funeral home, and then made the same loop back to where he started, back to the exact same place where Jim had given him the bike. He stopped the bike, his leg propped against the curb. It took him a minute to notice that he was smiling. He loved getting back to running, but he missed running his bike through the hills of his home. There were no hills in Brindle, but the feeling was the same. It had indeed been too long.

His thoughts drifted back to his old life. Yes, he hated the commute to work, and Kathleen was sometimes a pain in his ass. *Overall, though*, he questioned himself. Was *it really that bad that you had to go to these lengths? You've had to create a whole new life just to fit in.* Then he thought a little more. *If you take the 'f' out of life, you get 'lie'. And that's what you're living. One big lie. Just because you had to "get the 'f' out."* He smiled. *But you're having fun, admit it.* He shook his head, lifted his leg from the curb, and began to pedal the bike around the town and then to the store. When he got there, he checked the time, just to be sure he didn't break Jim's early curfew. It was ten minutes past noon, so he knew he was safe from any wrath. He laid the bike up against the outside wall and noticed the sheriff's car was parked in the back lot. He walked around the front of the store and through the front door, and found Jim at the cash register as usual.

"How's the bike?" Jim asked, looking up from a newspaper spread across the cash register counter.

"Pretty good," Will said. "In fact, I can't find anything wrong with it. Not so far anyway." Will walked toward the counter and looked around the store. The fact that the sheriff was there gave him a bad feeling. He didn't want to be in the pocket of the sheriff because of the coaching job, and he didn't want to be in the crosshairs of the man, either. *Hopefully, he isn't here to arrest me*, Will thought. He didn't see the sheriff anywhere, so he asked Jim about it.

"What's uh," he stammered. "What's the sheriff doing here?"

"Oh, man. I don't really want to tell you," Jim said.

"What do you mean?" Will asked.

"What did you do?" Jim asked.

"What are you talking about?" Will was perplexed.

"How long have you been in town?" Jim asked.

"Why are you answering my questions with questions? Just tell me."

"Man, I will let Utter tell you. Just wait," Jim said.

Will sighed. "Where is he?"

"Back in the terlit. He should be out directly." The door chime made a ding-dong sound as a man Will had seen before came into the store. He wasn't sure where he had seen him, but he knew the man looked familiar. Will watched as he went to the cooler in the back, picked up a twelve-pack of beer, and then came back to the front of the store.

"Just getting' off, Mel?" Jim asked.

"You know it," the apparent Mel stated. "I don't go back in until the day after tomorrow, so I'm gonna chill for a bit and drink some beer."

"I hear ya," Jim said, giving Mel his change. Mel left the store, and Will still could not figure out from where he knew the man.

"Okay," Will said. "I know he's Mel, but where do I know him from?"

"He works over at the Speedy Mart. Midnight to noon. Shitty shift."

"Ahh," Will said. "Okay, I'm going to get started. I'm sick of waiting on the sheriff to finish shaking his...you know." Jim looked at him and laughed, shaking his head. He returned his attention to the newspaper on his desk.

Will was on his way back to the storage room when Sheriff Utter met him at the narrow doorway. Will stopped short and then backed up a few steps to let the sheriff pass him.

"Hello, young fella," Utter said.

"Sheriff," Will said, a little nervously.

"You're just the man I'm looking for."

"Is that right?" Will asked, wondering if he could break for the door and get out if so needed.

"Yes, sir," Utter responded. "Why don't we head towards the front of the store?"

"Uh, okay," Will said.

The sheriff held his arm open, pointing towards the cash register. "After you, Mr. Lomax," he said from under his poofy mustache and with arched eyebrows. They moved toward the front of the store, and when they got there, the sheriff continued pointing to the door. Will looked at Jim, who was feigning interest in his newspaper. Will opened the door, ignoring the *ding-dong* noise, and they walked out to the sidewalk and then around the side of the building to where the sheriff's car was parked. He opened the right-rear passenger door and motioned for Will to get in and sit. He closed the door when Will was seated, and then moved to the driver's side of the car. He opened the front door and climbed into the driver's seat, and then closed the door, fastened his seat belt, and started the car.

"Can I ask where we are going, Sheriff?"

"It's time we had a chat, Mr. Lomax, and I just thought I'd drive you around the town of Brindle for a little bit, before you have to leave it." The sheriff gave him a rearview mirror full of eyeballs.

"Why would I leave?" Will asked, now more nervous than before.

"Mr. Lomax, what should I know about you?"

"Excuse me?" Will asked.

The sheriff pulled the car out into the street and began a medium-paced cruise. "What do I need to know about you?" he asked. "Are you a smoker? Do you drink too much? Are you a compulsive shoplifter? Do you wet the bed? Do you gamble? Do you do drugs? Do you have any warrants out for your arrest back in Philadelphia? Do you have children? What do I need to know about you?"

Will shifted uncomfortably in the seat and caught the sheriff's eye in the mirror once again. "Uh, no smoking, I have beer every now and then and hard liquor even less, I don't shoplift, no bed wetting since I was ten, except for college, which goes back to the drinking thing, I don't do drugs, and—." Will thought for a minute, trying to think of anything but the final question about the arrest warrants. "What else?"

The sheriff looked at him in the mirror again. "Gambling and arrest warrants," Utter said.

"Oh, yeah, arrest warrants in Philly. No, none of those either." *Technically not a lie,* he told himself. *You don't know about New York, but there's probably nothing in Philly.* "I've gambled in football pools and things like that, but I'm not a casino junkie, if that's what you mean."

Utter continued his tour around Brindle and was quiet for a moment. Then, after making a turn onto Acorn, he spoke. "What do you think of our town, Mr. Lomax?"

"It's fine," Will said. "I have enjoyed my time here so far. Why do you ask?" Will wanted to get to the bottom of this visit with the sheriff. He was getting more and more nervous the longer the trip was taking.

"Just curious, Mr. Lomax, why you chose here."

"I was out on the West Coast and fate stepped in. I guess that's the long story short. I drove through Brindle on my way out west, and I remembered it on my way back."

"You drove through it?" the Sheriff asked. "You don't have a car, Mr. Lomax."

"No, sir, I left it in Washington."

"What was in Washington?"

"The fire that engulfed it," Will said. "Burned to an empty shell."

"You didn't burn it, did you, Mr. Lomax?"

"No, sir. There was a fire in my landlord's house, and it spread to the garage."

"Do you have any questions for me, Mr. Lomax?"

"What's this all about, Sheriff?"

"Hmm hmm," Utter said. Will thought it might be a laugh, but wasn't sure. "I need your help, Mr. Lomax."

Will was relaxing a little more, but was tiring of the game. "What can I help with, Sheriff?"

"You ever thought about a career in law enforcement?"

"Ha!" Will yelled, a lot louder than he wanted. Utter looked back at him through the mirror. "Are you serious?" Will asked.

"As cancer, Mr. Lomax," Utter said, and pulled the car to the side of the road near the fairgrounds and came to a stop. He unlocked the doors from the inside and exited the vehicle. Will wasn't sure if he should get out or not, but thought that if he did not, Utter might view it the wrong way. He reached to pull the handle of the door, but then realized there was no handle. Probably good, as far as keeping arrested individuals confined was concerned. Utter was at the door now, and opened it from the outside and beckoned Will to exit as well. "Come on out, Mr. Lomax."

"You can just call me Billy if you want."

"I'd like to keep things formal for now, whether on or off the job. It cuts down on the confusion." He shut the door once Will was clear and began to walk toward the edge of the horse corral and leaned on the fence. "Mr. Lomax, you met Deputies Oglethorpe and Cortez the other night. Did you happen to meet Deputy Mulholland yet?"

"Can't say I'm sure one way or the other, Sheriff," Will said. "What does he look like?"

Utter snorted under the walrus mustache. "She, Mr. Lomax. Deputy Mulholland is female." He took his hat off and then replaced it again, using it to fix his hair. "And she's pregnant."

"Sheriff, you can add that to the list of things I didn't do as well. Now, please, what does this have to do with me?"

"Deputy Mulholland will go on leave in a few months, and I need a replacement for her. I need someone dependable, someone who has a good feel for what is right and what is wrong, and someone young and agile enough to do the job. Mr. Lomax, I'm a pretty good judge of character, and I think that someone I need is you."

"You want me to be a cop?" Will asked.

"Sheriff's Deputy, Mr. Lomax. What do you think?"

Will thought of any excuse he could muster to effectively say 'no,' but anything he thought would work escaped him. He tried anyway.

"Well, I have my spot at the liquor store, and you also got me the coaching slot at the high school."

"Don't worry about the high school," Utter said. "I have already taken care of that."

Will thought back to what Jim said about Utter having all the pull in the town. Utter had gotten Will a job at the high school, and then just as fast, found his replacement while recruiting Will to be a 'sheriff's deputy'. He thought about Sun Tzu. At least he thought it was Sun Tzu. If he had an enemy in Brindle, it would be the sheriff. So, why not keep his friends close and the sheriff closer? *Extremely close*, Will thought.

"What do I need to do?" Will asked.

"Nothing," Utter said. "Except go to training for three months."

"What kind of training?"

"Law enforcement training, Mr. Lomax." Utter motioned for them to head back to the car. "You'll run the gauntlet. You'll do everything from cardiovascular training to target practice. You'll study laws, you'll learn the local codes, and you'll know our traffic laws like the back of your hand. You'll learn how to save lives, and you'll learn how to take 'em, if necessary."

"What about—."

Utter cut Will off. "Don't worry about background checks or paperwork. I'll take care of all that. You just need to get out to Grand Island for training."

Will stiffened. "Grand Island. New York?" *Going back to New York is NOT a good idea.* Utter opened the rear door of the car and herded Will back into the back seat once again.

"Grand Island, Nebraska, Mr. Lomax. That's where the training facility is located. Any questions?" Utter shut the door before Will could answer. When Utter opened the driver's door, Will found his voice.

"When and where do I go?" he asked.

"You leave the day after tomorrow, Mr. Lomax," Utter said, getting back into the car. "Five o'clock in the morning. A bus will be here to pick you up on Acorn and Third. It's about 300 miles, so I suggest bringing something to keep you busy on the ride." Utter began to drive again, heading for the liquor store.

"Anything you suggest?" Will asked, still completely blindsided, but playing along. *Maybe Dante's Inferno?* Deep down, he knew he really didn't have a choice. If he turned down the job, Utter would either start digging into him or make his life in Brindle a walking Hell. *Maybe both.*

"This is a good start," Utter said, and tossed a book into the back seat.

Will picked it up and read the cover aloud. "'City Code of Ordinance and Laws – Brindle, Nebraska.' Sounds like a page turner."

"Mr. Lomax, I am offering you an opportunity that zero to few others have ever been presented. Now, if there is a reason that you don't want to grab that opportunity by the bullhorns and ride it, please tell me now so we don't waste any more of each other's time."

"Sheriff, please don't think that I am not thankful for the opportunity. It's just that this is all happening very fast. I just arrived in town a few days ago."

"I am aware, Mr. Lomax." Will wasn't exactly sure how to take that, and then Utter began speaking again. "You arrived on October 30, dropped off on the corner of Third and Acorn by Edgar Mathias, who picked you up from a bus and truck stop in Cheyenne, Wyoming. You live in a camper trailer you rent from a man named Gil Tolar, and picked up a stray cat for a pet. You frequent Rocky's Pizza Oven, and Jimmy at the liquor store likes you enough that he traded one Ryan Busch's liquor store tab for a bike, for you." Utter cleared his throat. "Now, Mr. Lomax, is there anything else that I need to know about you?"

"Other than me being your newest deputy, sir, I don't think so," Will said, hoping he didn't lose the chance. *How about that? You actually want the job now?*

"So it is, then," Utter said. He pulled the car up to the curb at the liquor store. "Get in there and fix Jimmy's books today. He knows you'll be gone for a while."

"Thanks, Sheriff," Will said. Utter got out of the car, walked around the rear of the vehicle, and opened the door for Will to exit. Once he was out, he had a question for the sheriff. "Can I ask a question?"

"Another one, or was that it?"

"Another one," Will said, rolling his eyes. "Why did I have to ride in the back seat for this little chat?"

"Look in the front seat," Utter said, walking around to the driver's side again. Will looked in what would be the front passenger seat and saw a rack mounted to the dashboard that held a shotgun. He nodded and turned, but heard the sheriff as he got into the car. "Nobody rides shotgun, except for the shotgun." Utter closed the door, and Will watched as he drove away in a cloud of dust.

Chapter 57 – Champ

The paperwork was just a formality. Detective Greco filled out the necessary forms, and Sergeant Harding signed where needed. Behind the paperwork was a heated argument where Greco had requested more time to work on the Kelly case, and Harding had flat-out refused. Greco called Harding 'short-sighted,' and Harding referred to Greco as a 'hot head with a water-thin theory.' It ended when Harding lengthened Greco's leave of absence from two weeks to an indefinite length of time. Harding also told Greco to leave the evidence from the Kelly case in the office. That was fine with Greco, but only because he had Maryanne Woods copy all of the documents, identification cards, and notes he had already taken, and put them into a file that he had taken home the previous day. It sat on his kitchen table, just waiting to be rifled through. Greco knew he was right, that Kelly was indeed alive, and living on nearly a half-million dollars that he had stolen from the company for which he worked, but something was missing. He was going to find it.

He left the office empty-handed, as directed by Sergeant Harding. On his way out, he had contemplated stopping by Michael Ilario's desk and asking him to resume his search for the source of the fake identification cards, but he couldn't risk Ilario saying the wrong thing to the wrong person, and then Harding getting a whiff of it. Greco was already putting his career on the line by defying the sergeant's orders, but he was hoping to find a solid lead that would temper any wrath the sergeant may have about Greco's insubordination. If he didn't, and Harding did find out, Greco would either be knocked down to wearing a uniform again or fired outright. He was taking a big risk by continuing the search for Kelly.

Greco left the station and made his way over to the hospital. He parked in the garage and took a series of hallways and elevators up to Steve's room. He poked his head into the doorway and saw a woman standing over the bedside. But it wasn't Steve who was in the bed. It was a young man who looked to be sleeping. The woman at the bed turned around and saw Greco peering in and asked if she could help him. He politely declined, saying he was in the wrong room, and left the woman to her purpose. He circled back to the nurse's station and asked where he could find Steve's room, and he was directed to the eighth floor. Once he got to the correct room, he found Steve, and anything he could have imagined was not as bad as what he saw when he arrived. Steve was propped up on a pillow behind his back, his eyes were closed, and there was a tube coming from somewhere that Greco could not see, but the other end of it was taped to Steve's face, and it went into his mouth. A machine was now breathing for Steve, Greco noticed. Not surprising, based on what Harding had told him, but still difficult to see. He stayed there for about two hours, just watching Steve. His chest would rise and fall rhythmically, without any variance in its cadence. Oxygen was forced in, then exhaled out. Greco thought about it being something that so many do without thinking about, but since Steve couldn't do it on his own, the machine was doing it for him. When he got up to leave, he put his hands on Steve's head and said a small prayer for him, asking for his recovery.

As Greco made his way home, he stopped at a deli and grabbed a sandwich and a bag of chips to eat for dinner. He envisioned his next few days with evidence spread all over his dining room table and possibly the breakfast bar that separated the kitchen from the dining room. He thought that laying everything out in the open might help him connect the dots and move the Kelly case forward, even though Harding forbade it.

When he got to his house, Greco parked the car in the driveway and made his entrance into the home. He announced himself in his usual manner by yelling, 'Honey, I'm home!' But there was, as always, no answer. The only acknowledgement of his arrival was Honey the dog lifting her head up from the arm of the couch where she had slept most of the day. She got to her feet and jumped from the cushions to the floor and met Greco in the kitchen, where he had put his sandwich on the counter. He grabbed a leash from a basket on the surface of the bar and attached it to Honey's collar, and took his lone companion out into the back yard to relieve herself. Greco felt fine letting her out of the back door without her leash, or he would have, if not for the annoying neighbor behind his house. His name was Bill Chaser, but everyone, at his own request, called him Champ. Champ Chaser. Even if he already told someone to call him Champ, and that someone still called him Bill, he would remind that person to call him Champ. Even worse, he owned two dogs as well. Two little poodles. The dogs' names were Chauncey and Chandler. Champ Chaser, and Chauncey and Chandler.

Greco never had a real problem with his neighbor or his neighbor's dogs until he caught the dogs doing their business in his backyard, and either Champ never kept a close enough eye on them to know what was happening, or he turned a blind eye to it. And there was the one time that Honey crossed over the border into the domain of the 'Heavy C's', as Greco called the lot of them, and Champ nearly lost his head and not so politely asked Greco to keep his dogs on his own property. Greco countered with the soiling of his own yard by Chandler and Chauncey, and then it turned out to be a quiet little war, of which Greco wanted no part, so he kept his distance and his dog on a leash.

Once Honey had irrigated the lawn a little, they went back inside, and Greco unclipped the leash from the collar and placed it back into the basket. He looked at the box on the table, which held the copies of the forms that were copied, and the photos that were taken of the physical evidence, such as the identification cards and Greco's personal notes. A heavy sigh escaped him, and he went to the bar and opened his sandwich. He took a large bite, and as he chewed, he opened the refrigerator door and grabbed a bottle of beer from the inside of the door. He twisted the top off and was rewarded with a refreshing 'psshhhht' sound, and the chilled gases escaped from the narrow opening in a spooky fog-like emission. Greco took a long drink from the bottle to wash down the sandwich. He walked over to the table and began to lay out the items from the box, one by one, inspecting each as he did to refresh his memory. He doubted he needed any refreshing, but he wanted to be thorough.

When he had gotten the last item out of the box, he spread it all out over his dining room table. The sandwich was now history, as was the first beer, and the second beer was about halfway into its impending doom. He sat on a chair next to the table and slouched against the back of it, and ran his hands over his head and through his hair. He sat back up and looked over the mass of paperwork and evidence, and then through his notebook. He flipped through the notebook and looked at each piece of corresponding evidence, and everything all pointed and ended at one point, and that was the taxicab ride. *Where the hell did he go?* Greco thought to himself. He wasn't able to get any copies of the videos from any of the security cameras at the banks or at the Quick-Key storage facility, but he did have some screenshots printed out, thanks to Michael Ilario. But so far, all of it ended up as nothing. He was losing hope.

Greco's mind began to wander, and he thought about Steve. Up there, in an otherwise vacant room, in a hospital bed, a machine is doing his breathing for him. Greco cursed himself for his self-pity about the case. Stevo would tell him to snap out of it and keep working the case until something popped. *I was working the case*, Greco thought. *And they took me off of it. I need you here, Stevo. I need your brain. Mine is tried, fried, and eggs up sunny side.* He laughed at himself for thinking of Steve's old line he would spout when he was tired. 'Tried and fried' was the negative part, when Steve was tired and at a dead end, but 'eggs up sunny side' was his way of always finding the positive in everything. Greco could not find the positive in this. He still felt like Kelly's wife had something to offer. Some little scrap of something, *anything*, he thought. She has to be the key.

Honey rose from her spot on the floor and came over to him at the table. She rested her head on his leg. He looked down at her and lightly scratched her head, and she let out a small whimper.

"Already?" he asked her, without much hope for a response. "We just came back in a few—". He looked at his watch and then the clock on the wall. They both agreed that nearly four hours had passed since the two companions had re-entered the house, and Greco started his sandwich, his beer, and his work. "Okay, well, come on, girl." He threw on a jacket to fight off the chill that had set in as the night approached, and snapped the leash onto Honey's collar once again. They went out the front door this time, and Honey squatted almost immediately when she crossed the sidewalk and hit the grassy lawn. She completed her task, and they continued down the sidewalk for a short walk, *maybe just around the block*, Greco thought. He was exhausted, but didn't know it until Honey pulled him out of his research trance to conduct her business.

His mind continued to focus on the Kelly case while they walked. Every now and then, Honey would stop and sniff the ground, or a tree, or any other random object she may have stumbled across in their walk. They passed a few houses on the street, which were parallel to Greco's house, and then Greco noticed they were next to Champ Chaser's sidewalk, and Honey seemed excited. She probably smelled Chaser's two dogs, but then Greco thought that Chaser's attitude towards his other neighbors was the same as Chaser's was to Greco's; there wouldn't be anything to smell on Chaser's lawn. That business would all be concluded on the lawn of his neighbors. Greco halted his walk, and Honey continued to sniff and then squatted on Chaser's lawn and dispensed some solid waste. Greco looked at Chaser's house and noticed that there were no lights on inside. Hopefully, no one was home, but knowing Chaser, he was probably sitting in the dark with night vision goggles eyeing the whole ordeal. Greco took a quick look around the street, up and down both sides, and saw no one. Attached to Honey's leash was a small plastic container that dispensed little baggies, which Greco used to pick up after Honey when they went on walks. *Not today*, Greco said. *All out of bags today, Champ,* he thought, even though the small container was nearly full. *Sorry, catch you next time. Maybe.* He praised Honey for her timely work, and they continued the remainder of their walk, and Greco felt oddly better about himself after the recent lawn soiling activity perpetrated by him and Honey. *Serves him right,* Greco thought.

They got back to the house and Greco, thinking that Honey had done her work for the evening, locked the front door, traversed the living and dining rooms of the house, and locked the back door as well. He looked at Chaser's house behind his and saw there was a light on in one of the back windows. *Probably just a light for security,* Greco thought. *Oh, but I wish I were there to see you when you see Honey's little present that she made especially for you!* Greco laughed at his own childishness and then came back to reality. He folded the leash and put it into the basket on the bar. He grabbed a small box that sat next to it, opened the lid, and turned it on its side, shaking it gently. *One, two, and three,* he thought. He held up each dog treat one by one, gave each to Honey, one at a time, and told her to take it easy and to chew slowly each time, and each time, Greco was wondering if she even tasted them. He flopped down in his chair at the dining room table and looked over the mass of information that lay before him once again. In his peripheral vision, he noticed the light from the answering machine blinking, blinking, blinking. He exhaled and drank the last of the beer that was in the bottle on the table. He stood up and tossed the empty bottle into his trash can, where it clinked against the other one that was already in there.

He hit the button on the answering machine, and it beeped and booped for a minute, and then the message began. It was Maryanne Woods from the station, and she was speaking in a hushed tone, as though she wanted only Greco to hear what she was saying. Greco listened as Maryanne's message played, and she told him that Kathleen Kelly had called the station looking for him, and luckily, the call was eventually passed to Maryanne. Kathleen had tried to reach out to Greco because she had some news on the case of her husband.

When the message was over, Greco pushed the red button on the phone, and then just stared at the surface of the bar that separated the Kitchen from the Dining Room. Then he pushed the red button and listened to the message again. As Maryanne's voice came through the box, and he digested what she was saying, a small smile began to spread over Greco's face.

"That's all I needed," he said.

Chapter 58 – The Spider

Will woke up earlier than usual the next day. He had a lot to do, and knew that he had not a lot of time in which to do it. He put on a pair of shorts and a sweatshirt and went out for a run through the streets of Brindle. He made it an extra-long run that day because he didn't know exactly for sure when he would be able to do it again. As he ran, he thought about what he was going to be facing in the next few months, and while he had an idea of what it would be like as far as educational training and physical training, he really had no idea of what he would be facing outside of that. Then the craziness of what he was about to do hit him hard, like a punch in the gut. He was a criminal, guilty of stealing nearly half a million dollars, and now he was going to go to training to be a cop. It felt, to him, like something out of a movie.

He finished his run, went back home, fed the cat, and then took a shower to wash off the sweat from the morning run. He decided that he would give the cat a name, and he chose 'Kat." Seemed easy and simple enough, and was gender ambiguous. He actually thought about the same name, but doubling the letter 't' and the end, for 'Katt,' but didn't think it necessary, and then he laughed at himself for even thinking about how to spell the name at all. And then he wondered if he chose Kat because it reminded him of Kathleen. He shook that thought from his head. The cat's name was 'cat,' no matter how it was spelled. On top of all that, it wasn't even his cat. It was what he presumed was a stray that now shared his residence. At least it didn't stink anymore and was actually looking healthier after a few days of getting some real food, and not whatever it had found in its travels throughout Brindle.

But what to do with Kat for the next few months? He thought about buying a few bags of food and slicing them open, and then putting them under the trailer for Kat to help herself, but then didn't think it was really fair to Kat to leave it outside for months at a time, and Winter was coming as well. No, he needed a place for Kat. Or he'd need someone to check on Kat every now and then to make sure there was food and water to be had when needed. And definitely clean the litter box that he had yet to purchase. The problem was, he only knew a few people in town so far, and asking someone to watch his pet for the next few months was not an easy ask. Jim and Daria were out as possible candidates because Jim was allergic to cats. He told Will that his sister had a cat, and when they visited, the cat would affect Jim's allergies so badly that his eyes would swell shut and he'd sneeze for hours afterward. He thought about Gil, but didn't think their relationship was strong enough based on just the rent and eventual purchase of a camper.

Will got dressed in a golf shirt and black jeans and put his jacket on. It was almost eleven o'clock, and he knew he was going to have to face something for which he was really not ready. Kat came outside with Will and darted under the trailer, as it had done for the past few days when Will would leave. Will surmised that Kat was an outdoor cat that liked to sleep indoors. It just needed to get out during the day, but would come back at night. Will was fine with that. He got on his bike and pedaled through the town, past the liquor store and so many other places he tried to find work. He thought that was funny. He was told there were very few jobs available in the entire town. Then he lucked into one, and it brought on the possibility of two more. *For a town with no work, there sure were a lot of jobs available*, he thought.

Will parked his bike up against the wall of Rocky's and went inside. A chime on the door that he did not remember being there before announced his arrival. The restaurant had just opened, and he appeared to be the first visitor of the day, as it was quiet and empty. He noticed there was no music playing, as it usually did, pouring from the speakers in the ceiling. At that exact moment, the speakers came to life and began to perform their daily function of providing background music for those patrons who would eventually arrive to eat their pizza, meatballs with pasta and sauce, or whatever they would choose to have that day. Will looked around, and there was no one in sight. He peered around the corner to the hallway, which led back to the kitchen door, and just then, Rocky appeared from the double doors carrying a tray of salt, pepper, parmesan, and crushed red pepper shakers on a tray. The sight of Will peering around the corner at her must have startled her, because she almost dropped the tray.

"Jesus H. Christ, you scared me!" she yelled.

"Eh, sorry about that," Will said. "The doorbell did ring when I came in. Let me help you with those." Will went to try for the tray, but she pulled back with a frown, letting Will know that all was not forgotten about the other night.

"I've got it," she said, and Will backed off with his hands in the air. She walked past him and out to the floor of the restaurant and began placing the various shakers on each table. "What do you want?" she asked when Will followed her out.

"To apologize," he said. "For the other night. I didn't mean to get so defensive with you. I should not have asked you out if I wasn't ready."

She eyed him and continued her task, but it looked to Will as if she was softening. "So, what's your deal?" she asked.

Will wasn't sure how far he wanted to go into it, but figured that maybe honesty was the right thing right now. He continued to follow her around the room. "Uh, honestly, I'm married."

She stopped what she was doing and looked at him. "Well, doesn't that figure. Where is she?"

"It doesn't matter where she is. It's over. I can't go back, and she doesn't want me there anyway. I just didn't know how I felt about being romantically involved with someone while I was still married to someone else. It just didn't seem right."

"I'm not asking you to get married, Billy. But you have to think about what you want. If your relationship with her is truly over, there shouldn't be anything stopping you from moving ahead with your life."

"With you?" he asked.

"With anybody you see fit, Billy." She finished her table prep and walked by him, heading back to the kitchen again.

He stopped short of following her. Space was important right now, and so was time. She emerged from the kitchen again with a second tray of shakers and began her work again.

"Listen," he said. "I'm going to be gone for a few months, and I don't want to leave things in a bad place with you."

"Where are you going now?" she asked.

"Utter wants me to join his department."

"You're gonna be a deputy?" she asked.

"That's the plan, I guess."

"Do you want to be a cop?" Rocky asked, laughing.

"I never thought about it before," he said.

She rolled her eyes at him. "Then what are you doing it for?"

"I don't know, really. Mostly, I guess, because I don't want to get on Utter's bad side."

She stopped placing the shakers on the table and looked at him. "What's the downside of getting on Utter's bad side?" she asked, as if she had not already schooled him on the topic.

"Let's just say that I don't need any jaywalking tickets. Like you said, I'd rather get along with him than go to war with him. Besides, what else am I going to do, be a wrestling coach at the high school?"

"I thought that was the original plan," she said.

"Me too. But Utter came calling, and Jim said Utter's got all the power, and you seem to agree. I don't really want to buck the system."

"He is the system," she said, with a heavy sigh. "All right."

"'All right' what?

"You. Me. We're all right. Or we will be under one condition."

"And what's that?" he asked her.

"When you get back from your training or whatever the hell it is, you tell me everything. You've got secrets. And I'm putting it on you. If you want any kinda relationship with me, I gotta know it all. No secrets between us."

He thought about that for a minute. He wondered if he could actually tell Rocky the truth. The truth was, if he did, it might scare her away. But if he didn't, she would shut him down anyway. "Okay," he said, thinking he had nothing to lose. "Everything."

"Well, all right," she said. "Now, did you come here to eat?"

"No, I came here to talk."

"Mission accomplished, Deputy."

"And to ask a favor," he said.

"Shit, this day keeps getting better and better already." She stood with her left hand on her hips and her right hand out towards him. "Well, whataya got, Copper?"

"How do you feel about cats?"

"Cats? Like 'meow' cats?"

"Yes, cats."

"Why?" she asked.

"Because I have one, and it needs to be looked after while I'm gone. I was hoping maybe you wouldn't mind."

"I know nothing about cats," she said.

"Neither do I, except that they eat and crap. Kat is an outdoor cat, mostly. It just likes to sleep inside. It leaves the house when I do and then comes back sometime after I get home. I feed it, give it water, and it sleeps."

"The cat's name is–."

"Kat," he said. "With a K. K-A-T."

"You said 'it'. Is it male or female?"

"Not sure," he said.

"Well, it's either got one set of parts or the other."

"Yeah, I can't really tell," Will said.

"Poor cat. All right. Bring it over tonight when I'm leaving, with its food and whatever else it needs. What about the box?"

"The box?" Will asked.

"Yeah. Don't they crap in a box?"

"Not this one. I believe it conducts all of its business outside."

"Hmmm," she said. "Yeah, bring it over later. I'll watch your cat. But you owe me."

"Sure...as long as you don't kill it."

She disappeared behind the wall again for a minute, then came back out, saw him, stopped, and looked at him. "Are you still here?" she asked.

"I'm going," he said, and gave a quick wave as he opened the door to the outside. He grabbed his bike from the wall and pedaled to the Pit Stop. He ran in and bought a bag of cat food. He would have liked to bring Rocky the super-sized bag, but carrying that on the bike might prove dangerous. He'd get her started with the small bag and leave her with some money to buy more when it was needed. He understood what a large ask it was to ask her to watch Kat for months, a cat who, days ago, was a stray, but Will didn't want to put it back out on the street, and he really had no one else to ask. He arrived at the trailer and unlocked the door, and to his surprise, Kat was not around to be found, but it was still early. Once in the house, he grabbed his duffel bag and threw all of his clothes except those he was wearing inside of it, and then went back outside and made the twenty-minute walk to the laundromat. As he waited for the laundry to cycle through the washing process, he thumbed through the book of laws and code from Brindle that Utter had given him.

What are you doing? The voice within him had surfaced again. *Are you nuts? You're the last person who should be going after a job as a cop. You're the criminal!* Will knew who he was and didn't need himself to tell himself that. It was already weighing on his conscience as it was. *And agreeing to tell Rocky the whole truth when you get back? What was that?*

"Shut up," Will said aloud, and two elderly ladies turned to look at him. "Oh, sorry...I was reading." One of the ladies shook her head and went back to her magazine while the other continued to look at Will. He could feel her staring at him, so he shifted in his chair a bit to make himself face away from her. She still stared.

"You're Billy Lomax, aren't you?" she finally asked.

"Excuse me?" Will asked, on guard.

"You're Billy Lomax. You're going to be the new deputy."

"Um, I'm sorry, ma'am, you have me at a disadvantage."

"Oh, I'm Felicia Utter. The sheriff is my husband," she said, extending her hand.

"Oh," Will said. "It's nice to meet you." He took her hand in a light handshake. "How did you know who I was?"

"My husband and I talk, and I saw the book. We must have a dozen of those or so lying around the house. I think there are two in the same bathroom. He said he was bringing on a Billy Lomax as a deputy, some new guy in town. I just put three and two together and came up with a five," she said with a slight chuckle.

"I see," he said. "What are you doing here?" he asked.

She looked around the room and then back at Will. "Laundry," she said. "The same thing you're doing."

"I'm sorry. That came out wrong. I know I use the laundromat because I live in a small trailer that does not have its own washer or dryer. I wouldn't expect a long-term citizen of the town to have to use the laundromat. I would think that you had your own machines at home."

She smiled. "One of the first things you're going to learn as a deputy is not to make assumptions, Mr. Lomax. A lot of 'long-term citizens' of Brindle use this laundromat. That's why it stays open. But your assumption, Mr. Lomax, is correct. We do have our own machines at home, but our washing machine is broken. So, right now, I wash the clothes here, and then take them home to our functioning dryer."

Will put his eyes to the floor for a second to digest her comment. "I apologize for making assumptions, Mrs. Utter. I'm just a little caught off guard, actually, by a lot of things. Ever since I came to Brindle, things have been happening so fast. Five days ago, I was working in a liquor store. Three days later, I was supposed to be a coach at the high school, and then yesterday I learned of your husband's plan to make me a deputy. It's all just a little overwhelming." He stopped for a moment and then asked her if she would need help with her laundry.

"No, I can manage it just fine. Let me assure you, Mr. Lomax, that the overwhelming part is probably over for you once you leave the training facility and come back to us to be sworn in as a deputy. My husband is not a lazy man, by any means, but I think this town and the surrounding area for which the Sheriff's Department is responsible is suited well for him at this point in his life. I could not imagine him in a big city role, especially now with all that's happened. I think you'll find that your time with the department, once you're settled in, will be a breeze for you. Especially since you're so athletic."

"I just think it's odd that everyone seems to know everything about me, and I've not been in town that long." He stood and walked across the aisle to the dryer that had just finished drying his clothes. He opened the door and piled the clothes back into his duffel bag.

She shook her head slowly. "Mr. Lomax, I know you come from a big city, Philadelphia, right? This is a small town, and everyone knows everyone. Our children play together, they grow up together, and the boys and girls eventually will date and marry, if they don't leave first. We go to church together, we go to our fair together, and we have our picnics together. When someone who is usually not a part of our 'together' comes into town, we notice, and we make it our business to find out what we can." She paused for a moment. "Imagine if you were camping, and you were in a tent. Then you looked into the corner of the tent, and you saw a spider. You consider that spider an intruder, don't you? You want to keep yourself and everyone with you safe from the intruder."

"Hmm," Will said, smiling at her. "With all due respect, ma'am, the spider was there first, before I put up the tent."

"Maybe in my analogy, Mr. Lomax, but you get the idea."

"Yes, ma'am, I do. And I may be the spider now, but when I get back, you're going to be glad I'm here catching flies."

She smiled as he approached the door to leave. "I think you finally understand, Mr. Lomax."

He turned to her and smiled back. "Ma'am," he said, and left the laundromat. He went back home, folded his clothes as neatly as possible, save for one set of underwear, jeans, and a shirt for the trip, and then put them back into the duffel bag again. Later that night, he did as he was asked and brought Kat and the food over to Rocky's as she was leaving for the night. They said a cordial goodbye to each other, and she wished him well and told him she would see him when he returned. He stopped by the liquor store on his way home, grabbed a six-pack of beer, said goodbye to Jim, thanked him for the opportunity, and then went home to drink his beer. The next morning, he was on the bus to the training facility in Grand Island, Nebraska.

Chapter 59 – You're Mine

The next day, after being up most of the previous night searching through every last bit of evidence that he had, Greco awoke refreshed and felt like he had a new purpose in life. The call from Kathleen Kelly, he hoped, would be the spark he needed to refire the heat under the Kelly case. He ate a quick bowl of cereal and took care of Homey's food and nature needs, and then reorganized all of the evidence that lay upon the table like an abandoned junkyard. He looked it over once more and then grabbed his travel mug, which contained his coffee, and left the house.

He traveled out of the neighborhood where his house was located, on Rugby Road in Prospect Park. He drove up Flatbush Avenue, across the Manhattan Bridge into the city, and made his way to the hospital to see how Steve was doing. Once he parked and got up to Steve's room, there was no one there except Steve, and he looked exactly as he had when Greco had last left him. He sat down in a chair, sipping on his coffee from the travel mug. He noticed a spot on his pants and cursed the supposedly leak-proof mug for its failure to do its job properly.

After an hour of watching Steve do nothing, Greco fell into a sort of trance, where he held his coffee and just stared down at the floor. He flashed back to the day he brought Steve here. *That* day. The day when the world was falling down around them, and they walked from the crash site to get to the hospital, until Greco had to pick Steve up and carry him the rest of the way. Greco looked back and thought about how the day could have been worse. He failed after a few tries and then settled on nuclear war as something that could have been worse. He was so deep into his transfixed gaze on the floor during his thinking that he didn't realize that a nurse had come into the room. She was checking something on a machine when it clicked, and it drew Greco out of his trance and back to the current reality.

"Oh, hi," Greco said.

She looked up and smiled at him and said, "Hello."

"How's he doing?" Greco asked.

"Are you family?" she asked.

He let out a small laugh. "Pretty much," he said. He pulled out his badge to show her. "He's my partner."

She exhaled at him, but then smiled, which then faded. "Unfortunately, he's had no changes. He doesn't show a lot of activity. Right now, we're doing what we can to keep him stable and alive." She walked over to him as he continued to look at Steve. She put her hand on his shoulder. "I'm sorry," she said, and then left the room.

Greco lowered his head back to the floor. He kept it there until the tear drop that had formed in each eye had fallen onto the white tile floor, next to a quickly drying drop of coffee. He ran his shoe over all three of them, stood from his chair, tossed his leak-proof cup into the garbage can, and left the hospital. He drove through the city and through the Holland Tunnel, and down into Staten Island until he got to the small apartment complex where Kathleen Kelly was living. He approached the apartment building and knocked on the door to Kathleen's apartment. After a few moments, he knocked again, and he was getting ready to call the phone number that she had provided when she left her message, but then she opened the door, wearing a bathrobe and a towel around her head.

"Sorry, Detective," she said. "I just got out of the shower when I heard you knock."

"No problem," he said, standing there a bit awkwardly in the doorway.

"Oh," she said, opening the door wider. "I'm sorry. Please, come in." Greco followed her into the apartment. She invited him into the living room and asked him to sit on the sofa. "Thanks for coming out, Detective. Can I get you a coffee or a soda? I think all I have is diet."

"No, no thanks," he said, thinking he might disappear into the couch. "I'm fine." He didn't dare add any more weight to his body for fear of not being able to extricate himself from the cloud of sofa in which he sat.

"Water?" she asked, still moving around in the kitchen.

"What can I help you with, Ms. Kelly?" Greco asked, getting impatient.

"I'm sorry if I didn't seem cooperative the last time we talked, sir, but I just could not believe that my husband could be involved in anything like what you were talking about."

"That's understandable, Dr. Kelly. You wouldn't believe the number of crimes we see where the significant other has no idea what the perpetrator is involved in. You believe differently now?"

"I don't know, Detective. I doubt if I have all of the information you have, so I cannot make an informed decision on the topic."

"Okay, so why am I here, Dr. Kelly?"

"Detective, I have a strong feeling that Will is still alive."

Greco stiffened. "Why do you say that? What would make you think that your husband is alive?"

"The day before yesterday, I got a call from the Newark airport. They found a briefcase in one of their storage lockers. It was empty, except for a business card."

"Go on," Greco said.

She paused for a moment. "It was Will's card, sir," she said.

Greco sat motionless for a moment, staring at Kathleen's mouth, and watching as if the words slowly poured out of it like syrup from a bottle. He could almost see it, letter by letter. "Okay," he said. "That's certainly interesting. Did you positively identify the briefcase as your husband's?"

"I never saw it," she said. "They told me, and I have now told you."

"Dr. Kelly, let me ask you a question. Let's assume that your husband is alive—"

"Pssht," she exhaled, and waved her hands upward, and then back down again.

Greco thought for a moment and decided that his question was not relevant. But curiosity got to him. He continued his question, thinking that he had an ally in the good dentist. "What do you think should happen to him?"

Kathleen sat for a moment and looked at the floor for a moment, and then she spoke. "Detective, that was a terrible day. A lot of people died that day, and if what you think has happened, and what I am starting to believe has happened, has actually happened, my husband used that day to escape the life he was living, the job he was working, and the wife to whom he was still married..." She paused again and then raised her eyes to meet Greco's. "He should burn for it."

Later, after leaving Kathleen's apartment, he sat in his car looking at a map he had pulled out of his glove box. The map, through multiple pages, showed New York City, and when Greco turned to the page indicated on the left margin of another, he found New Jersey, and barely off the left side of that page was Newark Airport. He figured he would take 278 into Jersey, then Route 9 through Elizabeth, where he could follow the signs to the airport. He started to fold the map away, but then thought for a second. He turned a few pages back in the road atlas, and then forward another page. He traced the roads with his finger from the World Trade Center to West Street. He noticed that the route took him past North Moore, the location of the Quick-Key, and decided it would have been pretty easy to stop there on the way to the airport.

On his route to the airport, traffic was terrible. The bridges were packed, and the off-ramps were a slice-and-dice of who could be the most aggressive driver and win one more spot in front of someone else to go nowhere fast. It was just before three in the afternoon when he got to the airport. He tossed the magnetic red light he carried in the car up onto the dashboard with one of his business cards, hoping no one would tow his car. He didn't have the time or patience to park in the regular parking lots and take a shuttle over to the terminal, so he used the service vehicle entrance and found an area that looked not-so-busy. He put his hazard lights on, just in case.

Greco walked into the terminal and looked for an information desk or somewhere he could get help. When he found nothing, he proceeded to a check-in window for one of the major airlines. When he asked where he could find the director of the airport, the woman behind the counter gave him a puzzled look. He showed her his badge and explained that it was a legal matter, and she directed him to security. When he finally got to the security area of the airport, he knocked on the door and waited. A few minutes passed, and then he knocked again. There was still no answer. Finally, a large black man in a bright yellow t-shirt came up to him and asked if he could help. Greco explained the situation, and the yellow-shirted man, whose name was Jackson, took him to another room where the airport police were stationed. Once again, he explained the situation and was escorted by one of the officers to the other side of the terminal, through a door that required the swipe of a plastic card, down several long hallways, and finally into a busy hub of people performing various duties at an incredible rate of speed. People and paper were everywhere. Greco was asked to take a seat on a padded bench and wait for the officer to return. He looked around the room and saw and heard people speaking in many foreign languages as they watched the screens in front of them. Greco always thought that cops had a tough job, but one look around this room made him glad he did what he did, and not whatever this was that was going on around him.

The officer finally returned and took Greco down another hallway and into a smaller, quieter office, and led him to the door of Robert C. Chisholm, Airport Director. Greco was led inside and asked to sit. Mr. Chisholm would be with him shortly. Greco looked around the room, and every picture that hung from the wall was either of an aircraft taking off or landing, or of Mr. Chisholm, or someone Greco thought might be Mr. Chisholm, shaking hands, getting awards, or presenting large cardboard checks to charities. Chisholm's desk was spotless, Greco noted.

The door opened, and a man walked in and said, "Detective Greco, I'm Rob Chisholm. What can I do for you?"

No hand of greeting was offered by Chisholm, so Greco got right to the point. "Mr. Chisholm, I'm looking for, hopefully, something in your security footage, perhaps, that may help me with a case I am working on. How well covered are your drop-off areas by security cameras?"

Chisholm put down a piece of paper he had carried into the room with him. Greco was surprised that it actually touched his desk. "One hundred percent, full image quality down to about forty to fifty feet."

"Clear enough to read a license plate?"

"Of course," Chisholm said.

"How far back do your security recordings go?"

"We keep everything. If it's over five years, it's in storage."

"Excellent. I need to see your drop-off areas for the morning of September eleventh," Greco said. He saw a response in Chisholm's face that was not all-accepting of Greco's request.

"Not too much happened that day after that morning, Mr. Greco. What time are you looking for?"

"I don't know yet, but I will know it when I see it."

Chisholm frowned, but he exhaled and picked up his phone, and for the next fifteen minutes, negotiated with different directors around the airport to give Greco the access that he quietly, yet firmly, demanded. When Chisholm finally hung up the phone, he folded his hands in front of himself on his desk and bowed his head. He was silent for a moment, and Greco thought Chisholm may have been praying. But finally, the head arose, and Greco was no longer staring at the hairless spot on the top of Chisholm's head.

"Mr. Greco, I'm going to give you an access badge, which will grant you access to our security facility on the other side of the terminal. Please work with the folks over there, and when you're done and you have what you need, leave your badge there as you leave."

"Are you throwing me out of your airport, Director?"

"No, Mr. Greco–"

"Detective," Greco said frankly.

Chisholm smiled a facetious smile and exhaled. "Detective Greco," he said, correcting himself. "I'm not kicking you out of my airport. I'm kicking you out of my office. Truth is, you're an out-of-state cop and I don't have to give you a damned thing. But I'm extending this courtesy to you. Don't make me regret it or withdraw it. Have a nice day. Detective." With that, Chisholm went back to the papers he had brought into the office with him. Greco picked up the badge that Chisholm had provided and put the lanyard around his neck.

"Director," Greco said in a hard goodbye. He turned and let himself out, found his way through the maze of hallways, and then back over to the other side of the terminal, where the security area was located. He used the badge to make his way into the security office and told them what he needed. He reviewed the recordings of each camera for hours, but he could not find Willem Kelly in any of them. Eventually, however, his persistence did pay off. At about the ten-thirty mark on the recording of September 11th, a minivan taxi pulled up to the curb, and Greco thought it looked like the one from the images he had seen on the videos from the Quick-Key, but he wasn't sure. He continued to watch, and a man emerged from the rear of the taxi and then walked toward the terminal.

Greco watched and had the security team hit buttons and swap views, and for about the next hour, he watched Willem Kelly walk around the Newark airport, sitting on benches, eating food, and using the restroom. *He is alive*, Greco thought. *There's my proof.* As he watched Kelly's videoed walkabout continue, Greco almost lost him after watching him walk into the restroom. However, backing up the tape a few times confirmed to Greco that Kelly had definitely come back out of the restroom in different clothes. He followed Kelly around the airport for a while, and then Kelly headed to the exit and went out to the pickup area. Greco watched as Kelly tried unsuccessfully to get into a taxi the first time, but found success on the second try.

Greco smiled and said, "I need a printout of that image of that cab, and I need a clear shot of the license plate. Blow it up." And then to himself he said, *I have all the pieces, now, Kelly. You're mine. I've got you.*

Chapter 60 – A Whisper In A Hurricane

Michael Ilario walked into the store and approached the counter. He was wearing a dirty pair of jeans, a t-shirt with a hole in the seam of the neck in the front, and a ragged flannel shirt over the t-shirt. He had let his facial hair grow as much as it could and still be within the limits of the rules of the NYPD, or at least no one noticed it enough to say anything about it. The beard hair was thin and scraggly, and the mustache was almost non-existent. His head was covered by an old baseball cap that he had dug from his closet. He knew it had to be at least ten years old, because he knew that the last time he wore it, he was a benchwarmer for his baseball team when he was still in Junior High School. The hat was dirty, carried sweat stains on the bill, had a fold in the front panel, which was adorned with a large script 'C,' and looked like he had actually dug it out from the bottom of a closet.

Ilario had taken the day off from work and had been traveling from store to store, asking veiled and clandestine questions to owners, employees, and anyone else he could find, including a few folks who were just hanging around outside of the stores. He believed himself to be seeming a little more and more conspicuous to those he addressed, the further along in his task he progressed. However, he shook off that feeling and continued, though he really had no idea what he was going to do or whom he was going to tell should he actually uncover some useful information. He doubted himself in this situation. If you were to put him behind a keyboard and a monitor, and something needed to be discovered, he was *the guy*. What was better was that he *knew* he was the guy, and it gave him the confidence to do what he needed to do and to feel confident about his results, no matter who his audience would have been. But *this*, this was way out of his comfort zone. Talking to actual people was not his flavor of ice cream, and the fact of them being strangers was the cherry on top of his awkward sundae.

A pimply-faced kid behind the counter greeted him with a dry 'Hello,' and a well-rehearsed line about Boob Tube Service and Sales being the top location to fix your old television or find your next one. The kid looked younger than Ilario, and probably was, but that was really saying something, as Ilario looked like he was still in college instead of four years out of it. Ilario squirmed at the situation he was in, and he stammered a bit, with some 'Uhs' and 'Ums'. Finally, the kid rolled his eyes and told Ilario to wait a minute. Pimple-face went around the corner and down a hallway that appeared to run the remaining length of the store. Ilario looked around at the televisions that were perched on the racks and others that were mounted to the wall, and wondered what the full inventory value of the store might be. He was looking at a large Panasonic widescreen that Ilario imagined he could have driven his car through, when a finger tapped his shoulder.

"She's a beaut, isn't she?" a voice said from behind. Ilario wheeled on one heel and nearly fell into the large television he was admiring. "Whoa, kid, take it easy! Are you okay?"

"Yeah, uhh, I'm fine. Sorry about that." Ilario stumbled again and struggled to make his brain connect with his mouth. His nervousness was showing.

"Good. Do you know what you're looking for?"

"I, uhh, I'm not, uhh, not here for—"

"Hold on, kid. Hey, Carl, get out on the back deck and help Mitch with the stock. Get all that stuff cataloged and into the stock room!" He shook his head and then turned back to Ilario. "Sorry about that. Now, what can I help you with?" Ilario listened and decided during Carl's banishment to the back room that he wasn't going to be weak and sputter and stammer anymore. He would just say what he needed and let the chips fall where they may. That was his plan, anyway. But the nervousness didn't disappear with Carl.

"I'm uhh, I'm not uhh, I'm not here for a television, actually," and Ilario's eyes went to his shoes. He'd done this multiple times that day, but it wasn't getting any easier. He felt like he already had the fake ID and was trying it out for the first time.

"I didn't think so. What's your name, kid?"

"Paul," Ilario said, remembering the name on the fake driver's license he had already created with his picture on it. "I found you on the list-serve."

"Follow me, Paul. You can call me Archie."

For the next half-hour or so, Ilario sat nervously in the same chair next to Archie's computer where Will Kelly had sat just months before on September tenth as Archie gave him his new identity. Archie thought about that very fact as he watched the picture print out for Ilario's fake ID for 'Paul.' He wondered where Will had gone and what he was doing. He didn't even really know if Will had gone through with it, considering the events of the next day. He thought, watching Ilario's face appear line by line, that even with what happened, Will would have had to go ahead with his plan. After all, he was a criminal who stole nearly five hundred thousand dollars. A lot of companies wouldn't let that go without punishment, and even if the company did, the cops wouldn't. Archie was brought back from his thoughts as the printer came to a stop and spit out the final product: a perfect replica of a New York driver's license, which made Paul Olsson, who looked a lot like Ilario, a perfect twenty-one and one-half years old.

"Wow, that looks great," Ilario said.

"Yep, just need to laminate it now," Archie said, lighting a cigarette. The smoke poured from his nose, and Ilario immediately pictured some mythical dragon, sneering and snorting, with smoke billowing from its nostrils just before it reared its head back and let loose with a furious fire that laid all in its path to waste. Within minutes, Ilario had his brand-new identity card, the third one he had received that day, tucked into his wallet. Then came the unpleasant part of the experience, where he would have to pay some ridiculous amount of money for the ruse, also for the third time that day. "Okay, kid, a hundred and twenty-five."

Ilario was astonished. One of the others he had gotten earlier in the day was only fifty dollars, and the other two were only seventy-five. "Wow," he said. "That's a little pricey."

"Well," Archie responded, again filling the room with smoke, "if you want a quality product, you have to pay for it."

"I see that," Ilario said, handing Archie the cash. "Hey, listen, do you ever do any other types of things?"

"What kind of things?" Archie asked with his eyebrows raised.

"I don't know," Ilario said, playing the nervous kid again. "Larger scale stuff. Like, if I wanted to completely redo my life and become another person. Something like that?"

Archie leered at him and took a long drag on the cigarette, and then crushed the butt into a well-used ashtray. He chuckled, and when he did, the last of the smoke left his lungs and surrounded Ilario. "No, kid...nothing like that. I'm just small time. Now, get out of here, and don't go telling anyone about this. I know your name and I know where you live."

Ilario walked through the door from the back office and out to the sales floor, where Carl was trying to pitch a Sanyo to a young couple with a baby in a stroller. He made no eye contact with any of them and made his way out the door. In his four attempts to acquire fake identification cards that day, he succeeded in three of them. Three driver's licenses, all with his picture on them, and all with different names. He felt like he had to get this information to Greco, but he wasn't sure how, or even if he could; he wasn't sure if he should. He wasn't very keen on getting under Sergeant Harding's skin or getting on his bad side, especially because he was working way out of his job description. Technically, Ilario knew that he had committed three successful crimes that day, which he was not eager to spread through the station where he worked. It would, most likely, be frowned upon.

Back in the Boob Tube store, Archie Eklund came out of his personal bathroom about twenty minutes after he had finished his business with Ilario. He dropped his newspaper on his desk and sat down with a huff. He felt that something wasn't right. Instinct, intuition, bad vibes, a sixth sense, whatever it was, he was feeling it, and it did not feel good. He thought back to Ilario's nervousness when Ilario was 'Paul', and then the young kid's gall when he asked about other services. It didn't sit right, and Archie's stomach made an odd sound. Mitch, the kid that Carl was helping on the dock, poked his head in and advised that all the new stock was put away. Archie advised him to go out to the front of the store with Carl and handle any customers that might come in.

He scooted up in his chair, poked a few buttons on the keyboard, and clicked his mouse on an icon on the screen. A modem connected to the computer made a dialing noise, and then a screeching sound came from the box, followed by some electric boings, and then finally was quiet. A window opened up in the corner of the screen, which Archie used keystrokes and mouse clicks to navigate to what he wanted to see. In this case, it was a file attached to a comment string on a list-serve that was updated whenever it needed to be. The list-serve was hosted by someone who had no real name that anyone reading the string would know, but it said the person's name was 'kID Shade 4712.' Archie was logged in under his name, which was also not his real name. His name on the screen said 'Fauxtaux phynysh.' Archie looked at the screen and found what he was looking for. He clicked on an icon, and a file began to download to his computer. Once it was finished, he opened the file and scoured its contents. He scrolled to the bottom of the file using the wheel on his mouse, and when he got to the bottom, he saw it. A photo ID for someone named Richard Hovater, and the picture on the ID was of none other than young 'Paul', who had just been in the store. Archie's stomach fell into his shoes. He continued to search the file, and he saw an image of 'Paul' again, this time as 'Michael R. Simpkins.' Archie knew he was in trouble.

He stood up and looked at the time. It was nearly five o'clock in the afternoon. He looked around his office, as if not sure what to do. But he calmed his nerves, went to his safe, and used the combination to unlock it. He fished out the cash in an envelope, one thousand dollars to be exact, and then exited the room and walked out to the sales floor to find Carl and Mitch watching something on one of the many televisions in the room. The place was empty of customers.

"Hey guys," he said, walking out to Mitch and Carl. "It's bonus day! You guys did great work putting all that away in the back. Sales are up this month, and I'm giving you two a little piece of the pie. Here's five hundred dollars each. Don't forget to pay your taxes." They both thanked him as they took his handout, Carl a little more wary than Mitch. "Also, those new flat twenty-five-inch SoundSonix over there? You each get one of those as well. And while we're at it, I know it's a little early, but why don't you both go ahead and knock off for the day? Sound like a plan?"

The boys knew better than to look the gift horse in the mouth, so they agreed, and each of them helped the other load their new flat screen televisions into Carl's car, which would eventually take each of them home. They came back in the store and said their 'thank yous' to Archie again, and he told them not to worry about it, and he would see them tomorrow. The boys left through the front door, and Archie locked it behind them, waving through the glass as he did. He turned and went back into his office area. He went into the bathroom, splashed some water on his face, and dried it with a towel. He put the stopper into the drain of the bathtub and turned on the water, watching as it filled slowly. He left the bathroom and went out to his office again, where he kicked open the slightly ajar door of the still unlocked safe. He grabbed a canvas bag from the back of the safe, opened it, and began to empty the contents of the safe into the bag. He went to the front of the store, opened the two cash drawers, and brought them to the back room. He took the cash from each drawer and stuffed it into the canvas bag. He opened the drawers of his desk and took the laminating packs and the rest of his stock of forgery and falsifying material and shoved it into the bag as well.

Finally, he removed the drawer from his desk and set it on the floor. He reached to the back of the bottom of the desk and detached a letter-sized envelope, which was stuck to the bottom of the desk by silver tape. He opened the envelope to reveal multiple driver's licenses with different names on each, as well as a passport. Archie took one look at the licenses and passport, and then closed the envelope and tossed it into the bag as well. He then looked over his shoulder and into the bathroom to check the water level in the bathtub. It was about half full. He took the computer monitor off the main central processing unit and placed it on the desk. He turned off and unplugged the brains of the computer, and carried it into the bathroom, where he plugged it into the wall. He turned the machine back on and then dropped it into the bathtub, where it sparked and smoked, and eventually shorted out the power to the store, as well as the rest of the stores that were connected.

Archie pulled out his lighter and used it as a light source to find his way back to his desk, where he lit another cigarette, picked up the keys to the store and the canvas bag, and walked to the back of the store. He opened the door at the back of the building, which was located next to the loading dock. When he got out there, the Asian couple who owned the laundry next door were already outside, and the man asked him if he knew what had happened to the power.

"No, sir," he said, taking the cigarette from his mouth and exhaling into the air. "Mine went out, too. So, I'm taking some stuff here and sleeping at a friend's house tonight. You guys have a good night and be safe. I'll see you later." He let the door slam behind him, which automatically locked it, and he walked down the steps to the alley behind the stores. When the Asian couple returned to their store and the door shut behind them, Archie took the keys from the store and tossed them into the creek that ran parallel to the alley. And then, like a whisper in a hurricane, Archie Ecklund disappeared.

Chapter 61 – Han And Chewie

Maryanne Woods picked up her ringing phone and pressed it to her ear with her shoulder as she shuffled papers on her desk. She spoke quite brashly when she identified herself and her department, and waited for the response from the other side. Who wanted something from her now? The stack of files and papers on her desk was just getting larger, and it seemed that at one point, one day, she would be engulfed by the mass of dead trees and paperclips. She had imagined they would find her body someday, maybe after someone noticed the stench of death, or hopefully before, when someone noticed she did not answer her phone, or provide the results of a request in a timely manner. Either way, she had a strong suspicion that it would be her demise. She imagined what would be written on her headstone. *What headstone? Who is going to get you a headstone?* Then she thought that at least someone would submit an obituary to the newspaper. *Maryanne Woods. Single. Lonely. No surviving relatives. Good enough to date and sleep with (if she was lucky), but not one to ever be married. Hidden hero of the Police Department. Did all the legwork while others got the credit. Died while filing. May She Rest In Peace.*

"*Maryanne,*" the voice on the other end of the phone said. "*Keep this quiet. It's Greco.*"

"Oh," she said, surprised. "How are you doing? Are you okay? How is Steve?"

"*I'm fine, Steve is—Stevo is about the same. Unresponsive and breathing by a machine.*" Greco took a breath to reset himself. He didn't want Maryanne to hear his voice crack. "*Listen, I need your help, but you cannot tell anyone what I'm doing.*"

"Okay, Mom," she said aloud, looking around. "What's up?"

"*I need you to research a tag for me,*" he said.

"Uh-huh," she said. "So, your medicine is ready at the pharmacy? What's the name of it?" Greco couldn't help but laugh a little, which she felt all the way on the other end of the phone, and it made her smile. He read the plate to her, and she wrote it down on the piece of paper under the top sheet of her pad. "Uh-huh. Can you, uh, can you *state* which pharmacy, Mom, so I know where to go?"

He laughed again, but silently commended her on her performance. "*Jersey,*" he said. "*It's a cab. I need to know the cab company and the operator of the cab, if you can.*"

"Got it, Mom. Anything else?"

"*No, dear, just be careful and buckle up when you drive, and look both ways crossing the street,*" he said, not completely getting it out of his mouth before he started laughing.

She lowered her voice. "Hey, Ma, you're an asshole," she said, and hung up the phone, maybe a little too harshly. She looked around, but no one took notice. At noon, the rest of the 'digging pool,' as she called all the assistants and dirt diggers that did all the behind-the-scenes work that allowed the police force to do their jobs and catch the criminals, went to lunch. Maryanne went into the motor vehicle administration database and found the license plate for the cab. It took her about an hour to deduce that the car was registered to the Newark Cab Company, which was located just a few blocks away from the Newark Airport. She looked up the company in the phone book, and the half-page advertisement for the company's services seemed to suggest that everyone needed transportation from the bus station to the train station or the airport, or from the train station to the bus station or the airport, or from the airport to the bus station or the train station. In small print near the bottom of the page were the words 'We Also Do Residential Rides!' Maryanne thought that was odd for a second, and then the thought passed her by as the office began to fill up with those returning from their lunch break. She was trying to think of a clever way to avoid any listeners-in as she tried to give the information back to Greco without it being an issue. All she could come up with was another phone call. She dialed Greco's home number, and he picked up on the second ring.

"Hello," she said. "Is this the *Newark* Pharmacy?"

Greco laughed as he wrote 'Newark' in his notepad. "*Why, yes, it is. How can I help you?*"

"I need to pick up a prescription for my mother." She listened as Greco continued snickering. "Her address? Yes, it is 416, Route 1, Newark." She paused for a second to make it seem as though a real conversation was happening, or perhaps the Pharmacist was looking in his computer for some information. Also, to give Greco time to write down the address. "Oh, I see, yes. Well, it doesn't get much simpler than that."

Greco decided it was time to throw her off the rails. "*Want to go to dinner tonight?*" he asked.

"What?" she exclaimed, loud enough to draw attention from her office mates. She noticed the looks and quickly composed herself. "Well, that is, uh, a shockingly large amount of medicine for mon—I mean money for medicine." She was flustered by Greco's question. But then, in classic Maryanne fashion, she regrouped. "Well, I guess that would be just what the doctor ordered. Uh, what, uh, what time do you close?" Greco took this to be her asking him what time they would be going to dinner. When he told her around seven, she simply gave an 'Uh-huh,' and then asked the address for the 'pharmacy' where she could pick it up, and Greco responded with his own address, and told her she was driving. "Great. I'll pick it up there. Thank you!" She hung up the phone and looked down at the yellow pads in front of her. The ruses that she had pulled off in the past hour that day had left her exhausted.

She looked up and found Sergeant Harding looking down at her in front of her desk. She immediately became nervous and fidgety. She always had a feeling that the phone lines were bugged, and now that Harding was here, she was sure of it, and she was also sure she was in deep trouble for the clandestine call with Greco.

"Sergeant, how can I help ya?" she asked.

"Ms. Woods," Harding exhaled. "We don't ask too much of you around here, do we?"

Maryanne wasn't really sure how to answer the question. A lie was the safe route, or was it deflection? She decided neither. "I guess I'm busy enough, Sarge."

"I'm not talking about workload, Ms. Woods. I'm talking about rules and guidelines." She wasn't sure where Harding was going, so she just let him speak. "That phone call you just had, Ms. Woods. Who was on the other end of the call?"

She gulped. "Sir?"

"It was not a business associate, I think. Your personal time is your time, Ms. Woods, and your work time is just that, time for work. Please keep your personal phone calls to your personal time. That's why you have a lunch hour. Please respect the rules, Ms. Woods."

She relaxed and made a 'tsk' sound. "You got it, Sarge. Sorry about that. Won't happen again. You see, my mom—"

"See that it doesn't, Ms. Woods. Have a fine afternoon." Harding walked away and headed back to his desk.

Maryanne focused on the yellow pads in front of her again. When Harding was safely back in his office, she mocked his admonishment. "'See that it doesn't'" she said in a lowered tone, riddled with sass. "'Have a fine afternoon.'"

The rest of Maryanne's afternoon was, in fact, just fine. There were no irrational requests from any of the detectives, and her phone was actually rather quiet. As the clock approached five, she found herself getting giddy for two reasons. One, she didn't want anyone to bring her any late afternoon 'I need this now!' work, and the second reason was her impending dinner with Greco. *Greco,* she said in her head. *You've only ever called him by his last name.* She knew his first name was Brian, but everyone called him 'Greco'. *Do I call him Greco or Brian tonight as we eat? Oh, where are we going to eat? And what did he mean by 'dinner?' Was it fine dining? Relaxed atmosphere? Fast food? Hot dog cart? What should I wear? How do I know what to wear? He never said where we were going. Ohhh...and then, later, you know, afterward, what–.* She stopped herself. *I don't even want to think about afterward.*

One of the rules that Sergeant Harding was so fond of quoting and enforcing was that co-workers cannot date or be romantically involved. Everyone knew the rule, and most everyone tried to obey it, but every now and then, there was...*a story.* Someone bragged about a conquest, or there was a sighting of two who should not be together, and the word would spread through the office like the Spanish Flu. Maryanne tried to stay away from the gossip, but it would find her anyway. Now, it appeared as if she might be the gossip, and she wasn't sure how she felt about it.

"Hey, Maryanne, you working late?" Trudy Mayweather's voice broke Maryanne from her thoughts and brought her back to reality.

"What?" Maryanne said.

"It's five after five. We made it through another one. Let's go get a drink!" Trudy said.

Maryanne thought that a drink might be a good idea, and then realized it would be a terrible idea. That's all she needed was to get tipsy and make a fool of herself in front of Greco and possibly a restaurant full of people. "Uh, no thanks," she said. I have to run across the bridge and get my mom's prescription." She was still living the lie, but it saved her from having to make another bad excuse. There was always the truth, she thought. *No, ladies, thank you, but I have to go home and freshen up and get dressed and let my dogs out so I can have dinner and hopefully more with Gre—Brian.* She thought that would go over like a lead balloon.

"Okay," Trudy said. "Maybe next time."

"Yeah, next time." Maryanne pseudo-cleaned her desk, which was to say she opened a drawer and shoved all of the yellow legal pads inside it, and then slammed it shut. *Perfectly presentable,* she thought. She wove her way through the mass of desks that ran along the wall of offices that bordered the outside of the building. *Offices. Windows. Must be nice.* She angled herself into her car, careful not to ding the door of the car next to hers in the tight parking lot. She wheeled out and headed for her little apartment above Roxy Delicatessen on Seventh. She liked her apartment, so close to both Central Park and Carnegie Hall, and Times Square as well, although she usually avoided it, and had never been there for the New Year's Eve shenanigans, as she called it.

Maryanne had two dogs as her companions. There were two little Dachshunds, both male, both from the same litter. She had lucked into getting the equivalent of about two thousand dollars' worth of pure-bred Dachshunds free of charge when her sister, who bred them as a means of living, had three litters to deal with all at the same time. She simply could not sell them all before she needed to do so, so Maryanne became the proud owner of two little black and tan dogs, which she had named 'Han' and 'Chewie.' She took them to a small park a few blocks away every morning before she left for work, every evening when she got home after they ate, and once again before she went to bed. On Saturday, they stayed in the park for a while, and the little dogs romped and ran all over the place, tangling themselves and each other in their leashes, and sometimes they tangled Maryanne in them as well.

When the dogs were fed and walked, and their evening business conducted and cleaned up by the ever-vigilant Maryanne, she looked at her watch and saw it was just past six in the evening. She gasped and realized she had less than an hour to shower, dress, and drive over to Prospect Park, where Greco's house sat on Rugby Road. She began stripping as she walked through the apartment on her way to the shower, which she felt was way too short, but it served its purpose. She was one who liked a long, hot shower, which in her building was available surprisingly often. She toweled off, powdered herself in her proper places, and took the second pair of underwear from a new pack that she always kept. *You know, it's been so long since, well, these probably aren't even a style anymore.* She cursed herself for cursing herself, and donned a black bra that was sheer in some places and not so in the places where a discreet person would say there should be coverage.

Now, she thought. *The hard part.* What was she going to wear? She opened her closet door, expecting to find only doubt and confusion, but instead, found the answer staring her right in the face. It was a royal blue one-shoulder cocktail dress that zipped in the back, one that she had not worn in quite some time. She took the plastic cover off of it, and from experience, looped a coat hanger through the zipper pull, and then stepped into the dress. She pulled on the coat hanger, and the zipper slid easily up until it reached her neck. *It still fits!* She was ecstatic. She looked at her watch and saw it was half-past six. Five minutes later, she was done with her jewelry and makeup and had her hair pulled back into a tight low ponytail. She gave the dogs a final pet goodbye for the night and headed out the door.

Chapter 62 – Intelligent, Attractive, Well-Mannered, Dog-Loving Foodie

Maryanne cruised in her Honda Accord through the evening traffic surprisingly easily and made it to Greco's neighborhood nine minutes before seven in the evening. She wanted to be early, but not that early. She did not want to seem too eager, so she drove up one block and then back down another in the other direction until she finally turned onto Greco's street, and as she counted the houses until she would find his, she realized she didn't need to find the house. Greco was waiting out front. He was wearing a charcoal gray blazer with matching pants with no tie. She looked at him as she approached and was glad that she wore what she did. Neither was overdressed, and neither was underdressed for the other. She slowed the car and came to a stop at the end of his sidewalk, where he was waiting.

"A little anxious, are we?" she asked.

"No," he replied. "I just didn't want you to have to deal with my dog." He opened the door to the passenger side of the car and eased his way in. It took him a minute to notice her in her blue dress, and after he did, he wondered why it took him so long. "Wow!" he said, his eyebrows nearly hitting the headliner of the car. "You—uh, you look—uh, incredible!" She blushed a little, but he never saw it. He was too busy looking at the single pearl earrings she was wearing and the matching choker that adorned her neck. It had one large pearl in the center and two pearls on each side of it, decreasing in size as they spread from the center's star of the show.

"Well, thank you, Greco. You look very nice as well."

"Thanks. But tonight, Maryanne, I'm Brian." She didn't even realize she had cut to the chase on one of the things that she had pondered for hours earlier. The name. She habitually called him 'Greco,' and he laid down rules for addressing each other.

"Okay, Brian." She pulled away from the curb, and they drove in silence for a few miles. The tension, he thought, seemed a little thick for two people who normally talked to each other multiple times each day. He tried to think of something to say, but all he could think of was work topics, and he wasn't going to do that. Finally, the lightning bolt of ideas hit him.

"So, where have you chosen for us to dine this evening?" he asked, happy to break the silence. He noticed that he drew out the question as long as he could. He didn't mean to do it, but he couldn't stop it, either. It just rolled out very slowly.

"We, my friend, are going to one of the premier Italian restaurants in New York City." Greco waited for more and also decided not to contemplate her use of the word 'friend' too much. However, she divulged nothing further. He decided to play a game.

"So, what if I am not a fan of Italian food?" he asked, with a little sheepishness in his tone and delivery.

"Then I would tell you that you can eat that giant plate of 'BS' in front of you. I work with you, I see what you eat, and I've ordered your lunch for you. Two out of five days per week, that I can tell, you eat something Italian."

He let out a chuckle. "When you're right, you're right. What's the name of this place?" He found himself feeling a little more relaxed in the situation, just as if they were at work. He wasn't sure why he was nervous in the first place.

"I'm surprised you haven't figured it out. Maybe you're not such a great detective after all," she teased.

"One clue? I'm supposed to get the restaurant name just from 'Italian?' What are we doing, going to Il Mulino or something?" She turned her head and looked at him as the car continued in a forward direction. He looked at her and then back to the road ahead of them. He saw the light ahead turn from green to yellow, and noticed that she was still looking at him. "Maryanne?" He nodded toward the front windshield, but continued to look at him with arched eyebrows. "Maryanne!"

She looked at him and said, "What?" He nodded towards the windshield again. She turned and slammed on the brakes of the Accord, stopping just short of the rear bumper of the Chevy Lumina in front of them. "How did you know that?"

"Know what?" he asked, catching his breath.

"Where we were going for dinner. How did you figure that out?"

"Because," he said, with a little bit of panache, "I am a great detective!" He laughed, and then she laughed as well. They made small chit chat until they got to the restaurant, which was located on West Third. She rounded the block and luckily found a parking spot as another car exited one. She angled the car into the spot with little effort, and within minutes, they were nearing the door to the restaurant, which was opened for them by a man in a tuxedo as they approached.

"M'Lady," Greco said, as he motioned for her to go first.

"Why, thank you, Mr. Greco. You are both a gentleman and a scholar." They both laughed and continued on their way inside, and they were seated at a small table next to a very large wine rack. "Pretty impressive," she said. "Too bad I'm not a wine drinker."

"Nor am I," he said. "Seems like a waste of a wine rack."

They were seated and immediately brought glasses of water, and when their server appeared, they both said they would begin with a glass of beer, which was brought before them in a matter of minutes. Greco said he would like to have a few minutes to look over the menu, and she agreed. They made up their minds in a few minutes and decided that she would have Mushroom Ravioli and he would have Chicken Parmesan, and they each would share with the other.

They sipped their beer and sat in somewhat of an awkward silence for a few moments. They each took turns looking around the restaurant, trying to notice something that would get a conversation started. He thought it was odd, since they never had a problem chatting at work, and they were very relaxed in their conversations in the car, even when she almost rear-ended the car in front of her. He finally decided he had had enough of the silence and would dive right into the conversation.

"Why did you ask me out for dinner?" he asked.

She looked at him with an odd expression on her face. "Um, you asked me out, if I remember correctly, and I do, because that's what I do. I remember things that all you defectives—I mean, detectives, forget."

He laughed at the joke. "Not the first time I have been called 'defective,' Maryanne," he said, smiling.

"I doubt that," she laughed, taking another sip of her beer. "Actually," she said, setting the glass back on the table, "I'm wondering why it took you so long to ask me."

He sat back in his chair, cocked his head, gave her a crooked smile, and brought out his best Sergeant Harding impression. "Now, you, Ms. Woods, of all people, should know that relationships in the workplace are frowned upon."

"Ugh! Stop it!" she said, laughing. "I just heard it again today from him!"

"About what?"

"You."

He stiffened in his chair and asked, "What do you mean?"

"Relax, Detective. He thought I was on the phone with my mother."

"He was listening to that?"

"Yeah," she said. "I'm not sure how much he heard of it, though. He just told me that personal calls were to be made on personal time, and that's why I get a lunch break."

"Ha," he said. "I thought eating lunch was the reason for the lunch break."

"Lunch? What is that?" she asked, jokingly. They both laughed, each having been the victim of so many 'working lunches'. When the laughter subsided, they found themselves in an awkward silence again, each waiting for the other to say something. This time, it was Maryanne who spoke up.

"So, what kind of dog do you have?"

He stopped his drink from his beer mid-sip and set the glass back down. He pulled his napkin from his lap and wiped the corner of his mouth to catch the little bit that had escaped through the side of the glass. Their server then appeared from nowhere with some steaming dishes on a tray. He laid them gently in front of them, hers before his, and asked if he could bring them anything more. They both responded with a refill on their beer, and he disappeared as quickly as he arrived. He let his head drift over his plate until the smell of the food penetrated his nostrils, and it immediately made him smile. She watched him and then did the same to her plate.

"This smells wonderful!" she said.

"Agreed." He picked up his knife and fork, cut a few slices of his chicken, moved them to the edge of the plate, and then he lifted the plate and offered it to her. She grabbed her fork and lifted her plate to meet his, and scraped the cut pieces onto the plate, right next to her ravioli. She then turned her plate and scooped a few of the ravioli onto the side of his plate. They each returned their plate to its normal position on the table and began to sample the food. Their responses were similar, with delightful eye-rolling and ecstatic exhaling as the delicious food passed over their tongues, was completely destroyed by their teeth, and then continued on, eventually making its way into their stomachs.

"Mutt," he said.

She held her finger over her lips and continued to chew until her mouth was free of ravioli debris.

"Excuse me?" she said, with a confused look on her face.

"Mutt," he said again. "The dog. The dog is a mutt," he answered. "I believe part German Shepard and part Beagle." He took another bite, and they continued eating and chatting, each at its appropriate time. The waiter returned with their beer.

"Yikes," she exclaimed. "I hope the Beagle was the male!"

"Hmmm," he said with a grin. "Hard to imagine unless the Beagle was on a step-stool!"

She laughed at his joke and let the moment pass with another sip of her beer. "I have dogs, too," she said finally.

"Really?" he asked, after swallowing his food more quickly than he should have, which induced a small cough. He took a sip of his beer to clear the debris, and after a moment, was able to continue. "What kind and how many?"

"Dachshunds," she said. "Two of them."

"Wonderful," he said. "Such cute dogs. They always seem to get right to the long and short of it."

"Wow," she said with a chuckle. "That's a terrible joke."

"I know it."

"And you still told it," she said.

He laughed and took a bite, and from the corner of his mouth came a 'Yup." And they both laughed a little. He finished his bite and took a drink. Then he looked at her. "You have to meet my dog," he said. "Since you're such a dog person. And how did I not know this before?"

"Well, I mean, we don't get really personal with work stuff," she said. "I know that sometimes you flirt with me, but—"

His eyes doubled in size. "*I* flirt with *you?*" he asked, with his voice going up a few octaves.

"Yes!" she said. "You flirt with me."

"*You* flirt with *me!*" he said, smiling.

"You're terrible!" she said.

"Yeah, well," he said. "I try." Then he looked at her. "Tell me," he said. "How are you still single?"

"Well, that was blunt," she said.

"I didn't mean it the way it sounded," he said. "You're very attractive, you're intelligent, you have decent manners, from what I can tell, and you have great taste in dogs and food. How is it that no one has taken you off the market?"

She exhaled. "Well," she paused and used her tongue to remove a piece of oregano from her teeth that she felt on the inside of her upper lip, and then continued. "I guess not everyone likes intelligent, attractive, well-mannered, dog-loving foodies. That, and the right guy never came along, I suppose. Timing was never right for anyone." She took a moment for him to let that digest, and then she turned the tables on him. "What about you, Brian? Why are you still single?"

He let the question hang in the air for a moment and tried to decide the best way to answer it. He liked dating, when he had the time, and he dated a lot, at least once or twice per week, usually a setup from one of his friends. They were never just... *right.*

"Well," he said, wiping the corner of his mouth with his napkin before placing it back into his lap. "I would have to say that maybe, *just maybe,* I've never come across the right intelligent, attractive, well-mannered, dog-loving foodie."

She looked at him, and they both began to laugh. He liked her laugh. They finished their meals with much of the same banter, and when their waiter came to ask if they wanted dessert, they both politely declined. He paid the check, and they left the restaurant, got into her car, and drove together to his house. She pulled up to the front of his house and stopped the car, but left the engine running. He got out of the car as she waited in her seat, and he then poked his head back into the car.

"What are you doing?" he asked.

"What do you mean?"

He smiled. "You gotta come in and see my dog."

"Oh, you were serious," she said, turning the car off.

He walked around the car and opened her door. "Yeah, I was serious. I'm a dog person and my dog is a people dog who loves dog people!"

She exited, and he shut the door behind her, and he led her up to the front door. Once inside, he made his standard announcement.

"Honey, I'm home!" A thunderous noise came from the floor above, and Greco shook his head and smiled. "She was on my bed," he said. "That's a no-no, but I ignore it anyway." They followed the noise across the ceiling until they heard Honey make her run down the steps. "Hey, girl!" he said, and Honey jumped up on him with her paws on his thighs. He rubbed her head for a second and then held his hand out toward Maryanne. "This is my friend, Maryanne!" The dog put her paws back onto the floor and gently walked over to Maryanne, held her head against Maryanne's leg, and looked up at her with the puppy-doggiest of eyes.

"Well, aren't you a little sweetheart?" Maryanne said, and she scratched the dog lightly behind her ears, and then placed a hand on each side of her face. "She's adorable!" Maryanne said to Brian, who was just watching the two of them together.

"Beer?" he asked.

"No thanks," she said. "I should really be going soon." She didn't really want to go, but felt like she needed to go. She was lightly tugging on a small, knotted rope that Honey had brought over to her. He unscrewed the cap from the beer he had pulled from the refrigerator, tossed it into the trash can, and watched her as he leaned against the wall that made one-half of the entrance to the kitchen. She stayed for a few minutes longer, playing with the dog and chatting with Brian about the dinner, but they never spoke about the Kelly case, which was okay with her, even though she really did want to know more about it. After all, she was doing the dirt-digging. After a quick goodbye, she grabbed her purse, and as he escorted her to the door, he insisted on walking her to her car. When they got to the door, she stopped.

"Brian, I have to ask you something. If we didn't work together, and you were on a regular date, and found that she was an intelligent, attractive, well-mannered, dog-loving foodie, what would you do?"

He laughed. "Honestly, right now, I don't know. I'd probably want to get to know her better."

She made a 'tsk' noise and continued her line of questioning. "Let's say, for the sake of argument, that you knew her like you knew me."

His face got serious. "I'd have to ask her to stay," he said, and he looked into her eyes, and then blinked hard. "But we do, Maryanne. We work together, and you know the rules."

She looked at the floor. "You're right, Brian. I do know the rules." She grabbed his hand from the door handle and didn't let it go. "And I probably know them better than you. The rules say that active co-workers shall not engage in romantic relationships."

"Right, I know this," he said. "Where are you going with this, Maryanne?"

She smiled at him. "You're not active, Brian. You're suspended," she said, and closed the door, locking it from the inside.

Chapter 63 – Kalisa

When his alarm went off at five-thirty the following morning, Greco woke to a bed that had both halves occupied for most of the night, but he noticed he was alone now. He kicked his feet over the edge of the bed, stretched, dressed in sweatpants and a hoodie, and made his way down the steps to the main floor. He looked around, but there was no sign of Maryanne. He peered out of the window and saw that her car was gone.

"Hmph," he said, and then called for Honey. She came rolling into the kitchen, and he grabbed the leash from the basket and clipped it to her collar. "Come on, girl," he said, and they went out of the back door and into the yard. He walked her around the perimeter of the yard, and then cursed himself for not making better choices. Champ was in his backyard as well, with Chauncey and Chandler, neither on a leash, but still staying within the confines of their own space. Greco cringed when he heard Champ's voice.

"Hey, neighbor!" he yelled, much too loud for before six in the morning, Greco thought.

"Morning, Champ," Greco said, still walking with Honey.

"Man, I had a hell of a night last night," Champ continued to bellow, walking closer to Greco. Honey bristled at his approach.

I bet not as good as mine, Greco thought.

"Yeah, the bowlin' league team took home the trophy, and then we celebrated big time! I got hammered and had to be driven home, but I think my bud was as drunk as I was. Took thirty minutes to get home and, you know, the bowlin' alley is only about fifteen minutes away!"

"You probably shouldn't be telling me that your friends drive while intoxicated, Champ," Greco said. *Idiot.*

"Hell, I know, but it was last night, so I think he's safe now. Hope he is, anyway. I'll have to check on him."

Greco looked at him. "You're a good friend, Champ," he said with inner sarcasm. Honey found a good spot to add some moisture to the already dew-covered grass.

"I try, buddy. Anyway, short story long, he parks along the street to let me out, and I get out and I'm carryin' this big ass trophy, you know, 'cause we won the championship and all, and I start walking up toward the house, trip on my own shoelace, or somethin', and fall onto my lawn. The trophy broke into about five or six pieces."

What a shame.

"And then, I'm pickin' up the pieces of it, you know, 'cause I gotta glue it together, 'cause I'm Champ, and Champ deserves trophies, right? And then as I'm walkin' up to the house, I smell somethin', and it turns out that when I fell, I fell into a pile of dog shit. Right on my lawn! Can you believe that?"

Greco had to try extremely hard to suppress his laugh, but he failed. "I'm sorry, Champ," he said, still laughing and thinking about the events of the late afternoon before Maryanne picked him up. "I shouldn't laugh, but it's a little funny. I can picture it!" *Wish I had been there to see it.* He finally was able to control himself and seize an opportunity. "Well, I guess just make sure you clean up after your dogs," he said.

"Wasn't my dogs," he said. "Too much shit. My dogs leave little shits. This was a lot of shit, so it had to be from a bigger dog, like yours. Maybe it was one of them Dobermans, or that Retriever up the road. Anyways, so, that was my night. How's yours?"

"Oh, just a quiet night for me, Champ. Nothing like yours. Listen, great chatting, but I gotta go. I have some work to do. Take care."

"You too, neighbor," Champ said, and turned toward his house.

I need to put up a privacy fence, Greco thought. *But that story, though, I need to remember that story to make me feel better when I'm having a crappy day.* He laughed at his own joke, and then he and Honey aimed for the back door of the house. When he got to the back door, he saw a small piece of paper tucked into the door between the metal and the screen. He took it out, and walked into the house, and laid the paper on the table. He got Honey settled with some fresh water and her treats.

Greco looked back towards the note on the table and wondered if it was a message from Champ about his evening. He walked over to the table and unfolded the note, and was pleased to see it in a handwriting that he could not possibly believe was forged by Champ. He recognized it. It was Maryanne's handwriting. He read the note.

Hey Brian,

Sorry to leave without saying goodbye, but I have to get home to my dogs and get them walked and fed before I go to work. I had a great time last night, and not just here. I enjoyed the dinner as well, and just talking to you, outside of work-talk. We'll have to do that again, if you want, sometime before you get reinstated! Hope you have a great day!

Hearts,

Maryanne

He smiled at the note, folded it back up, and laid it back onto the table. He believed he would read it again later. Right then, he had work to do. He went upstairs, took off his sweatpants and hoodie, then showered, shaved, and put on a suit as he would on any other workday. He went back down the stairs and pulled out the big yellow phone book that was dumped onto his front porch every six months. He opened it and looked for taxi companies, specifically, the Newark Cab Company, but he found no listings. *Must not be that big of a cab company to not be listed,* he thought. He would have to figure out the best time to get to the cab company's location to talk to someone who might be able to help. He decided that the earlier he got there, the better his chances would be.

The clock on his dashboard read seven twenty-eight in the morning when he arrived at the Newark Cab Company. He parked his car out in front of the business, exited his vehicle, and looked around. There wasn't much to it from what he could see, and it looked deserted. It was basically an old gas station with the fuel pumps removed, and a service lift added to one side of the building. He walked to the front door and gave it a tug. The door opened, to his surprise, and he walked into the small room, which appeared to have previously been a waiting room, but now served as an office. The room was divided in half by a wall that went from the floor to about halfway up the ceiling. The rest of the way up it was a see-through material, which Greco guessed as plexiglass at first glance. He approached the window, and behind the transparent separation between them, he saw a small black woman sitting in a chair. She wore horn-rimmed glasses with a black frame, and they were secured to her by a chain that connected from each earpiece and went around the back of her neck. She did not seem to notice his approach. She was diligently copying numbers from a stack of small papers into what appeared to be a bookkeeping ledger. He removed his sunglasses.

"Excuse me," he said through a small hole in the window, which was actually made of real glass that just happened to be rather dirty.

She held one finger up in the air as if to ask him for patience. She continued jotting down numbers with the other hand and seemed content to make him wait until she was finished. He looked around the small room at the bare walls that were paneling on the bottom, and dull paint, which he assumed was white at some point, the rest of the way up. He heard her clear her throat and turned around to see her peering at him over the top of the glasses.

"'elp ya?" she said, in an island accent which he could not immediately identify.

"Yes, ma'am," he said. He pulled his badge from his pocket, showed it to her, and identified himself. "I need some information on your fare logs and records.

"What kind of de information," she said.

"I basically need to know who was driving a certain car at a certain time on a certain day. Would that be something with which you could help me?"

"What day you lookin' for, mon?"

"September eleventh of this year."

"Ah, bad day, mon," she said. "Very bad day."

"Yes, it was," he said. "Would you have the information I need? I need to speak with one of your drivers regarding a possible crime."

"What crime?" she asked, indignantly. "We commit no crime here."

"No, it wasn't one of your drivers. Possibly a fare."

"Well, Mista, we only have de three drivers. Me husband, and me two sons."

That statement explained a lot, as far as Greco was concerned. The small, run-down garage, the lack of any real information about the establishment, and the lack of a fleet of cars. He put his hand on the bridge of his nose and rubbed the small indentations of where his sunglasses used to sit.

"Your whole driver roster is three drivers? How many cars do you have?" he asked.

She signed and put her pen down on the ledger and looked up at him. "Three," she said. "And you want to speak with me husband, Cleo. He was de only one working on de nine-eleven."

"Great. How and when can I speak with him?"

"He's out all of de day, from six in de morning to 'round midnight. He don't stop. He drive all de day."

"I really need to speak with him. It's very important."

She looked at him and then grabbed a microphone on the desk. She tapped one of the black buttons on the base of it. It crackled for a second. Then, she spoke into it.

"Cleo, I need you back at base. You have a fare."

The radio crackled, and then a voice came from the other side. "*Okay, Kalisa. Ten minutes away.*"

"Dere you go, mon. He be right here soon."

"Kalisa," Greco said. "Is that your name? It's beautiful."

"Ya," she said. "My mother gave it to me."

"Does it have a meaning? It's wonderful."

"She looked at him over the glasses again and smiled. "It means, 'The One Who Has Given Herself To God.'"

"That's very nice," he said in a soft tone. "I have to ask you, is Cleo going to be upset because you told him to come back for a fare, and he finds out it's just to talk to me?"

Kalisa looked at him and exhaled. "When he come back, you go, somewhere, wherever, but not here. So, you are a fare, Investigator mon." Then she chuckled a little and smiled at him, picked up her pen, dropped her head, and went back to her ledger.

Greco smiled back at her and thanked her, and then turned toward the door. He walked outside into the bright morning sunlight and took in a breath of what he had hoped would be fresh air, but it was mostly exhaust fumes from the road on which the taxi company was located. He turned around toward Kalisa again, and now she wore a concerned look on her face. For a while, he sat on the edge of a large concrete flower pot, which was now filled with only dirt and an old soda can, and watched the traffic go by. He wondered aloud where some of the vehicles were going. If there were a parent and a child, he imagined it was a ride to the child's school. Two or more adults would have been in a carpool to work or some other business function. There were some things his imagination could not keep up with, however, so he just let them pass without another thought. He was musing about his most recent assignment when a young man, about late teens, Greco thought, approached him.

"Hey," the kid said. He was wearing stained blue jeans and a black denim jacket with holes in it.

"Hey," Greco said.

"He out?" the kid asked.

"Excuse me?" Greco asked.

"CB. He out somewhere? I don't see any cars."

Greco decided to play along. "Yeah. I'm waiting for him."

"Damn," the kid said. "I need to get my shit before school. I can't handle today straight."

Straight, Greco thought. *The kid can't handle school* straight. *What did that mean?* Then he figured it out. *Cleo is dealing. Leverage time,* he thought.

"Well," Greco said. "In the short term, I might be able to help you out. What do you get from Cleo?"

The kid eyed Greco for a second. "Nah, I'm good," he said, but then looked at his watch.

"Suit yourself, Greco said. "Don't be late for school, though, and go in smelling like weed or high on coke. They'll burn you down." The kid puffed out his breath and scratched his head, and then turned to look up the road as if he expected Cleo to appear from thin air. There was a patch that ran the length and width of the back of the jacket for what Greco guessed was a musical group he had never heard of. There were skulls, blood, and bubbling beakers of bright green liquid.

"Okay," the kid said. "I just need some pot for now."

"Ah," Greco tisked. "Sorry, I don't have any pot, but I do have this." Greco pulled his badge from his coat and showed the kid, whose eyes got large, and whose feet began running immediately. He turned the corner of the building and nearly tripped over the downspout from the building before he disappeared from sight.

"Stay in school!" Greco yelled, laughing to himself. He was thinking about how fortunate the encounter with the kid was, based on what he had learned, when a familiar-looking vehicle pulled into the lot and parked beside him. Cleo Baptiste put the car into park and exited from the driver's side, crossed from behind the car, and opened the rear passenger door.

"'ello, mon," he said, gesturing for Greco to enter the car. Greco got into the car and waited as Cleo crossed behind him again and got back into the driver's seat, and then closed the door. "So, where we goin' today, mah friend?"

"Well," Greco said as he pulled out his badge and flashed it at Cleo. "We don't really need to go anywhere. You can go ahead and turn on the meter, but we can stay right here if you want." Cleo bristled at the sight of the badge, but then calmed.

"Whatever you say, mon," he said. "Whatchu want." It came out more of a command than a question, but Greco let it pass.

"Mr. Baptiste," Greco asked, holding up a photo of Will. "Do you know this man? We have reason to believe you have met him before."

Cleo stiffened, but remained calm. "Mon, I don't remember who get into mah cab from one day to de next. I just drive mah cab from 'ere to dere."

Greco began looking at his notepad. "Mr. Baptiste, would your landlord, a Mr. Donald Randall, be interested to know that you sell and habitually use marijuana? You wouldn't be dealing and be under the influence while you're on his property, would you? You wouldn't be dealing and be under the influence when you're driving this cab, would you?"

Cleo dropped his head. "Aww, c'mon mon, I'm just trying to make some extra money for mah family. It's only pot!"

"It's still illegal, Mr. Baptiste. But, if you cooperate with me, I might forget that." Cleo shook his head slowly. "So, have you seen this man before?"

Cleo exhaled and acquiesced. "I remember dis man. 'e 'ire my cab, twice in a day. 'e say 'e is done with de city life and was gettin' away as soon as 'e can. It was on nine-eleven, and 'e say dat 'e cannot fly away, so, 'e ask me to drive 'im to de bus station."

"Which station?"

"'e ask me to take 'im to, uhhh, Jersey City station, and den, a few minutes later comes back out and 'e ask me to go to Newark. I'm eatin' mah lunch and I tell 'im dat, and 'e gives me a hundred dollars to take 'im. So, I put down mah san'wich, and I take 'im dere, to de travel plaza. Dat's all I know, mon."

"Newark travel plaza, correct?" Greco asked.

"Das what I said, mon. Anything else I can 'elp yah with, mon, or are we done?"

Greco smiled. "Sure. What kind of bags did he have? How many?"

"Mon, I tink 'e 'ad two bags. One was a big duffel bag, and one was a regular-size bag with the Giants logo on it. Can I get back to work, or will ya be takin' me to jail?"

"No jail today, Mr. Baptiste. But don't let me hear about you dealing drugs anymore." Greco got out of the car and removed his wallet, pulling out a twenty-dollar bill. He held it out to Cleo, who made a face at it, but then took it anyway. "Thanks for the ride, Mr. Baptiste," Greco said with a smile.

For the rest of the day, following his chat with Cleo Baptiste, Greco followed the breadcrumbs that Will had left behind on his journey from the East Coast to wherever he went. Wherever that was, Greco did not yet have an idea. He left the cab garage and went to the Newark travel plaza, where he had to wait until eleven o'clock for the Director of Operations to arrive for her shift. After waiting and introducing himself, Greco began this chapter of his investigation by requesting security camera footage, which, when he viewed it, could be described as grainy at best. He asked for any credit card transaction history available from that day, and after hours of searching, Will Kelly's name was nowhere to be found. It made sense because Greco didn't think that Will Kelly would have left a credit card trail for anyone to follow.

Greco then had to get down to some gritty details and search for cash transactions. He estimated that the time frame had to be somewhere between eleven o'clock and two o'clock that day. Knowing what he knew about criminals in flight, he also eliminated all transactions with destinations that were less than a full state away. That narrowed the search down to thirteen transactions. Greco noted the time of each cash transaction from a large green-and-white-bar paper report that had been provided and then reconnected with the Director of Operations.

She led him back to the security center so they could check the video surveillance again. Greco looked closely at the unclear picture and watched each transaction closely. He looked at the approach of the person to the counter, as much of the transaction as he could see, and then even closer as the person left the counter with their tickets, and which direction he or she was headed. He thought about not even giving the women a second thought, and just focusing on the male patrons, but he didn't yet know how crafty Will Kelly could or would be. *Maybe he dressed as a woman*, Greco considered. He watched them all closely, with one disappointment or lack of clarity following the previous one. He looked back at the green-and-white-bar paper and counted that he had eliminated eight of the thirteen transactions. He was down to three when he saw something that caught his eye. The customer was carrying two bags, and one was a large duffel bag. Greco kept watching. The figure turned away, and then he saw it. The other bag. Emblazoned on the side of the second bag was the logo of the New York Giants. He looked at the report again and found the time stamp. His finger followed the line across the paper. He looked away from the paper for a moment and then back to it again.

"Indianapolis," he said.

Chapter 64 – Clock Clock

Greco woke up at five-thirty the next morning and grabbed the suitcase he had packed the night before from the end of his bed, and made his way down the steps and into his kitchen. He let Honey out into the backyard and didn't care if Champ Chaser saw it or not. Honey stayed in the yard and did not wander, and when she was finished with her business, Greco let her back into the house. After a few reward treats, he slipped a spare key under the mat by the back door.

Greco had made the decision as soon as he figured out that Will Kelly had gone to Indianapolis that he was going to try to follow the same route and hunt Kelly down, and bring him to justice. He also decided not to waste time and to leave the next morning. He had called Maryanne and told her his plan. She was supportive of his decision, told him to be careful, and agreed to make sure Honey was well taken care of while he was gone. She would come over later to let Honey out, and then she would take the dog to her apartment and make sure she was fed and had plenty of water while Greco was gone. She hoped that Honey would enjoy her time with Han and Chewie.

Greco gave Honey some extra attention before he left, and he walked out of the house with his suitcase in hand before the sun came up. Will Kelly had taken a bus from Newark to Indianapolis, but Greco didn't have that luxury. He needed a car wherever he was going. He needed to make the trip in his own car, and leaving early was the best way to make the most of each day. He had thought about stopping in the hospital to visit Steve, but he didn't think it would do anyone any good, especially himself or Steve. Still, Greco felt bad about not making the visit.

He navigated his way out of his neighborhood and through others until he was able to access I-278 and then into New Jersey, where he picked up I-95 and headed south. He figured that with the stops and perhaps sleep, the trip to Indianapolis would probably take about thirteen hours. But once he got there, where would he go? What would he do? It was basically a thirteen-hour trip down a dead-end road. Or maybe it was going to be a thirteen-hour trip that would open up into a thousand different options when he arrived. Greco had to admit to himself, he was a little excited by the unknown factor of this chase he was on.

He was just south of Trenton and stopped on the side of the road to relieve himself. The timing was perfect as he had to get off of I-95 and onto the 76, which would take him out to Harrisburg, Pennsylvania, and points further west. He pulled off the Interstate near Carlisle and got a cheeseburger and fries from a fast-food restaurant. He was about three hours into the drive and needed to stretch his legs anyway, but he didn't waste any time. He ate as he walked and shook his legs and stretched, drank his water, and used the restaurant's restroom before he was back out onto the road. The stop cost him less than twenty minutes of time.

When Greco got back out onto the Interstate and continued his drive, he began to think about this case and where it started and how it had progressed. And then he wondered, what was yet to come. What would he do when he actually confronted Will Kelly, assuming that he would find him in the first place? The search was going to be about as regimented as Swiss cheese. When he got to Indianapolis, he would start with the bus station and see if they had any surveillance video of Will Kelly. If so, Greco might at least get an idea of which way Kelly went when he got off the bus. Greco imagined himself in the shoes of a criminal who was on the run and traveling by bus on a multi-day schedule. Sure, you could sleep on the bus, but what kind of quality sleep would it be? Greco had also considered the time of Will Kelly's travel and the route the bud had taken. The schedule that he saw for Kelly's path to Indianapolis would have him arriving there at around two forty-five in the afternoon on September twelfth. Greco figured that after many long hours on the road across multiple buses, there would be two things on Greco's agenda when his ride was complete. The two things were, depending on what he ate on the trip and how well he had slept, food and somewhere to sleep and get cleaned up.

That's where Greco believed he would start, after his investigation at the bus station.

He wasn't sure when it happened, but I-76 merged into I-70, which was fine, because that was part of his travel plan. Greco did realize, though, that since he was unfamiliar with the roads and the complete course to Indianapolis, he would need to pay closer attention to his driving and not get lost in his thoughts. This proved to be difficult. His tires made noises when he rode over seams in the highway's surface. They were spread evenly along the highway, and they turned into a droning of *clock-clock* noises. His eyes were tired from the unchanging scenery: a long highway with trees on both sides, sometimes broken up by an off-ramp, or some other distraction from the endless road ahead. *Clock-clock, clock-clock, clock-clock.* He rubbed his eyes, one at a time, so he could still see the road ahead. First the left, then the right. *Clock-clock, clock-clock, clock-clock.* His legs were getting tired from being in the same position for so long. *Clock-clock, clock-clock, clock-clock.* He grabbed his cup of water from the cup holder in the console for a drink, but all he got for his efforts was the annoying slurping sound of a straw in an empty cup. *Clock-clock, clock-clock, clock-clock.* He needed a rest stop.

Greco was south of Pittsburgh and continued on until he saw signs for Washington, Pennsylvania, which advised of food, fuel, and lodging, all of which Greco would have taken. He had a quarter-tank of fuel still, so he made that a second priority. The first was a restroom, some food, and a fresh drink. He signaled at Exit 17 and pulled off a long off-ramp, and took a right turn at its base. He immediately saw a few gas stations and an ice cream place, but off in the distance, he saw a familiar red and yellow fast-food sign. That would be his first stop. He pulled into the parking lot and parked as far away from the door as possible. He needed the walk. *Kelly, you asshole,* Greco thought. *You're going to make me get varicose veins from driving so much!* He walked in the front door of the restaurant and bee-lined for the restroom. Then he needed some food, but he wasn't super happy about eating another cheeseburger and French fries. He chose a chicken sandwich and saw that apple slices were an option for a side order. He placed his order and added a large coffee and an extra-large ice water.

He walked back to the car with his food and drink, all placed nicely in a cardboard rack provided by the restaurant, which he decided that he would utilize in the car, since he only had the one cup holder. He stopped to fill up the gas tank, got back onto the highway, and continued his trek with a sip of coffee here and a bite of sandwich there. He didn't want to stop again, so he kept the water only when he was feeling parched. *Clock-clock, clock-clock, clock-clock.* The noise continued, but before long, he was out of Pennsylvania and into Ohio, and in a little over two hours, found himself in Columbus, where, against his will, he once again stopped to stretch and use a restroom.

In another two hours, Greco crossed the state line from Ohio into Indiana. He knew he still had a long way to go, but also felt that he was in the home stretch. But it was not a pleasant drive, right now. The sun was trying to set, and it was shining directly in his face. He didn't want rain, but a few clouds would not have bothered him in the slightest way. At least he was in the state in which he was supposed to be. *Well, that's not really true,* he thought. *I should still be in New York. Harding's gonna fire me for all this.* He put the thought of Harding's wrath out of his mind and tried to focus on the drive, which the closer he got to his destination, the further away it seemed to be. He cursed himself for thinking that he was 'almost there' when he reached Indiana.

He did, however, finally reach his destination of Indianapolis, and he used his road atlas to locate the main bus station there, located on Illinois Street. He looked at the clock in his car, and it was nearly eight-thirty. Not the best time to get in touch with whoever was in charge of the bus terminal for questioning, but he was going to try anyway. He parked and walked into the main building and sought out a ticketing agent or a service desk. He found the former and waited in line until it was his turn. He asked the woman who was behind the desk if he could speak to the highest-ranking person currently in the building. He was directed to a white door cut into a white wall with a large red line running parallel to the floor and the length of the wall.. He knocked on the door and was asked to identify himself, and when he did, he was admitted through the door. He was led down a hallway by another woman who directed him to sit in a room and wait, and someone would be right with him.

Greco looked around the room. It appeared to be an employee breakroom as it had several vending machines, three refrigerators, two sinks, an office-style watercooler, and several microwave ovens. He looked at the vending machines, desperately hoping they offered coffee, but none of them did. He took a cone-shaped cup from a tubular dispenser on the side of the cooler and pressed a blue button to fill the cup. His mouth expected a refreshing drink of nearly ice-cold water, but it received an unrewarding room-temperature version of the liquid instead. Greco grunted and tossed the cup into the nearby trash can. He was about to check the vending machines for a cold soda when the door opened and a man of about forty years old, Greco estimated, walked in. He walked over to Greco and stuck out his hand.

"Matt Tucker," the man said. 'What can I do for ya?"

"Greco," Greco responded. "NYPD."

"You're a long way from home, ehh, Sergeant? Lieutenant? Officer?" Tucker motioned his arm toward one of the small tables in the room, and both men took chairs opposite each other.

"Detective is fine," Greco said. "Or just Greco if you want. I don't want to take up too much of your time, but I'm looking for a possible fugitive from my precinct. I believe he came through this bus terminal."

"Oh my," Tucker said. "How can I help?"

"Well, I'm wondering if I can get a look at your video surveillance footage from September 12th."

"I'm not sure I can do that, partner. I'm just the night manager here. The Director won't be in until the morning. She's the head honcho around here. Just between you and me, I don't think she's my biggest fan, if ya know what I mean."

Greco nodded. "I understand," he said and leaned forward in the chair. "It would only take a few minutes to see what I need to see, and it's really important that I stay on the trail of this guy. It's been a few months now, and I need to stay on his trail while it's still warm if I want to catch him."

"Yeah, I getcha, man, but I just can't, right now. Why don't ya come back in the morning and talk with Brenda. Brenda Carlin is her name, and she's the top dog." Tucker immediately shuddered. "Uh, don't tell her I called her that, please."

Greco nodded. "Our secret," he said dryly, standing from his chair. "I guess I'll be back tomorrow. Can you leave her a heads-up that I'd like to have a word with her?"

"Will do, Detective," Tucker said, rising as well. "Anything else?"

Greco stopped, turned his head back around, and said, "Yeah. Can you recommend a hotel in the area?"

"Sure can. Are ya looking for cozy, comfy, and pricey, or coarse, common, and penny-pinching?"

Greco thought for a minute about his trip and how long he had been in the car. "Let's go with the first one," he said.

"That's easy," Tucker said. "The Revere, right around the corner and down the road two blocks."

"Thanks," Greco said, and made his way out of the room and into the terminal, and then out to the street. He thought about calling a cab, but decided to walk the distance and stretch out his legs a little more. He got to the hotel safely, paid for the room with his credit card, and headed up to the third floor. He opened the door to his room and stood there in the open doorway for a moment after he turned on the light. The room was beautiful. He had not stayed in many hotels in his life, but this one had to be the best he'd ever seen. He laid his suitcase on top of one of the dressers in the room and opened it up so his clothes could breathe. He undressed down to his underwear and put on a t-shirt that he had taken from his suitcase. Then he pulled out his toothbrush, brushed his teeth, swallowed a glass of water, and then crashed onto the bed. He was sleeping within minutes.

Chapter 65 – Steve Angelucci

Greco awoke the following day refreshed, but still feeling his thirteen-hour journey from the day before. He showered, dressed, and then sat at the desk in his room and formulated his plan. He would check hotels and motels in the area to see if anyone remembered Will Kelly or if he left any trace of himself behind, and if so, could provide any information on where he was or where he was going. He doubted that Kelly would completely change his name, as it was Greco's experience that when people did this type of thing, and changed their first names, they tended to get caught because they wouldn't answer when called by someone, because they were not used to answering to that name. More often than not, when someone was called by his or her new name, the person would not answer; it would lead to questions, and the story would begin to unravel.

But Will Kelly seemed not to be your everyday criminal. He was intelligent, calculating, a planner, and a footprint hider. He had taken many steps to conceal his disappearance, his getaway, and his plans for his future. Greco realized he was a few states from home and had done well tracking Kelly to this point, but he knew in his heart that Kelly wouldn't stop in the first place he landed. He'd keep going. He'd find somewhere sustainable, but not too large, and also just large enough so he could comfortably fit in. He'd live a quiet, probably sheltered, lonely life. He'd hide in plain sight.

Greco took the large phone book from the desk and flipped through the pages until he got to the "Lodging" section. He ripped the pages from the book and folded them, so they fit neatly into his pocket. He thought it might very well take him weeks to perhaps find the hotel where Kelly had stayed, assuming he did stay anywhere in the area. It would be like finding a needle in the haystack, but he had to try. He really didn't have anything else to go on. Kelly's trail was getting colder.

He found the first hotel about a half mile from the Revere. No one there, however, seemed to recall seeing Will Kelly.

Nor did they at the next one, or the one he tried after that. He kept going, though, and he had to if he was going to find Will Kelly. In all, that first day, Greco visited eleven hotels, motels, and inns in the city of Indianapolis. None of them gave him any leads, and at the end of the day, he was more than a little tired. He had chosen to walk to the hotels that were close to the Revere, but the next day, he decided he would drive. He got back to the Revere and stopped into the connecting lounge for a drink. He sat at the bar and had a beer, which quickly disappeared and was just as quickly replaced by another. When he finished the second, he asked for his check from the bartender. He opened his wallet and pulled out a credit card to pay. That's when it hit him.

Greco remembered that he had needed to use a credit card when he got his room at the Revere. He doubted that Will Kelly would have used a credit card, so Greco thought that maybe, *just maybe*, he could eliminate the hotels that required a credit card. That would be his plan the next day when he went searching once again. He stopped at the front desk to ask when the general manager would be in, as he was told that she would be available the next morning.

When he stopped at the desk the next morning, he was greeted by Jennifer Cody, The Revere's general manager. He introduced himself to her and explained why he was in Indianapolis, and asked her if she wouldn't mind answering a few questions.

"Absolutely," she said. "Do you want to come back into my office?"

"That will be fine," Greco said, and he followed her back through a door and into a hallway. The office was the first room they encountered, and she offered him a seat across from her desk.

"What can I do for you?" she asked.

"Let's assume you had a visitor from out of town, and they only had cash. I noticed you require a credit card at the time of check-in. What would you do if someone came in who did not have a credit card?"

"Well, now we'd direct them to another hotel in the area. Not as nice as the Revere, but similar."

"Now?" Greco asked. "What about 'then?' And when was there a change?"

"To be honest, it doesn't happen that much. Most of our guests have reservations which require a credit card. We get very few walk-ins. I wasn't aware of it happening at all because one of our former employees was running a scam with her brother, and she would direct guests to his motel across town. If your guy came in here in September, and Noel was working, and didn't have a credit card, it's a pretty good chance that is where she sent him."

Greco was dumbfounded. The one break he needed, he may have just gotten. "So," he said, "do you know the address of the brother's motel?

"Absolutely." She grabbed a notepad from her desk and wrote down the address, talking as she wrote. "Yes, we had a big investigation into it and everything. Turned out she was sending customers there for years. He also drives a taxi, and she would use her position here to increase his business. Folks needed a cab, she called him." She handed him the piece of paper from the notepad, which he took and put into his pocket.

"That's a great scheme," Greco said. "Believe me, I have seen a lot of them, and that one's pretty good."

"We didn't really appreciate it," she said.

"No, I cannot imagine you did. You've been very helpful. Thank you."

"Anytime," she said. "Be careful if you go to the Big Star. It's in a pretty bad area."

"Thanks for the heads up," he said, and he left her in her office and found his way out. He went back up to his room and decided to give Maryanne a call to see how she was doing.

"*Maryanne Woods,*" she said, answering the phone.

"Hey, you," he said.

"*Greco, oh my God. Where are you?*"

"Indianapolis," he said, "and I just got a lead on my guy."

"Brian, you have to listen to me," she said.

"What?" he said.

"Brian, it's Steve."

"What about him? Is he getting better?"

"No, Brian. He's not. It's worse. He's dying."

"What?!" Greco yelped. "What happened?"

"They think he might only have days left," she said. *"His body is just giving up."* She was crying as she spoke. *"Brian, it's so sad."*

"Oh my God," Greco said in disbelief. "I'm coming home. I'm leaving in a few minutes, and I'll drive straight through. I'll see you tonight."

"Be careful," she said, trying to hold back her tears.

Greco hung up the phone and grabbed his suitcase. He pulled all the clothes from the closet and drawers that he had put away just a day ago and dumped them all inside the suitcase. He zipped up his bag, took a final look around the room to make sure he had everything, and then left the room, closing the door as he left. He stopped at the front desk on his way out and advised that he was checking out early, but was informed that there were no refunds for his short stay. Greco could not have cared less, and in minutes, he was in his car and driving back to New York. He was going home.

He stopped at a convenience store and bought a bottle of water and a large coffee with extra sugar. The ride home would be worse than the ride out to Indianapolis. At least with the ride to Indy, he was looking forward to something. Furthering his case. Making strides. But now, as he drove back home to New York, all he had was dread. The next few days would be pure torture, he thought. If Maryanne was right, and Steve Angelucci was close to expiring, Greco dreaded the waiting, the sitting by the bedside and hoping his friend and partner would pass peacefully, if indeed that was the only remaining path for him. In truth, Greco was hoping for a miracle. Modern medicine should be able to help a healthy, vibrant man like Steve. Then Greco found himself cursing the doctors for their inept ability to save Steve, but that quickly passed, as he reaffirmed to himself that it was not their fault. Steve knew what he was doing that day. He knew what he was getting into every day that he put on his badge. Even as bad as September 11th was, Steve, Greco, and everyone else who wore a badge signed up for it.

As the miles passed, Greco thought back to his conversation with Steve in the hospital. Steve accepted his fate. He had told Greco that if this was how it was going to be, he was at peace with it. Greco shook off the feeling of guilt he was beginning to have. He never should have left Steve that day, but everyone had to do what they thought was the right thing in that terrible situation. But still...

Four hours into his trip back to New York, Greco needed to make a stop to refill his coffee, get more water, and relieve himself of the water and coffee he had purchased earlier. He grabbed a premade sandwich from a cooler as well, and a bag of trail mix to munch on as he drove. He made quick work of the water and was wondering if he was dehydrated. He tried to make sure he got enough water each day, but the long hours of driving had thrown him off his normal balance. He told himself he'd have plenty of time to drink water and electrolyte beverages as he sat with Steve, just waiting for the inevitable. He told himself he would not leave Steve's bedside as long as Steve had breath in his lungs, as long as his great heart would still beat. His greatest regret was leaving Steve that awful day, and he'd never do it again.

His thoughts drifted from Steve to Maryanne, who had sounded so upset on the phone. What a terrible thing it had to be for her to be the one to give him the news about Steve. He hated that she was in that situation—no, that *he put her* in that situation, by traveling halfway across the country to search for basically a ghost. He told himself that if his first trip to Indianapolis had been unfruitful, he would have dropped it and gone back to New York, not to return, unless there was a break in the case which led him back. But there was something, now. Noel. The Big Star Motel. The cab-driving brother. The dishonest working relationship. They all had to point somewhere. Willem Kelly was *out there, somewhere.* Greco was determined to find him. He had to find him, or all of this was for nothing. In his mind, he blamed Willem Kelly for what was happening to Steve. The two situations were not directly related, but Greco was not in New York for Steve because he was chasing Willem Kelly, who seemingly just happened to vanish into the dust cloud that would ultimately cost Steve Angelucci his life.

The sun had set behind him, but was still causing a glow in the sky that he could see as he entered New Jersey. He was getting so close now. He remembered how he had cursed himself when he crossed into Indiana and thought he was almost to his destination. He wasn't going to do that this time. He was making good time, shaving nearly an hour off of what he estimated to be another twelve-to-thirteen-hour drive, but he was at around ten hours now, with about one more to go. He would go straight to the hospital with no more stops. He had to go to the bathroom again, but wanted to keep going. Unfortunately, it got the best of him, and he had to stop on the side of the road. He just pulled over onto the shoulder of the highway to conduct his business. He didn't want to take the time to find an off-ramp and a restaurant or gas station to use. Within minutes, he was back on the road, and before long, was pulling into the parking garage near the hospital.

He asked at the front desk which room Steve Angelucci could be found, and was told room 622. He was given a visitor's badge, which he clipped to his shirt. He took the first available elevator up to the sixth floor and followed the signs on the wall until he turned the corner and found himself looking at so many of his co-workers at the station. Everyone was crying, and Greco had a horrible feeling. Maryanne was there, and she looked up and saw Greco, and ran to him, meeting him halfway down the hall. She reached him and threw her arms around him, sobbing uncontrollably.

"Maryanne, what's happened?" he asked.

"Brian," she said through the tears. "Steve is gone. He just passed away. Just a few minutes ago. You just missed him."

Chapter 66 – I'll Tell You Everything

Will found himself, four months later, on a bus back to Brindle. He had completed his training at the Academy and was actually looking forward to beginning his new career as a Sheriff's Deputy in his new hometown. He had excelled at the Academy, learning various forms of martial arts and self-defense, the laws of the state, the rules of the Academy, CPR and first aid, weapons training, tactics of negotiation, interviewing methods, stealth practices, search and arrest practices, sobriety testing, fingerprinting, crowd control, vehicle stops, patrol scenarios, and several other topics. He was rather comfortable with his time at the Academy after the first few days. Utter had not properly prepared Will for the full experience, and several things, like soap and shampoo, towels, toothbrushes, and toothpaste, and even a pillow and pillowcase for his bed, were things that Will had to make an immediate shopping trip for on his first day at the Academy. Leaving the campus, of course, was another issue, as anyone who desired to do so needed written authorization. Will looked back at that time when he wondered if he was doomed from the start.

Fortunately, however, the trainers understood his issues and gave him a pass for the day, and Will was able to get what he needed as far as his personal items. Then, of course, there was his sidearm. One more thing Utter had neglected to tell Will was that everyone was to bring their own sidearm, whether it was one obtained by each person through proper channels or whether it was one issued to each trainee by his or her respective department. Will's second day consisted of explaining to his trainer that he had no idea that he was supposed to have brought his firearm with him, and he had not yet been issued one. This was where Utter actually came through for once. He had called ahead, and when it was discovered that Will was who he was and without a firearm to use, he was temporarily issued one from the Academy's armory that he could use until he graduated. He was also issued a flashlight, handcuffs, a belt and holster, an expandable baton, safety glasses, earplugs, and a cleaning kit for the firearm. He was also issued whatever ammunition he needed, but each day it was a hassle for him to acquire it from the armory. Everyone else already had their own.

During training, the trainees would run for miles every day. Of course, Will had no problem with this and aside from his knee which still bothered him every now and then, he was in top condition for the task. He also did fairly well on the firing range, the self-defense courses, and the field tests, but it was in the classroom where he really excelled. His scores for the courses were equal to some of the best in the history of the Academy, and his final exams were nearly flawless. Will thought that maybe some of the best criminals might make the best cops, although he wasn't ready to call himself one of the best criminals. Even after graduation, as he stood there, in his uniform, taking an oath to serve and protect, he couldn't help but think that even though he was starting a new life as a peacekeeper, he'd never be able to rid himself of the knowledge that he was a thief. He felt odd about that. In his old life, he was on one side of the law, and then he took a step across a line from which he could never return, and he was on the other side. Now, he was on both.

He made mental notes about what he needed to do when he got back to Brindle. He needed to check in with Utter. He needed to see Rocky and retake ownership of Kat, assuming it remembered who Will was after these few months. He was pretty sure he would need to fumigate his trailer for bugs. He hated spiders and figured that as the weather got colder, they would crawl into the trailer and make a home there. Then he would have to clean the trailer from top to bottom to make sure he got rid of any pesticides left over from the bug bomb. There was a lot to do.

Although he was anxious about starting his new career as an officer of the peace, that wasn't what worried him the most. He made a promise when he left, a promise to Rocky, that he would tell her *everything* when he got back, assuming he wanted a relationship with her. In his head, he thought he did, but in his heart, he still felt it was wrong, because, after all, he was still married to Kathleen. *Or was he?* Technically, *technically*, Willem Kelly was married. *Billy Lomax was not.* He played around with that idea in his head for a while. His two sides battled back and forth for quite a while, and in the end, the criminal in him won. He did have feelings for Rocky, that was certain. He decided, in that moment, when the criminal won the internal struggle, that he would honor Rocky's wishes and he would tell her the truth. His truth. Whether or not it would be the full truth, he had not yet determined. But he felt like he at least owed her something.

The bus pulled into Brindle around five o'clock in the evening after stops in three other towns. Will waited at the side of the bus for the driver to open the storage containers underneath, and when Will had his bag, he began walking toward the trailer park, but he only made it about five hundred feet. The siren of a police vehicle made a short bloop-bloop noise, and Will nearly jumped out of his skin. He turned around and saw Utter creeping slowly behind him. Will stopped, and Utter pulled alongside, rolling down the passenger window.

"Get in," Utter said, peering over his mirrored sunglasses.

"Sheriff," Will said in greeting. He instinctively reached for the passenger door, but found it locked, and remembered that the only thing that rode shotgun with the sheriff was the shotgun. He opened the back door of the car and climbed inside, and shut the door behind him. He felt like a child.

"Is there something you might think you need to tell me?" Utter asked, looking into the rear-view mirror at Will. From Will's point of view, it was a dangerous question, and he would have to choose his answer very carefully.

"Not that I'm aware of, Sheriff. Other than I graduated from the Academy and I'm ready to start working. What are we talking about?"

"I got a little word about you, Mr. Lomax. A little birdie called me and dropped some information about you. I have to tell you, I'm a little surprised." Utter continued to look in the mirror at Will, waiting for him to speak. Will said nothing. The sheriff looked at him and laughed. "They said, 'High intelligence, a fast mover, quick thinker, problem solver, and possible future negotiator. Possibly a detective. Your test scores were some of the best in the history of the Academy.' I knew what I was doing when I sent you to the Academy, and you didn't disappoint."

"Well, that's good to know, Sheriff," Will said, relaxing a little. "I just paid attention and applied myself. The athletic parts were easy. The academic stuff, that's what I had to focus on."

"Well, you did well, son, and I'm proud of you. You start in a week. You work from three in the afternoon to three in the morning, Saturday, Sunday, Monday, and Tuesday. Between now and your first day, you'll study our local codes and laws, and you'll take a test on Friday, the day before you work your first shift. I don't doubt that you'll have no trouble passing it."

Will sat in silence for a moment, and wondered if these 'do you have something to tell me' chats with Utter would one day be the one when Utter knew Will's real past. *That would certainly be an odd conversation,* he thought. He decided he would have to answer Utter.

"I'll do my best, Sheriff."

"I'm sure you will," Utter said. Utter kept driving at a leisurely pace until he reached the trailer park where Will's home was currently sitting. "Which one is it?" Utter asked.

Will scooted up in the seat and pointed to his trailer. "That one. There."

Utter aimed the car towards Will's trailer and parked in front of it. "You ever thought about getting something more permanent?"

"Eh, maybe. Right now, that's all I need. A roof, a bed, a shower, and someplace to keep the beer cold."

"I don't suppose I have to tell you that there is no drinking while you're on the job. Wednesday through Friday, you do what you want, but for those four days you're on, keep it dry. Even when you're off. I don't need anyone showing up to work with a hangover."

"Not a problem, sir," Will said.

"Alrighty then. You have your book to study from, correct?" Utter asked.

"That I do," Will said, anxious to get out of the car.

"Best get to it, then," Utter said, and Will took that as his cue to get out of the car, but he had to wait for Utter to open it for him. Once free of the car, he grabbed his bag and shut the door and watched Utter drive off in a cloud of dust. He fished his keys out of his pocket and opened the door to the trailer. It didn't look too bad, but smelled a little musty, he thought. The spiders were not nearly as bad as he thought, either. He moved to the narrow path between the sink and stove and the dining room table/guest bed, and wheeled his bike to the outside of the trailer. It looked as it did the day he left for the Academy. He chained it to the dying tree that was borderline on his property, but there was no neighbor with whom to argue, so he cared very little.

He needed to do so much and had very little time in which to do it. He needed to go shopping. He needed to go see Rocky. He needed to go get Kat. The truth was, his world was still spinning a little bit from when he first arrived in Brindle. He had never really settled in completely, with everything happening so quickly after he arrived, and he still had a few things to take care of before home became home.

Will thought that he could really use a car, but buying one was almost out of the question, unless he bought someone else's car, but he knew he would inherit the problems with the car at the same time. He thought he might get a car to use from the Sheriff's department, but he wasn't sure if he would get to hold onto the car or if he had to turn it in at the end of each shift. He made a mental note to ask Utter that very question the next time he saw him, but he wasn't trying to go out of his way to bump into Utter, either. Will also needed some things for the trailer as well. All those little things that aren't essential to life, but things that any self-respecting homeowner would have. He needed a broom and a mop to take care of the floors that were not carpeted, and maybe a small vacuum to take care of the ones that were. A set of dishes would be useful, instead of him just using the rewashed take-out containers he had acquired. Kitchen towels instead of paper towels to dry his dishes. Real sheets for his bed. The *little* things.

He could ride his bike to the store, for sure, but he could not picture himself weaving all over the road trying to balance whatever he bought, including the broom and mop, as he rode back home. He remembered how difficult it was for him as a kid to ride his bike and carry his baseball bat at the same time while riding home from practices and games. He decided that he would just take a run to the store, get what he needed, and walk it all home. *Speaking of walking,* he thought, *you need some new shoes. Cheap shoes,* he reminded himself. The first thing he needed to do that night, however, was to let Rocky know he was back and go get Kat from her. He put on a heavy jacket and locked the trailer door behind him. The bike was unchained next, and in a few minutes, Will was cruising down the dusty streets of Brindle on his way to Rocky's restaurant. When he got there, he parked his bike next to a flower bed and walked inside. Rocky was at the cash register and saw him as soon as he walked in.

"Well, if it isn't Buford T. Justice," she said. "I thought you had run off and joined the Navy, or maybe the circus."

"You're not that lucky," he said, with a laugh. She did not laugh, and Will caught it. He thought she had said they were fine, but she still seemed to be harboring some ill feelings. "How are you?"

"Living the dream," she said, counting out a customer's change and providing a receipt. "If I were anybody else, I couldn't handle it, so it's a good thing I'm me."

"You being you is a good thing," he said.

She walked away to a soda fountain behind the counter and drew a large cola, popped a lid onto it, grabbed a straw, and then thrust it all at her customer, wishing him a happy evening. She came back to the register, grabbed another receipt from an empty pizza box, and began keying information into the register.

"It's good to see you," he said.

"Good to be seen," she said, coolly.

"Should I come back when you're not so busy?" he asked, without realizing that he was loading the gun that she would use to shoot him.

"Why would you do that?" she asked. *Boom.*

"Well, to see you. To talk to you. To be with you. I'm back now, and I'm ready to move ahead with my life."

"Well, look at you all grown up and ready to take control," she said.

"Rocky, what's going on? I thought you said we were fine when I left. What has changed?"

She stopped and turned. "Months," she said. "Months. No calls, no contact, no nothing. I seriously thought you moved away and left me with your stupid cat."

"Rocky, we were not able to have outside contact! It was like being in a sequestered jury. No contact with anyone on the outside, nothing to distract us from what we needed to do. I might as well have been in basic training for the military. If it makes you feel any better, you were my first stop, until Utter got a hold of me first. Right off the bus."

"God, what did he want?" she asked, filling a napkin dispenser.

"Just to chat," Will said, fibbing a little. He didn't want to gloat about his success at the Academy. Not right then, anyway.

"About what?"

Will sighed and realized she wasn't going to let it go. "He wanted to tell me that he was right about me going to the Academy. Apparently, someone there called him and told him how well I did."

She stopped stocking the napkins. "You did well?" she asked.

He looked at the floor. "Yeah," he said. "Well, pretty good. I graduated."

"How good?" she asked. "And don't lie. I'll know if you do." Will stuttered a little, but managed to get out something like 'The top of my class,' but she didn't hear him. "What was that?" she asked.

"Something like the top of my class," he said again.

"Really?"

"Yeah," he said. "Actually, since I'm not lying, and because you'd know if I was, I got some of the best scores in the history of the Academy."

"Really?" she asked again, smiling now, with her chewing gum between her teeth.

"No more lies," he said. "I meant it when I left, and I mean it now. If you want to hear everything, I'll tell you everything. Then it will be your choice."

"What's my choice?" she asked.

He looked her directly in the eyes. "Whether or not you still want to have anything to do with me anymore."

Chapter 67 – His Purpose

Greco stood up from where he sat, straightened his jacket, and began a short walk to the front of the rows of chairs, which seemed to stretch endlessly across the lawn. When he turned around to face everyone, he thought he could see the end of the rows, but he wasn't sure. There was a weird morning fog that was hanging about one to two feet above the ground, creating a spooky effect that seemed only appropriate for a cemetery. He pulled a piece of paper from his chest pocket, unfolded it, and stepped up to the microphone.

"I wasn't there when Steve died," Greco began. "I should have been. He was my partner. He was my partner for thirteen years. I should have been with him. I should never have let him run into that building that day. I never let him leave my side any day before that. I should have never left his side that day, nor any day since." Greco cleared his throat before he continued. "The thing about Steve was, he wouldn't have it any other way. He would want me to continue on with the job. He wanted me to keep on doing what we did together for all those years. He told me just that in his hospital bed. He also told me that if he didn't survive, he was going to be satisfied that he fell during his time on the job, doing his job, serving this great city to the best of his ability. I don't think a lot of people in the force really knew Steve. I don't think they knew his intellect, his sense of humor, and I know for sure, they didn't know how big his heart was. All they truly knew was that he was a great cop, and that he did his job unfailingly, unselfishly, and honestly."

Greco turned over his piece of paper to the other side and looked out at the attendees. A sea of cops, all in their dress uniforms, had come out to mourn Steve Angelucci. Greco tried to look each of them in the eye at some point as he talked, but there were far too many. So, he did the best he could. He made sure to spend extra time speaking directly to Steve's wife, Brenda. She and Steve had met when Steve was a rookie on the force, and had two children; one boy, Heath, who was ten years old, and a girl, Heather, who was eight.

Greco returned his eyes to his notes. "I remember this one day, Steve and I were called to a 'B&E' at a building down on 64. We got there, and it was a restaurant, which is long gone now, but it was a little burger diner, family-owned, Mom and Pop kind of deal. So, we get there, and the couple who owned the place had gotten there before us. We take down all of the information, and I'm ready to go to start finding out what we could find, but Steve keeps asking them questions about the business and their personal information. How long had they been in business? Was it the same location? How long had they been married? Just a lot of extra information. He was actually getting on my nerves a little bit, because it was past lunch time, and if you know me, you know that if I'm hungry, and I'm around the corner, you can hear my gut rumble before you ever see me." A few small chuckles came from the crowd, and then Greco continued on.

"So, anyway, we were there, and Steve had asked them for so much information that they really appreciated his interest, and they made us a very hearty lunch before they would let us leave. Great burgers, all the toppings, fries, shakes, you name it. They even had these little apple pies that were so crispy, I think they deep-fried them. I kinda miss that place now that I think about it. So, we finally get out to the car with all the food and the drinks, and Steve starts chowing down, but I'm stuck driving, so I can't eat, which makes me more frustrated as we go on. Finally, I look over at Steve, and he can't even eat because he's laughing so hard. I ask him what's so funny. He looks over and tells me that he stayed so long because he knew I was getting upset, but now I'd better let him drive because my stomach was so loud. He said it was making so much noise that if needed, we'd never be able to sneak up on anyone!"

Greco let the laughs die down before he went on. "A lot of you guys know that I used to umpire Little League games over in the park on Saturdays. What you may not know is that now and then, there would be this obnoxious guy in the stands who would heckle me for balls and strikes calls. He wasn't anyone's parent; he was just there. He'd say the most ridiculous things, telling me I should upgrade my phone service, because he could make better calls from long distance. He'd yell out that the dirt had better eyesight than I did, just the most random stuff. Yeah, that was Steve as well. Such a great guy. I'm going to really miss him." Greco let that sink in for a moment before he continued. "So, before I go, I received a phone call one night. The guy on the phone said he was from the Times and wanted me to get a subscription. I told him I already had one, but he kept going, telling me that he could get me a better deal, I just had to up my subscription to premium, and I would get two papers every day. I asked him if he was talking about an evening version of the paper, and he told me that was not the case. I would get two papers at the same time. I asked why I would want a second paper every day, and he said silly things like maybe the news would change between the two versions, and that I should be fully informed. Then he told me I could use it to wrap glasses if I was moving, or paper the table if I was eating messy seafood. He even told me that I could use it with vinegar to wash my windows. So, this guy has me on the phone for about twenty minutes, with all this B.S. about why I should get a second paper. I finally told him my wife wouldn't appreciate two newspapers every day. The guy finally started laughing at me and said, 'You'd have to be married first!' That's when I knew. It was Steve.'"

Greco took a second after the stories and became serious. "One thing about Steve, though. If you didn't know him away from work, you'd never believe these stories. When he was on the job, he was on it. Even when he was 'tried and fried,' he was still, always,..." Greco made a motion toward those in the seats, and in near-unison, they responded with 'eggs up, sunny side.' Greco let the noise die down a bit and then continued. "Rarely did he have any jokes or anything like that when he was working. His focus remained on the cases until he was done with them. He was that on-point. As far as I know, there wasn't anyone better. And I should know. Steve was my partner. And he was my brother."

Greco folded his paper and tucked it back into his pocket. He slowly walked away from the podium and crossed the row of seats in front of his seat, and then sat down. He considered his thoughts that he had earlier in the day, and the day before, and each day since Steve had died. He was going to resign from the force. There were too many memories, good and bad. He couldn't get the vision of Steve running into the growing pile of dust and rubble, and he couldn't let go of the fact that he wasn't there for Steve when he died.

He sat in his chair and considered everything he had just said. He buried his face in his hands and cried softly for the rest of the service. He didn't hear most of what was said, not by the preacher, not by Sergeant Harding, not by anyone. He only heard the echo of his own words as they continuously rang through his head. When the time was appropriate, he was able to stand and salute his fallen partner, friend, and brother as a group of seven officers fired their rifles three times each. His body shuddered at each firing, and the sound rang in his ears afterward. He sat back down and returned to his thoughts of his friend. He pondered so deeply that he didn't feel the hands upon him when the service was over. Many had reached out to him to see if he was okay, but they never knew. His thoughts consumed him, and then, after a while, as if he was given an electric shock, he escaped his thoughts and came back to the now. He looked around the cemetery, and the chairs that surrounded him were all empty. The service was over, and his friend was gone.

Greco rose from his chair and walked slowly across the grounds of the cemetery until he reached his car. On the ride back to his house, all he could think about was Steve and the talk they had in the hospital room. He replayed it to the best his memory would allow, painstakingly trying to remember the entire conversation. He fought back tears and cursed at himself, but when he parked his car in front of his house, he had weighed all the factors and found a new outcome. He wasn't going to retire from the force until it was time for him to do so, and until that time, he would continue his work, and he'd do it to the best of his ability, and he'd do it in Steve's memory, as a tribute to him and the work that he did.

He closed the door to his house and sat down on the couch. His home was desperately empty and quiet without Honey there to help occupy his time and his thoughts. He took a look at the front page of the newspaper he had brought in with him, but the news did not interest him at all. The only thing he could think about now, the one thing that filled his head, his purpose, was getting back to work, and the first thing he was going to do was find Willem Kelly and bring him to justice.

Chapter 68 – Willem Kelly, Freeze!

Rocky sat back in her chair and began shaking her head slowly. *You sure know how to pick the winners,* she told herself. She picked up the burning cigarette from the ashtray and took a long drag, and then blew the exhaled smoke up into the air. She looked across the table at Will, who had just finished his story. He told her about Kathleen and the marriage when it was new and good, and then later when it wasn't. He told her about his plan to escape it all, and the lengths he had gone to make it happen, from the planning to the execution, and the fake customer accounts to getting his high school friend involved in making the fake identifications for him. He told her how he had planned to make his escape the day after he thought he'd been found out, and how that day just happened to fall on September 11, 2001. He told her about his trip across the country, his work on the fishing boat, how he lost nearly all the money, and how he ended up in Brindle.

Will looked across the table, which was adorned with the standard pizza restaurant red-and-white-checkered tablecloth. He tried to gauge her possible reaction and thoughts on his activities, but she just sat there, shaking her head. She took another long pull on her cigarette, and he took a drink from his beer, which he had previously not touched since she set it in front of him about forty-five minutes prior. The restaurant had been closed for about three hours, the servers, bussers, and kitchen staff had all left long ago after their duties were completed for the night, and the total number of people in the restaurant at about twelve-thirty in the morning was two. Those two people just sat and looked across the table at each other. Finally, Will couldn't take it anymore.

"Are you going to say anything?" he asked.

She exhaled. "I'm not sure what to say. You basically told me you're a married, lying, cheating ex-fisherman criminal on the run from his family, his employers, what else? Oh yeah, the police." She paused for a second, then continued. "Now you ARE the police. How does that even happen?"

"Okay, I get it," he said. "It's a lot to take in. But you asked me to be honest and tell you everything. That's everything, I promise. Or at least all that I think matters," he concluded.

She looked at him and crushed her cigarette in the bottom of the ashtray on the table. "Honestly," she said, blowing the last of the inhaled smoke up into the air, "I've probably made worse choices as far as friends."

"Friends?" he asked, and began to wonder why he was even compelled to tell his true story to her.

She laughed. "Friends, boyfriends, mates, lovers, friends who occasionally have sex, whatever you want to call it. Look, I'm no pushover and I don't see the world through rose-colored glasses, so to speak. I know there are good people, bad people, people in between, people who can change and won't, people who should change, and won't, and people who I thought could never change that do. You, sir, are a mixture of some of those. I'm classifying you as a good person who went bad, and then changed for the good again. The question is, would you ever go back to being a bad person?"

Will wasn't sure how to answer that, or even if he accepted being 'classified' by Rocky. He was now sure that, if their relationship did progress, he was going to have to ask her for *her* story. Maybe he wasn't quite ready for that, though, he thought.

"Listen," he said. "I was in a bad situation, and I didn't know how to get out of it without it costing me everything. It did anyway, but I didn't know that until later. I just wanted out, and the way I did it, sneaking off like that, Rocky, that made me a bad person, and I'm not sure I can shake that, but I will tell you, I don't have any plans to do anything like what I did to get here."

"Well, that's a load off my worry list, Butch Cassidy," she said, half chuckling. "Look, you got a weird past, I get it. But, it's probably no weirder than anything else I've seen out here. You know that once I dated a guy who had six fingers on his right hand? You should have heard all the weird things he wanted to do with that extra finger."

Unfortunately, at the time of her story's punchline, Will had just taken a gulp of his beer. The terrible result was that the table, Rocky's shirt, and face were now covered in Will's beer, which was ejected from his mouth like a fighter pilot in a failing aircraft. Rocky just looked at him with an incredulous expression, and he stared back in complete horror, for what seemed to be half of eternity. But then, she began to smile, and then laugh, and then he smiled, and he laughed, and they carried on with that for a few seconds, even as he walked to a nearby bus cart and pulled off a few napkins. He gave them to her, and she, while still laughing, managed to clear away the liquid debris.

"I have to get out of here," she said, "and that means you have to go as well. No one sleeps in my restaurant."

"Sounds good to me," Will said. "But listen, I don't start work until next Friday. Think you can get a night off between now and then?"

"For what?" she asked.

Will stood up and started towards the door. "For a dinner that doesn't come in a pan, cut it into eight triangular pieces and stuffed into a box?" He was walking away from her and had the door halfway open when he heard the command.

"Willem Kelly, freeze!"

Will stopped with the door halfway open. He hadn't heard the name in quite some time, and the din of it ringing in his ears was enough to make his neck sweat immediately. He went cold. Then he turned. "Rocky, please, don't call me that. I know you're just joking, but I don't need anyone hearing it, not even by accident."

Rocky made a half-frown, then she smiled. "Tsk, last time, I promise."

"What's up?" he asked. She moved closer to him and stopped when she was less than a foot away. She leaned in a little and offered him her right cheek. He leaned in slowly and kissed her softly, and then said goodnight.

He was almost on his bike when the door opened, and Rocky stuck her head out. "Hey," she said. Will stopped and turned, and looked at her with arched eyebrows. "You know," she said, looking ornery, "that's not the only thing I offer." Will immediately thought back to the kiss on the cheek and wondered what she might be suggesting.

"Uh," he said nervously. "What do you mean?"

"Pizza," she said. "Not just triangles. I also offer a Chicago-Cut style pizza," she said, and laughed, knowing that she got him with her joke. He shook his head, hopped on the bike and peddled out of the parking lot.

The next week went by in a blur for Will. He spent his days clearing and tidying up his property of the weeds and branches that had accumulated while he was gone. He also got a long-handled brush and scrubbed the outside of his trailer. At night, he spent his time studying the book of laws and codes that Sheriff Utter had given him. He wanted to make sure he did as well or better on his department test as he did at the Academy. Rocky wasn't able to get a night off from work, so their dinner date had to wait until another day. He had checked the classified section of the newspaper for cheap cars, but found nothing in the area that was cheap enough to serve his meager needs as a runabout. He just needed something to get from here to there, now and then, but nothing seemed to fit.

He decided he could wait it out, and he still had the bike, and was pretty sure he could use the patrol car for some emergent personal uses if push came to shove. Utter wasn't on duty the other day when he had picked Will up as he was walking from the bus stop to his trailer. Will figured it wasn't that big of a deal, as long as he didn't buy any beer while in uniform. Then he remembered one of the deputies buying beer after the skirmish at the liquor store.

That Friday, Will arrived at the Sheriff's Department at about eleven forty-five in the morning, fifteen minutes before his test was supposed to begin. He announced himself at the front desk to Deputy Ricky Oglethorpe, who took a long look at Will as if he recognized him, but didn't say anything. Will decided to let him off the hook.

"Hey, Ogre," he said. "Oh. I'm sorry, can I call you 'Ogre,' or would you prefer me to wait until we get to know each other better?"

Ogre looked at him again and cocked his head to the side like a confused dog. "Do we know each other already?" he asked.

"Yeah, the D&J Liquor Store robbery a few months back. I kind of got involved. Billy Lomax."

Ogre smiled and slapped his own forehead. "Oh yeah...the wrestler! You're taking Mulholland's place. Welcome, welcome, uh, let me get you started here. You're here to take the test, right?"

"Affirmative, Deputy," Will said.

Ogre looked at him and smiled. "I guess we'll be calling you that, soon, too. Wes Tim told us all you were top of the class at the Academy. Congratulations."

"Thanks," Will said. As Ogre shuffled around the front desk, seemingly not finding anything, Will wondered how difficult the actual tests might be, and if Ogre was able to pass them and keep his job as a deputy, hopefully, Will would have no problem. Will put his predetermined thoughts about Ogre to rest, though, and decided to give him the benefit of the doubt. Ogre finally returned with a small booklet, a pad of lined paper, and two sharpened pencils.

"Follow me," he said. Will walked around the side of the front counter and followed Ogre down the hallway. "Need to pee?" Ogre asked.

"Uh, no, I'm good."

Ogre laughed. "I have to ask," he said. "I have to lock you in a room, and you can't get out until you've finished the test."

"Oh, no, I'll be fine," Will said.

"Superdee dooper," Ogre said, and then he opened a door to a small office and placed the booklet, pad, and pencils on the table. "Okay, here we go. So, you have one hour from the time I close the door to finish the test. You good?"

Will took a seat at the small table and scooted in his chair. "Yeah, I think I'm good. Thank you, sir."

"You can call me Ogre, Billy," he said, and shut the door of the office. Will began the test immediately, and as he proceeded through it, he found that he knew most of the answers without really thinking about them. He looked at the booklet from the side and figured he was over halfway through it, and he'd only been at it for about fifteen minutes. He sat back in his chair and once again thought about the craziness of what had happened to him, or more accurately, what he made happen to himself, in the recent and not-so-recent past. He looked out of the window of the office in which he found himself. He looked at the buildings outside, none of them more than three stories tall, and all he could think about was the one thing that he kept thinking about ever since that last day in New York. *How different the world feels when the skyline changes.*

He finished the test with fifteen minutes to spare, and he waited for Ogre to come in and get him. When the door finally opened, Will stood with the stack of papers and pencils in his hand. It wasn't Ogre, however, who opened the door, but Sheriff Utter instead. Utter had a stern look on his face as he motioned for Will to sit back down at the table. He held out his hand for the test booklet and pad of paper and sat down on the other side.

"Well, hello, Sheriff," Will said.

Utter didn't answer. He sat down and looked at the pad of paper where Will had written out his answers to the test questions. Utter had his lips pushed out as he read through the answers, and every now and then, his eyes came off the paper and met Will's, but the expression never changed. Will thought he looked like a walrus-mustached duck, but he kept that to himself. Utter continued to look through the answers and flip pages, and Will was beginning to get a bit antsy. But then Utter closed the booklet and put it on top of the pad of paper, and then picked them all up together. He sat back in his chair and let out a long exhalation of breath, all while still looking at Will.

"Who do you think you are?" Utter asked. Suddenly, Will had that feeling again. Utter knew something. Maybe he knew *everything.*

"I'm sorry, Sheriff?" Will said in a confused tone.

"You know, I've seen people from all walks of life. They come through this town, and they stick around for a few minutes, and they think they know everything about us, and they leave," Utter said, still eyeing Will, who began to feel uneasy once again.

"Buy ya know what? They don't know anything." Utter slammed down the stack of paper, and the wind blew the pencils off the desk. "And now, *you* come in here, *you* stick around for a few minutes, and *you* think *you* know everything." Utter picked up the stack of papers again. "You think you're different from any of those other idiots that came through and through they knew everything?" Will was scared to answer. Hopefully, the question was rhetorical. It was. Utter stood up, walked over to Will, and motioned for him to get up. Utter got up into his face. "Well, it turns out that you *are* different from them, and not only that, but you also do know everything." Utter exhaled and then restarted. "I've never seen this before, son, and I've been doing this a long time. You answered every question correctly. Unbelievable." Utter shook his head and held out his hand to Will. "Welcome to the Sheriff's Department of Brindle."

Will was dumbfounded. He had not gotten even one question wrong? Out of one hundred and twenty questions? Will found it a bit unbelievable himself, but he wasn't going to contradict Utter. Instead, he stood and took Utter's outstretched hand and accepted his hearty handshake.

"Okay," Utter said. "Go back out front and have Og—uh, Deputy Oglethorpe show you to the uniform closet. Find something that's close to your size. We'll get you measured later, but there should be something in there to fit you. Get three sets of pants, shirts, and socks, and a hat and a tie. There's a logbook in there. Just make sure you sign everything out. Oglethorpe will show you. I'll introduce you around to everyone tomorrow. I'll see you then." Utter turned to walk out the door, and as the door began to close, he heard Utter's voice once again. "I'll be damned. Perfect score! Sheesh!"

Chapter 69 – First Day

The next day, Will arrived for work a full thirty minutes early, dressed in his uniform that someone else had worn before, he was sure, but that was okay. He thought he looked good in it. He couldn't help but think that one of the first things he would do when he got out on his own would be to stop at Rocky's and get a few slices for dinner, and she would see him in his uniform.

Utter was at the front desk with several other deputies standing around, and Will recognized Ogre and walked over to him to shake his hand.

"Hey, Deputy," Ogre said with a large grin on his face. "Welcome to it and congratulations. I heard you aced the test!"

"Yeah," Will said. "Apparently, I couldn't get one wrong if I tried. There were probably a lot more correct guesses than answers!"

"Nah, don't sell yourself short. You're a natural at this. You're gonna do great!"

"We'll see," Will said, and he walked over to Utter. "Sheriff," Will said in greeting. Utter turned around to face Will.

"Deputy Lomax," Utter said. "I'd like to introduce you to some of the other staff and deputies you'll be working with. This is Alli Morrow, she works dispatch, and when you're out on the road, in addition to your normal patrol, you get radio calls from her, or Stan Bigbee, who will come in at midnight."

"Hey there," Alli said, and shook Will's outstretched hand.

"Nice to meet you, Alli," Will said.

"You already know Ricky Oglethorpe, and you met Deputy Juan Cortez." Cortez looked on from a clipboard on which he was filling out some forms.

"Deputy," Will said.

"Hey," Cortez responded, and took Will's handshake, but released quickly, and then cast a wary eye at Will, and then returned his attention to his forms. Will wasn't sure what had just happened, but he didn't like it.

Utter pointed across the room to a middle-aged woman sitting at a desk and filling out some paperwork. "That's Jill over there. When you need to do paperwork, see her. She'll walk you through it. That's about it for now. Let's get you fitted and armed, and then out on the street to serve and protect. Follow me." Utter walked down the hall, and as he passed, he could almost feel Juan Cortez staring at him, and he was glad when he and Utter were out of sight around a hallway corner. Utter unlocked the door, and they entered a small room with a cage that ran along one wall. Utter used another key to unlock the cage, and yet another key to open a smaller cabinet within the cage. He removed a black revolver with a brown handle. "This is your service weapon," Utter said. "You'll know when to leave on your side at a threat and when you'll need to actually take it out of the holster and use it. We like to use our words first and weapons last. Here is your club, also to be used sparingly unless needed. Your cuffs, keep the keys on you at all times. Here's your belt; it's got all the compartments you'll need for your firearm, cuffs, et cetera. Finally, here's the most important piece: your badge. Deputy, when you put this on, you're not only representing this department, but this entire town, county, and the surrounding areas. You ARE Brindle."

"Understood. I hope to do it proud," Will said.

"That's what I like to hear," Utter grunted as he shut the door to the cage and locked it. "Over here," he said, and Will followed him to a smaller cabinet on the other side of the room. "This is the ammo locker. We hope you never have to use it, but you will need some to start. Your weapon is a Smith & Wesson Model 29. It is a double-action, six-shot revolver with a five-inch barrel. It uses a .44 Magnum cartridge manufactured by Remington. You will start with the six cartridges that are already loaded for you, and six more will fit into your service belt. Should you ever need more, Jill has the key. She tracks every single round that comes in and goes out of this office. Should you need to fire your weapon in the line of duty, you will replace any rounds used immediately. Understood?"

"Perfectly. I hope to never have to use the weapon as well, sir."

"Good deal," Utter said. "You share your shift with Oglethorpe tonight. He'll show you the ropes and get you acclimated to the job, show you what you need to do, and so forth. Good luck, Deputy. Be safe out there."

"Thank you, Sheriff."

Utter cleared his throat. If we're not around any civilians, you can call me Wes Tim, or just Utter, if you prefer. Hell, I'll answer to most anything."

"Sounds good," Will said, and he headed back to the front of the building where Ogre was waiting. "Are we good to go?" Will asked Ogre.

"Yeah, you ready?" Ogre asked.

"Ready as I'll ever be." Will followed Ogre past the front desk, where Alli was sitting and typing something.

"Have a good first day, Rookie. Come back safe," she said. She seemed to be flirting with Will, or at least he thought so.

"I'll do my best," he said. He followed Ogre around the room and down another hall, where they went out a side door of the building to a parking lot where five patrol cars sat waiting for someone to drive them in service of the community. Ogre pointed to the second car along the fence.

"That one," he said. "Don't worry, I won't make you sit in the back of the car like Wes Tim. You can sit up front."

"That's refreshing," Will said, and climbed into the passenger seat.

Ogre plopped his ample frame into the driver's side of the bench-style seat in the front of the car. He put his seatbelt on as Will did the same. He exhaled, looked at Will, and shook his head. "Well," he said, "Alli likes you."

"I was going to ask you about that," Will said. "She seemed a little flirty."

"Yeah, she does that, especially to the new guys." Ogre adjusted the seat and then put the car into reverse.

"Really? All the new guys?" Will asked.

"Well, just all the guys, really. I don't really know how to put this delicately, but let's just say she's a little fast. Well, a lot fast."

"Oh," Will said. "So, she dates a lot?"

"I don't think there's a lot of dating involved. It's really just the end result of a really good date!" Ogre said, laughing. "She and I have had a few rounds."

"I see," Will said, making mental notes. He decided he would focus just on Rocky for now and try to keep that relationship above water. He didn't need to rock the boat any more than it already was, even though they left everything on a good note when they were last together. "So, what do we do? Just ride around and wait for something to happen?"

"Mostly. We have some actual tasks that need to be completed every night," Ogre said.

"Sounds interesting. What type of tasks?"

"Well, for one, unless we're otherwise engaged, between eleven and midnight, and one and two in the morning, we will do a perimeter check of the fairgrounds."

"What's at the fairgrounds?" Will asked.

"Right now, nothing," Ogre replied. "But we still have to do the check, because sometimes folks will go in there when no one is around. Nothing crazy, just hooligan nonsense. You can imagine things that happen under the bleachers. The County doesn't fool around with that stuff. Usually, I will do the check around eleven, have my lunch from midnight to one, sitting in the fairgrounds parking lot as a deterrent, and then walk it again at one. It's like three hours of coverage."

"You do that every night?"

"Every night that I work the three-to-three," Ogre said.

"You ever catch anyone doing anything?" Will asked.

"Yeah, used to happen a lot. Like I said, mostly sex and drugs. It doesn't happen that much anymore."

Will thought about that for a second and said, "Do you think they might be picking other times to get into their activities because they know your schedule?"

Ogre gawked at Will with a quizzical look on his face. Then he arched his eyebrows, pursed his lips, and said, "Maybe. Yeah, I guess they could." Ogre continued driving until he came to a stop sign on Third Street, where it connected with US Route 30. "Maybe we should try a different time."

"Up to you, Ogre. This is your show. I'm just here to learn." Ogre made the turn and continued to drive around the town on their patrol until about five-thirty in the afternoon. He crossed over the railroad tracks and pulled into the Rusty Rails Tavern. The Rusty Rails was an old motel that had been closed down, but then was bought by two brothers who lived in the next county eastward. Their home county denied their liquor license, so they purchased the motel and turned the motel kitchen and lobby into the Rusty Rails Tavern. "What are we doing here?" Will asked.

"Food," Ogre said. "Best burgers and fries around. I wouldn't hang out here, though. We'll get it to go." They walked in the front door, and the chatter that was filling the room seconds before turned into a few whispers, and Will could only assume the place was not cop-friendly. He didn't think much of the place the first time he saw it, either. The place was dark, with paneling on the inside with a lot of neon signs advertising any beer or spirit one could think of, and dim lamps hung from the ceiling. Ogre walked up to the bar and flashed a hand signal to the woman standing behind it. He held up two fingers showing the palm side of his hand, and then turned his hand around to show the back side.

"What was that?" Will asked.

"Two and Two. Two burgers, two fries," Ogre said with a smile. "They only come one way, so I hope you're not allergic to anything."

"What's on them?" Will asked.

"Cheese, ketchup, mustard, mayonnaise, lettuce, tomato, onion, and some sort of seasoning they put on it. It's spicy. Great burger!" Will turned his back to the bar and leaned against it, and soaked in all that the Rusty Rails had to offer, which wasn't much. The bar patrons sat in small huddles around the tables and kept to themselves. A jukebox in the corner played a country song sung by someone that Will did not recognize. A pool game that appeared to be in the middle stages was now abandoned by its players. A dartboard hung on one wall, but there were no darts and nowhere to stand to throw them, as the floor in front of the board was covered by a table. One television hung in a corner behind the bar, but it was not turned on at the moment. "Come on," Ogre said. Will had not realized that the food had been delivered, and Ogre had already paid.

"Oh, sorry. What do I owe you?" Will asked.

Ogre headed to the door, and as he opened it, he said, "Don't worry about it. It's on me. But you have to promise the first time you train someone, you do the same for them. It's kinda like a passed-down tradition."

"I think I can handle that," Will said, walking out the door and letting it close behind him. Ogre got into the car, as did Will, and Ogre drove to the vacant lot across from the Pit Stop and parked the car. He opened the bag that held the food and distributed one bag of fries and one of the burgers to each of them. Will picked a fry out of the bag and ate it. "Hmm, not bad fries," he said.

"Freedom Fries," Ogre said.

"Indeed." Will said as he unwrapped the burger from its foil packaging and opened it up to look inside. He rolled down the window of the car, picked off two huge rings of raw onion, and flung them into the parking lot. "Yuck," he said.

"Litter!" Ogre screamed.

"Oh... sorry," Will said. "I didn't think it was litter if something would eat it."

"I'm just kidding. Not an onion man, huh?" Ogre asked.

"Not really. Sometimes I can take them in small doses, but that's onion overkill right there. This is a super sloppy sandwich. I'm surprised you'd want to tackle this while wearing your uniform."

"I'm a pro," Ogre said, smiling, and then he patted his belly. "I've been training for this my whole life!" Will carefully wrapped his burger back in the foil it came in, and only exposed enough of it to take a bite. The burger wasn't bad in

Will's opinion, but he had definitely had better. If this was the best that Brindle had to offer, he was thinking he might have to open a restaurant.

They stayed in the lot until both had finished eating, and then drove around for a while, waiting for a call on the radio or something else to happen, but neither came. At nine o'clock, when the sun had gone down, boredom was setting in for Will.

"Hey, why don't we go check out the fairgrounds?" he asked Ogre.

"Good idea. Let's go." Ogre put the car into gear.

"Wait," Will said. "How far away are the fairgrounds? Just a few blocks, right?"

"Yeah."

"Let's roll up on it quietly and see if we can catch someone in the act of doing something they shouldn't be doing. Park about a block away."

"And walk all that way?" Ogre asked.

"You can do it. I believe in you." Will gave Ogre a nudge in the belly. Ogre drove until Will told him to stop, and they went on foot from there. They walked across the grass until they reached the arena floor, which turned to dusty dirt. "Hey, check that out. It rained last night, right?"

"Yeah," Ogre said.

"Those shoe prints are fresher than that. Someone has been here since then."

Chapter 70 – He Went To Seattle

Greco didn't want any part of driving back out to Indianapolis, so he took a flight and rented a car from the airport. The increase in security at the airport was impressive and comforting to him, although the process did take a lot longer than it had before. When he landed in Indianapolis and picked up his rental car, he picked up right where he had left off before being called back for Steve Angelucci's downward turn, death, and eventual funeral. Greco was still struggling with Steve's passing, but getting back to work, whether it was official police business or not, was helping him cope. He was glad to be back on the chase, and he was armed with new information.

A few days after Steve's funeral, Greco met up with Maryanne to try to find more information. They used all of their resources and experience to think about how someone on the run could trip himself up. They came up with ideas together, and Maryanne, in the office, searched vehicle registrations, large cash purchases, and crimes that fit the same fraud profile that Willem Kelly had used. It was when they were digging into the fraud aspect that they found a strange credit card purchase in Stockton, Kansas. Deeper searching found that the purchase was for a pair of boots at a sporting goods store, where the credit card transaction was tried and approved, but there was no information on the buyer. There was no name associated with the card, nor was there a home address, credit limit, or associated bank. There was never any actual purchasing transaction shown on the credit card history, though. There was a hold, but never any debit made on the account. And then they found another one at a car rental place in Seattle, Washington. None of it helped them very much, though, since they couldn't connect any of it to Kelly. He took some books from the bookshelves of the Kelly home to read as he traveled, hopefully to maybe find some sort of clue that would help in the investigation. There were books on finance, poetry, and travel.

Greco drove from one side of Indianapolis to the other, crossed the railroad tracks, and turned onto 17th street, and found the Big Star Motel exactly where the manager of the Revere said it would be. He parked the rental car in the dusty lot and headed for the shack that was labeled 'Office,' and opened the door. A man came from the back of the small office and stared blankly at Greco until Greco decided that he should be the one to speak first.

"Hi there," he said. "I'm looking for Leon." The man behind the counter reached under the desk and pulled out the black gun that was pointed at Will Kelly months ago. What Nole didn't expect was that Greco was quicker on the draw, and was pointing his own gun right back at Leon, and his badge was in his other hand. "Put it down, and no one gets hurt," Greco said. "I just need some information." Nole dropped the gun onto the desk, and Greco took it and stuck it in his belt around his back. "I'll hold on to this for now," he said.

"I have a permit for that," Nole said.

"You'll get it back, but not right now. Right now, I need you to answer some questions. What's your name?"

"Nole West."

"Mr. West, have you seen this man before?" Greco held up a picture of Willem Kelly.

"Not sure. He looks kinda ordinary."

Greco pushed the picture closer to Nole's face. "Think harder," he said. "I know he was here."

"Man, I don't know. If he was directed here by Noel, you'll want to talk to Leon."

"Where's Leon?" Greco asked.

"He's out on the road on a fare," Nole said. "But I can call him and tell him you need to see him. Is he in some kinda trouble?"

Greco put the picture back into his pocket. "Not yet. I just need to talk to him. Get him on the phone and get him here." Nole picked up the phone and did as he was told. Greco waited in the one chair that was in the office until Leon arrived. When a car, appearing to be a taxi, pulled into the lot, Greco went outside.

"You Leon?" he asked.

"That's me. What's this about?"

"Have you seen this man?" He held out the picture of Will.

"I was wondering when this would come back to haunt me," Leon said.

"So, you have seen him?"

"Yeah," Leon said. "I've seen him. What's this about?"

"Detective Brian Greco, NYPD. When and where did you see him?" Greco asked, ignoring Leon's question.

"Here, last September. A few days after the attacks."

"What was he doing here?"

"Not sure... he rented a room for a few days and then he left. I drove him around all over the place, though."

"Where?" Greco asked.

"Uh, a store for some supplies."

"Which store, and what supplies?"

"Uh, the Super-Jack's. He got a lot of weird shit. Pillows and sheets and stuff, because he didn't trust what we had in the motel. He also got a mobile phone and some random other stuff. Toiletries, and whatnot."

"Where else?"

"What?" Leon asked.

"Where else did you take him?"

"Oh. Umm, let's see, restaurant for food, uh, oh yeah, some optician in town. I think that's about it."

"An optician? Where?" Greco did not recall seeing any pictures of Willem Kelly wearing glasses, but then he thought about contact lenses. Maybe Kelly was trying to change his eye color?

"Uh, let's see, where was that?" Leon thought out loud. "Umm... West Washington, I think?"

"Anything else you can remember? Name?" Greco asked.

"He was calling himself Joseph something, but I found out that his real name was something else."

"What was it?"

"His last name was like, Loman. I can't remember his first name. Maybe Billy? Or Bobby?"

"Thanks," Greco said. "Anything else?"

"Yeah. I sold him my car."

"He bought your car?"

"Yeah," Leon said. "He paid cash for it. He said he wanted to go home. But I don't think he was talking about going back to Philly."

Greco raised an eyebrow at Leon. "He said he was from Philadelphia?"

"Yeah, but he told a lot of lies, too," Leon said.

"Do you have the VIN number for the car you sold him?"

"Yeah, but I don't know what good it will do you."

"Why is that?" Greco asked.

"Probably a month or so after he left, I get a call from Motor Vehicle Administration telling me they found my car, and it was basically burned to the ground."

Greco perked up at this piece of information. "Where did they say they found the car?"

"Seattle. Washington. He drove the car across the country, and then torched it."

Seattle, Greco thought. *He went to Seattle.* "Thanks for your cooperation. Anything else you can think of that might help?"

"Not at the moment. Do you have a card? I can call you if I remember anything." Greco pulled a business card from his wallet and handed it to Leon. "Thanks," Leon said.

Greco got into his car and was a few miles away from the Big Star when he remembered he still had Nole's gun in his waistband. *Oh well,* he thought. He decided to get a room in a motel for the night, but he wasn't going to stay at the Big Star. If he ever saw that dirt motel again, it would be too soon.

Before he settled down for the night, however, he was going to check out the optician that Leon had mentioned. He marked it on the GPS device in the rental car and followed the path until he found Spectrum Optical on West Washington. He parked the car in the oddly shaped parking lot and went into the store. A bell chimed when he walked in, and a small Asian man peered up above his glasses as Greco advanced on the front counter.

"Help you?" Míng jié Zhang asked from behind the counter. Greco introduced himself and produced the picture of Will Kelly, and asked if he remembered seeing him. "No, no know him," and Mr. Zhang began to walk toward the back of the store.

"Are you sure? I was told he was in this store last September," Greco said.

"I already tell you, I no know him." Greco looked around the store and notices small cameras in each corner of the room.

"Do those work?" he asked.

"No. Only there for deterrent. No stealing. Mr. Zhang very busy. You go now." Greco exhaled and took another look around, wondering what would have brought Will Kelly to an optician's store in Indianapolis, but he could not make any connections. He turned and left the store, got into his rental car, and drove to the Revere, where he treated himself to a nice room with a comfortable bed. He would need the rest. It was going to be a long trip to Seattle.

Chapter 71 – The Doobies

Will and Ogre continued walking as quietly as possible across the dirt oval that was the fairgrounds arena. Will was afraid that Ogre's heavy breathing would give them away before they were able to conclude his first investigation. It was rather dark, as there was no moon, and they were able to easily make it across the ring without being seen by anyone. When they were closer to the edge of the ring, Will stopped.

"So," Will said, "I don't want to overstep any boundaries here, but let's assume we catch *someone* doing *something*. What do we do?"

"Not sure. I've never caught anyone yet."

"Ogre, how long have you been on the job?"

"Six years."

Will exhaled. "Does anything ever happen in this town?"

"Uh, be careful what you wish for. Wait until summer. As for tonight, we'll play it by ear." They continued across the ring until they reached the area between the fence and the grandstand, when Will stopped again.

"Ogre, stop. Do you smell that?" Ogre sniffed the air and gave Will a knowing look. They scanned the grandstand but didn't see anyone in the seats. Ogre was about to begin climbing the steps when Will stopped him. "Wait," Will said, and then he directed his voice toward the announcer's booth at the top of the stands. "Mind if I take the lead?" Will asked. Ogre shook his head. "Sheriff's Department," Will called out. "Y'all come on down out of there." There was no response from the booth.

"Maybe there's nobody up there, Billy," Ogre said, shaking his head. Will repeated his command. "You're wasting your time." But then, one by one, two teenage boys and one girl of about the same age came out of the door to the booth and began making their way down the steps toward Ogre and Will. When they reached the two Deputies, they stopped.

"Whatcha all doing up there?" he asked, knowing full well what they were doing.

"Nothing," the girl said.

"Yeah, just talking," one of the boys said.

"Now, you know I don't believe that for one second," Will said. "You all smell like a three-day-old dead skunk on the roadside. Do I need to ask you these questions down at the station?" The third of the trio, and the youngest, Will gauged, spoke up.

"Please, sir, it was just a little pot. I've never tried it before." Will crouched in front of the boy and looked him in the eye.

"Is that a fact? What's your name, son?"

"Jason, sir."

"Jason, what?"

"Hubley, sir. Jason Hubley."

"How about you?" Will asked the other boy. The boy just looked at the ground and said nothing.

"You," Will said to the girl. "What's your name?" She looked at the silent boy, then at Will, and then at the ground. "Okay," Will said to Jason Hubley. "What's her name?"

"She's my sister, Marcy," he blurted out, which elicited a backhanded slap across the chest from the girl. Jason fell backward into the dirt. Will estimated his weight at under one hundred pounds, and he went down easily.

"That's enough of that," Will said. "Now, you all are in some trouble here. Do you want to be in more? Name?" he demanded from the third one.

"My name is Trip, sir. Trip McCaslin," the third one said.

"Okay, now we're getting somewhere," Will said. "Marcy, Jason, and Trip. Where are your parents?"

"They're all at Mr. Gil's barbeque," Jason said. "They'll be there until at least midnight. Please don't call them!"

"Gil. Gil Tolar?" Will asked. *Thanks for the invite, jerk,* Will thought. *I bought my house from you.* "Where's the stash?" Will asked, but none of the kids said a word, and they just stood there. "Easy way or hard way, kids. Your choice."

Trip spoke up first. "Up in there," he said, pointing to the announcer's booth. Will nodded at Ogre, who took out his flashlight and started up the stairs towards the announcer's booth. Will continued with his questioning.

"So now we know where it is, and we know what it is. The big question is, where did you get it?" Jason, Trip, and Marcy all said nothing, but Will could see that Marcy and Jason's eyes were beginning to look towards Trip. Will moved in closer and lowered his voice, almost to a whisper.

"Come on, Trip. Tell me where you got it, and this goes so much easier." Trip began to squirm, and Will applied more pressure. "Where do you live, Trip? So I can go find your parents and tell them to come to the station to get you out of jail. Where?" Trip began to cry.

"P-Please don't tell my parents," he finally said through his tears, and then he looked up at Will. "Please," he said again. "I'll ne-never do it again!"

"Where did you get it, Trip?"

"I don't know his name... he said to just call him the All Blues Man."

"Okay, calm down. Take a breath. How do you know how to find this All Blues Man?"

"He found me, well, us, a few days ago, just after school. He was waiting by the backstop at the baseball field and started walking with us as we walked by. He just gave it to us. We didn't buy it."

Ogre came back down the steps with a small bag in his hand. "Two joints, unlit. There's another piece of one somewhere, I'd bet, the way that booth smells."

"We threw it out the side window when we heard you guys yell," Trip said. Ogre began his second search of the evening.

"What does this 'All Blues Man' look like?" Will asked.

"I don't know, like, normal. Dressed all in blue. Blue jeans, a jean jacket, a baseball hat, and sunglasses," Trip said.

"And he had a mustache," Marcy added. Ogre came back with the slightly used joint and added it to the bag with the other two.

"Well, that's a good start," Will said. "Now, let's get you guys to the stations for processing." Ogre shot him a surprised look, which Will returned with a wink. Will's statement was returned with three immediately crying twelve- and thirteen-year-olds. Will stopped and looked at them. "What have we learned this evening?"

"We're done. We promise," Trip said. "We just decided to try it together."

"Trip, Jason, Marcy... go home," Will said. "Go now. And take a shower. You all stink." The three immediately ran off toward the exit of the fairgrounds, presumably to their homes.

Will turned to Ogre. "So?"

"Not bad," Ogre said. "Not bad. You scared some kids, got the drugs, and got a description of the supplier."

"Would you have done anything different?"

"I would have made you climb the steps," Ogre said with a winded laugh.

"Fair," Will said. "But, with all due respect, if they took off running, would you have been able to catch them?"

"Good point," Ogre said. "Let's go."

The rest of the night went without incident, but Will kept his eyes focused for anyone wearing blue jeans, a jean jacket, a baseball hat, and a mustache, but he found no one of the sort. He wondered if he should be worried about a small-time small-town pot dealer, but then he also remembered an oath he had taken to protect and serve, and that included those who were the targets of the "All Blues Man."

At two-thirty in the morning, technically Sunday morning, Ogre pulled the car into the parking lot at the station. He explained to Will that they should try to come back early to get started on any necessary paperwork from the evening's activities, should there be any. The only thing they had to do was log the two-and-three-quarter joints they had lifted from the kids into evidence. They walked through the side door of the station adjacent to the parking lot, waved to Jill on their way past, and headed to a small office with a cabinet on the wall. Ogre used a key from his key ring to open the cabinet, and selected a ring of keys with the number eight written on a key fob. He tossed the keys to Will, who caught them in mid-air.

"What's this?" he asked.

Ogre smiled at him. "Not that it's going to be that much of a surprise to Utter, but I'm going to recommend to him that you go solo from now on. You did well tonight, and I'll tell him what you did. Your car is outside. Utter doesn't care if you use it for personal use, but if you do, you should be in uniform, and don't use it for personal stuff during your shift, unless it's to get something to eat or something. Like, no grocery shopping or dates."

"Thanks," Will said. "The car is in the side lot?"

"Yep," Ogre said. "It's the one right next to where I parked. Just take note of the plates so you know which one yours is going forward. You can head on home now. I'll take care of the doobies."

"Fair enough. Thanks, and thanks for showing me the ropes. Looks like an easy town to keep safe."

"Well, like I said, summer's coming," Ogre said.

Chapter 72 – Manhunt

Greco swore at himself for making the decision to drive to Seattle instead of flying, but he didn't want to leave any stones unturned. He would stop along the way, as much as possible, and ask around, showing Will Kelly's picture to anyone he could find. He decided he would take the most direct route to Seattle, which was Interstate 70. He stopped in Terre Haute, he stopped in Effingham, and he stopped in St. Louis, but no one could remember seeing anyone who looked like the picture Greco had of Will Kelly. He stopped in Kingdom City, Columbia, and Kansas City, but still no luck. He tried in every city in which he stopped, but no one had ever heard of Will Kelly or anyone with the last name of Lomax. Same with Topeka, Salina, and Denver. Greco felt like he could say the trail was getting cold, but the fact was, there was no trail. There was just Indianapolis and Seattle, until he remembered the credit card report he and Maryanne had run.

He turned the car around in Denver and angrily traveled to an area he had already passed. He cursed under his breath, telling himself how stupid he was for not remembering the credit cards earlier. Hours later, when he arrived in Stockton, he found what he thought would be the only sporting goods store in the town. He walked into the store and approached the front counter, and found a small man in a white button-down shirt and an apron, also wearing glasses.

"Hi there," Greco said. "I am Detective Brian Greco, NYPD, and –"

"New York! Well, aren't you a long way from home!"

"Yes, it's been quite a trip, but I got to see a lot of the country."

"And a beautiful country it is," the man said. "What can I do for you?"

"Well, I was wondering if you could help me. Have you seen this man by any chance?" He held up the photo of Will, and the man studied it.

"Hmm," he said. "Not sure if I remember seeing him or not, but I don't have the greatest memory sometimes." Greco looked around the store and didn't see any camera.

"No security cameras, huh?" Greco asked.

"No, not out there, no, sir. But there is this one back here, behind the fishing lures. I thought it was pretty clever because I could 'lure' any crooks into thinking there were no cameras!" The man nearly got the entire statement out of his mouth before he started laughing hysterically at his own joke. Greco smiled out of politeness, but was ready to move on.

"How far does it go back?" Greco asked.

"I usually change the tapes about every Sunday unless I forget. How far back should we be looking?"

"September," Greco said. "Sometime after the eleventh."

"I should have that," the man said. "Follow me." The man, whose name Greco learned was Stanley High Eagle, a descendant of a Native American tribe in Oklahoma, led Greco to a small office in the back of the store. He showed Greco the pile of tapes he had and how to work the viewer, and Greco found it very similar to how the viewers in the banks back in New York had worked. Stanley excused himself to go back and run the store, while Greco perused the tapes. He started on September 13th, just to be sure, even though he knew that would have been way too early. What was he looking for anyway? A needle in a haystack was far too simple a project compared to this. He was looking for one thing and one thing only, and that was an image of Willem Kelly buying items from this store.

About forty-five minutes after he had left Detective Greco in the office to review films and was doing inventory of the items he kept in front of the counter, Stanley High Eagle heard a shriek from the back of the store and a happy version of a declaration of a son's relationship to his mother of questionable repute. Stanley dropped his clipboard and skittered as fast as he could to the office in the back of the store.

"What's wrong?" Stanley asked in an excited tone.

"Nothing is wrong, Mr. High Eagle. In fact, it couldn't be more right. I found my guy, from New York, through Indianapolis, and all the way out here to Stockton, and eventually to Seattle. Can you tell me what this man bought?"

Stanley looked at the screen and noted the time and date, and then turned to a large cabinet and opened the door. He talked to himself as he searched.

"Well, let's see, there's September... and there... and let's see, there we go... and this looks like it... Yes, ah, here we go," Stanley muttered. "Looks like a tent, a sleeping bag, some random camping supplies, a cooler, oh, and uh, some western boots. Justins."

"Who is Justin?" Greco asked.

"Oh, uh, sorry, that's the brand of boot he bought."

"And he paid with a credit card?" Greco asked.

"Uh, let's see..., no, he paid cash, but reserved the boots on the card. Standard practice for anything we have to special order. But then he came back and paid cash for them when he picked them up."

"Did he say or do anything that seemed odd?"

"Well," Stanley said, "I don't really recall, not so much, but he did ask me where he could go camping, and something else... what was it? Oh, laundromat. He wanted to know where the laundry mat was."

"Okay, Mr. High Eagle. I need you to do me a favor. I need you to work with your local authorities, the police here, and figure out where the call for the credit card authorization goes. I need to know the source of that card. There has to be some money behind it, or it would decline. Can you do that for me?"

"Oh, uh, I guess I could. Just call the police?"

"Exactly right, Mr. High Eagle. Tell them everything you can about the transaction for the boots, the Jerry's –"

"Justins," Stanley said.

"Right, Justins. Tell them everything, and tell them you need their help in finding the source. When you do, here is my card. I'm putting my cell phone number on the back of the card. When you know something, call me. Any time of the day. Will you do that?"

"Well, sure," Stanley said.

"Thanks, Mr. High Eagle." With that, Greco left the store and got into his rental car, for which he was well over his mileage threshold on the rental agreement. He cared little about that, though. He was happy that he was putting the pieces together, but also felt that he needed to move faster, so he drove even further away from his target, and back to Kansas City., He turned in his rental car and booked a flight to Seattle. While he was waiting for his flight to depart, he called Maryanne to check in with her. She told him everything was fine, but Sergeant Harding regretted giving him all of this time off after Steve's death, because cases were piling up. The worst part was that Harding seemed to zone in on Maryanne for updates on Greco. He would ask her if she had heard from Greco recently, and she would of course deny it, even though they spoke nearly every day. She thought that was odd, and it worried her that he might know that they had some sort of relationship. *I don't even know what to call it,* she thought. *It was one great date, and now we're in a long-distance relationship.* It was what it was.

Greco also called a rental car company at the airport in Seattle so that his car would be waiting for him when he landed, and also contacted the local police and advised them of his imminent arrival and his purpose for visiting. He spoke with Sergeant Maxwell, who advised Greco to come see him at the station when he was ready the following day. Finally, he made a reservation at a hotel near the airport.

Greco formulated his plan of what he was going to do and what he was going to ask, and to whom he was going to ask his questions. His flight was uneventful, nothing special, just a small bag of peanuts and a bag of cookies that boasted that it was only one hundred calories. *Only a hundred calories in all three of these little cookies?* he jokingly asked no one in particular in his mind. The plane landed at ten after eleven at night, and Greco was exhausted. He retrieved his baggage and picked up his rental car from the garage near the terminal. As he drove to the hotel, he saw a twenty-four-hour diner, and he stopped to get something to eat. He read a local newspaper that the restaurant provided as he ate a sandwich with a cute name. The whole menu was filled with named sandwiches that described what they were. He avoided the fried chicken sandwich, which was called the Mother Clucker, and settled on the Geneva Gobbler, which was a turkey and Swiss cheese on a roll. His fries were cold, but he wasn't really interested in them anyway. He had not had a real meal in quite some time and was aching for some New York food. He had come across some different types of food as he traveled across the country, but he missed New York.

The next morning, Greco awoke to a rainy Seattle day and called Sergeant Maxwell to see when a good time would be to come see him.

"First thing. Soon as you can get here," Maxwell said.

Greco quickly showered and dressed and drove to the west precinct police station to meet the sergeant. Sergeant Maxwell was a tower of a man. Greco estimated him as just a few inches short of seven feet tall and around the three-hundred-pound mark. He was Black, had a short flat-top haircut, and a well-groomed mustache. The two men shook hands when they met, and Maxwell led Greco into a small office with windows on the west side of the building. Maxwell motioned for Greco to sit in the chair nearest to the desk, and Maxwell took the seat on the other side. Greco took a look outside to see if he could expect a change in the weather any time soon, but the sky was the same color of gray as far as he could see. He thought about asking Maxwell about the weather, but it seemed like trifle small talk, and he was anxious to get down to business.

"Thanks for seeing me," Greco said.

"Not a problem. How can I help?" Maxwell's voice fit his body. It was a deep baritone and reminded Greco of Michael Clarke Duncan in *The Green Mile*. Greco went on to explain the story of Willem Kelly, and how he had stolen nearly half a million dollars from the financing company for which he worked, how he had made his escape in the midst of chaos, and how he had been on the run and was traveling under a new identity. Maxwell listened intently as Greco told about trailing Kelly to Indianapolis, and finding the man who sold Kelly a car, and how the car ended up in Seattle.

"And that's where I am now," Greco said. "I'm hoping I can pick up the trail here."

"I see. Well, if the car was burned, we should have a report on it." He hit a button on a speaker that was attached to his phone by a wire. "Burnie, can you come in here, please?" A moment later, a young man in a police uniform walked into the office and addressed Sergeant Maxwell.

"Sir?" he said.

"I need you to pull a file from the end of last year. A car fire, from–, when was it, Detective?"

"Probably October or November from last year," Greco said. "Here's the VIN for the car." Greco handed the young man a piece of notebook paper.

"You may have to search other districts for the information, so don't just limit it to ours," Maxwell said.

"Got it," the young man said.

"Thanks, Glen," Maxwell boomed. "He a good kid," Maxwell said when the door closed. "He's not really street cop material yet, so we're keeping him close until he's ready."

"Good deal," Greco said. "I can't tell you how many young rooks I see coming into the force now. Hell, my partner wasn't but twenty-one when he joined, and –." Greco fell silent for a moment as thoughts of Steve came flooding back through his mind. He had to adjust himself in his chair, and he turned his head and looked out the window.

"You okay, Detective?" Maxwell asked in a softer voice. Greco was silent for another moment until he felt he could speak clearly. He stood and went to the window.

"Yeah," he said. "Sorry. My partner died recently."

"On the job?" Maxwell asked.

"Yeah."

"Hmph. Terrible," Maxwell said. "How, if you don't mind my asking?"

Greco was still struggling, but managed to get out, "Nine-Eleven."

"Oh my God," Maxwell said, exhaling heavily and shaking his head. "I'm so sorry, Detective. How long were you partners?"

"Thirteen years. Steve was a rookie at twenty-one, I was already four years in, and we got paired. We were both on the street back then, and got promoted to Detective at the same time. That's how good he was. He was four years behind me and made detective at the same time I did. Steve was a great cop, and an even better detective."

"I'm sorry, Detective," Maxwell said again. Maxwell sat in silence, watching as Greco continued to look out of the window at the gray sky and the rain that fell from it. He watched the droplets fall into puddles, making them unnoticeably larger. There was a knock at the door, and then it opened, and Officer Burnie was back.

"Got lucky, Sergeant. I couldn't find it in the car fires. It was in the property flire friles—err, fi-re-fi-les," Burnie said, getting tongue-tied. "It was part of a house fire. The house, garage, and car all went up in the same blaze."

"Let me see that, Glen," Maxwell said. Burnie gave him the file, and Maxwell flipped through the pages. "Detective, you're going to want to talk to a Mr. Charles Travis. He was the fire investigator in charge of that case." Maxwell wrote down the number on a notepad and ripped off the sheet, handing it to Greco. "Here's his phone number."

"Can I get a copy of that file?" Greco asked.

"I don't see why not. Burnie, can you make the Detective a copy of the file?"

"Sure can, Sarge. Be right back," Burnie said.

"'Preciate it, Sergeant," Greco said.

"Let me know if there's anything else I can do to help, Detective."

"Will do, sir, will do," Greco said. Greco walked out of the office and waited for Burnie to return with the copied file. Once he had it, he left the station and sat down in the driver's seat of his rental car. He was hanging one leg out of the car with the door open, and dialing the number for Charles Travis. He connected with Travis' office and was told he could stop by in the afternoon. Greco had a few hours to waste until then, so he looked up the address of the fire where the car was burned, and followed the path on the GPS unit in the car.

He arrived at the address of the fire, and it didn't seem like too much had been touched since the fire. There was a burned hulk of a building with a garage, just as burned. Greco took a peek at the debris, but he didn't find a car. He moved around the pile of rubble and found what used to be the driveway. There were black scrapes cut into the concrete as if something heavy had been dragged across it. *The car was towed*, Greco surmised. At that moment, Greco's phone rang. He flipped it open and pressed the button to accept the call.

"Greco," he said, and listened as someone on the other end of the phone spoke. "Yes, sir, thanks for calling me. I'd like to ask you a few questions if possible." There was a moment of silence on Greco's part before he spoke again. "You can meet me out at the site of the fire, if you don't mind," he said, and then listened again. "Sounds good, sir. I'll see you then."

About ten minutes later, Charles Travis pulled up to the curb on the road where the Kearney house used to be, and he parked directly behind Greco's car. Greco opened his door and exited his vehicle, and they met between the two cars.

"Detective Greco?" Travis asked.

"Yes, thanks for meeting me, Mr. Travis," Greco said.

"Call me Charlie," Travis said.

"So, what happened?" Greco said.

"You've got the report, Detective. Exactly what it says. Mr. Kearney doused the house with gasoline and lit it, killing himself and burning everything on the property, except that set of stairs."

"What about the car? Did you know that a car registered in Indiana was found here, burned all to hell?"

"Mr. Kearney had a tenant who lived on the second floor. A man named Lomax. The car was his," Travis said.

"Was the tenant a victim of the fire as well?" Greco winced.

"No. Mr. Lomax was unharmed."

"Did you question him?" Greco asked.

"I did. He was at work at the time of the fire. All his belongings burned, as well as the car. We had the car towed out. Demolition crew hasn't gotten here for the house yet," Travis said.

"Where did he work?" Greco asked, a little surprised that someone with nearly half a million dollars would need to work. *It does make sense if you're trying to fit in.*

"Worked on a fishing boat," Travis said, flipping through a notebook. "A fishing vessel called *The Seafarer.* Why all the questions, Detective?" Greco told Travis the story of Will Kelly and his escapades, and then continued asking his questions.

"Do you know where Mr. Lomax is now? Greco asked, hopeful.

"I do not. Could be anywhere."

"Where can I find this fishing boat?" Greco asked.

"'Bout a mile that way, Detective," Travis said. "It's right across from the cannery. Follow your nose."

"Thanks, Inspector," Greco said. "You mind if I reach out to you if I have any other questions?"

"Not at all," Travis said. "Good luck with your manhunt."

Greco made his way to the docks and parked in the lot across the street. He walked along the bulkhead until he found the entrance to a building which said "Cannery." He tried the door, but it was locked. He turned and searched the docks, looking for a boat called *The Seafarer,* but did not find one. What he did find was a flyer stapled to a pole outside the Cannery. It was a help-wanted flyer to work on *The Seafarer,* and there was a phone number, which Greco dialed immediately. He was presented with a recorded response advising that *The Seafarer* would return in two days.

Chapter 73 – Crazy Train

For the first few weeks that Will was on his own as a Sheriff's Deputy in Brindle, Nebraska, he wondered if he could not have taken a more boring job, not that he really had the choice. Wes Tim Utter had brought him in as a Deputy nearly without an option. He wondered what it would have been like to be the wrestling, football, and baseball coach, at least for a while, but it seemed as if those days were long past him. Now, he was, in the simplest terms that he could use, a cop. He was a criminal, a fugitive, a deserter, and a cop. He really had no idea of what to make of the happenings of the last nine months.

He wore his uniform with honor, though, and his star with pride as he patrolled the streets of Brindle in the late afternoon into the darkest hours before the dawn. He didn't follow Ogre's direction of coming back into the station thirty minutes early to complete any paperwork, because there never was any paperwork. It was as if the county, for the most part, rolled up the sidewalks at ten o'clock at night and didn't unroll them until six in the morning the next day. Sure, the farmers and pump-jack operators were up well before that, most when Will was getting off of work, but Will never heard a peep from anyone. Ogre insisted that it would change, but Will wasn't sure Ogre was the best judge of how crazy things could be. "Just wait," Ogre would say, and Will waited. And he waited, but nothing ever happened.

On May 18th at three o'clock in the Morning, Will opened the side door of the station to end his shift. He walked into the big, beaming face of Ogre staring back at him. Ogre was dressed for his shift, which had rotated to the three-in-the-morning until three-in-the-afternoon shift. Ogre didn't really care when he worked, so Utter would move him all around the schedule to fill in while the other deputies took time off for whatever reason.

"What are you so happy about?" Will asked Ogre tiredly.

"Because this is the day I have been waiting for," Ogre said, still smiling. "This week, the fair comes to town, and you're going to get what you've been asking for!"

"Sounds like you're wishing bad on me, Ogre," Will said, squeezing past Ogre in the hallway.

"I wouldn't do that to you, Billy. It'll happen all by itself!" Ogre chased Will down the hall. "You'll see. When you come in on your shift on Saturday, it's going to seem like a different world."

"Ogre, I've been watching these people for a few months now and hardly a one of them has shown me anything that makes me think they're more dangerous than a mosquito."

"It's not the town folk you have to worry about, Billy. It's the folks that come from out of town, and it's the fair folk themselves."

"I'm sure it'll be fine, Ogre. Thanks for looking out for me." Will turned to leave, but then stopped. "Hey Ogre, when does the fair start?"

"Friday night. They'll wheel in today, get their stuff set up today and tomorrow, and then at noon on Friday, they'll open."

"Thanks, Ogre," Will said, ready to find his pillow. He thought since he was not due back on until Saturday afternoon, he might see if Rocky wanted to go to the fair for a while on Friday. He'd ask her later that day when they would meet for dinner at the Hungry Horse Restaurant, the site of their first date. He thought it would be weird asking her to go to something of which she was probably very familiar, and he knew nothing about, but he would do it anyway. They had been seeing each other regularly when Will wasn't working. In fact, on most of Will's off-nights, they could be found at Rocky's house, watching movies or baseball on television, and sharing a bottle of wine. They had spent a few Friday nights watching movies in the park which were shown on the wall off a storage building, free to anyone who wished to attend. The films were family-oriented, nothing too risqué, and were usually comedies. They had seen _Ghost_ one night, and were treated to _Short Circuit_ on another. When they had dates, the following mornings would usually find Will driving back to his trailer-home, where he would find Kat waiting for him at the door.

Will's workdays were static. He would go in at three in the afternoon and get off at three in the morning. He would get home, make his lunch for the next night, feed Kat, take a shower, and go to sleep. He'd usually wake up around eleven in the morning, no later than noon, feed Kat, take care of whatever chores or tasks or errands needed to be done, and then he'd go back to work. On his off days, he'd take on the larger chores, such as laundry or cleaning his trailer, and then around ten o'clock at night, he'd wander over to Rocky's restaurant and hang around, waiting for all the patrons to leave, and then he'd help Rocky clean up and close for the night, and then they would go to her place. Rocky never took a day off, as far as Will could tell. All of their nights together started late and finished early in the morning when Will would go home. That Friday night, however, was different.

Rocky agreed to take the night off and allow Will to escort her to the fair. They walked the entire grounds together, holding hands. They shrieked on a few of the rides and played a few games as they covered the grounds. She beat him in a game where she tossed a ball at some milk bottles, knocking them all off the pedestal on which they sat in a pyramid formation. Will didn't even knock all of his down, and she cleared them all. The prize was a small pink bear, and the game attendant said that to get the big prize, she just needed to do it again. She politely declined, took her bear, and gave it to Will.

"Little Billy Bear," she said, smiling at him.

"Is this mine now?" he asked.

"Yep."

"Good. At least I have something to show for all this money I kicked out tonight."

"Don't worry," she laughed. "You'll get paid back in full later on."

The next night, Will showed up at the station for his shift thirty minutes early, like he usually did. Ally was at the front desk to greet him as he walked past Jill's desk on the side and grabbed a pen on his way by. He had an impressive collection of pens from the station in a cup on his counter at home. He could never remember to grab one of them as he left for work each day, so each day, he grabbed a new one from Jill's desk, and his collection of pens would grow again.

"Hey, Rookie," Ally said, tilting her head and smiling at him.

"Hi Ally," he said, walking by and not stopping.

"I saw you at the fair last night," she said. "You with that pizza woman?" She was still smiling at him.

"We were there, she was just showing me around," he said, sarcastically. "I'm not really familiar with that kind of thing, so it was good to get to learn the ropes a little. Ogre said it can be a little bit of a problem sometimes. I just wanted to scope it out, and she was helping me."

"Uh-huh," Ally said, rolling her eyes a little. Will continued down the hallway and found Ogre in the break room, where he could always be found after his shift, having a coffee. No matter when his shift ended, he had a coffee.

"Hey, Ogre," Will said, walking over to the coffee pot.

"Hey, Billy. How's everything going?"

"Can't complain."

"Right? No one listens anyway."

"What was that?" Will asked, joking.

"I said, – Oh... I got you. Good one."

"Take care, Ogre. Have a good one. Get some rest." Will left the break room with his coffee and almost bumped right into Deputy Juan Cortez. "Oh, sorry, Juan. Didn't see you there."

"Watch yourself, Rookie. You almost stained my uniform!" Cortez barked.

"Yeah, sorry about that. I'll try to watch where I'm going," Will said.

"You better."

It was clear to Will that Cortez didn't like him. Will wasn't sure why, but it was fairly easy to see. He went into the briefing room and checked out the news on the bulletin board, and there was nothing new, except the wrap-up of Will's seizure of the marijuana from the kids at the fairgrounds. He took a seat and waited for Utter and the rest of the team to come in and take their places. Cortez came in and stood at the back of the room. A few other deputies followed and took seats in various random places around the room. Ogre was last, yawning as he walked in, and continuing until he found his seat at the front, one seat away from Will. Utter walked in next.

"Afternoon, people," Utter said as he walked into the room. "Please forgive the rare use of this briefing room for this update, but you all know what week this is. The fair brings in extra people and extra nonsense. Keep your eyes and ears peeled because shenanigans do not go unpunished in my county. Anything you see outside of legal boundaries, you are to put a stop to immediately, and extract the perpetrator from the situation. This goes for the fair itself, or anywhere else that you see something going on that runs afoul of our laws. You will keep our citizens safe." Utter cleared his throat. "Now, assignments."

Will thought this was odd. For as long as he's been a deputy for the county of Brindle, he'd never had an assignment other than to check the fairgrounds every night. There was also never more than one other deputy working during his shift. Sometimes he was out there alone with no backup, which he didn't mind.

"Cortez, Ogre, Escobar, and Jarrett," Utter began, "Thanks for working the day shift. Get out of here and go home, get some rest. Lomax, you have the fair. Breece, Foresha, you're on support and patrol. That is all. Get to it."

Will stood and hung around quietly until the room had cleared, and Cortez cast his last side-eyed glance at him. When Ogre, the last to leave the room, stopped hanging around to see if he could be the last to leave the room, disappeared, Will approached Utter.

"Sheriff," he said. "One question?" Utter cleared his throat again, and his mustache puffed when he responded to Will.

"What is it, star pupil?"

Will laughed for a second just to be courteous, but inside, he hoped the name would not be permanent. "Is there anything in particular I should be looking for when I am at the fair?"

Utter smiled like a happy walrus. "As the saying goes, it's like pornography. You can't define it, but you'll know it when you see it." With that, Utter left the room. Will left the building and got into his car, driving directly to the fair. He parked his car alongside one of the side roads and entered through the gate to the fairgrounds. The fair was a conglomeration of skill games, seemingly rickety rides, odd stationary talent shows, and walk-around clowns and performers that did whatever they could to draw attention to themselves. Will understood the reason for the rides, the shows, and the games, and that was to make money, which each required for a patron to enjoy. The walk-around performers and clowns were just annoying. Will did not care for clowns at all, and these were no different.

For the first five hours, Will patrolled the fairgrounds, seeing what he could see, and putting his eyes on as many people as he possibly could as much as he could. He was looking around so much, he began to get a headache, but he pushed through, and the night remained quiet and lawful. And then it happened. At a quarter after ten o'clock that night, what Utter and Ogre had foreshadowed actually happened. Will was about fifty yards from a game that used guns to squirt water into a frog's mouth, which would inflate a balloon in front of each player until one of the balloons popped. It was in the middle of a game when Will saw it, and all he could get out of his mouth was, "Wha?" He called Sheriffs Breece and Foresha for backup, and took off at a run toward the game.

A few minutes before eleven o'clock that night, Will marched a man into the Sheriff's Department, through the lobby, down the hall, and into one of the three holding cells. He locked the door and told the man he'd be back in a few minutes. Will walked back out to the lobby and stopped by the front desk, where Ally was sitting, staring at him. He felt her looking.

"What?" he asked.

"What did Looney do now?" she asked.

"You know him?"

"Oh yeah," she said, smiling. "Everyone knows old Crazy Train."

"I feel like someone could have warned me about 'old Crazy Train.' How do you know him?" Will asked, and immediately regretted it.

"How don't I?" she said, with a small laugh and snort. "What'd he do?"

Will exhaled and grabbed a report form from the assorted papers and envelopes in an organizer on the wall. "You're not going to believe this. Well, maybe you will. Anyway, Mr. Casey Looney, at the water gun game, is aiming his water gun at the frog's mouth, just like everyone else. The bell rings to start the game. He drops the gun, and he stands on the stool, he drops his pants, he pulls out his, dare I say impressive personal squirt gun, and proceeds to urinate into the frog's mouth. Urine splashes everywhere, little kids are screaming and being traumatized, some adults are laughing, some are angry, and it was a mess. So, I got him for public intoxication and indecent exposure. I'm pretty sure I can get him for destruction of property, because those little plush frogs that are the prize are probably ruined."

Ally laughed and looked at him with a sly smile. "Wish I'd been there to see that," she said. "I do love me a good naked guy."

"Why do they call him 'Crazy Train'?" he asked.

"Lot of reasons," she said. "His first name is Casey, like Casey Jones, and his last name is Looney, so that's the crazy part. And I'm guessing you got a good look at the 'train' tonight."

Will arched his eyebrows a bit, maybe unknowingly, and walked back to the cell to get a statement from Looney, but Looney had nothing to say, other than a few loud snores as he lay on the thin mattress inside the cell. Will left the building again, this time through side rooms so he could avoid Ally, whom he really thought was nothing more than annoying.

He snuck out of the side door of the building and made his way to his car, and headed back to his post at the fair, relieving Deputy Buddy Breece to go back to his patrol. The rest of the evening went without incident, which was fine with Will. He had seen enough, actually, too much, for one day.

Chapter 74 – Needle In A Haystack

Greco sat on a low dock for a good part of the day with his pants rolled up and his feet dangling into the water. He had no idea when he woke up that morning what time *The Seafarer* would return to the dock. He only knew the day that the boat was scheduled to arrive, so he got there early and stayed. He packed a sandwich and some chips he had gotten from a vending machine in the motel lobby, where he had been staying for the past two days. The little brown bag was sitting right next to him on the dock. Greco watched as the boat came in and others were heading out. There were passenger boats, and commercial fishing vessels, and they all had somewhere to go. In fact, Greco thought, it seemed that he was the only one around that wasn't going anywhere.

Around one o'clock in the afternoon, Greco opened the brown bag and pulled out the sandwich. It was a pre-packaged cold cut that he opened and added the mustard from a small one-serve packet he had gotten at the store when he bought the sandwich. He took a bite and immediately regretted nearly every choice he had made that morning. The sandwich was terrible. He put it aside and, while snacking on the contents of the bag of chips, a crumble of one rolled down his jacket and into the water. He watched it float for a minute, and then it began to move. Small fish with which he shared the water were beginning to nibble at the chip. He grabbed the sandwich and tore off a small piece of the bread, and tossed it into the water. More fish gathered, and he soon had a small feeding frenzy right at his feet as the fish attacked the bread. He took a piece of the lunch meat and tossed it into the water, but the fish were unconcerned with it as it floated for a minute, and then sank to the bottom, or was swallowed up by something else he could not see. The water was not very clear. Some Mallard ducks began to take notice and hung around nearby. Greco stood from where he was sitting, and the ducks moved closer. He tossed a piece of the bread in their direction, and it was swallowed up quickly, and the ducks came closer.

Greco considered it a bonus that the sun was shining that day, as the previous three were filled with rain and clouds. He looked up into the sky, shielding his eyes from the sun, and saw birds flying overhead, and realized that he missed New York. He would often take walks through his neighborhood and see squirrels and birds all about, and then there were the pets everyone was walking as well. He felt like he was living in hotels, motels, and often his car, as he was driving across the country, and he was missing home. He cursed Will Kelly under his breath for making him chase him all over the country.

The ducks began to swim away, feet kicking beneath them, and Greco became vaguely aware of a noise that entered into his stream of consciousness. He had plenty of background noises going on, birds, boats, traffic, but this was louder. He focused on the now, and from the left side of his vision, a boat appeared, slower and looming larger than what he had seen earlier in the day. As the boat got closer, he could see that the name on the bow was his day was instantly better. The name on the bow read *The Seafarer*. Greco mused to himself that his ship had finally come in.

He got up and put his shoes and socks back on, rolled his pant legs back down, and straightened them as best as he could. Luckily, they were dark in color, so the newly formed wrinkles did not show up too much. He walked across the street from the marina and leaned against the pole at the cannery, and watched the boat dock, and the men on the boat doing the work they needed to do. After a while, four men disembarked from the boat, walked across the street, and approached Greco's position near the pole.

"You guys from *The Seafarer*?" Greco asked as they approached, already knowing the answer.

"Yah," Jelly said. "You looking for a job? We're a man short, and it sucks."

"No...I'm looking for Captain Russell Pearce," Greco said.

"Him," Jelly said, aiming his head backward without stopping. "With the white beard."

"Thanks," Greco said. When the captain got closer, Greco addressed him. "Russell Pearce?"

"That's me," Pearce said, stopping and dropping his duffel bag to the ground.

"Detective Brian Greco, NYPD," Greco said, holding out a hand.

"You're a long way from home, Detective. What can I do for you?"

"I'm looking for someone," Greco said. "Someone who I think used to work for you. Goes by the name of Lomax. Billy Lomax."

"Oh yeah," Pearce said. "The one that got away."

"Pardon?"

"Kid had some real promise. Took to working on the boat like no one I had ever seen before. He was a natural. Worked for me for about two months, maybe, then just upped and quit and disappeared."

"You don't happen to know where he went, do you?" Greco asked.

"I do not," Pearce said. "Seemed like he was leaving in a hurry, though. Didn't give me any notice. Been short-handed ever since. I know he didn't live too far from here. Couple of blocks, maybe. Always walked to work, always walked home."

Greco sighed at the newest dead end in a journey full of them. "Well, thank you for your time, Captain. Good luck out there."

"Uh, hold on a second, Detective," Pearce said. "I'll be right back." He walked into the small office where Chief, Jelly, and Stump were all waiting for their paychecks, and returned a moment later with a cardboard box. "If you find him, these belonged to him. He left them behind."

Greco opened the box and took a look at the contents inside. "Umm, okay," he said. "But, why?"

"Seemed too nice to throw away," Pearce said. "And in the short time I knew him, I really liked him."

"Fair enough," Greco said. "Thanks again for your time." Greco held the box under his arm and carried it toward his rental car, but in the middle of the parking lot, he stopped short. He thought about the box under his arm, some of Will Kelly's belongings, and he looked at his rental car, and thought that even if he did only have a few belongings left after the fire, he'd still need some way to get them from one place to another. *I bet he rented a car,* Greco thought. He called Maryanne and had her look for odd credit card purchases, similar to what they had previously found, but this time, to narrow the search to car rental places in the Seattle area.

"*Discovery Car Rental,*" she said. "*It's on Elliott.*"

"You are a peach, Maryanne. How do you track all this stuff down?"

"*Magic,*" she said.

"That I don't doubt," Greco said with a laugh. "I know you're going out on a limb for me, searching for all of this. Don't get in trouble."

"*I won't. I believe in what you're doing, Brian. I miss you, everyone does, but you're doing the right thing. Let me know if you need anything else.*"

Greco hung up the phone and used his local map to find Elliott Avenue, and traveled the most direct route he could find, but not being familiar with the streets of Seattle, he took a wrong turn and ended up on an expressway. By the time he found his way to Discovery Car Rental, they had closed for the evening. Dejected, he found a restaurant with a bar, had a cheeseburger and two beers, and then found his way back to his motel and fell asleep watching the Mariners eventually losing to the Orioles, three to two.

The next morning, Greco awoke and checked the yellow phone book for Discovery Car Rental and saw that they opened at eight o'clock in the morning. He showered and dressed and headed to the motel lobby for a coffee, which he immediately dumped in the flower bed outside after he tasted it. He dropped the cup into a trash can and looked down the street towards the specialty coffee shop. He decided against it, though, and hopped into his rental car and headed for Discovery. When he got there, he spoke to a man named Fahar, who was more than happy to look through the rental records in his computer and found that a Billy Lomax did indeed rent a car last November, reserving it on his credit card, but paying in cash when the rental was complete. He has no idea where the young man was going when he returned the car, but security footage showed that he walked off on foot heading south.

Greco spent the remainder of the day on foot as well, showing Will Kelly's picture to every business all along Elliott Avenue until it merged into Western, but he had no luck finding anyone who remembered seeing Kelly. He turned and made the walk back to his rental and drove back to the hotel. He was exhausted and decided he would order in some food and spend yet another night at the motel.

As he was entering his room with a six-pack of beer under his arm, his phone rang. He flipped it open and pressed the green button and said, "Greco."

"*Detective Greco, this is Stanley High Eagle. We spoke at my store in Stockton about your fugitive and his credit cards?*" This was not a call that Greco was really expecting. He had considered it yet one more dead end in a long string of them.

"Yes, Mr. High Eagle. I remember. What can I do for you?"

"*I'm sorry to call you so late, but I just got some interesting information. Do you have something to write on handy?*"

"I do," Greco said, and sat down on the bed and dug the pencil and small pad of paper from the motel nightstand. "Go ahead."

"*You're going to want to call a man named Winston Davis. He handles credit card fraud for the Sheriff's office here. Let me give you his number, and you can call him now. He said he would wait for you.*"

"Thank you, Mr. High Eagle. I appreciate the help," Greco said, writing down the phone number provided by Stanley. He cleared the call and dialed the number, and it was answered on the second ring.

"*Davis,*" said the voice on the other end.

"Mr. Davis, this is Detective Brian Greco, NYPD. I was told by Stanley High Eagle to call you."

"Yes, Detective, I was waiting for your call. Mr. High Eagle told me of your manhunt, and I was very intrigued. He gave me the information on the credit card charges, and I was able to track the credit cards to an account held by a Mr. Míng jié Zhang in Indianapolis, Indiana. It's very interesting, Detective. If you had not looked into this, no one would have been the wiser, because the cards don't actually move any money if the transaction is settled with cash. Your man could have gone on and done this forever if you didn't look into it."

"Well, he still might. I don't have any idea where he is."

"Are you still in Seattle, Detective?"

"I am," Greco said. "Why do you ask?"

"Well, when I did some digging, I found he used one of the credit cards to reserve a car at a rental facility."

"Yeah," Greco said. "I knew about that one. I just don't know where he went after that. Our list kind of ended there."

"Maybe lucky for you, we can do a deep dive on these reserves. You might want to check the bus station in Seattle. He may have purchased something there as well. We're showing another hit on the credit card."

Greco sat up from his slack position in the bed. "I should have thought of that," he said.

"Needle in a haystack, man," Davis said.

"I appreciate it, Mr. Davis. More than you know," Greco said. He hung up the phone and stared at the carpet for a minute. He had a new lead. He laughed and shook his head, picked up the motel room phone and dialed the number of the pizza place the motel advertised, and ordered a large sausage and mushroom with extra cheese. When the order was completed, he hung up the phone. He smiled and picked it back up and dialed four-one-one. An operator picked up on the other end and asked if she could help him. He looked down at the pad and saw where he had written down Míng jié Zhang's name, and smiled.

"Yes, can you give me the Indianapolis Police Department in Indiana? Non-emergency number, please. Preferably, credit card fraud, if you can find it." He was back on the trail, and he was happy.

Chapter 75 – Lila

Will kicked a bucket on the floor over to the girl on the cot, who immediately vomited into it, and continued to spit into it well after she ran out of fluid. The girl was in her late teens, probably out of high school, but Will wasn't sure yet. She had blonde hair that was straight and ran nearly halfway down her back. It was caked with dried vomit around each side. He looked at her, slightly amused, but not really. She was far too young to be drinking, and everyone is too young to drive while intoxicated, he thought.

"So," Will said to the girl, "You wanna tell me where you got the booze?"

"I told you I got it from home," she said, sniffling and wiping the remnants of the vomit from her face. Will handed her a napkin, which she used instead of her sleeve.

"Not buying it, kiddo," Will said. "The receipt in the bag says it was all purchased from D&J Liquors, and that was earlier tonight." It was nearly one o'clock in the morning, and Will had not had this much activity during his shift since the week prior at the fair. He had been parked a few blocks away from the park when he spotted a Volkswagen speeding down one of the side roads. He quietly followed it out into the street and saw that it was sidewinding a little, so he turned on the lights and pulled the car over. Will had no trouble determining that the girl was definitely intoxicated, as the car smelled of booze, or maybe it was her. Her eyes were glassy, and when she engaged with him during routine questions, she slurred her words. He got her license from her, found out her name was Lila Blankenship, and her license said she was nineteen years old.

"Oh, God," she said, and grabbed the edges of the bucket. Will smiled again.

"Where, Ms. Blankenship?"

"Eat a dick," she said.

"Wow. Okay. Have it your way." He grabbed a bag from the table inside the small cell and opened it, producing a giant cheeseburger sub that he had picked up from Rocky's earlier in the night. He unwrapped it slowly. Took a large bite and began to chew as loudly as possible.

"Ugh," she said. He set the sub down on a table that just happened to be next to a fan that he had brought in to hopefully make her feel better more quickly. Since she wasn't being helpful, he decided to use it as a weapon. The smell from the sub hit her almost immediately, and she vomited again even faster. He picked up the sandwich to give her a break from the smell.

"Where," he said, when she was finished, but she said nothing. "Okay," he said, and placed the sandwich in front of the fan again.

"Okay–" she said, but was interrupted by a burp and a hiccup, and then she expelled some flatulence from her rear end. Will scooted his chair back a foot or so and re-aimed the fan. "Oh, God," she said again, starting to cry. He handed her another napkin and retreated to the safety of his chair across the cell. He let her compose herself before asking again. She sniffled and said, "The All Blues Man." He bought us the booze. He told us he'd buy it if we took his weed to a party and gave it out."

"Did you give it out?" Will asked.

"No. I was too afraid. I'd never done anything like that. I don't even smoke it. I just told my friends I could get the bottles for the party, and when I got carded, I got desperate, and he was there."

"Where's the marijuana now, Ms. Blankenship?"

"In my purse," she said. Will looked over to the table where her belongings were being stored. *Dummy,* he told himself. *You searched her car but not her purse. Good job, Deputy.* He decided it might be best if he left that out of the report, but he wasn't sure how. In the end, he would write that the girl willingly disclosed that she had the marijuana in her purse, which was not really a lie.

Will opened the purse and found a small plastic container that, oddly enough, he could not smell, but the contents inside were unmistakable. He put it in his pocket and set the girl's purse back onto the table, and then thought about what she had said. *The All Blues Man.* His mind flew back to his first night when he and Ogre had caught the kids smoking in the arena announcer's booth.

"Ms. Blankenship, is this the last time you drink while you're underage?"

"I hope so," she said.

"And is this the last time you operate a vehicle while under the influence of alcohol?"

"Yes," she said. "May I go home now?"

"I'm afraid you'll have to have a guardian come and pick you up."

"My mom is out of town," she said.

"What about a father or grandparent? Aunt, Uncle?"

"Never knew any of them," she said.

"I see. When will your mother return?"

"Next Monday," Lila said. "She travels for business. She does sales for the grain company. She's not home too much." Will began to feel some sympathy for the girl. He remembered growing up for most of his life without his mother. This girl had no one.

"Make me a promise, Ms. Blankenship." She looked up at him. "Promise me that when you get home tonight, you will not leave the house until noon today, at which point you will take a nice leisurely walk to this address and pick up your keys, and then take another walk over to High School Street and pick up your car, and hope that it has not been towed."

"Okay," she grumbled. "I promise."

"Don't make me regret this, Ms. Blankenship," he said. He emptied the vomit basket into the trash can, washed it out, and put a new bag in it while Lila gathered her things. He led her out of the side door and to his car, which was parked in the lot, and he drove her to the address on her license.

She looked up when the car stopped and then looked around. "This is not my house," she said, still a little groggy.

"What do you mean?"

"I live two blocks over. That way."

Will cleared his throat. "That's not what your license says."

"What does it say?" she asked.

"905 Madison."

"That's right," she said. "Maybe I do live here." She opened the door of the car and stepped outside, and he was careful to watch her as she walked up the driveway to the sidewalk and to the front porch. She stood there for a minute, all while he was watching, and then turned back around and came back down the driveway. "I need my keys," she said.

"Oh, sorry." Will got out of the car and escorted Lila up the driveway and to the front porch, where he asked her if the key he was holding was the correct one to unlock the door.

"Yes," she groaned. He opened the door and let her into the house. She flicked a light on and looked around. "I do live here," she said. Will took a look around and decided that the house was in decent shape for being mostly run by a teenage girl.

"What are you doing tomorrow, Ms. Blankenship?" Will asked.

"Sleeping until noon, walking to the address you gave me to get my keys, and then walking to the school road to get my car. I promised."

"That you did. I hope you can honor that promise. Have a good night. Lock the door behind me." Will exited the house and waited until he heard a clicking noise to step off the porch. He returned to his car and sat for a minute until he saw the lights go out. He thought he could get over to D&J Liquor before they closed at two o'clock, and hoped he could make it, because he wanted to know more about The All Blues Man. He got to the door of the liquor store and pulled on the handle, but found it locked. He looked inside and saw Jim at the counter, and he lightly tapped on the glass. Jim looked up and smiled, and came around to the door.

"Well, the prodigal son returns," Jim said with a laugh. "What brings you here? Come to shake me down for back pay?"

"No... I was in the neighborhood and thought I'd drop by, see how everything was, and I have some questions."

"Okay, fire away, Deputy."

"Well, I ran across a girl tonight who was intoxicated and driving under the influence. The bag of alcohol in the car said that it was purchased here."

"Okay," Jim said. "You know, that's what we do!"

"This girl was nineteen," Will said. Jim frowned and pulled his body back from the counter on which he was leaning.

"Nope. I don't sell to minors," he said. "I card everyone."

"This girl had a fake ID," Will said.

"Wait... younger girl, pretty, blonde hair down her back, wearing a tight red shirt with the rack pushed up?"

Will cocked his head sideways. "Sounds like the girl."

"I turned her down and took her ID and told her never to come back. Here." Jim opened a small plastic box that looked like it was designed to hold recipes or index cards. He pulled a card from the box. "This is the ID I took from her." Will took the ID card, and it was a driver's license for one Lila Blankenship, living on 905 Madison, and it was an exact copy of the one Lila had presented him with previously.

"I'll take this with me, if you don't mind?"

"Sure," Jim said. "Need a sixer to go?"

"After the week I've had, not sure I should turn that down, but I have to. Let me ask you another question."

"Shoot."

"Do you remember the guy who came in and bought all this?" Will handed Jim the receipt that he found in the bag Lila had in her car.

"Nope," Jim said, and Will looked down at the ground before Jim continued. "But the camera might. Grab a six-pack of *Anfitzipation* and meet me in the back. Will searched the cooler in the microbrew section and found the beer, and headed into the back, finding Jim in the office. "Here, sit down," he said. Will sat in the chair next to Jim, and they watched the video of the evening's activities. They watched as customer after customer came in and bought their refreshments, saw Lila Blankenship try to buy alcohol, and Jim taking her fake license, and about twenty minutes after that, a man came up to the counter in blue jeans and a jean jacket. Will tried to look closely at him, but he kept his back to the camera, facing the back of the store as he leaned on the camera. Will could only tell that he had shoulder-length hair.

"Well, thanks, Jim. That's the guy, I guess. I just have no idea who he is. Do you know him?"

Jim leaned back in his chair. "You know," he said, "I'm not sure if I've ever seen him before. I can look back through some older camera videos, but I don't recognize him."

"Do me a favor, Jim? If you see him again, call me?"

"Will do, Deputy."

Chapter 76 – Going To Denver

Greco woke up early the next morning and called the front desk to advise them that he would be checking out that day. He had decided the night before, after informing the Indianapolis Police of the credit card fraud sourced from an optician in their city, that he would not spend another evening in Seattle. He had a lead for the bus terminal, and even if that came out to be a dead end, he knew he had to go somewhere else, because Will Kelly was most likely not in Seattle anymore. But where was he? Hopefully, Greco thought, the bus terminal would point him in the right direction.

He dressed and grabbed his recently repacked suitcase, dropped the key for the motel in the office, signed his credit card bill, and headed to the rental car return at the airport. He caught a shuttle bus from the airport to the bus terminal, and at about eleven-thirty in the morning, arrived to hopefully find the next piece of the puzzle. Greco walked through the front door of the terminal and headed directly for the security station. He was getting better at knowing where to go in different places when he needed information, not that it should have been new to him. But this was a different kind of investigation. This was a manhunt like no other he had ever endured. This was like chasing a ghost, holding the needle in the haystack.

He explained to the security desk who he was and what he was doing and why, and one of the security officers escorted him to a side room where another officer listened to his story and took him to another side room where there was a library of video recordings all along one wall, all sorted by year, and then sorted by month, and then sorted by week. Greco was in his glory. He started at the logical starting point and continued to watch the video until he saw the familiar figure of Willem Kelly. He called the security officer back in and found out how he could check his purchase records based on the date and time of the security recordings, and he found out that Kelly had reserved a ticket with his credit card, but paid cash for it when he arrived at the terminal. He took a bus trip from Seattle to Cheyenne, Wyoming, and that's where Greco would soon be headed.

He took a taxi to Discovery Car Rental, where he had just been the day before, and tried to rent a car to take to Cheyenne, at least, but soon found out that Discovery would only rent local, and did not have an office in Cheyenne. He left Discovery and called one of the national companies and found a car that he could drive to Cheyenne, and that car could be found at the Seattle airport. Greco continued his circle of the city of Seattle, and the waste of most of a day. He was only happy because he had made it to the bus terminal, located Kelly in the security recordings, and found out where he was headed. Beyond that, though, he still had nothing. What would he do when he got to Cheyenne? Was Kelly the kind of person who would take a bus to a location nearest to where he wanted to go, and then continue his journey using another form of transportation? Or would he double back once he reached Cheyenne, and end up in someplace like Laramie, or head south to Denver??

Greco got his car and decided that he could leave no stone unturned, no possible witness untested. He would stop in several places along the way to Cheyenne. He had gotten a map from the security officers at the bus terminal, and they pointed out the route the bus would take and the places it would stop. Greco decided he would stop in Rawlins, Sinclair, Walcott, Elk Mountain, Arlington, and Laramie on the way to Cheyenne and see if anyone knew anything. He could not take a chance on skipping a location that Kelly may have revisited after getting to Cheyenne. He had a notebook full of plans and places to stop, and he was sick of writing the word "Cheyenne," but he didn't want to take anything about his notes as a given. It took him two days to get to Rawlins, which he had underestimated. He stopped at every rest station, and had gotten turned around in the mountains, and it took him half a day to get going in the correct direction again.

Once he was in Rawlins, he stopped at every gas station, bus stop, convenience store, fast food restaurant, and random business he could find, and would show Kelly's picture, but he came up empty. He slept in his car at the end of a street in the Circle Cross Trailer Court. He set his watch alarm for five o'clock in the morning so that he wouldn't alert any of the neighbors, which might result in a call to the police about some vagrant sleeping in a car. He was back on the road in minutes, but he needed to stop and use a bathroom and get a coffee, both of which were available pretty quickly at a gas station and convenience store. He filled his gas tank while he was there and took his coffee and a bottle of water for his trip. Food, or any food he would have eaten, was non-existent at the convenience store, so there was another stop at one of the national burger joints that served a sort of breakfast.

In Sinclair, the only places he could find to stop were a small café, a towing company, and an oil refinery, and he stopped at all of them, but no one had remembered seeing Kelly before. Walcott was the next town on his list, but when he got there, he stopped at one of the two gas stations in the town, asked his questions, and then kept on going. In his notes, he wrote down that Walcott was only slightly larger than a village. In Elk Mountain, the only place he could think to stop was at the Elk Mountain Trading Post, where he had a sandwich and fries, which he found rather tasty. However, apparently, Kelly had not been there to anyone's knowledge.

He arrived in Laramie, which was decidedly a larger town than he had thought it would be. He began at the west end of the town, where there were many businesses, and he showed his face and Kelly's picture to every one of them. It took him the better part of two days before he found his first lead.

He stopped in a bar and liquor store on Third Street, and was in the midst of asking the man behind the cash register if he had seen the man in his photo when a young woman standing behind him said she remembered seeing him a few weeks ago in a restaurant. Greco turned his attention to her.

"You're sure it was this man?" Greco said, holding up the picture.

"Pretty sure," she said. "He was over at the restaurant having a beer and a sandwich."

"Have you seen him any time after that?"

"No, he said he was leaving that day. He was headed to... oh, where did he say, oh! Denver. He said he was going to Denver."

"Denver," Greco repeated. "Denver, Colorado."

"I guess that's the Denver he was talking about. He finished his beer and left."

"And this was three weeks ago?"

"Yeah," she said. "About that."

"Do you know anyone else who may have seen or talked to him at around the same time?"

"Eh, not sure," she said.

"Thanks," Greco said. "You've been very helpful." He left the store and stopped at a convenience store and bought a map of Colorado with an enlarged map of the Denver area. What he didn't hear was the conversation at the liquor store between the woman who said she had seen Kelly a few weeks prior.

"It's crazy," the man said.

"What's that?" she asked.

"That you recognized the guy he was looking for."

"Oh," she said. "That. Well, honestly, between you and me? I've never seen the guy before. I'm in a hurry, and that guy was in my way, slowing me down."

Chapter 77 – Odd Job

That Saturday night, Will was working his standard shift and patrolling around the town. He had checked out the fairgrounds earlier and then stopped at Rocky's for a slice of pizza. He decided he needed to stop doing that for a few reasons. Should Utter happen to perform a ten o'clock check-up on him, he shouldn't be hanging around Rocky's when he should be protecting and serving. The second reason was personal. He felt his pants getting a little tighter since he began his career as a deputy, and he had to feel that it was Rocky's extra cheese special that was doing it. He had also not gone for his daily run in quite some time. Weeks, he thought. He'd have to get back to that and start eating more salad or lean proteins.

Will pulled the car up to the stoplight and sighed as he watched nothing happen, anywhere. The main streets were quiet. He ventured out of the town, as that was part of the patrol, and turned out onto the main road, and then parked the car across from the Rusty Rails Tavern. He turned the headlights off, and with the bright streetlights above him aimed at the tavern, no one could see his car unless they shielded their eyes from the light, and for a reason to do so, most of the time, there was none. Everything seemed quiet at the tavern, and he was about to get moving again, when some movement caught his eye. A young man and woman, both of barely legal age, seemed to be having a disagreement. When he shoved her, Will hit the lights on top of the car and pulled it across the road to where the two were standing. He got out of the car, and the man and woman instinctively backed up against the outer wall of the tavern. Will approached them and shone his flashlight in their faces, not because he needed the light, but just to give himself the advantage.

"What's going on here, kids?" Will lowered the flashlight.

The man spoke first. "Nothing," he said, lowering his hands.

"He shoved me!" the woman yelled.

"I know," Will said. "I saw it. Why did you shove her?" he asked the man.

"It's none of your business," the man said. "We're just having a disagreement."

"May I see some ID, please?" Will's tone was not that of a question, but more of a demand. The man reached for his wallet and pulled out his driver's license. Will looked at it under the beam of the unnecessary flashlight. "Miles Davis'?" Will asked.

"Yes," the man said.

"Hmmm," Will said. "And how about you, Betty Lou? Any ID?"

"It's in the bar," she said.

"Her name is Lucy Atwater," Miles said. "And she owes me money."

"And for what does Ms. Atwater owe money to you?" Will asked.

"It's none of your business!" Miles said, almost shouting.

"I'm making it my business, Mr. Davis. Now you can tell me about it here, or we can all go to the Sheriff's Department and work it out there."

"It's for pot," Lucy said. "I owe him the money for drugs." With this statement, Miles grunted, turned, and kicked the dusty parking lot.

"I don't sell drugs!" Miles yelled. "I have my own stash, and I gave her some, and she owes me for it."

And then, for Will, it clicked. *Ball cap,* he thought, *and jeans, jean jacket, and mustache. And he sells marijuana. Miles Davis. The All Blues Man that the kids told me about at the fairgrounds. It's gotta be him.*

"Ms. Atwater?" Will asked.

"He's right," she said. "I owe him two hundred forty dollars."

"It's three hundred now, you skank!"

"Hey, hey, hey, now, let's keep this civil," Will said. "No name-calling. Ms. Atwater, do you want to press charges against Mr. Davis for shoving you?"

"Um," she said. "I don't know. It kinda hurt, and it's not the first time he did it."

"You have twenty-four hours to decide. Here is the number for the Sheriff's Department. If you choose, call them and give them your statement." He turned towards Miles. "She owes you three hundred dollars?"

"Yes," Miles said.

Will looked at Lucy. "What other drugs has he sold you?"

"Nothing," she said. "Just the pot."

"Must be quite a habit to be three hundred dollars in the hole," Will said. "And you," he said, handing Miles Davis his license, "You don't sell drugs, you say, correct? Just to her?"

"Yes!" Miles said again, angrily.

"Ms. Atwater, do you have the money that you owe Mr. Miles?"

"No," she said meekly. And then Miles muttered something under his breath that sounded to Will a lot like 'dirty whore.'

"Now I do want to press charges," she said, and Will was immediately on Miles.

"Hey, what are you doing?" Miles screamed.

"You're under arrest," Will said.

"For what?!"

"Battery. You shoved Ms. Atwater. I saw it happen, and she wants to press charges."

"You pig piece of shit!" Miles said, and brought his foot back and up into Will's groin. It was just a glancing blow, but it was enough for "The All Blues Man" to make a break for it. Will got back to his feet and ran after him, around the corner of the Rusty Rails. He had to navigate a pile of empty beer kegs that Miles had apparently knocked over, either on purpose or because he ran into them, and they fell. Will cleared the kegs and could see Miles about fifty yards ahead of him, running on foot. He never had a chance, though, as

Will closed on him quickly and tackled him just before Miles was about to jump a split rail fence into some almost unfortunate farmer's land.

Will brought out his handcuffs and slapped one onto Miles' right wrist, and pushed him up against the ground face-first. He grabbed Miles' other wrist and pulled it back, securing the remaining cuff around it, and then pulled Miles up to his feet.

"Come on, let's go," Will advised Miles Davis of his rights as they walked back to the bar and to where Will's car was parked. Surprisingly, Lucy Atwater was still there waiting. Will walked by her and began to stuff Miles into the back seat. "Ms. Atwater, you have a nice evening. Straighten out your life." He was driving the car with his quarry in the back seat when Miles began speaking.

"You can't hold me on this," Miles said in a cocky tone.

"You're probably right," Will said, but followed it with silence.

"So why are you taking me in?"

"Because I can hold you for twenty-four hours without charging you."

"So, you're going to what, leave me in the pokey for twenty-four hours and then let me go?"

"Hmm. Maybe," Will said, internally laughing about Miles' used of the word "pokey." "But I'm guessing I'm going to be able to produce some witnesses that will identify you as someone who tried to sell them some marijuana."

"Good luck with that," Miles said. "No one is going to pick me out of a line-up."

"No line up. I'm just going to march them into the Sheriff's office, let them see you in the jail, and tell me that it was you."

"Come on, man. It's just pot!" Miles said.

"But it's illegal, and you're selling it to minors. Now, you can admit to me that you're selling it, and I'll try to get the judge to go easy on you when it comes time for whatever penalty will be handed down, probably a fine and some time. But maybe I can get it down to just a fine. You admit it, spend the night 'in the pokey' as you say, and you can be out tomorrow afternoon on bail. You continue to deny it, and my witnesses identify you; you're not going anywhere for a while. Now, what's your name?"

"Miles Davis," Miles said. "I already told you."

"Nope," Will said. "Not that one. What's your other name? What does everyone call you?"

Miles sat back in the car and exhaled heavily. "Come on, man," he said. Will just looked at him in the rearview mirror. Miles rolled his eyes. "The All Blues Man," he said as he exhaled, and then he softened. "You're not from here, Deputy. I know this. You've only been here a few months. Where are you from?" Will just eyed him through the rearview mirror. "You're not from a small town. I can see that. You don't know what it's like to be from a small town, and what you need to do to make ends meet around here. Half the town is out of work for half the year, and the other half is made up of retirees, broken-down military veterans living in shit-shacks, and people on welfare. People take odd jobs to make extra money, and when those odd jobs are gone, there's nothing left for the rest of us. I didn't graduate from high school, sir. I had to make money so my mother and I could live in our house. If I don't sell pot, we lose the house. This is my odd job."

"There have to be other ways than selling drugs. You could have been me. The Sheriff picked me out after being here for a few weeks. You could have gone after the same job before I even got here. Instead, you chose to grow and sell marijuana." Miles mumbled something that Will could not hear.

"Say again, please?" Will said.

"Nothing."

"I can't help you if you're not going to help me," Will said. Miles looked at him in the mirror.

"I don't grow it. I just distribute it." Will looked at him through the mirror as he continued to drive, but then stopped the car and put it into Park. "Where do you get it?" he demanded.

"I pick it up."

"From where?"

Miles shook his head. "They'll kill me if you go after them. They'll know it was me who told you, and then I'm dead. They told me that."

"I can protect you if you tell me where you get it. You tell me, and I'll make sure they are off your back."

"You're going to get me killed!"

"You've dug your own hole. Let me help you get out of it," Will said.

"I don't know who they are. I don't meet them. I just pick up the stuff."

"Where?"

"Different places. They call me once each week, and I have a certain amount of time to get to the location."

"How long?"

Miles let out another long exhale. "Depends on the location. Once it was right outside of town under the seventy-seven bridge, and they gave me ten minutes. Another time, it was out by the old movie theater, they gave me a half-hour."

"When do they call you?" Will asked.

"Every Monday at two in the afternoon. They call and tell me when and where. I dump the cell phone, go to the spot, drop off the cash, pick up the package, which is usually the stuff, and there's another cellular phone with it that they use to call me the next week."

"How much are you supposed to give them each week?"

"Five-hundred. I keep the rest."

Will said nothing more on the ride. He contemplated the information he had gotten from The All Blues Man and decided that Utter should be brought in to talk about the next steps. Will would try to talk with him on Monday. For now, he had gotten what he wanted, information, and he was getting a drug dealer off the streets of Brindle.

Chapter 78 – Holes

Sheriff Wesley Timothy Utter had come into the station that Sunday afternoon when Will was scheduled to work his next shift. Utter had called Will earlier that day and asked him to come in about thirty minutes early so they could discuss The All Blues Man, and when Will arrived, Utter, Ogre, Cortez, and Deputy Sharon Reyes, who had previously worked as a police officer in San Diego. Utter asked questions, which Will answered with the events of the previous shift, and after the conversation was finished, Utter agreed that Will had acted properly. The other deputies agreed, and even Cortez said he was impressed by Will's ability to extract the information from the perpetrator so well in his young career as a deputy.

Utter decided that the next course of action would be for Will to work until midnight that night, instead of his usual three o'clock in the morning shift end. He would go home, get some rest, and then follow Miles Davis, who had been released on his own recognizance. Davis was released, subject to his cooperation in the next exchange of cash for supplies in whatever location he was given by his suppliers. He reluctantly agreed, just to get out of the cell.

The deputies disbanded, and some began their shifts, and some went home to rest, or wherever they went when they were off duty. Will began his shift by filling his insulated cup with coffee from the breakroom and exiting out the side door of the building, where he got into his car. The first thing he did was head to the fairgrounds for his initial check. He parked alongside the split rail fence that wrapped around the grounds except for where the entrances and exits were located. He walked along the fence until he reached the first opening into the grounds, and then walked the inner perimeter, through where the thoroughfare would be located, where "Crazy Train" exposed himself during the fair itself, and eventually to the stables and barns where livestock was kept to either be shown or sold. Ever since his first night when he caught the kids smoking in the announcer's booth, he had not had one instance of trouble as he scoured the fairgrounds.

It was about five o'clock when he finished the fairgrounds patrol. He returned to his car and did a drive around what could be considered the inner perimeter of the town itself. This was basically a preemptive move for him, as people of the town not only felt safer when they saw a deputy's vehicle cruising around, but they were less likely to get into trouble if they thought they might get caught in the act of doing something wrong.

It took him about an hour to complete the circuit around the town, and then he would cross up and down some of the streets, noticing whatever he could that might seem out of place, but there was never anything. At ten o'clock, he crossed to the north side of the town and stopped at Rocky's for dinner.

'Hey, Deputy," she said, as he walked in and removed his hat. "Two slices of double cheese?" As good as that sounded to Will, he decided that he'd be better off sticking with the plan of the salad. He would actually sit down and eat a salad, instead of driving around and taking a bite of pizza at each stop sign.

"Not tonight, My Dear. I'll have the Greek Salad, no onions."

"Wow," she said. "Going healthy?"

"I've always been healthy," he said. "Until I started eating your pizza every day!" He took a seat where she pointed.

"Don't blame me for wrecking your bad habits," she said. "Be right back." She disappeared around the corner, and Will looked around the restaurant. It wasn't crowded at all, and Will had to believe that was because it was late on a Sunday. A few minutes went by, and Rocky came back with his salad and a breadstick. "Anything else?" she asked.

"No, this is good. Sit down and chat if you have time."

"I have all the time tonight. Sunday nights are always slow. It's good though, because we can detail clean and stock up on things that we let run down on Friday and Saturday."

Will swallowed the bite of salad that he was chewing as she talked. "You could close earlier," he said, taking another bite.

"I don't want to cut anyone's hours more than I need to. If I can stay open and pay the staff to do the work, I'll do it."

"Makes sense, I guess," he said.

"What do you have going on tonight?" she asked. "Anything big?"

"No, afraid not. Everything is calm and quiet, but I'm sure you already knew that."

"Everything is calm and quiet, all the time, every time," she said, taking a drink of her soda.

"Seems that way, except for the drunks," Will said, scraping the last of his salad onto his fork with the breadstick.

"Drunks?" she asked.

"Well, yeah, I told you about the dude at the fair who played the squirt gun game with his own squirt gun."

"Yeah, who else?"

"Some girl I pulled over the other night. She was weaving down the street, so I stopped her. I took her into the jail to chill for a while, and then took her home."

"Anyone I know?" Rocky asked.

"Off the record, Lila Blankenship?"

"Wow. Her mother used to work for me. Now she's some sort of traveling salesperson."

"Interesting," Will said, and then he had a thought. "You don't happen to know where they live, do you?"

"Over on Madison. Nine-oh-something. I used to drive her home after work. Why?"

"Just curious," Will said. "The daughter had a fake ID. I just wanted to confirm I dropped her off in the right place."

"Seems like you did well. As far as the drunks, well, there's not too much to do in a small town a lot of the time. That's why there are three liquor stores, three bars, and four restaurants that serve alcohol in such a small area."

"Perils of small-town life, I guess?"

"Something like that," she said. "Okay, you gotta go. I have to get cracking."

"Fair enough. What do I owe you for the salad?"

"On the house, Deputy. Have a safe night." She gave him a quick kiss on the cheek.

"Will do, Dear. Will do." He grabbed his hat from the table and put it on top of his head, and she locked the door behind him. He got into the car and started it, and began another round of road checks. He had gotten used to spending time around the Rusty Rails as it got later in the evening and earlier in the mornings. He thought his presence there was certainly working as a deterrent. The only flare-up was the issue with Miles Davis. He was getting ready to head over there again when his radio crackled. Ally's voice came over through the static.

"BC-8, come in, BC-8."

Will grabbed the CB microphone and pressed the button on the side. "BC-8," he said. "Go ahead."

"We have an apparent dead body."

"Oh, wow. Okay. Where?"

"In the cemetery," Ally said.

"Well, there's probably a lot of them there."

"You know, I love having you on the job more and more every day."

"Can't see how you couldn't."

"Okay, smart guy. This body is above the ground. Will you go check it out, please? Cortez is on the way."

"10-4. Who reported it? Are they still on the scene?"

"Far as I know," she said. *"A man named Jacob Lynch found the body and called it in."*

"Alright," Will responded. "I'll go check it out." He aimed the car back out onto the main road and drove toward the edge of the town, past the old drive-in theater, and turned into the cemetery. He looked around, but didn't see anyone anywhere. He got out and looked around, and finally, in the distance, in the back corner of the cemetery, he saw what appeared to be someone holding a flashlight. He got back into the car and drove down to the screen, towards the flashlight, and he stopped about five hundred feet from the scene, trying to preserve any evidence that might be around. He grabbed his flashlight and turned it on, and began making a sweeping pattern back and forth across the road. He didn't find anything of note and finally approached the old man with the flashlight.

"He's over here," the man said. Will approached slowly.

"Did you call this in?" Will asked.

"Yep."

"Can I have your name, sir?" Will asked.

"Jacob Lynch," the man said.

"Mr. Lynch, can I ask what you're doing here at this hour?"

"I work here. I maintain the grounds, place flowers, dig the holes, and prep them for the service the next day."

"I see," Will said. "How did you find him?"

"Just like he is. I just put the sheet over him."

"When did you find him?"

"Right before I called it in. Maybe thirty minutes ago?"

"When was the last time you were in this area of the cemetery?"

"Oh, not since yesterday. I work nights mostly. Prep work."

"Anything special you know about what happened, Mr. Lynch?"

"Uh, he looks like he was shot, to me."

"Did you hear any gunshots, sir?"

"No... No, I didn't. But I just got here not too long ago."

Will put his notebook back into his belt and aimed his flashlight over at the dead body. "Okay," he said. "Let's see what we have." He pulled the sheet back, and the body was face down in the grass of the cemetery. There was one hole in the back area of the victim's clothing. Will had a bad feeling right away just by what the man was wearing, but he needed to know for sure. He rolled the body slightly to one side. "Dammit!" he said aloud.

Jacob Lynch moved closer. "Do you know him?" he asked.

"Yeah," Will said. "I know him." He took a closer look at the body and the wounds. Three holes in the center of the chest, and two in the head. It was Miles Davis, The All Blues Man.

Chapter 79 – Blood

Will watched as the ambulance pulled away from the scene where the body was found by Jacob Lynch. In the middle of being angry about his best witness and mole in the drug operation being dead, Will thought the crazy thing was that Jacob Lynch had found the body, and within a few days, would probably be digging another hole for the body that he found. His lead was dead, and he had nothing to go on.

"Cheer up, Rookie," Deputy Juan Cortez said, slapping Will slightly on the back. "You got one of them off the street. You just have to wait for it to start again, get the right guy in the wrong place, and get him to roll over on his suppliers, without them finding out so they don't kill him."

"Gee, thanks. I feel like I was really on to something."

"You were, kid, and you did well. You put the pieces together and were on your way to finishing the puzzle, so to speak."

"Thanks, Juan."

Cortez let out a heavy sigh as they began walking back to their respective cars. "I gotta tell you, kid," he said. "I didn't like you very much when you first got here. I thought there was something weird about you, and I'm usually a pretty good judge of character. But I was wrong. You've turned out to be pretty great at this. You've taken to it faster than anyone I've seen. You should have been a deputy as soon as you turned twenty-one years old. I think you were born to do this. I don't know what you did before this, but it was a waste of time." Cortez stopped and then turned towards Will. "What did you do before this?"

Will snickered a bit and took two steps forward, and put his arm around Cortez. "What do you think I did?" he asked.

"I don't know, that's why I asked,"Cortez said with a smile.

"Guess." Will thought he might be treading a dangerous path, but he couldn't help himself.

"Well, we all know about your wrestling background, but I'm guessing you never took that pro, right?" Will smiled and shook his head. "You were going to be a coach at the high school, so you must know a lot about sports, you're athletic, but I don't think you made a living from it." He looked at Will. "Stockbroker?" Will looked at him sideways. "No?" Cortez asked. They were now stopped at Cortez's car, and Will's was right behind his. "Investment banker?" Will stiffened and hoped Cortez didn't see it, but he was turned toward his car, unlocking the door.

"What would make you ask that?"

"Well," Cortez said with a laugh. "You have an athletic body, but you got an office ass. You've spent some time sitting on something other than dugout seats!" They both laughed. Will mostly covered himself, but he still found Cortez's comment fairly funny.

"That's fair," Will said. "Get out of here. Go get some sleep."

"Oh, I intend to, kid. Dead bodies should be the only thing you wake up the acting Deputy in Charge, so I assume we'll have no more tonight."

"Uh, hopefully not," Will said, opening his car door. Cortez smiled and angled himself into his car, backed out, nearly hitting an old headstone, and then drove away. Will got back into his car and then realized something wasn't right. They had missed something. He got out of the car again and walked over to where the body had previously lain. He looked around at the scene from all angles. He looked from the eight main compass points, he looked from ground level, and he looked from over the top, as much as he could without disturbing the grass. It was then he figured it out. He ran back to the car, turned it on, and picked up the CB.

"BC-8 to BC-2, come in." There was static, and then nothing. Will figured it was too soon for Cortez to have gotten back to his house already, so he tried again. "BC-8 to BC-2, come in BC-2." More cracking.

"*BC-8, BC-2, go ahead.*"

"Juan, I found something at the scene!"

"*What did you find, kid?*"

"Well," Will said, and then stopped. It sounded weird in his head, but he still said it. "It's more like what I didn't find."

"Make up your mind, did you find something or not?"

"There's no blood," Will said.

"What?"

"Juan, there's no blood on the scene. A man has five bullet holes in him, three in the center-mass and two in the head. There's no blood."

"That means–," Cortez started, but paused, and Will cut finished off the thought.

"The body was moved after. They killed him somewhere else and then dropped him in the cemetery. That's why no one heard any gunshots."

"You're probably right."

"Juan, do you know if anyone near the cemetery has any security cameras that might show who dumped the body?"

"Not that I'm aware of, but we can canvas tomorrow."

"10-4. Have a good night, Jaun." The radio crackled and then went silent. Will's mind went back to the events of the night, and the fact that his witness, *his* witness, was dead, and the fact that Will had told his witness that he could protect him if Miles gave him the information he wanted. Will felt guilt. This was his first major success and his first major failure as a Sheriff's Deputy. He remembered back to the time when he told himself that what he really wanted to do with his life, his *new* life, was to make a difference. He didn't know if his making a difference was something he had already done in Brindle, or something he was yet to do. In his heart, however, he did not feel like he had achieved his goal. One drug pusher off the streets did not constitute a difference, at least not in his thinking. There had to be something more.

Will continued his shift, what was left of it anyway, and patrolled the streets of Brindle. Thankfully, at least in his mind, the rest of his shift went without issue. He turned in his paperwork, which took longer than normal because there was the uncommon dead body to address. He barely replied with a "fine" when Ally asked how the rest of his shift went.

He grabbed his keys from the desk and left for the day, happy that this was his last bit of work for the next few days. He was looking forward to a few days of nothingness, assuming forces of nature and the universe complied.

He pulled the car into the parking lot at the trailer park and navigated to his slot, parking the car in front. He locked it, as usual, and found Kat waiting at the steps, also as usual. He went inside, and Kat followed, meowing all the way. He fed Kat her usual can of smelly, wet shreds of whatever brown meat was written on the side of the can. He had noticed months ago that the fish-flavored food, the beef-flavored food, and the chicken-flavored food all looked and smelled the same. In his weakened emotional state that night, he wished he had a fresh catfish or perch for her to eat, instead of the processed stuff in her bowl.

She finished her food and went into the bathroom to her litter box, and Will began to take off his deputy's uniform. He heard the shriek of screeching tires, but made no other thought about it. However, when the bullets began to pierce the side of his trailer and travel through the other side of what could be considered his dining room, he took full notice. He belly-crawled off the bed and onto the floor. He heard what sounded like machine-gun fire and also shotgun blasts, but that , along with a noise from Kat, was all he could identify through the din of the event. He reached for his gun and held it up to the shattered window over his bed, and emptied six shots from it. He crawled across the floor and found Kat, grabbed her, and rolled under the kitchen table to avoid getting hit.

The onslaught lasted under a minute, but to him, and probably Kat as well, it felt like a much longer time to experience something as horrific as it was. Finally, when the shooting stopped, tires screeched, and then there was silence, broken only by the smoke detector in the kitchen, whining its incessant wail. He checked himself for injuries and found blood on his white t-shirt, but didn't sense any pain. Then, he saw it. The blood was from Kat.

Chapter 80 – Little Bear

Greco spent two weeks in Denver looking for Willem Kelly and came up with nothing. He had checked in at the office several times with Maryanne, and she said that Sergeant Harding was getting more and more frustrated with Greco's absences and the chasing of his fugitive. Maryanne said she thought he was going to pull Greco back to New York sooner or later, and Greco's chase was so far in that it was actually visible in the station's budget.

Greco had been back to work for the NYPD since he was in Seattle. He had convinced Harding that Will Kelly was alive, and he was hot on the trail. He had chased him from Indianapolis and all the way across the country until he landed in Seattle, and he felt he was so close there that he could smell Kelly. He had him. He just needed to catch up to him. He convinced Harding that it was something that he could do.

He still had Cheyenne as a target for Will Kelly, and every other point east from there, and he would search them all until he found him. Kelly was one man, relatively new in a town somewhere, out there, and Greco was going to catch him, one way or another. He was driving back towards Laramie, which was taking him far longer than he wanted, to pick back up on Kelly's trail. As he drove, he found his mind wandering to Maryanne, to Honey, and to his home and career in New York. He was tired of traveling, tired of driving, but he had nothing else to go on other than checking in each town.

He pulled into a motel in Laramie and parked the car for the night, balancing his suitcase and a sandwich and fries he had purchased from a convenience store a few blocks away. He got himself settled into his room, which, for a motel, was pretty nice. It had a little kitchen complete with a microwave, stove, refrigerator, and sink. Some of the places he was staying, he felt as if he was fortunate to unlock and open the door and find a bed.

He ate his sandwich and fries and cracked open a cold beer, and set it on the edge of the table next to the bed. He dialed the phone and, after a few rings, heard Maryanne's voice on the other end.

"*I thought you stood me up,*" she said.

"Never," he said, taking a drink of the beer. "How was your day?"

"*Fantastic. Harding is all over the place with you right now. I think he's going to reel you back in soon.*"

"So that was a sarcastic fantastic?" he asked.

"*Oh yeah.*"

"Well, we'll see. I'm close, Mar, real close. I can smell this guy. I just need more time."

"*You're close to running out. I want you to get him as well, because you'll never rest until you do, but Brian, not at the expense of your career. When Harding calls you back, you need to come back.*"

Greco exhaled. "I know," he said. "I just need to keep going. I can't quit. Not until I find him." He took a sip of the beer as she sat silent. "How are the dogs?" he asked, changing the subject.

"*They are fine,*" she said. "*They seem to get along well together.*"

"I figured they would. Thanks for taking care of Honey for me. Does she look like she even misses me?"

"*I miss you,*" she said.

"I miss you too. I'll call you tomorrow." He hung up the phone and sat back on the mattress of the bed. He would drive straight through to Cheyenne the next day, without stopping, and hope he would find some sort of a lead there on Kelly. He would worry about that day when it came with the sunrise. At that moment, that night, he was exhausted. He drank down the rest of the beer and then grabbed another one from the little refrigerator, popping the top and drinking nearly half of it. He opened his suitcase and pulled out the shirt and pants that he would wear the next day, and hung them in the bathroom. The rest of the beer was next on his list of accomplishments, and he ended it quickly and then lay down to go to sleep. He didn't even turn on the television.

The next morning, he woke up before the sun rose and found himself rather refreshed. He didn't wake up during the night, that he could remember, anyway, and he felt good. He stopped at the convenience store again on his way out after leaving the motel, and grabbed a large coffee and a bottle of water, and he was reminded of the first time he left New York in his quest to find Kelly. When he left New York, thinking he was invincible and would not be stopped in his task, which he thought might not take more than a few days, if that long. His eyes were open now. Kelly was not stupid, and he was not an easy chase. He was naïve to think otherwise, especially for a veteran detective in the NYPD.

He drove up through Laramie, without stopping, as tempted as he was to find the woman who said Kelly was headed to Denver. He was pretty sure she was lying, and if he had any jurisdiction in Laramie, he probably would have stopped. He drove up through Bossler and then on to Whiting, and there was no sign of Kelly anywhere. He decided that he'd better get onto Cheyenne and see what he could find there. Time was getting short. From Whiting, he drove south on Interstate 25 past Slater and through Chugwater, again without stopping. If a lead brought him back in that direction, he'd go back. But for now, it was forward to Cheyenne, until he saw a sign for a place called the Little Bear Inn. He realized that he really hadn't eaten all day, so he decided to stop.

He pulled the car into the little parking lot and made his way to the front door. There were only three other cars in the parking lot. He opened the door and walked in, and needed to let his eyes adjust to the dim lighting, and then he took a seat at the bar. He was checking out the decorations around the restaurant, and had to smile when he saw what was labeled as a "Wyoming Catfish." It was a horrible combination of the front half of a cat and the rear half of a fish. He decided to stay away from the seafood if they offered it. A middle-aged woman behind the bar came over to him and slid a menu in front of him.

"Know what you want to drink, dear?" she asked.

"Draft beer, please."

"We got a couple," she said. "Which one you 'ant?" Greco looked over at the beer taps.

"The blue-handled one is fine."

"I'm Connie. Need a minute with the menu?"

"Yes, please," he said. She winked and walked off to pour the beer, and returned a few minutes later with the drink. "How's the steak here?" he asked.

"Hon, this is Cheyenne's original steakhouse, we been here since 1958. If we've served a bad steak, I haven't seen it yet."

"I guess I'll have the strip."

"Baked tater and veggies?"

"Sounds good," he said, and he looked at the catfish on the wall again.

"You got it." Greco took a long drink of the beer and then also asked Connie for a glass of water.

"You're not from around here, are ya?" she asked.

"What makes you say that?" he said, smiling.

"I don't know you, and I've been working here for twenty-six years. I pretty much know everyone in the county if they've been here, and everybody in the county has been here, I think. And you talk funny." He choked on the water a little, thinking it was funny that someone with Connie's accent would call out someone else for talking funny.

"Well, Connie, you win the prize. I'm not from anywhere close to here."

"Let me guess. New York."

"That's right. How did you know?"

She exhaled, rolled her eyes a bit, and her hands went to her hips. "Are you here for the dude ranch?"

"Dude ranch? No, I'm here on business."

"I see," she said, her hands leaving her hips. "Let me go check on that steak." She returned a few minutes later with the steak on a platter, the baked potato wrapped in foil in a side dish, with the vegetables in a side dish. There was also a dinner roll with butter provided. "Refill on the beer," she said, not so much a question, nor did she remain for what may have been an answer.

He cut into his steak and found it perfectly done to his liking, and the butter was melting all over the baked potato already. A dish of sour cream was to the side, but Greco left that alone. The first bite of the steak was ridiculously delicious, and it reminded him of New York. He was biased, but he felt that New York had the best steak. This was a very close second place. Before he realized it, half of it was gone, and the bread he was using to soak up the juices was completely gone, and he was extremely full.

"More than you can handle, dear?" Connie asked.

"Seems that way, Ma'am. Can I have a take-home box?"

"You got it." She disappeared for a few minutes and then returned with a Styrofoam box and a plastic bag. "Any dessert?"

"No thanks. Can I ask you a question?"

"Shoot."

"Can you recommend a decent motel to stay in tonight? Nothing too fancy?"

"There's a Heaven Seven right down the road toward past Cheyenne, at the crossroads of I-80," Connie said.

"Can I ask you another question?"

"You mean after that one?"

"Yeah, sorry." Greco reached into his jacket pocket and pulled out Will Kelly's picture. "Have you seen this man recently? Last six months or so?" Connie looked at the picture closely.

"I don't think so. No, but you might want to check Cheyenne. If he's not local, and I guess he's not because you're not local and looking for him, most travelers don't make it up this way. They usually stick to the bigger towns."

"I'll do that," Greco said. "What do I owe you?" Greco settled up with Connie and took the thirty-minute drive south and found the motel she recommended, which luckily, had vacancies. He checked in, put his food in the mini-fridge, and called it a day. He called Maryanne, and they chatted for a while, and the main idea that Greco got when he hung up the phone was that he was out of time. He needed to find Will Kelly *now.*

Chapter 81 – The Safe House

Will grabbed a piece of an old t-shirt he had ripped apart and wrapped it around Kat's head to try to stop the bleeding. Fortunately, neither of them was shot, but Kat received a nasty cut on her head from some shattered glass. Will's home, however, was destroyed. The light from the streetlamp outside shone through the holes in the side of the trailer and illuminated the smoke that was lingering in light streaks across the room. Shattered glass was all over the place, a cabinet dangled from the ceiling above the sink, and the top of the door was bent inward from the force of the gunfire.

Juan Cortez was first on the scene, with Ogre and Deputy Owen Linkletter following shortly after in their patrol cars. Cortez surveyed the damage and took notes, shaking his head about what had happened. Ogre questioned the residents of the RV park, but at three o'clock in the morning, all of them said they saw nothing as they were sleeping at the time of the attack. Cortez came over to Will and shook his head.

"You pissed off the wrong gringos, kid," he said.

"I guess so. You ever seen anything like this before?" Will asked.

"No, not like this. Used to have a biker gang run through town and raise some hell every now and then, but this," he stopped. "This is crazy." He paused and looked at the trailer, which was beginning to lean to one side as the air leaked slowly from the damaged tires. "You got somewhere you can stay?"

"I think I'll check out the motel for tonight and then work on something long-term in the morning."

"Good," Cortez said. "Get your rest. Utter will probably want to talk to you tomorrow about all this, and then he'll most likely force you to take some days off to recover."

"Recover from what? I'm fine."

Cortez exhaled. "Any deputy who shoots another human gets time off. Mental break."

"What?" Will exclaimed.

"Yeah. We think you shot someone. There's glass out by the road near all the shell casings, and there's blood on the glass, so unless someone cut themselves on the glass, it's probably that you hit whoever you were aiming, or not aiming, for."

Will digested that information with a deep breath. "I don't need to recover, and I don't need time off," he said slowly.

"We'll see. I'm about done here. I have what I need." He looked at Will's patrol car, sitting there with glass shattered and two flat tires. "Need a lift to the motel?"

"No, I'm going to pack some things, and then hoof it."

"Suit yourself, kid. Try to get some rest."

"Thanks, Juan." Will waited for Ogre and Linkletter to clear out of the park as well and went into the trailer. *I shot someone?* he thought. He grabbed his duffel bag, filled it with clothes, and went for the remainder of the cash that he had from his illegal escapades in New York. He opened the bottom drawer, and the bag was there, but when he opened it, he found it empty. "Son of a bitch!" he yelled. He had not looked for it in a while because he did not need it. He was employed and doing fine as a deputy, but he always had this in the back of his mind, especially if he needed it to help him get on the run again.

Ke had not so much forgotten about the money; it was just that he didn't need it. He was comfortable in Brindle and had stopped looking over his shoulder. Coming clean with Rocky was a big part of that. Now, the money was gone, and it brought up questions. Who had found it? How did they know about it, and why did they think he had such a large sum of cash just lying around in an RV? Now he was nervous again.

He grabbed his duffel bag and realized locking the door was a futile effort, so he left it hanging open. He tucked the injured, yet seemingly normal, Kat under his arm and began his walk to the motel.

Old Man Perry was behind the desk of the Motel Brindle as usual, and Will wondered if he ever slept more than a few hours each day. Will paid cash for the room, told Perry he didn't know how long, but maybe for a few nights. Will said he would let him know. He got into the room, got Kat settled on the bed, and really wished he'd had some beer. Instead, he took a shower, threw on some clean clothes, and crawled into bed. He fell asleep almost immediately, and at some point during the night, Kat had crawled up and snuggled behind his knees.

He woke the next morning to a pounding on his motel door. He put on his t-shirt and opened the door to find Wes Tim Utter standing in his doorway holding a bag and two Styrofoam cups with lids. Will didn't say anything, but just pushed the door aside and motioned for Utter to enter.

"Rough night, huh?" Utter asked.

"To put it mildly," Will said.

"Damnedest thing I've ever heard of," Utter said. "May I?" Utter motioned to the still-made bed as a possible seat.

"Of course, I'm sorry." Will rubbed some crust from his eyes and eyed the coffee, which Utter handed over after he sat.

"I'm not sure how you like it," Utter said.

"Hot," Will said.

"It is that," Utter said. He opened the bag and took out two small packages that contained breakfast sandwiches. He gave one to Will, who took it and immediately unwrapped it and took a bite.

"Thanks," Will said with a mouthful of ham, egg, cheese, and biscuit.

"Thought you might be able to use something," Utter said. "Listen, I know Ogre and Owen were out there last night asking around, but I went back over this morning and threw my weight around a little bit, and one of the neighbors, uhh, what was his name. I left my notebook out in the car. It was like Dusty Rhodes or something, but that wasn't it."

"Sandy Shore," Will said, still chewing.

"That's it," Utter said. "You know him?"

"Yeah, we've talked a few times in passing. Seems a nice enough guy."

"Yeah, he does. Turns out Mr. Shores thinks he saw a red pickup truck squealing wheels through the trailer park, then a whole lotta ruckus, and then the same red pickup squealing out of the park."

Will took a sip of the coffee to clear his mouth of biscuit debris. "Did he get the plates?" he asked.

"First couple digits, but that wasn't the best part," Utter said. Kat crawled under Utter's leg and rubbed against his shin. He reached down and patted her. "The truck had no tailgate and a black door," Utter said, then paused. "And the window in the back was shattered."

"A shattered window and a black door?"

"Yep, like it had to have a door replaced at some point, and all that was available was black. Plus, the window we think you shot out."

"Well, that should make it easy for me to spot."

"True," Utter said. "But, it may not be that you're looking for them, Billy. Getting involved with that Blues Man has opened up a can of something fierce here. If you took one of them out, it might get worse. I'm afraid that if they find out they didn't get the job done on you the first time that they are going to come back again. I can't have my town getting all shot up, Billy."

"What do you want to do?"

"I think you should leave the town for a little while, Billy. Let things cool down."

"Sheriff, that's just going to make it worse around here! Come on, help me. Let's go find these guys. Get that description out to the other counties and see what comes back!"

"Billy, I get what you're saying, but I think it's for the best. Whoever they are who came looking for you before, if you're not here, they won't know where to look. It's not up for debate. We'll put you in a motel for a week or so in the next county." Will looked at Utter and shook his head, and the two men sat in silence.

Finally, Will looked up. "Sheriff," he said, "What if we went the other way?"

"What do you mean, Billy?"

"Let's bait the hook. Get it out that the hit was a failure, and that we have an expert witness in the case. Someone no one knows about. And then we draw them in, and then we get them."

"No, Billy. End of story. Listen. Shooting someone, even if you didn't see it, is a traumatic experience. You need time to deal with it in your head. Now, there's a safe house out on Rt. 772. It looks like a barn, but it's got everything you need inside. Belongs to a farmer I know who used to have some hands living in it. Just hang there for a while. There's food in the fridge."

Will exhaled. What choice did he have but to acquiesce and do not only what his boss was telling him, but the county Sheriff, too? "How long do I have?"

"Go see your friend from the pizza shop for a while. I'll pick you up at six o'clock and drive you to the safehouse," Utter said.

"I don't suppose she could come with me," Will said.

"I've known Rocky a while. I don't think she's fallen this hard for someone in quite some time. I know you spend some time together. But, I've also never seen her give up being at her restaurant when she could help it. Plus. I don't think it's a good idea for her to go. You need to be focused, just in case."

"All right, Sheriff. I'll go, but I don't like it."

"I understand. Now, get yourself straight. Get to the station and pick up a spare car for the day if you need it, and then meet me there at six. Enjoy your coffee." Utter got up from the edge of the bed and left the room. Will wasted no time in getting to the station to pick up the spare car, and he spent a large part of the afternoon with Rocky before she went to work at 5 o'clock. They had a long conversation about Will's night and the events that happened. Rocky turned fairly hysterical when he told her about the shootings, and her thoughts ranged from Will quitting the force to getting out of town and using the money he had left to start over somewhere else. She swore she would keep in touch, and they could still be together. He nixed those options and told her what the plan was, and that seemed to settle her down, but she wasn't happy about it. She did agree to watch Kat as it healed. At six o'clock, he met Utter at the station as designed with his duffel bag over his shoulder. They drove out to where the highway met Rt. 772, and Utter turned the car to the left and headed up the road for about a mile before turning onto a dusty road that wound up a small hill until it ran into a ranch. Utter drove straight to the barn and stopped beside it. He was checking the mirrors when Will broke the silence.

"Do I need to tell anyone I'm here?"

"No," Utter said. "Everything is all set. Just go inside and hang low. There's one thing I forgot to tell you. There's no toilet inside. There's a shit-shed behind the barn. Sorry about that. If you gotta take a leak, find a tree, or use the sink, or something."

"Sounds great."

"Billy, I'm sorry," Utter said. "But it's for the best."

"I get it. Thanks, Sheriff."

"Billy," Utter stopped him. "You're on my force now, and I consider you a friend. When it's informal, call me Wes Tim, or W.T. if you prefer."

"Will do. Thanks." Will shut the door of the car and slung his bag over his back, and walked toward the door of the safe house as Utter drove away. The door was unlocked, and the lights were on when he opened it. There was a small kitchen inside and a table in the middle of the room. Towards the back of the area were four sets of bunk beds, each made neatly. There was one window, above the kitchen sink, but it was blacked out with paint. There was a sofa and a lounge chair in the middle of the room, sitting atop an area rug, and a table against the wall, which held a television. A bookshelf sat next to it, the top row full of books he's never heard of, and the bottom shelf full of video cassettes of movies from two decades before.

He inspected the remainder of the building, but there was nothing more of note that he could see. The freezer and refrigerator were full of food, and there was a cabinet filled with snacks. He glimpsed his immediate future, and it looked like an evening of stove-top popcorn and *The Breakfast Club.* When he considered what had happened the previous night, that seemed like an upgrade. He sighed and resigned himself to being there, and went into the back room the check out the beds. They were thin mattresses on a spring frame, barely enough to support him. He hoped the previous ranch hands weren't much bigger than he was, or they might have been resting on the floor.

He walked back into the main room and took one look around before going to the fridge and pulling out a beer. He flopped down on the couch and opened the beer, and took a long swig. He looked at the bottle and realized it was a beer he had never heard of before, and it tasted odd to him. He looked in the refrigerator for another brand, but that was all there was. He downed the rest of the beer and grabbed a lemon-lime flavored soda, and went back to the couch. He turned the television on and realized there was no reception on any channel, and he knew why the videos were there. He found a copy of Goodfellas and popped it into the VCR. After about twenty minutes, the beer kicked in, and he had to go to the bathroom. He decided that he wasn't going to go into the sink as Utter had suggested.

He turned off the lights and the television and opened the front door a crack. He didn't see anyone outside, especially not in a red truck with a black door, so it seemed safe enough to him. He walked around the side of the building towards the outhouse, but when he got close to it, he realized why Utter would steer him away from it. It smelled horrible, but the part of it that really got Will was that the roof was caving in. He pictured himself underneath a pile of outhouse rubble, stuck, and not able to get away from the stench. He leaned his hand up against the outside of the barn and relieved himself.

He completed the task and headed back to the door. As he turned the corner, he felt an arm go around his neck from behind. His first instinct was to fight off the attack, but he felt the cool pressure of a gun at his side.

"Move," his assailant said, and forced Will back around the side of the building.

"Something I can help you with?" Will grunted, and they moved towards the back of the property and a large stack of bales of hay.

"I'm helping myself, Deputy. The same way I helped myself to that cash you had in your bottom drawer. You cost me money, you jackass, but now we're square. Well, we will be here in a few shakes. I'm getting you and the Brindle sheriff off my back so I can do my business in peace. You should have left well enough alone. Now, you're going to die." Will couldn't be sure, but he assumed that this had something to do with the All Blues Man case. The man pushed Will down and into the bales of hay. He pulled a heavy-duty zip-tie and tried to wrap Will's hands together. Will fought against it, but the man slammed the butt of the gun against Will's forehead, opening a cut, and rendering him helpless. The zip-tie went on with no issues this time, and the man put one around Will's feet as well.

This was not how Will imagined his life would end. He thought someone would catch him and he'd finish off his life in prison, because someone would certainly kill him there. In New York, he was always scared of getting hit by a bus or a taxi when he crossed the street. But even when he was going through deputy training, and even the previous night when his trailer was getting shot to pieces, he never really thought about getting shot. However, this seemed to be the end of his road.

"Who are you?" Will asked, his head pounding from the butt of the gun.

"Doesn't matter, Lomax. You're not going to be around to tell anyone. But lemme tell you that you stirred this pot the first time you took my weed off the street from those kids. And then you arrest my distributor and make me kill him to keep him quiet. And then...and then you killed my brother last night! We had something going, he and I, and you've made it your job to screw it up! Now, I'm not a dangerous man on a normal day, Lomax, but you're pissing me off. So, I hate to spoil your night, partner," the man said. "But you're gettin' to be a bee in my bonnet." He dragged Will to his feet.

"Well, I tend to do that when someone attacks the hive," Will said, standing up straight.

"Hmm, well, it's time for a little busy bee to get squashed." The man backed up a few steps to point the gun at Will's face. "This ain't the first time I've had to do this," he said. "You scared?"

"I don't want to disappoint you," Will said. "But this is not my first time either."

"It's gonna be your last, Deputy." He pulled the hammer back on the gun, and it made a dramatic click. "This one's for my brother. So long, sucker."

The gunshot rang out and echoed in the hills and off the side of the barn. Will felt no pain. He checked himself for holes and blood again, but only found what was on his forehead already. Then he looked at his aggressor, who had a blank look on his face, and then dropped to his knees and fell forward onto his face. Will turned to his right to see Utter standing with Ogre. The smoke was coming from Ogre's gun.

Chapter 82 – Carry Out

"I'm sorry, Billy, to keep you in the dark, but we couldn't risk you knowing what was happening and still have it go according to our plan." Utter had an odd smile on his face, or at least Will thought it was a smile. It was hard to tell under the walrus mustache. "You did everything we needed you to do."

"I'm not sure I understand, Sheriff," Will said, wringing his wrists, trying to lessen the pain from the recently removed zipties.

"Billy, you were spot-on when you said we should bait the hook. We were doing that anyway, but I couldn't let you in on it. It might have blown the whole bust."

"Tell me what I'm missing, because I've got gaps and possible questions."

Utter smiled again. "The man you shot last night in the red pickup truck was Terrell Montgomery. He was the twin brother of the man who tried to kill you tonight, Darrell Montgomery. Cops in the state have seen the red truck before, but we didn't know where to find it or the person who owned it. The Montgomery boys have been wanted for several bank and liquor store robberies, and two murders in Russell and Alston, Kansas."

Ogre chimed in. "Billy, you took down one of the most wanted criminal brothers in the multi-state area, and helped us take down the other. You're a hero."

Will almost fell backward, but the wall of the barn held him up. His life had been a whirlwind for quite some time, but the last seventy-two hours were like a tornado. He had taken down a drug dealer, had the drug dealer killed, been nearly shot on two occasions, and taken down two wanted criminals. *Who are you, Billy Jack, and what the hell are you doing?* He pulled himself away from the wall and gave Ogre a dismissive look.

"I'm no hero," Will said angrily, and began to walk toward the front of the barn. "Sheriff, can we get out of here, please?"

Utter exhaled under his mustache, and it blew in a forward direction. "Sure. Get your gear." Will entered the door of the barn, walked to the bunk area, and grabbed his bag, slinging it over his shoulder as he walked. He turned off the light in the barn as he left and closed the door behind him. Utter was waiting in the car, and Will climbed into the back seat. He said nothing for most of the ride. "Talk to me, Billy. What's on your mind?"

"Nothing," Will said.

"Horseshit. You're pissed. About what, not including you in the plan? I told you, Billy..." Utter's words trailed off, and Will began to think about his journey to where he was today. From his unhappiness at home with Kathleen, to his plan to escape, his coward's way out. He thought about his planned day of escape and the terrible things that happened that day. He flashed back to his cab rides, and then his bus trip, and then his car rides across the country. His landing in Seattle and his eventual exit. His trip back to Brindle, and eventually that path he took to become a Sheriff's Deputy, up to the events of the past few days. He knew he wanted to make a difference, and maybe he had as a deputy in Brindle. The truth was, he wasn't sure if he wanted to do it anymore. Maybe it was time for him to move on. *Move on,* he thought. *Move where? You don't know anyone anywhere and have very little money.* He shook his head and resigned himself to a life of servitude to the Brindle County Sheriff's Department. He began to get out of his own thoughts, and Utter's words were coming back to him.

"...why we had to do it that way. You have to understand that, Billy." Utter looked back at him as they stopped in front of the motel.

"I get it, W.T. I do. I guess if I had known about it, it could have gone down differently, but it turns out it all worked out in the end."

"I believe in you, Billy," Utter said. "You're the best new deputy I have had in a long time, maybe since Cortez first came here. You may be ahead of him, even, and I swear, he was born to be in law enforcement. Now go on. Get some rest."

"I will, thanks," Will said. He got out of the car and shut the door, and then knocked on the passenger side window. Utter rolled the window down less than halfway. "Hey," Will said. "Uh, W.T., you think I can get another car to borrow tomorrow?"

"No, sir," Utter said. "You've got tomorrow off. Get some rest." Utter drove away and left Will standing outside the office of the motel room. Will watched him go and then found the door to his room. He flopped back onto the bed and tried to sleep, but the only thing that he could think about was Darrell Montgomery and the rest of his stolen money. He wanted to find out where the Montgomery's lived, or lurked, as it may be, and he wanted to see if he could get his money back. He'd need a source, and he'd probably need a car. He thought about calling Edgar, the old man who actually brought him to Brindle in his car, but Will was sure Edgar would ask too many questions about where they were going or what they were doing.

The next day, he woke up and took a run around Brindle, and he felt great when he was done. Then, he took a swim in the motel pool. At around eleven-thirty, he got out and took a shower, and took a nice walk to the town library, which was shared with the high school. He walked in the front door of the library and over to where the computers were located. At that moment, he realized that he had not used the Internet since September 10, 2001, nearly ten months prior.

He sat down in front of the screen and typed on a website he used to use in New York to determine if his prospective clients were actually real. It was rare that he came across any that he could not find in the online phonebook. In fact, he had probably created more fake clients at his job than any other person had. He searched for Darrell Montgomery in the Brindle area but didn't find anything. Nothing for Terrell, either. He did just a search for any Montgomerys in the area as well, but the search returned no results. He remembered Utter or Ogre saying something about "multi-state area," so he widened his search.

There was a Darrell Montgomery listed in Goodland, Kansas, and three in Tulsa, Oklahoma. He did a search for Terrell, but only found a "T. J. Montgomery," and the address matched the one he found in Goodland, Kansas. It seemed as good a place as any to start. He left the library and began his walk back down to the Sheriff's Department to see if he could change Utter's mind about borrowing a car. He walked in the front door and found Ally at the front desk. She immediately began batting her eyes at him. He walked up, rested his elbow on the desk, and stood sideways.

"Hey, you," she said to him.

"Hey, yourself. What's going on?"

"Nothing," she said. "Just another boring day here in Brindle. It seems the only excitement that happens around here is whatever you're involved in," she said with a giggle.

"Yeah, well, that's not by design. I'd rather live the quieter life." He started to ask if Utter was in his office, but Ally cut him off.

"Quiet's nice," she said, and began to twirl her hair. "Speaking of quiet, what would you think of a nice quiet dinner, just you and me, someplace real dark and cozy? Some drinks, some food, some...adult conversation?" He stopped leaning on the counter and gave her a polite smile.

"Ally, I just got shot at the other night, and nearly killed last night. Nothing personal against you, but I'd like to keep things uncomplicated for a while." She looked disappointed, but quickly recovered.

"I'm not asking for complications, sweetie. I'm just offering dinner, and maybe...some dessert." She leaned forward on the counter, facing him so that her breasts nearly spilled out from the top of her shirt. He fought the urge to look and straightened his stance to be fully upright, so that he moved away from her without actually moving his feet to step back.

"Thanks, Ally, but not now. Is Utter in?" She huffed a little and sat back in her chair.

"Doubt it," she said, coldly. "Go look."

He nodded and walked around the corner and down the hall to Utter's office, but the sheriff was not in there. He took the shortcut through the briefing room to get to the side door so as to avoid interacting with Ally again. He came out of the side door and looked longingly at the extra cars from the motor pool that no one was using at the time. He was thinking that he might try borrowing Jim's car if his old employer would be willing to part with it for a while. He made his way on foot from the station to D&J Liquor and opened the door to find not Jim behind the counter, but his wife, Daria.

"Well, look at you, Wyatt Earp," she said. "Got any extra holes in you today?"

Will smiled at her. "Not that I'm aware of," he said.

"I guess that's a good thing. What can I do for you?" she asked.

"Is Jim around?"

"No," she said. "Day off."

"You're here alone?" Will asked.

"No, Joey Barleycorn is working here now that school's out. He does stock and cleaning for me."

"Why does that name sound familiar?" Will asked.

"You'll know it when football season starts again. He's the right tackle for the Pronghorns, and he's a monster blocker. Our quarterback only got sacked four times last year, and that's when the rush wasn't from Joey's side. Colleges are already looking at him, and he's only a sophomore this year. If he stays healthy, they are talking pro. We'll see."

"Let's hope he stays healthy. Alright, thanks," Will said. "Be careful, I'll see ya later." He left the liquor store and began his walk to Rocky's restaurant to see if he could use her car. Hopefully, she let him, especially when he told her why.

Will walked into the front door of the pizza restaurant, and immediately the smell of cooking dough and bubbling cheese filled his lungs, and it was glorious. He fought the urge to sit down and order and remained standing, waiting until he saw Rocky. It was only a few minutes before she walked out of the kitchen carrying a pizza to an awaiting table. On her way back, she stopped when she saw him.

"Hey, Deputy," she said.

"Hey, Rocky. You busy?"

"Not super-busy. I have some carry-out orders coming up. Is that why you're here?"

"No, I came to see you," Will said.

"Oh, there's the pick-up order from the department. Should be ready soon."

"Hey, can we talk for a few minutes?"

"Sure," she said. "Hold on a sec." She went to the back for a few minutes and then came back out with two soft drinks. "Come on over here to the quiet corner." She led him over to a table that was separated from the door by a partition. "Sit down. What's up?" The doorbell ding-donged in the background.

"Do you have to get that?"

"No, Sandy is back there. I told her I was taking a break. What's going on? You look worried."

He leaned forward and lowered his voice to almost a whisper. "Uh, not sure how it happened or when, but my money is gone."

"What do you mean?" she asked.

"The money that I stole when I was in New York. It's gone. Someone stole it from me."

"Do you know who?"

"Yeah, same jackass that shot at me the other night and tried to kill me yesterday."

"He's dead now, too, right?" she asked.

"Yeah, thanks to Utter and Ogre."

"So, what now?"

"I found out where they live. Well, lived. It's in Kansas. I want to go see if I can find anything there, at least maybe they didn't spend all of it. But I don't have a car. That's another reason I stopped by."

"You want to use my car? For what, to go on some wild goose chase for money that you stole and then someone stole from you?"

"Pretty much," he said. "If I can get out there today, I can be back in time tomorrow for my shift.

Listen, Rocky. I'm not planning to run anywhere anytime soon. But if I need to go, I need cash to do it, and I don't have a lot of it right now."

"What about what you draw as a deputy?" she asked.

"I haven't really been saving too much of that. You're an expensive date, girl," he said with a smile.

"You shit, it's not all me!" she said, and hit him with her towel.

"I know, I know... I'm just kidding. It would just make me feel better to know I had more if push came to shove."

"And if we get to shove, what about me?"

"I'll figure out a way to get back to you," he said. "No matter what."

"Mmm hmm," she said. She pulled out her keys from her apron pocket. "Go," she said. "Don't leave me with no gas."

"I promise," he said. "I'll have it back tomorrow. You're going to be okay getting around while I'm gone?"

"Yeah, Sandy can take me home and bring me back in tomorrow. No big deal. Now go, before I change my mind!"

"You're the best," he said, and stretched across the table to give her a soft kiss. The doorbell ding-donged again. "You'd better get back to work," he said. "More customers."

"Nope," she said. "Same customer that came in when we sat down just left. The chime came before the door opened, so it was someone leaving. Sandy must have taken forever to get whoever that was their order, so, yeah, I have to get back to work."

"Have a good shift and be careful," he said, and kissed her again.

Rocky was correct. The first and second chime on the doorbell was the same person. When Will went outside to find Rocky's car, he didn't notice, but Ally was also climbing into her car. She had come to pick up the carry-out order from the Sheriff's Department, and between those door chimes, she had heard almost everything Will and Rocky had said.

Chapter 83 – Grandpa Edgar

Greco awoke to a warm Saturday morning in June in Cheyenne. He showered and dressed, and grabbed a warm cup of coffee from the motel lobby before getting into his car to get out on the road. He had not gotten very far when a soft 'ding" rang out in the car, and he looked at the dashboard to find out that his gas tank was nearing empty. He looked at the road signs for help as to where to find a gas station to refill the car.

Greco drove along the roads following the signs with the gas pump icons until he reached a gas station with a convenience store attached. He parked at one of the pumps and filled his tank until the pump popped, indicating the tank was full. He decided to get a fresh coffee and a bottle of water, hoping the coffee was better than what he had gotten from the motel. He crossed the lot and went into the store, and found the coffee service in the back near the fountain soda machine. He grabbed a large cup, filled it, sweetened it and topped it with a lid, and took it to the front of the store. He was fifth in line.

A few minutes later, when he was third in line, he was looking out of the window of the store and saw a large bus out in the parking lot emptying passengers. It didn't occur to him to think about it until he was at the front of the line.

"Buck-thirty-nine," Teddy said. Greco dumped a dollar bill and two quarters on the counter and looked back out of the window.

"Where's that bus coming from?" he asked. "Any idea?"

"Prolly out west somewhere. This is a transfer spot from some of the big bus lines. They drop off an' pick up here." Greco stared out the window, watching people get onto the bus. They were all going somewhere, and they all came from somewhere. "Mister," Teddy said again. "Your change?" Greco took the change and dropped it into a dish next to the cash register with a picture of a sick child taped to it. He took out his badge and showed it to Teddy.

"I need to see your security tapes," Greco said.

For the next forty-five minutes, Greco waited as Teddy told his supervisor there was a cop from New York in the store wanting to watch videotapes, and then waited for the manager to arrive. For an hour and forty minutes after that, Greco watched as the manager of the store, a man named Winnie, short for Winston, operated the tape playback machine because he didn't trust Greco to work it. Greco finally hit paydirt when he watched Willi Kelly walk off a bus and into the store. Greco watched carefully and made a note of every step Kelly made, and everyone he talked to, including Teddy at the cash register. Then an elderly man sat at a table with some others, and he watched Kelly walk out of the store. *Another damned dead end*, Greco said to himself. *So close.*

"Do you have outdoor cameras?" he asked Winnie.

"Yeah, here." Winnie switched the screen over to the outside of the front of the building, but the camera was facing in the opposite direction from what Greco wanted to see.

"Can it zoom out?"

"Nope," Winnie said. It's just a recording."

"Wait, stop!" Greco nearly yelled. Winnie froze the picture. "Back it up," Greco said, and Winnie complied. In the lower corner of the video was the head of someone who Greco thought looked a lot like Will Kelly, wearing a Baltimore Ravens hat, but he was headed in the opposite direction this time. "Now, switch back inside," Greco said. At the table where there were once four men sitting, there were now three. The man Kelly had talked to inside the store was now gone. "Now back outside," Greco said. Winnie swapped the view again and looked at Greco, who didn't take his eyes off the screen. There was nothing for a minute, but then a car was moving across the parking lot, and Greco could see the older man through the side window, but the front windshield was glared by the sun. As the car continued to move, Greco watched carefully until he softly said, "Stop." Winnie stopped the tape again, and for perhaps one single perfect frame in the video, the glare moved aside, and in the passenger seat of the car, which was being driven by the older man, was Willem Kelly, in the black Ravens hat.

"Back up the tape for about two minutes," Greco said. "And show the inside of the store."

"Okay," Winnie exhaled, tired of the chase. He got to the part of the video that Greco wanted to see.

"Stop. I need to know who that man is, right there," Greco said, pointing at the screen. Winnie looked at him for a moment and then leaned back in the chair of the office and pushed the door open.

"Teddy," he yelled. "Get back here." A moment later, Teddy arrived at the office door.

"What's up?" he said. "I do something wrong?"

"Teddy," Greco said. "Do you know this man?" Greco was pointing at the screen.

"Yeah," Teddy said. "That's my Grandpa Edgar."

"I need to talk to him," Greco said.

"Can't," Teddy said. "He died two months ago." Greco winced.

"Listen, Teddy," Greco said. "The man I'm chasing, he was in this store last year, and your grandfather gave him a ride. Do you know anything about that?" Teddy nervously looked at Greco, and then Winnie, and back to Greco, but said nothing. "This is very serious, Teddy. If you know something and don't tell me, you can get in as much trouble as the man I'm after."

Winnie chimed in. "You'd better tell him if you know anything about it, Teddy."

"I used to h-help my grandfather earn e-extra cash," Teddy stammered. "I'd let him sit in the store and pick up random people off the buses that needed rides. We'd split the money. We thought it would be a lot of extra money, but there really weren't that many people coming off the buses with no plans of where to go."

"Do you know where he took this man?" Greco asked, holding up the picture of Will. Teddy shrugged and just said one word.

"Brindle."

"Where's Brindle?" Greco asked, forcefully.

Winnie spoke up. "Maybe less than an hour or so down the road. Maybe a little more. "Here." Winnie reached behind him and grabbed a folding map. He opened it up and showed Greco where Brindle was in relation to Cheyenne.

"Anything else you can tell me?" Greco asked.

"He tipped my grandfather extra," Teddy said.

Greco exited the store and got into his car, which he had forgotten was still at the gas pump the whole time he was inside. He cared not about it, nor the angry glances from others waiting in line behind him. He started the car and headed in the direction of Brindle, based on the map that he saw. He was almost excited, or maybe he was nervous. Assuming he did find Willem Kelly, how would Kelly react? Was he dangerous? Would there be a confrontation? A last attempt at freedom? All of these thoughts weighed on his mind as he made the trip.

Chapter 84 – Self-Investigation

Will guided Rocky's little red Honda across the three state lines to get to where he needed to go. He crossed out of Nebraska and into Colorado, and then out of Colorado and back into Nebraska, and then back out of Nebraska and into Kansas. He stopped every two hours or so to fill up the gas tank, because that was one thing that Rocky had warned him about. The needle on the gas tank indicator always said it was half-full. He didn't want to take any chances, but all the stops were slowing him down. He was bored with the road and tired of looking at lines speeding by him on the blacktop below and beside him. *Miles,* he thought. *More miles.* It got him thinking as he was driving, if he thought about it, he could probably hit pretty close to the bullseye if he had to guess how many miles he had traveled on the road since his escape from New York.

He left New York and went to Jersey by cab, and then from Jersey to Indianapolis on a bus. Traveled around Indy in a cab, then bought the cab and drove to Seattle. Then from Seattle, it was a bus ride to Cheyenne, and then an odd car ride with an old man to Brindle. Now, here he was on the road again, traveling from Nebraska to Kansas by way of Colorado. He was tired of the road and was thinking that, if he were lucky enough, he could stay in Brindle for the rest of his days. Just him, Rocky, Kat, a career as a deputy, and a great pizza restaurant. It sounded too good to him.

The afternoon sun welcomed him to Kansas, and it was about another hour to Goodland. Again, the trip seemed to drag on, and he wondered about the wisdom of taking such a trip, especially since he had to get back home to work his shift tomorrow evening. Still, he ventured on. He told himself he had to know, and if there was a chance that the money was still in the Montgomery's house, he had to look.

He traveled the main highway through Goodland and then turned off onto Rt 21, heading south. The road crossed a set of railroad tracks, and he turned left onto Rt. 64, and followed that out of the main part of the town and into where there was nothing but farmland as far as their eyes could see. He kept going until the addresses started to make sense to him, and he finally found what he was looking for. Route 1-A was a dirt road that was a left turn off of 64, and it wound through some farmland until it dead-ended into a small bank of trees, which surrounded a mobile home. The tires on the home were flat, and it did not appear to be mobile any longer. Will decided he shouldn't judge. His place wasn't much better right now. He would ask Rocky if he could stay with her for a while, just to see if it worked in the short term. Then, maybe for the long term.

Will parked the car and got out slowly. The place appeared to be deserted, but he didn't want to take any chances. He wished he could have brought his gun. Someone might be hiding somewhere with a shotgun. He snuck around the back of the structure and neither saw nor heard anything from inside or outside. Then he heard a snapping sound, but it was himself, stepping on a twig from one of the dying trees.

He put his heart back in his chest and moved around to the front of the building, making sure to watch his step as he moved forward. He climbed the rickety and rotting steps to the door of the trailer, and immediately smelled something terrible, but he didn't know what it was. He knocked lightly on the door at first, and then a little harder when no one answered. Finally, he placed three heavy knuckle raps on the door. If there was anyone home who wasn't legally deaf, they would have heard it.

He looked around his location, but there was nothing else to see anywhere, and there was no one around to see him, either. He put his hand on the doorknob, and slowly turned, and to his surprise, it kept turning, and finally released the bolt that was holding it closed. The door opened, and another nasty whiff of whatever was in the house came out of the house to meet him at the front door. He opened the door a little more and peeked inside, and still saw no one. He left the door open as he entered in hopes of letting the place air out. The smell was wretched rot and putrescence, and he could hardly stomach it. He walked into the kitchen area and looked around, but saw nothing of note. He opened drawers and cabinets, cupboards, and closets, but found nothing.

Apparently, the Montgomery boys didn't hide anything in their kitchen.

He walked through the living area of the trailer and found two recliners, nearly ripped to shreds and down to the foam padding. There was a television with no screen against a wall, and a radio against another. There were lights, but none of them worked, and Will doubted there was any electricity for quite some time. The smell was getting worse.

The living area led to a narrow hallway down the right side of the trailer. There was a small bedroom on the left, which Will searched thoroughly and found nothing. He even looked under the bed, which he regretted when he found a pair of dirty underwear. The drawers were empty, and there was nothing in the closet. He continued down the hallway to what appeared to be another bedroom, but on the left, there was a bathroom. That was the origin of the stench, he believed.

He pushed the bathroom door open and almost vomited at what he saw. Lying in the bathtub, which was full of some liquid, was a dead deer. It appeared to have been gutted and then placed into the bathtub. There were empty bags of ice laying all over the floor. Will guessed this was how the Montgomery brothers kept their kill meat cold until they could eat it. This time, however, no one was left to add more ice. Will's lucky shot and Ogre's calculated one made sure of that. Will stepped out of the bathroom with one room left to check.

"What are you doing in here, Billy?"

Will froze. It was Utter's voice behind him.

"Uh, Sheriff," Will stammered. "What, uh, what are you doing here?"

"I followed you," Utter said. "Now, what are you doing here?" Will tried to think quickly for an excuse, but was coming up empty. "What would make you drive hundreds of miles to break into the home of two men who tried to kill you?"

Will just stood there, saying nothing. He had nothing to say, really. He wondered what Utter knew. He stood there, staring at Utter, and slightly shrugged his shoulders. "I don't know. I guess I just wanted to know more about what's behind all of this."

"Billy," Utter exhaled under the poof of mustache. "I hope we don't have a problem. I gave you that badge, and you said you'd honor it. I'm not sure that's what you're doing right now. To honor that badge, you have to follow the orders of your superiors, namely me. When I tell you to take time off, you take that time off. It's for your own good."

"I'm... I'm sorry, Sheriff. I'm not sure what I was thinking," Will said.

"Oh, I know what you were thinking. You decide to come up here and start your own... Dammit, what is that smell? Let's go outside." The two men left the trailer, and all Will could think of was how unlucky he had been that Utter had followed him and he wouldn't be able to get the money if there was any, and how lucky he was that he didn't find it and have Utter catch him with it. Utter sat on the step and looked up at Will, who was standing just a few feet in front of him. "Billy, you can't go off on some half-cocked self-investigation. If there was anyone here, you'd probably be dead. You came here with no weapon and no backup. You have to be smarter than that. You could probably be sheriff of this town, one day, Billy, if you live long enough. Remember when I said, 'You are Brindle?'"

"Yes, sir," Will said.

"I meant it. You need to get the Philadelphia out of you and get the Brindle in you. Do you get what I'm saying?"

"Yes, sir. I think I do," Will said. And he meant it. The events of the day had made his decision for him. He would stay in Brindle as long as he could.

"Good. Now go home, Billy. And tell your girlfriend to get her gas gauge fixed. It's hard as hell to tail somebody when they stop every two hours for gas and piss breaks."

"I'll do that, Sheriff. What about you? Are you coming?"

"Well, you dragged me out here. I'm going to call some local boys, and we might as well start digging around in here to see what we can find."

"Understood, sir," Will said. "I'm sorry I let you down."

"Billy, you're doing all the right things, you're just doing some of them the wrong way. Now go home. You have to work tomorrow."

"You got it. W.T.," Will said with a smile, and he got into Rocky's car and drove back to Brindle that night.

Chapter 85 – It's Over

Greco pulled into Brindle around seven o'clock in the evening and decided to look around to see what he could find. His first goal was to engage the local police to see if they knew they had a fugitive living in their town, assuming he was still there. He looked around the town, driving up and down the streets until he found the Sheriff's Department. He parked the rental car out front and looked at it as he walked away. He couldn't imagine what the bill from the rental car company was going to be like.

He walked up the steps to the front door of the Sheriff's Department. He noticed the name of Wesley Timothy Utter, identified as the sheriff, written in gold lettering on the door. He opened it and went inside. He was met by a young, attractive girl who was working at a counter in front of the office. She was on the phone with someone and was twirling her hair as she talked, something of which Greco was never a fan. He waited patiently as she talked on the phone, but she continuously made eye contact with Greco, smiling as cutely as possible. Greco didn't bite. He stood there waiting politely, expressionless. Finally, she hung up the phone, turned away from the front of the desk, and grabbed a piece of paper from a rack. She wrote down a few words and circled some things, and then finally turned back towards Greco.

"Can I help you, sugar?" she asked.

"I need to speak with Sheriff Utter," Greco said. "Is he in?"

"Not right now, sweetie, but he should be back later tonight. He's on the road doing an investigation of some sort." Greco grumbled under his breath at this news.

"Okay," he said. "I will try again later. Do you know where I can get something to eat in the meantime?"

A few minutes later, Greco was back on the roads of Brindle, keeping an eye open for the mysterious and elusive Mr. Willem Kelly, but he never saw him. He passed a nasty-looking bar called the Rusty Rails, which must have been so bad that there was a Sheriff's Deputy's car parked in the lot, presumably as a deterrent for nefarious activities. Greco was surprised that Ally, the girl at the Sheriff's Department, would recommend such a place to a visitor. He passed the Hungry Horse restaurant and decided against it as well. It looked better than the Rusty Rails, but a Hungry Horse wasn't exactly appetizing. He finally found Ally's last recommendation and pulled into the parking lot. He looked at the sign, and it made him think of New York. *Rocky's Pizza Oven*, he thought. *It even sounds like New York*. He parked the car and headed into the restaurant, with the door ding-donging as he entered.

"Can I help ya, hon?" A woman with blonde hair and too much eye makeup greeted him at the door.

"Table for one, please?"

"Sure, follow me," she said. He followed her through the restaurant to a table next to a window looking towards the west, and the sunset he was seeing was beautiful. It was a few minutes before another woman named Jodi stopped at his table.

"Hey there," she said. "Something to drink?"

"Iced Tea? Unsweetened?"

"You got it," she said. "Be right back." She walked away, and Greco began to look around the restaurant. It was about half full, and he wondered if a place this big in a town this small ever was completely full. It didn't seem like much to look at, with the booths and tables all covered in classic pizza restaurant tablecloths and drinks served in the same translucent red cups that most pizza places in New York used. Jodi returned with his unsweetened iced tea and placed it on the table.

"What can I get for ya?" she asked.

"Uhh, let's see," he said. He had forgotten to look at the menu while she was gone. "How about a small meatball, mushroom, and extra cheese?"

"Stuff the crust?"

"Sure," Greco said. He thought, no matter what, he was probably headed home soon anyway, so he might as well splurge.

"You got it. Be about ten minutes." Jodi took his menu and walked away. Greco began to focus on why he was there. If this restaurant was half-full in a town this small, maybe Kelly was here. He looked at his hands and decided they might need a wash before eating with his hands. He got up and located the sign for the restroom, and pointed his body in that direction. He began to walk, but kept his head on a swivel, checking every male face he could find. He took care of his business and decided to travel back to his seat via the longer way around the restaurant. He looked at every face again, but Will Kelly was nowhere to be found. Dejected, he sat back down at his table and began to drink his iced tea. A few minutes later, Jodi came out carrying his pizza on one hand, placing it on an elevated rack in the middle of the table.

"Here you go, dear," she said. "Anything else?"

"Yeah," he said, and reached for his picture of Will Kelly. "Have you seen this man around?"

"Here?" she asked.

"Anywhere," he said.

"Umm, I'm kinda new here, so I don't know too many people. Let me get the manager for you." Jodi turned and went towards the kitchen. Greco waited a few minutes and then decided to get into his pizza. He grabbed a slice and bit into the point, and was instantly transported back home. *How in the hell*, he thought, *did they manage to capture almost, if not exactly, a classic New York pizza?* Even the slices were big, and he couldn't help folding them. After another slice, a woman came out to his table.

"Hi, I'm Rocky. This is my place. How can I help you?" She asked.

"Mmm," he said, swallowing his bite prematurely. "Hi, Rocky. First of all, this pizza is fantastic. Reminds me of home."

"Oh yeah," she said. "Where's home?"

"New York." Rocky's head turned a little sideways when he said this.

"You're a ways from home," she said. "What brings you to Brindle?"

"That's what I wanted to talk to you about." He pulled out his badge, and she stiffened. "My name is Detective Brian Greco from the NYPD. I was wondering if you might be able to help me."

Inside her heart, Rocky felt that she knew what was coming. "What's that?" she asked.

Greco showed her the picture of Will. He didn't look exactly the same, but she could tell it was him. Have you seen this man around Brindle?" Greco asked. She looked at him, and then at the picture of Will. She cocked her head sideways at the picture again.

"Detective," she said, "I see a lot of repeat customers in here, so I know a lot of people from the town, but we also get a lot of people who just pass through and stop for good pizza. With all the new faces I see, I'm not sure I'm the best person to ask. What makes you think this person came through Brindle?"

"My ongoing investigation. That's really all I can say about it, but I've followed his trail up to here, in Brindle. If you haven't seen him, I'm guessing he didn't hang around, or he doesn't like pizza. So, you're sure you haven't seen him?"

"Hmm," she said, looking at the picture again. She shrugged and gave the slightest indication of a head turn. "Hmm," she said again. "Excuse me, Detective, I have to get back to work now. Good luck finding your guy. Probably, he moved on somewhere else. Try Cheyenne, or Denver?"

With that, she walked away, calmly at first, but when she got through the kitchen door, she increased her pace and looked around, and finally found Jodi in the storeroom grabbing a package of napkins.

"Jodi," Rocky said, trying to sound as calm as possible. "The guy, th-the cop, the detective..."

"Who?" Jodi asked.

"Ugh, table 21!"

"Oh yeah, the meatball mushrooms extra cheese stuffed crust. What about him?"

Rocky stammered. "He, uh, he's good for now. He doesn't need anything for a while. He said to just check on him in about fifteen to twenty minutes."

"Sure," Jodi said.

"Thanks, Jodi." Rocky went to her office and grabbed her cell phone. She dialed Will's number and waited as it rang five times before the voicemail picked up. She waited for the voicemail to end and began to speak. "Billy, it's over! Get out of here now! They found you. A Detective from New York is here, in Brindle, and he's looking for you. Take my car, get out now. Find me later if you can. Go to Cheyenne and get on a bus or something! I know you're at the Rusty Rails, so I'll be headed over as soon as I can get out of here. I love you."

Meanwhile, Greco had checked the hotel at the highway crossing, but it was closed for renovations. He was tired, annoyed, and disheartened. All this time. All this way. All this work. He was pretty sure he was getting called back to the office soon, and all of this would be for nothing. He spied a liquor store just up the road and made the turn into the parking lot. He wasn't looking forward to sleeping in the car that night, but a six-pack of beer would make it nearly tolerable. He walked into the liquor store and back to the refrigerated section. He pulled out a six-pack of beer and put the cool cans to his head, and felt instant relief. He took the cans up to the front of the store and put them on the counter near the cash register.

"Anything else?" Jim asked.

"I don't think so," Greco said. "Is it always this quiet around here on a Saturday night?"

"No, sometimes it gets kinda rowdy, but nothing too crazy."

"I have to be here probably at least until tomorrow. Is there a motel around here that might have a vacancy?" Greco asked.

"Sure. You can check the Motel Brindle right out on the main road. They usually have some rooms except when the fair is in town."

"Is the fair in town?" Greco asked.

"Nope."

"Thanks. Have you been working here for a long time?" Greco asked.

"I'd say so," Jim said. "Yeah, for a while."

"How long?"

"As long as we've been here. Nine years. I'm the 'J' in 'D&J'."

"Oh, maybe you can help me then." Greco showed his badge and extracted a picture of Will from his coat, and showed them both to Jim. "Do you know this man?"

Jim looked at the picture for a second. "Oh, yeah," he said.

"Where?" Greco asked.

"Here in town, for a few months. That's Billy. Deputy Lomax."

"Deputy Lomax?"

"Yeah," Jim said. "Billy. Good dude. He's only been here, like I said, for a couple of months, but has done some great things. He used to work here."

"Do you know where I can find him?"

"Well, he works nights, and he's probably out on the road right now. But on Saturday night, I'd bet he's trying to keep the peace over near the Rusty Rails."

"Great," Greco said. "That's that rough-looking joint, right? I think I saw it on my way into town."

"Right down the road here, a mile or two, just across the railroad tracks."

"Thanks," Greco said.

"Everything alright?" Jim asked.

Greco smiled. "It is now. I don't need this. Keep the cash, thanks for your help!" He left the beer on the counter, exited the liquor store, and got into his car, aiming it in the direction

Jim had pointed. He cruised along slowly until he saw some lights in the distance. He slowed even more and stopped just on the near side of the tracks. He looked across the parking lot of the bar but didn't see anyone matching Will Kelly's description. Then he looked to the left, and across a dirt road just over the railroad tracks, he saw a patrol car he had spotted earlier, and someone leaning against the door. Greco took out his binoculars and adjusted the eye pieces, doing an awkward scan of the area until he found the car in his sights again. He zoomed in on the man standing next to the car. Greco slowly pulled the binoculars away from his face, revealing a mouth agape. He couldn't believe it. It was Willem Kelly.

Greco removed his mobile phone from his pocket and dialed four-one-one. He sank lower into the car to keep his eye on Will but not be seen. "I need the number for Brindle, Nebraska Sheriff's Department," he said. Will seemingly was not going anywhere at the moment and was content to lean on his patrol car outside of the bar. When his call was connected, he was given the dispatch office. "I need either the Sheriff, or... or whoever ranks highest on duty. My name is Detective Brian Greco, and I am with the NYPD." A few minutes passed, and Greco never took his eyes off Will.

"*Sheriff's Department, Deputy Cortez,*" came Juan's voice over Greco's phone.

"Deputy Cortez, my name is Detective Brian Greco from the NYPD. I need you to listen to me."

Chapter 86 – The Showdown

Will watched for most of the evening as patrons went inside the Rusty Rails and then back out again, some there to kickstart their Saturday night drinking, and some for food. He was beginning to have more suspicions about the place, though. Often, people would walk in the door, and walk back out around five minutes later, and be on their way to wherever they were going. Will could understand that maybe a few people went in for a quick shot and a drink, maybe, but it seemed too many people in and out that quickly. He was wondering if there might be a new drug dealer in Brindle, filling the gap left by the demise of the Brothers Montgomery. He made notes in his pad, and over the next few days, would compare the notes and see if there were any patterns developing by the same people. He would speak with Utter about it tomorrow in the briefing room and get his thoughts on the idea. He folded up the notepad, put it back in his back pocket, and leaned back against the car to survey the comings and goings of others. Other than the increased foot traffic, it seems like an unusually quiet night that the Rails, he thought.

"Deputy Lomax."

Will turned around to see Greco standing next to his car on the other side of the railroad track. He had never seen the man before, not that he could remember, and certainly not around Brindle. "Yes, how can I help you?" Will asked.

"You can put your hands in the air, you son of a bitch." It came from behind Will, and he knew the voice immediately. He also figured out what was happening, and it wasn't a good thing. At this point, he decided running was not an option. They had him.

"Juan," Will said. "What brings you out of the station on a night like this?"

"You know why I'm here, you lying, backstabbing thief. I knew you were trouble the first moment I met you!"

"Aww, Cortez, that's why I love you. You have all the right things to say at the right times. But, with all due respect, you didn't know shit. You praised my work constantly and called me by endearing terms."

"Fu—" Cortez started, but was cut off by Greco.

"Easy, gentlemen. Let's not let this get out of hand. Willem Kelly, my name is Detective Brian Greco, NYPD, and you're under arrest. I need you to remove your sidearm, slowly, and lay it on the ground. Deputy Cortez, I've got this. Please holster your weapon."

Will turned and saw Cortez behind him. Now Utter was standing there as well. "Hi, Sheriff," Will said in a greeting.

"Billy, help me out, here. What's going on?" Utter said, hands on his hips.

"Long story, Sheriff," Will said. "But in short, back in New York, I stole a bunch of money from some places that really didn't need it that much, but somebody found out, and I had to bolt. Apparently Detective Greco, here, figured it out. Here we are."

"I see," Utter said, his face falling.

"And I'm awfully sorry to disappoint you," Will said. "You asked me when we first met and several times after that if there was something you needed to know about me. Every answer I gave you to those questions was true. But this is what I guess you needed to know. I did some not-so-legal things and I just happened to land here in your town."

"Enough! Drop the weapon, Kelly!" Cortez yelled and pulled back the hammer on his gun.

"Easy, Deputy," Will said. "Wait your turn. The Sheriff and I are chatting. Don't be rude."

Greco was taking in the full scene and was slightly amused by Will's relaxed state of mind and calm demeanor. A train whistle wailing in the distance only added to the drama. Greco knew it was time to take control of the situation. "Mr. Kelly, lower the gun to the ground, slowly, and walk back towards me."

Will ignored Greco's request. "How did Cortez find out, Sheriff?"

Utter harumphed. "Ally told us. She said she heard you and Rocky talking yesterday when she picked up the lunch order. She was spitting venom. Sounded like she had a grudge against you."

"Well, I wouldn't go out with her."

"Well, that would do it," Utter said. "'Hell hath no fury,' I guess."

"Tell her I said 'goodbye. Truthfully, Sheriff, this was the best job I ever had, and I'm sorry to lose it. When I left Seattle, I knew I wanted to do something that would really make a difference. I think I did that here, and my past aside, I want to thank you for that opportunity." Will took a breath. "For what it's worth, I think you should check out the Rusty Rails. I think we–, well, uh, you have another drug supplier in Brindle."

Utter chuckled. "I always liked you, Billy," he said. "You turned out to be a real good deputy." Then he turned to Cortez. "This is out of our jurisdiction, Juan. Let's leave this to the Detective. He's got a handle on it. Let's go."

"Sheriff!" Cortez yelled. "He's been portraying himself as a Deputy. That's a crime, and it's in our county!"

"No, Juan, he didn't," Utter said. "He was a real Deputy." He turned to look at Greco. "And a good one," he said, shaking his head. "No matter what he did before he put it on, he honored the badge afterwards. Let's go, Juan." Cortez looked like he could spit fire and glared at Will, who only looked at his former co-workers. Will watched them go and then lowered his head, and then turned back to Greco and lifted it.

"Now, uh, excuse me, Detective, was it?" Will asked.

"That's right."

Will nodded. "And you're here to arrest me?"

"Also correct. Time to pay up. You used a tragedy that cost me my partner to cover your tracks and make an escape. I couldn't let it go after that."

Will met Greco's eyes when he spoke of Steve Angelucci, and then shook his head. "Your partner was killed in the nine-eleven attacks?"

"Yeah, and he was a good man," Greco said. Will nodded slightly, exhaled heavily, and contorted one side of his mouth in disgust and sympathy.

"I'm sorry," Will said. The two men then stood in silence for a moment. Listening to the train whistle in the background.

"I don't have the money anymore," Will finally said. "I lost it in a fire in Seattle after I left New York."

Greco put his hand on his hip, looked at the ground, and then back up at Will. The house fire, Greco thought. Then, cocking his head to the side, he said, "I don't care. That's not my concern. My place is to bring you back. I know about the fire. It's part of what helped me actually track you down."

"Hmm," Will said. "I bet that's some kind of a story."

"It is that. Now, enough chatter. Take off your sidearm and drop it."

"I'd love to hear it someday."

"Come with me quietly and I'll tell you all about it," Greco said, tensing.

Will had his hand near his holster on his own hip. "Well, you followed me across the country and halfway back, made it to Brindle somehow, and here we are, I guess," he said, looking at the mountains in the distance, and the desert at his feet. He used his other arm to gesture at what he was seeing. The sun had set, but there was still residual light in the sky. In the distance, the train wailed again.

Greco looked around as Will motioned. "Yeah," he said. "Here we are," and cast a wary eye at Will, not sure what to think of his foe.

"After all this time, and" he paused, "and after all these miles, you tracked me down, Detective Greco. How does it feel?"

"It feels the same as it does any other day when I get to bring someone in and hopefully to justice. This is just further away." They stood with the railroad tracks between them, about twenty feet apart. He looked at Will in his Deputy's uniform, and a thousand questions ran through his head. But he decided and hoped he would be able to ask them later.

Instead, he volleyed Will's question back at him. "How do you feel?"

"How do I feel?" Will asked and let out a small chuckle. He put his hands on the front of the car and popped himself up to a sitting position on the hood with his feet danglin below. Greco flinched ever so slightly, but remained calm, and then relaxed. "I'd feel a whole lot better if you were in your car five hundred miles away and headed in the wrong direction." The distant train was getting closer. "I actually feel pretty good. I spent a long time running, and now that I know it's over, I think I can relax a little." The two stood in silence, taking in what Will had said, and both were unsure of the next move. "I really am sorry about your partner," Will finally said, his tone serious and sympathetic. "I'm guessing if it was the two of you working together, you would have found me a lot sooner. Two heads being better than one, and all." The light from the front of the train began to illuminate the track as it got closer and closer. It would soon bisect the two men, yet neither was certain what would happen before or after it passed.

Greco studied his adversary, not knowing which direction this altercation was going to take. He then looked at the ground. "Probably," he said, his volume increasing to adjust for the noise of the train. "He helped me on your case from the hospital bed until he died. He was a true cop."

Will looked around and then spoke. "Indeed, sir. Indeed," he said, hand coming off of his sidearm, and he crossed his arms in front of him. The move made Greco tense up again for just a second. He was giving Will a lot of leeway in this exchange. Probably more than he had ever given anyone else in this type of circumstance. He had been in standoff situations before, but had no idea if Will had been in one, nor how he would react to being in one. For Greco, most were like a cornered animal, with few options left. "Beautiful night," Will said, looking at the million pinpoints of light in the sky. He recited:

"When the radiant morn of creation broke,

And the world in the smile of God awoke,

And the empty realms of darkness and death

Were moved through their depths by his mighty breath,

Greco interrupted:

"And orbs of beauty and spheres of flame

From the void abyss by myriads came,—

In the joy of youth as they darted away,

Through the widening wastes of space to play."

Will joined in. *"Their silver voices in chorus rung,*

And this was the song the bright ones sung."

Will looked on in wonderment, and when Greco had finished, he turned back to the sky and quietly said, "William Cullen Bryant. You're a fan?"

"Not really," Greco said, checking the sky as well. "I don't get into too much poetry. But you had the book on the shelf in your old house, and I remembered it from that."

"You memorized a poetry book? That's industrious of you," Will said.

Greco nodded and smiled. "It made for good reading during the chase. Now, you gotta come with me, Kelly," Greco yelled. "I can't go home until you do. And I'm really ready to go home. I'm tired."

"Hmm," Will said. "I guess," and he stood up from the hood of the car, and his hands went back to his hips. At that moment, the train was upon them, blinding and loud and dirty. It passed in between them, and Greco cursed himself for not moving faster to apprehend Will before the train arrived. He was trying to look between and under the cars, but the train kicked up so much dust that he couldn't see under it, and it was moving too fast to see between the cars. The noise was deafening, and finally, Greco backed away.

The train kept going, and after another sixty seconds or so, Greco could see the end of it approaching. He hopped into his car and counted the seconds painfully as it passed, anxious to know if he'd be able to track Will's patrol car from the scene if he fled. The last car finally passed, and as Greco peered through the settling dust, he could still see the patrol car. Will was about ten feet back from where he previously stood, and he leaned against the side of the car with his hat down over his eyes, chin to his chest. Greco, though he looked like one of those wooden silhouettes of the cowboy that people put up at their houses. He stepped out of the car and cautiously approached the tracks and crossed them this time.

"I should have warned you about the dust," Will said. "Sorry about that."

Greco took a few steps closer. "You didn't run," he said, waving his hand in front of his face to try to dissipate the dust in the air.

"I'm tired of running. I've been on the run since nine-eleven. The day before, practically. Maybe even three months before, when I hatched this genius plan. I'm tired of lying about who I am." He turned his head to see that Rocky was standing there. "Rocky, I'm sorry that this has caught up to me, and that you're involved. You deserve better than that. I'm so sorry. I love you. Please take care of Kat for me?"

"Oh, Billy," she sobbed, shaking her head. "I tried to get to you." And then she nodded. "I will. And I love you, too!"

Greco looked over at Rocky with a stern look on his face. She'd lied to him, and if she could have gotten to Will, Greco was sure that he would have disappeared into the wind with her. But he also understood why she lied to him. "As I was saying," he said, "you have to take your fall for this. I need you to remove and put down your sidearm."

Will looked around. The train tracks. The dusty air. The bad guy. The good guy. The woman. The scenery. The showdown. He thought it looked like a scene from an old western film he had seen on late-night television. Or maybe it was a Johnny Cash song. Or a poem he had read somewhere. Maybe, he thought, it's a combination of all of them, and he'd found it in Brindle.

"Well," Will said, breaking the silence. "Are you ready?" he asked.

Greco tensed. "Ready for what, Kelly?" the detective asked.

Will's hand went to his sidearm again. "Let's go!" he said, and Rocky let out a gasp.

Chapter 87 – Sold Out

Greco spoke a few words to the Emergency Medical Technician and watched him shut the rear door of the ambulance, and then climb into the side door of the vehicle and shut the door behind him. He watched the ambulance drive away, lights still flashing, kicking up rocks and dust from the dirt road as it began to disappear in the distance. It rounded a corner and was gone. Greco had his hands on his hips, and then they fell to his side, almost lifeless. He was tired, and this eventful evening did nothing but make it worse. He felt like his breathing was labored, but it was not. He was just exhausted.

He crossed back over the railroad tracks and slid into his car, and then started the ignition and turned on the windshield wipers to clear the dust from his view. It reminded him of September 11 all over again. On that day when Sergeant Harding finally told him he had done enough and ordered him to go home, Greco had turned on the wipers in his car to clear his view for a very long ride home. Now he was staring another long ride home right in the face, and he wasn't ready for it. He needed to sleep. But he closed his door and put the vehicle in drive, and headed towards the edge of town to jump onto the highway. The trip would be over fifteen hundred miles, and that was by air. He had no idea what it would be like to drive it. He would need coffee. Serious coffee. *Like Jimmy's coffee from* Pulp Fiction, he thought. He turned the radio off in his car. No more music from the car's radio, and no more chatter from Brindle's Police Department channel. He wanted to drive in silence for a while and digest what had just happened. He had shot people before, as it was part of the job, and he was glad he didn't have to do it more often. It always stung afterward. The exchange between him and Will ran through his mind again. Both were tense. Both with their hands on their firearms at their sides. Both were at the end of a long road. And for what? For Will's need to escape his job, his wife, his life? For Greco's insatiable need to collect his adversary? It all seemed like a very small scene in a very big play, and he and Will had played the smallest of roles. It kept running through his mind until he said, almost in a whisper, "I didn't think you were going to draw on me."

"Hmmph," Will said, apparently waking from a short nap in the back of the car. "What's that?"

"I was just thinking to myself, out loud I guess, but I said, 'I didn't think you were going to draw on me,' back there."

"No," Will chortled and shook his head, half to say 'no,' and half to clear the cobwebs. "No, I'm in the wrong and I accept it. Plus, I'm thinking that you would have had the jump on me, factoring in your experience." He laughed and shook his head, and greatly exhaled. "No, sir, that was not my intention, and I apologize if I gave that impression. Honestly, once you found me, I was almost relieved."

"I bet. You've been on the run for a long time. I guess it's hard to keep up the lie for so long."

"That about sums it up," Will said, looking in the darkness outside as they travelled on the interstate.

"You spoke of experience, before. How the hell did you end up as a Sheriff's Deputy?"

"Apprehended a thief coming out of the liquor store I was working in. Took him down with some wrestling holds and held him until the deputies came. A few days later, the Sheriff, Utter, the guy with the poofy mustache, hunts me down. By the way, I thought I was caught then, but he was there to offer me a job in law enforcement. I took five months of training in Grand Island, –"

"New York?" Greco asked in a non-believing tone.

"No, no," Will laughed. "Not Grand Island, New York. Grand Island, Nebraska," Will replied. "I graduated at the top of my class, had no issues with the physical aspect, I guess due to my athletic background, and the academic stuff was just, well, academic. I was always good in school when I applied myself."

"And you've been a Deputy ever since." Greco let that sink in, and then a thought hit him, far off the topic. "You don't talk like someone from New York," he said. "I know when you left, and I followed your trail, just missing you by what seemed like days in a few places. It's hard to believe that you picked up your current accent just by being out here for the time that you have."

"Well," Will said. "I'd like to say it was just all part of the act, but the truth is, you can't help but pick it up. I guess I'll lose it in time, but I like this one better." They rode in silence for a while, and Will nodded off to sleep again. When he awoke, the scenery was the same, just one dark ribbon of highway in front of them, and everything they had been going through to get to this point behind them. He wasn't sure if he should talk to Greco. After all, he was given the right to remain silent. He decided to speak anyway, and if Greco didn't like it, he could tell Will to shut up. Will cleared his throat. "I'm not sure many would have the commitment to see this, though, like you did. In retrospect, it's not a lot of money to a company like Pickwick, so I'm surprised they even chased me, and you followed me all over the country to catch me. Why the dedication?"

"Pickwick didn't chase you. They knew the money was gone and figured you took it, but also thought you died at Ground Zero. I chased you. You broke the law, and it pissed me off."

"I guess that makes sense," Will said.

"Honestly, the longer the trail became, the more interested and determined I became. You left this trail of breadcrumbs so faint, but so dedicated, like the fake flight. The cabbie, Cleo Baptist –"

"Oh, Cleo! Ol' CB... he was a nice guy."

"Yeah," Greco said. "For a drug dealer."

"Really?" Will asked.

"Yeah, but just pot, really."

"Still against the law," Will said.

"That's what I told him," Greco said, and the two adversaries shared a smile. "Anyway, it was Newark Airport that got the investigation started again."

"How is that?" Greco really had Will's curiosity going now.

"The Newark Airport called your wife, and she called us."

Will leaned forward in the seat. "You talked to Kathleen? How is she?"

Greco laughed. "Yeah. I talked to her. She's fine. However, it may not be what you want to hear. She's engaged. I talked to her once when we thought you were dead, and once again when we thought you weren't. I thought she may have been involved in the crimes. She was pretty pissed at you, by the way. Anyway, they told her they found your briefcase in a locker there. You left a business card in one of the pockets. Restarted the whole investigation. Found your image on security cameras all across the country to find you." Greco was quiet for a moment and allowed that to sink in, and then decided to change the subject. "I've got your boots, by the way," he said.

"What?"

"Your boots, that you bought in Stockton, Kansas. You left them in Seattle. Your boat captain, uh, what's his name—"

"Pierce," Will said.

"That's it!" Greco said, snapping his fingers.

"Russell Pierce. He was a good guy. Especially when I told him I had to leave on short notice," Will said. Greco looked at him in the rearview mirror and sighed heavily. He may come to regret what he was about to say, but he was going to say it anyway.

"You know, I read your rights back there, remember?"

"I remember," Will said.

"Okay, just reminding you about the things you say and how they can be used against you."

"I'm not telling you anything you don't already know, Detective."

"Probably true," Greco said. "Just saying." They drove along in silence for quite some time before Will had some questions, even in his tired state.

"Detective?"

"Yes, Mr. Kelly?"

"How did you find me?"

"What do you mean?"

"In Brindle. How did you ever find me there?"

Greco exhaled. "It's a long story," he said.

"We have time," Will said, "and it may help you stay awake until we get to wherever we're going."

Greco considered his options. "Well," he started, "I followed you to Jersey, checked the security cameras, and found you took a bus to Indy. I drove there, lucked out by finding the hotel you tried first, and the manager told me about the scam that the brother and sister had. The guy you bought the car from, the motel owner and cabbie."

"Yeah, Leon," Will said.

"Yeah, Leon. Gol...you seem to have a great memory. He told me about you, and that's where I learned about you going by Lomax, and I got a lead on the fake credit cards. I checked with the Asian optician, but he was no help. Leon told me about the car and that Motor Vehicles contacted him and told him it was found in Seattle, charbequed. Apparently, that's when the money went up in smoke, so to speak."

"Yeah, most of it, and that was a punch in the gut," Will said.

"I bet. Anyway, I get to Seattle and speak with the fire investigator, who told me where you were working on the boat, and that's how I ended up with the boots. I ran the fake credit cards when I was out there and found the rental car and eventually the bus station, and repeated the steps with the security cameras. Found out you went to Cheyenne. Hit a lot of dead ends there. Went to Laramie, Denver, and probably dozens of other towns. I was getting ready to get back on the road and do blind searching again, and the car needed gas."

"The bus stop convenience store?" Will asked.

"Yeah," Greco said.

"Edgar has got a big mouth."

"Well, to be the bearer of bad news, Edgar's dead."

"Oh, really?" Will asked.

"Yeah, a few months ago. His grandson ratted you out. I got to Brindle and tried to talk to the Sheriff, but he was out of town on an investigation."

"Ahh," Will said, tiredly. "My attempted murder."

"What?" Greco asked. "Someone tried to kill you?"

"Twice."

"What for?" Greco asked.

"Another time, Detective. Please, continue."

Greco eyed Will in the rearview mirror for a second, and then nodded slightly. "Well, I spoke to the dispatcher at the front desk at the Sheriff's Department, who ultimately ratted you out, it seems. Ally, I think it was. She's clueless. I'm not sure she knows what day it is."

"Agreed," Will said.

"She did tell me about places to eat in town, though, and I ended up at your girlfriend's pizza place. Great pie, by the way."

"The best," Will said.

"Reminds me of New York," they said in unison, and they shared a chuckle.

"Seriously, though," Greco said, "I should have arrested her, too, for lying to me about knowing you."

"She's a good girl," Will said. "She deserves better than me."

Greco let that pass without comment. "Then I stopped at a liquor store to buy some beer, and –"

"Wait... which one?" Will asked.

"D&J... something like that."

"Hmmm," Will said. "Big guy behind the counter?"

"Yeah," Greco said.

"Jim... I got sold out by Jim."

"He didn't sell you out. He talked you up. Said you did good things since you got there."

Will exhaled. "And bad things before that." There was a long silence again before Will spoke. He scooted up towards the dip between the headrests of the two front seats of the car.

"So," he said. "What happens now?"

Chapter 88 – Arraignment

Greco removed the handcuffs from around the seat of the airplane, which Will had occupied for the last few hours as the plane left Nebraska and landed at LaGuardia Airport. Will thought it was odd that he was in handcuffs on a commercial flight. He thought there would have been some sort of prisoner transfer airplane that moved people on the run back to where they were supposed to go to jail. But there he sat, for what seemed like forever, in the window seat, next to Detective Greco.

Will was appreciative of what Greco had done for him, whether it was standard protocol or not. Greco led him onto the plane from the tarmac instead of marching him through the terminal in handcuffs, where all the other travelers could see. They were the first ones on the airplane and were seated all the way in the back, next to the bulkhead, which separated the passenger area from the service areas of the plane. He was able to see nearly everyone who boarded the plane. It reminded will of when he sat in the back of the bus on the way out to Indianapolis. He knew everyone's bathroom schedule and was sometimes presented with unfavorable aromas.

After the plane landed, the process was nearly the same, except in reverse. This time, they were the last ones off the plane and took a shaky set of steps that were attached to a truck to the tarmac, where a car awaited them. An officer got out of one car and opened the back door, where Greco reapplied the handcuffs and put Will in the back seat. The officer then retreated to another car, driven by yet another officer, and the car sped away. Greco got into the front seat and started the car, driving off the tarmac via a service road and then out onto the airport loop. Will looked around and decided he didn't really want silence as they drove.

"They've really beefed up the security now, huh?" he asked.

"Hmph. You got lucky. You should see it when you have to go through the terminal. Lines out the ass."

"Probably for the best now," Will said. "Bastards." They drove in silence for a while again, and Will felt that Greco wasn't really in the mood to talk, but they had that conversation on the plane. Will had brought it up, mostly because he wanted to hear more about how Greco had tracked him down. Greco simply told him that it was not often that he would arrest someone who wanted to talk. They usually just clam up and sit in the back seat, thinking about their first phone call. Will didn't even ask for a phone call. He just went along quietly. This time, it was Greco who initiated a conversation.

"You know," he said. "I was wondering."

"About?" Will asked.

"Why did you choose Billy Lomax? For a name."

"Pfft," Will said. "It sounded like Willy Loman, from <u>Death of a Salesman</u>. I read the book years ago, and then I saw it a few years back on Broadway. Brian Dennehy played Loman. I thought he was great. I wish I could have seen Dustin Hoffman play the role in the eighties."

"Interesting," Greco said. "I'm not sure I would have put that together, but now that I think about it, I remember seeing that book on your bookcase. I should have taken that instead of the poetry."

"I don't know, the poetry recital was pretty cool."

"Yeah, it was," Greco said, and they both chuckled. "You know, you might be the most interesting perp I've ever collared," Greco said.

Will sighed. "I'm sure that will help in court," he said.

"You never know, man," Greco said. "You get a few character witnesses in there, magic can happen." They continued the drive for a while, dealing with traffic and making small talk until they reached the station. Greco led Will down the steps into the processing area of the building and left him in the hands of the officers there. Before he left, Greco turned back to Will and watched the cell door close between them. Will was looking around the cell, at the little commode that was stuck to a wall, and the bed, which was nothing much more than a bench seat with thin padding. Greco saw the look on Will's face and came back towards the cell. When the officers left them, Greco looked around and lowered his voice. "You know," he said. "I don't often have much sympathy for the people I bring in here, and I can't say that I'm sure I have any for you. From what I know, I can't say that you're a bad person now. But for who you were *then*, you're getting what you deserve, and there's going to be more to come, and it's not going to be easy on you. I don't envy you. There's a million different kinds of criminals, some can do hard time, some can't. I don't envy you right now."

Will looked around the cell again. "I've slept on the ground, in my car, and on a boat on the ocean that had a worse bunk than here. I can handle this hard time, I guess."

Greco scoffed. "This isn't the hard time, man. Don't forget your phone call."

Early the next day, a Friday, Will was sitting on the bunk with his back against the wall when an officer approached the cell with a set of keys. He was a large Black man with a bit of a belly, and towered over Will by nearly a foot, Will estimated. He opened the cell and beckoned for Will to come out.

"What's going on?" Will asked.

"Time for your phone call," the officer said.

"I'm not sure I have anyone to call."

"You got a lawyer?"

"Not really," Will said.

"Family?"

"None to speak of."

"Any friends?"

"Just you," Will said. The officer tsked and rolled his eyes, and shut the door again.

"Let me know if you think of someone in the next hour. After that, you're going to head over to the courthouse for your arraignment and bail, and see if you can get out of here."

"Thanks," Will said. *Get out of here,* Will thought. *No one to call. Nowhere to go. Bail? Forget it.* He thought he could call Rocky back in Brindle, but doubted that his one phone call could be long-distance. The only other person he could think to call was Kathleen. She was the only other person he could really think to call. He knew it wasn't going to be pleasant, but he felt like he needed to do it. He felt like he owed it to her. Maybe this is where his hard time really started.

"Excuse me, Officer?" he said.

"What can I do for you?" he asked.

"Officer... Keller," Will said, reading the tag on the man's shirt. "I think I'm ready to make that phone call, sir." Keller put a set of handcuffs on Will's wrists, opened the door, and led Will down the hallway to a room with a table with a metal loop attached to it and a telephone on a wall. Keller moved Will into the hallway and over towards the phone. He locked the handcuffs through the metal ring in the wall and snapped them shut again.

"You got ten minutes," Keller said and left the room, shutting the door behind him. Will picked up the phone handset and took thirty of his six hundred seconds to remember Katheen's phone number. He dialed the number and counted three rings before the phone clicked.

"*Hello,*" came from a male voice on the other end of the line. The voice took Will by surprise as he was expecting Kathleen's.

"Uh, hi," Will said. "Is uhh, is Kathleen there?"

"*Who's calling?*" the voice asked.

'Uh, this is uhh, her ex-husband, I guess. Can I speak with her?"

"*You son of a bitch,*" the voice said, in a lowered yet more aggressive tone this time. "*Will Kelly? Why are you calling here?*"

Will was taken aback again that a male answering Kathleen's phone knew his name. "I'm sorry," Will said, "I didn't mean to..."

"*Didn't mean to what? Drag up the past from something that it took her forever to get over?'*

"I wanted to call her to apologize," Will said. "What I did to her, no one should do that to anyone. No one should have to deal with that."

"*No shit,"* the voice said. "*I'm not letting you talk to her.*"

"Please, I only have a few minutes. She's uh, she's my only phone call."

There was a moment of silence from the other end of the phone, and then the voice cleared. "*So, they got you, huh?'*

"Yeah," Will said. "They got me."

"*Good.*"

"Can I please talk to her for just a few minutes? Please." Will wasn't sure his last plea was heard, as it sounded like the phone was muffled. He heard voices in the background, one definitely female, and then the phone cleared again, and all Will heard after that was a click. They hung up on him. It was probably more like *she* hung up on him, Will thought. He put the receiver back onto the cradle on the phone and rested his head against the wall. Officer Keller returned to the room, freed Will from the restraint on the wall, and led him back to the cell, which was no longer empty, which made Will cringe. There was a man in ripped jeans and a t-shirt that had some stains on the front. Will assessed the man and assumed that he was a drunk and was sleeping it off.

About thirty minutes later, another officer came to the cell and directed Will to put his hands through the bars and attached another set of handcuffs to his wrists. He led Will out of the cell, down the hallways, and up the steps. The officer said that his name was Officer Daniels, and he would be taking Will over to the courthouse for the arraignment and bail hearing. Will was as pleasant to Daniels as he was to Keller, walked without issue, and did as he was told. In truth, inside himself, Will was happy having someone give him direction instead of having to make all of the decisions regarding his future. Daniels led Will to the area outside the courtroom where a young man in a grey suit stood and met them at the door.

"Mr. Kelly?" the man asked.

Will looked up. "Yes?"

"Hi, I'm Leonard Kirk," the man said. "I'm your lawyer."

"I didn't know I had a lawyer," Will said. "Are you a public defender?"

"You got it," Kirk said. "Nice to meet you. I wish it were under better circumstances. You're in quite a bit of trouble."

"Understatement," Will said.

"You're charged with embezzlement of nearly half a million dollars, flight from a warrant, credit card fraud, defaulting on a mortgage, criminal possession of forged instruments, forgery, falsifying business records, and..." Kirk paused for a moment. "Oh," he said. "Abandonment of your spouse."

"Wow," Will said. "I'm not sure I contemplated all of that."

"Most people don't when they are contemplating committing a crime, Mr. Kelly," Kirk said, still looking at the paperwork. "Small-time crooks just usually get one charge unless they get out of control. It's the planners that really get the business."

"Can I ask you a question?" Will asked.

"Another one?" Kirk said with a chuckle. Will did not laugh. "Go ahead," Kirk said dryly.

"How long have you been a lawyer?"

"Uhh, just over eight months," Kirk said, still flipping pages.

"I'm the worst case you've seen so far?"

Kirk ignored the question and shut the folder, then he opened it up again. "Wait, you became a cop?"

"Sheriff's Deputy," Wil said. "How screwed am I?"

Kirk shut the folder. "Mr. Kelly, do I need to read you that list of charges again?"

"No," Will said. "I don't guess you do."

"Time to go," Kirk said. They walked with Officer Daniels through the doors of the courtroom, and Kirk and Will were seated with some others in the jury box. He leaned over toward Will. "Look," he said. "We haven't had a lot of time to talk, but we have a little while before they go through all of these other cases."

"Okay."

"I've seen this judge before. You need to plead not guilty by reason of insanity. It's our only chance, or they are going to put you away for a long time."

Will looked at him. "I'm not crazy. I knew what I was doing."

"Do you want to go to prison for most of the rest of your life?"

"Not really, but I deserve whatever I get," Will said.

"Nobody deserves all of that," Kirk said, holding up the folder. Will looked at him and shook his head.

"I can't do it. I'm not going to lie."

"Man, you're not lying. No one in their right mind would do what you did. Something must have been making you do that. Crazy wife, work stress? Kids? Pets? Bills?"

"None of that, really," Will said.

"Listen. When the judge asks what your plea is, I'm going to say 'not guilty' and keep you out of jail forever."

"You will not, or I will fire you right now," Will said. Kirk shook his head and looked at Will.

"Look, I get it. You're a stand-up guy. You take responsibility for your actions, and you became a cop! It's obvious that you wanted to do something to make up for what you did, something nice, and it appears you did. Don't you want to get out of jail when you're still young enough to keep doing good things?" Will looked at Kirk and started to speak, but was interrupted by someone in the court.

"The People Versus Willem Kelly," a man in the corner of the room said in a booming voice.

"Come on," Kirk said. They moved toward a table on the right side of the courtroom. Will motioned towards the chair as if he should sit, but Kirk slightly shook his head. The judge put one hand under his chin and placed a finger across his lips as he read Will's file. When he was done reading, he looked up at Will, and then back at the papers, and then back at Will.

"Mr. Kelly," he said, removing his hand from his face. "The charges against you are as follows: embezzlement, flight, credit card fraud, intentionally defaulting on your mortgage, criminal possession of forged instruments, forgery, falsifying business records, and abandonment. Do you understand these charges that have been brought against you?"

Will looked at Kirk, who nodded. "Yes, Your Honor," Will said.

"And how do you plead?" the judge asked. Will looked at Kirk, who looked back at him and slightly shrugged. Will wasn't looking at Kirk for a response; he was remembering what he said about doing good things. About *making a difference.* He had made a difference, and he had made a better life for himself, and he had helped others in the process. In fact, in the few days since he was arrested and brought back to New York, he did miss his uniform, his car, and the ability to make things better. He didn't know what he could do in jail to help people, but he could figure it out. And he didn't know how he could help people if he ever got out of jail, but he could figure it out. "Mr. Kelly?" the judge said, snapping Will from his thoughts. He looked at Kirk and up at the judge.

"Not guilty, Your Honor."

Chapter 89 – Welcome to Washington

Greco looked on as the proceedings went on, amused that Will Kelly had chosen to plead not guilty by reason of insanity. He thought the public defender putting that bug into Kelly's ear was an interesting move, especially considering the conversations that he had with Kelly on the drive from Brindle to the airport, on the airplane, and then again on the drive through New York to get to the station.

"Mr. Kelly," the judge said. "You have pled not guilty by reason of insanity. Do you have anything else to say?"

"No, Your Honor."

"Very well. Counselor?"

Leonard Kirk, standing next to Will, chimed in, "We would like to request bail, Your Honor."

"Mr. Prosecutor?" the judge said.

A man in a black suit at the other table in the courtroom rose from his chair. Kirk told Will the man's name was Michael DiCiccio, the lawyer for the prosecution responsible for putting Will in prison for a long time.

"Your Honor," DiCiccio said. "We oppose any bail for the accused. We believe he is a flight risk and could disappear again at any time."

"A flight risk?" Kirk said, as loud as Will had heard Kirk's voice so far that day. "Your Honor, I don't believe my client is a flight risk. He did not resist arrest, and has been nothing but cooperative since that time."

The judge shook his head. "Mr. Kirk, your client is accused of disappearing into thin air, so to speak. If that isn't a flight risk, I don't know what is. Bail is denied. Anything more?" Will elbowed Kirk slightly, and when Kirk looked at him, Will slightly shook his head.

"Not at this time, Your Honor," Kirk said.

"Very well," the Judge replied. "Court proceedings are set for Monday, July twenty-ninth, at nine o'clock in the morning. We'll begin with Jury selection, then. Dismissed."

Kirk led Will back through the door of the courtroom from which they came in, and Officer Daniels was there to take Will back to the station. As they rode in the car, Will became curious.

"So, what happens now? It's three weeks until the trial starts."

Daniels looked at him in the rear-view mirror of the car. "You'll get transferred to a minimum-security holding area until the trial starts. It's not that bad, there. Private showers, at least, and two to a cell. You should be fine."

"Can we make phone calls there?"

"Twice per week."

"Great," Will said. They drove in silence for the rest of the way back to the station, and Will was shortly back in his holding cell. About thirty minutes later, Daniels came back. "Kelly, it's time."

"Time for what?"

"Your transfer came through," Daniels said. "Your destination is Washington Correctional Facility."

"Sounds great," Will said.

"It's clean, and like I said, private showers and a quiet cell. No bars. You got cinderblock walls and a metal door. Cots are pretty thick, too. You can handle it."

"I've probably handled worse when I was out west," Will said.

"Yeah, so I heard some of your hearing earlier. That's quite a list of offenses. What was the motivation behind it?" Will thought for a moment and then decided that he'd already said too much to too many people. He explained to Daniels that it would all be out in the open soon, and he didn't really want to talk about it without his lawyer present. Daniels said he understood, and in a few minutes, Will was handcuffed in the back of the patrol car again and on his way to his new home for the next few weeks.

The entrance to the facility did not seem like minimum security to Will. They drove through multiple gates and through fenced areas next to where men in orange clothing were lifting weights, playing basketball, and standing around talking and smoking. Will wondered if he'd need to pick up the smoking habit now that he was going to go to prison. He didn't really want to, but it just seemed that that was what everyone in prison did. They smoked, played basketball, and lifted weights. He hoped he wouldn't find out the truth about other rumors of prison life.

Daniels stopped the car in front of a smaller building, got out of the vehicle, came to the back seat, and helped Will out of the car. Two men, whom Will could only assume were guards at the facility, were there waiting on either side of a doorway into the building. Daniels escorted Will to the two guards, handed them a folder, and turned Will over to them.

"Good luck," Daniels said.

"Thanks," Will responded. The guards escorted Will into the building where his paperwork was filed, and he was transported to another small room. He was told to remove all of his clothing, and then was told to stand tall, then stoop, then cough multiple times, and then told to put on a shirt and a pair of pants, which were a horrible shade of yellow. There was no mirror for him to review his appearance, but he assumed he looked like an over-ripe banana. One guard handed him a pillow, a set of sheets and a blanket, and a pair of rubbery shoes, which, for some reason, he was not allowed to put on his feet yet. He was marched down a long hallway with metal doors on each side. He guessed they were cells for other unfortunate lawbreakers, but could not confirm that fact. They turned and started down another hallway that looked just like the last one. He noticed how quiet it was. Eerily quiet, he thought. Not like anything he had ever thought that a crowded jail would be like. They finally stopped him at one of the doors and forced him to take a step back as they opened the door. Once the door was opened, he was guided to the inside of the cell. One of the guards stayed outside the cell, and the other entered the cell with Will.

"Welcome to Washington," he said. "You'll leave your cell for breakfast, lunch, dinner, and recreation time each day. On Mondays and Thursdays, you get phone time. The rest of the time, you're in here. On Tuesdays and Fridays, you go to Laundry to get clean bed sheets, and on Fridays, you get a clean blanket. Lights out at ten o'clock. Any questions?"

"How do I know when to do all of this?" Will asked.

"We'll come get you, or you'll hear an announcement."

"Got it," Will said.

"Anything else?"

Will looked around the cell. "Not right now," he said. The guard said nothing, but turned around, exited the room, and the door closed behind him. Will looked around again and noticed that the sink and the toilet were the same contraption. It made him feel odd about possibly drinking the water from the sink or even brushing his teeth. There was a half-used roll of toilet paper on a table next to the toilet. The table had two drawers, and he couldn't help but open them. The top one was empty. The bottom drawer, when he opened it, held what he considered to be odd objects to be found in a prison cell. There was some soap, some chewing gum and candy, a few magazines, and a book on Origami. The odd item, though, was a small stuffed pineapple with glued-on eyes and a pink tongue. The tongue sat on one side of the mouth of the pineapple, and the eyes were the type where if you shook the toy, the eyes googled all around and then resettled in their original position.

He left the pineapple and other assorted items in the drawer as he had found them, and looked at the bunks on the left side of the room. The bottom bunk was made and had a pillow, but the top bunk was empty, with just a mattress. If he had not figured it out by this time, this was Will's verification that he did not have the cell to himself. He looked at the way the bottom bunk was made and tried to emulate it with his own set of sheets, blanket, and pillow. When he was satisfied, he climbed up to the top bunk and sat on the edge with his legs dangling over the side. He sat there for about twenty minutes before he started to get bored, and the novelty of his situation began to wear off. He thought about raiding the bottom drawer and borrowing one of the magazines or the origami book, but he didn't want to rock any boats regarding his yet-to-be-known cellmate. It was that exact moment when the door to the cell opened, and Will raised his head, but was still looking down on the man who walked into the room. The door shut and their eyes met for a second, and Will looked on as the eyes of the other man narrowed, and his mouth turned into the form of a sneer.

"Get your ass out of my bed," he growled.

Chapter 90 – Happier Than Miserable

Will looked at the man and decided to remain where he stood. "Looks like the bottom bed is taken," Will said. "I think this is my bed, so if you're going to sleep in my bed, and I'm going to sleep in it, too, who is going to sleep in the bottom bunk?" He eyed his new cellmate and greeted him with an equal sneer. The man furrowed his eyebrows and just looked at Will for a few seconds, and then spoke again.

"Man, I'm just messing with you. You're fine up there. Actually, you can have the bottom if you want it. I don't really care."

"I'm good up here," Will said, not exactly sure what to say. But then he stepped off the side of the bed and onto the floor to meet his man face to face.

"Tracey Allgood," the man said, and stuck out his hand. "Everyone calls me 'Tracks.'"

"Will Kelly," Will said, and shook the outstretched hand.

"Kelly. Irish?"

"Something like that," Will said. "Kind of mutt, I guess."

"How long you gonna be here?" Tracks asked.

"Not sure," Will said. "Three weeks until my trial starts, so at least that long. Then, who knows? How about you?"

"Two years down, three to go. I was a heroin addict. I'm clean now, but I got busted for breaking and entering. I got caught in the act, punched the cop, and then bolted. They got me a few blocks away. What did you do?"

"It's a long story, and we've got some time, it seems. I'll tell you, I just don't feel like spitting it all out right now." Will climbed back up to the top bunk and resumed his sitting on the edge position. "So, what's it like here?"

"Not too bad," Tracks said, sitting on his own bunk. "The food sucks, but you can supplement it with snacks from the commissary. You get an hour of exercise every day. The nights are quiet, and the rest of your time is, well, time. Do you smoke?"

"No, you?"

"No, never caught on. At least that clears the air."

"So, to speak," Will said.

"And there's the other thing," Tracks said.

"What other thing?" Will asked.

"That."

Will looked down and saw Tracks pointing at the toilet. "You have bathroom issues?" Will asked.

"The food here, man. It tears up my gut something fierce. Every morning, right before breakfast, I uh, empty the keg."

Will thought Tracks was friendly enough for a prison cellmate and was willing to glean as much knowledge from him as he could to make his stay more comfortable, but the toilet talk was a little too much for him. "Hey, Tracks, just do your thing, man. Don't worry about it. It'll work out." Tracks seemed the take this fairly well, and they didn't speak for a while, but then Will had more questions. "What do we do about showering, shaving, and things like that?"

"Ah," Tracks said. "Did you put any money into your commissary account when you got here?"

"No," Will replied. "I didn't have any money on me when I got pinched."

"What do you need?" Tracks asked. "I can hook you up until you get some money."

"Uhh, I'm not sure. What do you buy to just survive?"

Tracks laughed. "Just about what you said. Soap, for sure. Deodorant, toothpaste, toilet paper, and shaving cream. You don't need to buy razors. They'll give them to you, but they'll watch you shave and then take them from you when you're done."

"Makes sense," Will said. "I don't know that I'm going to be getting any money. I don't really have anyone to give me any to put into my account."

"I'll buy you soap, toothpaste, and deodorant, just so you're not stinking up the cell after a week or so. We can share the toilet paper. I'll get more." Tracks said.

"Thanks, man. I owe you."

The next few days for Will were a blur. He woke up each morning before Tracks and had nothing to do but sit on the bed and stare at the wall. He was thankful when the bell for breakfast came, even though the food was terrible, just as Tracks had warned. As far as Tracks and his bathroom issues went, Will was even happier to leave the cell for breakfast, because Tracks would stay behind for a while and take care of his personal business, and then join him for breakfast afterward. The breakfast period was thirty minutes, which didn't seem like a long time. Tracks explained to Will that the kitchen ran in shifts, and went by what color clothes you wore. Orange was first, then yellow, then blue, then red. Tracks also explained that there were people wearing gray, but that Will would never see them because they were in solitary confinement. The breakfast food was usually an egg product, probably powdered, two sausage links, and a piece of dry toast. On some days, there was oatmeal and fruit, which seemed to draw flies.

After breakfast, it was back to the cells to stare at the walls. Tracks let Will read his magazines, and tear a few pages out of them to try his craft at origami from Tracks' book. Will was only successful at making a frog and a paper balloon. He'd need more practice if he was going to be any good at it. Between breakfast and lunch, there was the opportunity, depending on which day it was, to either make phone calls to your lawyer or your family, go to the laundry for fresh clothing and bed sheets, or go to the commissary to get whatever it was you needed to make yourself comfortable or slightly happier than miserable.

Lunch was also run in thirty-minute shifts, and consisted usually of cold sandwiches, or sometimes a hamburger, which was also cold, as well as dry. The only condiment was mustard. Tracks explained that they used to have mayonnaise, but too many of the inmates were stealing it to use as a lubricant for extracurricular activities. Will thought about that when Tracks told him and guessed that mustard just wasn't as sexy as mayonnaise in those situations.

After lunch was the recreational period, when the inmates could go outside if the weather was cooperating, or gather in a common area to play cards, board games, watch television, or read books if the weather was foul. On his second day in the facility, Will stepped outside into the sunshine for the first time in a while, and it felt good to him. He also noticed those inmates in the different colored clothing that Tracks had mentioned. Tracks said that they keep the inmates separated by crime severity and color coding. Minimum security, like Will and Tracks, wore yellow. Anyone serving longer than a five-year sentence wore orange. Over ten years was blue, and the lifers wore red. Each prisoner wearing a certain color was kept segregated from other prisoners wearing different colors. Yellow-wearing inmates stayed with other yellow-wearing inmates, and an inmate wearing one color never mixed with an inmate wearing a different color. This kept the hardened criminals away from those spending only a short time in prison. This logic made sense to Will, and he was thankful for it.

Dinner each night was some sort of formed meat patty, chicken or beef, potatoes each night, without fail, a vegetable, and a roll which could have broken a window if thrown correctly. After the dinner shift, it was back to the rooms for the night for whatever entertainment the inmates could find for themselves, and then at five minutes to ten o'clock each night, a buzzer buzzed twice, alerting the inmates that lights out was imminent, and five minutes later, the place went dark for the next eight hours.

Chapter 91 – Goodbye Presents

On his third day in the facility, Will was told he could use the telephone to call a friend, family member, or lawyer. Tracks told him not to waste his phone calls on his lawyer. Use the call for a friend or family member, and tell them you want to talk to your lawyer. "Two birds with one stone," he'd say. Will said he didn't really have anyone to call.

"What about your old lady?" Tracks asked.

"She doesn't want to talk to me. She hung up on me the last time I called."

"So?" Tracks said.

"So, what?" Will said. "She's going to hang up on me again. It's a waste of time."

Tracks snickered. "Like you have so many more important things to do right now," and he rolled over in his bunk to face the wall. Will sat there for a minute and thought about what Tracks had said, and decided he was right. He hopped down onto the floor, put on his rubbery shoes, and headed down the hallway to where the bank of inmate phones was located. There were eight phones all along one wall, and then eight on the other side of the wall as well. Each inmate was supposed to be limited to five minutes, but the guards kept a close eye, and if you got disconnected or had to redial or no one picked up, they usually floated the inmates a few extra minutes.

He really wanted to get in touch with Rocky, but long-distance calls were not allowed to be made on an outbound basis. He wanted to call Sheriff Utter and apologize to him again for being misleading, but for the same reason, he could not. He decided that he was going to try to call Kathleen again. Maybe he could get her to give him a small window of her time to explain himself and to apologize to her as well. He didn't think there were enough apologies to give her, as she deserved much more than what he could offer.

He waited in line for an open phone in the bank of sixteen that were attached to the wall. He knew the phones would probably be monitored, at least that's what Leonard Kirk had told him, so he would need to be careful with what he said. A phone finally opened up for him to use, and as he walked past the other inmates to get to it, he heard bits of their conversations. Some of the inmates were angry, and some of them were crying. He picked up the receiver and dialed the number for Kathleen's apartment. The phone rang once, then again, and then three more times before he heard a click, followed by Kathleen's voice on a recording.

"Hello. You reached the home of Doctor Kathleen Kelly and Mister Ezra Rice. We're not home right now, but please leave us a message and we will get back to you as soon as possible. Have a great day."

As he listened to the message, his heart sank into his stomach. *Ezra?* He thought about hanging up, but decided instead to leave a message after he heard the beep from the machine.

"Uhh, hi, Kathleen. It's, uh, it's Will. I'm not sure what to say right now. I'm not even sure you'll get this. I'm assuming if Mr. Rice gets the message before you do, you'll never hear it. Then again, maybe you'll delete it anyway. I don't know. I just wish I had to opportunity to talk to you. I'm not proud of the bad things I've done, especially leaving you alone. I didn't know what else to do, really. You just became so distant..." Will stopped himself, as his voice cracked over the phone. "Well," he continued, "after. I felt like I couldn't connect with you anymore, Kathleen. We had separated anyway, but leaving the way I did, that was," he paused for a second, and then continued. "That was wrong. It was wrong, and I'm sorry, even though I'm sure that doesn't mean much to you right now, but hopefully, one day, somehow, you can find it in yourself to forgive me. I'm not asking you to forget what I did." He felt a tear roll down his cheek and quickly brushed it away before anyone could see it. "I'm guessing they might call you as a witness during the trial. I'm sorry about that, too. You don't deserve to get mixed up in all of this." A guard came over to where he stood and pointed to his watch. Will nodded, acknowledging that his time on the phone was nearly finished. "Anyway," he said, "I hope you get this message, and I hope you listen to it. Be well." He hung up the phone, turned back down the hallway, and returned to his cell. Ten minutes later, the cell doors were closed, and it was back to some quality time with Tracks.

They filled the time as Will told his story to Tracks, a little bit at a time, each day, as they were locked in the cell together. Will told him how he stole the money, and how he was found out by the people at Pickwick, and how he made his escape. He described the events of September 11th and how they interacted with his plan. He told of his trip across the country, half by bus, half by car, working on the fishing boat in Seattle, and then his eventual landing in Brindle, stopping a liquor store robbery, and eventually becoming a sheriff's deputy. It took Will the better part of a week to complete the entire story, up until he surrendered to Detective Greco. He had just finished telling of the showdown he and Greco had, being bisected by the train that evening, and his eventual surrender, when a knock came from the other side of the cell door, which then opened. A guard poked his head in.

"Kelly, you have a visitor. Let's go." Will couldn't think of who would be coming to visit him, but settled on the fact that it was probably Leonard Kirk wanting to talk about his case and the upcoming trial. The guard led him down one of the hallways with cells on each side until they reached a room that was longer than it was wide, with a row of partitioned seats on each side, separated by what Will thought might be a plexiglass divider. "Seat twelve," the guard said. Will followed the seats down the row until he reached the twelfth seat. He peeked his head around the edge of the partition and saw who was visiting. It was Kathleen. He couldn't take his eyes off her as he sat down. She was still incredibly beautiful to him. He picked up a phone receiver that was on the side of the partition. He was looking at her, and she was staring right back at him. Almost through him. Finally, she moved to pick up the phone on her side of the glass.

"Hello, Will," she said, seemingly emotionless.

"Hey, you," he said. "I'm surprised to see you."

"I'm surprised to be here," she said, coldly.

"It's good, though," he said. "It's very good to see you."

"Say what you need to say," she said. He looked down at the small table in front of him, which was attached to the clear separator between them. He knew she was going to make this difficult, but he accepted that. He felt like he deserved it.

"You got my message," he said. She said nothing, but continued to stare at him, impatiently. "Okay," he said. "Listen, Kathleen, I'm so sorry for putting you through all of this. I was selfish, and thinking only of myself, and I did not take your feelings into consideration when I did what I did. It was not fair to you, and it was mean. For that, I am sorry."

"You're an asshole," she said.

He absorbed the insult and nodded slowly, slightly. "I'm not really sure that quite covers it," he said. She looked at him and shook her head.

"Was it that bad, Will, really? Was it so bad that you planned to steal money just so you could cut out like a thief in the night? So you could run away and disappear? Start a new life while just leaving me behind?"

"I guess I wasn't thinking too clearly," he said.

"I suppose not," she said. "I don't get it, Will. You didn't want to be with me anymore, fine. You wanted to roam the country and move out west, fine. But the theft? The planning? I mean, false identifications, fake credit cards, pretending to be someone you're not? That's not the Will Kelly I know. Not the man I fell in love with those years ago. I don't understand it."

"I know," he began, "I suppose I was misguided by my own thoughts. Nothing was making sense. I guess I needed an adventure, and went about it the wrong way." He stopped and looked at her for a moment before he continued. "Remember 'Pacing The Cage?' he asked, and then recited the beginning of last verse:

"Sometimes the best map will not guide you

You can't see what's 'round the bend.

Sometimes the road leads through dark places,

Sometimes the darkness is your friend."

"So, you needed a friend and found it in the darkness," she said. She exhaled audibly and shook her head. "I know," she paused. "I know I wasn't the easiest person to live with for the past couple of years. I'll give you that. What I went through—what *we* went through, no one should ever have to deal with that. It was a terrible thing, Will, and it changed me. I guess it changed both of us." He nodded slightly, still looking for the right words to say, but never finding them. They sat in silence for a minute or so, and he decided he would not keep her any longer.

"I guess I was just pacing," he said, then sighed heavily. "I'd better let you go, Kathleen. The guard is giving me the eyeball," Will said.

"How are you doing in here?" she asked, suddenly concerned for a man she really had nothing but hatred for in the previous minutes.

"Uhh, I can get by. There's things to do, and they let you out to play every now and then so you don't go crazy. I'm just trying to fit in."

"I made some phone calls and did some research on how things work in here, and I put one hundred dollars in your commissary account," she said. "You shouldn't be going without some essentials. I also left something for you at the desk with the guard."

"You didn't have to do that," he said. "But thank you, seriously. I'll pay you back first chance I get."

"I don't think you can ever pay me back, Will," she said. "Consider it a goodbye gift. I don't really ever want to see you again." She looked him in the eyes when she said this, and it stung him deeply. She hung the receiver up onto the cradle attached to the wall, turned around, and left him there to hurt. A few seconds passed, and he hung up his phone as well. He wiped another tear from his eye, and it surprised him how emotional he was getting when thinking about Kathleen, a woman he ran across the country to get away from. He stood from the seat and walked down the hallway to the guard's desk, and asked if there was something for him. The guard turned around and fumbled through a desk drawer until he pulled out a book and gave it to Will.

"*A Painted House*," he said, reading the cover. "Thanks," he said and nodded to the guard, who just sat behind the desk with his arms folded across his chest. He worked his way to the exit of the room, and another guard led him back to his cell.

"Lawyer?" Tracks asked.

"Wife," Will said. "Ex-wife, really, I guess. I don't know. I guess technically we're still married."

"Wow. How did that go?"

"Uhh, rough," Will said. "Not what I expected, but I earned every bit of it, and maybe got some closure. At least I know where I stand."

"Where is that?"

"A very cold street corner with a biting wind, and no coat. She did put money in my commissary account, so I'll pay you back for the stuff you got me. Thanks for doing that."

"No worries," Tracks said. "What's with the book?"

"I'd say it was a long story, but you'd drag it out of me anyway."

"True," Tracks said, sitting up in his bunk. "Let's have it."

"I knew I was leaving at some point," Will said. "I just didn't know when. But then I got an email from the loss prevention team where I was working, saying my numbers didn't match up. They found some irregularities. I was supposed to meet with them the next day to explain what was going on, but I had no intention of doing so. I planned never to step foot in that office again. I was going to leave that night, as soon as I got my money and my new identity. I was gone. But, stupidity reigned, and I forgot the key to my storage unit where the money was hidden, so I had to go back the next day, but you know all that. What you don't know yet is that night, September tenth, I had a phone call with Kathleen. She was telling me about a book she was reading, just finishing it up, actually, and asked if I wanted to read it. We both loved reading books, and sometimes we would even read to each other. We loved John Grisham's books, and this was the one she was reading. She had asked if she could bring it over to the house the next day, and I told her that she could, even though I knew that I was going to be gone. Just one more mean thing I did to her. I think the book and what she said was her closure, and two ways she could zing me for the last time."

"What did she say?" Tracks asked.

"She told me the book and the commissary money were goodbye presents, and she never wanted to see me again."

"Ouch," Tracks said.

"Yeah."

Chapter 92 – Trial

The next two weeks went extremely slowly for Will. His trial date was fast approaching, for sure, but not fast enough. He and Tracks got along fine, and for the most part, made each other's lives tolerable as they shared them. They burned through a lot of magazines, tearing the pages out to work on the origami. Will used some of the money Kathleen had given him to buy a chessboard, and while Tracks knew the basic moves for each piece, he lacked strategy, and that made Will the winner quite often.

Will woke up earlier than usual on Monday, July 29th, 2002. It was going to be the first day of his trial, barring any unforeseen legal issues. He had spoken with Leonard Kirk on three of the previous five days, and they launched a strategy on Will's not-guilty plea. Kirk said that they needed to prove that Will was under undue stress from both work and home, and that's what made him do what he did. Kirk also felt that jury selection was going to be paramount for them if they were going to have a chance at winning the case. Kirk felt that a male divorced and overworked jury would be the friendliest to their cause, and they should try to avoid women jurors if at all possible. Also, they wanted to stay away from anyone in upper management in business. In short, they wanted single or divorced men who get their hands dirty in their job, and wanted to take it out on their bosses.

Will was granted an early private shower that morning, as were most of the inmates who had trial appearances, and by eight-thirty in the morning, he was ready to go. The facility had a bus used to transfer inmates to and from court, and Will wasn't the only inmate with a court appearance that day. There were four other men on the bus, and Will was content to ride in silence, but one of the other inmates was rather chatty and struck up a conversation with him. They talked about it being Will's first day, but Freddie, the chatter, was on his sixth day, and this was his third trial, so he let Will know that he knew everything about the process. "*This is going to happen, then that, then a witness will speak, and then another witness, and then a recess, and then more witnesses, and then they'll get you up on the stand and try to confuse yo ass, but don't let 'em,"* he said. Will was honestly ready to just move forward as fast as possible. The faster he was convicted and sentenced, or found not guilty, the faster he could get back to what was left of his life.

Finally, the bus pulled into the back parking lot of the courthouse, and the accused were led to a room where each was taken by a pair of guards to their respective courtrooms. Will was led into his and saw that Kirk was already there, seated at the table for the defense, with a briefcase, nine legal pads, about a dozen pens, and a flexible folder that he kept taking papers from and putting papers into. He was nervous, Will could tell, and the shuffling of the papers seemed to be a coping mechanism.

"Good morning," Will said.

"Hey," Kirk said, not straying from his shuffling.

"Are you okay?"

"Yes," Kirk said. "I'm just getting everything organized. Big day today. We need to pick the right twelve people."

"I hope you do," Will said, and sat back in his chair. The bailiff announced the judge's appearance, and all stood as he found his seat.

"Be seated, please," the judge said. "The court proceedings will now begin for the People versus Willem Kelly. We'll begin with any motions to be heard. Counselor?" The judge was looking toward Michael DiCiccio, the prosecutor for the state. A slight head shake was all DiCiccio provided. "How about you, Mr. Kirk?"

"Not at this time, Your Honor."

"Very well. Let's move ahead with the juror selection. Earl, please bring in the first group." Will gathered that the bailiff's name was Earl, as he was the one to leave the room. He returned less than a minute later with twelve unfortunate souls in tow. They each took a seat in the jury box and waited, already looking bored and a little perturbed. Michael DiCiccio was the first to question the witnesses. He asked them questions about their jobs, their backgrounds, and whether they felt there was any reason they should not serve on the jury. He then informed the judge of the potential jurors he wanted to strike or excuse from the proceedings. More jurors were brought in to replace those who left, and the process started again, but this time it was Leonard Kirk who was asking the questions. After six refills of the jury box, there were twelve individuals left.

Some luck was involved, as when Kirk was making his final round of cuts, there were six jurors to replace, and five men and a woman came in to fill the seats. In truth, Kirk did a great job with what he had to work with as far as the jury. At the end, there were nine men, only one of them in upper management, and three women, only one of them divorced.

The judge called for a recess for lunch after the jury was selected, and then began the actual trial proceedings. This seemed odd to Will, as in most of the movies he had seen and books he had read, there was usually time between the jury selection and the start of the trial. He didn't object, as it meant he wouldn't see his cell until later, at the earliest, which for Will, was fine. When the judge was announced once again and took his seat, he read to the court the offenses Will had supposedly committed, and then turned the court over to DiCiccio.

"Opening remarks, Counselor?" he said.

Michael DiCiccio rose from his chair and buttoned his suit jacket, walked across the courtroom, and never took his eyes off of Will until he approached the jury box. "Ladies and Gentlemen. What you're going to hear over the next few days is a story that is a web so well-woven that you may not believe it. But I assure you, it's all true. Now, I'm going to give you the facts about Mr. Kelly here, about what he did, and how he did it. When I'm done, defense counsel, Mr. Kirk here, is probably going to tell you that I'm distorting the facts, maybe even outright lying, about the tale of Mr. Kelly. But don't let his tales of Mr. Kelly's good behavior and becoming a model citizen sway you. Mr. Kelly is, in fact, a criminal, facing all of the charges that His Honor read to you earlier. I ask that you listen to the facts, and when asked, to return a verdict of guilty. Thank you." DiCiccio went back across the room with a smug little smile on his face, keeping his eyes on Will. Will returned an emotionless gaze.

"Mr. Kirk?" the judge said. Leonard stood up from his seat, put a hand lightly on Will's shoulder, and walked over to the jury box.

"Ladies and Gentlemen, first I want to thank you for sacrificing your time to perform your civic duties, and I promise I will try to keep you here not any longer than is absolutely necessary. Now, you've heard what the prosecutor has to say. He thinks he has this all wrapped up; he's going to present you with the facts, and he wants you to convict Willem Kelly of these charges. Well, I'm here to tell you that any man who performed the acts that Willem Kelly has been accused of cannot be in his right mind. It is my belief, and it is what I will prove to you, beyond the shadows of any doubt, that Willem Kelly was most assuredly not sane when he committed these acts. Now, I ask you to sit back and listen to what transpires here in this courtroom. You may find yourself bored at times, and you may find yourselves entertained at others. All I am asking you to do is keep an open mind, and I guarantee you that by the end of this trial, you're going to understand that our plea, of not guilty, by reason of insanity, is just. Thank you." Kirk crossed the room, turned at the table, put his hand on Will's shoulder again, and sat down.

'Thank you both," the judge said. "Mr. DiCiccio, your first witness."

"Thank you, Your Honor. The Prosecution calls Mr. James Higgins." The bailiff disappeared for a moment and returned with Higgins, who took his spot at the witness stand and was sworn in by Earl. Higgins looked at Will and shook his head in disbelief. "Mr. Higgins," DiCiccio said. "You are the head of security and loss prevention at Pickwick Finance, correct?"

"That is correct," Higgins boomed into the microphone.

"And what does that position entail, sir. What do you do?"

"I oversee the group of employees whose duty it is to review transactions to make sure that the dollar figures match the accounts and that the accounts are straight. I often follow up with the customers to make sure they have what they need financially."

"I see," DiCiccio said. "And was part of that review function reviewing the accounts that were set up by Willem Kelly?"

"We did review Mr. Kelly's accounts," Higgins said.

"And what did you find?" DiCiccio asked.

"For years, nothing. Everything was fine. His accounting paperwork always matched to the penny."

"And then?" DiCiccio asked.

"And then," Higgins sighed. "Then the team dropped the ball. Mr. Kelly was so accurate with his account that we stopped reviewing his to focus on some other accounts. By the time we found what we found regarding his accounts, it was three months too late."

"And what did you find in Mr. Kelly's accounts?"

"Discrepancies. On Monday, September tenth, of two-thousand one, we found that there were accounts with dollar amounts that did not make sense, and there were accounts with bad phone numbers and invalid addresses. It reeked of fraud, but due to his history with the company, we wanted to give Mr. Kelly the opportunity to explain himself."

"In fact, Mr. Higgins, were you not supposed to have a meeting with Mr. Kelly and F. Roger Dickey, also from loss prevention, the very next morning?"

"That is correct," Higgins boomed. Will thought the flags behind the judge were going to fall over every time Higgins spoke into the microphone.

"And to remind the court, what day was that meeting scheduled?"

"Tuesday, September eleventh, two-thousand one," Higgins said.

"Did that meeting ever take place?"

"No, sir."

"And why not, Mr. Higgins?"

"Because some asshole flew an airplane into our building." Kirk thought about objecting, but to what, he wasn't sure.

The courtroom began to rumble with low whispering and groaning, and the judge asked for order, and also asked James Higgins to watch his language, and Higgins apologized.

"And what happened, Mr. Higgins, to Mr. F. Roger Dickey?"

"He died in the building," Higgins said.

"Objection!" Leonard Kirk sprang to life. "Relevance?"

"Sustained," the judge said. "I will ask the jurors to ignore Mr. Higgins' response to that question."

"Mr. Higgins," DiCiccio continued. "What happened next?"

"We never had the meeting. We thought Willem Kelly died in the building as well, and the secrets he has been keeping died with him. There was nothing left to pursue at that point."

"Thank you, Mr. Higgins. No more questions, Your Honor."

"Mr. Kirk?" the judge said. Leonard Kirk rose to his feet.

"Mr. Higgins, how long had you known Willem Kelly before that meeting was to take place?"

Higgins inhaled and exhaled, and the microphone picked it all up. "About six years," he said.

"And did you ever spend any real time with him?"

"Real time?" Higgins asked. "I would say no. I usually don't hang around with co-workers."

"I see, and did you notice anything odd about Mr. Kelly the morning you were supposed to meet with him?"

"I'd never met the man in person, so I would have to say no."

"So, you wouldn't know if he were happy, sad, distressed, frantic, anything like that?" Kirk asked.

"Other than by his expression, no."

"Thank you, Mr. Higgins. I have no more questions, Your Honor."

"Redirect, Mr. DiCiccio?" the judge asked.

"Not at this time, Your Honor, but we reserve the right to recall this witness if needed."

"Mr. Higgins, you may step down," the judge said. "Call your next witness."

"We would like to call Ms. Jeanette Raines, Your Honor," DiCiccio announced. Will rolled his eyes. *They pulled poor Jeannie into this,* he thought. When Jeannie was sworn in, DiCiccio continued. "Ms. Raines, you were the administrative assistant for Mr. Kelly. Is that correct?"

"Yes," she said.

"And what did you do for Mr. Kelly?"

"Answered the phone, typed, filed forms, set appointments. The usual stuff," Jeannie said.

"And were you aware that Mr. Kelly was allegedly stealing nearly half a million dollars from your company?"

"I was not," she said. "I'm still not sure I believe it."

"Can you describe your relationship with Mr. Kelly?"

"Professional, I guess," she said.

"Did you have any romantic encounters with Mr. Kelly?"

"Objection, Your Honor. Relevance?" Kirk said.

"It goes to credibility, Your Honor," DiCiccio said.

The judge exhaled. "Overruled. Continue."

"Well, Ms. Raines?" DiCiccio said.

"Never. Mr. Kelly was always professional, and I'm old enough to be his mother. You should be ashamed of yourself, sir." A small bit of laughter spewed forth from the gallery, but was soon quieted by the rapping of a gavel.

"I beg your pardon, Ms. Raines. I apologize if I insulted you. Now, you said you set appointments for Mr. Kelly. Did you set the one he was to have had the morning of September eleventh?"

"I did," she said.

"What were Mr. Kelly's instructions to you regarding setting that appointment with Mr. Higgins and Mr. Dickey?"

"Mr. Dickey wanted the meeting at eleven in the morning, but Mr. Kelly told me to make it for eight forty-five, so that's what I did."

DiCiccio walked across the room and looked at a legal pad on his desk, and then came back to Jeannie at the witness stand. "Why do you think he made the meeting earlier?"

"Objection, speculation," Kirk shouted.

"Sustained," the judge said. "Get to the point, Counselor."

"Do you know why Mr. Kelly asked you to make the appointment earlier?"

"I do not," Jeannie answered.

"I tender the witness, reserving the right to recall if needed," DiCiccio said.

"Mr. Kirk," the judge said.

"Ms. Raines, did you happen to notice anything about Mr. Kelly in the months, weeks, or days leading up to his disappearance?"

"Well, he did seem to be stressed out there towards the end, and I'm pretty sure I heard him talking to himself in his office."

"Objection, speculation," DiCiccio said.

"State of mind, Your Honor."

"Overruled," the judge said. "Continue, Mr. Kirk."

"Could you hear what he was saying?" Kirk asked.

"Not really," she said.

"And how often did you hear talk to himself, Ms. Raines?"

"Objection! Your Honor, speculation," DiCiccio stated again, louder this time.

"State of mind," Kirk stated again.

"Overruled," the judge replied, and directed his attention to Jeannie

"I don't know," she said. "More than a few times."

"I see, thank you, Ms. Raines, no more questions."

"Let's take a fifteen-minute recess," the judge said. We'll reconvene at two-thirty." The gavel hit the table, and the courtroom emptied as everyone rushed to the restrooms. Will thought he spotted Kathleen as she was walking through the double doors out into the hallway.

Chapter 93 – The Right Thing

For the next day and a half, Michael DiCiccio brought everyone he could find to the witness stand who had interacted with Will during his crime spree and eventual escape. He brought in the managers from the banks that Will had visited to get the money, and they told of being swindled out of their cash by a master criminal. He called Cleo Baptiste, and Leon Anderson from Indianapolis, he called Stanley HighEagle from the sporting goods store, and he called Charles Travis, the fire investigator from Seattle. They all told their part of Will's story, and DiCiccio managed to make them weave a story so intricate and full of twists that it could have been penned by one of the great writers.

For his part, Leonard Kirk did the best with DiCiccio's witnesses as he could, but couldn't quite un-spin the marvelous tale that DiCiccio was pulling off. Will felt it, and he knew he was doomed to spend a whole lot of time in prison. DiCiccio called Kathleen, which was painful for Will. She refused to look at him. DiCiccio focused on how she had felt when she thought Will was dead, and then when she found out he was alive, and had chosen to go on the run to get away from her. Kirk declined to cross, but reserved the right to call her as a witness later. DiCiccio called Sheriff Wes Tim Utter, who told the truth, but managed to do it in a way that made Will appear heroic, which seemed to irritate DiCiccio. However, Utter ended on a sour note that it was a shame that such a good lawman was a criminal at the core. Will didn't think that helped his cause any, but he was grateful for the sheriff's kinder words. On the third day, DiCiccio called Detective Brian Greco as his witness. Greco was on the witness stand for four-and-a-half hours telling his part of the story, from chasing leads to eventually capturing Will Kelly more than halfway across the country.

Will held no animosity towards Greco for his testimony. He thought Greco was fair in his recounting of the events, and even managed to make Will sound good when he said he was impressed that Will had stopped a robbery and then had become a sheriff's deputy, and from all accounts, he made a good one. Greco said that someone of Willem Kelly's character, shaded past or not, was rare. DiCiccio tried to quiet Greco, but the judge instructed Greco to continue. He told of how Will had a chance to run once he was found, but he didn't, and he could have gone down in a shootout, but he didn't. He surrendered quietly on his own accord. When Greco finished telling his story, DiCiccio said that the Prosecution rested its case. The judge called for a lunch recess, and everyone was to return in an hour's time.

Will didn't think the trial was going to be as bad as it was. No one did anything dirty; they just told the truth. He was also unlucky when he got Leonard Kirk for a defense lawyer. It wasn't Kirk's fault. He was just inexperienced and got tasked with facing a shark like DiCiccio. Will was thinking about all of this while eating a sandwich in a small cell in the basement of the courthouse when a guard came and asked to speak with Kirk. Kirk excused himself and followed the guard through the door and up to the main floor. Will could not imagine what could be happening now, but it probably couldn't get any worse than it was. Will waited and waited, but Kirk never returned. When it was time to return to the courtroom, a guard walked Will from the basement cell into the courtroom and to his seat. He saw Kirk talking with DiCiccio and felt his stomach hit the floor. The judge walked in, and Earl the Bailiff told everyone to rise, and they did. Kirk was still over at the Prosecutor's table. The judge banged the gavel and called the court to order. Kirk and DiCiccio looked at each other, and Kirk asked if they could both approach the bench. The judge granted the request, and the two men crossed the bar and had a quiet conversation with the judge as he covered the microphone in front of him. Will sat impatiently, wondering what was going on.

The judge nodded his head, and Will heard him say "proceed" as he took his hand away from the microphone. "Counselor?" he said.

DiCiccio looked at Will and then to a smiling Kirk, and shook his head. "Your honor," DiCiccio began, "in light of testimony given today, some of the charges against Mr. Kelly have been dropped. The charge of flight has been dropped by the NYPD and the State, the State wishes to drop the charges for the credit card fraud due to lack of evidence as Mr. Zhang was never located, the former residence of Mr. Kelly was resold, therefore the mortgage company has dropped the charge of intentionally defaulting on the mortgage, and the spouse wishes to drop the charges of abandonment. Only the charges of criminal possession of forged instruments, forgery, falsifying business records, and embezzlement still remain. In an effort to speed up these proceedings, and in light of said testimony, the State will drop all charges except the embezzlement, which the Pickwick Finance company still wishes to pursue."

Kirk looked at Will with raised eyebrows, and Will was dumbfounded. As bad a job as Kirk had done during the cross-examination of each witness, it was possibly DiCiccio's ego and his confidence with his witnesses that may have backfired, and actually helped Will more than it hurt. The courtroom was full of chatter and murmuring, and the judge snapped the gavel to calm the noise.

"Mr. Kirk," the judge said. "It's your show now. Call your first witness." Kirk looked at Will with a sly smile.

"Here we go," Kirk said quietly to Will. "Your Honor," he said louder. "The defense wishes to recall Kathleen Kelly to the stand." Will looked up at Kirk with a quizzical look on his face. Kirk looked back at him and mouthed, *Don't worry. I've got this.* Kathleen was led back to the witness stand and sat in the seat so that she was not looking directly at Will at the table. He didn't blame her.

"Ms. Kelly," the judge said, "I am reminding you that you're still under oath." Kathleen nodded and looked ahead, but still not at Will.

"Ms. Kelly," Kirk began. "When you met Mr. Kelly, were you already a dentist?"

"No," she said. "I went to school after we were married."

"I see. So, Mr. Kelly supported you in your quest to become a dentist."

"Yes, I suppose he did," she said. Will listened intently.

"And did you purchase the residence at 1917 Foot Hill Road together?"

"No," she said again. "I moved in after we were... married."

"So, you moved into Mr. Kelly's house, a house he had purchased on his own, after you got married. Interesting. Now, when you were going to school to become a dentist, how many hours were you away from Mr. Kelly's home?"

DiCiccio stood to object, but the judge held up his hand.

"I was working and going to school at the same time," she said. "I was doing my best to help us make a life where we wouldn't need for anything."

"How many hours?" Kirk asked again.

"I don't know, twelve, fourteen?" she said, annoyed.

"That's a hard schedule, Ms. Kelly. And when you became a dentist, what hours did you work?"

"I beg your pardon?" she asked.

"Hours, Ms. Kelly. How many hours of each day were you at work?"

"I don't know. A lot." Kirk walked over to a table and grabbed a stack of paper.

"Isn't it true," he began, "that you sometimes worked fourteen to sixteen hours each day?"

"I was trying to build a practice," she said, slightly ruffled. Will was getting agitated himself. He couldn't see where Kirk was going with his line of questioning.

"Yes, I see," Kirk said. "And then, there was January eighth, 1999." Will shot a look at Kirk, but Kirk didn't see it. His focus was on a struggling Kathleen.

"How dare you," she said.

"What happened on that day, Ms. Kelly?" Kirk asked. Kathleen turned away from him and wiped a tear from her face. "What happened, Ms. Kelly?"

"The witness will answer the question," the judge said. Will clasped his hands together with his elbows on his knees and lowered his head to the table.

Kirk asked again. "What happened, Ms. Kelly!" he demanded. She whispered something that no one could hear. "Louder!" Kirk said.

"I miscarried our son!" she shouted into the microphone. The air was sucked out of the courtroom as nearly everyone in attendance took a gasp. Will sat with his head down, but he couldn't hide his sadness or his building annoyance at Kirk.

"Yes, and after that, isn't it true that you became more and more distant, Ms. Kelly? More and more subdued, and withdrawn?"

"I was heartbroken," she said through tears. "You can't know the feeling. I couldn't handle it... I didn't know what to do! I buried myself in my work."

"You became so withdrawn that you drove your husband into a spiral that he himself couldn't escape, and it drove him into an alleged life of crime!" Kirk said.

"No," she said, softly, almost inaudibly.

"Stop," Will said softly, but no one could hear him over Kirk's yelling voice.

"The death of your unborn child, caused by you working too much and spending too much time away from home, is what drove Mr. Kelly to do these alleged acts, Ms. Kelly!"

"Stop, Kirk," Will said louder, but to no avail. Kirk continued. Kathleen was crying loudly on the stand.

"Admit it, Ms. Kelly, you are the reason your husband did what the prosecution says he did."

DiCiccio stood from his table. "Objection!" he shouted. "Badgering!"

The judge began to speak, but no one could hear him over Kirk's frenzied accusations.

"Ms. Kelly, why don't you admit it! He didn't abandon you, YOU abandoned HIM long before he ever left!"

"STOP!" Will yelled, standing above all the noise. Then he lowered his voice when the entire courtroom was staring at him. "Please, Leonard, stop." Kathleen was destroyed on the witness stand. The only noise in the courtroom at that time was her sobbing. Will stood at the table and looked at Kathleen. "I'm so sorry," he said. And then he turned to the judge. "Your Honor," he said quietly. "I want to change my plea. I plead guilty to the remaining charges against me."

Kirk came over to the table. "Your Honor," he said. "A moment to speak with my client." It wasn't a request. He approached Will and whispered, "What are you doing? We've got her on the ropes?"

"This is wrong, Leonard," Will said sternly. "What you're doing to her is wrong! She doesn't deserve that."

"Come on, we've got this," Kirk said, excitedly, his volume increasing. "This is our way to win. Don't you see? What this bitch put you through is wrong! What are you gonna do –"

Kirk never finished his question. Will reached back and punched him square in the face, and the courtroom erupted into chaos.

Will looked down at Kirk and then up at the judge. "What am I going to do? The right thing, for right now, at least," Will said, shaking a hurting hand. "You're fired," he said, still looking at Kirk. The judge's gavel reigned the courtroom back into a quieter state. Kirk, who had fallen like a sack of flour onto the floor, stayed there, blood gushing from his nose. Will turned to the judge. "Your Honor, I'd like to represent myself going forward. And I," he paused, then continued. "I plead guilty to the remaining charge." He looked down at Kirk, and then back to the judge. "And I guess I plead guilty to the forthcoming assault charge as well," he said, nodding at Kirk.

Chapter 94 – New Perspective

The judge called a recess until the next day so that Kathleen could collect herself and Leonard Kirk could collect his body, his blood, and his belongings from the courtroom after his violent firing by Will. Will was taken back to his cell in the Washington Correctional Facility, and he filled Tracks in on what had happened during the courtroom proceedings.

"Well, I guess that's one way to go," Tracks said with a laugh.

"Yeah, I guess it wasn't the smartest thing to do," Will said. "I just couldn't take him assaulting her like that anymore. He never even discussed his strategy with me. He just went after her."

"That's some crazy stuff about the rest of the charges being dropped," Tracks added.

"I couldn't believe it," Will said, shaking his head.

"I guess this is your last night here, unless they send you back here after your sentence is delivered."

"Do you think they'll just keep me here with you, or would they move me somewhere else?" Will asked.

"I'm not sure. If you get more than five years, they'll probably move you and change your rags to a different color. Less than five, who knows?" Tracks said.

The impending sentence, which Will knew could always come at some point, was now a reality.

"I know I can't take it back," Will said. "Everything I have done, it's done. Some of it was good, and some of it was terrible, and I guess there was a lot of it that was somewhere in between."

"Would you take it back if you could?" Tracks asked him.

"I don't think so," Will said. "Honestly, for all the bad that it was, I think I'm better because of the experience. Not that I would do it again, but I wouldn't want it to have never happened."

Tracks cleared his throat. "Well, man, whatever happens, I wish you luck. If we don't get to get to be roommates after your sentencing, I think I'm better for knowing you."

"Why is that?" Will asked.

"They say this place is for rehabilitation, they give you all the time in the world to reflect on what you did and who you did it to, and what the final outcome was. But what I think most people miss, and why they go back to their old ways, is that they don't listen to the stories of the other inmates. They do their time and try something else, where I think if they listened to everyone else and reflected on that as well, they'd probably not go down that road and end up back in prison."

Will thought about that for a few seconds. "And now, because you know my story, you're not going to steal money and run and live someone else's life, and abandon your house and your wife?"

"Not a chance in the world, brother. When I get out of here, I ain't doing any of that shit, or anything else on the wrong side of the law."

Will laughed. "Well, then I guess our time here together was worth it," he said. A buzzer sounded throughout the prison.

"Five minutes to lights out," Tracks said.

"And yet we sit here illuminated in knowledge and self-growth," Will said.

"Well, I don't know about all that, but when you're gone, I'll miss our time. Thanks for teaching me how to play chess. I'm gonna have to find a smart inmate around here to play with. Probably harder than you'd think it is."

"I don't know," Will said. "There's probably a good deal of people in here who were calculating and using strategy."

"Yeah," Tracks said. But since they're in here, wouldn't that mean they're no good at it?"

"That's a good point," Will said, and they both laughed. At that moment, the lights in the prison cells shut off, and Will and Tracks were left alone in the darkness.

"Good night, Bud," Tracks said.

"Good night, Tracey. And thanks."

The next morning at nine o'clock sharp, the judge walked across the room and took his seat at the bench. Everyone was directed to sit as he adjusted the microphone. He peered over his glasses at the courtroom and shook his head slightly. He began: "Mr. Kelly. Before we proceed, I need to make you aware that, as you are now representing yourself, you cannot use that as a reason for claiming a mistrial once these proceedings have concluded. Do you understand?"

Will stood alone at his table. "I understand and accept that, Your Honor."

The judge clasped his hands together in front of him. "Are there any more witnesses from either the prosecution or the defense?"

"Nothing, Your Honor," DiCiccio said.

"Mr. Kelly?" the judge asked.

"Nothing more, Your Honor," Will said.

"Then we will move on to the sentencing stage of these proceedings," the judge continued. "Assuming Mr. Kirk wishes to press charges, you may face court proceedings for that at a later date, and any punishment requiring served time may be added onto your pending sentence from these proceedings. Is that clear, Mr. Kelly?"

"Yes, Your Honor," Will replied.

"Let's get to it then," said the judge. "Let's take a thirty-minute recess." When all required parties were back in the court, the judge resumed his place on the bench. He adjusted his glasses and fixed his gaze on Will, who was now standing, based on the directions of Earl the Bailiff. "Mr. Kelly. It is not often I find myself conflicted in such a way during a criminal trial when it comes to sentencing a guilty party. The story I have heard over the past few days has been nothing short of riveting. Someone should write the book. Your conniving and calculating methods of embezzling money through your employer disgust me. Your cowardice in running away from your problems makes me wince. Your disregard for the law and for those who care about you, and whom you obviously still care about, astonishes me, especially after what I saw in this courtroom yesterday. Your transformation from criminal to upstanding citizen, however, even under the shroud of lies, impresses me. And your ability to make one small corner of the world a better place because you chose to try to do the right thing, gives me hope." The courtroom was completely silent as the judge continued. "Don't get me wrong, Mr. Kelly. I am not a fan of any of this. You do deserve to be punished. Do you have anything to say for yourself?"

"Your Honor, I have no excuses and take ownership of everything I have done, and I am ready to be held accountable for my actions. I readily accept whatever punishment you decide to hand down."

"Admirable, Mr. Kelly. As most of the charges were dropped, the only remaining charge is that of the embezzlement of four hundred and fifty-five thousand dollars. That number could be crippling to some businesses, but luckily for you, not to a large financial company like Pickwick. The crime equates to Grand Larceny, and is punishable by a sentence in a New York State prison of not less than five years and no more than fifteen. Mr. Kelly, based on your actions, both bad and good, I hereby sentence you to five years and six months in a New York State prison, with eligibility for parole in not less than thirty months. This court is adjourned."

The judge rapped his gavel on the judge's bench and the crowd in the courtroom groaned and chatted as Earl came over and stood next to Will until an officer was able to get to their position. The officer handcuffed Will and began to lead him out of the courtroom. They were at the door when Will heard Kathleen's voice.

"Will," she said. He stopped and turned to see her looking at him, which surprised him. She took a few steps closer to them. "Thank you," she said softly. "And good luck." She turned and left them and made her way through the doors on the opposite side of the room. He watched her go and found himself slightly smiling. Maybe they had both found the closure that they needed. He knew they would never be together again, but at least their relationship could be civil. He valued that.

The officer escorted Will back to the car and then to the Washington Correctional Facility to gather his belongings. Tracks wasn't in the room when he returned, so Will didn't have a chance to say goodbye. He felt like he owed Tracks a lot for what he had done for him while they shared the room. He left the chess set for Tracks and all of the origami projects he had done over the past few weeks. He owed Tracks more, he knew, but had nothing left to give. The guard escorted Will to the area where he was first processed. They gave him back his clothes and other belongings, and fifty-three dollars and twelve cents.

"What is this?" Will asked about the money.

"The balance of your commissary account. It's what you didn't spend," the guard said.

"Oh. Uhh, can I give it to another inmate?" Will asked.

"You may," the guard said. "Tracks?"

Will's eyebrows raised at the suggestion. "Yes," he said. "Tracey Allgood."

"I'll take care of it," the guard said. "May I make a suggestion? If you have no other source of money, you should keep some of this so you can start an account wherever you're going. You're going to need things there," she said.

"I'll be okay," Will said. "I came in with nothing, I can leave with nothing."

"Suit yourself," she said. The guard led Will outside and to a bus with three other inmates who had all been previously sentenced. They rode in silence for what Will guessed was about an hour. The bus stopped in the secured lot of a large facility surrounded by fences topped with razor wire. The door opened, and a man in a guard uniform stepped aboard.

"Inmates!" he snapped. "My name is Guard Cruz Cage. You will address me as 'Guard Cage.' Not 'Mister Cage,' not 'sir.' 'Guard Cage.' Know it, and remember it. I am responsible for you four shitheads and several others. Do not piss me off, or I will make your life in here a living hell for the time you're here. Now, follow me." Guard Cage led the four men off the bus, and Will was last in the line of the four, followed by two more guards behind him. That was fine with him. He was happy to follow everyone else around for a while until he got acclimated to the schedules and processes. Cage led them to a small office where their paperwork was processed, forced to shower in the open, and a body cavity check. Then they were given clothing, shoes, sheets, a blanket, a pillow, and a pillowcase. They were on the move again, walking through access door after access door, each opened with a swipe of a card that hung from Cage's neck. Cage stopped in a hallway and began yelling at no one.

"Cage, 7432, cells one-two, one-three, one-four, and one-five." There was a buzzing sound, and four doors swung open. Cage turned to the four men. "Petroski, cell 1-2! Jimenez, cell 1-3, Kelly, Cell 1-4, Jackson, cell 1-5." Each man moved toward and into their cell. "Cage, 7432, close cells one-two, one-three, one-four, and one-five." Then, he lowered his voice and directed his speech to the newest inmates at the facility. "Welcome home, shitheads," he said as the doors shut.

Will looked around the room. The first thing he noticed was the same type of odd sink/toilet combination attached to the far wall that was in his previous cell. There was no bunk bed here, just the one bed. It appeared as if he would not have any roommates this time. There was also a small set of shelves next to the toilet that Will assumed was for personal items. One thing Will noticed about the room was that it was short. The ceiling could not have been more than seven feet from the floor, and when he reached up, he could touch the ceiling, and his arms were still bent at the elbows. He sat on the bed and looked around the room. This was going to be his home for the foreseeable future.

It was a seemingly endless string of days of routines for Will. Wake up, clean up, eat breakfast, exercise, spend time in his cell, eat lunch, exercise, spend more time in his cell, eat dinner, lounge around the common area playing Solitaire, spend more time in his cell, and then go to sleep, only to do it all over again the following day. It was two weeks before he had a visitor, which didn't surprise him. When he did get his first visitor, it surprised him that he *did* have one. He walked down the long corridor of cells on each side of the room and reached the area where he was directed to go through a set of doors that opened to the outside. The guard directed him around the corner to an area with metal picnic tables cemented into the ground. Will poked his head around the corner to see who his visitor was, and was shocked to see Detective Brian Greco on the other side. Will snickered and looked around the area, and then approached the table where Greco sat.

"Well, Detective, and I have to say I'm surprised to see you here. Isn't this some sort of occupational hazard for you? To come see the convicts?"

"We don't really have any rules against it, but then again, it's not encouraged, either," Greco said. "Sit down."

"You look better," Will said, taking a seat on the opposite side of the table. "Finally getting some sleep?"

"More than I was when I was chasing you all over the country."

"That's understandable," Will said. "Sorry about that, by the way."

"It's the job," Greco said. "How are you holding up in here?"

"Bored as hell. I'm waiting for them to give me a job or something so I can earn some commissary money. Right now, it's just food, exercise, and sleep."

"What exercise do you get?" Greco asked.

"I run every day, just laps around the yard," Will said. "It beats sitting and doing nothing. I don't know how some of these guys do it. They just sit and watch time go by."

"You'll get used to it," Greco said. "The job should be coming soon. They move people in and out of here all the time. Something will open up. In the meantime, I'll donate some money to your commissary funds while you get on your feet."

"You don't need to do that," Will said.

"It's fine," Greco said.

"Why?" Will asked. "Why would you do that after what I've done?"

"Mr. Kelly," Greco began, but then changed. "Will, if I may, there are a lot of things I've seen through my years, first as a street cop, even now as a detective, but I've never in my life have I seen or heard a story like yours," Greco said.

"Yes, call me Will, please. And people turn over new leaves all the time, Detective."

"Usually only when they are forced to, Will," Greco said. "You did it on your own, without being punished and forced to do it. I had several long conversations with Sheriff Utter. I know what you did out there, and what you're capable of. When you were sentenced, what did the judge say? He said you gave him hope. I have hope, too, Will, that you're going to do your time, get out of here, earn your freedom, and go on to do that thing, whatever it is, that's going to give you the satisfaction that you're making a difference. That's why, Will."

Will sat back in the metal seat of the table and exhaled. "Freedom. You want to know what freedom is? I wake up each morning, and I forget where I am, and then, I figure it out, and I'm actually relieved that I'm in prison. I'm honestly happy that I'm not a fugitive anymore and that I don't have to hide anymore. That's freedom." Will looked up at the clouded sky, pausing before he continued. "And hope? That's a lot to put on a guy who sits in a metal box for most of the day, Detective. Hope is not an oft-used word around here." He cracked his knuckles over his head and looked down at the grounds. Greco said nothing, so Will continued. "Hope," he said. "I had hope last year when I hatched this ridiculous plan. Hope of getting out of my old life, and hope of getting into a new one. That's why I bolted, Detective." Greco still said nothing and let Will speak. "I don't know, man. Maybe hope was what I found in that skyline I could see every day at sunset in that little city, no matter where I was. I could get out of my car or come out of my trailer and just watch the sun melt into the earth. I could go out on the edge of town, and there were no buildings, a few trees, just the sun and the earth, like a baseball going over the fence for a home run. Slowly, just going, going, gone." He looked around the yard they were in, which was surrounded by walls topped with razor wire, and trees that reached into the sky. "You know, I said something on September eleventh last year that stuck with me, and throughout this little journey of mine, I've oddly been able to say it multiple times, and it meant something each time. I said something about how different the world feels when the skyline changes. Now, I'm here, and you're talking to me about hope," he said. "Look what hope got me, Detective. Now there is no skyline. At least not that I can see."

Greco stood up and buttoned his jacket. "Find a new perspective, Will. You have a way of looking at things that many others don't. Think about it. The good thing is, if you play by the rules, you'll see a skyline again someday, whichever one you want to see. You'll have your freedom again."

Epilogue (Skyline)

<u>Six years later...</u>

Police Commissioner Raymond Gallagher stood at the podium and looked out at the masses of police and citizens that were in attendance. The sun shone brightly that morning, and it reflected in the dew that was still wet on the lawn. He looked down at his note cards, but decided he didn't need them, and put them in his pocket, and moved closer to the podium.

"Ladies and Gentlemen, fellow officers, distinguished guests, and the Ramirez and Greco families, welcome to this joyous ceremony. It is an honor," he said, "when I am fortunate enough to decorate and acknowledge the sacrifices made by one of the brave men and women under my command. This is, indeed, a great day." There was applause from the crowd, and Gallagher looked to his left and smiled at the guest of honor.

"This man," Gallagher continued, "I often struggle with his, shall we say, unorthodox methods, but he always seems to get the job done, and he does it well. He reminds me so much of another man I had the great opportunity, and the honor, to command, and many of you knew him. His name is Steve Angelucci, and it's hard to believe it has been seven years since we lost him."

Greco smiled from his seat on the side of the stage and nodded approvingly, and a large portion of the audience cheered. He had no idea that Gallagher was going to say those words, but he could not disagree with his commissioner. Greco had actually thought the same thing.

"This man that we honor today," Gallagher said, "is more than a great cop. He is a tenacious investigator and a true hero. Three weeks ago, while following a lead he uncovered, he not only found and captured Tito "El Toro" Minoso, a major player in one of the largest heroin distribution rings in our fine city, but in the process saved the lives of two of our great brothers, Sergeant Brian Greco, and Detective Paul Ramirez."

There was more chatter and applause from the crowd, and Gallagher let it go until it passed. "When the criminal and his cohorts had the two detectives in a compromising position, this man entered into dangerous hand-to-hand combat with the perpetrator and took him down before the others were harmed. His actions allowed Sergeant Greco and Detective Ramirez the opportunity to pursue and subdue two other members of the heroin distribution ring. In this man's heroic efforts, he was unfortunately injured himself, sustaining a puncture wound in the shoulder by his assailant. I am happy to report that he has fully healed and is now back on duty. Ladies and Gentlemen, it is my honor to award the Police Combat Cross and the Medal for Valor to Officer, and future Detective, Willem Kelly!'

Will rose from his seat and walked to the podium. He stood tall as Gallagher presented him with the two bars, one green, one blue, and Will accepted them with a handshake from the commissioner. He turned toward the crowd and showed the medals, and was urged to make some comments. He declined at first, but Gallagher's urging changed his mind. He didn't really want to say no to the police commissioner. Gallagher moved aside, and Will stood behind the podium.

"Uhh," he said, "public speaking..., this is not my strong point, so I hope you'll forgive me for ruining this ceremony." He stopped and took a breath. "Uhh, some of you know how I got here, and for those of you who don't, my only advice to you if you want to be a police officer is just to apply. Don't take the same path I took." There was some laughter from the crowd by those who knew Will's story. "Seven years ago, I didn't know what I wanted to do with my life. I was lost, literally and figuratively. There were times that I had absolutely no idea where I was. But I knew one thing. I knew that whatever I decided to do, or in my case, whatever I was forced into, I wanted to be able to make a difference. It's been a strange seven years since then. There have been a lot of ups and downs, and a lot of changes. Changes to this city, which I love, and changes to me as well. I mean, who would have thought that I would be training to be a detective, shadowing the man who arrested me, and did so in Nebraska of all places?" Most of the crowd laughed, and Will looked over at

Greco, who was smiling. He gave Will a nod to continue, and Will became emotional. "I stand here, on this stage today, and I look at these citations, and I'm not sure I really deserve them." Will used the tip of his finger to wipe a tear that was rolling down his cheek. "These citations seem heavy, not in weight, but in the responsibility to continue to strive to have earned them, and to continue the daily fight which we fight." He paused for a moment and then continued. "But I look to my right, and I see my mentor, Sergeant Greco, and Detective Paul Ramirez, and I see them today, sitting next to their wives, Maryanne Greco and Petra Ramirez, and I see them with their children, little Katie and little baby Pete. I see them, together, and I am," he paused for a moment to find the right word. "Whole," he said. "I am whole. I am fulfilled, and I am satisfied to know that my journey, though odd and difficult, has not been for naught, because I know that now, I have made a difference. That's all I ever wanted to do. Now, it's time for me, for all of us, to continue that fight. Thank you all." He turned to Greco. "And thank you," he said.

The crowd stood and applauded as Will walked across the stage to where Greco was sitting. Greco stood up, and the two men shook hands and then hugged.

"I'm so damned proud of you," Greco said. "You make me proud."

"Thank you, brother. That means so much to me," Will said. Ramirez stood up, and he and Will shook hands and had a short embrace. "So," Will said. "Lunch today?"

"Sure," Greco said. "Where?"

"Usual place," Will said.

"Ugh, really?" Ramirez asked. "Don't you ever get tired of the same food?"

"Not really," Will said. "I love everything about it!'

Greco looked at Ramirez and shrugged. "What the hell," Greco said. "But you're buying."

"Done," Will said. "I'll see you around twelve-thirty?"

"Sounds good," Greco said, and returned to Maryanne and their daughter Katie. After the ceremony, Will went back to his apartment and set his new medals on top of the hutch with the others he had received in his short time as a member of the NYPD. He got out of his dress uniform and into his regular officer's uniform and drove to the station for his shift. He got a call for a possible burglary, but it turned out to be an overanxious cat clawing around in a crawlspace.

At twelve twenty-eight, he pulled his car up into the alley between the dry cleaner and the restaurant, parking right behind Greco's car. This parking was technically illegal, but the owner of the restaurant never called a tow truck because they were such good customers.

"Let's see what kind of heartburn I can get today," Ramirez said, laughing.

"Only the best kind," Will said.

"You're getting a different heartburn than we are, Will," Greco said.

"Probably true, but I like it." Will pulled the door open and allowed Greco and Ramirez to enter before him. They took a seat at one of the tables as a busy waitress dropped off a set of menus. Her nametag said her name was Beth.

"Hey guys, what are we drinking today?"

"Diet," Greco said.

Ramirez echoed. "Diet."

"Two diets," Beth said, "and I know you want a water," she said to Will.

"You got it," he said. Beth nodded and left them to the menu. Will began arching and craning his neck as if he were looking for something, or someone.

"Relax, man," Ramirez said. "You're on your way to becoming a detective. So, deduce for us how you know she's here."

"Well," Will said. "The sign out front says 'open' and if that's true, then she's probably here. Also, since I saw her this morning, and she confirmed that she was definitely working today, so, I know she's here. Third, I'm here, and this place smells fantastic, so I know she's here."

Greco laughed. "You could have stopped at the first one," he said. "If this place is open, she's here."

"Who's here?" a voice from behind Will asked. He turned around to see Rocky smiling down at him. She bent over and they shared a quick kiss. "Beautiful ceremony this mornin'," she said. "Made me cry a little."

"Me too," Will said, a little embarrassed.

"Yeah," Ramirez said with a chuckle. "We all saw that. Sentimental bastard!"

"What are you all getting' today?" Rocky asked. "I know you're in a hurry. I'll fast-track it." She paused for a second. "Let me guess, usuals all around? You two," she said, nodding at Greco and Ramirez. "Deep dish or pan?"

"Surprise us, Fibber," Greco said.

"You really hold a grudge, don't ya, Detec—sorry, Sergeant?"

"That's how I do my best work," Greco said. "I forget nothing."

Rocky let that pass. "Katie looked cute this morning," she said, and remembered Ramirez was there. "I couldn't see Pete, but I'm sure he was precious." Ramirez nodded and beamed.

Greco laughed. "That's all, Maryanne. I can barely get the collar on Honey to take a walk now, you think I can dress my kid?" A laugh was shared by all, and Rocky disappeared to put their order in. She came back and tugged Will on the sleeve.

"A moment, Officer?" she said, not so much a question.

"A moment?" Ramirez asked. "Is that all it takes, Kelly?" and he began to belly laugh as if he had been the first man to ever crack a sex joke.

"Ha-ha, Funny Man. We're just going outside for a minute." Will said, scooting his way out of the booth.

"Hey," Greco said in a serious voice. Will turned to look at him. Then Greco began to laugh. "Public nudity, no matter how short a period of time, is still a crime!" And then Ramirez joined in the laughter.

"You guys keep scooting closer together in that booth," Will said. "People are going to talk," he said with a cheesy grin.

"Go see your girl, kid," Greco said. Will walked out of the front door and left Greco and Ramirez to their jokes.

"Why do we come here for lunch with him when he always ends up having lunch with her?" Ramirez asked.

"We desire punishment, I guess," Greco said. "I don't know. I just like watching them. Two criminals living the straight life now. You gotta love it. It has to give you hope."

Will closed the front door and found Rocky at the corner of the building. The neon sign blinking "Rocky's Nebraska-Style Pizza" buzzed overhead, and it reminded Will of the neon signs in the liquor store back in Brindle. "Hey there," he said.

"Hey, yourself," she said. "How was the rest of your morning?"

"Uneventful," he said. "I can only take down one drug kingpin per month. If I do any better, it makes the others look bad."

"Smart ass," she said. Then she got serious. "You could have been seriously hurt, Billy." She still called him Billy, and he didn't mind. It was a name reserved for her though. To everyone else, he was still Will. "Promise me you're not going to do anything like that again?" Rocky said in a pleading manner.

"Ahh," he started. "You know I can't do that. I have to do what I have to do. It's my calling," he said.

"I thought I was your calling," Rocky replied.

"No, *I'm* your calling," Will said with a laugh. "Keeping people in this city straight is my calling. You keeping me straight is your calling."

"I can accept that," she said. "Only because I know I can't change your mind about it."

"Wisdom beyond your years," he said. He looked out through the canyon between the skyscrapers and brownstones and admired the tops of the buildings cutting into the sky. He wasn't aware that he had stopped talking, so Rocky reminded him.

"You okay?" she asked.

"Yeah," he said. "Just thinking. All that time I was in prison, the recreation yard was surrounded by trees. That's all you could see. Trees everywhere. Now," he started, "now, it's hard to believe," he said.

Rocky looked at him as the traffic whizzed by on the street. "What's that?" she asked.

He smiled and looked back at her, and put his arm around her. "How wonderful the world feels when the skyline changes."

Notes From the Author

First off, thank you so much for taking a chance on an unknown author and giving his dream an opportunity to live and breathe. I am, and will be, eternally grateful for your support. Next, if you haven't read this book yet, and do not want to see any spoilers, STOP READING NOW and read the book first!

To begin, here's a little backstory. I first thought of writing a book when I was in my teens. I started an autobiography, but quickly realized that I was not interesting enough, not even for myself, to continue with it.

I wrote short stories and poems, but nothing special, and I thought that so many of them sounded so familiar. When I was working as a security guard in my early twenties, I started writing about a security guard who found that there was a parentless teenage girl with her two young siblings living in the water treatment plant he was guarding. I mean, what else are you going to do on a twelve-hour shift guarding an empty water treatment facility where you're alone and there's nothing to do? You pull out the typewriter from the trunk of your 1990 Dodge Daytona. (Yes, I am that old.) After a few chapters, I realized I had nothing more than a story with no ending and more plot holes than a block of Swiss cheese at the local deli.

In my late twenties, I started a story about a man whose life was so promising, and his future was very bright, yet it began to unravel piece by piece, year over year, lost loved one by lost loved one, until he could no longer take his sadness, and was left only with the thought of suicide. I had the beginning and the end of that one, and as I began to fill in the pieces, it stalled, and remains yet another file in the Incomplete Works of James Bruce Fitzgerald, Jr.

For about twenty years, spanning from my twenties to my forties, I also wrote for multiple websites about NASCAR. For a few years of that span, I was able to score some press credentials for the races in Dover, Delaware, which was exciting, and finally made me feel like a real writer. In 2012, I even had the opportunity to interview future NASCAR Champion, Kyle Larson. NASCAR was my writing focus for quite some time, actually, up until the early 2020s. Yet, it really did not satisfy that writing bug that I felt.

When I was forty-eight, I had an idea for a story, but unlike other times, I did not begin writing it immediately. This time, I gave it some thought. Thinking! What a great idea! I took notes when my brain would kick out an idea. I had a pile of emails that I had sent to myself with ideas. My phone still has random text messages to myself with ideas.

Then came November 17th, 2021. I developed an infection in my left leg, spent three weeks in the hospital, and finally came home at the end of the first week of December. Being laid up in a hospital bed for three weeks did wondrous things for my feet. It made them unusable. I could not put any weight on my feet without excruciating pain. So, I was bedridden until I could rebuild my strength and get better. Physical therapy, rolling tennis balls around under my feet, and some exercises to keep the blood flowing were, truthfully, just what the doctor ordered. However, there was that time in between. From when I got home from the hospital to the time I surprised my wife with dinner because I felt well enough to crawl from the bedroom, across the floor, up the stairs and to our front door to get the food that I had delivered to our house, it was a painful, soul-crushing/searching test, with a lot of tears. But what else could I do with that in between time?

I had a laptop computer, a lot of notes, and a head full of ideas. So, I began to put it together. Page by page, I began to give my outline life. I remember telling my sister, who was my first proofreader, by the way, along with my Mom, reading this book, chapter by chapter, as I emailed them to her. I remember telling her that writing the book was like putting a puzzle together. When you do a puzzle, you start with the corners and the edge pieces, and you make the border. Then, little by little, you fill it in, sometimes attaching pieces to the border, sometimes focusing on a certain part of the puzzle, such as a bouquet of balloons, or flowers, or something that when you look at the picture on the box, you know what it is and where it goes and which pieces have the colors or designs that you need to fill in the gaps.

Writing this book was just like that. I had the beginning, and I had the end, and I had so many parts that I knew I wanted to put into the middle. So, I started with the frame, and then the bouquet of balloons, and then the flowers, and then I just filled in the rest of the pieces. There was no struggle with this story. No gaps, no writer's block. It flowed out of me like water in a bag full of holes. The only thing I struggled with was finding the time to write it. Then, in April of 2024, I finished this book. One day, I may fully tell you about the struggles of getting it published, but not today.

Back to the book. It is truly a work of ninety-nine percent fiction. If you've read it, you know what part of the one percent of reality was. Honestly, I did struggle with making that terrible day part of the story, but after a while, I acquiesced and moved forward. I hope, in your eyes, that I did justice to the events of the day, the heroism shown by our first responders, and the unfortunate aftermath that we all witnessed, and I hope you feel that I did it with honor and respect. That's all I wanted.

The remaining part of that one percent, well, that's some of you, the people who I hope are reading, have read, or will read this book. You know who you are. I used many of the first and last names in this book as a tribute to people who have had a positive impact on my life. If you find your name in this book, thank you. This is my shoutout to you.

While there are mentions of actual people in this book, such as John Grisham, Kurt Angle, Gary Busey, and others, there are two real people that also exist in this story of this book. One of them is my literary version of me, Jim, and also my wife, Daria. You may have put together that we are the D and J in D&J Liquors, the owners of the liquor store in Brindle, where "Billy Lomax" worked for a short time. Daria really is a Registered Nurse and shines in her field, enough to have been honored with a Nurse of the Year Award. I do not own a liquor store, but I have spent some time in some!

Brindle is not a real town, but it is based on a real town, and one I have never visited, other than through the images of Google Earth. The real town is Kimball, Nebraska. If you look at Google Earth and find Kimball, you can see the school where Will almost worked. You can see the trailer park where he lived. You can see the fairgrounds where he visited on a regular basis. If you look at the corner of South Webster and West Third, you can see the building of a national pizza chain that, at least in my mind's eye, was Rocky's restaurant.

Some of the other locations in the book are, or were, real as well. Many of the restaurants, truck stops, gas stations, convenience stores, and other places are actual places. Some of them are named differently, and some of them use the actual name. Most of the time, if I said Will pulled off the expressway to fill his gas tank, there is an actual exit on the actual expressway that leads to an actual gas station. I tried to make it as real as possible, so it would seem real to you, because if it actually exists, then I didn't make it up, and it can't be that far-fetched. I used an actual house as Will and Kathleen's house when I needed to work a scene out in my head. If this is your house, I'm sorry, but thank you.

Now, I will tell you that I did make some things up. I did a tremendous amount of research for this book, and some things are factual, but there were just some things that I could not find enough information on to make sure they were factual, so I just went with what made sense to me. I hope you can suspend your disbelief should you know something to be inaccurate. Welcome to storytelling!

First, I know very little about amateur wrestling. Let's get that out of the way. I know more about professional wrestling than I do amateur, but it just seemed like a logical path for an athletic person such as Will to have a background in sports. Plus, because I knew where I was going with the story, it made sense for him to be able to take someone down should he need to do so.

The Nebraska Sheriff's Academy. I know there is a State Patrol Training Center in Nebraska, and it is in Grand Island, next to the airport. Again, thank you, Google Earth. I do not know how long the training program is, or if Sheriff's deputies are trained there. So, I went with five months, and "yes" as the answer to the question about the training of deputies. There may be some sort of handbook for the members of law enforcement from which to study, as described in these pages, but I'm not certain.

I don't really know if a "Fair" comes to Kimball, you know, the kind with the games and the rides, but if you're going to have a Fairgrounds, I think you need a Fair. Do I know if the pressure of a human urine stream is enough to trigger the little tab in the clown's mouth that will fill the balloon with air in a carnival game? No... no, I do not, and I hope I never really find out, but I thought it would lighten the mood of the book a little.

Do you know, in the State of New York, if a felon can become a police officer? Good question. Some sources say it is not possible, while others say it is. I went with the answer that would make the book better.

So, yes, there are some actual factual "things" in this book, and some of them came from my imagination. I just hope you enjoy it. I also hope to have another "Eureka" idea one day, because I loved writing this book. (Actually, as of the publishing of this book, I am actively writing the sequel, so if you enjoyed the story and the characters, stay tuned.) More than just loving the writing of the book, I loved finishing it. It gave me a great sense of accomplishment. It's a bit strange, you see, how wonderful it feels...